ANNA WAS ALL THAT A WOMAN CAN BE. . . .

THE DAUGHTER—Fiercely determined to bring her immigrant family out of poverty, yet never understood by those who thought they knew her best. . . .

THE LOVER—On fire in his arms, she gave to the man who was the true love of her life all the passion her husband never knew. . . .

THE WIFE—The model helpmate, she enjoyed her cold, ambitious husband's status and embraced him with all her strength, if not quite all her heart. . . .

THE MOTHER—Providing her children with every advantage, she adored them, but for one—her difficult child —she may have given too much . . . too late.

THE GRANDMOTHER—Proud matriarch of a successful clan, she would leave a legacy of material wealth, an indomitable spirit . . . and a stunning secret of love.

⊠ Sandra Bregman

Reach for the Dream

A Dell Book

Published by
Dell Publishing
a division of
Bantam Doubleday Dell
Publishing Group, Inc.
666 Fifth Avenue
New York, New York 10103

Dedicated to Stanley, with gratitude and love

ISBN: 0-440-20650-2

Printed in the United States of America
Published simultaneously in Canada
June 1990

10 9 8 7 6 5 4 3

RAD

⬣ Acknowledgments

I would like to acknowledge the gracious assistance rendered to me by the staffs of the United States Senate Library, the Library of Congress, the YIVO Institute, and the Montgomery County Library System. This novel could not have been written without the oral history records gathered by the Washington Jewish Historical Society.

I appreciate having had the opportunity to interview members of the Anna and Max Bregman family, now either deceased or elderly, who remembered life in the old country, who remembered "Mama being slapped by the cossack," and the crossing to Germany in the hay cart.

Finally, I am grateful for the guidance and enthusiasm of my dear friends in the Upper Montgomery County Critique Group. Jerry Rice has been extremely generous with her time in helping me prepare the final manuscript. My agent, Adele Leone, and my editor, Maggie Lichota, have believed in this project since the beginning and have provided wise counsel and exerted strenuous efforts on my behalf.

To all of the above, and to my understanding family, I say a big thank you.

S.E.B.

⊠ Contents

"I think," said Anna, toying with a glove she had removed, "I think that—if there are as many minds as there are heads, then there are also just as many kinds of love as there are hearts."

Leo Tolstoi, ANNA KARENINA

⊠ Part 1

The Deepening Shadow, 1988

Washington, D.C.

◈ Chapter 1

Anna squinted a bit as she looked down at the Georgetown University crew team practicing on the Potomac. Her son Charles had been right, as he always was, about moving their offices to Washington Harbor. Now, at the end of a hectic day they could watch the sun set over the Potomac, sending jagged shafts of orange and silver glistening and sparkling off the water and the mirrored buildings of Rosslyn. And to have the top three floors—it was sheer heaven!

Today is the first day of spring, she thought, and the birthday of my mother of blessed memory.

Spring! Glorious spring! Nowhere in the world is it as magnificent as it is right here in my city. Now, if only I didn't have these damnable pains in my abdomen.

And even though I asked for it, I dread this confrontation with Gilbert, child of my loins, bane of my existence—the one tragic relationship in my life.

She walked across the room to the wet bar and checked the two carefully prepared trays. One held pastries suitable for late afternoon tea, green grapes, and a wedge of Brie with water biscuits. On the other tray her secretary, Barbara, had placed Charles's favorite sherry, Gil's cognac, Baccarat glasses, and an Old Imari teapot with freshly brewed tea for her.

Such elaborate preparations I make for tea with my two sons! she thought as she turned back to her desk, sat down, and opened the center drawer. She looked in the cleverly concealed magnifying mirror, touched up her lipstick, powdered her nose, and patted her soft French twist to smooth two offending tendrils.

I'm as vain as ever. Old age and illness remove none of one's vanity.

As if on cue, Barbara's voice sounded over the speaker phone. "Senator, your son Gilbert has arrived. Shall I send him in?"

"Yes, Barbara, and please buzz Charles and ask him to join us." No matter how often she asked Barbara to call her Mrs. Dunay, she could be sure that at certain times she'd hear the old "Senator" slip out. As if Barbara needed to remind Gilbert that he was only a *state* senator, while his mother had held the coveted title of United States Senator. Ah, Barbara, such loyalty is gratifying to an old woman!

She wiped her hands against her skirt to dry the clamminess that had been there since lunchtime. *Damn it, why am I so nervous today? Why do I let my son intimidate me?*

Gilbert burst through the door, and she stood up and walked toward him, offering him her cheek to kiss, astonished once more to see how devastatingly sexy he still was at fifty-three.

Unlike many businessmen, Gil refused to use hair spray. Consequently, his dark brown, slightly wavy hair always seemed to need combing. Somehow, Anna thought, *it adds to his roguish quality, which women find so charming. That, and the teasing twinkle in his almost-black eyes.*

"Mother, you look glorious—more like Audrey Hepburn every day!"

So typical of Gil, charm oozing out of him like venom from a rattlesnake's fangs! But no sooner had that thought crossed Anna's mind than she chastised herself for it. *I've got to stop thinking about my son like that. It only makes matters worse between us.*

"Hmm. I don't think Miss Hepburn would appreciate hearing that, my dear, since she's young enough to be my daughter, and her hair isn't quite the color of cotton—at least not yet."

"Actually, she was quite charmed when I told her last summer that she bore a striking resemblance to my famous mother."

"Gil, you didn't!"

"Of course I did. We met her at one of Helene Rothschild's Paris dinners." He held her at arm's length and looked her up and down. "You look wonderful in blue, Mother. Is it Adolfo?"

Two of the things she disliked most about Gilbert and his wife, Winslow, were their constant name-dropping and their obsession with status symbols. Had she been like that once herself? She cringed at the thought. "No, my dear, it's Chanel. One of the pleasures of not being in politics anymore is being able to shop abroad. I suppose that's one luxury Winslow can't enjoy now, with you running for the Senate."

At that moment the door opened to admit Charles. Calmly, deliberately, he walked toward Gil and offered his hand. Reluctantly, Gilbert quickly shook his brother's hand.

Anna's heart fluttered at the sight of Charles. He was the

mirror-image of his father: identical chestnut-colored, wavy hair, deep blue eyes, confident stride. Do they pass that commanding-officer attitude in their genes? she wondered.

"It's been a long time. How are you?" Charles asked his brother with genuine feeling.

So like his father, Anna thought. A straight shooter, overflowing with integrity. Sometimes too much.

"Okay. And you?" A dismissal, ending the small talk.

Gil sat down in the club chair beside the sofa. "Mother, what's on your mind today?"

"First," she answered as she turned toward the bar, "let me get each of you a drink."

"Here, let me help you with those trays." Charles rushed to her side, carrying the heavier tray to the coffee table in front of the sofa.

Anna followed with the pastry. How tense we all are, she thought as she sipped her tea after they had all been served. "I've asked you to meet with me today," she began, but then started over. "Well, it has been a while, Gil—since last Thanksgiving? The only reason I know about your political plans is because I follow Maryland politics in the *Post.*" She paused, looking at their faces. "It's a shame I see so little of you and Winslow. Of course, I keep up with you through your children."

Gilbert strained to produce a pleasant tone. "What exactly is on your mind, Mother? I was very busy this afternoon, had to cancel two meetings to be here. Barbara said it was something very urgent."

"Yes. I haven't revised my will in twenty-six years, and after all, I am eighty-one now. It seems that the time has come to do it, to include specific bequests for each of your children." She looked from Gilbert's face to Charles's. They waited for her to continue.

"It's not just the businesses. I've four homes and jewels."

"Yes." Gilbert nodded, his eyes narrowing. "Exactly what is your net worth, Mother?"

Anna sighed as an immense wave of sadness passed through her. She had no heart for this meeting. "Charles can probably answer that better than I."

"Five hundred million," Charles announced matter-of-factly.

"Enough for generations to come—invested properly, of course."

Gilbert looked Anna squarely in the eyes. "You'll do exactly what you want to, Mother. I've no doubt of it. You'll turn everything over to Charles." The bitterness in his voice was almost shocking.

Anna imagined the steel glint in Charles's eyes at that moment, but because of the way they were seated, she could see only the back of his head. She watched Gilbert flinch under his brother's cold scrutiny—and was furious with herself for having let their relationship degenerate to this level.

"Actually, I've a special project that has been on my mind for a long time, and I'd like to get it started this week. That's why I said it was urgent for you to come today. I want to start a foundation."

"Oh, shit! You mean you want to give away our inheritance!"

"Hear me out, Gilbert. I want to take a small portion of the Dunay estate, fifty million, and establish a foundation to support worthy causes in Israel and Jewish charities like the Holocaust Museum here in this country."

"For chrissake, that's the worst idea I've ever heard. When did you get so religious? For a lifetime you've avoided being Jewish, and now you want to advertise it to the whole world."

"Mother, I think it's a splendid idea," Charles said. "How can we help?"

"Thank you, Charles. I appreciate your support." She turned her attention back to Gilbert. "I'd like you both to be on the board of directors, along with one of your children and my niece Sidney. Five people, in case it's necessary to break a tie vote. You'll meet twice a year to determine how to distribute the funds. It's really quite simple, and it won't take up much of your time."

"Damn it, Mother, what are you trying to do? Destroy my political career?"

"I fail to see how giving money to Jewish causes can hurt you in Maryland."

"Winslow and I belong to St. Francis Episcopal Church in Potomac. Everyone thinks of us as Wasps. How can I suddenly give away millions to Israel?" Gilbert had stood and was pacing back and forth, gesturing with his brandy snifter.

"But Gil, the Jews are one of the largest voting blocs in

Montgomery County. And Baltimore County too. I should think it would be to your advantage."

"Absolutely not! I wash my hands of the whole thing. What about the voting power of the fundamentalists? If you've got so much money to give away, why don't you establish a fund for my political career? I could use a steady source of political money."

Charles stared at his brother, commanding him to return the look. No one said a word for a long time. Then Charles said quietly, "About three weeks ago, I looked at the books, Gil. You drew twelve million out of Dunay International last year. That should be enough to live on splendidly, pay your gambling debts, and still have plenty of money left over for politics."

"But how do I know the money will always be there for me to draw on? You know, Mother, my ambition doesn't end with the state senate. I have my eye on bigger things."

God help us, Anna thought. But he was her son. And she, of all people, understood political ambition.

"Mother, I have an idea that might solve your problem," Charles volunteered. "Instead of putting me on the board, ask Emily. She'd be thrilled, she'd make it her life's work, and you know how competent she is. Then ask two of Gil's children, and of course Sidney."

Anna thought of Charles's wife, her beloved daughter-in-law, Emily Bradford Loomis Dunay. A thirteenth-generation American who had chosen out of intellectual and emotional conviction—and no small amount of love for Charles—to convert to Judaism. Emily put all the Dunays to shame.

"Why didn't I think of that? We'll make Emily president of the foundation. And then perhaps your Brad will serve with her, and Larissa and Scot can represent Gil's family since he doesn't wish to participate directly."

"I can't control my children—you know that, Mother. Not where you're concerned. You've already been beatified, and soon they'll promote you to sainthood."

"You've got your religions mixed up, old boy!" Charles quipped sarcastically.

"What I don't understand is why you've suddenly found religion. You haven't been inside a synagogue since Landow died, and the only reason you went with him was to further his political career. That's about as hypocritical as a person can be."

Anna flinched at Gilbert's reference to his stepfather, the late U.S. Senator from Connecticut, but she recovered quickly. "Then I'm to believe that you and Winslow attend the Episcopal Church out of religious piety." She couldn't resist a wicked smile.

Charles laughed, thoroughly enjoying his mother's put-down of Gil.

Gil forcefully placed the empty snifter on the table, causing the crystal to chime. "Is that *all*? I've got to be going."

"No, it is not." Anna's voice was suddenly imperious. "I haven't seen you since Thanksgiving, Gil, and I think twelve million a year should buy me more than thirty minutes of your time. Sit down. I want to give you a serious answer to your question." She felt her full confidence return, her nervousness evaporating.

"About three years ago I had the privilege of dining with Elie Wiesel. We talked about your grandparents, and the time they spent in the Warsaw ghetto. They were eminent doctors and had been living a completely assimilated, cultured life in Warsaw. They were part of the intelligentsia, participating and contributing to the well-being of their fellow citizens, and by their teachings and writings, to the practice of medicine worldwide." She pressed an escaping tendril of hair back in place, then continued.

"They, too, had not been inside a synagogue in years. In 1937 I spent some time with them in Paris, and I asked them if they were fearful of Hitler. They told me Hitler would persecute only religious Jews, not those who had become agnostics. I can only tell you, they were dreadfully, fatally wrong."

"All that happened years ago, Mother. It's time we forgot it."

"Elie Wiesel said to me, 'It takes courage to be a Jew. It takes courage to acknowledge *what you are* in this century.' I have been a long time arriving at that kind of courage, I have spent a lifetime trying to avoid the hard truth of my roots. But it's never too late. Emily, God love her, and my grandchildren have set the example for me.

"And now I think maybe I have as much courage as they. I want to do this. I want to do it for your father Claude's parents and for dear Douglas." She looked fleetingly at Charles, tears welling up in her eyes. "But most of all, I need to do it for myself because it's the right thing to do."

"I'm sure you'll do whatever you want," Gilbert said coldly. "You always have."

Anna nodded, feeling his bitterness. And yet for years she had tried to make life easy for him, to be certain he had everything he needed or wanted. Maybe that had been a mistake. At least his children hadn't absorbed his bitterness—they were a joy, every one of them. "I presume you and Winslow will be coming to dinner Sunday? Black tie at eight at Pennyfield Manor."

"Mother, have you gone bonkers? Who gives black-tie parties at home on Sunday night? And what's so special about this Sunday? It's not your birthday."

"I want to have all my loved ones, my heirs, together, looking their best, to tell them about my revised will. Surely you and Winslow are interested."

"We may be interested, but we have two other engagements."

"Cancel them," Charles interrupted.

Gilbert looked at Charles with all the scorn he could muster. "Look, I don't know what you two are cooking up, but if I'm not treated fairly in your will, Mother, I promise I'll contest it. When I do, the scandalous sex life of the famous Anna Dunay will be spread across the front pages of every major paper in the world. Do you really want that?"

Charles rose threateningly. "That's enough, Gil!"

"What're you going to do, hit me?"

Charles towered over Gilbert menacingly. "I think you've said quite enough."

Gilbert walked toward the door. As he turned the knob, Anna said, "I'll be expecting you Sunday, Gil. And please tell Winslow to wear her prettiest dress. Give her my love."

"Mother, why this urgency about your will?" Gilbert asked impatiently. "Are you sick or something?"

"Yes. I have intestinal cancer. Surgery is scheduled for two weeks from Thursday."

"Oh!" He paused and looked hard at her, then added, "I'm sorry." She didn't miss the slight lilt of happiness in his voice, as the door closed behind him.

He wants me to die.

It was as if a hammer and chisel had chipped away one more piece of her heart.

She sat still, trying to gain the strength to stand and walk to her desk where her pocketbook held a handkerchief. She didn't want to cry in front of Charles.

He turned to her just as she stood up. "Mother," he said as he wrapped his arms around her, "I'm so sorry, so sorry he's—such a bastard!"

He held her while her body shook for a few moments, as if she were suddenly freezing cold. "Can I get you something? How about some sherry?"

"Yes, that would be fine."

Charles lowered her back into the chair and quickly crossed the room to the bar. "He has one hell of a nerve threatening you with a sex scandal, when he's been involved in every possible kind of love affair."

"Oh, I don't know. Everyone seems to sleep around these days. He does. Winslow does. All their jet-set crowd does. But it's only a threat, don't you think?"

"Damn it all, Mother, he makes me so mad! You and I spend a lifetime getting him out of trouble—literally keeping him out of jail, out of the newspapers, propping up his political career. And look at the way he treats you! It was all I could do to keep from beating the shit out of him right here in the office!"

"My goodness, such language! Charles, you'd better calm down. You're not a young man anymore. We don't need to have the chief executive officer of Dunay International in the hospital, along with his mother!" She lifted a frail, blue-veined hand to her lips and sipped her sherry, then reached for a grape.

Charles watched her. "You really can't bring yourself to be critical of your son, can you, Mother?"

"What I *think* about my children and grandchildren remains inside my head and heart; what I *say* to anyone else, including you, Charles, is another matter. And you know I love and trust you dearly."

"Yes, Mother, I know." He smiled affectionately.

"You know, sometimes I wonder about Gilbert's attractiveness to voters. Every four years he gets reelected in spite of his life-style, his gambling, Winslow's incredible jewels and clothes, and their homes. I'm surprised it hasn't backfired."

"Are you kidding? Look at the Kennedys! Look at the Reagans! What are the most popular soaps on TV? The more glamorous the life-style, the more the public adores politicians and stars. And if their life-styles and friends have a slight twist of wickedness about them, so much the better!"

"Maybe you're right."

"And now I think it's time for you to call Marc and head home. It's been a taxing day for you."

"Actually, I'd like to be alone for a few minutes to collect my thoughts and pack my briefcase. You run along now—and do tell Emily I want her to be president of my foundation."

"You can tell her yourself tomorrow, when she takes you to the doctor. I'm sure she'd rather hear it from you. She adores you, you know."

"Yes, dear, and the feeling is quite mutual. Now, you get back to work, or I shall have to fire my CEO!"

He stood, gave her a mock salute, then bent down and kissed her forehead. "I love you, Mom."

Anna sat facing the massive expanse of windows and let the late Tuesday afternoon noises wash over her. She could hear the occasional honking of cars and the constant swooshing of traffic, and from her vantage point, she could see planes coming in to land at National Airport, at least one every minute.

Weary and shaken she was, but the elegance of her office soothed her. It was furnished, like all her homes and offices, in a blend of French and English antiques, oriental rugs, and European and American Impressionist art. Her sister Sasha's daughter, Sidney, had been her interior decorator for the last eighteen years. It was Sidney who had searched out the glorious objects and paintings that had come to mean so much to Anna.

One of my character flaws is my outrageous love for things.

She finished the last drop of sherry and placed the glass on the bronze table—an original by Philip La Verne, one of her few concessions to contemporary craftsmanship. But then it wasn't really contemporary, filled as it was with carved scenes of the Orient. *Such beauty, such workmanship, such joy things like this table give me! I wish I weren't so wedded to things. But in truth, contemplating beautiful things—and owning them—gives me more joy than the knowledge of my wealth and power.*

This glistening navy-blue Kirman, for example, she thought as she eyed the carpet with pride. *One of the last shipped from*

Iran before the shah's fall. It measured fifteen by twenty-three feet, and when Sidney had showed it to her, they had decided to do the whole room around the rug. All the upholstered pieces would be the same shade of ivory, the second most prominent color in the rug, and the sofas would have navy-blue-velvet pillows for accent. Two Mary Cassatt oils adorned the walls, and a marble sculpture by Brancusi stood on a pedestal between the two massive windows.

Her secretary had instructions to play classical music tapes, especially Tchaikovsky, Rossini, and Debussy, throughout the day. Now the music and the scene calmed Anna like a soothing balm.

She picked up the phone by her chair and pushed a button. Instantly, her butler, Antonio, answered at her Kalorama residence. "Yes, Madame?"

"Antonio, I'll be home in about an hour and a half. Please ask Rosa to have some of that wonderful minestrone for me. But first I'd like a nice Jacuzzi, and . . . a fire in my bedroom, I think. I'm feeling chilled today."

"Then you won't be going to the symphony this evening."

"No, I'm too weary. Marc delivered the tickets to Sidney. Also, I've canceled cocktails with the Brickmans. So I'll be home about six and then off to bed."

"Madame, all the grandchildren have been calling. I told them they could reach you at the office. They're most anxious to speak with you."

She thought of her grandchildren, scattered as they were to the four corners of the country—and abroad. "After a bit of soup, I'll phone them back. Any other calls?"

"Yes, Madame. Mrs. Winslow Dunay and Mrs. Emily Dunay have both called."

Anna smiled. Bad news traveled fast. Winslow hadn't phoned in years; Emily she spoke with several times a day.

"I'll call them all back this evening. Good-bye, Antonio."

A few minutes later, Anna was ensconced in the back of her limousine, again listening to the soft music of Debussy, giving her driver Marc directions.

"I'm feeling very nostalgic this afternoon, Marc. How about a sight-seeing trip?"

"Anything you'd like, Mrs. Dunay."

His soft Italian accent pleased her, just as his wife's pleasant way as her personal maid suited her.

"I'd like to drive around the Mall, then past the White House, down Pennsylvania Avenue to the Capitol, ending up on the Senate side. Then we'll stop for a quick visit at the National Gallery. I promised Antonio I'd be home by six. Can we do all that by then?"

"Depends on the traffic. So far it isn't too bad."

As Marc deftly maneuvered the long black car, Anna's mind traveled backward to the war years. How ugly the Mall had been then, with all those hastily built office barracks!

Her earliest memory of Washington, though, had been watching President Wilson ride up Pennsylvania Avenue in a horse-drawn carriage to his first inauguration. It had been March 1913. Her mother, her sister, and two of her brothers had huddled together, refugees from Russia's anti-Semitic policies. Her mother had been awed to the point of tears as she watched "the President of the United States of America" ride past them on his way to the White House. That a Russian immigrant could find freedom and a new life in the United States—and see the new President too! It was a treasured memory that her mother had carried with her to her grave, perhaps one of the most important days of her life.

What fun it had been years later, when her sister, Sasha, had been old enough to go with them on Sunday-afternoon excursions. Their favorite visit had been to the outer perimeters of the White House lawn. They would stand with their noses between the iron rails, watching the sheep munch on the grass. Once, only once, they caught a glimpse of President Wilson and his wife taking a Sunday-afternoon stroll inside the fence. He had waved to them. Their mother had repeated that story for years.

In later years, so many times they had walked the length of the Mall and back, dipping their toes into the wading pool, watching the ripples fan out. Then, just before World War II, the ugly temporary buildings had gone up, and it had seemed forever before they came down and the Mall was restored to the beauty L'Enfant had planned.

Yes, this was her city, the only place on earth she had ever wanted to live permanently.

"Oh, so many memories this avenue holds for me!" Anna

said, as much to herself as to Marc, as they drove down Pennsylvania Avenue, now clogged with rush-hour traffic. So many inaugural parades she'd watched, and funerals too. She had flown home from her post as ambassador to Austria to be here for President Kennedy's funeral, one of the saddest days of her life. Many terrible things had happened to her during the war, but Kennedy's death had hit her harder than some more personal events.

Marc came to a stop under the portico at the entrance to the Senate side of the Capitol. "Will you be going in, Mrs. Dunay?"

"No, I think not. But if you'd just pull around and park over there, so I can see the Capitol in all its splendor." It may be the last time, she mused, that I ever see this magnificent building, my working home for so much of my life.

What a shame, she thought as she looked at the concrete barriers. After Kennedy's assassination and Martin Luther King's, we had soldiers with machine guns. Now we have permanent concrete barriers. And electronic detectors and pocketbook searches, even of former senators like myself! What terrible things have happened in my lifetime!

And what wonders! To think that I've led the marvelous life I have—and it may soon be ending. This magnificent institution, the Senate. I love the Senate with a fierce love. It is mankind's greatest deliberative body, our government one of mankind's great achievements. Oh, there are rogues and womanizers and thieves, just as in every other institution or corporation. But for the most part, the Senate is made up of our finest men and, thank God, now a few women.

It would be a travesty for Gilbert to be elected to the Senate! A disgrace, a black day in the history of Maryland. It mustn't happen.

Brusquely, Anna directed Marc to take her home. "I'm wearier than I thought. I'd best get home and make those phone calls."

When Marc looked in the rearview mirror at Anna, she saw his look of concern. So they know, she thought. All the servants know I'm ill.

"Right away, ma'am."

"Sonia darling, I'm delighted to find you home! You're so hard to track down." As she spoke into the telephone, Anna visualized her favorite grandchild in New York. She would be barefoot, in faded jeans, an oversize T-shirt with some crazy emblem printed on it, and her long copper hair would be flying in every direction unless she had it tied back in a ponytail. "How did filming go today?"

"We had a great day, Bubby, but that's not what I want to talk about. Mom told me you're . . . not well. I'm so upset, I could hardly concentrate today. . . ." Her voice trailed off suddenly, and Anna knew she was crying.

She spoke in her sternest voice. "Look, Sonia, if President Reagan can recover from the same thing and run the country, I guess I can recover and run Dunay. Now, you stop worrying, and that's an order from your 'old bubby'!"

"Well, at least you don't sound sick."

"Did Barbara tell you about dinner on Sunday?"

"Yes, I'll be coming in on the late shuttle Friday. Can I stay with you at Pennyfield?"

"I'd be delighted, if it's all right with your parents. I expect some of your cousins will be staying with me too."

"Terrific!"

"Now, I want you to do a special favor just for me. Humor an old lady you love."

"Anything, Bub!"

"Go to Martha's tomorrow and pick out the most elegant dress you can find, one that makes your opal eyes sparkle. I want you to look splendid, regal, the way your aunt Winslow looks when she really dresses. *Comprenez-vous?*"

"Jeez, Sunday night's dinner is gonna be that fancy?"

"I want you to look like a regal heiress." As she said the words, Anna thought, If I could leave you everything, heart of my heart, I would. But that wouldn't be fair to all the others. So I have to choose from among all my things those I think you want most, and I daren't even ask you.

"Bub, I hate all this talk of wills and stuff—it's so morbid. I don't need anything to remind me of you. But I do want you to get well. I want you to always be there for me."

"I'll try, sweetheart, but that's not the way life is. So I must be prepared." She heard what sounded like snuffling on the other end. "Now tell me, why haven't I seen more of you in *W* and *Vogue* and *Bazaar*? Public relations is fifty percent of the game—I've been trying to teach you and Karine that for years!

You must concentrate on more publicity—especially with the Oscars coming up."

"C'mon, Bub! You don't seriously think *Stolen Moments* will be nominated, do you? Only a grandmother would imagine that!"

"Nonsense! The critics compared you to Ingmar Bergman— and you're only twenty-seven. Imagine! Yes, I fully expect to see you in Hollywood next winter getting the Oscar for best picture —and best director. Both!"

"Great. That means two events where I'll be able to wear that dress you want me to buy tomorrow! Bub, I do love your fantasies."

"Historically, let me remind you, we Dunays have a way of making our fantasies reality. Don't forget that, darling! And don't forget you are speaking to your biggest financial backer. Thirty-three percent of Colossal Pictures, right?"

"Well, if you put it that way," she said, laughing, "I wouldn't dream of disappointing my biggest fan and backer. I'll look like a goddamned movie queen on Sunday night."

"Wonderful! Cheerio now. I love you."

"And I love you, Bub."

As she put the phone down, Anna chuckled to herself at the Yiddish title for grandmother. She had not wanted to be called Bubby—she thought it too ethnic, too old world, and she had never looked the part. But Charles and Emily had rigorously insisted that their children call her Bubby. And Gilbert and Winslow had just as rigorously insisted that theirs call her Gram.

The phone jingled.

"Gram, it's me, Karine." Anna smiled as Gil's daughter's breathless enthusiasm came through the phone. "Mom tells me you're having a party Sunday night and we're all supposed to be there."

"Right."

"Will you wear one of my dresses if I bring it down Friday night? If it needs altering, I'll fix it myself on Saturday."

"Of course. I'd be thrilled to wear one of your designs."

"I knew you'd say that. I began it today. I saw this gorgeous lace, the exact color of your tanzanite necklace and earrings, so I bought enough to make you a long gown. Now, let me describe it. . . ."

Doesn't this child ever breathe? Anna thought as Karine continued her nonstop chatter.

"An illusion top with a very low neckline, almost off the shoulder. Long sleeves, like you prefer. A nipped-in waist and a full skirt to the floor. Or would you like it midcalf length?"

"It sounds magnificent, but I think such a wonderful dress should be floor length. Perhaps I'll wear it to the Academy Awards next winter. If it's as beautiful as it sounds, I think I will."

"I can't wait for you to see this dress. It's the most beautiful lace I've ever seen. I just *had* to make it for you!"

"You must let me pay you for the lace, Karine."

"No way, Gram, absolutely not! This is my present. You've given me so much. Are you still a size six? Mom says you might be losing weight."

"If the dress fits you, it'll fit me to perfection. Unless *you've* gained weight! Now, what will you be wearing?"

"Oh, it's so gorgeous! Royal-blue-silk organza, to the floor, in six-inch ruffles that cascade diagonally from the waist. A strapless sheared bodice. It's to die for! And guess what? Your friend Martha is going to carry three of my designs this summer. Isn't that fabulous?"

It exhausts me just to listen to you, my dear sweet talented grandchild, Anna thought, but she said, "That's wonderful!"

"Gram, I've a favor to ask."

"Yes?"

"Please loan me your sapphire ring and earrings, just for Sunday night, to go with the gown."

"You don't think they're a bit—overwhelming—for someone as young as you?"

"I don't mean *those* sapphires. I mean the studs surrounded by diamonds and the ring you never wear. They're in one of those boxes of jewelry you never open."

"My goodness, I'd totally forgotten those! Yes, your grandfather, Claude, gave me those sapphires just before he left for the war. I'd like you to have them. Permanently."

"Oh no, Gram, I couldn't."

"Nonsense. I haven't worn them in years, and you should have them because Claude gave them to me. I'll find something equally nice for your sister Larissa. Then you'll both have a piece of jewelry that your grandfather gave me."

"Cool! That's wonderful. I can't wait. Can I stay with you, Gram? Or is your house full?"

"We'll have a full house, I expect, but there's plenty of room, you know that. You can share the lavender suite with Sonia. How's that?"

"Terrific! See you Friday."

It's going to be quite a weekend—exactly what I wanted. To see them one more time, maybe the last time . . . and hear their laughter and hopes and dreams. . . .

When the light on the telephone flashed, she picked up the phone and punched the button.

"Bub, it's Elliot," she heard. "Now, what's the scoop about this weekend?"

"Hello, darling! I need you to coordinate with your sister Jennifer about time and place. She has a rehearsal Saturday, so I'm sending the plane to Albuquerque to pick up you and Cheray and Jen and bring you here on Sunday. The problem is, she has to be back in Santa Fe by Monday evening for another rehearsal."

"Fine. I'll work it out with Jen. Let's just hope my bride's feeling good enough to make the trip." Anna could hear him smiling when he said "my bride."

"What's wrong? Is she ill? Emily didn't say anything."

"I don't think it's anything to be concerned about." Elliot chuckled. "She's been suffering from nausea. In the morning. And she needs late afternoon naps. And her breasts are sore. But I'll get killed if I breathe another word to you, Bub, so you'd better act real surprised. Okay?"

"Oh, Elliot, I can't tell you how happy that would make me, to live to see a great-grandchild. Give Cheray a big kiss from me!"

"Bub, you don't know anything, okay? I haven't even told Mom and Dad."

"I understand. You can be sure I'll be a great actress. If only your grandfather were here!"

"Hey, is your party really black tie? I can't wear my cowboy boots?"

How he loved to tease her! Her errant oldest grandson had needed to prove himself away from the rest of the family, out in the hinterlands of New Mexico. In truth, it was a glorious part of the country, and she could now, at long last, fully appreciate why he'd made the decision he had. At the time it had nearly killed her very soul.

The light on the phone was flashing again. "Elliot, I've a call waiting. Will you be staying at Pennyfield or with your parents?"

"We'd like to stay with you. Cheray loves your house and can't get enough of you, so it would make her very happy if you've got bedrooms left. I understand everyone is staying there."

"Of course. Like old times. And tell Jennifer I'll expect her to stay here too. It'll be like old times at Rehoboth Beach."

Anna pushed the button and heard the caressing voice of Winslow, her flamboyant, flashy, and conniving daughter-in-law—who was nonetheless the mother of her beloved grandchildren Larissa, Karine, Scot, and Rick.

"Anna, I wanted to reassure you that Gil and I have canceled our other plans and will definitely be there Sunday. And to say" —her voice softened even more, almost to the point of a whisper—"how dreadfully sorry we are to hear that you're ill. What can I do for you between now and your surgery?"

"How nice to hear from you, my dear. I've just finished speaking with Karine. She sounds so happy."

"She does, doesn't she? Have you talked with Rick yet? He's in London recording, and I haven't been able to reach him."

"My secretary spoke with him yesterday. He's arriving Thursday evening, and he'll be staying at Pennyfield."

"I see."

Anna detected resentment in Winslow's voice.

"Well, I'm delighted to know you've reached him. I do hope he gets a haircut. His father is so offended by the way he dresses."

"It's all part of the act, Winslow. If you're going to be a rock star, you've got to look the part. At least, that's what he tells me." Why am I defending her son to her?

"His father wishes he'd have more consideration for his political career. After all, Gil is running for the U.S. Senate."

"Yes, it seems to me I read that in the paper." The silence on the other end punctuated Anna's sarcasm.

"Anna, do you think you could have lunch with me before next Thursday? I'd so love to see you."

"No. I'm terribly busy between now and then. Doctor's appointments and tests. Meetings with my bankers and lawyers. I'm sure you understand."

"Yes, but—"

"I'll be seeing you Sunday evening. After the surgery, you can come visit me at Pennyfield, and Rosa will make us a wonderful lunch. How's that?"

"Fine, I guess. In the meantime, if there's anything I can do to help you prepare for Sunday, do call me."

"Certainly. Cheerio!"

That bitch! The nerve of her! To pretend she's concerned, when she hasn't called me for lunch in fifteen years!

The phone was quiet, the house was still. It was only ninethirty, but Anna felt utterly done in, exhausted. She turned out her lights, watched the logs in the fireplace glow, and thought of her whole life—how glorious, how tragic, how unfinished.

▧ Chapter 2

"Bub, it's Sonia. Sorry to wake you. I'm calling from the studio, but I had to talk to you before I called everyone else, and besides, we start filming in thirty minutes."

Anna looked at her bedside clock. It was seven in the morning. Her butler had strict orders never to put a call through before eight-thirty. But he also had orders to put her grandchildren through immediately, no matter what time of day or night. She struggled to a sitting position and ran a hand through her hair, as if Sonia could see her at the other end of the phone in New York City. "My goodness, what is it, child?"

"I had a brainstorm around midnight. Let's have a cousins' party Saturday night—only the young generation—at Pennyfield. Ask Antonio and Rosa to make one of their wonderful Italian buffets. You know, manicotti, veal with green peppers, the way Rosa makes it, the works."

"But darling, Elliot and Jen and Cheray won't be able to make it. Jen has rehearsal Saturday."

"Bub, that's ridiculous! If her general manager understands that you want her in Washington, there'll be no question about her missing a rehearsal."

"Well, Jen hates to take advantage of—"

"She can do it this once. I'll talk to her. Let me work it out. Everyone's to wear jeans—even you, Bubby!" Sonia giggled, knowing her grandmother possessed nothing remotely resembling jeans.

"Oh, then I'm to be included in this party for the younger generation?"

"Sure, Bub. You're the youngest one of all."

"I don't know, dear. It'd be such a drain on the staff, with the big party Sunday night."

"Hire extra help. Listen, Bub, if it's too big a drain on *you*, then we won't do it. But if it's the *staff* you're worried about, I'll handle them. I'll talk to Antonio—you know he'd do anything for me."

Anna sighed in resignation. Sonia was right—Antonio had always doted on her. Her slightest wish would be his priority. "All right. Work it out with your brothers and sister and cousins."

"And Bub, not a word to the grown-ups. We don't want them butting in! I've got to get to work. Talk to you tonight."

Anna replaced the phone and lay back. Sonia, the organizer, the manager of all the cousins. Sonia and her brainstorms! God, I love that child. And won't it be fun to have all of them to myself!

Emily arrived promptly at nine and parked her white Jaguar in the driveway, knowing that Marc would be driving them to the hospital. Antonio was waiting for her at the front door. "Madame is expecting you. She's in the solarium."

"Ah, here you are." Anna put down *The Wall Street Journal.* "How nice you look, my dear! Coral's a great color on you. It cheers me just to see you. A breath of spring."

Emily bent to kiss Anna's forehead and tried not to show the alarm she felt. Charles had not prepared her for Anna's appearance. Her mother-in-law looked as if she had lost ten pounds in three days. She was dressed in a heavy wool suit to go to the hospital, and even though she was sitting directly in the bright sunlight, a mohair throw was covering her lap and legs.

As Anna slowly stood up, Emily saw her grimace and hold her abdomen. Quickly, Emily reached for her elbow to steady her. How frail this indestructible dynamo had become, almost overnight! Tears came to Emily's eyes, but she determinedly blinked them back. *I must be strong—it's the only way I can help her.*

Slowly, they made their way to the waiting car. Anna cautiously slid inside, settled herself, then patted Emily's hand and said, "I'm so glad you're going with me. It's not the kind of thing I want the men to suffer through."

"I know nothing about a colonoscopy, except what I read in the paper when President Reagan had cancer, and I've forgotten most of that. Will they put you to sleep?"

"No, only intravenous Valium. I guess I'll be in a sort of haze but conscious. The doctor will pluck some of the polyps and get a better idea of how much of the colon they'll have to remove in the surgery."

"There's no chance they'll get it all and you won't have to have full-scale surgery?"

"No, it doesn't seem so. But this ordeal will be over in a few hours, and I'll be back home in bed. I've an appointment with Charles and Hal Morganstern at four. I hope the grogginess will have worn off by then."

"You probably should've scheduled those appointments for tomorrow, Anna."

Anna smiled. "My dear, I've too much to do, and too little time between now and the surgery to do it. When I think of all the things I've accumulated over a lifetime. . . . I seem to be making endless lists trying to decide how to dispose of it all. I daresay I shouldn't have been so acquisitive."

"Is there any way I can help? I take pretty good shorthand. Maybe I can help you make lists."

"No, I've got Barbara." Anna turned slowly and sat sideways to face Emily. "What would you think if I gave Pennyfield Manor to Sonia?"

Emily's heart lurched. Triumph and fear flooded through her. To have her very own Sonia inherit that grand estate—it would be glorious! But could she deceive Anna that way? Anna, who seemed to have been her own mother her for all her adult life. . . .

"I'd give it to you and Charles, but your own home is so lovely, and you've put so much time and attention into making it perfect."

"Oh, Anna, I can't tell you how thrilled I'd—we'd—be for

Sonia to have Pennyfield . . . but what about the other children?"

"I have four homes and four granddaughters."

Emily was overwhelmed, ecstatic. To think that Anna would give her grandest home to Sonia! Even though Gil's Larissa was the oldest granddaughter! I must be honest with Anna. How long I've dreaded this day! But she's been so good to me, she deserves the truth. "I would have thought you'd give Pennyfield to Larissa, the oldest."

"No. Larissa's an intellectual—a writer, a dreamer. She doesn't care where she lives. Sonia, on the other hand, has the style to be mistress of Pennyfield. She'll do it justice."

Emily watched Anna squirm in the soft leather car seat, trying to find a comfortable position. She hadn't realized how Anna was suffering. "Do you really think you're up to this big dinner on Sunday night? I hadn't realized how much pain you're in."

"I want it very much. Having the children with me will be the best tonic ever." Anna hugged her arms close to her chest. "Marc, do turn up the heat a bit. I'm chilled."

"Of course, Madame."

Anna gazed out at Massachusetts Avenue, at Embassy Row, at the blooming forsythia and daffodils. "Isn't Washington beautiful? It's too bad I'll miss the cherry blossoms this year, but I should be up and about in time for the dogwood and the tulips."

"I hope you won't try to do too much too soon. After all, Charles and Scot and Brad can handle things very nicely."

"Yes. It's comforting at a time like this that my son and grandsons are running my business affairs."

There were a few moments of silence as both women were immersed in private thought. But as they rounded the circle of Pennsylvania and Twenty-third Street, Emily felt she would burst if she didn't confront head-on the issue of Sonia's inheriting Pennyfield. "Anna, there's something I must tell you about Sonia."

Anna looked at her sharply and drew herself up straight in the car. "Don't be ridiculous! I know everything I need to know about Sonia! She's more like me than any of my grandchildren. She's both brilliant and street-smart, she's beautiful, she works like a demon. She's infinitely more creative than I am. She has a mind for business that runs circles around Charles and her brothers. It's a pity she didn't want to involve herself in running Dunay International, but if I'd had her creative talent, I might have done something different with my life too. No, Sonia has all of me in her, plus some. She'll have Pennyfield." Then, as if in an afterthought, Anna added, "And I couldn't care less how many young men she's captivated. I will not concern myself with the love lives of any of my grandchildren."

Emily looked out the car window, afraid to let Anna see her face. Anna had deliberately, deftly changed the subject. She felt Anna take her hand and stroke it softly, then say in a quiet, determined voice, "My dear, I told you when Sonia was small that my aunt Bessie in Russia had hair and eyes the exact color of Sonia's. She gets that glorious auburn hair from Bessie and her opal eyes and creamy skin as well."

Marc stopped the car under the portico of the George Washington University Hospital, opened the door, and carefully escorted Anna through the sliding-glass doors.

"Marc, I'll need you back here at one, at this entrance."

"Exactly, Mrs. Dunay. I'll be here."

Josephine, Anna's personal maid, tiptoed quietly into the master bedroom, looked dubiously at her sleeping employer, then went back downstairs to report to Charles and Hal Morganstern.

"Mrs. Dunay is sleeping. She hasn't awakened since Mrs. Emily Dunay and I put her to bed, sir. I really don't think I should awaken her."

"I'll go upstairs and speak with her. She insisted that this meeting had to take place this afternoon," Charles said to Hal as he set down his glass of sherry.

He walked into her pale blue bedroom suite and felt and smelled the stifling heat generated by the pine and cedar mixture burning in the fireplace. He watched his mother breathing softly as she slept. He looked at her pasty-white face. Her thin, blue-veined hand rested on the blue-satin coverlet. Tentatively, he picked up her hand. It was ice cold.

"Mother . . . mother, it's Charles. We're here for the meeting you wanted. Hal Morganstern and myself. Do you want to sleep a bit more? We can come back tomorrow."

Anna opened her eyes, blinked, closed them again, then

slowly opened them. She stared at Charles, thinking she was looking at his father—So tall, broad shoulders, brown hair flecked with silver—no, no it can't be. She tried to comprehend his message. "No . . . no, I need to talk today. . . ."

"Mother, I'm not sure you're alert enough. They've given you sedatives and pain-killers."

"Let me try. Give me a hand."

He held his hand out to her and as she tried to pull herself up to a sitting position, he supported her back with his other hand. She threw the covers off, then slowly swung her legs over the side of the bed.

"I'm so dizzy . . . must be the Valium . . ."

"Mother, listen to me. There's nothing so important that it can't be taken care of tomorrow. We'll be available over the weekend if you want us. Now, be sensible and get back into that bed until the drugs wear off. I'll tell Hal we'll meet here tomorrow morning at ten." Charles tucked the covers around her. Anna was too drugged to protest. "Are you warm enough?"

"Yes, love, thank you . . . for being so patient . . . and all that. . . ." She closed her eyes, then opened them and murmured to Charles, "Call Barbara and ask her to come here at eight-thirty tomorrow, prepared to take lots of dictation."

"Fine, Mother. I'll do it right now."

The next morning, Thursday, Anna was more alert, though she was restless and hurting. She welcomed her secretary with an intent, searching look.

"Barbara, over the years you and I have had a wonderful relationship," Anna began as she settled herself comfortably on the blue Scalamandré silk sofa in the library. It was going to be a long day. She adjusted the pillow behind her back, then asked Barbara to hand her the salmon-colored mohair throw, which she wrapped around her lower body. "I know I can trust you to keep things strictly between us, confidential. This morning I'm going to dictate some letters and memos that are more confidential than any I've ever done before. Can I trust you?"

Barbara looked momentarily stunned. She felt a slow blush creep up her face. "Of course, Mrs. Dunay. I wouldn't dream of revealing any of your business."

"Good. Then let's begin. This first memo is to go to our

comptroller, Philip Levine. One copy is to be hand-delivered to my son Charles."

Barbara picked up her steno book and wrote as Anna said, " 'From this day forward, March 22, 1988, absolutely no Dunay Corporation money is to be paid to Gilbert Dunay without my specific authorization in writing.'

"Type that on my official chairman-of-the-board stationery and bring it to me for signature this afternoon. You can hand-deliver it to Charles and Mr. Levine tomorrow morning."

Barbara nodded in understanding and sat poised for more dictation.

"This next series of letters is to be typed on my personal stationery, the blue parchment with the Dunay family crest. I want them to be formally addressed on the envelopes. The first is to my eldest granddaughter, Miss Larissa Dunay.

" 'My dearest Larissa,

" 'How proud I am of you, my dearest, for having set your own course so courageously and with such dignity. My wish for you is that you win the American Book Award, the Pulitzer prize, and eventually, after a lifetime of fulfilling, inspired work, the Nobel prize for literature.

" 'Such are the dreams of an old grandmother. I have tried to do what I could during my lifetime to make it possible for you to pursue your own dream.

" 'Though I know how unmaterialistic you are, how little clothes and homes and such mean to you, I nevertheless want you to know that you will inherit my Kalorama home, all the furniture, rugs, art, and—this I know will please you immensely —the full contents of the library. In other words, the Kalorama house and everything it contains. I am telling you this now— long before my death, I hope—so you may make your plans accordingly.

" 'Know always that I love you deeply and am so pleased I was able to be a patron of one of America's future literary greats.'

"Now, Barbara, stop that sniffling! I'm not dead yet, not by a long shot. We won't be able to get this job done today if you start crying."

"I'm sorry. It's . . . so sad."

"It is not sad! It's wonderful that I have such fine grandchildren to carry on the Dunay name. Now, the next letter is to Karine."

Barbara took dictation for nearly an hour, but Charles and Hal Morganstern arrived before Anna was half finished. She had many more letters to dictate, but she sent Barbara back to her office and welcomed Hal and Charles.

After Antonio served the men coffee and placed a tray of Danish pastry on the coffee table, Anna dismissed him and asked him to close the door behind him.

"Hal, I can make this short and sweet. Remember those nine municipal bonds I purchased eighteen years ago? Labette County, Kansas, bonds, I believe, each for one hundred thousand dollars, paying twelve percent interest."

"Yes. They're in your safety deposit box at Riggs."

"Fine. Charles"—she addressed her son, who was making notes on the small pad he carried in his suit pocket—"you'll need to go with Hal to get those bonds."

"Yes, Mother."

"I want them brought out to Pennyfield on Saturday with nine brown envelopes."

Hal nodded his head. Charles looked puzzled at his mother for a moment, then asked in a soft voice, "Who will you give the ninth one to now?"

"Charles, I don't appreciate questions like that. Allow me to surprise you once in a while—give me that small pleasure. After all, I'm not obligated to tell you everything."

"You sound like yourself today, now that the Valium has worn off! I love it!"

"Second," Anna said, turning back to Hal, "I want you to study my personal stock portfolio and liquidate two million. Today."

"What on earth for, Mother? That's crazy! If you need two million, take it out of the company!"

"No, this money must come from my personal stock portfolio. You two gentlemen get together this afternoon and decide which stocks to sell. I want two million dollars deposited in my personal account no later than Monday morning."

"Yes, Anna. I'll see to it immediately."

"Thank you, Hal. Now, if you don't mind, please take your coffee and wait for Charles in the solarium. There's a private family matter I want to discuss with him."

Hal picked up his briefcase and his coffee and left, closing the door behind him.

Charles looked hard at his mother. It was rare that she was abrupt with people, so he knew something was bothering her.

"Charles, I was aghast to learn that you gave Gilbert twelve million last year. That's obscene. Why wasn't I informed?"

"I thought I was carrying out your wishes. Years ago, while Dad was still alive, the last time Gil had serious—I mean really serious—problems, you instructed me in no uncertain terms to always make sure he had whatever money he needed and wanted." Charles's voice had become terse, angry.

"Yes," Anna said quietly, with less certainty, "I do recall, now that you mention it. I—I never guessed . . . or meant that it reach such outrageous—I mean really, twelve million is ridiculous. What on earth is he spending it on?"

"Jewels for his wife and mistresses. Homes. Renting a yacht. Villas. Gambling debts—"

Anna waved her hand at Charles to silence him. "I want it stopped! Immediately! Not another penny without my express authorization! I've dictated a memo to you and Phil. Barbara will deliver it tomorrow morning. Not one more penny without my authorization, for as long as I live. Do I make myself clear?"

"Mother, for chrissake, I thought I was doing your bidding. Do you think I liked signing those checks? I resented every last dollar of it! What has he ever done to earn one penny from Dunay corporations? Not one damned thing. All he's ever done is disgrace us—or try to."

"Okay, okay. I'm not blaming you, Charles. I never dreamed it had gotten so out of hand."

"Dad told me to do two things to protect you. That's all he was ever interested in, you know, protecting you. He told me to keep a dossier—literally to have a detective track Gil's activities. And he told me to make sure Gil had the money he needed. Somehow, Dad felt that would keep you safe from any harm Gilbert could cause."

Anna smiled, remembering her husband's love and protectiveness. It was true—sad, but true. He had never trusted Gilbert, and he had been right not to.

"You look exhausted, Mother. Don't you think it's time for lunch and a bit of a nap?"

"I wish. I've so much to do, so very much yet to do."

"You've got my curiosity up. What the hell do you need two million dollars for by Monday?"

Anna smiled a broad smile, and her eyes twinkled for the first time that morning. "I've a wonderful surprise for you, a wonderful surprise for all of us—and I shan't let you wheedle it out of me. Now, go back to the office and find that two million in my stock portfolio."

After a light lunch and an hour's nap, Anna greeted her personal lawyer, Adam Grenville. She had dozens of lawyers on her corporate payroll, including her grandson Brad. But the business of making a will called for someone outside the family, someone she had known and trusted for two dozen years. She had prepared herself for the meeting by making long lists on a yellow legal-size pad, for dozens and dozens of pages.

After they exchanged warm, affectionate greetings, Anna began. "Tell me, Adam. Can I leave Gilbert a specific sum of money and prevent him from contesting the will?"

"Very simple. We'll put in an *in terrorem* clause, which will prevent all of your heirs from contesting any part of the will in any court. If they contest it, they lose whatever you have bequeathed them. You're not planning on cutting him out altogether, are you?"

"No. But I'm leaving him considerably less than he thinks he should get. I want to be sure he can't break the will."

"No problem. Leave it to me."

"About the houses, the four of them. Does it make more sense to leave them to the grandchildren in the will or to turn over title now?"

"Might as well leave them in the will. You'll have to pay either gift taxes or estate taxes. Uncle Sam will get his due either way."

"Yes. That's fine. Now, about the jewelry. Can I simply give a few pieces away privately?"

"For the record, you didn't ask that question and I didn't answer it. But yes, in the privacy of your bedroom, give them individually anything you wish to give them. The sooner, the better."

"Fine."

"May I see those lists?"

Anna handed him the yellow sheets. She had outlined in detail various bequests to her grandchildren, to her niece and nephews, to her three brothers and her sister Sasha, to Charles, Emily, and Gilbert.

"I would like to videotape a summary of my will tomorrow morning. Will you arrange it?"

"My goodness, Anna, that's a bit quick."

"My doctors have told me I may not come home from the hospital."

"Oh, Anna, dear Anna, I'm so very sorry! But we must hope and pray for the best."

"Exactly. In the meantime, I want to videotape it so that I can explain in my own words why I have done things the way I have. Please, Adam, see if you can't arrange a videotaping? Tomorrow morning, as I must go to Pennyfield in the afternoon."

"I'll do my best." Adam sighed. "I have a friend, maybe I can get him to come over. . . . I'll call you this evening."

He stayed a few minutes more, then rose, kissed Anna's hand, and took his leave. She watched the fire glow in the fireplace and wrapped herself tightly in the mohair blanket. As she drifted into an uneasy sleep, her last thought was to devise a plan to prevent Gilbert from winning his Senate race. Cutting off money was not sufficient. . . .

"Charles, I'm sorry to bother you so late at night, but I've something I must discuss with you, or I won't sleep tonight. Please call me back on your secure line."

"What is it, Mother?"

"Don't be alarmed. I must ask you to do something that no one else can ever know about."

Two seconds later, the phone in Anna's bedroom rang. Twenty years before, when they had been faced with employee sabotage, they had installed secure phones in each of their homes and private offices. No one could listen in, and the lines were swept for bugs every other month.

"Now, what is it, Mother?"

"I hate to ask you to do this, especially because it will take up much of your personal time. You mentioned you had collected a dossier on Gilbert."

"Yes?"

"I want you to photocopy it tomorrow. Don't ask a secretary to do it. No one must ever know about this. Take one copy and put it in a three-ring black notebook. And if you wouldn't mind, do a two-or-three-page summary at the front, listing each 'escapade,' the date, witnesses, and so forth."

"Mother, what do you have in mind?"

"That's my business. Put your copy in your safe, and bring my copy to Pennyfield early Saturday morning. I will keep it in my own safe, after I read it."

⊠ Chapter 3

Anna woke up Friday morning free of pain for the first time in weeks. Today the children are arriving, she thought. Today I am going to Pennyfield Manor. She picked up the phone to summon Josephine to bring her breakfast and newspapers, then settled herself back against her pillows. The thought of going to Pennyfield made her heart soar. It was like getting ready to go on a vacation.

Shortly after lunch and after the videotaping session, Antonio finished packing the station wagon and Marc carried Anna's small bag to the limousine. They drove leisurely out Massachusetts Avenue to Goldsboro, then onto River Road. Anna gazed absently out the window at the early spring flowers while her mind flew back to the days in 1958 when she and Senator Albert Landow were planning their "country home" in Potomac.

At that time, the mansion was magnificent beyond anything that existed in the Washington area. The architect, famous for his Williamsburg restorations, had built a Colonial-style, dual-winged manor house of handmade brick high on a cliff overlooking the Potomac River. It had taken three years from the time they purchased the property until it was fully furnished and they moved in. She had never forgotten the tone of awe in Albert's voice when he had said, "Anna, this is your masterpiece! It is by far the most exquisite residence I've ever seen."

"We've built it for our grandchildren," she had replied, even though at that time only Larissa and Elliot had been born.

"We'll have holiday dinners and birthday parties and sweet six-teen parties. And we'll give weddings in the grand ballroom."

She had designed it with her hoped-for grandchildren in mind, creating one wing for the children and their nannies and one wing for adult guests. Her own second-floor master suite not only had a large bedroom with a small deck overlooking the river, but a sitting room, a bathroom with a sunken tub, and a private study. A staircase spiraled down to the magnificent cherry-paneled library, which she had filled with leather and gilt-edged editions of the classics.

Later, she had added a tennis court for Albert and Charles and a swimming pool for Gilbert, Winslow, and the grandchil-dren. Finally, she had added stables for the magnificent Thoroughbreds she and Emily had delighted in racing at Lau-rel, Pimlico, and Bowie, and occasionally riding themselves.

The two cars turned off River Road onto a two-mile-long private drive heading directly toward the river. It was lined on both sides with tall old sugar maples and a freshly painted white board fence.

Her heart leaped once more when they stopped in front of the classic, perfectly balanced Georgian mansion. She smelled box-wood and burning pine smoke, which drifted down from the six chimneys.

"Oh, it's good to be home!" Anna said as Antonio opened the door for her. She stepped inside the immense marble hall with its double-wide staircase and smiled approvingly at the huge vase of lilies in the center of the Lalique cactus table. *And to think this all belongs to me, a frightened little girl from Pinsk! Look at this home! I still have to pinch myself to make sure it's real!*

Josephine led her to the elevator at the rear of the entrance hall. "Would you like tea in your study, Madame?"

"No, I'd like my tea out on the terrace. I want to enjoy the birds and flowers and the peace of the river before the children arrive." She turned back to Marc. "You mustn't forget to pick up Sonia and Karine. They'll be coming on the six o'clock shut-tle."

While the young people were arriving, unpacking, and catch-ing up with one another, Anna spent most of Saturday poring over the dossier Charles had delivered early that morning.

She hand-wrote notes to be given out Sunday night to various family members, and she napped so that she would be fresh for the "jeans" party with the young ones that evening.

She fretted and stewed, thinking of Gilbert. He was her son. She loved him dearly. But she also understood him. Then suddenly, a plan, full-blown, formed: she knew precisely how she would prevent Gilbert from being elected to the Senate—without publicly embarrassing either him or the rest of the family.

And she also knew how she would prevent him from ever contesting her will.

For the first time in days she felt in control, and after a quick glass of Harvey's in her sitting room, she descended the marble staircase and made her entrance into the glassed-in porch, where a large circular table had been set with a red-and-white-checked cloth and candles in old Chianti bottles. Sonia had turned the room into an Italian trattoria.

The grandchildren were gathered around the white, weathered-wood bar at the far end of the L-shaped porch. They stood to greet her, kiss her one more time, and exclaim over her "jeans."

"Bub's definition of *informal* has always been different from ours," Brad announced as he hugged her and checked out her pearl-gray cashmere knit slacks, pullover, and knee-length cardigan.

"Wow, Gram, that's Gloria Sachs at her best!" exclaimed Karine.

"Right you are, Karine. How do you like my new jewelry?"

Elliot and Cheray looked at one another and grinned with pride. Anna was wearing an Indian necklace of coral, turquoise, and silver that they had brought her that afternoon, along with matching earrings and two Indian braclets they had given her previously.

As Scot kissed her cheek, Anna said, "I do hope you'll play for me tonight. I'd so love to hear some Gershwin."

"After dinner, Gram. Anything you want. We might even get Jen to sing some Italian love songs."

Sweet, petite, deep violet-eyed Jen stepped forward to kiss Anna. She had been able to get out of her Saturday rehearsal after all. She was the shyest of the group, but when she stepped on a stage and the music started, she became a different person:

animated and confident, with her voice that made your heart skip a beat. Claude would have been so proud of her.

Anna turned around to give Cheray a kiss. Dear girl, when she had walked into the house, the minute Elliot was out of earshot, Cheray had whispered her secret to Anna. Each of them had now told Anna the secret, and each didn't know the other had.

Meanwhile, Elliot had staked out his territory. "Bub, can I have the first toast after dinner tomorrow? As you know"—he winked—"I have a very special announcement to make."

"Of course. But your dad and Uncle Gil will want equal time." How did I manage to raise a family where everyone wants to give after-dinner speeches, even—no, especially—the women!

Anna eyed the huge display of shrimp, crab claws, and lobster that sat on the far end of the bar. Sonia and Elliot and Rick were devouring the shrimp.

"Sonia sweetheart," she began, trying to sound testy, "since when has this kind of seafood—from Luck's caterers—been Italian? Elliot and Rick, you shouldn't be eating so much shrimp—you know it's very high in cholesterol!"

"C'mon, Bub, no sermons tonight. After all, we don't eat like this every night," Elliot admonished her.

"Doesn't everyone look wonderful, Bubby? Even Rick?" Sonia enthused.

"Yes, indeed. The men look like *menschen,* and the women look like they should star in your movies."

"Yeah, I wish I could convince this big cowboy here to give me three months of his life." Sonia playfully punched her brother Elliot.

"Sonia, get real! Can you imagine the crap I'd take back in Albuquerque from the real estate people if I played in one of your flicks, not to mention the guys I hang out with at the rodeos?"

At that moment Brad joined the group. "I keep telling you, Sis, I'll do a screen test anytime you want. Every time you put out a casting call, I call your people, but they aren't interested. Do you know how miserable it is to be the only Dunay with no talent, not one drop of talent?"

"My heart breaks for you, little brother," Elliot teased as he looked up to his six-foot-four younger brother. "You're going to be general counsel of Dunay in two or three years. You're going to end up with the whole enchilada. Isn't that right, Bub?"

Anna put her arm around Brad's waist and squeezed him. "I don't have one iota of talent either, Brad, but together you and I will conquer the world!" Then she looked at Elliot and laughed. "Do you remember that I stopped speaking to you for a month when you turned down Harvard for the University of New Mexico? You wanted to be a professional baseball player, of all things! You're the one who turned down the whole enchilada!"

"And," Elliot rejoined, "if I hadn't been so stubborn, had some ideas of my own, we wouldn't own the properties we do in the Southwest today, either, Bub. So aren't you glad I was stubborn?"

"I have had . . . occasion to ponder it. You're even beginning to get back on my good side these days, Elliot. It's taken a while, but you're getting there."

They both knew she was thinking about that expected great-grandchild.

"I'm so stuffed, I may not fit into my dress tomorrow," Sonia announced as she put down her napkin. "Wasn't this a great idea? Hey, you guys—how about giving some credit where credit's due?"

"That reminds me, Gram," Larissa said quickly, "I still need to pick out a dress. I hope you have something that will fit me."

Anna smiled at her oldest grandchild. She was, at first glance, the least attractive of her eight grandchildren. But the other seven were magnificent creatures. By ordinary standards, Larissa was lovely-looking. She was what she was: a poet, a dreamer, a writer who thought not one minute about clothes. She wore her caramel-colored hair long and natural—wash-and-wear style, the girls called it. She didn't use a drop of makeup. Anna had always believed this was a reaction to her mother Winslow, who was always perfectly coiffed, made up, and dressed to the hilt no matter what time of day. And she knew it infuriated Winslow that Larissa would not make the slightest effort toward glamour or sophistication.

At that moment, Rick, her youngest and most outrageous grandchild—a rock star, for goodness' sake!—stood up to make a toast. As he was tapping his wineglass for attention, Elliot said to Anna, "At least he doesn't wear an earring—and he prefers females!"

And he's the most politically conscious of the bunch, Anna thought as he began his toast.

"Gram, as the youngest member of this family, I want to thank you for creating the happiest memories of my childhood. I can't remember a time when we didn't spend the summer with you and Gramps at Rehoboth Beach, and Thanksgiving and Christmas in Aspen. I know I speak for all of us when I say thanks for the wonderful time, for your never-failing love and understanding. Thanks for the memories—as Bob Hope would say!" Everyone clapped and sipped their wine as Rick sat down.

Sonia stood up. "Guys, I've had a bit too much to eat and drink. But I'm still sober enough to know that it's time for the girls to retire upstairs to Bubby's closet."

"Hurray!" Karine interrupted.

"You fellows can do whatever men did in the eighteenth century, when the women went upstairs to powder their noses."

Sonia then took Cheray by the arm and said, loud enough for everyone to hear, "Now the fun begins. We go shopping in Bubby's bedroom!"

Elliot, seated to the right of Anna, helped her up from her chair. "You'd better go protect your property from those scavengers."

"No, no." She laughed. "They can have whatever they want. I'm delighted I have things they'd like to wear." She watched Scot. He was making his way toward the piano in the family room, as promised.

Anna and the men followed Scot. He played several Gershwin numbers, a Chopin prelude, and modern jazz, then turned the piano over to Rick, who played his own compositions. Actually, quite well, Anna decided.

"How 'bout some poker?" Elliot asked the men, and Anna felt that was a cue for her to excuse herself. "I'd better see what those girls are up to."

As she reached the entrance to the elevator, she met Antonio coming from the kitchen, carrying a tray bearing two bottles of champagne.

"Where are you taking that, might I ask?"

"Miss Sonia called down to the kitchen. The young ladies need refills."

"If you ask me, I think they've had enough already!"

Antonio smiled, almost intimately, at Anna. With a plea in his eyes and a lowered voice he said, "Madame, the young people are taking your illness very hard, and they are trying to be brave. You must understand the pressure they feel, they are so very worried."

"Oh, all right, all right! Give them all the champagne they want. But mind you, I don't approve of all this drinking!" She tried to sound harsh and imperial, but she was having difficulty blinking back tears at the thought of the children trying to be brave. Had there ever, in the history of the world, been a grandmother more loved, more blessed, than she?

Antonio and Anna arrived at the "closet"—actually, a large bedroom filled with racks and racks of suits, dresses, gowns, and dozens of photograph albums—at the same moment. They heard shrieks of laughter and Karine's loud voice doing an imitation of Anna's affected British accent:

"Excellency, I've a word or two to say to you! What do you mean, wait until the Russian soldiers reach Berlin? That's outrageous! We'll bloody well march on Berlin immediately!"

"Can't you just hear Bub telling Litvinov off?" chimed Sonia.

Anna entered the room followed by Antonio.

"Actually, it was at a cocktail party at the Russian embassy, and I was a guest. Only half-joking, I told the Russian ambassador something like this: 'You goddamned Communists better get it out of your head that you're going to take over the world! After we saved you from the Nazis!' " Everyone gasped. She had their full attention.

Anna sniffed suspiciously, thinking she smelled cigarette smoke, which was strictly forbidden in her home. She surveyed the scene. Larissa and Jen were lying stomach down on the floor poring over photograph albums. Dressed in the suit Anna had worn the day she'd had lunch with Winston Churchill, Karine wore an old wig of Anna's and on top of that, Anna's black Persian lamb hat and matching fur muff. Sonia, meanwhile, was standing in front of the three-way mirror holding the gown Anna had worn to the White House to meet the King and Queen of England.

Cheray sat on a folding chair, taking it all in, with Anna's sable coat draped over her lap. Obviously, she had been trying it on.

Josephine hung up all the clothes as the girls took them off. And everyone, even Josephine, was drinking champagne. Antonio walked around the room refilling their glasses.

"Bub," Sonia broke the stunned silence, "this dress is horrible, ugly! I can't believe you wore it to meet the King and Queen."

"You must remember the times. It was 1939. King George VI and Queen Elizabeth came on a state visit, and it was the last really big festive party before the whole world was engulfed by war. But already fabric was scarce. And I didn't have any money then, none to speak of, so I bought copies of European magazines and took them to a little Italian seamstress at Fifteenth and Irving. She made my clothes—that gown, for example. At the time it was really quite lovely, and I felt good in it."

"Gram, this suit amazes me. It's so perfect, even today. David Hayes could have designed it!" enthused Karine.

Anna looked at the beautifully tailored glen plaid suit Karine was taking off. She had purchased it in 1941 and she had felt so special in it that she had asked one of the Capitol photographers to take a picture of her in it.

"Not only did I wear that suit the day we had Churchill for lunch, I wore it for Roosevelt's fourth inauguration, which, incidentally, for security reasons was held on the White House back porch." Her voice became quiet. "And then twelve weeks later he was dead and my dear, dear friend Harry Truman became President. What awful times those were."

"Was Truman your favorite President, Gram?" Larissa asked, her owlish glasses slipping from their perch on top of her head to her nose.

"I knew him best. I'd known him ever since he came to the Senate. He was a very personable man—always inquired about Claude, what was I hearing from him, and so forth. But I also felt great affection and admiration for Kennedy. And for Roosevelt, too—even though the way he abandoned the Jews during the war is unpardonable—a black mark on his presidency!"

"Gram, tell me about this dress. It's truly magnificent! I didn't think you liked Bill Blass."

Anna smiled in memory at the shocking-pink-satin-and-black-velvet ball gown Karine was holding. "I only wore that dress once, and it's a delicious story. President Johnson was nearing the end of his presidency. He'd announced he wouldn't run in 'sixty-eight because of the Vietnam war, and Humphrey was already busy campaigning. Lady Bird and Lyndon held a dinner upstairs at the White House to raise private money for the LBJ Library. They flattered us by keeping the guest list small and holding the dinner upstairs in the family living quarters. This particular night they had invited fifteen couples, we were included. So fifteen women had spent the day at the beauty shop. Each had chosen her most expensive, most elegant dress for this terribly special occasion. And three of us—three out of fifteen—showed up at that dinner wearing the exact same gown. I remember reaming Blass out the next day. And I've never bought another since. Can you imagine?"

"Gram, after you're well, completely recovered from the operation, could I come and stay with you and interview you on tape?" Larissa pleaded. "These are exactly the kind of anecdotes I love, and you'll never write them down."

"That sounds like fun. You'll have to jog my memory, though, I've forgotten so much."

Sonia chimed in, "If you do that, Larissa, please make a duplicate tape for me. It would be great resource material for my films."

"That reminds me—there's something serious I'd like to discuss with you girls. I've got so many books, records, diaries, letters—you know, I'm a pack rat, I've saved everything over the years, and I've got to decide what to do with it."

"Oh, Bub, don't talk that way. We know you're going to get well, and we only want you. We don't want your things." As Sonia's eyes filled with tears, she blinked them back.

Anna patted her hand, then said, "Look, you silly girls, I know I'm going to get well this time. But I *am* eighty-one years old, and I'm not going to last forever. So together we must decide how to dispose of . . . all this memorabilia."

"I want your books," Larissa immediately stated.

"You'll have to fight Brad and Scot and me, too, for some of them!" Sonia answered her cousin.

"Wait! There are thousands of volumes—some duplicates, even—between the Connecticut house, the Kalorama house, and the library here. I think Larissa should have first choice of all the fiction, including the first editions. Brad and Scot can split up the nonfiction—it's mostly history and politics. And I don't know what you want, Sonia."

"I'd like some of the fiction and some of the history."

"Perhaps what I'll have to do is ask your cousin Sidney to mediate the division of my library. But I do feel that Larissa, our very own novelist, should have first dibs."

Karine made her claim. "I'd like your clothes, Gram, especially the ones in this room. I love the way you've labeled them, so I know which events you wore them to and the year."

"Yes, Karine, I intend for you to have my clothes."

"But I could use some of them for my movies," Sonia interjected.

"Sonia, Sonia, what am I going to do with you? I'm sure that Karine will loan you whatever you need for a movie."

"I will, Sonia, don't worry."

"Now, what about you Jen? You're being mighty quiet over there in that corner."

"I'd like your records, especially opera, the real old ones of Caruso and Lily Pons. All those."

"That's what I thought you'd like. But I expect Scot and Rick will want some of the instrumental music, so maybe Sidney will help you sort it all out."

"And Gram?"

"Yes, Larissa?"

"I'd like all the photograph albums, the diaries, the letters, all the political stuff."

"Maybe we should hire an archivist to sort it all out, then leave it in your custody, with the idea that any of the others can borrow it when they have a need for it. I don't know what else to do, my dear. Both you and Sonia—and for that matter, the men too—have legitimate reasons to want those things."

"Cheray, what do you think Elliot would want?" It bothered Anna that Cheray was so quiet. She probably felt overwhelmed by all the Dunays.

"You should ask him, but I'd guess he'd like anything having to do with Gramps. Gramps is really his all-time hero."

"See, that's the problem," Larissa protested. "Elliot lives in New Mexico, I live here, and we both want the same historical material."

"Bub?"

"Yes, Jen."

"Were you in love with Gramps at Yalta?"

Anna's heart froze as she looked at Jen. She was studying the box of pictures taken at the Yalta conference. Then she locked eyes with Sonia, terror gripping her. . . .

Karine saved the day. "Of course not, stupid. If you'd ever taken a history course, you'd know that Yalta took place during the Second World War. Gram was married to Grampa Claude then!"

Karine doesn't know. None of the grandchildren know except Sonia. I must speak to their fathers about telling them the truth. They're old enough now to hear it and understand.

Just then, they heard a knock on the door, followed by Elliot's booming voice: "Are you all decent? I've come to claim my bride. It's her bedtime." Elliot sauntered into the room, and Cheray rushed over to join him.

"Bub, promise me you won't banish me to the basement servant's quarters tonight. We're officially married, see?" He held up Cheray's left hand, displaying her rings.

"Cheray, darling, don't believe any of those awful stories he tells you. I wasn't a warden. I was just trying to save him for you—for the right woman!"

"The truth is that Bub used to hire detectives to prowl the halls and make sure there wasn't any illicit bed-hopping when I brought a girl home."

"Bosh!" Anna said sternly, but with sparkling eyes.

"Yeah, and now she wishes some of us would bring some men home! Isn't that right, Bub?" Sonia teased.

"Sonia darling, the ballroom is awaiting your wedding. It has been for nearly thirty years now! Since before you were born. So get on with it!" Anna stood. "And now, my dears, I'm off to bed, and I suggest the same for you. And no more champagne. It gives one a horrible hangover."

"How would you know, Bub?"

Elliot's teasing voice made her heart glad. How he loved to rile her, to make her angry! He was the only one who could get away with it, and he knew it.

"I was young once, not so long ago, and I loved—absolutely *loved*—champagne." She kissed both Cheray and Elliot lightly as she passed them on her way out the door.

Sonia carried a tray of empty champagne flutes, two empty bottles, and an ashtray into the kitchen. Then she joined the others in the family room. Elliot and Cheray had changed their minds and come back downstairs. It was nearly midnight. Sonia was bone tired.

Brad looked up at her from his perch on the fireplace hearth as she sank into one end of the huge rectangular-shaped sofa beside her sister Jen. "How is Bubby? Were we overdoing it, with all our teasing?" Brad asked.

"She's awfully tired, but I tucked her in, and her major concern was that you and Scot spend the night here rather than try to drive back to your apartments after drinking so much. The butterscotch bedroom is available."

"Yeah," Scot drawled from the opposite side of the sofa, "I'm really too tired to drive tonight."

"That means we'd have to get up early to get the golf clubs," Brad answered, already yawning.

"It must be pussy paradise down there at the Watergate for you guys. Two great pads, a Porsche and a Jag to entice the women with. Oops! Sonia's giving me dirty looks, I guess I'm not supposed to talk that way in front of our little sister." Elliot, who had one arm draped around his wife and the other around Jen, slurred his words. He was more than a little drunk.

"Jen, tell me, please tell me," Rick teased, "that you're not a virgin, not *still* a virgin. I can't stand it. You're twenty-three, for chrissake!"

Jen threw a pillow at him, hitting him squarely in the face. "Mind your own business!"

"Hey, I like that!" Scot cheered.

"I've got an idea: let's play Truth, like we used to at Rehoboth Beach. Everyone's sworn to tell the truth, and my question is, 'Who are you sleeping with now?' We'll start with smart-ass Sonia!" As Elliot said it, he reached over Jen's shoulders to give Sonia an affectionate pinch.

"Like hell, I'll tell you! I wouldn't tell you if I was sleeping with Richard Gere!"

"Only you, Elliot," Karine said with disgust, "would be vulgar enough to suggest such a thing. Ugh! You're disgusting!"

"Fuck off, you guys. I was only kidding." Elliot shrugged, gave up on them, and nuzzled Cheray's neck.

"Well, aren't we going to speculate about the will? It's the only thing Gil and Winslow have on their minds these days." Scot's sarcasm reverberated through the room.

"You work there every day—you probably know more than anyone else," Elliot answered.

"No way. Dad calls me about six times a day, and Mom calls me at least twice a day to ask what rumors I've heard. It's wonderful—all this attention I'm suddenly getting from my parents."

"Nothing would make me happier," Rick said slowly and bitterly, "than if Gram cut them off without a nickel. I'd love it."

"That's not nice!" Karine admonished Rick. "You shouldn't say that. You shouldn't talk that way about our parents."

Sonia was surprised to hear Karine scold Rick. The two of them had always been close. Ever since they had all been toddlers, it seemed, the patterns of relationships that had formed in that family had not altered through the years. Larissa had always been the loner. Karine and Rick, both exuberant by nature, had been pals. When they were in the same physical location, they were inseparable. Karine always took up for Rick. And Scot, when he felt like being sociable, sought out Larissa. They were lonely children, all of Uncle Gilbert and Aunt Winslow's children were lonely.

"God damn it, I'm entitled to my feelings! And that's how I feel about Winslow and Gilbert!" The intensity of Rick's bitterness startled even Sonia. "We aren't even allowed to call our parents Mom and Dad like most children—it might ruin Winslow's image!"

Sonia didn't want to hear all this. "You know, you guys, Bubby is going to be fair to everyone. There's no reason for there to be any suspense over her will. She's going to preserve the assets of Dunay corporations for generations to come. All of us will be very well taken care of. But we'll be expected to work and make something of ourselves."

"Yeah, everyone in this family works—except Gilbert and Winslow!" Rick shot back. "So why doesn't she cut him off without a nickel?"

Sonia realized they were all looking at her, expecting her to know the answer. It had long been understood, though never discussed among them, that Sonia always knew what was going on in Anna's head and heart. Some kind of special bond seemed to exist between them—it did exist, in fact—and the entire family looked to Sonia to interpret Anna for them.

Cautiously, she formulated her answer. "Anna . . . would never hurt anyone in her family . . . needlessly. Nor would she do anything that would bring public disgrace or ridicule to any member of the family. And whatever you may feel about Gil and Winslow . . . he is her son. *He is her blood. We are all Dunays together.*" Then, as an afterthought, she added, "It's even possible that she blames herself for his character flaws. Have you ever thought of that?"

"What I don't understand," Larissa began tentatively, "is why Gilbert has always hated Gramps so much."

"Yeah," Scot joined in. "He always said Gramps married Anna for her money. But if that's true, why did he leave each of us a trust fund when he died? He could have left his entire fortune to his own children."

Am I the only one who knows? Is it possible none of them has ever guessed—or been told? Sonia asked herself.

"Rick," she said, to change the subject as quickly as possible," please don't smoke anymore. This room already smells terrible, and you know that the idea of any of us smoking really upsets Bubby."

"I hear enough lectures from her. I don't need one from you too!" Rick had become testy.

"I don't know about the rest of you guys, but I'm going to take this gorgeous creature up to my bed and ravish her." Elliot stood and pulled Cheray up from the sofa. "What's everyone doing tomorrow?"

Karine stood up, too, yawned, and answered, "Gram's made special arrangements for all the women to go to her beauty shop tomorrow, even though it's Sunday. She's ordered the works— hair, nails, toenails, facials."

Scot stood and touseled his sister's Liza Minnelli haircut. "And what, may I ask, will they do with this? Shampoo it and charge you thirty dollars?"

Karine hugged her tall brother Scot, then walked toward the foyer. "Tomorrow night should really be something! A drama! The stuff of soap operas!"

"Don't forget our rehearsal at four at Scot's apartment— that's Jen, Rick, Scot, Brad and me. Okay?" Sonia reminded them.

Elliot turned back to Sonia, who was gathering up dirty

glasses. "I've got business meetings with Dad all day. I trust you girls will not let Cheray get into too much trouble."

"Don't you worry," Larissa said as she put her arm through her new cousin-in-law's. "We'll give her a full briefing on your escapades before she met you!"

"Oh, God! I keep forgetting we've got a writer in the family. You're probably taking notes for your next novel."

"Right you are!"

How wonderful it is that we cousins love one another so much, Sonia thought as she and Jen carried the dirty glasses and ashtrays to the kitchen. And especially in our family, Elliot and Brad and Jen—and dear Doug, dear beloved Doug, how we miss you. And—in our family—we even love our parents, too, thank God! We are so blessed, and we take it so for granted. . . .

She reached over and hugged Jen. "Thanks for helping me. I didn't want the staff to see that mess tomorrow when they've so much else to do."

"Ah, c'mon, Sonia, you're just playing little mother, like you always have. I know you—you love it. You can't fool me."

Sonia loved her little sister. Jen was so innocent, so young, so vulnerable.

"Sonia, tell me, you know everything. Why *did* Uncle Gil hate Gramps so much? I thought Gramps was *so* wonderful!"

⊠ Chapter 4

Anna sat in the Queen Anne wing chair in front of the pale marble fireplace in the sitting room of the master bedroom suite, savoring the final, delicious moments of anticipation. Already she heard car doors closing, and then the muffled greetings in the great hall. She had instructed Antonio to send everyone upstairs to the ballroom, where cocktails would be served on the forty-foot terrace, four floors above the granite cliff overlooking the Potomac River. It was, to her mind, the most magnificent view of the river in Washington, her favorite place to begin an evening, especially at this time of year.

She smiled at the lovely bouquet of lavender roses that filled the Baccarat bowl on the table next to her chair. Emily, knowing they were her favorite flower, had sent them over that afternoon. They were the perfect shade to highlight her blue and lavender brocade bedroom suite. This room was one of her favorites, small and restful, one of the few truly intimate rooms in this huge house.

Lovingly, she caressed the lace skirt of her long tanzanite-colored gown. It was one of the most beautiful dresses she had ever owned, even if Karine, her very own granddaughter, had designed it. She looked at the seventeen-carat flawless pear-shaped diamond on her hand; she wouldn't give that one away, not anytime soon. It was her most precious piece of jewelry, her most emotionally precious.

She picked up the phone, and Antonio answered immediately. "Please ask my sister and her daughter to come up to my sitting room, Antonio."

So it begins.

"Exquisite!" Sidney gushed as Anna stood so that they could admire Karine's design.

"I must say you look marvelous tonight. I can't really believe you're ill!" exclaimed Sasha, looking trim as ever and not a day over sixty, though she was nearly eighty.

"The children do it for me. Having them here the last two days has been a joy." *How I do carry on—just like any Jewish grandma!* "I wanted to see the two of you before the party is in full swing. I have a gift for you, something very precious to me that I want you to have now, and then give to Sidney," she said to Sasha. She handed her sister a large velvet box and signaled for her to open it immediately.

"Oh, oh my!" Sasha exclaimed as she picked up a long necklace of black and imperial jade beads, interspersed with tiny rodelles of paved diamonds. Suspended from the center was a large, intricately carved imperial jade pendant, bordered on four sides by paved diamonds in art deco style. With the necklace were matching earrings: a carved leaf of imperial jade that held a strand of four round diamonds, which in turn held a two-inch-wide polished imperial jade cylinder. "Anna," Sasha began, her eyes misting, "I remember when Albert gave you this. I was so envious! I've always loved jade."

Moved, Anna responded, "I know, dear sister. Louis has seen

to it that you are blessed with everything the world has to offer, but I wanted you to have something of mine that I know you've always admired. And now for you, Sidney." She handed Sidney a large royal-blue box. Sidney opened it, gasped, and said, "Are you sure you want to give this to me? Now?"

"Yes, my dear Sidney. You've been so loyal, so fine a niece. Whenever I called, you always came running. You were always there for me, you always produced the impossible immediately . . . and I wanted to see . . . your pleasure. I know this has always been your favorite of my jewels." Anna picked up the heavy Bulgari design and placed it around Sidney's neck. Centered at the bottom was a huge emerald, suspended from four ropes of cabochon sapphires. Six cabochon rubies, surrounded by tiny diamonds, wound up the side of the necklace. "The problem with a dog collar like this is that it makes your neck ache when you leave it on for any length of time. I always get a headache when I wear it. But I hope you'll love it—and think of me—and remember my deep affection for you."

"Oh, Anna, how can I ever thank you? You've *made* my career—without you I'd never be the success I am. You're so terrific!"

She had to get them out of the room before she herself became overly emotional. "Now stop this, both of you, or you'll ruin your makeup! Run along, back upstairs, and ask Charles and Emily to come down."

While she waited for Charles and Emily, she poured herself a sherry and sipped it slowly, savoring the surprise and pleasure in Sasha's eyes. Sasha, who had had luxuries before Anna did without working for them. Sasha, who in their early lives had seemed destined to have everything Anna would never have.

"Come in," she called when she heard Emily's tentative knock. "Oh good, you've worn my favorite dress. I was hoping you would. I almost called you and asked you to." The dress was a confection of reembroidered white lace fitted to Emily's hips; a deep royal silk taffeta skirt billowed down to the floor.

"Mother, you're also stunning!" Charles exclaimed. "I can't believe this is the same woman I saw at eight o'clock this morning."

"Goes to show what makeup and a hairdo does for a woman. You should know that by now." She turned back to Emily. "Do

I have on too much blush? Karine insisted on doing my
makeup, but she may have overdone it. What do you think?"

"You look perfect, absolutely perfect. The children seem to
be having a hilariously good time, as always."

Anna silenced the small talk. "I have something for you,
Emily. I've been wanting to give these to you for a while, and I
decided tonight would be the right time. I want you to wear
these to the Opera Ball."

She handed Emily a deep-blue-velvet case, the kind Emily
had seen many times before, stamped TIFFANY on the top.

"Oh, my."

"Charles's father gave me these sapphires the year I was
chairman of the Opera Ball. Now, put them on—I want everyone to know I've given them to you. Besides, they're perfect
with your dress." Anna fastened the spectacular diamond and
sapphire necklace while Emily placed the matching earrings in
her ears and the bracelet and ring on her hand.

"And Charles, I have something for you too. But we need to
discuss it. Please pour yourself a drink, and let's sit a moment."

Emily hugged her quickly, then disappeared into Anna's
bathroom, clearly overcome with emotion.

Anna walked over to her desk and picked up a small envelope. She handed it to Charles. "This is the key and the combination to the door of a hidden vault in the wine cellar. You'll
need both to open it."

"I didn't know—"

"No one knew but your father and I. And the Pentagon."

Charles waited for Anna to continue. "In that small room
you will find all your father's logs, personal diaries, and World
War II papers. The Pentagon has already photocopied the ones
they want and confiscated the classified documents. There's so
much there—much of it of a very personal nature—notes on his
conversations with Presidents and foreign leaders, especially
military leaders when he was the Chief of Naval Operations.

"In his diaries he speaks quite candidly about his concern for
the future of our country, about Hitler and Stalin, his feelings
about Russia.

"You, Charles, are the only one in the family I feel safe en-
trusting these materials to. You decide whether you want to hire
a biographer, or maybe an archivist. You decide what to destroy. All the letters he wrote to me over a lifetime are there. I

can't bear to destroy them, but you may wish to. I rely totally on your discretion. Please make sure you remove that material from the house immediately if . . . if . . ."

"Yes, Mother, I understand. Don't worry about a thing, and" —he bent over and kissed her forehead— "I am deeply touched that you want me to be custodian of my father's place in history."

"That's it. Exactly!" She sipped her sherry. Emily had repaired her makeup and slipped quietly back into the room.

One more mission accomplished. There was still one last gift to give out before dinner. Then she would join the party already in full swing upstairs.

"Now, run along back to the party, and send that rascal son of yours and his bride in to see me."

Anna fought the urge to burst out with Elliot and Cheray's secret as she sent Charles and Emily back to the ballroom. Oh, how she would have loved to break the news to her beloved son that he was about to become a grandfather! But, no. That's Elliot's grand surprise, she thought, as the young couple breezed into the room.

"Jeez, Bub, Aunt Winslow's losing it over that jewelry you just gave Mom. She turned absolutely pea green!" Elliot was enjoying Winslow's envy. Anna felt a stab of pain in her abdomen. Was she being cruel? Perhaps it hadn't been a good idea— but what the hell, it was done. She had a perfect right to give her things to anyone she wished.

"You should see Aunt Winslow's dress. It's magnificent," Cheray gushed. "Givenchy. Red-silk organza. Strapless. She has the best body I've ever seen on a woman that age!"

"Please, Cheray, don't choose Aunt Winslow to emulate. She spends at least forty hours a week perfecting her face and body —aerobics, swimming, tennis, exercise, and diet. She's always tan and always thin. It's her obsession, the way most women today are occupied with careers. Her body *is* her career. But her mind is empty." I shouldn't say things like that. Behave yourself, Anna.

"I think she's mixed in a face-lift." Elliot snickered.

"Hush!" Anna scolded him.

She put her arm around Cheray's waist and led her over to her desk. "I have a small gift for you, my dearest, a very special gift. On our first wedding anniversary, Elliot's grandfather gave me this ring." Anna placed a seven-carat square-cut ruby ring on Cheray's right ring finger. "Now I want you to wear it and remember me."

Elliot picked up his wife's hand and looked at the ring. Softly, very softly he said, "Thanks, Bub, thanks. That means a lot to me."

Anna kissed them both, then added, "One more thing. I want my great-grandchild to live in the style a Dunay should. I'm planning on giving my homes to my granddaughters, Elliot. I'm telling you this now. Since you choose to live in New Mexico, I know you'd sell it if I gave you one. So I'm giving you this instead." she handed him a small white envelope. As he accepted it, he winked at Cheray. "See, I told you this was going to be an envelope party!"

On her seventieth, seventy-fifth, and eightieth birthdays, Anna had given each of her grandchildren a substantial check. They called such occasions "envelope parties" behind her back, but she had overheard them once, and now she understood what Elliot and Cheray had been anticipating—a check, perhaps for five thousand dollars.

Elliot looked stunned. "My God! Bub?"

"You should build a lovely home and furnish it."

"Bub, this would build ten mansions in Albuquerque!"

"Well, then invest what's left over, for your child. But first I want to be sure Cheray has exactly the home she wants. Don't you dare spend one penny of that money on investments before your home is absolutely complete and furnished. Do you understand me Elliot? Or I'll . . ."

He grinned his wicked grin at her, the grin he always turned on when she lectured him. "You'll what, Bub?"

"I don't like the way you take a wedding gift and invest it when you should be using it for a nice home for Cheray. Notice, my dear grandson, that that check is made out to Cheray too!"

"Okay, Bub, I promise. Not a penny in land until the house is finished. But it doesn't exactly have to be Pennyfield Manor."

"Of course not. But a nice home, a nice place to raise a family. A place to entertain your friends. With Dunay style. Damn it, Elliot, you know what I mean." She pinched his cheek. He could always rile her, and she loved him dearly.

At that moment Sonia burst into the room. "Bub, you'd better hurry up and join the party before it degenerates into a war!

Winslow is looking daggers at everyone and waiting for her royal summons!"

Anna laughed, put her sherry down, took one last look in her mirror, and sprayed a bit more Ferré perfume on her wrists. Locked arm in arm with Elliot, she made her way to the elevator.

He's still a devil, that one, she mused as she studied Elliot in his tux. Even a finely tailored tux couldn't mask his raging sexiness, the wicked raciness that emanated from him like musk. No one had ever exactly told her, but she had picked up enough family gossip to know that a steady procession of young women had made their way through his bedroom during his bachelor days—which had gone on entirely too long, to her way of thinking.

His wicked smile was followed a second later by a wink, the kind that had always melted her attempts at disciplining him and that reminded her of his grandfather—the sexiest, most charming and brilliant man she had ever known.

Somehow it had skipped a generation. Charles, for all his charm and intelligence, had a quieter, less disruptive personality. Elliot, like his grandfather, had a disturbing effect on every female he encountered.

Anna's glance passed to Cheray, resplendent and voluptuous in deep purple taffeta, which molded her curves, then flared out into a trumpet skirt. Her blue-black hair, deep-brown-velvet eyes, and light olive skin attested to her ancestry. She was a true Spanish beauty, and she seemed overly subservient to Elliot in Anna's presence. But others had told her that Cheray possessed a fiery temper.

Perhaps she had that perfect combination of glamour and personality that would protect Elliot from temptation. *God willing!* It's so hard for two people so attractive not to find temptation lurking around every corner.

Finally, her gaze rested on Sonia. Tonight she was every inch an heiress, a star. She had chosen a fantasy by Zandra Rhodes, a hand-painted silk chiffon gossamer gown in melting colors, ranging from pale blue to deepest turquoise, shot through with a dash of shocking pink and lightly beaded in aurora borealis crystals.

"Your gown is perfect for the Oscars!" She smiled up at

Sonia. "Only for that occasion, I think you must borrow my opals. You're old enough now to wear serious jewelry."

"But I love these earrings." She patted the small black opal studs that Anna had given her on her eighteenth birthday.

"Yes, my dear, but we can do better. And I do love your hair tonight. It's truly regal!" Sonia's flaming auburn hair had been sleekly combed up into a Gibson girl look, with a few tendrils escaping here and there. In the center of the topknot she had fastened a ceramic cabbage rose in opalescent aurora borealis. "Wherever did you get that hair ornament?"

"Do you approve? It's my one concession to fun. I got it at a little boutique in SoHo."

Anna smiled her approval just as the elevator door opened. Gilbert and Winslow were standing directly in front of them. "We were on our way to come and get you, Mother. We thought something might be wrong." Gilbert looked flustered.

Anna offered her cheek to be kissed, then turned to Winslow for her greeting. "That's some dress! I daresay it's French. Shame on you, Winslow! You should be wearing one of Karine's creations. All the best boutiques on Madison Avenue are carrying her designs now. And Neiman-Marcus is going to have a few things this spring." Before Winslow could say a word, she continued, "How do you like this dress? Karine designed it."

"It's beautiful. I'm so proud of her, Anna. But I like your necklace even better."

Instinctively, almost protectively, Anna reached for her necklace. The large tanzanite stone, ninety-six carats, was set in platinum and suspended from a necklace of a hundred and twenty diamonds. Her ear clips, with perfectly matched twelve-carat tanzanites, were held by diamond clips containing fourteen pear-shaped diamonds. Anna considered it the most perfectly designed jewelry Tiffany had ever created. It was the last major gift Charles's father had given her before his death.

"Oh, my goodness, Winslow! You have a jewelry collection that is unparalleled! You can't possibly want anything of mine." And with that, she whisked away into the ballroom.

The first thing her mind registered was the blazing Waterford chandeliers, then the sixteen matching sconces that lined the ivory walls. It was a ballroom in the grand tradition, right out of a European castle. She loved it. For a moment Anna imagined the room was filled with dancing couples, dressed in white tie and splendid ball gowns. Oh, the glittering parties she had given in this room! Every President except Nixon—no way would she ever invite that weasel into her home—had dined here. Heads of state, ambassadors, journalists, media stars— invitations to her home had been coveted second only to the President's invitations. Such gaiety and warmth and sumptuousness had filled this room. She heard and saw the past vividly. The music of Peter Duchin, the laughter, the mingled perfume of jasmine and roses and lilacs. But she hadn't given a party that elegant since . . . since . . .

She blinked back tears and at the same moment spied the video cameras, klieg lights, open Steinway, and ballroom chairs set up theater style. Anna knew instantly who to blame. "Sonia! What are you planning?"

"Oh, just a tiny program, a little surprise for you. And I decided to film it for posterity, that's all."

Anna tried to sound stern. "I hope you're not spending my investment in Colossal Pictures to do this! This is ridiculous!" Sonia and Elliot both laughed at her and led her across the ballroom, out onto the terrace, where all the guests were waiting.

When she entered, conversation stopped for a second, then applause and cries of "bravo" broke out. She mock-curtsied, beaming with happiness; then, seeing Karine watching her, she pirouetted like a model so all the crowd could admire her gown. In a very loud stage voice she announced, "Any of you ladies who would like to own dresses by America's hottest designer should speak to me. I can get it for you wholesale!"

They broke into laughter, clinked their glasses in salute to Anna, then continued their conversations. Antonio brought her a fresh sherry. She stepped to the left to greet her brother Joshua and his pudgy wife, Florence, whom she liked a great deal.

As she accepted their hugs and greetings, she heard the cascading sound of ethereal harp music. Antonio had remembered! For a dozen years now, she had hired a harpist to play during cocktails. Somehow the rippling music perfectly fit the scene of the meandering river, whatever its level of turbulence or quietude, and the soft rustling of the leaves of the very old, tall trees. A familiar emotion washed over her: Up here on this glorious terrace we are on top of Washington, on top of the Potomac, on top of the world.

"A magnificent sunset. Too bad you missed it!" Louis Bernstein announced as he kissed her. Louis, Sasha's husband, was one of the few male family members who had never played a direct role in Dunay corporations. Only when she had first formed the Trans-Continental Travel Agency in 1947 had she gone to him for financial help. Since then, she had never needed him; instead, they had limited their relationship to trading stock tips and occasional family trips together. He was, after all, the father of her favorite niece, Sidney.

She kissed her brother Samuel, a serious, deeply dedicated man who had for years overseen Dunay Hotels. Now, however, he was semiretired and Sasha's son Joel had taken the reins of the hotels.

And finally, her oldest brother, Al. Both Al and Sam were widowers now. Both had spent a lifetime with Dunay corporations, and both had made fortunes because of their devotion and loyalty to Anna.

"Bub, it's time to begin the program. Come, take your seat so we can get started." Sonia had her parents in tow, as well as Gilbert and Winslow. She led the five of them to the front of the ballroom, where she had placed name cards on the seats of the gold chairs. Anna sat front and center, flanked by Charles and Emily on one side and Gilbert and Winslow on the other. Shortly, all the other guests took their seats in the rows behind. Waiters refilled drinks, the chandeliers were dimmed, and Brad, at a signal from Sonia, stepped forward and picked up the microphone. It appeared that he was going to be master of ceremonies.

He looked directly at Anna and began. "Bubby, on this very special night, with all those you love most in the world assembled here, we've created a special entertainment. Now, don't worry. Antonio has known for days, and the staff is timing your banquet for after our performance. You see, we knew Dad and Uncle Gilbert would hog the spotlight after dinner, so we felt the only way the younger generation could get equal time was to plan our little surprise for now."

Anna shook her head in mock disgust, as if she were angry. She turned to Charles and said in a loud whisper, "Your Sonia thinks she's already running Pennyfield, giving orders to my staff! The nerve of her!" Then she broke into a wide smile.

"Bub," Brad continued, "we've brought in great entertainment from all over the world, as you'll see in a minute. But first, I'm going to introduce a man of great talent, but a talent the world will never recognize. Because you conscripted him for service with Dunay."

Anna nodded her head. Yes, Scot did have great musical talent. She remembered the arduous decision over whether he would go to Juilliard or get an MBA from Harvard. She had talked him into Harvard—had she done the right thing?

". . . will play two of Anna's favorites, *Rhapsody in Blue* and 'Claire de lune.' "

Scot entered from the right service entrance of the ballroom, looking exactly like a Wall Street executive should look. Then he smiled broadly at the audience, especially at Anna, and a bit of Gilbert's roguish look crossed his face. He took his blond coloring from his mother, and his tall, trim good looks came from her side, too, Anna thought. But his musical talent—ah, that he clearly had inherited from Claude.

Here he was, twenty-five already, and not a serious girl in sight. That bothered Anna. She would like to see all her grandchildren happily married, on their way both professionally and emotionally. Scot, like Brad, was every inch a businessman, a workaholic. It felt good to know she was leaving the control of her corporations to Charles, and after him to Brad and Scot. They both had good business sense.

As Scot stood and bowed after the Gershwin piece, Anna reached over Gilbert to pat Winslow's arm. "Aren't you just bursting with pride? He's so handsome and so talented. A wonderful son!"

Winslow smiled her first genuine smile of the evening. "I'm very proud—very, very proud of all of them."

Anna thought she detected a touch of mistiness in Winslow's eyes. So, she has feelings like a mother after all!

The quiet, beguiling opening of "Claire de lune" washed over Anna. She closed her eyes. Oh, when Claude had played that melody, it was as if he were making love to her—except his lovemaking was never that tender, that rhapsodic. Scot was much more musically talented than his grandfather Claude had been. . . . Yes, when she remembered Claude at all, she wanted to remember him playing that music.

". . . all the way from Santa Fe, one of America's great new opera stars. I have the joy, Bubby, of announcing to you and all our family that my very own little sister Jennifer has this past week signed a contract with the San Francisco Opera Company to sing the role of Micaela in *Carmen* next season."

The audience burst into applause, and Anna jumped up to hug Jennifer, who had made her entrance dressed in an exquisite yellow Japanese kimono and wig, complete with oriental combs. After the hug, Anna took the microphone from Brad: "And now *I* have an announcement to make: Everyone in this room is invited to Jen's opening performance. We'll take both company planes, and you'll all be my guests!"

She handed the microphone back to Brad. He pretended to look at Anna harshly: "Scot and I will have to look at the books and decide if you can afford that extravagance!" While the audience laughed, Anna sat back down and Brad continued his introduction.

"Tonight, Jennifer will sing Bubby's favorite aria, 'Un Bel Di' from *Madama Butterfly.*"

Jennifer was barely five foot two. Her eyes were the color of Anna's necklace, her skin was milky white, and her hair the darkest black—the same color, in fact, as the wig she was wearing.

" '*Un bel di vedremo* . . .' "

It was heaven. To think that her grandchildren had this kind of talent! To hear that soaring angelic voice—if only Jennifer's grandfather could hear her tonight!

Of all the performing arts, Anna's favorite had always been opera. The glorious music, the fabulous costumes—yes, Jennifer had been right to sing in costume—the spectacle, the drama, the dance—for her, opera combined the best of everything.

And I remember so vividly when I asked little Jen what she wanted for her eighth birthday, and she said, "Would you take me to the opera?" I took her the next Saturday, to see Madama Butterfly *in fact, and as we walked out of the opera house, with the profound seriousness of an eight-year-old, she looked up into*

*my face and announced, "When I grow up I'm going to be an
opera star."*

*And I had—so foolishly—answered, "But my dear child, a
voice like that is a gift from God. Only one person in ten million
can sing opera!"*

"I will, Bubby!"

And she had never wavered from that course.

"And now, all the way from London," Brad began as Jennifer rushed off, "we have one of the great rock stars of the
present day, one of the stars, you may recall, of the Live-Aid
concert for starving Ethiopians. I'm told by my sister Sonia that
he's the sexiest eligible man in the family—our very own super-
star, Rick."

Rick sauntered slowly toward the microphone. His walk was
arrogantly confident, and his smile, at first tentative, grew large
as he looked at Elliot. Anna turned around and watched Elliot
make a face at Rick from the second row.

"Shame on you!" she hissed.

When he reached the front of the piano, Rick took the microphone from Brad and smiled calmly at Scot, who was seated at
the piano ready to accompany him. "Gram, I don't want you to
get upset"—he paused—"or nervous." He paused again. "Dad
and Mom, I promise you'll like what I'm going to do—you'd
better, I've never practiced anything so much in my life."

Nervous laughter filled the room. Anna could feel the tension
that had descended over the front row begin to lift. *It's no
secret—we hate his music.*

"Scot and I have been practicing all afternoon. I'm told this
is one of your favorite songs from a show you saw back in the
fifties. And now I'll do my Ezio Pinza act."

The piano introduction began. Anna recognized it: "Younger
Than Springtime." There wasn't a sound in the room, nothing
but sighs, as Rick, standing directly in front of Anna, sang with
husky passion and perfect voice, the tender Rodgers and Hammerstein ballad.

*It's as if . . . foolish old woman that I am . . . it's as if
he's making love to me.*

Anna wiped that obscene thought out of her mind, understanding instantly the attraction he held for all the female fans
who screeched and reached and tugged and sighed and
screamed when he performed.

" ' . . . to me.' "

Gilbert was the first person on his feet, applauding with gusto, while his great-aunt Florence called from the second row, "Why don't you sing those songs all the time, Rick?"

"My sentiments exactly," Anna said as she turned to smile at Florence.

Rick bent down to kiss Anna's forehead, and then he shook hands with his father. "You were wonderful, Rick, really wonderful," Gil enthused.

Brad took the microphone back and held up his hand to quiet the applause, "Now, for the frosting on the cake. Jen"—who was that moment reentering the ballroom dressed in a one-shoulder Grecian chiffon in buttercup-yellow, her long black wavy hair brushed back off her face and lightly caressing her shoulders and back—"and Rick have agreed to sing a medly of three of Anna's favorite show tunes."

After lusty applause, Jen and Rick began singing "People Will Say We're in Love."

What a stunning couple they make. He's a "hunk," as the girls say, and she's such a petite, vulnerable little thing. . . . I'm so glad Sonia is filming this. . . . I'm bursting—just bursting. . . .

After more thunderous applause, they sang "I Have Dreamed" from *The King and I*, then ended with Brad introducing "Anna's all-time favorite song. She was at the National Theatre with Senator Landow on opening night back in 1957— 'Somewhere,' from *West Side Story*."

It is my favorite song. Favorite musical.

Anna closed her eyes, remembering the night she first heard it performed. She had been holding Albert's hand. But the song spoke directly to her heart. It spoke of her illicit love for Kurt.

Kurt—oh Kurt, if only you could be here tonight . . . you'd be so proud! Oh, Kurt, I love you so. I always have.

The applause was deafening. Everyone was standing. Anna reached into her evening bag for a hanky. How could they do this to her, really? How could they get her all emotionally worked up like this? And before dinner too! How would she ever make it through dinner?

"Mother, the show's over. Let's go downstairs. You can

thank the children later." Charles reached for her elbow to help her to her feet.

As she stood, she felt a sharp pain in her abdomen, then a dizzy whirling sensation in her head. And then everything went black.

▦ Part 2

Choose Life! 1909

Anna Dunay, the former U.S. Senator and founder of Dunay International, was rushed by helicopter to the George Washington University Hospital last evening, after she collapsed during a family dinner. A hospital spokesman reported her condition as critical but stable this morning.

—The Washington Post
"Style" Section

Chapter 5

Give me your tired, your poor,
Your huddled masses yearning to breathe free,
The wretched refuse of your teeming shore.
Send these, the homeless, tempest-toss't to me:
I lift my lamp beside the golden door.

—Emma Lazarus,
"The New Colossus"

Pinsk, Russia, the Second Night of Passover 1909

"May the spirit of this festival remain with us throughout the coming year, and may we be imbued, at all times, with its lofty and exalted teachings.

"May Zion be blessed with peace, and may our brethren and all mankind live in harmony and contentment. Amen."

Reb Joshua Siderman closed the prayer book, laid it down on the white-damask-covered dining table, took off his wire-rimmed spectacles, and smiled warmly at his family. Then he added the age-old dream: "Next year in Jerusalem!"

He sipped the special holiday wine and turned to his two grandsons, who were seated on his left. "Now, Albert and Samuel," he began, his brown eyes sparkling, "you may search for the matzo. Mind you, be careful! You will not get a groschen if you break any of Bobbe's nice things."

Reb Joshua put his glasses back on and looked lovingly at two-year-old Anna, who was confined in the treasured highchair that her other grandfather, Moshe Aronowitz, had made. He was Pinsk's master cabinetmaker, and he had made it for the Sidermans when Albert, the first grandchild the two couples would share, was born.

"Anna, you and I will look for the matzo together." He winked at her.

"Good Yuntif—Happy Pesach." These words signaled that the Passover feast and solemn prayers were finished. The family was now free to laugh and gossip and drink more wine or tea.

Six-year-old Albert and four-year-old Samuel, dressed in tailored knee breeches and coats with velvet trim, climbed down from the tall, ornately carved dining chairs and scampered around the dining room looking in Bobbe's usual hiding places for the matzo.

Sarah, always apprehensive when her children were set free in her mother Rachel's elegant home, admonished them one more time: "Stay in the dining room, boys, and be careful around Bobbe's china cabinet!"

"Me, too, Mama," Anna pleaded as she lifted her arms to permit herself to be lifted out of the confining chair.

"Yes, my dear. You've been such a good girl—two hours is a long time for such a little one. Zayde will help you find the matzo." Sarah lifted the petite black-haired, blue-eyed toddler, then turned to her father seated at the head of the table. "Here, Papa, here's your little princess." She deposited the wiggling child in his lap and bent to graze his cheek with an affectionate kiss.

It was hard to find a spot to kiss him. His black felt skullcap came down to his bushy white eyebrows, and the rest of his face seemed to be covered with hair: a neatly trimmed moustache and a flowing, snow-white beard that matched the full mane of long hair on his head. For years now she had teased him that he looked like Saint Nicholas. "Please, Papa, don't spoil the holiday by arguing with Jacob tonight," she urgently whispered in his ear.

His smile faded, only to be replaced by a stern glint in his eyes. She bit her lip, realizing that she had only reminded him of his displeasure with her husband.

Reb Joshua turned his attention to Anna. *"Shaine, shaine medela,"* he cooed, nuzzling her soft neck while she stood on his thighs and tried to take off his glasses. "A beautiful, beautiful girl! And now we will look for the matzo." He stood her on the floor, then took her by the hand and led her toward the heavy brocade-draped windows.

Sarah sat down again and fixed herself more tea with strawberry preserves. She glanced nervously at her husband, tried to reassure him with a forced smile, then looked pleadingly at her in-laws, Moshe and Suevia. Everyone knew that Reb Joshua was angry with Jacob again—it seemed a perpetual state of affairs between the two men she loved. Her father had ordered time set aside after the second seder for a family conference.

The night before, at the first seder, the Sidermans had invited all their children and grandchildren: Sarah's two older brothers and sister, their spouses, and seventeen grandchildren. Tonight, her mother had told her, was reserved for Jacob and Sarah only and the Aronowitz grandparents, who had a strong interest in what Reb Joshua was determined to discuss: Jacob's activities.

At that moment, Samuel and Albert shrieked. They had discovered the matzo. Anna, with her zayde in tow and a hand full of matzo, returned to the table. Reb Joshua sat down. The three children stood lined up by his chair.

"Bring me my money box, Bobbe!"

Laughingly, Rachel brought the tin box filled with coins.

"Now, let me think. How old are you? Ten groschen for each year—that's sixty groschen for you, Albert!"

Dark-haired Albert, a miniature of Jacob minus the beard and moustache, grinned wide-eyed as his grandfather counted the coins. "Don't spend it all on candy, mind you. It's not good for you."

Sandy-haired Samuel watched eagerly as the old man counted his forty groschen. Then Anna, imitating her brothers, held out her tiny hands.

"Me too, Zayde!" she demanded.

"A regular Hayyah Lourie you're raising, Sarah!" laughed Moshe, then broke into a hacking cough. Hayyah Lourie, Sarah knew, was a legend, the wealthiest woman in Pinsk. She shrewdly bought and sold corn and timber and had guided her family into brilliant investments.

"And what will you do with your groschen, Anna?" Reb Joshua asked in a mock-serious voice.

"Save it in my money jar," Anna answered seriously as she looked up into her grandfather's dancing eyes.

"Very good, very good! Your mother is raising you well!"

He gets such pleasure out of giving away Mother's money, Sarah thought bitterly. She was annoyed with her father because she knew what was coming. She allowed herself to think something that she could never say to his face: that he could pursue his life of study and writing and lecturing and meditation only because her mother, Rachel Eliasberg, had brought a portion of her family's great fortune to her marriage to Reb Joshua.

On the other hand, Sarah was proud of her husband, Jacob. He worked with his hands and his brains and his ability to lead men. He was the chief foreman at the largest timber mill in

Pinsk. And timber was the town's leading industry. No, there was nothing lazy or sedentary about her Jacob.

And her father-in-law, Moshe, had spent a lifetime crafting magnificent furniture for the wealthy families of Pinsk and Minsk and sometimes a special order from St. Petersburg. Moshe had made her own mother's splendid china cabinet—to house the green and gold Meissen china and Bavarian crystal—even before Sarah had been born.

Sarah thought both Jacob and Moshe Aronowitz were hard-working, solid family men. Yet she understood—and resented—the fact that her father, by virtue of his prominence as a Talmudic scholar and religious judge, and her mother, by virtue of her inherited wealth as an Eliasberg, ranked several rungs higher in Pinsk's stratified Jewish world than the Aronowitz family.

And what does that make me?

She was the wife of a highly respected man—in his circle—and she supplemented his quite sufficient income with generous gifts from her mother. The truth was—and Sarah was bitterly aware of it—that the Jewish community concurred that she had married beneath herself. Her betrothal announcement had set tongues wagging. How could Reb Joshua have agreed to his daughter's imperious demands, her insistence that she be permitted to marry the man she had loved since she was twelve? It was unthinkable!

And yet it was happening again and again in some of Pinsk's finest families. The younger people were refusing the matchmakers' suggestions, refusing to obey the centuries-old traditions. And her father, who prided himself on his openness to new ideas, to new ways of thinking through religious issues, and who had even told the married women in the family to stop wearing wigs and to let their hair grow naturally, had relented and permitted Sarah to marry her handsome, bright, industrious, and very independent Jacob.

Since that day, there hadn't been a moment's peace between the two men.

The old servant, Harmel, served the three men schnapps, offered them cigars, then left them in the library. Reb Joshua seated himself in the worn leather chair behind his desk, which was piled high with aging parchment manuscripts and finely tooled, leather-bound volumes. He lit his pipe, watched Jacob light a brown cigarette, and waited for Moshe's coughing fit to subside. "You should see a doctor, Moshe. I know a lung specialist in Minsk."

"You breathe sawdust for a lifetime, so you cough, what else is new?" he responded with a shrug of his shoulders.

Reb Joshua looked at Moshe's dark, now-shiny suit. It was the same suit he had worn to Jacob and Sarah's wedding and to every dinner he had ever attended in their house. It was probably the only suit he owned. He had lost so much weight, the coat hung limp on his gaunt, tall body. His hands, Joshua noted, were callused and black-nailed; obviously his hammer had missed its target many times.

Reb Joshua cleared his throat and tugged on his white beard. "Jacob, Sergeant Layvick came to see me last week with dire warnings." He watched Jacob closely as he spoke. "There's a price on your head. If you weren't my son-in-law, the cossacks would have killed you months ago."

Jacob refused to flinch as he stared back into Joshua's eyes. He puffed on his cigarette and nodded his agreement.

"You're under constant surveillance, have been for years, ever since the Arnadsky affair. They have informers planted everywhere, even among your men at the factory. The czar has sent agents to infiltrate the Bund, three undercover men."

Jacob stood up, nearly knocking over his chair. He began to pace in front of Reb Joshua's desk. He puffed again on his cigarette. "So what are you asking me to do? Quit?"

"No. It's too late for that. Seven years ago, I pleaded with you to cease your organizing activities. Every strike you staged cost the Eliasberg family. That's your mother-in-law's, your wife's, and your children's money." Reb Joshua pointed his finger at Jacob, who looked as if he were about to explode. "Hear me out! When you labor leaders succeeded in changing the workday from fourteen hours to ten, even though it cost our family money, I applauded you—your ideals, your results. Not your methods!

"I don't like the czar's policies any more than you do. But you're endangering your wife and children. All of us are at risk of being beaten or killed by the cossacks. *Because you are part of our family!*"

Moshe nodded his head in agreement with Reb Joshua, then began coughing again.

Jacob inhaled deeply, then crushed his cigarette. Calmly, deliberately, in a throaty voice, he bent over Joshua's desk. "Is it my turn now?"

Reb Joshua nodded.

"Reb Joshua, you're a brilliant, learned—even, I'll admit, a modern thinker—for a Talmudic scholar. And you know the history of government-sponsored anti-Semitism. In 1793, when Russia partitioned Poland and made Pinsk a part of Russia, thousands of Jewish families like ours were forced to live within the Pale of Settlement. Either that, or convert to Christianity.

"And since 1881 it has been the official policy of the government to promote pogroms, to promote pillaging, looting, rape, brutal assaults, even cold-blooded murder. If the peasants can focus their pent-up frustrations on the Jews, it takes the heat off the czars!

"Look at what's happening in all of Russia, not just in Pinsk. Here we have it good: Jews are eighty-three percent of the population, we've always gotten along fine with the non-Jews. The fact is, even though the government has tried to start a pogrom here, it has always failed. The peasants will never rise up against the Jews in Pinsk. They wouldn't dare. Forty-nine of the fifty-four factories in this city are owned by Jews!" Jacob hitched up his pants, then paced a few more steps. He turned back to Reb Joshua. "In Pinsk, it's the rich Jews who are exploiting the poor ones. The labor force is ninety percent Jewish."

"Yes, I know, and conditions can stand improvement. I grant you that, Jacob. But where else in the world does every factory have its own *shul*, so the men can stop for prayers? Where else in the world does a whistle blow an hour before sundown on the Sabbath and holidays, so everything closes down? Pinsk is a good place for Jews to live, and you and your revolutionary friends are threatening all the Jewish families here with your activities."

"Yeah, it's great to be a Jew if you're a Lourie or a Levin or a Halpern. Or an Eliasberg! But it's not so great if you're a sawmill operator with eight children to feed. You"—he pointed a finger at Reb Joshua— "are part of the elite group that calls the shots here, and you don't want your fiefdom destroyed! How can you justify what the czar's people did to the Jews of Kishinev?

"You pay bribes as a way of life: to keep your nine-year-old grandsons from being torn from their mother's arms for the czar's armies; to get your grandchildren into high schools and universities," Jacob continued. "But how can the man who cuts logs for me keep his son from spending the next twenty-five years of his life in Siberia?

"Think of it, Reb Joshua, only ten percent of the Jewish children in Pinsk are permitted to get an education. And you say this is a good place for Jews?"

"No, I don't defend the czar's policies," Reb Joshua stated. "But if your Bund overthrows the czar, how do you know that the Bolsheviks—or whoever else comes to power—won't treat the Jews worse?"

"Anything would be an improvement for the Jews." Exhausted, Jacob dropped back into the leather sofa.

Moshe cleared his throat, then spoke up. "Jacob, Reb Joshua and I agree with you about the czar's policies. But we're talking about your life! You're under a death threat! The cossack who kills you and makes it look like the revenge of a peasant will receive a promotion and hundreds of rubles!"

Reb Joshua shook his finger at Jacob. "Of all God's commandments, the most important one, Jacob, is 'Choose life!' You must save your own life and your family."

Jacob looked from Reb Joshua to his father. In both their faces he saw understanding, love, fear, and pleading. "What . . . what would you have me do?"

The room was silent. He could hear his father's raspy breathing. Reb Joshua put his pipe down, spread his hands out in front of him on the desk studying his fingers, then flexed his hands into tight fists. When he relaxed them, he looked squarely at Jacob, and Jacob saw the beginning of tears behind Reb Joshua's spectacles.

"Go to America. Take your family. Take my beloved Sarah, light of my life. Take Albert and Samuel. Take beautiful little Anna. Make a new life in America." Quickly he pulled a handkerchief out of his coat pocket, took his glasses off, and began wiping them.

Jacob looked at his father.

"Yes, my son, you must go. As soon as possible."

Jacob stared. He looked back and forth at the two men, astounded. They were telling him to leave Russia—to never come back. His anger rose up like bile in his throat. Again he began again to pace.

"I won't do it! I won't go to America and be exploited by the German Jews. Everyone knows the German Jews meet the boats and hire all the Russian Jewish greenhorns at slave wages. You've heard the stories from the ones who've come back. Reb Joshua"—he stopped in front of the desk—"the streets are *not* paved with gold in America!"

"I know, I know. But you'll be alive. And well. You don't have to go to New York. There are other communities—Cleveland, Philadelphia—"

"You could go to Washington. Your two cousins live there, you've seen their letters. They have a bakery," Moshe interrupted, then coughed again.

"I can't—I can't think of taking Sarah away from her mother. And from you, Reb Joshua. Sarah couldn't stand being uprooted."

"Better she be uprooted, make a new life in America, than be a widow, or worse, see her children slaughtered and herself raped and beaten by those monsters. My prominence, our rubles, even Sergeant Layvick can no longer protect you or your children from them."

Jacob laughed sarcastically. "You don't really think the authorities are going to grant me, a revolutionary with a price on my head, the legal papers a Jew must have to leave the Pale and travel to Hamburg? Even your money won't buy those papers."

"No, of course not. You'll have to go under cover. But I've made plans for you. I have a map here"—he rose and reached over the desk to hand it to Jacob—"a route across the Polish territory with safe houses marked. . . ."

In the parlor Rachel Siderman, Suevia Aronowitz, and Sarah Aronowitz sat doing needlework, but they were actually eavesdropping on the heated conversation in the library. Anna was sleeping on the burgundy-velvet sofa next to her mother. Albert sat under the oil lamp, staring up into it with a kaleidoscope. Samuel built towers with dominos.

Desperate for the men to finish their argument, Sarah was also impatient with the boys and couldn't begin to carry a decent conversation with her mother or mother-in-law. Is the rest of my life going to be like this, she wondered, simply because I dared to marry the man I love? Why must Father always try to dissuade Jacob from his beliefs? Can't he see how much his ideals mean to him? Jacob's right—he's really working for the good of all the Jewish people. Why is Father so afraid of change?

But Jacob, for his part, was rigid too, she thought. He knew when he married Sarah that she came from money. He understood that she would never be willing to live on his income alone. Yet he resented anything her parents did for her. Jacob and Sarah played a game, a transparent game. She kept several dozen chickens at their home—a far less pretentious home than her parents'! It had a real floor, although the majority of homes in Pinsk had dirt ones. When she ordered clothes for her children and herself, she told Jacob she had paid for them with her egg money. He pretended to believe her, though any rational man would know that a year's worth of egg money wouldn't pay for even one of Sarah's dresses.

Jacob had even resented her dowry, though it was certainly in keeping with her family's position in Pinsk. To smooth matters over a bit, her parents had wisely ordered the furniture for the newlyweds' home from Jacob's father's shop. As was the tradition among the wealthy Jewish families in Pinsk, her parents had provided a home, furniture, and an ample trousseau for her, plus a large amount of cash. Jacob, a secret revolutionary even when they had married, wanted to forswear it all and live humbly like his workers in the timber factory, but she would have none of it. At least she had won that battle.

And others too. On Sabbath and the High Holy Days, they sat with her parents on the east side of the Great Synagogue of Pinsk—built in 1640 and renowned throughout Europe for its architecture and opulent interior. On the holidays they dined with her family. Only occasionally did they travel to the outskirts of Pinsk to visit with his parents.

All this Jacob resented, yet he managed to live with the knowledge that his children would receive a public education and would never want for anything. His love for Sarah—and the passion with which she responded—was the soothing balm that made his compromises possible.

Sarah understood this. Anticipating an argument between her father and her husband, she had lied to the rabbi that very afternoon when she went to the ritual bath. She had subtracted two days from the required number of days since her last menstrual period had begun. Having gone to the mikvah, she could now spend the night in Jacob's bed and try to heal the wounds her father would have surely opened.

Suddenly, the women were startled out of their reveries by repeated loud knocks on the door. In burst two uniformed cossacks, followed a few seconds later by a somber and terrified-looking Sergeant Layvick.

The elderly servant, Harmel, rushed in from the kitchen and stopped dead in his tracks and began to tremble. Instinctively, Suevia grabbed the two boys to her lap. Rachel ran to the library door to alert Reb Joshua, and Sarah gathered Anna in her arms and walked over to face the intruders.

"How dare you burst into Reb Siderman's house like this? What is your business?"

The taller, heavily moustached soldier shoved Sarah aside with a mean glint in his darting eyes and strode into the parlor. "We've come to count the Jews. Give me your passports! Seems like there's too many of you here, and it's past curfew."

Sarah stared at him. "Get out of here! This instant! You've no right to come bursting into a private home."

The second cossack lifted his arm and smacked Sarah's face, then shoved her out of his way as he followed the first cossack into the parlor. Anna began to wail. Jacob had stepped from the library door into the parlor just in time to see the cossack slap Sarah. He rushed toward him, but Sergeant Layvick stepped between the two men as the cossack pulled his gun.

"There, there, Jacob. Calm down. Sarah's not hurt. Let me handle this."

"If you were able to handle it, they wouldn't be here!" Jacob shouted angrily as he strode toward Sarah and took the baby Anna from her arms. "You'd best get some ice."

"Now gentlemen, let's see if we can settle this peacefully," Reb Joshua began in a modulated voice, his hands visibly shaking. "What is it you want?"

"We're here to search your house. Aronowitz's horses are outside. He must be having a meeting of his rebels here tonight."

"That's not true! We are celebrating the second seder. Surely you know that!"

"Give me your passports!" the first soldier demanded.

Quickly the women searched their purses, and the men reached into their coat pockets. Reb Joshua went back into the library to get his.

They handed their passports to the tall cossack. He opened each one, looked at the names, saw the bright red stamp JEW on each one, then threw each of them on the table, spitting out the words '*Jew, Jew, Jew, Jew* . . . ,' which resounded like a death knell.

That finished, he harassed Reb Joshua. "How many more Jews you got upstairs in your attic?"

Shaken, Reb Joshua answered as calmly as he could, "None. You know we don't do that kind of thing."

"Liar! We know you kept a family here only last week. We got them crossing the border near Brest. They had a map, a list of all the places they had stayed between St. Petersburg and Brest. We've got good informers these days."

"Don't you dare call my father a liar!" Sarah shouted at him.

"Don't you dare raise your voice to me, you little tart, or you'll find out what a real Russian man is like!"

Sarah shrank back in terror and huddled close to Jacob.

"Ah . . . everything seems to be in order here, don't you think?" the police sergeant suggested in a pleading voice to the cossacks.

"Look, Layvick, we know you're on the take from Siderman, we know you're gonna try to protect him. Now, let's see . . . are all of you staying here tonight? It's way past curfew, and we can't vouch for the safety of any Jew this time of night."

"I will personally escort Mr. and Mrs. Aronowitz home," Layvick volunteered. "I will guarantee their safety."

"It's not the old ones we're concerned with," the tall cossack said as he stared at Jacob.

"My daughter and son-in-law and their children are spending the night with me," Reb Joshua announced, his hands still shaking.

Jacob started to object, but Reb Joshua silenced him with his piercing eyes.

"Aronowitz, we're watching you!" the tall cossack warned again.

Then, as suddenly as they'd burst in, they left, slamming the door behind them.

Harmel, who had watched the entire scene from the doorway, mopped his perspiring brow with his handkerchief, though it was chilly in the house. Suevia reached into her bag for smelling salts, and cautioned the boys not to breathe a word. Rachel walked toward Reb Joshua and took his hand soothingly.

Sergeant Layvick broke the silence. "I'm sorry, so sorry, Reb Siderman, to have ruined your seder. I tried, but I couldn't get them to continue on after they saw Jacob's horses outside. I'm so sorry."

"I understand. I know you tried. Do you think you can get Moshe and Suevia home safely at this time of night?"

"Yes, I'm sure of it. It's Jacob they want."

Quickly, Moshe and Suevia gathered their coats and overboots and kissed their grandchildren good night. They thanked the Sidermans profusely, then solemnly took their leave of Jacob and Sarah.

"My son, you must consider everything we've said tonight. And what you've just seen. I believe Reb Joshua has the best idea—especially now."

"I'll consider it, Pa," Jacob answered as he shook his father's hand, then hugged him. He kissed his mother and held her tight, as if he would never see her again.

Now he had to discuss the idea with Sarah.

Rachel asked Harmel to make more tea. Reb Joshua poured another schnapps for himself and Jacob, and the two men again disappeared into the library. Carrying their tea glasses upstairs, Rachel and Sarah quickly dressed the children for bed and tucked them in.

Sarah, exhausted and emotionally distraught, asked her mother to forgive her for not going back downstairs. She wanted to get undressed, lie on her bed, and gather her thoughts before Jacob came upstairs.

We are not safe anymore. They could kill him any day.

These two thoughts repeated themselves in her mind as she undressed and prepared for bed. And, she thought, *my children are not safe. My family's rubles can no longer protect them.*

The answer was staring her in the face, bursting from her unconscious. She had tried to contain and control the thought, had not dared to mention it for years now: *We could go to America.*

Many Pinsk families, she thought, had fled to America since 1903, when a Russian agent provocateur named Arnadsky, who had infiltrated the Bund, had been bludgeoned to death in a back alley by three youths. Many of the revolutionary leaders had been brutally beaten and sentenced to long prison terms in Siberia. Others had successfully fled to America. In the intervening years, Jacob had climbed further up the ladder of leadership, and his activities were no longer a secret to anyone, Jew or non-Jew.

The government had tried to incite a pogrom in Pinsk, so the cossacks had arrived in 1905. Wholesale arrests, accompanied by brutal beatings, followed. A curfew had been imposed after eight in the evening. All meetings of groups, large or small, were banned, so Jacob had begun to hold his meetings in the woods outside Pinsk on Friday evenings, when religious Jews were in *shul* praying. Even so, the meetings had been infiltrated by Russian agents. It was only a question of time.

Jacob entered the room quietly, thinking Sarah was already asleep. Instantly, she stood and wrapped her arms around him. "Jacob?"

"My darling Sarah, I'm so sorry . . . what happened to you tonight . . . I'd like to kill that man with my bare hands."

"Hush! You mustn't do anything foolish. We have enough trouble already."

He kissed her once softly, then again more passionately. "Are you . . . clean?"

"Yes, my darling, I went to the mikvah today."

"Wonderful! I need you so much."

After their passion was exhausted, they lay awake holding hands, watching the moonlit shadows of the tall tree outside the window make designs on the bedroom wall.

In a hoarse voice, Jacob whispered, "We must go to America."

"Yes, my love. We must."

⬛ Chapter 6

Pinsk, Russia, Early Spring 1911

She drove the cart full of children down the bumpy, rutted road faster than she'd ever imagined the horse could go, furiously lashing it with the whip, fearful that the cart might overturn and kill her children. The cossacks were closing in! They shouted and brandished their rifles, closer, ever closer.

Suddenly, the horse stopped. The cartwheels jolted and screeched. Her heart beat as if it would burst through the walls of her chest. Her body was drenched in perspiration.

The birds' loud calls woke her. Sarah opened her eyes, then shut them against the daylight that was filtering into her bedroom. A nightmare—only a nightmare, thank God. Sarah willed it to recede into blackness.

It was peaceful that morning; no winds were blowing. Soon Sasha would awaken, urgent for her breast. Fear rose again in her throat: Today is the last day of my life in Russia.

Boruch ata Adonai . . . *Blessed art Thou, O Lord our God, King of the Universe. . . . Give me the courage, give me the strength to do what I must. Give me the courage to be strong, even cold and unfeeling. For my parents' sake. All day long. For this one last day.*

Seventeen-month-old Sasha began to whimper. Slowly, groggily, Sarah changed her baby's diaper, cooing to her all the while, as if this morning were just like any other day. "Do you know, *tsatskeleh,* you little doll, you are the reason we didn't go with your father to America, because I was pregnant with you! Now hush—don't wake Anna. Not yet."

She settled herself in the rocking chair and chubby, golden-haired Sasha eagerly grabbed for her breast.

The rocking chair. Made by her father-in-law. Moshe had died seven months after Jacob had left for America. He had lived only two days to welcome his newest granddaughter into the world; then his lungs had given out, worn out from a lifetime of struggling for breath.

Death giving way to life. So it has always been, so it will always be. Blessed be God.

And tomorrow morning by this time, we will begin our journey to America. But first to Germany, in a hay cart filled with one trunk—and four little children. Dear God, don't let the cossacks catch us!

Sasha satisfied her empty stomach while random thoughts ricocheted through Sarah's head. What would her new home in Washington be like? Jacob had written that he lived on a beautiful cobblestone street, lined with elms, with tall red-brick houses, all alike, lined up wall to wall, one against the other. "The schools are free, and the children will learn English quickly. We have two synagogues, and every Jewish family knows everyone else's business. We take care of one another, like always. It's a great place for children to grow up."

But he had said very little about his work. First he had worked at his cousin's bakery to save money to start his own store. Now he ran a neighborhood grocery out of the front room of a corner house that he rented. The arrangement seemed a bit dubious to Sarah, but she was determined to take the children and join him. Whither thou goest, I will go. . . .

But, oh the pain of saying good-bye today! How will I get through it? It's like a living funeral.

Reb Joshua knew that the authorities would like nothing better than to capture them and make an example of what happens to a revolutionary's family, even after Jacob had escaped to the United States. So he had carefully plotted a new route across the Polish territory for them. He had sent letters and money to his acquaintances and fellow rabbis to insure that she and the children would be welcomed in each small *shtetl*, or Jewish enclave, hidden for a day or two, supplied with a fresh horse and food. He hoped that this way, she would be able to continue for a few more days, a week or two more, until she reached Germany. Then she would be safe.

Their planning had been a closely guarded family secret. Her relatives and friends were aware she would be leaving soon, now that Sasha was old enough to travel, now that the worst of winter was behind them. She had to hurry while the ground was still frozen, before the heavy thaw set in. If she didn't leave now, the wagon could get stuck in the deep muddy ruts in the backroads she would be traveling.

Reb Joshua had hired one of Harmel's granddaughters, who was a Catholic Pole and could therefore travel freely, to serve as a maid for Sarah's family. This peasant girl, Mara, would accompany them to Hamburg in the horse-drawn hay cart, then return to Pinsk by train. Thank God, she spoke both Russian and Polish. If questioned, they would say they were traveling to visit relatives in the next town. Reb Joshua had even supplied them with a list of local Christian residents that they could name. Forged passports would state they were Catholic. And they would make a point of traveling across the dangerous borders on the Sabbath, when no self-respecting Jew would consider riding in a wagon.

Reb Joshua had planned Sarah's trip even more carefully than Jacob's. He declared that God would excuse them for breaking certain laws in order to save their lives. God's ultimate law, which they could not break, he reminded her, was to survive, to choose life.

Sarah dreaded seeing her mother's face at breakfast. Every morning for weeks, Rachel had greeted her tearfully. "Must you go now? Why not wait another year? Sasha will be older."

"Ma, it's settled. I must join Jacob. The children need their father. I need my husband. He needs us. The Law commands it."

And her father agreed—for still another reason: "If she doesn't leave for America soon," he declared, "it will appear to the community that Jacob has abandoned her, cast her off as his wife, perhaps that he even intends to divorce her. No, Sarah is right, Rachel. She must leave this spring, exactly as planned. It is time for Albert and Samuel, and even little Anna, to go to American schools."

Sarah had saved all her farewells for this final day, lest careless gossip or a remark overheard by a servant alert the authorities.

· The people she would confide in were few: her sister and brothers, her now-widowed and ailing mother-in-law, and Grandmother Eliasberg.

Not even the children knew they were going. Sarah sent the boys off to school, then dressed Anna and Sasha in their velvet dresses and fur-collared coats. She gently fingered their hand-embroidered underclothes and felt a moment of anguish. She would have to leave their lovely clothes behind. Too many trunks would alert the authorities to her real intentions. She slammed the drawer. What were clothes compared to her children's lives?

She and the girls drove to the outskirts of Pinsk, where her mother-in-law still lived in back of Moshe's cabinetmaking shop, now rented by one of his former assistants.

Since Moshe's death, Sarah had taken the children to visit their Bobbe Aronowitz at least once a week. Suevia was doing poorly, suffering from rheumatism that was aggravated by Russia's bleak, frozen winter. Her only joy, it seemed, was hearing her read Jacob's letters from America. Suevia could neither read nor write, so Sarah always read Jacob's letters to her, hoping her mother-in-law also had one for her to read aloud.

After hugs and kisses, Suevia made fresh tea in the brass samovar and hastened to warm some currant-studded hallah for the girls. While Suevia bustled about the kitchen, Sarah's eyes dropped to the dirt floor. Suevia had lived all her life in a home with no real floor. Sarah had never lived in a home that didn't have wooden floors and fine Persian rugs. What would Jacob expect of her in America? Did his house there have a real floor? He had said something in his letter about a water pipe in the house. Imagine, in Washington they didn't have a village water-carrier!

Sarah read Jacob's latest letter to Suevia. He described his new store but prudently made no mention of her forthcoming trip because the czar's government frequently opened, read, and sometimes destroyed letters to Jews. Sarah then quickly told Suevia she was leaving the next day.

"Ach! Ach! You're taking the boys? My grandsons?" Tears streamed down her weathered, parched face. "My last memory of Jacob! Why not take only Samuel, and leave Albert here in your mother's house?"

"No, no, Bobbe, both boys need their father. We must be together as a family."

Her mother-in-law collapsed into the hard wooden chair. She wiped her eyes, laid her head in her arms on the table top, and moaned, a loud, heart-rending death moan. Desperate to alleviate her sorrow, Sarah patted her shoulders and stroked her upper arm.

"It's for the best. Really it is. The children will get an education. They will have great opportunities. All of them will go to a university, I promise you. They will be safe from the czar's recruiters and the cossacks."

Suevia looked up at Sarah, straightened herself in her chair, and wiped her eyes, struggling to regain her dignity. "Yes, of course you must go. I've always known you would." Then her voice cracked again. "But why so soon? They won't come for Albert until he's nine . . . next year."

"It's not only the army. We want to be a whole family again."

"You are right." Suevia now patted Sarah's hand and reached over to tearfully hug Anna, who was picking the currants out of her egg bread and eating them.

Suevia's eyes misted up again. "I will never see my grandchildren again. Never again."

Sarah felt her own eyes begin to fill, but she willed the tears back. She could not permit herself the luxury of breaking down.

The tears streamed down Suevia's face. "Who will read my letters from Jacob? From you and my grandchildren?"

"My father has promised to come read your letters. Perhaps you wish to move to my parents' home?" Sarah wished she could add that Suevia might even come to America, but that was impossible. Suevia was too old, too ill, and too fragile to consider making such a journey.

"I must be going, Bobbe. I've so many people to visit." Besides, this is too painful. I cannot watch you grieve so.

Suevia grimaced as she struggled to her feet and tried to stand straight. "Wait. I want to give you something.". She shuffled into the parlor and came back carrying a large brass candlestick, ornately carved with Hebrew letters. "My Yom Kippur candle. May you burn it every year in peace and health and happiness." She paused to wipe her eyes. "And may you teach your children about their old grandparents back in Russia."

Sarah accepted the offering, knowing she could not do otherwise, but she wondered how much she would be endangering herself and her children by packing it. What if her trunk were searched by cossacks?

"I have something for you too," she announced as she produced a new portrait of herself and her children. "I will send you more every year so you can watch the children grow."

"Good." Suevia studied the picture. "Send me a picture of Jacob in his store. And your house—a picture of that too."

The old woman bent to kiss her granddaughters one last time, then fiercely hugged her daughter-in-law. "I will pray for your safe journey."

As Sarah drove the wagon back toward Nevsky Avenue,

Anna asked "Where are we going, Mama? What did Bobbe mean about going on a journey?"

Sarah smiled at her precocious Anna. Perhaps it wasn't too soon to tell her. "We are going to America to find your Pa!"

"Oh, goody! Do I get to ride in a big boat?"

"Yes, my little one. A very big boat."

"When, Ma?"

"Tomorrow morning, very early."

As her great-grandmother unbuttoned her coat, Anna burst out, "Bobbe, we are going in a boat to find Pa!"

The elegant white-haired woman, dressed in navy wool with Venetian-lace trim though it was only noon, looked severely at Sarah. "So. You've told the children?"

"Yes. A few minutes ago, at Bobbe Aronowitz's house."

"This would not be happening if you'd listened to your parents years ago and married a more suitable man." Bobbe Eliasberg let a wiggling Anna off her lap and stared imperiously at Sarah. "Why don't you just let him divorce you? There are lots of women in America. He'll be married in no time, and your father can arrange—"

"No, Bobbe! I'll not have you talk this way in front of the girls." Sasha whimpered to be fed, but Sarah was of no mind to nurse her while arguing with her domineering grandmother.

"Your mother and I never could talk any sense to you."

Theirs had always been a troubled relationship. Sarah had spent a lifetime simultaneously loving and hating this woman. She had so many good qualities—she was cultured and educated and well read, she read Tolstoi and Chekhov and Dostoevski and wasn't the least shocked by modern ideas. But she believed her wealth entitled her to order people's lives.

She pulled a lace handkerchief from the belt on her dress and fidgeted with it before she put it back. Suddenly, she folded her pudgy, white, bejeweled hands on her lap and smiled broadly. "If I were thirty years younger, I'd come with you. Now, what do you think of that?"

"I wish you could, Bobbe. We'll miss you so."

She rang for a servant to bring lunch and take the little ones to the kitchen to be fed. Then she turned back to Sarah. "I trust your mother has given you my gift. Be very careful how you sell those diamonds. They aren't large—only a carat or so—but they are flawless and of the finest color."

Having known for months about her granddaughter's plans, Bobbe Eliasberg had had her jeweler take apart one of her diamond brooches. Sarah's mother had removed the second, fifth, and seventh covered buttons on the sleeves of Sarah's navy serge traveling dress. The six loose diamonds, covered by three layers of cloth, had become "buttons," to be discreetly removed and sold whenever Sarah needed money.

"I hope you won't need to dispose of them between here and America. There you can make some investments." She patted Sarah's hand. "Buy land. Jews can own as much land as they can afford in America."

"Yes, Bobbe. I hope I can."

"And be sure to look up my nephew, who's a big shot on Wall Street in New York City. And Yetta, who lives in Connecticut, and Faigle, who lives in Cleveland. . . ." She rattled on a long list of relatives and friends who had left for America during the last dozen years and had written back urging her to come.

Only after they finished a leisurely lunch and the girls were in their coats did tears come to the old woman's eyes. "God be with you, my child. I love you—and I must admit I like your chutzpah. Be sure to write me everything! Write me about Broadway!"

Sarah drove the girls home and put them down for naps, then drove toward the Pina River, the town marketplace, and secured her horse. She walked slowly, smiling and chatting with acquaintances, greeting Chaim Weizmann and Saul Gittleman, Zionist friends of her father, and all the while she wanted to scream out, "I'm leaving, you will never see me again!" Yet she dared not even whisper it to her best friends.

When she reached the Lourie match factory, she asked for her brother Ben, who worked in the accounting and shipping office. Ben, who was married to a distant cousin of the Lourie family, had always been her favorite brother. But because of Jacob's Bund activities, they had grown apart as adults: Ben represented management, Jacob the laboring men and women of Pinsk. After Jacob's departure for America, Sarah and her brother had grown close again. Even so, he was surprised that she came now to the factory.

"On a gorgeous spring day like this, with the ice breaking up on the river, why are you looking so serious? Is someone ill? Bad news from Jacob?" Ben, like several others in the family, nourished a hope that Sarah would not go to America. With Jacob, the troublemaker, gone, the cossacks had ignored her.

"I've come to say good-bye." Suddenly she reached for his hands to steady herself, feeling faint.

Ben's ruddy face turned ashen. "Come with me into the *shul.*" They entered the small synagogue, a part of the factory, now empty and quiet. "Sit," he ordered.

"But . . ." she objected, knowing only men were allowed here.

"God will understand." He sat facing her, still holding her icy hands. "When?"

"Tomorrow, before sunrise."

"On the Sabbath? No!"

"Pa says it will be safe that way. We have Catholic passports."

"I don't believe it! I'll never—"

"Shh!" Sarah silenced him with her finger on his lips. "Don't say it, Ben. I couldn't bear to hear it from you. You'll come to visit us. I know you will. Or maybe you'll come to stay."

"Oh, my dear, dear, brave sister." He cried into her hair as he hugged her. "I'll be waiting every day for news of your safety! Go now, before my emotions make a baby of me!"

Quickly, quietly, she slipped out of *shul*, while he remained behind to say the ancient prayers.

After an unusually solemn Sabbath dinner of roast chicken and noodles, Reb Joshua walked to the Great Synagogue of Pinsk. The women stayed behind for a last visit. Rachel's youngest sister, Bessie, had come to say good-bye and bounce Anna on her knee one last time. It was obvious to Sarah that Bessie was trying to keep the conversation light and frivolous in order to help Rachel get through the evening.

"I want you to send me a picture of the people with black faces that Jacob writes about. Can you believe it, black skin? Really!"

"Tante Bessie, why is your hair different from Ma's?" Anna asked as she fingered Bessie's curls.

Bessie reached up to push back the flaming auburn ringlets, which never stayed put, no matter how many combs she wore.

" 'Cause a Tartar climbed in bed with 'Madame Eliasberg,' I expect!" Bessie winked at Rachel and Sarah, and all three women burst into laughter at the thought of any man daring to get into bed with "Madame Eliasberg."

"Maybe someday, little Anna, you'll have a daughter with hair like mine," answered Bessie in a serious voice, "and you'll think of me when you look at her. It could happen, little one!"

There was a tap on the door, then David, a friend of Jacob's, cautiously opened the door.

"My men are here, Mrs. Aronowitz, with a new wagon and horse; we'll load it for you and leave it in the stable. And I'll be here at five in the morning. I'm to take you across the first border. It's the way Jacob and your father want it."

"Fine." Sarah clutched her stomach as sharp pains dove toward her feet. It's all real. This isn't a game. "Tomorrow morning, early . . . I'll be ready."

After that, there was no escaping the few chores left. The three women bathed the four children—they should at least start off their trip to America clean—even though Harmel, the old servant, looked skeptically at this heating of water on the Sabbath!

All the children were sleeping, their wicker bags packed, their clean, simple clothes laid out awaiting the morning. Reb Joshua had dictated that the children wear and take clothes of the laboring classes, and that Sarah choose her simplest, oldest dresses for the trip. They could not take much, not even much money, for fear of discovery, and thus could not in any way draw attention to themselves. "You can have new clothes made in America! Your husband wouldn't be sending for you if he couldn't take care of you."

Her father returned from Sabbath services late and checked the stable to satisfy himself that David and his men had done their job well. Then he came indoors and wearily hung his coat and hat on the coat tree. Harmel greeted him with a cup of hot tea. In the parlor he found Sarah in her robe sitting at his chess table. Her eyes were pink around the edges, and she was idly fingering the chess pieces.

"So. One last game, then?"

"Pa." Sarah heard the choking sound of her own voice. She stood and wrapped her arms around him. "I tried . . . I tried so hard all day long—not to cry. But when David brought the wagon . . . when we bathed the children—it's so real Pa! I'm so frightened!"

He held her away from him, to study her face. Tears were brimming in his eyes too.

"And I don't want to leave you and Ma."

"My child, I can think of no burden God will ever lay on your shoulders—or mine—that will hurt more than what you must do tomorrow. But you must do it. You must.

"You must do it for the sake of your children and your grandchildren and your great-grandchildren. Because life is never going to be better for Jews in Russia. Not in my lifetime, not in yours.

"Much as it tears my heart out to say it, you must go. At least some of our family must be saved from what is coming. And America is the only place on earth where Jews are welcome.

"You must go. As your father, I command it!"

▣ Chapter 7

Sarah concentrated only on washing and dressing and pushed all thoughts of what lay ahead to the back of her mind. Her fingers were like ice; the early spring temperatures made the room bitterly cold. She donned her fine linen and lace undergarments, then the coarse black stockings and shoes of a maidservant. At least the underwear was her own, she thought bitterly as she lowered the much-washed, coarsely textured gray shift over her head. She had borrowed two dresses from her Polish maid, Mara, to wear on the drive across Poland. When she arrived safely in Germany, she could dare to be herself again. She fastened her hair with combs and tied on a tattered old babushka.

Then she woke the children, hours earlier than their usual waking time. As she dressed them, her father and David carried a wicker bag for each child to the wagon. The men had already laid out goose-down quilts for the children, crates of eggs, oats and hay for the horse, and various parcels of food—enough to last them until they crossed the border, near Brest.

Unable to contain her emotion, Rachel had not volunteered to help with the children. Finally, when everyone was assembled in the kitchen, Reb Joshua led Rachel into the room. She had summoned all her willpower, Sarah realized, so as not to frighten the children.

Rachel kissed each child tenderly, admonished the boys to help their mother—"Be a *mensch*!"—and told them to write letters and send pictures from America.

"Bobbe, why don't you come too?" Anna asked when it was her turn. "We're going on a great big boat!"

"I'm too old, my child, too old. But you will have everything. I know that. Your mother will see to it."

At last it was Sarah's turn. Fighting tears, she wordlessly hugged her mother, then Reb Joshua. She could not bring herself to say good-bye.

They went outdoors where David and Mara stood anxiously waiting beside the packed wagon. David looked at Sarah's dress with approving eyes but frowned at her hair. "Take your hair down, then put the babushka back on. For the next few weeks, you must look like a peasant."

She looked at her father questioningly.

"Do as David says. He has helped many refugees escape. Trust his judgment."

She took the combs out angrily, wondering why she had let herself be talked into this. She settled the children on the quilts. Mara climbed in beside them, Sarah climbed up beside David, and with one final wave and one last admonition from Reb Joshua—"Write as soon as you are safely in Germany!"—they were on their way.

One final glimpse of the onion-domed cathedral, one final pass by the Great Synagogue, then they plunged deep into the dense forests surrounding Pinsk.

Late the next afternoon, by prearrangement, they met with four rough-looking men on horseback. David conferred privately with them, then explained to Sarah, "We're crossing the border about a mile from the guard house while they divert the guards with whiskey, gambling, and women," he explained. "No one will ever know you crossed."

"Are you sure it's safe?"

"Yes. We've given the farmer Jules Polaski three rubles per head to let us cross his farm. Tomorrow he'll repair his fence. Again." David chuckled.

"My father said to trust you, so I will. I remember how Jacob spoke of you."

"Don't worry. By sundown, we'll be five or six miles inside the old Polish territory. I've made this trip dozens of times."

Several days later they reached Bialystoki and Rabbi Lipshitz's home, and it was none too soon. The children were exhausted and chilled; Rosa's temper had flared more than once, and they were out of food and water.

The tired refugees were welcomed warmly by the old man and his wife. "Your father is one of the bright lights in Talmudic scholarship. I am honored to be of assistance to his family."

After being served tea and hot bread with preserves in front of a fireplace, the Aronowitz family welcomed the warmth and coziness of real beds with real pillows. Sarah settled the children in the attic bedroom, then returned to the parlor to bid farewell to David. He would buy a horse from Rabbi Lipshitz with her father's rubles, she was certain, and leave to return to Pinsk before dawn.

"Remember me to Jacob. Tell him the 'movement' misses him," David said as he bowed formally to Sarah.

"We thank you so much. Please go see my parents and tell them we're fine."

"I will, I will. First thing, you can be sure!"

"Shalom."

They slept late the next morning and then, after a hearty breakfast, took a long walk around the Jewish section of Bialystoki. Sarah realized as she strolled past the tailor, the blacksmith, the baker, the shoemaker, and the synagogue that Jewish villages were the same all over. The people dressed the same, the countryside looked much the same, they ate the same foods, and they even spoke one common language—Yiddish.

She felt herself relax. This trip would not be nearly as terrible as she had imagined.

For weeks, Sarah and Mara, looking like sisters, drove the children from village to village. They followed a pattern of traveling for several days, then resting for two or three days in a safe house. Then with a new horse and fresh food and water, they would set out again.

When Sarah drove, the children played games and slept. When Mara drove, Sarah told the children stories and quizzed the boys in math. When everyone was exhausted from the bumpy cart, they would stop by a river bank to fish and enjoy a picnic. Sarah tried to make this part of the trip a gay adventure, knowing the Atlantic crossing would be tedious for such active children.

They stopped for long rests in Orneta and Gdansk and Koszalin. They presented their forged Catholic passports at the German border, and without a moment's hesitation, the guard waved them on.

At last we are in Germany. The worst is over. There is nothing more to fear.

When they stopped in Friedland, in Germany, Sarah posted a long letter to her parents and to Jacob telling them everything was going exactly as planned. They stopped to rest one last time in Güstrow, then continued on to Hamburg, where they would take the steamship to Liverpool.

Arriving in the bustling seaport of Hamburg before noon, Sarah asked directions in Yiddish and took her family directly to the Jewish Aid Society. She picked up their prepaid tickets for the boat to Liverpool, determined the sailing date and time, and located the address of a pension in which to stay. Her plan was to send Mara back to Pinsk by train and sell her wagon and horse.

She had discarded the forged passports in Güstrow, changed into her own clothes, dressed her hair elaborately on top of her head, and in her own mind, reclaimed her real identity—that of Jacob's wife and Reb Joshua's daughter.

How shocked she was to discover, then, that being Reb Joshua's daughter meant nothing in Germany. When a German government doctor informed her that he would not accept a St. Petersburg doctor's certificate that Samuel, who had had surgery to cure trachoma, was indeed cured, she was distraught. "Madame, I must insist you stay here two months, then bring

Samuel back. If he shows no sign of trachoma, I will sign your papers."

She appealed to the Jewish Aid Society. They had seen thousands of similar situations. "Find a place to stay in the *shtetl*, do some handiwork, let the boys study. Two months will pass quickly."

Sarah had nearly exhausted the small amount of money she had dared to bring with her, but she was reluctant to sell a diamond. After a night of restless, dreamless sleep, she decided to keep Mara with her to care for the children. She, Sarah Siderman Aronowitz, would work!

She quickly wrote Jacob and her parents, posted the letters, and that afternoon found a job in a dressmaker's shop. Her fine hand with a needle would pay off.

Two months later, Sarah took Samuel back to the German doctor. He issued a certificate that permitted Sarah and her children to leave for Liverpool. After a tearful farewell to Mara, whom they had come to love dearly, Sarah and the children crossed to Liverpool. But to Sarah's great shock, this was not the end of the issue of Samuel's trachoma. Now she needed an English doctor's certificate!

"Dr. Drysdale, you don't understand," Sarah said to the English doctor, who understood Russian. "We've already been detained two months in Hamburg. I have certificates from our doctor in St. Petersburg, I have Dr. von Braun's certificate from Hamburg. They both say Samuel no longer has trachoma. He is totally cured!"

The elderly, graying man looked sympathetically at her, then at Samuel. "I am sorry, Mrs. Aronowitz, truly I am. But our laws are very strict, and those of the United States are too. If I don't keep you here in Liverpool for two months, they will surely keep you at Ellis Island." He ruffled Samuel's black hair affectionately. "I am so sorry. I must obey our laws."

This is craziness! Sarah thought. We expected problems in Russia and had none. Now, in England, after wasting two months in Germany, we must wait again. And Mara is not here to help me with the children. I have no place to stay.

"Can I help you find living quarters? Perhaps you will be more comfortable in the Jewish section."

She looked at him sharply. How did he know they were Jewish?

"Can your husband wire some money? Perhaps I can receive it at my bank and turn it over to you in pounds?"

She looked closely at him, beginning to trust herself as a judge of character. He was a caring, honest man. "Could you?"

"Yes."

"If my father in Pinsk were to send you money for me, how would he do it?"

"I see. Well, I have a professional colleague in Minsk, a Russian Orthodox man of liberal persuasion. Here, I will give you his address." Dr. Drysdale paused to write a name and address. "If your father gives him rubles, he can wire the money to my bank here in Liverpool, and you can pick it up in pounds here at my office."

Sarah smiled, liking this man immensely.

"In the meantime I will lend you enough money to live on for the two weeks or so."

Sarah started to shake her head no, then stopped. "Dr. Drysdale, why are you being so kind to me, a stranger and a Jew?"

"Because I have a Jewish daughter-in-law. I'm not sure she has your courage, but if she ever needed assistance, I jolly well hope someone would help her."

Sarah stared at him, astonished that he spoke kindly of a Jewish daughter-in-law. She had never known a Jew who had married a Christian. She decided to try again. "You're sure you can't sign the papers?"

"No. I won't break our laws. And I can't be bribed. But I do know what your people suffer, and I'll help you if you'll let me."

Sarah left Dr. Drysdale's office with conflicting emotions: frustration, anger, respect, even warmth for an honorable, caring man. She'd had few experiences with non-Jews, but most of them had been horrendously insulting and humiliating. She began to feel strong again and instructed a driver to take them back to the cramped room they'd stayed in since arriving in Liverpool.

It had been a murderous voyage, four days of storms and seasickness, four days that had caused Anna to declare over and over again, "I don't like big boats!"

Sarah had learned much about herself and her children. Children are adaptable to any situation, she'd decided, as long as the adult in charge controls her own fears and doesn't share them with the children. Her children made friends easily and learned new languages quickly. Samuel had actually been sorry to leave his new friends in Hamburg to board the ship for Liverpool.

Sarah had also discovered that she was good with money: saving it, bargaining with it, and dealing in several different currencies. She had also discovered she had a language ability that she hadn't known she possessed.

Yes, she and the children had enjoyed Hamburg. It had almost been a holiday, even though she had worked.

Now, in Liverpool, she had only enough money to last her until her father managed to get money to her through Dr. Drysdale.

"I trust these weeks haven't been too horrible," he said as he finally signed the papers declaring Samuel free of trachoma and the entire family healthy and ready to leave for the United States.

"Thanks to you and your bank's services, we've not suffered. Now, I must hurry over to the steamship office."

"You have your tickets?"

"I have five tickets for a ship that sailed sixteen weeks ago! But I believe they'll honor them for the next ship heading for New York."

Dr. Drysdale stood and offered his hand. Handshaking between men and women was new to Sarah; back in Russia, any touching between sexes, except that between man and wife, was forbidden.

She held her hand out in response. "Thank you, doctor, and good-bye."

"Mrs. Aronowitz, I wish you bon voyage and a safe crossing with no seasickness."

Her next stop was the steamship office. It was already the end of August—she should have been in America for several months by now!

"We're completely booked. The best I can do is take these tickets, refund you the money, and sell you five steerage spaces." The clerk looked at her as if he were certain she would wait rather than travel steerage.

Another wait! It was intolerable, frustrating to the point of madness!

Sarah had no idea what traveling steerage entailed, but she was determined to get her family on the next ship, no matter what class they traveled.

"All right," she snapped. "I'll take the money and the steerage tickets. And we leave the day after tomorrow?"

"Yes. The *Atlantic Prince*."

"Tell me," she asked, suddenly worried about her quick decision. "What is the food like in steerage?"

"Ah . . . I would recommend you bring as much as you can. Preserved fruit, preserved meats, cereal—bring as much as you can with you. Of course, they do serve three meals, but the food might not be to your liking."

He means it's not kosher, she thought meanly, but I didn't expect it would be.

Sarah spent the next day buying crates of nonperishable food.

Dressed in her fine blue serge traveling dress with the leg-of-mutton sleeves and a small black hat perched atop her carefully arranged pompadour, Sarah Aronowitz walked up the gangplank carrying Sasha. Samuel, Albert, and Anna, also dressed in their finest summer outfits, each holding the other's hand, followed immediately behind. Then came three young men whom Sarah had paid a pound apiece to carry their trunks, bundles, and crates of food.

The sailor directing traffic began to direct her toward the second-class level, then looked again at her tickets. "Has there been a mistake, missus? Are you traveling steerage?" He looked her up and down, then looked appraisingly at the children.

"Those are the only tickets I could buy. I'm told there's no other space available."

He looked at the tickets again, winced, and then directed the Aronowitz family down to the steerage section.

As she descended the stairs, head held high, she once again reassured the children and herself, "At last, at last, children, we are on our way to America. In fifteen days we will see your pa again!"

❊ Chapter 8

People traveling in steerage class quickly separated themselves into groups according to homeland and religion. So it was that Sarah made friends and carved out space for herself and her children with seventeen Russian Jewish families and eleven Russian Jewish men who were traveling to America, for one reason or another, without families.

Jewish refugees from Latvia, Lithuania, Poland, and Germany also crowded into the limited steerage space. Catholic farmers from Germany and Ireland, and a handful of English families—all seeking a new life in the promised land of opportunity—filled every last inch of space on the bottom of the overloaded ship.

Initially, Sarah, like a mother hen with chicks, tried to keep her brood within eyesight. But each day, Albert and Samuel wandered farther away to find friends among the Yiddish-speaking children. The women exchanged gossip and stories about their families "back home" and told one another all the rumors about life in America. They did needlework and nursed their babies and chased after their toddlers. The men smoked and played cards and chess and told stories about how they had outsmarted the cossacks. For the first five days of the voyage, Sarah thought it wasn't so bad. Then, on the sixth day, hope turned to fear.

A Yiddish-speaking sailor named Danny, not more than nineteen years old, who had boasted of having made the Atlantic crossing eight times, came down to their group. He said, "The captain has asked that anyone with medical experience, any nurses or doctors, come to his office immediately."

One of the single men who'd worked as an assistant in a hospital in St. Petersburg, and two women who had been nurses, followed Danny up to the captain's office.

Late that night, they returned with the dreaded news: "Two cases of cholera. No question about the diagnosis. We must immediately take measures to protect ourselves."

Suspicion clutched Sarah's heart. Could this be a trick? But then she remembered the kindly Dr. Drysdale. This was a British ship, she reminded herself, not a Russian or a Polish ship. Surely they intended Jews no harm.

All around her, parents were holding their children. Tears

streamed down the mothers' eyes, while the men registered terror mixed with defiance.

Somehow we'll make it, pray God!

All the milk aboard the ship, Danny told them, had been thrown overboard. Human waste had to be disposed of immediately. All water must be boiled for at least five minutes before being consumed.

When the initial hysteria subsided, Sarah called Danny aside and asked, "Can you get us a big metal tub and some coal?"

He looked at her as if she were crazy.

"You must try. We will build a fire over by that air vent, cook our own food, and keep our children from dying. I have a five-pound note, and there's more. If you can help us, a bit extra."

Sarah barely slept that night. She felt awful fear in the pit of her intestines, then realized that the fear could bring on diarrhea and vomiting, and she could be falsely diagnosed as having cholera. "We must organize ourselves tomorrow," she mumbled to herself. "We must be busy every minute—too busy to worry."

The next morning, Danny brought Sarah a big steel tub, a bag of coal, and an iron pot. As if by magic, three samovars were pulled out of trunks, along with other large pots and pans and eating utensils.

Sarah, having procured the essentials, organized several women to cook for the group. Everyone would drink tea, lots of it, and eat oatmeal flavored with a drop of honey or preserves. Dried fruit, of which Sarah had bought a large supply, and fresh bananas, which Danny would bring them in quantity for a tip, plus hard-boiled eggs, which he would also supply, would be their daily fare. Bread, herring, and soup made from a chicken and whatever else was available would keep them from starving for the remainder of the trip.

Sarah organized the children into "lesson groups," which the fathers and mothers would teach according to their skills, and one of the fathers organized the smaller children into "game groups." In the midst of this happy organizing, word arrived that seven more cases of cholera had been discovered, and two passengers had died. To protect the health of the remaining passengers, the two bodies would be disposed of at sea.

Spontaneously, the entire steerage section seemed to become a synagogue. Loud voices chanted Hebrew prayers for the dead and more prayers for the continued health of the living. The prayers turned to singing and then back to quiet conversation.

"We must keep very busy. We must not let the children see our fear, or someone will be misdiagnosed," Sarah scolded as she walked from group to group. "You, Aaron—teach those boys over there how to play poker," she admonished a young father, who was staring at his wife and children with tears in his eyes. "Your premature tears don't do anyone any good!"

By day, she kept herself ceaselessly busy, haranguing anyone she caught doing nothing. By night, in her bunk with Sasha and Anna, she allowed herself the luxury of tears. For the first time in her life, she felt utterly helpless, beyond the reach of her father's reputation or her mother's wealth. Like an insect, she felt anonymous. No power she could invoke would save her children or herself from death at sea. She had never felt so bereft and lonely. *"Boruch ata Adonai . . ."*

The next day, Sarah realized that the group needed daily exercise and fresh air if they were to fight off cholera. "Danny, please take me to the captain. I will be the spokesman for our group."

At first Danny hesitated, but seeing her determination, he shrugged his shoulders and told her to follow him.

She held her head high and tried to imagine how her grandmother Eliasberg might handle such a situation. Simply remembering her grandmother's imperious ways gave Sarah a sudden morale boost as she knocked at the captain's cabin door.

In response to a shouted "Come in," she entered, followed by Danny. He would translate, as she could speak no English and the captain surely could speak no Russian or Yiddish.

"I've come to speak to you about the conditions in the steerage section, Captain Everett," she said, looking directly at the middle-aged blond man with the wind-battered skin. "My name is Sarah Aronowitz, and I am traveling with four small children."

"Yes. And what are your complaints?"

"Actually, not a complaint, sir. Given the fact that a cholera epidemic has broken out aboard ship, and given the fact that it seems to be occurring mostly in steerage class, I want to request that the passengers be given an opportunity—perhaps an hour each day—to exercise on the upper deck and get some sunlight and fresh air."

"Impossible. The rest of the passengers would be outraged. We can't have a bunch of ragamuffin refugees littering the upper decks, spreading disease."

"The doctor I've spoken to, sir, says fresh air and exercise are absolutely essential for the well-being of the below-deck passengers. I implore you, as a humane act—"

"I will think about it."

"Captain, I need not remind you that the lives of hundreds of people are in your hands on this ship."

"I know that, damn it!"

"I'm sure you feel the responsibility very intensely."

"Mrs. Aronowitz, I've heard quite enough. You should be pleased that I've let you get away with your cooking operation down there. Highly irregular, that!"

Sarah smiled at Danny. She didn't know the captain knew about her small infraction of the rules.

"The danger of fire is always very great on a ship. I trust you and your people will be very careful."

"Sir, you may be sure of it. I have lived all my life in a city where even the sidewalks are made of wood. I am fully aware of the danger of fire. We will be most careful."

"Thank you. Now if you'll excuse me . . ."

"Captain, if you would confer with the medical personnel on the ship, I'm sure they would advise you to let the steerage passengers up for exercise. Please, at least ask their advice, for the sake of your own conscience."

"Good-bye, Mrs. Aronowitz!"

The next morning at dawn, the Russian Jews were awakened by Danny. "Captain Everett has ordered all passengers to exercise for one hour, beginning in five minutes. Please get ready and follow me."

A cheer went up. Sarah promptly became the leader of their group as they promenaded around the deck six times. Afterward, they went below for a breakfast of black bread and herring and more boiled tea with preserves.

Meanwhile, Danny herded groups of the remaining steerage passengers upstairs for exercise.

In the next days thirty-two passengers, three of them from the Russian group, were buried at sea. Everyone was thirsty and hungry; even water was now rationed. On the fifteenth day,

Danny came down to announce that on deck they could see the shores of America.

"Mrs. Aronowitz, if you would follow me, Captain Everett wants a word with you."

Sarah winced at the fetid odor as she passed a slops jar and followed Danny up three long flights of stairs.

This time, the captain welcomed her into his office, invited her to be seated, and poured her a cup of English tea.

"We . . . ah . . . we have a problem, and I understand you are more or less the leader of your group, organizing them. As such . . . I thought you might be able to help me."

"Yes? What problem other than the cholera?"

"That's it. You see, the United States authorities won't permit us to land and offload the passengers."

"I don't believe it!" Sarah's hand flew to her mouth.

"We are to receive a shipment of food and water in a matter of hours. But the authorities may not let us disembark."

"We must wire the Hebrew Immigrant Aid Society in New York. Surely they will find a way to help. I insist, Captain!"

"Yes, indeed, Mrs. Aronowitz, send a wire to anyone you think can help. I want to dock this ship as much as you do, believe me."

"There are more important Jews than me on this ship. Bring the wealthiest Jews out of first class in here, and we'll send wires to relatives in New York."

Twenty-four hours later, word came that fresh food and water would be delivered every day, but the seven hundred-odd passengers must stay aboard for fifteen days, idling off Manhattan. The Red Cross notified all relatives that the passengers would then be taken to Hoffman Island for a five-week quarantine after the fifteen days.

The Jewish passengers counted: they would spend Rosh Hashanah on Hoffman Island but, if they were lucky, Yom Kippur with their families.

The next day, Sarah asked Danny for another meeting with Captain Everett. After making polite conversation over tea, she got to the point. "We deeply appreciate your making it possible for us to get an hour of fresh air every day. But under these quite extraordinary circumstances, might it be possible to increase the exercise time to two hours a day, one in the morning and one in the afternoon or evening? I'm sure the other passengers would understand."

"It would be quite extraordinary."

"But these are quite extraordinary circumstances."

"Yes, I see. By the way, Mrs. Aronowitz, I have an empty cabin in second class, just the right size for you and your children. It's been cleaned well, and it's quite safe."

"There's an elderly couple in our group who need it more than I. Now, about the exercise—I'll be happy to write a wire to your superior requesting it."

"Let me think about it."

"Captain Everett! Both you and I know you have the authority to do this! Stop playing games when hundreds of lives are at stake!"

Three hours later, the steerage passengers were led upstairs for their second hour of exercise that day.

It was late October before Sarah Aronowitz and her four children, along with seven hundred other weary passengers, were told they would be released to their relatives. They never understood exactly who had been feeding and clothing them and communicating with their relatives. The most they could determine was that it was some combination of the government, the steamship line, the Red Cross, and the Hebrew Immigrant Aid Society.

Sarah had organized life for her little community of Russian Jews on Hoffman Island exactly as she had on the ship. The boys and girls could now add and subtract and speak Yiddish and Russian—some could even read in both languages. They had heard all the old fairy tales innumerable times, and their imaginations had been stretched to make up new stories. They had become accomplished actors after putting on performances to break the boredom.

Sarah had recruited Danny to tell them about life in America and drill them in English words. Everyone was busy practicing English and desperately trying to stay healthy for the final, crucial physical exam at Ellis Island.

Sarah was told that her husband had come, for the second time, to New York from Washington and would be waiting for them when they cleared immigration. As she bathed and dressed herself, Sarah wondered what he would feel when he saw her and the children. Lice had invaded their hair, and the boys' heads had been shaved on the ship. It had nearly torn her heart out to see those beautiful boys made ugly. Her dress had been ruined, first by the horrors of the trip, then by the government's insistence on fumigating their clothing. Luckily, she'd had enough notice to snip off the second, fifth, and seventh buttons on each sleeve and hide them in her bag. Now she must greet Jacob in a shapeless, faded cotton shift that had been sent in by some Jewish charity in New York. Her children looked poverty-stricken and gaunt. What would Jacob think? Would he have any comprehension of their ordeal? Could anyone who hadn't lived through it understand?

Jacob Aronowitz tapped the ebony cane he carried for effect against the pavement, keeping time to a popular tune that was playing in his head. Two hours already he had waited, scrutinizing each woman with children who had walked out the doors. Why was it taking so long? Surely nothing else could have gone wrong. Only two days ago, before leaving Washington, he'd received a letter from Sarah saying the children were well. Praised be God!

Would she recognize him in his new suit, with his hair freshly barbered and his beard gone now for two years? He'd gained weight and a few gray hairs, but overall he knew he was still an attractive man. Many a mother at Adas Israel Congregation, not believing he was really married, had tried to interest him in her daughter.

His heart lurched. He thought he was dreaming. Outside the door, just now, stood a bewildered mother, her long black hair covered in a faded babushka and dark circles under her eyes. Two ragamuffin boys, and a dark-eyed, gaunt girl who looked a bit like his Anna—could this be them?

He stared at the hapless group.

They stared back at him.

At the same moment, they began walking toward one another. When they were close enough to reach out and touch, the frail, dark-eyed woman said, "Jacob? Is it you, Jacob?"

"Sarah . . . Sarah . . . my God!" He wrapped his arms around her, the realization of her ordeal sweeping over him like waves of nausea. Her letters had all been so hopeful. Could it really have been this bad?

He knelt down to greet the boys and Anna. Samuel was somber-faced, almost angry. "Couldn't you do anything, Pa?"

"No, son, the rules . . ."

"I don't like boats. I hate boats!" Anna declared, not sure who this strange man was.

"Where's our house, Pa?" Albert asked. Then, spying four black men sitting on a bench, he asked, "Does that color wash off, Pa?"

"Hush, hush, you mustn't talk about shvartzers like that. Not here." He kissed Sasha, who had insisted on being put down on the pavement. He had never seen her before. Then he stood up and hugged Sarah again.

This is a different woman, he thought. My wife! But I don't recognize her. Will she ever regain her youth and beauty? He searched his heart for love, but what he felt was sorrow and pity. Understanding that it was he who had put them through this ordeal, he felt enormous guilt. He pushed all those feelings to the back of his head.

"Here, we'll take this horse-cart." He motioned to the nearest driver to help load the bundles and trunk, then helped each child. As he assisted Sarah, he said triumphantly, "Welcome to America! I'm so glad you're finally here!"

To the driver he said, "Pennsylvania Station."

The children looked out the window of the speeding train eagerly, incessantly asking questions. So much was new! They had never been in a train before, had never had a soda pop, had never eaten a hot dog. Nor had they seen black people who walked back and forth through the car selling food, taking tickets, calling out the names of strange cities.

Jacob insisted they repeat the name of everything. They would learn English immediately.

"Your suit is elegant, Jacob. It must have been expensive." Sarah smiled shyly at him. All her confidence had deserted her since leaving Hoffman Island. When he removed his jacket, she was shocked to see a black armband. "Why are you wearing that? For your father, still?"

"No, dearest." There's so much I have to tell you, he thought. "It's for . . . my mother, Suevia. She passed away in July."

"Oh!" Sarah gasped, and tears filled her eyes at the memory

of their parting. "I'm so—so sorry. She wanted pictures—she would have liked to see you in your suit. But why, Jacob, do you not wear a hat or a yarmulke?"

"This is America! That's only for the old Jews. When you come here, you must dress like an American. We will buy new clothes for you and the children too!" As he looked at her tired, piercing eyes, he realized this was a different woman from the wife he'd left two and a half years before. She had lost her youth and her beauty—and her sophistication. The softness was gone. Along with her gaunt body, he sensed a woman hardened by experiences that he could only surmise.

"Pa, can I have another hot dog?" Albert sang out as the vendor made his way down the aisle.

"From hunger! I've never seen such hungry children." He ruffled Albert's scalp, which was just beginning to bristle with the growth of new hair.

"We *are* hungry, Jacob. We've been hungry for so long, we don't know what a full stomach feels like." She looked at him with chilling eyes. "Jacob, tell me truthfully. Are those—those hot dogs . . . *trayf?* Are they pork?"

Jacob felt his face redden. He'd been eating forbidden food for so long, he hadn't even thought to explain to her that he didn't keep kosher, he didn't follow the dietary laws anymore. "Yes . . . well . . . that's one more thing we need to discuss. We will keep kosher at home if you insist, but when we're away from home, eat like everyone else. It's the only sensible thing to do in America."

Sarah watched her children gobble up the novel sandwiches. It was a first. They had never eaten pork before. "Pray God my father never sees this," she whispered in a despairing voice, then turned away from Jacob and concentrated on the view of Philadelphia.

A couple of hours later, the Aronowitz family arrived at Union Station in Washington, D.C.

"The fountains are beautiful!" Sarah gasped when they walked outside the station onto the sidewalk.

"Look at the Capitol! That's the Capitol, Sarah!"

"Magnificent!"

"Tomorrow I'll show you where the President lives. A wonderful house."

"Yes. Tonight I only want to see my house, thank you!"

They climbed aboard another horse-drawn carriage for the short ride to Sixth and K in the Southwest, Jewish section of Washington. Sarah was pleased with what she saw. Unlike the poverty she had glimpsed from the train in Baltimore and Philadelphia, Washington was exactly as Jacob had described it. A splendidly beautiful city of broad avenues lined with tall old trees and friendly-looking shops.

She was excited. Her new life would now begin. Soon the carriage came to a stop in front of a tall redbrick house on the corner.

"Children," Jacob announced, "we are home. This is your new home!"

He unlocked the door and lit a gas lamp, which illuminated the front-room grocery store. He led the family through the grocery, cautioning them not to touch the glass cases—"We don't need sticky fingerprints."

The next room was furnished with a sofa, two large chairs, more gas lamps, and a table in front of the sofa. Sarah noticed there were no draperies or curtains, only a dog-eared window shade. But the floor was wood. She did have a wood floor after all!

The kitchen was the final room on the first floor. Jacob had furnished it with two sets of bunk beds that he had made himself, a gleaming white square metal table, four hard-back wooden chairs, a peculiar-looking stove, cupboards, and a sink.

"Let me show you the water pipe," Jacob enthused as he turned a knob. Water came gushing forth. "I told you we don't have water carriers in America!"

Under the sink, Sarah saw the corrugated metal tub that would be the family bath and laundry tub. "Is the water only cold?"

"Yes. So far, we haven't put a heater in the house. Someday soon."

"And where will we sleep, Jacob?" Sarah was still carrying a heavy bundle, wondering where to put it down.

"Oh, in the parlor. That sofa is a bed. I'll show you!"

"What about upstairs? Aren't there bedrooms upstairs?"

"I've rented the upstairs to the Epstein family. You'll like them. She's a wonderful cook."

Sarah carried her bundle back into the tiny parlor. She looked at the bilious green sofa, sat down in a brown overstuffed chair, and looked at the other chair: a faded, worn, dirty rose-colored brocade, obviously secondhand. Paint was peeling from the walls, and the floors needed refinishing. Her eyes rested on the crude rectangular table—a slab of wood with four legs—in front of the sofa. "Did you make the table, too, Jacob?"

"Yes. It's not much, but it serves a purpose for now."

"Ma, can we get undressed now?" Samuel asked. He was anxious to try out his top bunk.

"Yes, and please help Anna." She looked with pleading eyes to Jacob. "I'm so tired. Would you mind getting Sasha ready for bed?"

"Of course! Of course!" Jacob hurried back into the kitchen.

Sarah wondered how much longer she could hide her deep disappointment.

One day at a time, she told herself, lifting her bag onto the table. Like on the ship, like on Hoffman Island. I'll do it one day at a time.

When she was in her nightdress, she slumped back into the brown chair. Jacob was still talking to his new-found children.

For this, she thought as she stared at the offensive sofa, for this we came to America.

⊠ Part 3

The Promise of America, 1911

A spokesman for The George Washington University Hospital confirmed that Mrs. Anna Dunay is resting comfortably while extensive tests are under way. It is anticipated that she will be hospitalized at least one more week. Her room is "absolutely overflowing with flowers," the spokesman continued, "and the family is arranging for their transfer to various nursing homes around the city."

—The Washington Times
"Life" Section

⊠ Chapter 9

So, then, to every man his chance—to every man, regardless of his birth, his shining, golden opportunity—to every man the right to live, to work, to be himself, and to become whatever thing his manhood and his vision can combine to make him—this, seeker, is the promise of America.

Thomas Wolfe
You Can't Go Home Again

Washington, D.C., Yom Kippur Afternoon 1917

Ten-year-old Anna Arnold put down her library book—it was the third time she'd read *Little Women,* she liked Jo so much— and glanced at Sasha, who was sitting cross-legged playing jacks on the floor of the bedroom they shared. She decided to go downstairs and find Mama. As she passed the mirror above their dresser, she saw that her long black hair was mussed. Quickly she ran a brush through it, then remembered the comments of the women at the *shul.* She looked carefully at her eyes. Yes, she thought, they did match her dress, they were exactly the same shade of blue.

She ran downstairs to the dining room. "Mama? You're crying!"

Sarah looked up from her prayer book, untucked the handkerchief in her belt, wiped her eyes, and patted Anna's hand, which had come to rest on the damask tablecloth.

"What's wrong, Mama?" Anna was still dressed in her bluevelvet jumper and white lace-trimmed blouse. She hadn't changed since they'd returned from *shul* with Sasha and the baby.

"It's nothing. I'm remembering the old days back in Russia. I —I miss my mother and father on the holidays."

Anna stared at her mother. Why was she so unhappy?

Sarah broke the silence. "Do you remember them at all? Do you have any memory of your grandparents?"

"Yes. I remember Bobbe and Zayde very well. I remember Zayde's long beard and Bobbe's huge house. I can see it in my head whenever I shut my eyes. They had a wonderful house, didn't they, Ma?"

"Yes, indeed. It was beautiful. And beautifully furnished. Remember the deep red oriental rug? And Bobbe's china—Meissen, it was!"

Anna looked around the small room that served as their dining room and parlor combined, now that the Epsteins had moved out and the upstairs had been turned into three bedrooms. "Our house is nice now, too, Mama."

"Yes. But . . ."

"Do you think someday you'll go visit Bobbe in Jerusalem?"

"I doubt it. Who knows how much longer she'll live? She's fifty-one already, and she's been through so much . . . so much loss. First my father of blessed memory and then Bobbe Eliasberg, and then going with Weizmann to Jerusalem. They had to leave everything behind. They gave up everything. Everything."

"But Ma, at least she's safe there, and she's with two of her children and some of her grandchildren. Perhaps it's for the best. I wish you would cheer up. Bobbe wouldn't want you crying for her on Yom Kippur."

Sarah reached out and caressed the brass Yom Kippur candle that Suevia Aronowitz had given her as a parting gift. "Do you remember anything about the crossing on the ship, Anna?"

"I remember it all, every minute. And I'll never go on a ship again. Or a hay cart either. That was the most miserable summer of my life."

"I'm surprised you remember so much. You were such a little one, only four—"

"I remember the soldier hitting you."

"No."

"Yes. Sometimes I have nightmares. The soldier hits you, and I have a piece of matzo in my hand and try to hit him back with it, but the matzo crumbles. I have that dream all the time."

Yes, Sarah mused, I suppose the child does have nightmares about those days. It may have been harder on the children than I thought at the time. My bones, my body will never be the same again! Aches and pains and chills—one never recovers from something like that. But at least I have baby Joshua now, a namesake for my father of blessed memory. "Is Joshua asleep, Anna?"

"Yes, Ma. He went to sleep the minute I put him down. And

Sasha is practicing jacks in our room. She said to call her when you need help in the kitchen."

"Well, just looking at you has cheered me up, as it always does. You're such a good girl, I appreciate all you do to help, Anna, in the store and with Joshua. You know that, don't you, dearest? I think sometimes I'm so weary, I forget to tell you that. And your patience when you teach me English and read the papers to me . . ."

Anna blanched in embarrassment. She could handle only so much praise, Sarah realized. "Would you like to read your book now? Since you've spent most of the day in *shul*, you can go read your book. God will understand."

"How much longer before Pa and the boys get home?"

"Not till sundown, not till yizkor service is over. I'll call you and Sasha when I need your help. Now, run along. You might want to change your dress so you won't spill anything on it."

"Yes, Mama."

After Anna left the small parlor, Sarah tried again to concentrate on the words in her prayer book. She had left *shul* early in the afternoon when Joshua, now four, had begun to fuss. Now, in the late afternoon, she couldn't help but think of the wonderful holiday seasons she had enjoyed in Russia. She compared them with life here. There she had dressed in such fine clothes, and meals had been huge family gatherings—real celebrations. The entire city of Pinsk had seemed to close down for the High Holy Days. Here, they closed the stores on the holidays, but the family at her dining table consisted only of Jacob, herself, and their five children.

Everything in America was different and faster. Even their name was shorter. Jacob had changed it to Arnold. Now she was Sarah Arnold, storekeeper. She ran the grocery store in their front room six long days a week, closing only on Sunday. Jacob had turned it over to her within six months of her arrival in America; he had worked for his cousin at the Morning Star Bakery again for two years, then opened another grocery in Anacostia. Fourteen-year-old Albert worked for him after school and on Saturdays. Twelve-year-old Samuel, along with Anna, helped her run the small store in their front parlor. And Sasha helped take care of Joshua.

After a few initial arguments, Sarah had taken control of the family finances from Jacob. She had determined that the first order of business was to get the family out of debt, to pay off Jacob's loan from the Hebrew Free Loan Society. She had sold one of her grandmother's diamonds to buy what she considered the bare necessities for her family: decent furniture, dishes, Sabbath candlesticks, a Sabbath tablecloth, and some new clothes for the children and herself.

The next order of business had been to claim the entire house for her own family. This meant paying twice the rent they had been paying and then buying furniture for the upstairs bedroom. This had been accomplished by scrimping and saving every penny, for two long years.

With the advent of Joshua and the added laundry to be done in the corrugated metal tub in the kitchen, she hired a black woman, Maud, to come in one day a week to do her laundry and a second day a week to clean her house. She paid Maud a dollar a day, and Maud was delighted to have the work.

She stared at the candle as if in a hypnotic trance. Now she had to concentrate on saving for the boys' education. They had to go to college. She didn't know about the girls. It would be nice, but it was more important that they marry well. And to do that they needed clothes and a nice home to entertain young men in. They had to move away soon, out to Petworth, maybe up Sixteenth Street, she thought.

In Pinsk it would have been easy to make them good marriages, but here they were nobodies. In Pinsk they were considered people of quality, educated. It's Jacob's fault we had to leave. Why couldn't he leave well enough alone? Why did he have to organize the working people? And look at him now. He manages a small store—nothing big. A lot he's made of himself in America! Sarah knew Rachel would be shocked by the way her daughter was living. The work in the store, the drudgery . . .

The door slammed, and Jacob, Albert, and Samuel walked into the parlor.

"Still praying?" Jacob looked at her and saw the tears. "Well, it's time to break the fast! Time for a drink!"

Sarah stood up slowly, reluctant to interrupt her reverie. "I'll . . . get things ready. Just a few minutes." She went to the bottom of the staircase and called to Sasha and Anna.

Platters of gefilte fish, lox and bagels and cream cheese, cottage cheese and freshly cut fruit, herring salad, and a gelatin

mold were carried to the table. Jacob poured wine for everyone
and said a blessing over it and the hallah. Then the family
wasted no time filling their plates after the twenty-four-hour
fast.

"To a good year!" Jacob toasted, taking a second big gulp of
wine. "What do you say, Sarah? Don't you think this will be a
splendid year for the Arnold family?"

He's trying so hard, God bless him, she thought, to raise me
out of this moodiness.

"Albert will stay out of trouble with the police, and his
grades will improve, and he'll hit ten home runs. Samuel will
get a messenger job this summer with Western Union, right,
Samuel?"

Samuel, always anxious to please, smiled at his father, while
Albert ignored Jacob's remarks and stuffed his mouth.

"Anna will stick her nose in a book every time Mama turns
her back, and Sasha will become the champion jacks player in
all of Washington!"

"And what do you prophesy for Joshua, Pa?" Anna asked.

"Joshua will learn his alphabet and his numbers if you teach
him, my dear. And he'll be ready for school soon. Won't you,
Joshua?"

"And then, my dear," he said to Sarah, "you'll have more
time for the Sisterhood. Maybe you'll even want to teach over
at Amity Hall. After all, no one knows Hebrew better than Reb
Siderman's daughter!" he added with pride in his voice.

"I'd like that. Someday when the children are older. I do
miss the old ways. . . ."

"I know you do, dearest, but this is America."

Later that evening, after the children were in bed, Sarah sat
with her crocheting and a glass of tea with cherry preserves in
their small parlor. She was waiting for the last of the four
yahrzeit candles to burn down. As was their tradition on Yom
Kippur, she had lit a memorial candle for each of Jacob's parents, for her father, and for her bobbe Eliasberg. Though Jacob
had dozed off in the big chair across from her, the Yiddish
newspaper on his lap, Sarah was determined to concentrate on
memories of her family until the last flame flickered out.

Suddenly, with a start, Jacob awakened. He looked hard at
Sarah and brought himself out of a nightmare, back to reality.

He shook his head as if to clear it, then went to the kitchen and poured himself some schnapps.

When he came back into the parlor, he sat down next to Sarah on the small sofa and put his arm around her to comfort her. "I know, Sarah, I know," he said in a soothing voice.

"You miss the old country, too, Jacob?" She wiped her eyes again.

"You'll never know how much. I don't like to dwell on it. My parents, your family—the feeling of comfort just from knowing they were there." He sipped his drink. "In Pinsk I knew every street, every alley. I'd lived there all my life, like you, Sarah. It was home. Comfortable. Here—well, everything's so big, so confusing. The language . . ."

"I know, Jacob." She patted his hand. "You find English difficult. You should let Anna teach you. She's very patient."

"Ach! Who wants their children to be their teacher?"

"But in all the families it's the same. The children speak and read English perfectly, while the parents grope for the right word."

"Oh, Sarah, it's not just that." He sighed, wiping his face with his handkerchief. "I was *someone* in Pinsk. The men respected me. I was their leader. Here I'm a poor, ignorant shopkeeper."

"I've wondered why you haven't gotten involved with the unions here."

"Sarah, for God's sake." Jacob stood and began to pace back and forth, gesturing with his glass of schnapps. "It's bad enough to have to flee one country in a lifetime. I'll never—" He looked at her, and tears formed in his eyes. "I'll never endanger you and the children again. That day I saw you at Ellis Island, saw what my obstinate, hard-headed ways had done to you and the children, I promised myself I'd never put you in danger again."

"Oh, you mustn't feel that way! What you were fighting for in Russia was right! And we got here safely after all. It just took a long time."

Jacob sat down beside Sarah and took her face in his hands. "I love you, Sarah, and I'll never forgive myself for what I've done to you. You're—you're old before your time, overworked, and you don't let yourself enjoy life, and it's my fault. I never forget that, not for a moment."

He kissed her hard, then kissed her again.

"Jacob, I never knew . . . we've never talked about it. I thought you loved America."

"I put up a good front. What else can I do? I see your courage, your determination. But the truth is—and both of us know it—we didn't choose to come here. We were forced to come because of my activities."

"Jacob," she pleaded, determined to cheer him up, "life is good here. The children are so happy. And they can go to school. And we don't have to worry about the conscription."

"Yes, I tell myself that every day." He drained the last drop from his glass and put it on the table in front of the sofa. "You and I may never live as well as your family did in Pinsk, but if the children take advantage of all the opportunities here, surely *they* will."

"So we must cheer ourselves up, Jacob. Every day. By reminding ourselves of their future. Besides, life is safer and better for Jews here, everyone knows that."

"Yes, here it's the colored people who are treated badly. They are the objects of bigotry and scorn. If I were to fight for anything here, it would be for a better life for them. They're human beings too."

He stood and reached for Sarah's hand. "But as you've heard me say, I did enough fighting and organizing in Russia to last me a lifetime. No, here we're safe. And the well-being of my little family, the seven of us, is my only concern."

The last of the yahrzeit candles flickered out. Sarah picked them up and carried them into the kitchen. Then she forced herself to sound hopeful. She came back into the parlor, took Jacob's hand in hers, and said, "Come, let's go upstairs."

Sarah sat in the tiny yard in front of the corner store with her next-door neighbor, Edith Rappaport. The two women fanned themselves and watched Edith's two toddlers play. Sarah sighed, then said, "Do you think we'll ever get used to such heat?"

"We never had weather like this in Russia, that's for sure. But I like it here. This is a good neighborhood to raise children," Edith answered, putting her fan down and exchanging it for a sock that needed darning. "So Samuel isn't going to be working in the store anymore. A big-shot messenger for Western Union, I hear."

"Yes. I really don't need him anymore. Anna's wonderful in the store. She's there now, either reading or talking on the phone. She and Sasha always have their ears glued to that phone. We had it put in for the business, but it's nice for the girls to be able to talk to their school friends."

"I'll bet they don't have telephones back in Pinsk yet, or Victrolas. Or cars, for that matter," Edith said as she spied a Model T driving slowly down Sixth Street.

"Jacob can't wait to get one," Sarah said in an exasperated tone. "He's saving for a car. I'm trying to convince him we need a bathroom first. Why do we need a car when we have street-cars? But it would be so nice to have a bathroom."

"I agree. But the men love cars."

"And Albert and Samuel, and I guess even the girls, agree with their father. That's one argument I won't win."

"But wouldn't it be nice if you could drive over to Indiana Avenue to pick up your orders from the traveling salesmen, the drummers, rather than schlepp over there every Sunday night on the streetcar, you and all the children?"

"That's Jacob's main argument for buying a car. He's even thinking of borrowing again from the Hebrew Free Loan Society, though I hate to be in debt to anyone."

"It seems to me a car would make everything so much easier for you and Jacob," Edith commented. "With you running two stores and the children getting older. It won't be long before Albert will be able to drive too."

"I suppose you're right. But I'd like a bathroom." Sarah heard the phone jingle, then heard Anna's melodious voice answer it. Shortly, she came to the door.

"Mama, it's Footer's Delicatessen. They want four quarts of your herring salad by three o'clock Saturday afternoon. Okay?"

"Tell them to send someone to pick it up. I'm not responsible for deliveries on the Sabbath!"

"So," Edith chuckled, "your salad is becoming famous!"

"They offered me fifty dollars—imagine!—for the recipe. But I won't sell it. Why should I? People are coming from all over —even outside The Island—to buy it. I get calls every day."

"The Island" was what the Jewish residents called the self-contained area, isolated from the rest of Washington, where they lived. It was bounded by the canal, the Mall, and government buildings on the north; by the Washington Channel and wholesale markets on the west; South Capitol Street and the Anacostia River on the east; and by the arsenal known as Ft. McNair on the south. One hundred nineteen Russian refugee families had settled there since Sarah had arrived in 1911.

By her calculation, she served some ninety families with her small grocery operation, but the number grew each week as word of her special salads spread. She hired Maud to come each Thursday and Friday morning, two extra days, just to make fresh salads so the Jewish families could serve them on Saturday evening when they celebrated the end of the Sabbath.

"So you won't even tell your secret recipe to your next-door neighbor?"

"Why should I? So you can get the fifty dollars from Footer's?" The two women laughed, each knowing she could trust the other. "Besides, it's easier I should send Anna over with a gift of my salad every Friday afternoon in exchange for your pecan buns. It keeps my family happy—and my recipe a deep secret!"

"I've tasted Footer's imitation of your salad. What do they do wrong?" Edith asked, as she tucked a strand of dark hair back into her bun.

"That meshugga Footer puts mayonnaise and mustard in it. I use only sour cream—that's the difference. Now, I won't say another word!" Sarah winked at her friend, then smoothed her checkered apron over her blue-muslin skirt.

"Your Anna, she loves that opera music." They heard Caruso's tenor filtering through the screen door.

"Yes, and she plays it too loud. It drives her father nuts. Anna's determined to be the most cultured person in all of Washington. It makes me laugh—she's so much like her grandmother Eliasberg in Pinsk, and she hardly knew her. She was only four when we left."

"What I miss most is the Sabbath," Edith said as she wiped her little girl's nose with the handkerchief that was always tucked up her sleeve.

"Me too. There, we really looked forward. Here, it's the hardest day of the week. We work from before sunup till midnight."

"Well, it can't be helped. Business is business."

"My father of blessed memory would turn over in his grave if he knew." Sarah sighed and fanned herself.

"But you still keep kosher. Of that, he'd be proud."

"Ach! *I* do, but the children, the minute they leave The Island, they eat all kinds of *trayf.* I know it, they don't need to tell me. Not one of them will keep the old ways. Such a shame," she said, shaking her head. "When I think of how I could speak Hebrew even, and Anna and Sasha can't read a word of it. Such a pity."

"What does a girl need Hebrew for in America? Better she should learn how to put makeup on and get a rich husband."

The phone rang again, and Anna came to the door for her mother. Sarah stood with effort, fanned herself one last time, then bade good afternoon to Edith.

Eleven-year-old Anna, still dressed in the navy-blue-linen dress her mother had paid twelve dollars for at Kann's, removed the white-velvet band from her hair. It was too tight, and her head had been aching since early afternoon. She sat alone at the kitchen table this night. The house was quiet, and everyone had gone to sleep. She savored the feel of the linen against her palms, then opened her diary and began to write. She told herself that she couldn't not write about this important day in her favorite brother's life.

Dear Diary,

Today was Samuel's bar mitzvah. He did very well, according to all the old folks. I didn't understand a word of it 'cause it was all in Hebrew, but he sounded good and his chanting voice was strong and confident. And he looked ever so handsome in his new suit. He's the best-looking boy in the family.

Mama looked the nicest I've ever seen her look. She went to the beauty parlor to have her hair done. She wore a rose-colored silk dress and a matching hat—both new, from the best department at Hecht's—and new black patent-leather shoes and a new bag. It's the first time I remember Mama spending any money on herself. Pa was very proud of her and is trying to talk her into going to Colonial Beach for dinner at Mensh's Hotel next Sunday. I hope we'll go, every-

one I know's been there, and it's kosher, so Mama'll be able to eat the food. She's so silly about that.

Pa looked very good, too, in his new suit, fancy shoes, and walking stick. But then, he always looks nice when he dresses up. Pa appreciates how important it is to look nice. Mama says he's changed since the old days in Russia, but I don't remember what he was like then. To me he's always been the same—a lot more fun to be with than Mama, who's always so serious. Also, it's easier to get money from Pa for the movies or a new record, even new clothes. When I want money I go to Pa. He asks fewer questions and doesn't make me feel guilty. Of course, I know Mama's right about saving money. But once in a while it's fun to buy something like a book or a record.

Mrs. Rappaport told me to look all the boys over in shul and pick out my future husband. I know she was teasing 'cause I look so grown-up these days, but she was partially serious. So while Samuel was reading and davening and all that stuff, I tried to look at all the young men his age. I didn't see one that interested me—they all have bad complexions, and their clothes hang on them or their hair looks wild. None of them looks like what I dream of in a husband. Mama and her friends think all a girl can do with her life is get married and have children. It seems like marriage is the end of their lives. After marriage, all they do is have babies and cook and wash dishes and clean house. And I hate all those things—ugh! I'm going to work in an office. Maybe I'll never get married. Who wants to be bothered taking care of a man, anyhow? Now, Sasha's different. She's already boy-crazy—she and her gang all chase after boys something terrible. It's disgusting, the way she acts. And she can't wait to go to dances.

I had a new dress too: a white and navy "sailor girl" dress in linen, and I wore white small heels and a broad-brimmed white hat with a navy band. Everyone commented on it. I also had a touch of rouge on, and Mama didn't catch me—I laughed because she told me I looked "flushed" from all the excitement. She didn't realize that was makeup she was looking at!

"Here, Anna, hold the cookies and brownies on your lap," Sarah said as she tried to wedge their huge picnic lunch into the back of the Buick touring car that Jacob had brought home Friday night.

Anna, Sasha, and Albert were crowded into the backseat along with the food; Sarah sat in the front seat with Joshua on her lap. Jacob was taking them to Glen Echo Park, way out "at the end of the line" on McArthur Boulevard.

Samuel had to work on Sundays at Western Union, so he couldn't go on their Sunday excursions. He was saving money, with Sarah's help and guidance, for his college education at Ben Franklin University. Albert's college money was Jacob's problem, Sarah had declared, since Albert had been helping Jacob at his store in Anacostia for years now. She wondered, but didn't dare ask Jacob, if he had actually saved the money or if he was going to borrow again when the time came for Albert to go to college.

"Isn't this wonderful? Isn't it just great?" Jacob called out over the roar of the car's engine. He loved his new car, and Sarah hadn't even asked him where he'd got the six hundred dollars to buy it. After all, he had put a bathroom in their house last summer, and he was entitled to his new toy.

"Yes, it really is wonderful," Sarah added enthusiastically, pleased to see everyone looking healthy and happy. It had been a hard winter, and everyone had come down at one time or another with influenza and bad colds. Now, Albert was finished with Business High and ready to enter college in the fall, and Jacob was happy with his new car. So Sarah felt ready to relax and enjoy her Sunday at the park.

Jacob provided dimes and quarters to the children for rides on the carousel and the Ferris wheel and ponies. They ate the home-cooked picnic lunch Sarah had packed and bought only cream sodas to drink. Sarah wouldn't permit them to eat any "junk" in her presence.

Late in the afternoon, while the children roamed the amusement park and Albert spent his time at the dance pavilion, Jacob and Sarah sat alone on the blanket. Her back and legs had given out from so much walking.

"So, are you happy now? Have you gotten over your homesickness for the old country?" He reached for her hand.

"Oh, Jacob!" She beamed. "Of course I'm happy. Who

wouldn't be happy with such fine children, a healthy husband, two stores, and now a fancy car parked in front of my house?" She leaned over and pecked his cheek. "Yes, it is good. *Only in America.* And soon Samuel will go to college. Then we must begin to save for Joshua."

"You and your saving, Sarah. Sometimes it's good to spend and have some fun. We won't live forever."

"Ah, but I'm saving for something special—a new house." She winked at him playfully.

He smiled at her with deep affection. Sarah would always be Sarah. Never satisfied.

"I want to move out to Petworth or Brightwood, so the girls will have a nice home to bring a fellow home to. So they won't be ashamed."

"They've no call to be ashamed!" Jacob answered, suddenly defensive. "You've fixed the house up real nice. They have their own bedroom and now an indoor bathroom."

"But I want to move out of Southwest. I think we can afford it in a few more years. I've got a nice little nest egg saved up."

"Sarah, you're talking about ten to twelve thousand dollars for a house in Petworth or farther out."

"I know, but I think we can do it in a few years. If you'd only try to save a bit, Jacob."

"Twelve thousand *not* counting new furniture, and if I know you Sarah, you will want new furniture too."

"Tell me honestly, how much debt do you have?"

"Sarah, we've had this argument before. I manage my business, and you manage yours. I'll take care of whatever debts I have myself. Have I ever asked you for money? Well, not for years, at least."

Sarah reached over and patted Jacob's thigh. "Let's not spoil a lovely afternoon with arguments. I'm saving for the house, and you give the children all the spending money they need that they don't earn themselves."

At that moment Anna and Sasha and Joshua arrived back at their blanket carrying empty soda-pop bottles.

"I rode every horse on the carousel, Mama!" Joshua announced proudly.

"You should see Albert dancing, Mama. With a pretty girl with red hair," Sasha added.

"I don't approve of public dancing."

"Mama, don't be so old-fashioned. In America everyone dances. It's perfectly proper," Anna scolded.

"I can't wait till I'm old enough to go to dances. Pa, how old do I have to be?" Sasha asked her father, who could refuse her nothing.

"You can go to the Jewish dances when you are fifteen or sixteen. Then you can shop for a husband like you shop in Hecht's and Lansburg's all day Saturday! But first your Mama tells me she has to buy a new house for you and Anna to entertain your fellows in. I don't know where your Mama gets her ideas, but I think she's looking for a rich husband for her girls."

"No, only a decent man who will respect them and be able to provide for them. A Jewish man!"

"Mama, not even I would have the nerve to bring home someone who wasn't Jewish," Anna teased.

"I don't know. Today even good girls are dating *goyim* behind their parents' backs, and that sometimes ends in marriage. If you don't date them to begin with, you won't be tempted to marry them. There are plenty of Jewish boys in Washington, you don't have to look at the *goyim*."

"Here we go again," Anna said to Sasha, annoyed by her mother's constant sermonizing. "I'll bet that redhead Albert's dancing with right now isn't Jewish."

"Josh, you stay here and keep your mother company while we go check out who Albert's dancing with," Jacob said with a huge wink at Anna and Sasha.

"Come back soon," Sarah called to the disappearing trio, who were laughing and joking, probably at her expense. "I want to be home before dark. Besides, we have to go pick up things from the drummers." Well, she said to herself, someone in the family has to have standards.

Chapter 10

1921

Anna glanced at her reflection in the door window. The wind had blown the angle of her hat askew. She tilted it slightly more to the right, smiled, then lifted the gleaming brass knocker and knocked gently three times. What a magnificent house! she thought as she studied the pale beige-brick facade and the heavy carved-oak doors and smelled the boxwood and lilacs. Shortly, the door was opened by a hefty black man in a butler's white-cotton jacket.

"Yes, miss?"

"I'm Anna Arnold. My mother asked me to deliver this sample of herring salad to Mrs. Boland." The butler looked her up and down. Anna knew that she didn't look like someone who would be delivering a grocery order to a fine home on Massachusetts Avenue. She'd planned it that way.

"Ah, yes . . . Miss Arnold, normally we receive deliveries at the back door. But—well, since you're here, do come in."

"I understand I'm to wait while Mrs. Boland tastes the salad." She knew deliveries were made at the back door and had deliberately chosen the front.

"Ah, yes. Follow me to the kitchen."

Anna passed through the wide marble foyer, memorizing each elegant detail: the massive, curving staircase carpeted with an oriental runner held with brass rods, the magnificent, huge gilt mirror over the wood and marble-topped chest, the heavy gold candleholders on each side of the mirror. It was splendor beyond anything she had ever seen.

When they reached the kitchen, the butler invited her in and asked her to be seated. A fat black woman, peeling carrots and potatoes at the huge white sink, looked at her curiously, then went back to work. It was the biggest kitchen Anna had ever seen.

"I'll call Mrs. Boland." He picked up a telephone, pressed a button, and explained Anna's presence.

While she waited, Anna surveyed the kitchen: two huge ice-boxes, the largest cooking stove she'd ever seen, and two ovens. She wished she could really see the living room and dining room and library, which she'd only caught glimpses of from the foyer.

"Ah! Miss Arnold! Your mother told me you'd deliver the salad. How nice of you."

Anna stood and tried to decide if she should hold her hand out to shake this glorious creature's hand. Mrs. Boland was young. She seemed only a few years older than Anna herself. Dressed in a short afternoon dress of pale turquoise—was that silk?—with a rose-colored flower at the neckline, Mrs. Boland wore her blond hair in the new short fashion, crimped in waves close to her head. The butler offered Mrs. Boland a small plate with her mother's herring salad spread on a piece of Russian bread. When Mrs. Boland reached for it, Anna noticed the large diamond sparkling on her small hand. She was the most glamorous woman Anna had ever seen—and she was savoring her own mother's herring salad!

"Oh! It is delicious! Just as Margo said. Who would have thought of putting apples and almonds with herring? My goodness, yes—I definitely want to order some for the party on Saturday, Evans. And we must have some of this bread too. Does your mother bake the bread also?" Mrs. Boland asked.

"No, ma'am. She buys it from the Morning Star Bakery. We get a delivery every morning at nine."

Mrs. Boland looked closely at Anna, then walked to the table and sat down. "Tell me about yourself, Anna. Where do you go to school?"

"I'm a sophomore at Eastern High."

"I see. Do you have a job?"

"No. I mean, yes—I help my mother run the store."

"Do you think you might . . . would you consider . . . we do need one more person to help serve at the party Saturday. Would your mother be able to spare you?"

That means I could see the rest of this glorious house, I could see her friends, their clothes. . . . "Oh, yes Mrs. Boland, I'm sure my mother wouldn't mind."

"Well, fine. In that case, I'll send my man in the car to pick up the herring salad and black bread and you on Saturday at noon. The party begins at five, and you should be able to leave by ten in the evening."

Anna calculated her mother's reaction. She wouldn't like the idea of Anna going into a gentile home and working as a "ser-

vant." In fact, she knew her mother would be outraged. But she
wanted to do it, just once, to see how these people lived and
entertained and dressed—oh, she wanted it so much! "I'll be
ready at noon. How should I dress, Mrs. Boland?"

"Oh, don't worry about that. I'm sure we have a uniform in
the pantry that will fit you. Just wear stockings and black shoes.
Evans will provide a uniform, apron, and cap. You'll earn five
dollars—how does that sound?"

I'd do it for nothing, just to see one of your parties, Anna
told herself, but to Mrs. Boland she said, "That's most generous, ma'am."

"You know," Mrs. Boland continued as she looked closely at
Anna's face and hair, "you're very beautiful. I'm having some
of your people, some Jewish friends, to the party Saturday. In
fact, my good friend Margo is the one who told me about your
mother's salad. Who would have believed herring could be so
good? I've heard that Jewish women are good cooks—this
proves it."

Anna listened to her words with a cynicism she had developed over her years in public school. She's surprised to see a
Jew who doesn't have a hawklike nose. She's surprised to see a
Jew with blue eyes and a snow-white complexion. She's surprised to see the daughter of a grocery-store owner so impecca-
bly dressed. I don't look Jewish, therefore I'm acceptable as a
serving girl at one of her fancy parties. She's trying to tell me
she's not prejudiced against Jews like most the people in Washington. Jews are only slightly above blacks as far as most gen-
tiles are concerned. . . . "Ah, I must be going, Mrs. Boland. I
have some other deliveries to make."

"Yes, dear. Run along, and tell your mother I absolutely love
her salad, and I'll need three pounds and about two hundred
slices of these little breads—you call it Russian black bread?"

"Yes. I'll make sure everything is ready at noon."

Mrs. Boland escorted her to the front, she noted with pride,
rather than turning her out the kitchen door. She knows I'm
not really a servant girl!

"Absolutely not! I didn't bring you to America to become a
servant!" It was the reaction Anna expected. She would appeal
to her father.

Late that night, when Jacob and Albert arrived from Anacostia, Anna was waiting up in the small parlor behind the store. She explained the situation to her father.

"Tell me why you want to do this, Anna. It doesn't sound like something you'd want to do. I understand your mother's feelings. And how will you get home Saturday night at ten o'clock? Mrs. Boland didn't offer to send you home in her car, did she?"

"I was hoping . . . I was hoping you'd pick me up, and then we could drive back to Anacostia and pick up Albert at midnight. Please, Pa! I want to do it so badly."

"But why?"

"I want to see the house. I want to see her fine friends, their clothes. I want to see the rest of the food she serves. Maybe I can pick up some new ideas for Mama—and she does have Jewish friends coming to the party, she told me so. She's a nice lady. Please, Pa."

"I don't know."

"And I'll make five dollars! Think of it—that's half of what Samuel makes in a whole week of work."

"Maybe I can talk your mother into it, just once."

"Only once, Pa. I promise I'll never ask again."

Dear Diary,

Today I saw the way I'm going to live someday. I'm going to live in one of the big houses on Massachusetts Avenue. I'm going to have fine china—Royal Crown Derby, it says on the back—and heavy silver and fine tablecloths made by nuns in Spain. And I'm going to wear clothes made by Jean Patou in Paris. Mrs. Boland and her friends all wear their dresses at least eight inches above their shoes. And pale silk stockings and dainty heels, and oh, the gorgeous jewelry: diamonds, long ropes of pearls, I even saw one large square-cut emerald ring. Such wealth! I can't believe the Bolands receive Jewish families, but I heard names like Hechinger and Hahn and even Shapiro. That's very unusual here in Washington. But of course those are the rich German Jews, Mama says, not Russian Jews like us. They live out on Sixteenth Street in big mansions. They must have sons too, I wish I could figure out how to meet them.

Mrs. Boland's house is furnished beautifully. I told Mama about it—she was angry with me, but that didn't keep her from waiting up to hear all about it. She wanted to know everything. The colors are mainly a medium blue and beige, beautiful pale Persian rugs with furniture that she told me was Queen Anne and Sheraton and Hepplewhite. I really don't know what that means, but I'm going to find out! Everything at the Bolands' was lighter in feeling than the heavy furniture and colors in our house. And the draperies and furniture are beautiful pastel silk brocades and taffetas.

When the party was over and it was time to pay me, Mrs. Boland took me up to her bedroom. It was a fairy tale, fit for a queen. The bed has huge posts on each end, and they're draped in a pale blue chiffon fabric. The walls are covered in watered silk, and the table next to her bed has a magnificent crystal lamp and a huge crystal vase filled with deep red roses. Her closets are like a room, with a whole wall full of silk party dresses. And dozens of pairs of shoes. Such a life, I can only dream about!

The guests were what Pa wanted to hear about. He's always been interested in politics, Mama says, especially back in Russia. So I told him about the senators and congressmen and two Supreme Court justices, including Justice Louis Brandeis! They seemed old and not much fun. Mrs. Boland's young friends were dressed better and had nicer jewelry.

Mr. Boland must be at least twenty years older than Mrs. Boland. They have separate bedrooms, no children, and pictures of their racehorses all over the library walls. He smokes a pipe and talks a lot about Wall Street. I don't know what he does for a living, but I think they must have inherited their money. Anyhow, I don't know what she sees in him besides his money. She's so beautiful, and he's not good-looking at all. Just distinguished-looking, I guess.

It's three o'clock in the morning, tomorrow I can sleep late. What an exciting day!

"The retail business is quite a good business for a woman, I've always thought, Anna," Elinor Gleason explained as she folded and stacked the wool sweaters that had just arrived for the fall season. "You should work part-time during your last year of school. You have the talent to go far. In ten years you could be a buyer if you stayed here at Hecht's."

Anna smiled at her boss, her current idol. "I've been thinking about your offer, Miss Gleason. I'd love to continue working after school and on Saturdays, but I won't promise you I'll stay after graduation. I've always wanted to work on Capitol Hill, and I've learned shorthand and typing and bookkeeping."

"That's a man's world, seems to me. It's a shame we can't convince you to stay here. It's a lot more fun, believe you me, to work in a store than to sit behind a typewriter. And the money's the same, I expect, either place."

This discussion had been repeated several times during the last month. Anna and Elinor Gleason had become instant friends, even though Miss Gleason was her boss. They had discovered last May that they both loved classical music, the same books, and the same art galleries. Anna had emulated this British woman's taste in clothes and had even begun to imitate her British accent, to the distress of Sarah and Jacob, who had difficulty enough understanding English as Americans spoke it, let alone with a British accent. Her sister Sasha teased her about being a snob and her brothers ignored her, but Anna continued to pepper her conversation with whatever expression Elinor Gleason had taught her that day.

The idea of working as a saleswoman at Hecht's after graduation held some appeal. She could buy her clothes at a discount, she would be meeting new people and making new friends, and ultimately, if she stayed long enough to become a buyer, she would travel to New York and maybe even to Europe.

But another part of her wanted desperately to work on the Hill. She had spent three years preparing herself to be a secretary, getting nothing but A's in her business classes. She felt the work would be more interesting and her chances of meeting a really exciting young man would be greater there than in Hecht's department store.

And she had discovered that she shared her father's interest in political affairs. Though he resoundingly criticized his friends in the Communist party, he had become addicted to the radio news broadcasts. He had finally mastered English well enough to read several newspapers each day. Whenever Anna stopped by his Anacostia store, he was discussing the latest political news with his customers. Mama said she was glad he limited himself to heated discussions. "It's best for the family that way. Besides, a businessman can't be too outspoken about politics!"

Every day of her life, Anna read the newspapers to her mother and then spent time explaining various political stories to her. Gradually, Anna's interest in history and politics had become as great as her interest in literature and art. And she had come to realize that Washington was the center of the world, that this was where everything that was important happened. I want to be there, I want to see it firsthand. I want to be a part of it.

"Miss Gleason, I'll let you know by next April. That way you'll have time to hire someone else if I decide to apply for a job on The Hill. How's that?"

"It's a shame that you're not going on to college. With a mind like yours, you should be—that's what I think." She placed the carefully stacked sweaters on the shelf behind her and went over to a customer to ask if she might be of assistance.

That's the way I feel too, Anna thought angrily. She was by far the best student in the family. She had earned the right to go to college. Far more than her two brothers, who were only mediocre students. How could her mother be so old-fashioned to believe that a woman's only future was marriage?

Sarah looked at her family seated around the dining-room table for Passover dinner, devouring the roast turkey and tongue. On this night in 1923, everything felt worthwhile—all the hard striving, the penny-pinching, the cajoling, the pretending she sometimes had to do. Tonight they were eating their first holiday dinner in their new home on Otis Place in Northwest Washington. Albert, dressed in a navy-blue three-piece suit, looked every inch the businessman he would shortly be when he graduated from Ben Franklin University with his degree in business and accounting. Samuel, the light of her life, was equally handsome in a deep brown lightweight wool suit. Always a good student, he was two years behind Albert at the same school. They talked of starting their own accounting firm someday.

Anna, beautiful troublesome Anna—what's a mother to do when her most talented child has such great dreams? Sarah wondered. Jacob constantly told Anna not to set her sights so high, so she wouldn't be disappointed, but Sarah wasn't sure he was right. Maybe Anna was one person who *should* set her sights on the heavens. But wouldn't one think a girl that beautiful would have a beau? Her daughter's lack of interest in men bothered Sarah. They called and called, but Anna referred them all to Sasha—Sasha, who had more beaus than any mother could wish, Sasha, who would be married before she finished school if she didn't watch her.

And Joshua—her prize for coming to America. It was like having a second Samuel, a son whose only desire in life was to please his mother. *Tonight I feel blessed, truly blessed.*

"So tell me, Madame Arnold, how do you like being a lady of leisure? Are you finding it agreeable?" Jacob asked with a huge wink at his children.

He's so proud, Sarah thought, *so proud that we were able to buy this house and furnish it. And that I'm now free to spend my days playing bridge or doing needlepoint with Maud to do the housework.* . . . "I love every minute of it, Jacob. I'm thinking that every woman should be as happy as I am at this moment. Such a splendid family, all of you."

"I'll drink to that," Jacob said as he raised his glass.

"So what are you saving for now, Mama, now that you have your house all furnished?" Albert asked in a teasing voice. The children never ceased teasing her about her penny-pinching ways, but even they didn't know her secret—that she had finally sold the five Eliasberg diamonds and used that money, in addition to her savings, to pay for the house and the new furniture. Then they had sold the two stores and Jacob had become manager of the A&P supermarket. Now she could plan—they had a certain, steady income each month, and Jacob turned it over to her. "I'm saving for Anna's wedding, of course. And for Sasha's, and for Joshua's college education."

"Ohhh—is there something I don't know, Anna?" Albert teased.

"Don't bother to save for my wedding, Mama. You'll need it first for Sasha."

Sarah didn't miss the bitterness in Anna's voice. She blamed it on that Gleason woman at Hecht's, putting ideas into Anna's head all the time. First, the ridiculous British accent, then the constant begging to go to college. *I'd like to be able to afford that, but who sends their daughters to college? Only rich goyim,* Sarah thought, *not people like us who have to struggle for every* dime. Anna should be looking for a husband, not always sitting with her head in a book. She's too smart for her own good—Jacob's right about that. And she's so sure of herself, she's right about everything. No wonder no man ever asks her for a second date—she frightens them away.

"Pa, can I invite David Rabinowitz to go with us this Sunday to Marshall Hall?" Sasha asked.

"Aha! So he's your current favorite? yes, *shainele,* you may invite him. It's time I got to know this young man, find out what his prospects are."

"Pa, you won't embarrass—"

"Your father never embarrasses you, you know that, Sasha!" Sarah said as she passed the carrot *tsimmes* to Samuel.

"So. Anna, have you decided to give notice at Hecht's?" Jacob asked. "Shouldn't you take the typing exam first?"

"Next week, Pa. Next week I'm applying to the Senate for a job beginning June 1. After I'm sure I'll be hired there, I'll give notice to Miss Gleason."

"What do they pay at the Senate?"

"I believe it's fourteen dollars a week. About the same as I make at Hecht's, but the work is more exciting and the opportunities are greater."

"Are there many Jewish girls working on the Hill?" Sarah asked.

"Yes. The government is not allowed to discriminate."

"My dear," Jacob began kindly, patting his eldest daughter's hand, "the civil service doesn't discriminate, but employment on the Hill is not covered by civil service rules. I don't want you to be disappointed. There's still a great deal of reluctance in many offices to hiring our people. You should be prepared for that. You'll have to be twice as good as the Irish or German girls to get the kind of job you want. Too bad you don't have your sister's blond hair, you could pass."

"That's ridiculous. Why would she want to be anything she isn't? She should be proud to be a Jew!" Sarah exclaimed, angry that Jacob should be putting such an idea in their daughter's head. "Anna's so talented, she'll have no difficulty at all getting a job and keeping it."

▨ Chapter 11

June 1924

Shortly after lunch Pete O'Brien, the florid-faced supervisor of the Senate mailroom, called Anna back into his private office.

"C'mon in, kid," he grumbled as he stood at his file cabinet examining a folder. "The girls tell me you're catching on fast. That's fine." He did not ask her to sit, so Anna remained standing next to one of the chairs in front of his desk. "How d'ya like the work so far?"

"It's actually quite easy—monotonous sometimes, but quite simple." This was her first real conversation with her boss. Anna's hands were clammy, and she yearned to wipe them on a handkerchief, but she resisted the impulse.

"Yeah, well."

She wondered why he had called her in. Was there something special on his mind? He laid the file down on a table next to the file cabinet, and as he did several papers fluttered to the floor. He looked at her, and she knew he was waiting for her to retrieve them, even though he was closer to them. After a moment's hesitation, Anna deliberately walked closer to him, bent and picked up the papers, and handed them to him. As he took them, he stood directly in front of her and placed both his palms flat against the wall on each side of her face. "Ya' know, Anna, you're very pretty, you've got pretty eyes." His face loomed closer.

The smell of whiskey nearly bowled her over. Prohibition had been enacted—where had he gotten the whiskey? Anger surged through her at the thought of this huge, disgusting man trying to kiss her.

"Mr. O'Brien, you'd better not do that. My uncle, the senator, wouldn't like it if I told him." It was a bold lie, but she didn't care. He deserved it.

Instantly, O'Brien backed off. "What uncle? Who's your uncle—which senator? God damn! That sonofabitch Johnson in personnel sent a spy in here. Who's your uncle?"

"That's for me to know, Mr. O'Brien, and for you to wonder about. But I will tell you this much—he does oversee personnel. Actually, we look a good deal alike." Realizing she had established the upper hand in this little battle, she decided to exploit it for all it was worth. "May I sit down, Mr. O'Brien?"

"Yeah, yeah. Sit down. We need to get better acquainted." As he took his seat behind his desk, Anna demurely crossed her legs and willed her hands to stop fidgeting. Chin up, Anna. Look him square in the eye.

O'Brien wasn't as much in charge as he had been previously, but still he tried to hang on to his bravado. "Tell me, how's this senator related to you?"

"He's my mother's brother," she coolly lied.

"I see. Well . . . Arnold, what kind of a name is that? It's certainly not Italian or Irish or German. You're not a Yid, are you?" he spat out in disgust.

"Mr. O'Brien, have you ever heard of the poet Matthew Arnold? He's one of England's finest poets."

"No, but I've damn well heard of Benedict Arnold. You part of that traitor family?"

"No, sir."

"Well, okay, so you're English. Probably one of those families that came over on the *Mayflower,* from the sound of things."

"Yes, sir." My God, I can't believe I'm doing this. I never dreamed I could lie so easily.

"Ya know, we Boston Irish don't have much use for you English, not much use at all. In fact, I find your accent distinctly offensive."

"I'm sorry about that, Mr. O'Brien, but it's hard for me to shake an accent I've heard all my life. I'm certain you'll find my work satisfactory, though. I'll try not to be a bother. I'll just get the work done on time, and you'll not have to listen to my accent."

"Well . . ." She could hear the question in his voice: Is she or isn't she? He capitulated and smiled. "Here, take this file to Senator Simpson's office. That's why I called you in here in the first place. He wants it pronto."

"Yes, sir!" Anna stood, accepted the file, and marched out of his office, head held high. Then she went to the ladies' room and vomited her lunch.

The truth was, Anna loved her job in the Senate mailroom. Not so much the work—it was tedious and boring—as the surroundings. To be working in the Capitol! To be able to walk through the statuary hall every day, to stop for a moment in the visitors' gallery and watch a debate by the most brilliant men in the nation, to recognize various senators from the photos she had studied, to spot their wives in the gallery—it was sheer heaven, exactly what Anna had wanted.

Every evening she studied the previous day's *Congressional Record,* as well as *The New York Times,* which she bought at the newsstand on her way home from work. It was her one great indulgence, to spend money on newspapers, but she considered it an investment in her career.

She also made it her business to find out about cultural events that were free or to which she could obtain free tickets. She attended lectures at the Corcoran Gallery and at the Smithsonian. She requested free tickets to plays at the Folger Shakespeare Library, and every now and then she was able to get a ticket to a string quartet performance at the Library of Congress.

Quiet evenings with Mama and Pa seemed pale by comparison to the festival of culture that awaited her in the rest of Washington. She planned her leisure hours with the same care she gave her wardrobe and makeup and daily reading: she would make the most of every waking moment of her life—and the sky was the limit of her ambition.

Four months after she started work in the mailroom, Mr. O'Brien again summoned her to his office. Immediately, he asked her to be seated.

"Miss Arnold," he began, having called her Miss Arnold instead of Anna ever since their initial run-in. "Johnson from personnel has called me. He needs a clerk-typist for a crazy congressman from New York, Fiorello La Guardia, and he wondered if I had anyone ready to move up. He specifically asked about you since you did well on a typing test last spring. So, if you wanna go interview for the job, you can go over there right now. La Guardia needs someone next Monday, and Johnson's got a replacement for you here. So if you wanna move upward and onward, here's your chance."

"What do you mean, 'crazy congressman'?" Anna asked.

"Well, this guy's kinda nutty, can't decide if he's a congressman or a hero-pilot, a Republican or a Socialist. He left the Congress to be a flyboy in the war—he's a decorated dago, a big hero! Then he gets himself elected alderman of New York City, and now he's back here."

"I'd like to interview for the position, Mr. O'Brien, and I can't thank you enough for giving me this opportunity."

Anna excused herself, flew to the ladies' room to repair her makeup and hair, then rushed over to the office of Congressman Fiorello La Guardia, otherwise known as the "Little Flower."

"Mazel tov!" Jacob exclaimed, kissing Anna when she told him about her interview and her new job. Starting Monday, she was to be a clerk in Congressman La Guardia's office. Standing in the kitchen as Sarah pinned up the hem of a brown-tweed skirt that she was making for her, Anna listened closely to her father.

"He's one of the greatest men in the Congress, a real champion for the working man, for the labor unions and farmers, and especially for the Jews. Let me tell you, Anna, he's even worked at Ellis Island interviewing refugees as they came off the boat. He's a great man. I'm so proud of you!" Jacob kissed Anna again. She was surprised by his enthusiasm. "He has the guts to take on Henry Ford—not many men are that courageous. He's gone after Ford for that anti-Semitic newspaper of his. Just a couple of weeks ago in the Congress, La Guardia accused Ford of carrying on a war against the Jews, not only in America but in the whole world. He's got guts."

"Pa, not everyone shares your opinion. Lots of people think La Guardia's a bit off his rocker." Anna turned slightly to allow her mother to pin the back of the skirt. "And his cigars stink to the heavens. I can't stand them!"

"Well, you'll just have to get used to them. He's probably a bit crude and vulgar, but he's a man of the people. A great man."

"I'm finished." Sarah sighed, and Anna helped her to her feet. "We're so proud of you, Anna dear. Now, go get dressed and we'll have dinner. You must be hungry after such an exciting afternoon."

As Jacob had advised, Anna quickly became accustomed to La Guardia's salty language and smelly cigars. She learned his priorities: battling the high cost of food and rent for his constituents in New York City, fighting for the rights of wage earners on strike, for a redistribution of wealth through taxation, and for government aid to the poor and the minority citizens of his Twentieth District.

Hundreds of letters poured into his office each week asking him for help in getting jobs, in getting better housing or a more equitable rent, help in filling out naturalization papers. The congressman ignored none. "Bread and butter issues are the important ones," he said. "If you can help me deal with those, you'll earn your salary and then some."

Anna built her own network. She quickly learned exactly who in which agency of the government could process a given set of papers, investigate a housing claim, or help with citizenship papers. She reinforced this network by writing thank-you letters to the government bureaucrats who helped her. Each evening, when she presented Congressman La Guardia with the mail she had prepared for his signature, she also gave him several letters to various bureaucrats to sign that read: "Anna Arnold has told me of your efficient and compassionate assistance to my constituent . . . and I thank you from the bottom of my heart."

With each of these letters, Anna made a point to enclose an autographed picture of the "Little Flower," and soon bureaucrats all over Washington were hanging his picture in their stark offices. The next time Anna called that person for assistance, she got it faster than any other clerk. And always, a personal letter from La Guardia followed.

Anna's life centered totally on her job. The harder she worked and the more hours she spent at the office, the more La Guardia depended on her. She arrived at seven in the morning and usually didn't leave for home before nine or ten in the evening. She worked all day Saturday, and on Sunday afternoon. The only time she reserved for herself—largely to please her mother—was Friday evening. She made it her business to leave the office by six on Friday, never explaining to anyone why she always had a dinner engagement that evening.

Anna had become the office arbitrator on matters of grammar, etiquette, and protocol. Because of her rapid typing and shorthand skills, she quickly became La Guardia's favorite. He summoned her into his office whenever he felt the urge to write a newspaper column, a lengthy letter to the President, or a speech for the floor of the House.

Late in 1924, he became embroiled in a fight with the New York landlords, who were claiming they had a constitutional right to set whatever rents they wished.

"Anna, come in here. We've got to blast these lawyers and professors."

While Anna sat with steno pad and pen in hand, La Guardia chewed on his cigar and paced as he dictated:

"There is no argument that can prevail when a man with a weekly income and a family to support is compelled to pay out of his income such a large proportion that there is not sufficient left to properly care for and nourish his children. That is the condition in New York City; that is the condition in Washington, D.C."

He tugged on his suspenders, turned to Anna, and asked, "It is, isn't it Anna? Don't you see lots of poverty in this city, especially in the back alleys? S'terrible, the way Negroes live in this city, a damned disgrace, worse'n anything in New York, if you ask me."

"Yes, it is sad, and in the nation's capital."

"Yeah—well, you fix this speech up, make it sound good like you always do, and then do a letter to the editor for *The New York Times*. I'll need it Monday."

"I'll be in at seven tomorrow. Don't worry, it'll be on your desk Monday morning first thing."

"You're Jewish, aren't you?" He stopped pacing and looked directly at her.

Anna felt as if she'd been stabbed in the stomach. No one had asked her that since her first day in the Senate mailroom. Stunned, she didn't answer.

"I've wondered why you always leave early on Friday. Thought you had a sweetheart, but if that's the case, I figure you'd want to date him Saturdays and Sundays. But you're always here. Last week in church I was thinking about you, and it hit me—you're Jewish."

Anna looked at him, looked away, then remembered how many times her father had told her he was a hero to the Jewish people. Maybe he would understand.

"Anna, don't worry about it. I have lots of Jewish friends, they're fine people. No reason you should try to hide it, no reason to deny it. It certainly doesn't make any difference to me. Now, let's continue. 'As long as landlords are determined to exact a pound of flesh from their tenants . . .' "

He dictated for more than an hour. Anna nervously watched the large clock on his wall, hoping he would finish so that she would make it home in time for Sabbath dinner.

At long last he finished dictating, then had one final piece of business for Anna. "I've promised you to the New York State Society. Hope you don't mind, but you're the one person on my staff who has a sense of how things should be done—you know, etiquette and all that stuff. There's gonna be a big dinner next month, and a gal by the name of Naomi Hoffman from Senator Coleman's office and you are in charge of all the arrangements. So call her on Monday, and the two of you get to work on it."

Anna was enchanted with Naomi. She was a few years older than Anna and was perfectly groomed and dressed in the most beautifully tailored black-wool suit, floral-silk blouse, and red pumps, which picked up the red in the blouse. Her black hair was combed severely back into a large bun at the nape of her neck; her deep brown eyes were accented with kohl lining. Around her neck she wore a three-strand opera-length pearl necklace, which Anna thought might be real. On her right hand she wore a cabochon ruby surrounded by diamonds. Her nails were polished bright red, which matched her lipstick. She was the most sophisticated career woman Anna had met on Capitol Hill.

"Our special guests will be Al Smith, Franklin Roosevelt, and Jim Farley. They'll be seated at the head table, along with the members of the delegation and their wives," Naomi said as she ate cherry pie à la mode.

"Who is Jim Farley?" Anna asked.

"Oh, he's a friend of Roosevelt. He's the Democratic Party chairman for Rockland County. He was a member of the New York State Assembly last term, but he lost his bid for reelection. He's currently the chairman of the New York State Athletic Commission. But mainly, he's Roosevelt's close buddy. His wife won't be coming—she's having a baby soon."

The women chatted about flowers, candles, the menu, music, and place cards. Anna was sorry when the lunch came to an end, so taken was she with Naomi. But she would see lots of her in coming weeks as they put together the Christmas party. "Imagine, they've asked two Jewish girls to plan the Christmas party. Can you think of anything funnier?" Naomi quipped as they left the cafeteria.

Anna wondered how she knew. Had La Guardia told Naomi's boss, or did she look that Jewish? "Let's have lunch next Friday and decide what else we need to do," she suggested, anxious to have a reason to see Naomi again.

"Better yet," Naomi suggested, "come to my apartment. I'll have my maid fix dinner for us."

Naomi's one-bedroom apartment was on Sixteenth Street, one of the most prestigious addresses in Washington. Anna was all curiosity as she sat down in the small dining nook and watched Naomi uncork a bottle of red wine. How could she afford such elegance? Where had she purchased her black-market bottle? How could she afford to dress so expensively on her Senate salary, which couldn't be much more than her own?

As if reading her mind, Naomi quickly volunteered, "My beau, Steven Jacobsen, had a case of wine delivered last weekend. So enjoy!"

They planned the dinner-dance down to the last detail, going over a checklist Anna had prepared. When their work was finished, they turned to more frivolous matters.

"What will you be wearing?" Anna asked her new friend.

"I've a dress I wore last winter in New York. No one here's seen it yet. Bottle-green velvet, with a cape trimmed in ermine."

"Goodness! So elegant!"

"The Christmas party is always the most elegant party of the year. Most of the men come in black tie, and the women always wear long dresses. You'll love it; it's such fun. And you'll get to meet Steve—he's a doll!"

Steve, it turned out, was a lawyer in a New York firm, and Naomi and he spent every other weekend with each other. Anna wondered how intimate their relationship was, but didn't dare question Naomi more closely.

On the night of the party Anna donned a royal-blue-velvet gown—her first long gown—which her mother had painstakingly made for the big event. Anna noted with enormous pleasure that everything was going beautifully in the majestic Senate caucus room—exactly as she and Naomi had planned it. And she was thrilled by Congressman La Guardia's obvious pride in the job she had done.

"Whenever you need anything done in Washington, Anna

Arnold's the one to call," Fiorello La Guardia was saying expansively to Roosevelt and Farley between puffs on his cigar.

"She's talented as well as beautiful—is that what you're saying?" Farley asked as he shook her hand with gallantry. "If she's so smart, how come she's working for you, a Republican? Seems like you'd have the good sense, Miss Arnold, to come over to the Democratic side of the aisle."

Anna could think of no response, so she smiled broadly at both Farley and her boss.

"I understand you are responsible for this wonderful evening," Franklin Roosevelt said as he grasped her hand. "It's very nicely done."

"Do call me if I can ever be of assistance," Anna told the two men, finally having found her tongue.

"You can be sure we will. And if you ever come to New York City, be sure and call me. I'd love to show you around." The genial Irishman Farley passed her his business card, richly embossed with his title as athletic commissioner.

"One of these days I'm gonna bring her to New York and show her around myself," La Guardia responded, his arm around Anna in a fatherly gesture. "I'm not gonna let you guys get your grimy fingers on her, you can be sure of that!" La Guardia laughed and puffed again on his cigar.

"Anna, you done a good job here tonight. It's the nicest party we've ever had."

It was late February 1926, George Washington's birthday weekend, before Anna finally got her long-promised trip to New York. And when she went, it was at the invitation of her now-close friend, Naomi Hoffman, who had recently broken her ties with Steven Jacobsen and wanted Anna's company on a trip to visit her parents.

Nothing Naomi had told her prepared her for the opulence of the Hoffman home. They lived high above Fifth Avenue in an eighteen-room apartment filled with antiques and fine paintings. As she sat at dinner that first evening, Anna realized that Naomi's job in Washington was unimportant in the scheme of things; it was simply to pass time until she found a man her parents considered worthy of her hand in marriage—and Steven had not been such a man. He was hardworking, a Harvard graduate, but a Russian Jew, not a German Jew like

Naomi and her family. That, and that alone, was the reason her parents had insisted that she end the relationship. Anna found it more than a little shocking, considering that, as Naomi had confided to her, they had been intimate for more than a year.

The next day, a Saturday, Naomi took Anna on a trip through the major New York department stores, interrupted briefly by lunch with Jim Farley, who took them to the Plaza Hotel Palm Court. Naomi, it turned out, had told Farley that he should pay attention to Anna because there might come a day when she would be of great assistance to the Democratic party.

Anna, a bit bowled over by the attention of such an important man, promised him she'd be "his gal" in Washington: "Whatever you need, just give me a call."

Back in Washington after the heady trip to New York, Anna spent hours measuring her life against Naomi's. The difference was money. Naomi could flout sexual conventions, dress beautifully, live in her own apartment, and afford a maid—all because her father and mother had money. Money made the difference, and she was determined to have that kind of money someday.

No, she'd not give herself to any of the mediocre young men who pursued her through Senate hallways and at the Saturday-night dances, or found excuses to introduce themselves to her in the Senate cafeteria. She'd watch Naomi, learn from her, and emulate her style, her panache. And she'd rule out men as husband material based on her estimate of their future earning power.

In the late spring of 1926, while the Republican party was trying to convince La Guardia to become one of theirs instead of clinging steadfastly to his independence, Anna received a tearful call from her mother. "Please, Anna, can you come home early today? I need you."

It was the first time her mother had ever called her away from her work, and she gave no hint of what was behind the stressful call. After Anna made her excuses, she quickly took a cab to her Otis Place home. There she found her mother in her bedroom in tears.

"Sasha got married this morning! Can you believe it? Married —and with none of us present. I'm heartbroken. I would have liked to give her a nice wedding. What kind of girl does a thing like that?"

"She married Louis?" Anna asked, knowing that Sasha had been sweet on Louis Bernstein for months now.

"Yes. In Baltimore. That rabbi should be censured for doing such a thing—marrying a girl without even her parents' knowledge. And Sasha only seventeen!"

"Mama, I don't know why you're so upset. I'm nineteen, and you never stop harassing me about marriage. Lots of girls get married at seventeen. They'll be happy, you'll see."

"But she should have waited for you. You should have been married first."

"Maybe that's why. Did you think of that? She knew I wasn't going to get married anytime soon, so she eloped. Don't worry, Mama—it'll be fine. Does Pa know yet?"

"Yes, and he's upset too. Sasha shouldn't break tradition like that. She knows better. I just don't understand her."

"How do you know? Did they call?"

"Yes, they called. They're going to New York on the train for a honeymoon. I hope she knows what she's doing. Are you sure you're not upset, Anna?"

"No, Mama. Honestly," she lied, determined not to let her mother know that she was envious of Sasha. "If it's me you're worried about, stop. I've no intention of getting married until the right man comes along. And that's that."

"Well, what do you think? When they come home next week, should I make a party for them? You know, invite the family and the neighbors?"

"Sure, Mama. And I'll help you. I'm good at giving parties these days. I'll help."

Sarah wiped her eyes and suddenly cheered up. *"Shainele,* do you think you could do something for your brother? Could you get him a messenger job at the Senate?"

"Yes, Mama, I probably can. I'll get Joshua a job this summer."

"You're a good daughter, Anna. A daughter to make a mother's heart swell with joy!"

"Tell me, is it really good? I mean, what's it like?" Anna and Naomi sat digging their toes into the sand at the Hoffman beach house on the Cape during June 1927. She'd finally gotten up the nerve to ask her good friend about sex, which had already been a part of Naomi's life for four years.

"Depends on the guy. I've been in bed with—promise me, Anna, you won't think less of me—I've been in bed with five different men in four years. Isn't that just horrible!" She giggled, then whispered, "It's great, but better with some than with others. A more experienced man is always a better lover. But it's *always* good, always! I don't know what you're waiting for. You know Michael Strauss is dying to get you in bed. He told me last week you're a real chill!"

Anna felt her cheeks flame. Then, to cover her embarrassment, she laughed. "He really doesn't interest me that much. Oh, he's nice enough looking. And he likes good music. But who wants to be married to a veterinarian?"

"No, I don't suppose that's too enticing. What do you think of Bud Rosen?" Naomi asked, thinking about her newest conquest.

"He's okay—but what kind of a name is Bud?"

"Short for Theodore! Can you imagine?" Naomi began to rub more oil on her legs and arms.

Anna, who sat huddled in a long robe and floppy hat without an inch of skin showing, shook her head. "You're going to ruin your skin, Naomi. I don't know why you want to look like a *shvartze.*"

Naomi ignored her. They'd had this discussion before. "You know, Anna, I've been thinking. It's time you moved over to the Senate side. You've been in La Guardia's office for over three years now. There's an opening for an assistant clerk in the Naval Affairs Committee now, and there'll be another in a few months. I'm going to apply for one, and if I get it, I'll be able to influence them to hire you for the second. Wouldn't it be fun if we were working in the same office?"

"Yes, that does sound like fun. Naval officers always look so splendid in their uniforms."

"True. But they're not husband material. Did you ever hear of a Jewish admiral? No, they might be good for an affair, but they're not husband material. But it might be an easy job. If I get hired, I'll figure out a way to get you in there too."

Anna sat back on her beach chair, picked up *All the Sad Young Men,* Fitzgerald's latest collection of short stories, and returned to reading. Actually, she thought, it wouldn't be a bad idea to take a job with a committee. Working for La Guardia, though always a challenge, was exhausting. She could do with an easier, less demanding job—and one that paid better.

"Miss Arnold?"

Anna frowned at the paper in her typewriter, feeling harassed. She had to have Senator Hale's speech finished by four-thirty, but it was already after three. Even as she stared at her shorthand notes, hoping the deep-voiced intruder would take his business to one of the other assistant clerks, her peripheral vision took in a deeply tanned masculine hand trying to give her a thick manila envelope. The hand led to a dark-blue-serge sleeve adorned with the two gold stripes of a lieutenant in the U.S. Navy. *Darn! Not now!* She sighed and looked away from her steno book and up into dark-brown eyes.

"Miss Arnold, Admiral Hughes asked me to deliver this to you. It's the finding of the Court of Inquiry on the sinking of submarine S-4 when it collided with our Coast Guard destroyer *Paulding* last December."

A suave, ruggedly handsome officer stood in front of her. The loud roar in Anna's ears drowned out clattering typewriters, a ringing telephone, and muted conversations. Anna was so overwhelmed by the lieutenant's presence that even his voice was drowned out.

The roar grew louder. She could hear nothing but the thumping of her heart. Only when his lips stopped moving and he seemed to be waiting for a response from her—only then did she come out of her trance and recover her poise. She stood, mechanically reached out to shake his hand, and said the first thought that came into her head: "When did Admiral Hughes begin using lieutenants as messengers?"

He held her hand longer than necessary, his eyes roving down her body boldly, then returned her haughtiness with a teasing look of his own. "I'd be a messenger every day of the week, Miss Arnold, if you'd have a cup of coffee with me."

The nerve of this devil! It's positively indecent, the way he's looking at me!

His sparkling eyes were blatantly flirting with her—outrageously flirting—and with a shock she realized she loved it.

She appraised him from head to foot. Good Lord, he was the epitome of a Greek god! Something over six feet tall, she was sure. Perfectly turned out in his double-breasted serge suit with gleaming gold buttons. His black regulation shoes shone like onyx. His face was deeply tanned and slightly creviced—probably by sea duty. His broad shoulders tapered down to slim hips and a flat stomach. He was one officer who believed in staying in fighting trim. What was it about a naval uniform?

Every naval officer seemed handsome to her, and they were in and out of her office all day. By now, she should be immune to their practiced charm. But this man! This man was the most compellingly handsome man she'd ever seen.

"I'm terribly sorry, Lieutenant, truly I am, but I've got this long speech to finish for Senator Hale. I really can't leave my desk right now. I hope you'll give me a rain check?" Is something wrong with me? she asked herself as she felt overheated and goose bumps on her arms at the same time.

"I'm disappointed too." Something about his resonant voice made the balls of her feet tingle and her hands perspire.

He looked at his watch. "How about Monday morning? I'll be over here next week doing some briefing before the hearings begin. May I stop by Monday?"

"I'd be ever so pleased, Lieutenant," she responded, hearing a strange high-pitched sound in her voice. What's wrong with me? she wondered. I sound like a giddy schoolgirl. And I didn't even catch his name.

"Monday, ten-thirty, then. It's a date." He flashed another tantalizing smile at her, then added, "Have a restful weekend."

As soon as the committee staff door closed behind him, Naomi grinned and asked, "Who's that, Anna? What has Admiral Hughes sent over to seduce us now?"

Anna felt her cheeks turn scarlet. "I don't know. I didn't hear his name, it was so noisy in here."

Naomi laughed at Anna, then said, "If you ask me, he's a cross between Douglas Fairbanks and Valentino. He could seduce me anytime!"

⊠ Chapter 12

As Anna rode the trolley up Sixteenth Street toward her parents' home that afternoon, her thoughts returned again and again to the audacious lieutenant who'd invaded her work and her very being. He was indeed attractive, as Naomi had wasted no time pointing out, but there was something about his eyes—intelligent, fearless, and sensitive. She alighted from the trolley and began the long walk home in the April drizzle.

With Albert and now Sasha married and Samuel usually working late into the night, only she and Joshua now shared the special Sabbath dinner that her mother prepared on Friday evenings. In the years since she'd begun work, she'd pulled further and further away from her parents, even though she still lived at home. Their values seemed old-fashioned, even ridiculous, when measured against what was happening in America. Religion, which meant so much to Sarah, seemed utterly remote from Anna's daily life.

Even discussions of world affairs and daily political events had become futile. Her parents read the papers avidly, but they didn't possess the understanding that Anna found in even the most unsophisticated clerks on Capitol Hill. Sarah and Jacob were content to attend to business and focus their social life on the small Jewish community that had started in Southwest but had spread into the new middle-class neighborhoods of Northwest Washington.

Coolidge was still President, prosperity was everywhere evident and growing, and life was as good as it had ever been for them in this country. Anna didn't want to rock the boat, but she desperately wanted to move out of their house. Unfortunately, the only acceptable way for a "nice girl" to move out of her parents' home was to get married. She didn't crave marriage, even though Sasha seemed happy. But Anna wanted to get away from the provincial atmosphere she came home to every night. She especially wanted to get away from her parents' probing questions that arose every year on Rosh Hashanah and Yom Kippur.

That autumn of 1923 when she'd first worked on the Hill, she'd begun to lie to her boss. It had then become necessary to keep up the lie that she wasn't Jewish. So she told her parents she was attending services at a special *shul* on the Hill. That didn't seem too outlandish to them; they remembered the *shul*s in the factories of Pinsk. But no such *shul* existed near the Capitol, and even if it had, she wouldn't have endangered her image by absenting herself from the office on Jewish holy days. She had felt terrible guilt that first year, but it abated as each year passed. The constant hypocrisy, lying to her parents, assuring them she had spent all day in shul, fasting and praying, wore on her. She had to move out of their home. If only she could live in an apartment of her own and visit them on special occasions—that would be perfect! she thought as she walked up the front steps. Wonderful Sabbath smells greeted her: freshly baked hallah, roast chicken, and noodle kugel.

"So here you are—we've been waiting," Jacob said, rising from his chair to receive a kiss.

"Pa, I'm exhausted. Such a day! I had a major speech to turn out for the chairman, and so many interruptions—"

"Well, you're home now," her mother interjected as she kissed her. "Go wash up and we'll eat. You need to eat, you're too thin!"

On Saturday, Anna bought a red-linen suit and a teal-blue-silk dress from Elinor Gleason at Hecht's. As usual, Elinor had held them on a special rack in the back of the store for her. She'd seen them three weeks before and had told Elinor she liked them but would wait for a sale. Anna never bought anything at full price, and Elinor conspired with her to put back anything she had her heart set on.

No sooner had Anna left the store than she began thinking that she would wear the new red suit on Monday—he might really keep that coffee date. Why can't I stop thinking about him? I don't even know his name. And it's a cinch that he's an arrogant devil—a man that handsome would have to be.

That night she went to a Capitol Hill staff dance with Naomi, and though she danced with the usual eligible men she saw in the halls every day, she found herself comparing them all negatively with the nameless lieutenant.

On Sunday the two women went to the Corcoran Gallery for a special exhibit of paintings by the French painter Henri Mattisse. They treated themselves to supper at the Willard, then went back to the gallery for a concert.

At the end of a very pleasant spring day, Anna found herself back home in bed, impatiently thinking about how to enchant the debonair lieutenant—if he actually returned the next day.

"I'm new at this business of congressional relations, so you must educate me, Anna," Lieutenant Kurt Addison said as he held the chair for her in the Capitol cafeteria. "Isn't it unusual for the committee to hold two different hearings simultaneously?"

He's a disturbing man, she thought as she sat down. "It *is* unusual, but in this case it's dictated by the availability of the officers here in Washington. I've only been working for the Naval Affairs Committee four months now." She looked at the thin crow's feet spreading out from his rich brown eyes. I wonder how old he is . . .

"Do you have all the reports you need from us for the S-4 investigation?" He stirred his coffee, then took a swallow, his eyes never leaving hers.

"I believe so. Tell me, what do you think about that—was it the Coast Guard's fault or the Navy's?" She was determined to keep this conversation strictly professional . . . until she knew him better.

His face broke into a broad grin. "You don't really think I'm going to tell you it's the Navy's fault!"

"Honestly, off the record. What do you think?" She wanted to keep him talking, to prolong this coffee break as long as possible.

"These are the facts as I see them: On a Saturday afternoon in December, when most of the men were on shore leave and the weather was cold and windy off the coast of Massachusetts, the destroyer *Paulding* collided with submarine S-4, which was performing a scheduled speed test on a well-marked, long-used sea lane. The vessels sighted one another twelve seconds before the collision—too late for either to alter its course. The sub went down with forty men aboard."

All signs of amusement had evaporated from Kurt's countenance. His eyes filled with pain as he described the tragedy to Anna.

"A rescue mission was carried out for nearly a week, until the secretary of the Navy and the chief of naval operations called it off on the following Friday, when it was certain that all the men aboard were dead. The forty men had been in the engine room and the motor room. Autopsies indicate they lived for several days but eventually died of carbon dioxide poisoning and drowning. Bad weather hindered the rescue operation, but it's questionable that we could have saved them even with good weather."

"How ghastly! But what I don't understand," she asked, "is why the Navy hadn't warned the Coast Guard that they were conducting speed tests in those lanes."

Kurt looked at her with new appreciation. "That's precisely the question the committee will bore in on next week. One result of the investigation may be that rules will be established regarding that kind of communication. But the important thing to remember is that we have submarines at various places, from China to New York, all the time, and the only thing that will protect the crews from this kind of tragedy is good lookouts on both the subs and the destroyers. My own theory—and you mustn't quote me on this, Anna—is that the lookouts weren't doing their job on either craft. Admittedly, the weather was bad . . ."

Anna found her mind wandering from what he was saying. She kept examining his face, his eyes, his hands, as if some revelation would come forth, some exciting clue about his private life. What did she need to do to entice him? He stopped speaking, took another swallow of his coffee, then resumed his analysis.

"My feeling is that in this case the committee is simply exercising its muscle. When the hearing's over, the recommendation of the Court of Inquiry will be reversed, and Admiral Brumbry will not be disciplined. Basically, he's a damned good officer and we need more like him. But that doesn't mean the control force will continue to operate the way it always has. The Navy will clean its own shop without help from Congress."

He picked up his cup again, then set it down and said, "Anna, forgive me for being personal, but you are a truly beautiful woman. I simply have to say it." He glanced meaningfully at her left hand. "I can't believe you're not married."

Because I've only just met you—give me time! she thought, but she smiled coyly and answered, "Lieutenant, I really care about my work with the committee, and it would take quite a man to sweep me away from my career."

"Good for you! Hold out until you find exactly the right man!"

This personal conversation had caused her stomach to feel queasy. She felt impelled to turn the discussion back to professional matters. "Exactly what is your assignment, Lieutenant?"

"My job is to get as close to the staff as possible. I'm assigned here for four years, and I hope this is the beginning of a long and exciting friendship and collaboration with you, Anna, for the benefit of our country." He raised his coffee cup in a toast.

She responded by meeting it with her own. "To our friendship, Lieutenant."

"And the next order of business is for you to call me Kurt, since I've already taken the liberty of calling you Anna."

Twice more that week Kurt Addison stopped in unexpectedly to take Anna for coffee. Each time, Naomi waited back in the office, Anna knew, expecting to hear that he'd asked her for a date. But no such luck!

The following week, the two hearings began. Each day Anna and Kurt sat in the same stuffy hearing room, listening first to an account of the submarine accident, then later in the day, to Secretary of the Navy Curtis Wilbur debating the senators on the Dallinger amendment. Frequently Anna looked up from her note-taking and saw Kurt's eyes fastened on her. When their eyes locked, she read friendship, caring, and admiration—even, she thought, desire. Why hadn't he asked her for a date?

". . . the central issue is whether ships should be built in government yards or private yards. And I submit that even though the private yards pay lower wages and therefore can build the ships for less, it's important that we have efficient government yards so that the private yards don't dictate the price. . . ."

On and on it went, for days. April became May, and Kurt Addison continued to take Anna for coffee in an almost proprietary way, continued to look at her with what had to be total fascination, continued to flirt outrageously with her—but didn't ask her for a date.

When the hearings were over, the coffee breaks with Kurt were over too. Anna didn't hear from him in a week. Not a phone call, not a sudden visit—nothing. She pondered what to do. She lay awake at night calling his face to memory, wondering what it would feel like if he kissed her, if he undressed her. What could she do to get his attention again?

Finally, one morning on the trolley, she had a brainstorm. She needed a copy of a letter from Admiral Hughes to the Court of Inquiry to complete the committee report and send it to the printing office. She would call Lieutenant Addison! Just thinking about placing that call made her hands clammy.

"I've missed seeing you," she said with a coy smile as he held a chair for her at the Occidental Restaurant. She wore her new blue-silk dress, and she knew she looked absolutely smashing.

"And I've missed our conversations too. I'm glad you called yesterday. It gave me the excuse I was looking for to properly reward you for all your help."

"I don't know that I've done much yet, Kurt. Only little things."

"Yes, but I want to know that I can count on you in the future. We live in dangerous times and have fallen dangerously behind in our production of ships of all classes. The problem is that the entire country is tuned out, overrun by isolationists. No one wants to think seriously of security or the possibility of another war."

"You don't really think . . ."

"I think it's always a possibility—and we're becoming less and less prepared for that eventuality. I need your help, Anna. For the good of the nation."

She listened attentively as he brilliantly articulated the need for more ships, for more research money. And while she listened with one part of her brain, she schemed with the other.

"I'd suggest that you invite the members of the committee, a few at a time, for an afternoon or evening of informal conversation and dining. Don't you have a yacht that you can take out on the Potomac? Get Admiral Hughes to talk to them individually on a one-to-one basis."

"What a superb idea! Would you do a briefing paper on each senator—his preferences, ideas on the Navy, even his personal background, education, his wife, all that sort of stuff?"

"Yes, of course, I'll do that for you. But will you invite me along on the trips?"

"You can count on it! Anna, you're wonderful!" He reached over and took her hand and held it for a minute. Electric shocks ran up her arm, and she thought she would faint from happiness. It was the first time he had touched her.

Anna now had a definite project to work on with Kurt—a series of yacht dinners to be hosted by the chief of naval operations and the secretary of the Navy. She worked with Kurt on the menus and on the choice of jazz bands to play for dancing. She helped him decide which mix of senators and naval officers to invite to each party. She helped him prepare talking points to brief the naval officers with—all of this, and still he didn't ask her for a date.

During the second, very successful twilight dinner during the dog days of August, she sensed his presence in back of her as she talked with Commander Hoover. Most of the group had finished eating and were fox-trotting to "I'm Always Chasing Rainbows."

"Pardon me sir, but would it be terribly improper if I stole Miss Arnold away from you for a dance?"

"Not at all, Lieutenant, not at all." He waved them away.

At last, Anna thought, at last.

Kurt held her rigidly, at a proper distance, and as they danced they nodded and smiled to the officers, most of whom were dancing with senators' wives. When that number ended, the band began "Dardanella." Anna was nervous, almost afraid to speak, to break the magic of being in Kurt's arms, even if at a considerable distance. A tingling sensation had invaded her body, her heart beat in her throat, and her chest felt as if it would burst through her blue-silk-organza gown. When she dared look in his eyes, she was frightened by the unconcealed desire that revealed his thoughts—and she hoped, his intentions.

"I'm not ready to give you up yet," he whispered as they pulled together to let another couple pass them on the dance floor.

"I wish you never would," she heard herself answer.

A fleeting look of pain passed through his eyes, then he pulled her close and pressed his lips to the top of her forehead. They danced, neither of them speaking, neither of them willing to break the spell of the moonlight and the rippling water. To Anna, it seemed as if they were all alone on the boat, not surrounded by twenty other couples. She felt his body harden

against hers and marveled that he was finally responding to her
—after all these months. Finally.

The following week he did not call her office, nor did he come
by for coffee. Nothing, not a word.

"Anna, have you ever considered that he might have a girl-
friend already? For gosh sakes, he might even be married!"
Naomi said one afternoon as they walked toward the trolley.

Anna thought about Naomi's idea and measured it against
what she knew he had felt when they danced that night. No, it
was impossible that he had another girl. Absolutely impossible.
If she knew anything at all about men and women, she knew
that he felt toward her what she felt toward him—an intense
attraction. What then, was preventing him from acting on it?

A second week went by, and still not a word from Kurt
Addison. In desperation, Anna called his office. A secretary
informed her that Lieutenant Addison was on leave. "His wife
had a baby last week, and he's home helping her out. Can I
refer you to someone else, or should I have him call you when
he's back, Miss Arnold?"

All the blood in Anna's body drained and plummeted to her
feet. She felt prickly sensations in the back of her head. Everyone in the office looked frozen, but the room circled around her
in slow motion. It couldn't be! He couldn't be married! And a
father! "No, no . . . never mind."

Anna let the phone slip out of her shaky hand and drop onto
the cradle. Her fingers began playing with a paperweight.

"Anna, Anna, are you all right?" Naomi hovered over her
friend. "You look like a ghost. Has someone died?"

Anna struggled to comprehend what Naomi was saying,
what all this new information meant to her. "His wife had a
baby last week. He's home taking care of her. . . . Oh, Naomi,
I can't bear it." Anna reached for her purse and Naomi followed her to the ladies' room, where Anna proceeded to blame
herself and her wicked imagination for getting herself in this
mess to begin with. "Oh, Naomi, how could I have been so
stupid, so dumb . . . not to see."

"Anna, can you break away for a few minutes? There are a
few things I need to discuss."

Kurt stood directly in front of her desk. She couldn't look at him. "I'm sorry, Lieutenant, I don't have time. I can't leave my desk right now." Anna struggled to make her voice indifferent.

"Anna, this is me, Kurt. What's wrong? What've I done? This is getting ridiculous. Not professional behavior at all. I've called you eleven times and left messages. Courtesy dictates that you return my calls." He leaned over her desk. "I came over here to find out what's wrong. Now, come with me. We're going downstairs for coffee."

"I'm really busy . . ." She heard her wavering, pathetic response.

"Anna—"

Something in his voice, the level of anger and frustration and righteous indignation—and even pleading—something got to her, breaking all her resolve.

She stood up, and with a determined, regal posture, walked out with him. When they reached the elevator, he asked for the ground floor instead of the cafeteria. "I think we'll take a stroll outdoors instead. It's a beautiful day." She didn't respond but followed silently beside him. She couldn't speak, nor could she look in his eyes.

At each street, he cradled her elbow in his large hand to assist her. Her mind was awhirl. What would he say to her?

They came to a stop in a small park with a fountain. He leaned against a cool marble statue. With a quavering voice he began speaking.

"I questioned my secretary. She repeated every word of your conversation with her. She told me what she had told you. I understand why you are angry with me."

"You do?" She dared to look him directly in the eye for the first time. She saw anguish.

"I'm sorry. I should have told you long ago. It was just . . ."

"Just what, Kurt?"

"Anna, you've put me through torture. It's not your fault, and you couldn't possibly have known it. But I've been obsessed with you since the first day I met you. I think of you first thing in the morning and the last thing at night, I dream of you, I spend my days thinking of excuses to call you or come to your office. I hate weekends because there's no way to see you or talk to you."

Anna absorbed the pain—and the sincerity—in his eyes. Her

heart felt as if it had suspended its beating. What would he say next?

When he told her what she wanted to hear, tears filled Anna's eyes, and she forgot all inhibition. She reached toward him. He held his arms out, welcoming her into his embrace. She wrapped her arms around him and sobbed into his uniform, while he tightened his grip, then slowly ran his hand up and down her back, comforting her. She had never felt such warmth.

After a long time, Kurt held her back and tilted her chin so he could see her face. Tears filled his eyes too. "I love you, Anna. I'm so ashamed. It's not something I wanted. It goes against everything I've ever believed in."

"Oh, Kurt—if only you knew how long . . ."

"Shh—I know. Don't say it. I've seen the love and disappointment in your eyes for too long now. I've hated myself for the deception. I tried to tell you we can't have one another. I'm so goddamned miserable, I can't begin . . ."

He held her face in his hands, he kissed each eyelid and the tip of her nose, then he kissed her lips lightly. Her arms tightened around him, and she returned his kiss with all the passion she had bottled up for months.

Wicked fantasies rushed pell-mell through her mind. Couldn't they just run away together, away from the whole world? "What's going to happen to us?" she asked weakly as he led her to a park bench.

Kurt held her hand as he spoke. "We must remain the professionals that we are. We must do our work, day after day, and pretend we don't have these feelings. We must ignore them, shove them to the back of our minds."

"Kurt! That's impossible."

"Yes, probably. But I don't have a better solution. I can't get transferred away, especially since you're helping me do such a good job—not for four more years."

Anna looked at her hands. Unconsciously, she had been twisting a handkerchief.

"I believe in honor, in vows, in responsibility. I've never broken a trust. But then, I've never been tested before. I've never wanted anything as much as I want you, Anna. But it's out of the question. Even if I were weak and undisciplined, I couldn't do it to you, I couldn't turn you into my mistress, my illicit lover."

"Who would've thought that such a beautiful thing as love could be so wretched, so painful? What will we do?"

"Somehow we'll manage. We're both intelligent and disciplined. We'll just keep a stiff upper lip."

"Oh, I can't stand this! I'm going back to the office." Anna felt angry. He made it sound so simple, but she had never hurt so much, never felt such wretched despair. How could she continue to see him and not be able to love him? How could she readjust her whole inner world, all her hopes for the future? Could it be that she'd never be able to marry him? When all her fantasies for the past five months had centered on a future with him? How could destiny be so cruel? She had found the only man she'd ever love, and he was married! It felt as if her world had ended.

For weeks, Kurt avoided going near Anna's office. Perhaps, he rationalized, if he stayed away long enough, she'd meet someone and begin a real romance. It would be the best possible thing that could happen for both of them. But no sooner did he think this than his imagination conjured up a picture of Anna in all her exquisite beauty, making love to some faceless male body, and he felt such deep revulsion that nausea rose in his throat.

She continued to haunt his dreams and his fantasies. He sat in his office doodling incessantly, trying to concentrate on writing testimony for Admiral Hughes, trying to keep Anna from the forefront of his mind.

He reminded himself of the reasons he had married Betty: she was pretty, and she had adored him unequivocally at a time when he felt most vulnerable, his last year in Annapolis, before facing the real world on a destroyer. She was totally dedicated to his career, to being the perfect wife and mother for a man who, in her eyes, was clearly destined someday to be the chief of naval operations. No small dreams for Betty. And they had been happy in their little house in Arlington, Virginia—as happy as any man had a right to expect to be—until he met Anna.

Anna was the ultimate woman. Never had he seen a woman with such regal self-assurance, as if the world were hers to command. She must have been born with that grace and elegance, he mused, from splendid English bloodlines. She possessed that unmatched porcelain complexion—she looked as if her cheeks had been lightly feathered by roses each morning—that only British women seem to have. Her sleek black hair, always shining and done to perfection, and her sparkling dark-blue eyes, which held shimmering pools of love for him—it was too much. He couldn't help himself. He loved her. She had enchanted him, and there was nothing in the world he wanted more than to ravish her, to claim her as his own.

Yet that could never be. Not only because he believed in keeping vows, in keeping a family intact, but because on another level, Anna threatened his career, everything he had ever worked for. Betty had intuitively understood the reach of his ambition: he would one day be chief of naval operations. And as far as he knew, there had never been an officer who'd made admiral after a divorce, much less the highest office the Navy could confer. No, he had to give up all designs on Anna if he was to remain true to his own ambition.

"Damn," he muttered as he rolled another piece of paper into the typewriter and began the next section of testimony. Sooner or later, probably no later than the end of this week, he'd have to make another appearance at the Naval Affairs Committee staff room. Inevitably, he'd have to see Anna. And the wanting would increase and increase.

"All I can tell you is that I'm tired of being the butt of family whispers and jokes. I'm not in any rush to get married, but that doesn't mean I don't want my privacy, my independence. My own home. And Naomi is a nice girl. You know that, Mama!" It was late one Friday evening in October, and Anna was having a battle with her family. She had announced at dinner that she had signed a lease, along with Naomi, for a two-bedroom apartment on Sixteenth Street.

"But *shainele,* you have your own bedroom, and no one ever questions you about what time you get home or where you've been. How much more privacy do you want?" Jacob was in strong agreement with Sarah on this issue.

"It just doesn't look right. What will the neighbors think— my unmarried daughter living alone? The only explanation is—"

"Is what, Mama?" Anna was furious, determined to have her way. She had lived in her parents' home long enough.

"Well . . . what your Mama's trying to say is that nice girls don't live alone, unchaperoned."

"Do you want to date a goy? Is that it?" her mother asked with tears in her eyes.

"Mama, it has nothing to do with whom I date or don't date. In fact, what angers me the most is this constant harping on the fact that you don't think I date enough. I happen to prefer my life the way it is, and who I live with and who I date are not the neighbors' business. It's settled—I'm moving in two weeks. If you're interested, I'll take you to see the apartment tomorrow."

Anna stood to go to her room.

"You're breaking your mother's heart, Anna. Don't do it." Jacob wiped his forehead and blew his nose.

Anna stomped out of the room and hurried upstairs, slamming the door behind her. She was sick of their concern for her reputation. If only they knew how she was suffering inside—but no, they'd have no compassion for a woman stupid enough to fall in love with a married man.

Early on the Saturday morning after Thanksgiving, the phone rang in their apartment. Anna was reading the newspaper and finishing her second cup of coffee, and Naomi was expecting a call from the man she was having an affair with. Naomi grabbed the phone, sounded mildly surprised, said a few words, then announced, "Anna, it's for you." With her hand over the receiver, she whispered, "It's Kurt!"

Frantic questions raced through Anna's mind as she reached for the phone. How did he know she had moved here? How did he know their phone number? Why was he calling her on a Saturday, a holiday weekend? Was it some kind of national emergency?

"Hello! What a surprise! Did you have a nice Thanksgiving?" Her hands were icy against the receiver.

"It's a gorgeous day, like early spring. Could I interest you in a picnic in Rock Creek Park? I know a beautiful spot, complete with burbling brook. I'll bring the picnic—and a bottle of champagne."

His voice sounded carefree and suggestive. Challenging. What should she do? Her impulsive heart overruled her calculating brain. "I'd love it. I adore picnics! But what's an officer doing with champagne, sir? Don't you know that's illegal?"

"My darling Anna, everything I intend to do today is illegal." Then without giving her a split-second to reconsider, he added, "I'll be in front of your apartment in twenty minutes. Be there." He hung up.

She ordered her brain to stay in limbo and rushed into the bathroom to run a bath. What to wear to a picnic? Surely not slacks, I want to be sexy, I want to seduce him—or entice him to seduce me. She settled on a dark-blue-wool skirt, topped by a cornflower-blue-cashmere sweater. She would wear her hair down her back, brushed back off her face and held by a simple navy-velvet band. And she had new navy pumps. She wouldn't wear flat shoes, not when she was going out with such a tall, stunning, charming—were there words enough in her head to describe this Adonis?

Eighteen minutes later, she was leaning against the brick stairwell, fighting nerves, convinced that at any minute her mother or father would drive by and know exactly what her plans were for the day. Surely every stranger could read it in her face, her illicit intentions. But it didn't matter, nothing mattered anymore except that she was wildly in love with him—come what may.

"You look very fetching, Miss Arnold," he said as an amused smile played around his eyes.

Anna sat quite stiffly, a bit too far away from him, but it gave him the opportunity to enjoy her exquisite profile, to celebrate with his eyes her ample bosom, so beautifully outlined in the soft sweater. He sensed her intense nervousness, which echoed his own. He reached over, took her hand, and squeezed it. "Relax, darling. Relax."

She smiled at him tentatively, shyly.

"Do you know what I see sitting next to me? A gorgeous, stubborn, willful, magnificent woman. The smartest woman I've ever known."

"If I'm so smart, why did I fall for a married man?" She looked at him, warming to his banter.

He flashed a stunning, roguish smile her way. He was determined to hide his own feelings of guilt. "Fate, my darling. Fate."

The spot he'd chosen for their picnic was as advertised: peaceful, quiet, semiprivate, enchanting, with the sound of rushing water, the smell of autumn leaves, the dampness of early fall. They walked a long time, holding hands, chatting nonchalantly about office matters, gossiping about Naomi and her fellow. Then Kurt spread a plaid blanket on the ground, and they set to work unpacking the picnic basket: pâté and braided olive bread, apples and pears, a wedge of Brie cheese, two pieces of fried chicken, and two pieces of coconut cake for dessert. He produced two crystal champagne glasses and a bottle of Mumm's champagne—"Compliments of Admiral Hughes, my dear. Only don't tell him you're the one who shared it with me." Damn it, why did he keep reminding himself—and Anna—of his guilt?

They devoured the lunch and champagne, surprised at how hungry they both were after their long walk. Then Kurt lay back on the blanket and pulled Anna to his chest. He looked deep into her eyes, searching for a decision. He grasped her face in both his hands and kissed her lips, tenderly at first, then as if to devour her.

At first resistant, she gave in completely to her long-suppressed passion and felt herself surrender to whatever consequences there might be. He kissed her again, then drew her down against his chest so that the top of her head fit neatly against the bottom of his chin. He wrapped both his arms tightly around her small body, then caressed the back of her head with his right hand. "I've given up, Anna, given up trying to be an officer and a gentleman. I can't do it, not when you're involved."

"Kurt," Anna asked with great fear, "where does your wife think you are this minute?" It was an issue they had to face head-on.

"She believes I was called away to Norfolk for two days." Anna heard what almost sounded like a sob in his voice. "I know it's awful. A lie. But my whole relationship with Betty has become a lie. I make love to her and wish I were making love to you instead. Life has become unbearable."

And if I make love with you, Anna thought, I will be collaborating with you in cheating on your wife. We will be equally guilty. And yet . . .

She waited speechless for what he would say next.

In a hoarse voice from deep within his chest, he said, "I've tried so hard to put you out of my life. But I can't." He shielded his eyes from the light with his hand, as if protecting himself from an inner vision. "You know, Anna, I've never decided to do something that I absolutely knew was wrong. Yet here I am, holding you in my arms."

Anna could think of no response; she merely hugged him more tightly, feeling his distress.

"We're wasting time. We've only three years and three months before I'll be back on a ship somewhere in the Atlantic or the Pacific. We've only three years to love one another enough to last a lifetime. How do you feel about that?"

He was waiting for her to speak. He would not put words in her mouth, she realized. He would not make the decision for her. She had to make it for herself. She should be strong enough to give him up, she told herself. But she couldn't summon the will to stand and walk away.

"I guess . . ."

"Yes?"

"I think . . . three years is . . ."

He tilted her face up so he could look into her eyes. "I hoped you'd feel that way. I've reserved a room in a hotel in Alexandria, for tonight and tomorrow."

Slowly, ever so slowly the afternoon progressed—according to a mysterious timetable that Kurt had planned, Anna realized. They lay for a long time on the blanket, kissing occasionally, hugging, but also talking about their feelings, both happy and sad.

"I'm usually pretty good with words," he said quietly. "But the first day I saw you, I was blown away. Such dignity when you stood to shake my hand. Such a quick putdown, calling me a messenger boy. Women don't usually respond like that." He kissed her fingers while he talked, one at a time. Each kiss sent ripples of pleasure down her arm. "Tell me, my sweet, what did you think of me that weekend? Don't lie and say you didn't think of me at all."

"Would I lie to you?" Anna answered in a dreamy voice. "I thought you were probably the most conceited, arrogant, cocky womanizer I'd ever met. And the best-looking too!"

"And when did you realize you wanted to make love with

me?" He nibbled on her pinkie, then drew her hand over his mouth and played with her palm with his tongue. When she could stand it no longer, she pulled her hand away and reached for his face. She kissed first his lower lip, then his whole mouth, deliberately teasing him with her flickering tongue.

"Just now, Lieutenant. Just this moment. For the first time, this minute, I realize I want to make love with you."

"Hell, Anna, you're not a very good liar. But since you're in the mood, let's pick this stuff up and head for Virginia."

When he stood, Anna looked directly at the bulge in the front of his camel trousers. She had not been unaware of the state of his passions.

Her feelings of guilt returned when he left her to walk around the block while he checked into the George Mason Hotel. What was she getting herself into? Where would it lead? Would he understand he was her first?

And then she felt his familiar grip on her elbow as he wordlessly guided her into the hotel, toward the elevator, and into the suite he had reserved for them.

When the door was closed and bolted behind them, he took her fully in his arms, leaning down to kiss her lips as she stood on tiptoe to reach up to him. Hungrily, they devoured one another, attempting in a few minutes to slake the thirst they had felt for each other for eight months.

He scooped her up in his arms, carried her through the sitting room into the bedroom, and gently placed her on the large bed. Her body began to tremble, goose bumps broke out on her arms, and her hands were icy. He kissed her again, then—never taking his eyes off her—began to strip. He pulled off the brown turtleneck sweater, unbuckled his belt, and removed his shoes and pants. His eyes commanded her to look at him, look at him totally, completely. See the man you are about to get. Enjoy the sight.

Anna felt her face flaming, her eyes riveted to him indecently. Blushing, she turned away, and concentrated on the cabbage roses in the wallpaper.

He reached for her shoulders and forced her to look at him. "Anna, my dearest, can you begin to imagine how I've yearned for this moment? How I've rehearsed it in my mind thousands of times, night after night, at three in the morning? Say it,

Anna, say it!" His eyes bore into her, pleading with her for the ultimate surrender.

"I love you"—she laughed softly at him—"I love you so much, I'm about to do something I never thought I'd do. Why have you wasted so much time, you silly man? Didn't you know from the first moment that I was like putty in your hands?"

At that moment Anna felt whole again, as if parts of her had been split apart all day but had now reassembled in her person. Her body and her brain and her emotions were united again. With all her being she loved him and wanted to give herself to him totally.

He moved toward the bottom of the bed and slowly removed her shoes, softly rubbed the bottom of each foot, then pressed his lips against her arch. He reached up her thigh, unfastened her garters with what she realized was the experience of years of making love to women—other women. He drew her stocking down, careful not to tear it, and deposited it on the floor inside her shoe. He moved up to kiss her open mouth again, penetrated her with a teasing tongue, then lightly kissed her eyes and nose.

He unfastened the second stocking and removed it with equal care. Then he moved back to the head of the bed. Again he kissed her mouth, then with both hands gently slid the velvet band, freeing her glistening black hair. He pulled big handfuls around to the front of her shoulders.

"I love your hair down long. It's so sensuous, so much more erotic than when you put it up."

"Bedroom hair . . . isn't that what you're saying? I could hardly wear it this way at the office."

"Not unless you wanted every man in sight to be arrested for rape. Hmmm . . ." He buried his face in her hair and inhaled deeply while he began to raise her sweater from the back.

She caught her breath—it was really going to happen.

Slowly, trying not to unduly mess her hair, he removed her sweater, one arm at a time. He hadn't looked at her breasts, now covered only by a black-lace bra. Instead, he concentrated on each arm, kissing her from the tips of her fingers to the top of her shoulder. Then he held her away from himself and looked squarely at her bosom. "Beautiful, absolutely magnificent," he whispered as he looked from her breasts to her eyes, then back to her breasts. He reached around her back to unfasten her bra.

She felt her body stiffen momentarily, then relax again as his eyes caressed first one naked breast, then the other. How could it be that just his eyes, sweeping her nipples like that, could cause such delicious pain in her abdomen, such singeing sensations between her thighs? In her most vivid fantasies she had never had such overpowering physical feelings!

He bent to kiss her breast, nuzzled it softly at first, teased it with his tongue, then sucked deeply. Her whole body shuddered, and as his mouth reached for the other breast, she felt his hand slowly move down her abdomen. Can it get better than this? she wondered as he nibbled her left breast, then kissed the small of her neck and moved up to her mouth again.

"I think I'd better finish what I've started," he muttered. He tore himself away from her mouth and reached for the button and zipper on her skirt. "I'll need your help," he said as she lifted her hips and allowed the skirt to slip off. He removed her black-silk half-slip and then her garter belt. Only her panties were left—and his shorts.

He removed his underwear, placed it on the chair next to the dresser, and walked back toward her. She tried not to look, not to see that swollen pink shaft coming toward her. She didn't want to seem like a trollop—but she had never seen a naked man before, let alone an aroused naked man. Her eyes were glued to him, her face aflame.

He stood over her, as if commanding her to look at him, appreciate his fullness, his ripeness. He looked down at her body, up and down, caressing each inch with his loving, ravishing eyes. Slowly, his taut hands reached down and slid her black panties down her legs.

He sat down beside her, his back to her lower body, his eyes looking directly into hers. "Tell me, my darling, not that it's any of my business, but I don't want to hurt you. . . . Is this your first time?"

As he said the words and looked unflinchingly into her eyes, his left hand made its way between her legs, lightly touching, caressing her. She wanted to lie, she wanted to appear experienced, sophisticated, worldly-wise—but the words wouldn't come out. She continued to look at him, loving his naked body, his hairy chest, his lean hips, his wonderful rugged face, his large bronze hands. But no words came out of her mouth.

Meanwhile, his left hand probed deeper. Then he swung his body around so that he was lying, snug against her, and moved his right hand where his left had been. "Does that feel good? Do you like it?"

"Oh my God, I don't ever want you to stop," she gasped, "never."

"I won't my darling, I won't," he said as he rolled over toward her and again kissed her breasts.

His mouth and tongue moved downward in a circling motion, downward, ever downward, and Anna felt herself drowning in delicious swirling spasms. A heat she had never imagined built up in her abdomen, tingling sensations leaped up her legs, all feeling centered itself in her groin. He parted her legs with his head, and with his mouth and tongue he set her body on fire. She felt lost, transported to another world. Another being— someone she didn't know was experiencing this wild, unending pleasure. Then it came, one gigantic wave after another. And another. Her body tore open with pleasure, dissolved in hot pain, and came to life again with each touch of his probing tongue. She heard her voice call out his name, again and again, "I love you, Kurt, oh how I love you."

He moved up to her mouth again and kissed her deeply, then moved on top of her. With the experience of some former incarnation, she reached down to guide him inside her body, to unite him with her very self. It hurt. Oh, how it hurt, and then the pleasure began again and she was calling out his name. "Kurt, oh Kurt, I love you!"

▨ Chapter 13

Anna lay perfectly still, listening to the rain beat against the hotel room window, listening to the wind howl, and looking at Kurt. Day was breaking—a miserable day weatherwise, but Anna had never felt happier. She watched Kurt sleep, watched his chest move up and down, and looked closely at the bronze eyelashes guarding his dreams.

Her body ached. She felt a soreness between her legs, then remembered pleasure. They had made love to the point of exhaustion, then showered together as if it were the most natural thing in the world. Afterward, Kurt had ordered dinner sent to the room and had somehow obtained a fine bottle of Burgundy to go with their filet mignon.

They had turned on the radio and danced to the sounds of Tommy Dorsey. And then slowly, ever so slowly, they had made their way back to the bedroom again.

I'm a different human being today, Anna thought. There's no going back, no returning to that former state of innocence. Sex is so much better than even Naomi told me. Why have I wasted so much of my life waiting?

Kurt shivered, opened one eye, looked at her, and closed his eyes again. A smile began to play around the corners of his lips. With his eyes closed, he reached out and pulled her close. "It's heaven to wake up with you beside me."

She lay in his arms, content to breathe his masculine scent and study the hair on his chest. If only this day would never end. . . .

"What would you like to do today, Anna?" he asked, stifling a yawn.

She grinned up at him, wondering if she could shock him. "More of the same?"

"Hmmm—that's what I was hoping you'd say. Breakfast first?" A roguish look took over his face.

She answered by placing his hand on her naked breasts, moving the tips of his fingers against her nipples. "Are you that hungry? You can't wait?"

After breakfast and lunch in the hotel room, and after they had read the Washington papers and *The New York Times* from cover to cover, Kurt asked, "Anna, tell me. Where'd you go to school?"

Feeling as if he had hit her in the stomach, she answered, "Eastern High School. Why?"

"Where'd you go to college?"

"I didn't."

"I would have sworn—you read all those books in high school?" He'd put down the magazine section of the *Times* and stared at her in wonderment.

"Not in high school. Just on my own. I love to read."

"Why didn't you go to college?"

"My parents felt it was more important to educate my brothers. They couldn't afford to send me too."

"You know, it strikes me as strange—I've known you for eight months, and I know absolutely nothing about your family. I assumed . . ."

"What did you assume?" she asked, curious as to how he perceived her.

"Well, let's see. You carry yourself with such style and elegance. You have that wonderful British complexion and accent —I love to listen to you talk. The lilt of your voice is music to my ears. I guess—I guess I assumed you were from a fine old aristocratic family, your ancestors probably arrived on the *Mayflower*. I would have picked you for a Radcliffe or Vassar graduate."

"I wish . . ."

"What?"

"That what you thought was true." She sighed. "No such luck. And I don't know much about you besides the fact that you graduated from Annapolis in 1924. Where did you grow up?"

"In Oregon. Portland. My parents are both lawyers. My dad's the senior partner in a law firm, and my mom runs a small pro bono clinic for the poor."

"Why did you choose the Navy over your father's law firm?"

"My grandfather was a naval hero, and he influenced me. I wanted to be like him. Dad and Mom were all for it. I have one sister, and she's their daughter-lawyer."

"Tell me, how can you afford this"—she gestured to include the suite—"and room service and fancy wines and cashmere sweaters?"

"My grandfather got lucky years ago, made some money, and left me and my sister each a trust fund. That income permits me a few extras. It sure makes life on a limited Navy salary easier."

"I hope your trust isn't invested in stocks. Something horrible is going to happen, I can just feel it."

"I agree. No, it's in income-producing property on the West Coast. It's a steady, dependable income. Frees me to dedicate myself to my work."

Anna felt unaccountable twinges of envy—unworthy of her,

she decided. How can I be envious of the man I love because he's had an easier life, because he has security? What's wrong with me?

"How old are you, Anna?"

She didn't want to answer him, didn't want him to know the truth.

"Anna?" A puzzled frown covered his face.

"I'm twenty-one." She watched his eyes light up in surprise. "How old did you think I was?"

"At least twenty-four or twenty-five." He motioned for her to come sit beside him on the sofa. When she cuddled next to him, he asked more questions about her family. She told him about each of her brothers and her sister, what they were doing with their lives, and about her parents.

"Don't you wish you were married like Sasha?" he asked tenderly.

"Only if I could be married to you," she began, then realized she had touched on a taboo subject. "Actually, I'm not in a rush to be married. I like my career just fine."

He kissed her forehead and reached for her breast simultaneously. Then he said, "We have to check out in about an hour. How about one last time?"

"Ah! I see I have competition!" Kurt said as he eyed the dozen red roses in a vase on Anna's desk. "Who's your secret admirer, Anna? I'll kill him!" He grinned a wide, rakish grin down at her.

"You'll do no such thing, Lieutenant! He's one of my favorite people in the whole world—James Farley." She flashed a sassy smile up at him. "My goodness, you're here early this evening. I wasn't expecting you for a while yet, but—well, I can finish this tomorrow morning."

She closed her steno book, put a few things in her desk drawer, then excused herself to go to the ladies' room. Meanwhile, Kurt made the rounds of the office, joking and chatting with staff. When Anna returned, they walked out of the office and down the hall to the door.

"What a lovely spring evening, look at those gorgeous red tulips!" Anna enthused as she took Kurt's arm and crossed the street to his car. It was Friday night, and though she was disappointing her mother, she was thrilled that Kurt had invited her to dinner. Simply being in his presence, being able to look across a table and drink in his love, made her feel joyously alive and completely happy.

"If you're in the mood for crab imperial, we'll go to Harvey's," he said as he helped her into the car and closed the door. When he was seated himself, he reached over to kiss her. "I love you, darling. You look absolutely splendid in yellow—so feminine. I'm jealous of all the men who feasted their eyes on you today." He turned on the motor, then asked, "Why is James Farley sending you roses? Is there something I should know?"

"Don't be ridiculous! He's a married man with two children!" No sooner were the words out of her mouth than Anna's face turned scarlet.

"Exactly. Married men have been known to fall in love with you, Anna. I thought I'd point that out." He hated himself at that moment, hated the fact that he was so weak he couldn't give Anna up.

"Why, Kurt, I do believe you're jealous."

"Damn right! I don't need competition from—oh, never mind." The last thing Anna needs tonight, Kurt told himself, is to feel my frustration. And guilt.

She was astonished at his anger. "If you must know, my dearest, I did him a favor last week, a political favor, and he never forgets to thank me. Either a box of chocolates or flowers. He's very thoughtful that way."

"Hmm. And how many passes has he made at you? How many times has he invited you to dinner?"

"He hasn't. This is a ridiculous conversation. You're worried about me and another man, yet I have to live with the fact that every night you go home to your wife's bed! I'm the one who has cause to be jealous."

"You're right. I'm sorry. We should talk about it tonight. It's always best to clear the air."

They drove in silence the rest of the way to the restaurant, but Kurt helped her out of the car in his usual gallant manner, kissing her cheek lightly as she brushed past him.

After they ordered dinner, Kurt added some whiskey to Anna's soda from his flask. Then he asked, "Was your mother upset when you canceled out on dinner?"

"Well, I'm sure she was disappointed, but I promised her I'd drop in for Sunday dinner."

"Not the same as the Sabbath dinner, though, is it Anna?" He looked at her closely, his expression serious, his eyes unwavering.

She busied herself smoothing her napkin over her skirt, trying to think what to say.

"Why have you never mentioned you're Jewish? You told me all about your family but neglected to mention anything about that. Where does the British accent come from?"

"Does it matter, Kurt?" she asked with fear in her voice.

"What matters to me is that for some reason, something to do with what you think I might feel for you, something has prevented you from telling me you're Jewish." He paused, reached across the table for her hand, then continued, "Surely, by now you know me well enough, Anna. You should feel secure enough in my love to know that it makes not a whit of difference to me. You could be Catholic, Protestant, Jewish, Muslim, Hindu—whatever. I love you for all kinds of reasons. Knowing you're Jewish has only increased my respect for you."

"It has?" Anna asked, astonished.

"When I was at the Naval Academy, the brightest men were the Jews. They tried the hardest, had the best minds—great in math and science and physics—and they were treated with scathing contempt by most of our classmates. And the shame of it is that damn few of them will make admiral, due to prejudice. The Navy will lose its brightest minds."

In a quiet voice Anna answered, "Most non-Jews don't share your views. Hardly a day goes by when I don't hear someone making a nasty comment about Jews. I deal with it by not volunteering any information about my religion. It's no one's business anyway."

"I agree, but I thought you loved me, and I thought we shared all our most intimate thoughts. We've been making love for nearly six months now, and yet you didn't trust me enough to confide in me. I think that says something about what kind of a man you think I am."

"Nonsense. You're making too much of it. I'm not a religious person at all—there's no reason I would have discussed religion with you."

"I think it goes deeper. I think you're ashamed of being Jewish. You wish you weren't Jewish—isn't that right, Anna?"

"Oh, bosh! I don't know, I suppose, maybe it is."

He sipped his drink, then reached for her hand again. "The British accent is an acquired accent, intended to deceive people, isn't it, Anna?"

"What is this, a cross-examination?"

"I want you to think about these things. I find them disturbing. Even though I admit I find your accent most charming, I'm chagrined to discover it's a deliberate attempt to deceive. Such motives are unworthy of you, Anna. You're made of finer stuff!"

The waiter arrived with their crab imperial at that moment. Kurt saw relief in her face and decided to let up on her—he would return to the subject later. They chatted comfortably about Navy matters, committee gossip, and the erratic stock market. Then Kurt told her that he had use of one of his friends' apartments for the evening.

"Of course I want to," Anna responded, "If you promise to stop scolding me."

"It's a deal."

But Kurt didn't keep his end of the bargain. After they satisfied their passions and lay entwined on the large bed, Kurt, with his right arm raised so that his hand rested on his forehead, said, "Anna, I worry about you, worry about the fact that you're wasting the best years of your life in this illicit affair when you really should be out there dating eligible men. Surely you want a husband and family."

Anna listened, not making a comment, her mind idling. It was something she, too, thought of occasionally, but chased away to some dark corner of her mind. She had a wish—a hope —a belief—that if she could make Kurt love her enough, he would leave his wife and children and marry her. But she dared not articulate that wish. She didn't want to scare him away.

When she didn't answer, he pursued the issue. "What *do* you want out of life?"

"I suppose I want what every woman wants. But more. I want to be very wealthy. I want a beautiful home, decorated with antiques and fine art and oriental rugs. I want to be able to afford the finest couturier fashions, to travel to Europe and Asia."

"You're not going to get wealthy working in the Senate, not on a government salary, that's for sure."

"No, I probably won't stay at the Senate forever," she responded quietly as she stroked his chest.

"I'm kind of surprised. I thought you were dedicated to working for the country, all that sort of thing. But you want money. Well, maybe it's just as well I didn't meet you before—being wealthy has never been one of my goals."

"That's because you've always had your grandfather's trust fund. You've never wanted anything you couldn't have."

"Not true! I'm not that wealthy. There are lots of things I'd like to be able to afford. But making money for its own sake is not one of my priorities." He sat up and began to pull on his shorts. He turned and looked at her, a stern look in his eyes. "And it shouldn't be one of yours either, Anna."

Anna sat up, shrugged, and began to dress. Finally, she broke the awkward silence. "Face it, Kurt. We're different. I'm Jewish, and you're a Wasp. You pointed that out earlier this evening. And whether you want to admit it or not, that single fact in our lives causes us to have different experiences and different expectations."

Fully dressed in his imposing naval uniform, he walked around the bed and took her in his arms. "I'm trying to understand you, my darling. Isn't that what love is all about? And I do love you—more than anything in the world, don't ever doubt it."

A year or so later, Anna lay alone in her bed, alone in her apartment. Naomi was in New York trying to help her family come to grips emotionally with their reduced state. Ten days before, the stock market had crashed. On Black Tuesday the market had panicked. Naomi's father had sustained losses of at least four and a half million. Her mother had taken to her bed, and all over New York men were committing suicide.

Anna selfishly reflected that her own parents, because they had so little, had not been touched by the crash. Their life would continue as before: Jacob would continue as manager of the grocery store, Sarah would teach Hebrew and probably raise her maid's salary in a gesture of goodwill. Anna's own savings, stashed away at a rate of two or three dollars a week, amounted to only a little over a thousand dollars, safely deposited in Riggs Bank.

Her own job and her brothers' seemed safe. But panic prevailed all around them and seemed to pervade the very air they breathed.

In spite of Kurt's dire warnings about American military unpreparedness, Anna had to agree with the news pundits and the people that President Hoover's major job now was to rally public confidence in the economy. Much of what she did at the Naval Affairs Committee suddenly seemed irrelevant—to everyone but Kurt and his fellow officers.

Kurt. Tonight he's dancing at the Army-Navy Club with his wife. She's dressed to the nines, Anna imagined, vivaciously chatting up his superior officers, flirting with him on the dance floor.

While I'm lying here all alone, with no hope, on a Saturday night. Maybe Naomi's right. Maybe it's a no-win situation for me. But I do love him—oh, how I love him!

"Is Louis's business okay?" Anna asked cautiously as she sat opposite Sasha in the small bistro they had agreed upon for lunch.

"Not as good as it once was, but he says Washington is depression-proof. As long as the government is here, people will buy and sell property—and he'll make commissions."

Anna looked at her radiant, brown-eyed sister, who was blossoming visibly in the eighth month of pregnancy. Though her body was huge, her face never seemed prettier. "You look terrific, Sasha. Who would've thought . . ."

"I feel wonderful, too, though it's hard to sleep at night, hard to find a comfortable position. The little guy kicks and kicks."

"You're so sure it's a he?" Anna kept up the small talk, wondering why Sasha had insisted on having lunch with her.

"Anna, Mama asked me to have lunch with you. She's worried." Sasha moved her purse so the waiter could serve the chicken salad, then looked again at Anna. She could see that Anna was holding off an angry retort while the waiter was there.

When he left, she exploded. "What's Mama upset about now?"

"She says . . . well, she thinks . . . are you dating someone special these days, Anna? You can tell me the truth. I won't tell Mama." Sasha watched Anna's face flush, watched her squirm as if deciding whether to confide in her.

"Yes. I am seeing someone special." Anna took a bite of her salad.

Sasha studied her, waiting for more. Anna looked marvelous, slender and chic. Her hair and nails were perfect as always, and her pale-gray spring suit was the epitome of tailored elegance. But in her deep-blue eyes, Sasha saw pain.

Finally Anna said, "It's really no one's business but mine, whom I'm dating, what I do in my leisure hours."

"We don't mean to be nosy—honest, Anna. It's just—well, I can tell you're not really happy, or you'd tell me about it. You'd be bragging about him if you felt good about it. Is he a goy?"

Anna put her fork down. "Not only is he not Jewish, my dear little sister, but he's a married man with two children. Now"—Anna watched the horrified expression enlarge on Sasha's face—"are you going to tell Mama and Pa about that?"

"Oh, my God, no. I think that's exactly why Mama's so worried—I think she's figured it out. Oh, Anna, we love you so much. You must come to your senses!"

Anna looked at her crestfallen sister. "My business is my own. I didn't tell you who to marry. I didn't tell you to have a baby. I don't interfere in your life. I don't want anyone in my family interfering in mine. Is that clear, Sasha? There's no need for you to tell Pa or Mama anything. Tell them you had lunch with me and that everything's fine. Tell them, if you must, that I'm dating several men simultaneously—and they're all Jewish. That will make Mama happy."

"I can't lie to them."

"Sometimes, sometimes, my dear little sister, a lie is a blessing. Why should they feel my pain? Isn't it enough that I'm living with it? Why should they suffer too? Don't tell them, Sasha! Promise me."

Slowly, wiping her lips with her napkin, Sasha nodded in agreement.

She's never looked more gorgeous, Kurt thought as he watched Anna's animated face study the window displays in the shops in the lobby of the Plaza Hotel. "I love that dress, that fabric, darling. It clings to your curves so marvelously."

"Silk chiffon is wonderful. Do you like me in violet? This is the first time I've worn anything quite this color."

He could tell that she had never felt more beautiful, either, more loved and cherished. She had said as much at dinner that evening in the Oak Room. They hadn't wanted to leave the building after spending all afternoon making love. So they had showered and dressed, Anna in the dress she had bought especially for this night of dinner and dancing—her twenty-third birthday—and now they had decided to give up the idea of dancing and go back to their room. If they danced at all, it would be to radio music.

After Anna had seen all the shop windows, they slowly walked toward the elevator. Kurt held Anna's elbow in his usual possessive way. When the elevator door opened, out stepped James Farley. He recognized Anna first.

"Anna! Don't you look splendid!" he greeted her.

"Mr. Farley!" She was speechless. How could she explain the fact that she was waiting to board an elevator with a handsome lieutenant in a hotel in New York City?

"And who's this lucky man?"

Anna recovered her poise enough to make the introductions, then Kurt saved the day.

"I've heard a lot about you from Anna, Mr. Farley—and from your friend, the governor. Now, if you'll excuse us, we're late for my commanding officer's wedding reception—very late, I'm afraid," he coolly lied as he looked at his watch to emphasize the point.

"Well, Lieutenant, it's good to meet you. You take good care of my gal Anna, now, y'hear!"

After the men shook hands again and Mr. Farley kissed Anna's cheek, they boarded the elevator.

Kurt looked down at Anna, who was clearly distressed. "You can stop trembling, love. He didn't suspect a thing."

"Thanks to your quick thinking. I was so embarrassed."

"I know. When you're embarrassed, your cheeks turn the most delightful shade of deep rose, and your eyes get even darker." He squeezed her hand. She tried so hard to be sophisticated and invulnerable—and usually she succeeded.

As he turned the key in the lock, Anna held out her left hand and admired once again the ring he'd given her that afternoon: a large pear-shaped black opal, surrounded by two rows of small diamonds. "I had a friend bring it back from Australia. I thought it would match the fire in your eyes," he had said as he placed it on her finger. When I get back home, she thought, I'd best put it on the right hand or people will think—well, I don't know what they'll think.

They danced, then, to radio music, and they drank champagne, toasting Anna's birthday and their love. Kurt realized that Anna seemed more relaxed, totally open, and bursting with love for him. It was the first time in months he hadn't felt tremendous tension in their relationship. Only love, pure, free-flowing love. "I wish you could always be as happy as you are tonight, Anna," he whispered, then pressed his lips against her forehead. The music was "Am I Blue?" and Kurt wanted to suspend the moment and keep it forever fresh in his mind.

"I could be this happy if I knew you were really mine."

"Ahh . . . I wonder." The moment was over, he could feel the tension in her voice and body.

She pulled slightly away from him, stopped dancing, and asked, "Is there a doubt in your mind? I've given it a lot of thought, through a lot of sleepless nights. You know, Kurt, I'd give up everything to marry you. I'd walk away from my career on the Hill, leave my family, and leave Washington without a backward glance if I knew I could spend the rest of my life with you." She sat down on the sofa, looked at him with pleading eyes, and motioned for him to sit next to her.

"Anna, I wish it hadn't come to this. I know you believe what you say, that you could be perfectly happy married to me, keeping my home, having my children. But when I try to imagine you in that role, it doesn't work. The life of a naval officer's wife is boring most of the time. She follows her husband to a base, then sits at home twiddling her thumbs for six months at a stretch while he's at sea. I can't imagine you finding satisfaction in that kind of life."

"I would," she answered defiantly, "even though you can't imagine it. I'd find something meaningful to do, I'd keep my mind active."

Kurt stood up abruptly and walked toward the window, looked out, then turned back to Anna. "This is a pointless discussion." He softened his voice, then continued, "From the very outset I've tried—religiously tried—to make sure you understood that I will not leave my wife and children. I will not break up my family."

Suddenly his voice broke, his composure dissolved. "Shit, Anna, I hate myself for being so weak, for not doing the right thing and giving you up! It's just—you're the only meaningful thing in my life!" He turned back toward the window and pounded on the sill. Then, after a long moment, he turned back to her. He had regained his composure.

"And of course, that's not entirely true either. I love my children, I want them to grow up in an intact family. And I care deeply about our country's defenses and feel I can make a contribution. Maybe even make admiral someday."

"Kurt, I do understand. You've never misled me. It's my silly imagination. Wishful thinking. I've been deceiving myself." Anna loved him and hated him at the same moment. She understood she couldn't have him to herself. But she wasn't ready to give him up yet. Tears filled her eyes. "Kurt, we're making one another so miserable. Surely there must be a way, a solution."

He sat beside her and gathered her in his arms. "I've racked my brain." He sighed, then continued. "I'm not being fair to Betty either. She's a loyal wife, a truly good person, and she deserves better than this ugly deception.

"Fulfilling an obligation and being a responsible person are the most important values my parents and my education at Annapolis drilled into me. I can't forget that, and I don't think you'd like me nearly so much if I were the kind of man who took responsibility lightly."

"I know, I know!" Anna cried out and buried her face in his chest.

He felt her sob against him, and wished for a split-second that he had never let himself make love to her that first time. But no, I can't feel that way, he told himself. I love her. I've never felt this much love for any woman. "I'm so sorry—so sorry that our love has brought you unhappiness, Anna. Please believe that I never meant to hurt you."

"I know, and I'm acting silly, stupid. Forgive me. Let's go for a walk—it's a beautiful evening."

He looked down at her delicately clad feet: her violet satin heels matched her dress. "I don't think those are good walking shoes, but I'd love to be your date on a hansom carriage ride through Central Park. Would you like that?"

Her face brightened to a wide smile, and her eyes sparkled again with love. "Oh, yes."

"Then we're off, milady!"

Anna lay on the sofa reading Hemingway's *A Farewell to Arms,* occasionally sipping on some wine that Sasha and Louis had given her for Christmas. It was New Year's Eve, 1930. Everyone she knew was out partying or giving a party.

Sasha had invited her to her fancy new apartment on Massachusetts Avenue, Naomi had suggested she might go with her and her latest beau to a party, and one of the girls in the office was also giving a party. None of them appealed to Anna. She wanted to be with Kurt on New Year's Eve, and that, it seemed, would never be possible. He was dancing with his wife at the officer's club. Lucky her.

At precisely midnight, the phone rang. Hoping against hope that Kurt was thinking of her and had left Betty long enough to call her, she answered with an upbeat "Hello?"

For a moment there was silence on the other end. Then she heard her mother's hesitant voice. "Anna?" A long pause followed. "Anna, I was sort of hoping you wouldn't be home. I thought you might be out with one of those young men Sasha told me about. But—well, we're here at Sasha's house, a lot of nice people here, and you should see the champagne and whiskey and two waiters! I don't know how Louis does it, but everything is lovely. A real fancy party. Well, what are you doing, *shainele?* Why are you home on New Year's Eve?"

"Oh, Mama, I've a touch of the flu, a sort of intestinal upset or something. I had a date, but I broke it. He wasn't so special anyway. I'll probably feel better tomorrow. But thanks for calling."

"Your Pa is standing here. He wants to talk."

It's terrible the way I lie to my parents, Anna thought as she pictured them dressed in their finest at Sasha's fancy party.

"Anna, darling, I'm sorry you're not feeling good. But we want you to have the most wonderful year of your life this year, 1931. Something tells me 1931 will be wonderful for you. We love you, *shainele!*"

"Yes. Happy New Year to you, Pa. Maybe if I feel up to it tomorrow, I'll come by for dinner."

"Wonderful! It will make your mama glad. A *mitzvah!*"

"Good night, Pa." It was all she could do to keep tears out of her voice. Here she was, the only woman in Washington sitting alone without the man she loved on New Year's Eve. And it was all her own doing—her own stupid wishful thinking. "Oh, damn!" she muttered, then went back to her book and her wine.

"It's been three years since you first brought me here for lunch," Anna said to Kurt as she slipped into the booth at the Occidental Restaurant one afternoon in April.

"Three good years or three bad years?" he asked gently as he picked up the menu.

"On the whole good, I'd have to say. I love working with the committee. I've learned so much, especially from you. And of course, there's Naomi."

"She's really a good friend, isn't she?" He studied Anna's eyes, always so revealing of what she was thinking. Now, in deep thought, remembering, they were a darker blue than usual. Perhaps it was a reflection of Anna's stunning new navy-blue spring suit. "What do you think of her fiancé?"

"I'm happy for her. At last she's found a man who satisfies her parents. That's important to Naomi—especially with what's happened to their money in the crash. They feel they're newly poor, even though they still have much more than my parents do. But it's true, their circumstances are considerably reduced. They've sold their Fifth Avenue apartment and moved to Columbus Avenue; and their home at the beach is gone too. It's been hard on them, and they're good people. I like them."

"You didn't answer my question. What do you think of David Adler?" Anna frequently dodges a question, Kurt mused, rather than tell her real feelings, especially if they are negative.

"If you want the truth, I don't trust him. Something about him seems sneaky. He's good-looking enough, and he comes from money. Naomi thinks she loves him, and I guess that's what counts. After all, Naomi's getting up there in years—she's almost thirty. If she's going to get married, she'd better do it soon."

"And what about you, Anna? Are you looking?" He wanted her to be happy even more than he wanted her exclusive love. He knew he would be leaving her shortly, in January of the next year. There had been nights when he had lain awake trying to tell himself to break off their relationship even before he left Washington—for her sake, not his. But he couldn't bring himself to deny himself her love, not as long as he could still have it. What a bastard I am, he thought as he looked into her sad face.

"I'll start shopping for a husband after you leave. I've got more time than Naomi—I'm six years younger."

"And much, much more beautiful, I might add, and more intelligent. Which reminds me: the purpose of this lunch is to plot the hearings."

"Yes, Lieutenant. I've got news on that score. Senator Hale has agreed to hold hearings on our lack of military preparedness in early January. My assignment is to work up a long, detailed list of questions that will lead to certain conclusions—or at least opinions. By the way, he knows you're behind this."

"Terrific! You've made progress, Anna. Now we need to decide who should be called to testify."

"Exactly. And I need to know in advance pretty much what each man will say so I can plot out specific questions for each witness."

"You know, Anna, if these hearings take place and turn out the way I think they will, it will be the greatest contribution I can make to my country. Do you realize that Japan will have twice as many modern vessels as we do when the London treaty expires in December 1936?"

"But so will Great Britain, France, and Italy. Why are you so sure Japan will be our enemy?"

"I feel it in my bones—intuition, I guess. I'm cocky enough to believe I have the intuition about foreign and military affairs that you women seem to have about romantic affairs."

Anna smiled warmly at him—he was such a love! "Will Hoover support a naval buildup? I should think he would. Think of the thousands of men all over the country now standing in soup lines who could be working in naval yards."

"If he had an ounce of sense, he would. But all indications are that the secretary of the Navy will be unable to recommend building additional ships unless the Bureau of the Budget and the administration approve such a plan. And my guess is, they won't. That's why these hearings are so important. Admirals can't recommend a program the administration opposes, but Congress can require military men to give their best judgments about the state of our military preparedness. And Senator Hale and his colleagues can do their damnedest to educate the public after they get the facts from the admirals."

Anna sipped her tea, thinking about his plan, and said, "Yes. You work up a list of likely admirals to testify. We'll need some charts showing the relative naval strengths of Great Britain, Italy, France, Japan, and the United States."

Kurt eagerly agreed. "I'll put them together, along with tonnage and age. It's very important to differentiate between modern vessels and overage vessels. At the present time, we have two hundred three overage vessels, while Japan has twenty-three. We have only one hundred seventy modern vessels, and Japan has one hundred eighty-four. And since 1922, we've started only one-fourth the number of new ships that Japan is building. But no one in America wants to face that ugly fact. Our heads are in the sand—we really believe the propaganda that the Great War was a war to end all wars."

Anna responded in a quiet voice. "I really had hoped—perhaps you'll believe it naive of me—but I had hoped that if the United States stopped building new ships, the rest of the world would follow our example. I guess it didn't work out that way, did it?"

"Everyone shared your hope, especially in the heady days after the London treaty. But the reality is that we stopped building, while Japan and London—and even France and Italy —are building four and five times as many new vessels as we are. Someday, I fear, we'll pay a price for that naïveté."

Six weeks later, on a Thursday morning in June, Anna noticed a lot of whispering going on in the office. Staff members were gossiping about something, and she was being kept in the dark. At lunch with Naomi in the Senate cafeteria, Anna asked what was going on.

Naomi flushed, then said, "You may as well know, Anna. Kurt's wife gave birth to a nine-pound baby boy last night. That's what everyone's afraid to tell you."

Anna forced herself to take a bite of her Salisbury steak, then swallow it. She refused to let Naomi see her distress. She glanced at her friend, then back at her plate. She was momentarily speechless.

"Did you know she was pregnant?" Naomi asked in a soft voice.

"Of course I knew," Anna lied. "He's never pretended that he would ever leave her. That was only my wishful thinking."

"Perhaps it's time to end it, Anna. You're wasting the best years of your life. It's a no-win situation."

"Well, he's going to be transferred next winter anyhow. It'll have to end soon enough. If you'll excuse me, Naomi, I'm going for a walk around the block. I need some exercise." Anna stood and picked up her tray.

"Are you okay? Would you like to be alone, or should I come with you?"

"I'm fine. I'd—I'd like to be alone."

When Anna went outdoors, she took three deep breaths and headed for the nearest unoccupied bench on the Capitol grounds. Her mind was awhirl, a million echoes of his voice, his hands on her body, his breath in her ear, his eyes boring into hers.

Why didn't she die in childbirth!

My God, what a monster I've become! Wishing someone to die. How could I? I don't really wish her pain and suffering, or death even, she thought. I only want her to disappear from his life. I wish they had never met . . . or that we'd never met.

No, I don't wish we'd never met. I wouldn't give up the past three years for anything, not for anything. . . . I may never love a man again, or never quite like this, but I'll always have the memory. Oh, my God, I love him so very much . . . he didn't even tell me she was pregnant—wouldn't hurt me that way. . . . Where will it all end?

▧ Chapter 14

January 7, 1932

The chairman, Senator Frederick Hale, pounded the gavel, and the Naval Affairs Committee hearings on building up the Navy came to order. Secretary of the Navy Adams sat directly across from him. He was flanked on both sides of the long committee table by admirals and civilian aides.

Republican senators were seated on Senator Hale's right side, and Democrats on his left. Legislative aides and committee clerks filled the long row of chairs immediately behind the senators. Anna Arnold sat directly in back of Senator Hale, ready to pass him pertinent questions and other messages.

Lieutenant Commander Kurt Addison, recently promoted and preparing to leave for his new assignment in the Pacific as soon as the hearings were over, sat opposite Anna, behind Secretary Adams.

These hearings were not adversarial; rather, they were for the purpose of establishing a record that members of Congress could use to promote their legislation. The "rules of engagement" were clearly understood on both sides of the table. Kurt and Anna had carefully orchestrated and prepared their respective superiors.

If there was an adversary in these hearings, he was only there in spirit. But President Herbert Hoover was so beset with the problems of the Depression that he failed to grasp—according to Kurt and most of the members of the Navy hierarchy and the senators in the hearing room—the increasingly dangerous military unpreparedness of the United States.

Anna and Kurt had worked on little else during the previous six months. It was a bitter irony that the end of long-awaited hearings would also mean the end of their love affair. Kurt was scheduled to leave for Hawaii the following Tuesday, and Anna could think of little else as she glanced across the table and met his eyes.

He, on the other hand, was intent on Secretary Adams's answer to the chairman's probing question about the administration's stand on legislation mandating the building of new ships.

As expected, Secretary Adams said he could not take a stand.

The chairman then presented large charts detailing the buildup of naval forces by Japan, France, Italy, Great Britain, compared to that of the United States. These charts had been prepared by Kurt with suggestions from Anna. After the secretary admitted that the facts and figures were correct, he continued to say he could not recommend a course of action. Senator Shortridge then jumped into the discussion.

"You are at liberty, under the law, to make suggestions or

recommendations in response to a given bill that has been introduced, are you not?"

Secretary Adams answered, "We are limited in expressing our views by the Bureau of the Budget."

"In other words, by the President's policy. Isn't that correct? But you are not limited in giving to Congress upon its request any information you have in your possession, or any opinions as to what would be a proper construction program. You are at liberty to give information to Congress that it might ask for and that might be deemed proper to give."

The secretary answered as planned. "Yes."

Kurt smiled at Anna, the smile of two conspirators.

Chairman Hale pressed the Navy secretary on the figures of Japan's navy versus that of the United States: "We have been doing practically nothing in the way of keeping our Navy up to modern conditions, while Japan has built hers practically up-to-date."

"And it might be added that she did that with money borrowed from the United States," Senator Tydings added.

As the morning wore on, Anna found herself listening less intently to the back-and-forth of the hearings and turning increasingly inward to her own thoughts. Kurt looked so handsome sitting opposite her, in his new uniform with its two and a half stripes. And he looked so pleased with how everything was going. He had rehearsed the admirals, who would pick up where the secretary left off. He knew exactly which men would provide the arguments that the senators needed to present their case to the American public.

As she thought of their three years together and the pain she now felt, it was almost as if someone she loved had died and she was waiting several days for the burial. She had to get through these hearings, look across the room at him all day, then work with him each night to prepare questions for the next day and get them to the right senator. Then, when everything was over, he would say good-bye and leave. Walk out of her life.

This is my reward for having helped him be so successful a congressional affairs liaison officer.

I have only myself to blame, she thought as she absentmindedly scribbled the word *never* down the side of her yellow legal-size pad. Never, never, never again. Never again will I let my heart rule my head. I wouldn't be in this fix if I'd used my brains instead of letting my emotions take control. No, when he's gone from my life, I'll find a husband like Naomi's David and I'll begin to have some of the things I deserve. No more of this being the other woman.

She looked up and caught his eye. He winked. He's delighted, so delighted with how things are going, she thought as she resumed writing *never, never, never* down the left side of the page.

After ten that evening, the Capitol was quiet except for their voices and the occasional footsteps of a Capitol policeman outside in the corridor. Anna sipped cold coffee.

"Admiral Pratt will be terrific, you wait and see. He's got more guts than Adams. He won't mince words," Kurt said as he dictated questions, which Anna typed simultaneously.

"Question: If this bill were enacted into law, even without the Vinson bill, provided the budget showed a disposition to carry out the plan recommended by the Navy, the Vinson bill would not be necessary, would it?" Kurt sat down in the chair next to Anna's desk and picked up her yellow legal pad.

"What will he answer?" Anna asked.

"He'll say we need both pieces of legislation. Anna, what does this scribbling mean? 'Never, never'?"

Anna flushed bright red. "It's nothing. Just doodling—you know, when I got bored. My head's reeling with statistics about tonnage and age and kinds of ships."

"If it's only doodling, why are you blushing?"

"Let's finish, Kurt. I'm tired," she answered in a tight voice.

He reached over and caressed her arm, forcing her to look at him. "Anna, I love you. You do know that, don't you?"

"Yes." Her eyes began to fill with tears. "It's hard, it's so hard to look at you all day long and love you so much and . . . know you are leaving."

"Oh, Anna, dearest." He stood and pulled her to her feet. "If only there were some other answer." He kissed her deeply. At first she resisted, then she surrendered to his overwhelming masculinity. "That's enough for tonight," he said as he led her toward the brown leather couch in the reception area. "I know how exhausted you must be. The hearings are bad enough without all this emotional strain."

He sat down and pulled her down onto his lap, then kissed her again.

"We—we could go to my apartment, if you'd like," she stammered.

"Hmm. I really must go home tonight . . . but this sofa's nice and comfy." He eyed her with the mischievious look she always found so disarming. "Wouldn't you like to get laid in the United States Capitol? Doesn't that sound deliciously naughty!"

"Kurt! Do you think it's safe? I mean, what if the guard comes to check on us?"

"Simple!" He left her on the sofa, walked to the door, and locked it from the inside. Then he turned off the lights in the office, and the moonlight came flooding in from the large windows across the room. "Now, isn't this romantic? We should have done this long ago!" As he walked back toward Anna, he began unbuttoning his shirt.

"Thank you, Admiral Rock. The committee will stand adjourned." Chairman Hale pounded his gavel lightly, then stood. The men began shaking hands all around. Kurt flashed a big smile at Anna from across the room, then walked slowly out of the room with half a dozen admirals.

Senator Hale had invited the staff and Kurt back to his office for a "Coca-Cola party," he being a senator who believed in strict Prohibition. Anna knew that Kurt would join them as soon as he escorted the officers to their waiting cars.

"We got what we wanted, young man!" Senator Hale enthused as he patted Kurt on the back. "You did a fine job of preparing them, and I must say that Anna, here"—he draped his arm around her shoulder—"did a wonderful job scoping out the flow of the questions. Yep, we got exactly the testimony I wanted. Congratulations to both of you!"

"Thank you, sir," Kurt answered modestly, and beamed first at Senator Hale, then at Anna.

"And congratulations on that new stripe too! When are you shipping out?"

"Next Tuesday, sir."

"Must be busy packing, getting everything in order."

"Everything's pretty much in order. I was waiting for these hearings."

"Yes, well, now that they're over, you're off to sea. We're

going to miss you around here. The gals in the office all have mad crushes on you. 'Course, I'm sure you know that, probably been happening to you all your life."

Kurt changed the subject of the chairman's chatter, seeing Anna squirm under his arm. "You might like to make an inspection trip to Pearl Harbor. I'd be delighted to set it up for you, sir."

"Hey, not a bad idea—not a bad idea at all! My missus would like that a lot. She's always wanted to go to Hawaii. How about your missus—she excited?"

"Oh yes, and the children are thrilled at the prospect of being able to swim all year."

"Y'got any pictures of the kids?"

When the senator asked Kurt that question, Naomi's eyes met Anna's and she saw Anna's pain. Anna pulled herself out from under the heavy arm of Senator Hale, walked behind his desk, and looked out the window at the view of Washington.

Naomi joined her, and the two women stood silently staring out the window. Then she whispered, "Keep a stiff upper lip. It's only a few more days now."

"I know," Anna answered in a quavering voice. In the background they heard oohs and aahs as a picture of Kurt's three little children was passed around the room.

"Here's to everyone—all the staff, for a job well done!" Senator Hale announced, raising his soft drink as if it were a glass of whiskey and toasting and thanking them for their good work. "And to wish Lieutenant Commander Addison well in his new assignment."

Kurt's eyes locked with Anna's. A look of apology, of deep anguish crossed the room; then she heard herself say to Senator Hale, "I'm going to take Monday off and catch up on my personal life, if you don't mind, Senator. For one thing, I need some sleep."

"Anna, dear, of course. You must be exhausted! You were here until the wee hours every night. You deserve some time off. Of course!"

"I may even entice her out to the country this weekend," Naomi chimed in. "She needs a complete change of pace."

Monday morning shortly after ten, the phone rang in Anna's apartment. Even before answering it, she knew it was Kurt.

"May I come over?" His voice was husky.

"Yes. I was hoping you'd call. I'll make us scrambled eggs and salami, or something like that."

"I'll be there in thirty minutes."

She dressed and made up her face, fixed a chipped nail, then went into the kitchen to see what she had to serve him. We'll make do with whatever's here, she thought as she opened her refrigerator.

If I could only stop thinking, if my mind would only stop working! I want to be numb, devoid of feeling. I want to be somewhere I can't feel the pain.

Kurt arrived carrying a bottle of white wine and a paper bag from Brentano's bookstore. After he set them down, he held Anna for a long time in his arms, not saying a word. They walked over to her window and looked down on the traffic crawling up Sixteenth Street.

"I feel as if I have nothing more to say. I've had a horrible weekend. How about you?" he asked.

"Naomi and David did their best to cheer me up, fed me until I was ready to burst. I rode their new Arabian stallion, we went browsing in antique shops. It wasn't bad."

"I hope you'll keep very busy after I'm gone."

She sighed. "Yes, they say work will heal. Oh, damn, Kurt, why are we trying to be so brave? It hurts! It hurts so much!"

She pulled away from him and went into the kitchen to fix their lunch. While they ate, they talked about the hearings. Then Anna told Kurt about a call she'd had from James Farley the previous week. "He says he can fix it so I can work for him at the Democratic National Convention as part of Roosevelt's campaign team. But I have to save up my annual leave and probably take some additional time off. Exciting, isn't it?"

Kurt's face lit up. "Wonderful! You'll love being right there in the thick of things. I'm delighted for you."

Neither of them felt like making love one last time. They only wanted to sit and drink in one another's eyes.

"This isn't good-bye forever, Anna. Our lives are bound to cross again and again. You know that. I'll be back here at least twice a year—not that I'm telling you to wait for me. Next time I see you, I want you to be married."

She looked at him sadly. "I guess that would salve your conscience."

"I want you to be happy. I can't even imagine you with another man, but I know it would be right for you. And the truth is that I love you so much, I want you to be happy. Your happiness is more important to me than my own."

"If I were married, you'd have a certain peace of mind."

"That may be true. Oh, hell, Anna, there's no point in discussing it anymore. I've a gift for you. Something you can read on a cold winter's night when I'm standing watch out in the Pacific—something to remember me by. I'm going to go now. I'll stop by your office and say good-bye to everyone."

"Yes, you'd better leave," Anna said, telling herself not to become emotional, not now.

He put his hat on at that wonderful rakish angle she loved, pulled on his navy-blue trench coat, fastened the buttons and the belt, turned the collar up just so. . . . He was still the most handsome man she'd ever seen. He walked toward her slowly, took her in his arms one last time, and held her for a long moment. He tilted her chin up so he could see her eyes. He kissed each eye, then the tip of her nose, and then he kissed her lips resoundingly.

"I love you, my darling Anna. Always and forever."

And then he was gone.

She looked out the window and watched him get in his car and slowly drive away. Then she picked up the Brentano's bag and took out a heavy book. Ah, yes—*The Oxford Book of English Verse*.

She opened it to the first page.

To my dearest Anna, the greatest love of my life. As I watch the first evening star and the last morning star, I will think of you and hope that you have found the complete happiness and love you so richly deserve. Remember me. I will remember you always. I love you.

K. A.

⊠ Part 4

A Dose of Realism, 1932

Filmmaker Sonia Dunay, whose movie Stolen Moments *is rumored to be the true story of her grandmother Anna Dunay's life, confirmed last evening that the former U.S. Senator is scheduled for abdominal surgery to remove a malignancy.*

—Variety

⊠ Chapter 15

March 1932

"Miss Arnold, may I present our good friend and doctor, Claude Dunay." The Polish ambassador beamed at Anna. "He grew up in our country, but alas, he chose to desert us in favor of the United States."

The distinguished-looking young doctor took Anna's hand and bowed slightly while he simultaneously lifted it and grazed it with his lips. She stifled a giggle as she felt his moustache tickle the back of her hand. Although she had been to a number of embassy receptions, no one had ever kissed her hand before.

The ambassador continued his introduction, "Miss Arnold is a legislative assistant to Senator Frederick Hale."

"Ah, yes! I'm delighted to meet you, Miss Arnold. Please let me get you a drink," the young doctor said as he took his leave of the ambassador and guided her toward the bar at the far end of the ballroom. "One of the pleasures of these parties is the fine Polish vodka they serve. It's the only place you can get good vodka in Washington these days."

As he whisked her through the crowd, Anna sized him up. Early thirties; dark-brown hair, already beginning to thin; a self-assured, almost arrogant manner in his greetings to embassy personnel.

"They're all my patients!" he boasted as he stopped at the bar. "I'm the only doctor in town who speaks Polish."

"How long have you lived in America, Doctor?" Anna asked as she accepted a glass of vodka on ice, then turned back toward the crowd that was surging through the ballroom.

"Nearly a dozen years. I came here to go to medical school and liked it so much, I stayed." He looked into her deep blue eyes, her perfectly sculpted face, her shiny black hair done up on top of her head, and decided she was the most beautiful British woman he'd ever met. "Your dress is stunning. Is it French?"

"No, I'm afraid not. I designed it myself and had a wonderful Italian seamstress make it for me. The lace is imported from France, though."

"I thought so. It's splendid. I admire a woman who can take the best of the couture and translate it to fit her own needs and budget! The smartest French women do exactly that—have their own dressmakers copy the couture at a quarter the price or less. Very smart of you."

"I take it, then, that you've also lived in France?" Anna discovered she was enchanted with this debonair, worldly young doctor. He was definitely worth getting to know, even though it meant she wouldn't circulate the way she usually did at embassy parties.

"I attended what you Americans call high school and college in France. Actually, my parents are French. They moved to Warsaw after they finished medical school."

"Both your parents are doctors?" Anna was more impressed each minute.

"My mother's a psychiatrist—she studied with Freud. Father specializes in diseases of the nervous system. They're renowned throughout Europe—they present papers at medical conferences regularly. I had the joy of reading their work as an assignment while I was in med school in Arizona." Anna walked toward the comfortable-looking silk damask chair in the library. This young man was so interesting, she yearned to continue their conversation. After they were seated, she put her glass on the coffee table—she didn't like vodka—and turned to him. "What's your speciality?"

"I'm an internist, but I specialize in stomach disorders."

"Do you write papers too?" She studied his unflinching gray eyes. They were mysterious, questioning, appraising, calculating. What did he want to know about her?

"I'm busy building up my practice in Washington these days, but I try to do two papers a year and attend two medical conferences. More than that, I can't handle right now." He sipped on his drink, never taking his eyes away from her own. "And now it's my turn. How long have you been in this country?"

Stunned, Anna realized he believed she had come from England. She would not disabuse him of that notion. "I came here as a small child."

"Ah. Then you attended American schools."

"Correct." Anna changed the subject quickly. "I'm ravenous. Shall we see what's on the buffet table?" she asked as she stood.

He put his glass down. Thinking that she had remarkable poise and a regal carriage, he followed her out of the library. They both launched into conversations with other acquaintances while they munched on finger food, then lost sight of one another in the crowd. Anna was just thinking how miserable it would be to go back out into the spring snowstorm and hail a taxi, when the handsome doctor, dressed in a black homburg and velvet-collared overcoat, came up behind her in the foyer. "May I offer you a ride home, Miss Arnold? My car is parked in the next block."

"That would be ever so kind of you, Dr. Dunay. I hope it's not too far out of your way. I live on Sixteenth Street."

"Not at all." He took her elbow and escorted her out of the embassy. As they walked toward his car, he introduced himself further. "My name is Claude, and I know yours is Anna. Would you be offended if I called you Anna?"

She smiled at him—he was wasting no time. "Aren't the trees beautiful? Don't you love to walk in the snow?"

"Not really. If anything, I prefer the weather where I went to medical school, in Arizona. I had enough snow in Poland to last me a lifetime."

"Sounds like you don't like Poland much."

"I don't," he responded with barely concealed anger. "The Poles are a very narrow, prejudiced people. They don't compare with the French when it comes to culture." He paused, looked at her to see if she shared his opinion, then continued, "I would have nothing to do with them except for the fact that I'm a young doctor trying to create a practice. Generally, one embassy leads to the next. I made it a point to get to know the Polish ambassador, the French ambassador, the British ambassador—and it's led to business. They and their personnel want a doctor they can communicate with in their own language. In fact, most of my patients are foreigners, members of the diplomatic corps."

Quite a catch! Anna lifted her long hair and fanned it out over the pillow above her head. She lay on her back, staring at the light fixture over her bed, letting moments of the weekend wash over her memory. The day after the embassy party, Claude had shown up at her office unexpectedly. Had he been checking up on her, to see if she really did work for Senator Hale? No, it seemed his only intention had been to invite her to a concert at the Library of Congress. The next day he took her horseback riding in Rock Creek Park, looking handsome in his

jodhpurs and hacking jacket ("from Hermès") and his shiny
black boots. If she continued to date him, she'd have to buy
riding clothes.

And today the art gallery. It's like taking a tour with an art
professor, she thought, as she remembered his minilecture on
Claude Lorraine and the relative unimportance of the Impressionists. "I love the old masters—they're the only paintings
worth investing in. Mark my word, in twenty years no one will
hang Impressionists on their walls. They'll be relegated to the
attic or the basement."

When he made statements, he made them with such authority, she hardly dared dispute him. After all, he seemed so
knowledgeable. Yet she did prefer Impressionists, no matter
what he said.

He had taken her to Footer's deli for Sunday-night supper,
then drove her back to her apartment. He had quickly kissed
her good night at her door, and from the way he did it, he
didn't seem to expect an invitation inside.

Just as well, Anna thought. This time I'll do things the right
way, by the book. I won't mess up my life again. Good grief! I
never asked him if he was married! How could I have forgotten
to ask him! But surely he couldn't have spent the whole weekend with me if he had a wife waiting at home. Well, no matter.
He's coming to the Hill for lunch tomorrow. I'll find out. I'll
make it my business to find out, before this goes any further.

"Anna, for the life of me, I don't understand what's your
hurry. Are you afraid he's going to escape? Or evaporate into
thin air? For gosh sakes, you've only known the man seven
weeks! What's the rush?" Naomi argued as she set her tray
down on the table.

"We've decided, Naomi, and that's all there is to it. Don't
give me an argument!" Anna picked up her fork and attacked
her meal with a vengeance.

True, she thought, only seven weeks. But I do want a husband, I want some of the good things in life that Sasha has
simply because she's Louis's wife. And if I want Claude, I'm
going to have to catch him fast. Not everything about him is
perfect. He has such contempt for the poor. But maybe it's
good, maybe that's what spurs his tremendous ambition and

determination to be rich. The truth is, he's extraordinarily self-disciplined. And a touch arrogant. . . .

"Why are you getting married in Baltimore? Why not here? I don't understand you, Anna. You sound like you've taken leave of your senses. Let your mother give you a wedding! She'd be thrilled! He's Jewish and a doctor. She'll be the envy of all her friends. Give her the pleasure!"

"Claude doesn't want a big wedding. He feels very strongly about that. No fuss—a justice of the peace."

"Not even a rabbi? Anna, you can't mean it!"

"Naomi, either you're my friend or you're not. Now, will you or won't you be my attendant?"

"Oh, hell, of course I will. But I don't understand you, Anna. I really don't." Naomi stopped suddenly. "Anna, you're not—"

"No, I've never even slept with him, so don't worry."

"You're sure you're not doing this to get even with Kurt?"

Kurt will be pleased, it will ease his conscience, Anna thought, then said, "Naomi, listen to me. Claude is a brilliant doctor, a marvelously cultured man, a wonderful conversationalist, a son of two doctors. He's handsome and witty, and he wants the same things out of life that I do. We enjoy one another. What more could I want in a husband?"

"You forgot one thing, Anna. Love. Do you love him? Do you even begin to love him as you loved Kurt?"

Anna looked Naomi straight in the eyes. "More. I love him much more than I loved Kurt." As she said the words, she felt shooting pains in her chest. *I may be able to fool Naomi, but I can't fool myself. Never mind. I'll grow to love him more after we're married.*

"Okay. Oh, hell, Anna, you know I'll do anything for you. When and where?" Naomi broke into a broad smile.

"Terrific. Next Friday. If you and David can meet us at my apartment, Claude will drive us to Baltimore. The ceremony is set for three in the afternoon. Then we'll spend the weekend there."

"Ugh! Baltimore's a crummy place for a honeymoon."

"Yes, but I can't take any leave now if I'm going to the convention in Chicago next month. I've got to save up every single vacation day for that. We'll take a real wedding trip later."

"So you're still going to the Democratic Convention? Is Claude going with you?"

"Oh, no." Anna shook her head. "He can't leave his practice for two weeks, and besides, I'll be too harassed for us to have any fun together."

"And he doesn't mind you leaving him for two weeks?"

"No. He takes pride in his liberalness. He says we're going to have a modern marriage—whatever that is. And he doesn't want any children. He wants me to be a full-time career woman. Imagine that!"

"That's quite modern, I'll admit. But what about you? Don't you want children?"

"I don't know. I've never really thought about it. I guess I don't care that much."

"Sounds to me like he's talked you into it."

"Could be."

"What'll you tell your mother?"

"I'll just tell her that we wanted to elope. After all, Sasha did. Why not me?"

Naomi sighed, then said, "Anna, why do you continue to hurt your parents for no good reason? I don't understand you."

Anna's face blushed crimson. "It's my business, Naomi. It's the way Claude wants things. I can't help it. I really can't."

After they were married, Anna called her parents to tell them the news. Her father answered the phone. "Pa, I've got special news for you." She swallowed the lump in her throat and determined to go on. "I got married this afternoon—to a doctor, an internist named Claude Dunay. I know you'll like him. . . . Pa? Are you there?"

"My God! Anna—this is such a surprise! Sasha told us there was someone special . . . but we didn't—here, your mama is standing by me, tell her."

"Yes? What is it Anna? Are you okay?"

"Yes, Mama. I was just telling Pa my wonderful news. I got married this afternoon. We eloped, just like Sasha." Anna stopped when she heard her mother gasp and say, "Jacob . . . my smelling salts . . . quick!" Then Sarah spoke in a whisper to Anna again. "Tell me . . . about your husband."

"Mama, he's a doctor. He's French, but he grew up in Poland."

"A Jewish boy grew up in Poland! Poor boy—and his parents?"

"His parents are both doctors. They still live in Poland."

"But Anna, you're not going back with him?"

"No, Mama. His practice is here. In a nice office on Connecticut Avenue. He takes care of all the foreign diplomats." She heard a long sigh of relief from the phone.

"So when do we get to meet this wonderful man? Where are you, Anna?"

"We're in Baltimore. We'll be home in a few days, and we'll have dinner together. Yes, we'll have dinner at the Willard Hotel on Thursday night. How's that?"

"Mazel tov, darling." Anna heard a snuffling sound, and she knew her mother was struggling against tears. "And now your pa wants to congratulate you. This long-distance phone call is costing a fortune."

"Yes, Mama. Let me speak to Pa again."

"So. You've made us very happy after all. A Jewish man, you say? You're certain?"

"Yes, Pa, I'm certain. You'll like Claude a lot. And remember —from now on, I'm Mrs. Claude Dunay!"

"Mazel tov, mazel tov! I'll call your sister and brothers and tell them the news. And your mother will make a party to introduce him to the family."

"Thanks, Pa. I've got to go now."

"Yes, you go take good care of your husband. Have a wonderful time!"

Anna spied her mother and father before they recognized her. Her mother had a new dress on—she'd probably bought it just to meet her son-in-law-the-doctor. Her father was dressed in his three-piece black suit that he usually saved for funerals and High Holy Days. His hair was freshly barbered, and his moustache neatly trimmed.

Anna had dressed in a new raspberry-red-linen suit and a striking black portrait hat and black patent-leather shoes. It was the outfit she'd been married in, and she was especially proud of it. Claude stood beside her, dapper as always in a dark-blue suit, straw hat, and ivory-handled walking stick.

Anna watched her parents walk down the eight steps to Peacock Alley. They're aging rapidly, she thought. They have to take the steps so slowly. And Mama's hair is almost completely white now. How many of those white hairs am I responsible for?

After hugs and kisses, nervous introductions, and compliments all around, they were seated in the splendid oak-paneled dining room.

Anna instantly sensed that her parents were as nervous as she was. Her father tried to break the ice by asking Claude about Poland. The two men agreed that it was a terrible place for Jews to live. Then Claude spoiled everything for Anna by saying, "My parents don't practice the religion any longer. They stopped considering themselves Jewish long ago. It's the only way to survive as a professional in Europe these days."

"But," Sarah broke in, "you were raised Jewish, weren't you, Doctor?"

"I had a Hebrew tutor, and I studied the history of the Jews and other religions as well. That was the extent of my religious education."

"You weren't a bar mitzvah?" Sarah asked in a shocked tone.

"No, my parents didn't believe in drawing attention to our Jewishness."

"For shame!" Sarah shook her head in disbelief.

"Mama, people do things differently these days, especially in Europe. It's not like when you were a girl."

"My father of blessed memory was a learned Talmudic scholar. Didn't Anna tell you?" Sarah stated defiantly.

Claude looked at Anna, a flash of anger in his eyes, then turned to Sarah. "No, Anna hasn't told me much about her family."

After that they discussed the weather and the food they were eating, and Jacob asked a few questions about Claude's experience in Arizona. Anna was relieved when the dinner was finished and she and Claude were alone again in his car. She had sensed his growing anger all evening.

As he drove up Fourteenth Street, he exploded. "I feel as if you tricked me into marrying you! I don't know how to say this diplomatically, Anna, but somehow you led me to believe you came from a much more cultured, educated background than you do. Your parents barely speak English, for God's sake! And I'll bet neither of them reads or writes English!" He looked at her, waiting for her to deny it. She stared straight ahead.

"Where the hell does your British accent come from? Who are you trying to kid? And your fancy clothes and manners—you sure had me fooled!"

"Claude, I resent that! My parents haven't had the opportunities your parents had. Obviously they didn't have the education. But they're hardworking, honest people who've done a fine job of raising five children. They've scrimped and saved so my brothers could have opportunities they didn't have. After all, they grew up in the old country! I'm proud that they've accomplished what they have.

"As for me, well, you can't fault me for trying to improve myself! Yes, I talk like an educated woman. I've educated myself. You married me because of who I am, not because of my parents. And meeting my parents shouldn't change your feelings toward me. I am what I've made myself." Claude's reaction to her parents was exactly as she had feared it would be. It was just as well she hadn't introduced him to them before.

"Okay. Okay." He sighed, turned onto Sixteenth Street, and drove the rest of the way to her apartment in silence.

As they walked up the steps, she told him her plans for helping him build his practice. "We'll keep an index file—I brought the cards and file box home today—of people we meet at parties. Their names, their occupations, what they were wearing—so we'll remember them next time—and we'll have a large party two or three times a year and invite people who might become patients. Meanwhile, I'll take your cards with me everywhere. You know how many people I meet every day. Don't worry, darling—I'll be a great asset to you. You'll see."

"I'm sure you will, Anna," he responded in a resigned tone. He turned the key in her door—it was *their* apartment now. He had moved his few possessions from the dreary room he had rented before marrying Anna.

Anna went to the kitchen to make tea. Claude followed her, still wearing his hat. "I'm going out for a walk. I need to clear my mind, to think awhile. I'll take my key. Don't wait up for me."

"I feel like a walk too. Wait a moment, and I'll change my clothes."

"No, Anna. I need to be alone. You get some sleep."

After Claude left, Anna took her tea and sat on the sofa thinking about him, about the evening, about her parents.

Claude's reaction to them was exactly what she had feared it would be. That was the real reason why she had married him before introducing him to her parents. He felt nothing but scathing contempt for poor immigrant merchants. They were beneath him—and if they were, so was she, at least in his mind.

Not for one minute do I think Claude is superior to me. He may think so, but I'll disabuse him of that notion!

Her eyes passed over the stack of Van Gogh prints on the coffee table. I really must take those to the office and send them downstairs to be framed, even though Claude doesn't think they amount to much. Imagine, he gave six of them away to his women friends—"on their birthdays"!

Claude had explained to Anna how he came to have the prints Van Gogh had made of his best canvases. "Theodore Van Gogh sold them to my father many years ago, when Vincent was desperate for money. A dozen of them for less than one hundred dollars. When I was leaving to come to America he gave them to me, told me they were my inheritance. That shows you how angry my parents are with me—they give me a bunch of worthless prints as my only inheritance."

Anna picked them up and looked at them one by one. They were black-and-white copies of Van Gogh's oil paintings. But, she thought, Claude's probably right, he's clearly a minor painter. They're not worth much. Still, our walls are empty. I'll have them framed and hang them over the sofa.

So much for family, Anna thought. Claude didn't like her parents, and who knew what they thought of him? On Sunday he would meet Sasha and Al and Sam and Joshua, and chances were, he wouldn't like them any better. At least she didn't have to worry about getting along with his parents.

But what exactly does he mean by "a modern marriage"?

Anna took a taxi to Union Station—her bags were simply too heavy to try to manage on a trolley—even though Claude had lectured her early that morning on spending money. At least once a day, every day, they had a scene about money. Each evening she had to write down every penny she had spent that day in a little notebook and justify every expenditure to him. He did the same, explaining to her how he walked instead of taking a trolley or taxi. "Walking is the best possible exercise anyhow, Anna, and you spend most of the day in a chair!" But he had been out on a house call and couldn't drive her to the station, so she had splurged on a taxi. Well, so be it.

She passed group after group of Bonus marchers, those veterans of the war who had descended on Washington twenty-five thousand strong to plead for their well-deserved bonuses because they were hungry. She worried about the fate of the nation. Things were bad and getting worse. Fifteen million men were searching for nonexistent jobs. People were peddling apples on every street corner. Every day, she passed long lines of people in front of soup kitchens. And Hoover seemed impervious to it all, locked away in the White House, eating a seven-course dinner every night.

She bought two apples from two different peddlers outside Union Station, thinking as she did it that she'd have to justify it to Claude. It was hard for her to walk by a hungry person and pretend not to notice, but Claude had been drumming away at a theme that many people all over America seemed to share, that the poor are responsible for their own fate. It was not her problem. . . .

On her way to the convention in Chicago—it was Anna's first trip west—she saw hoboes and vagabonds and wandering groups of youths. She saw tents pitched near the railroad tracks, she watched starving children huddle close to their wretchedly dressed mothers. Dear God, she prayed, give Franklin Roosevelt the inspiration to figure out a way to put an end to all this suffering, help him drag this nation out of the Depression. But first, help him win the nomination!

When she arrived in Chicago, she took a taxi to the Congress Hotel, checked into a room she would share with Mary Dewson, then reported to Jim Farley and Louis Howe in Suite 1502. It was Sunday, June 19, eight days before the Democratic Convention was to begin. Chicago was still recovering from the Republican Convention, which only a few days before had renominated President Herbert Hoover.

The mood in Roosevelt's headquarters, connected by phone to his office in Albany, was upbeat. "Whoever the Democrats nominate will win the presidency," Farley announced, "and my money says we'll nominate Roosevelt." He then assigned tasks to the dozen aides he'd recruited from New York and Washington.

"Anna, you work with Mary. Make it your business to meet

and stick close to all the women delegates and party leaders. Have breakfast with them, buy them coffee, call them in their rooms—stay in touch on a daily basis. And keep me and Louie informed of any changes, any intelligence you can pick up. Once in a while, Louis or I might need you to type something. But mostly, your job is to glad-hand the women delegates."

Anna eagerly jumped into the fray, helped decorate the head-quarters, set up a hospitality table, sorted out stacks of literature about Roosevelt, and assisted Howe and Farley with their long lists of delegates. She listened to their phone conversations —they were systematically calling delegates all over the country —flattering, cajoling, even pleading with them to jump on the Roosevelt bandwagon.

Toward the end of the week, the delegates began to arrive in Chicago. More and more often, Howe and Farley invited delegation leaders, one at a time, into the back bedroom of the suite.

"What's your price?" Howe asked former Governor Harry Byrd of Virginia.

"I'd like to be senator," the wizened old man stated.

"Is that your price?" repeated Howe, as Anna took down their conversation in shorthand.

Byrd nodded his head.

"Very well. We'll put one of Virginia's present senators, either Senator Glass or Senator Swanson, in Franklin's cabinet."

Anna could barely suppress a gasp at the directness of it all.

Between meetings like this, Anna presented each female delegate with a personally autographed picture of Roosevelt and questioned her about her special interests. She asked her advice for FDR—a calculated bit of flattery she'd picked up from Farley.

On the eve of the convention Farley called his now-enlarged troops together for final orders. He introduced Arthur Muller as floor leader, several assistants, and a few more trusted lieutenants. "When Muller, Bill Howes, or Joe O'Mahoney gives you an order, consider it as coming from me. You'll be our troops on the floor—we're gonna win this one!"

Nothing had prepared Anna for the excitement, the raucous crowds, the crush of human flesh she experienced during that week. The next day, the national chairman called the convention to order, only to be drowned out by the roar of the crowd. "Delegates will please take their seats!" was repeated over and over again. Anna had never seen such flaunting of a gavel; this was a far cry from the stately decorum of the Senate. After the many sergeants-at-arms did their work, most of the delegates responded, and the music and singing and oratory of Senator Alben W. Barkley of Kentucky opened the convention.

Anna greeted and escorted Sam Rayburn of Texas back to Farley's "private office" in the Roosevelt suite. It was Thursday, June 30. Nominations would be made on the floor of the convention that afternoon. Anna seated herself behind Rayburn and opened her steno pad.

"There's no question about it. FDR has okayed it. He wants Garner as his vice president," Farley stated.

"What do you want me to do?" Rayburn asked.

"Get Texas to cast its vote for Garner on the first ballot, then switch to Roosevelt immediately after the roll call."

"Can't do that, Jim," Rayburn responded. "I've got to vote Garner two or three ballots at least. How long can you keep your people together?"

"To be perfectly frank, I can hold them for three ballots, possibly for four, maybe five."

"We'll just have to let the convention go for a while, even if we are interested in the vice presidency—and I'm not saying that we are. But one thing I don't want is a repetition of that convention at Madison Square Garden! We don't need one hundred ballots to choose a candidate!"

After the two men left, Farley cautioned Anna one more time that everything she'd heard was confidential. Then he picked up the phone and called Governor Roosevelt in Albany.

The names of nine candidates for the presidency were placed in nomination that afternoon. The nominating and seconding speeches continued long into the night. The glamour of the event and the enthusiasm of the delegates had long since evaporated. Many were napping, their clothes askew. Ties hung open, hats were wilting. Amid the general dejection, the bunting drooped, and the aisles were littered with the debris from demonstrations. Nevertheless, Jim Farley and Roosevelt determined that they wanted at least one roll call before adjournment. The clerk began to call the roll at four twenty-eight in the morning. "Alabama!"

"Alabama casts twenty-four votes for Franklin D. Roosevelt."

Anna felt her skin tingle as she marked her yellow legal pad. She'd expected Alabama to vote for FDR, but still it was a thrill. It's beginning now! It's finally beginning! She forgot her weariness and exhaustion. A sudden belief that FDR would win on the first ballot overtook her rational knowledge that it was impossible.

Two hours later, the first roll call over. FDR had six hundred and sixty-six votes, more than any other candidate, but he needed one hundred four more to win the nomination. Roosevelt picked up only eleven more votes on the second ballot. Though the Roosevelt forces tried for an adjournment, a third roll call began, and Roosevelt picked up five more votes. By then it was nine o'clock Friday morning; everyone wanted to adjourn.

It's over, Anna thought to herself as she made her way back to the Congress Hotel suite. We can't possibly hold our votes through another ballot.

When Anna opened the door to Suite 1502, she found Louie Howe lying on the floor in his shirtsleeves between two blowing fans. He was racked by a strangling asthma attack. If only Claude were here! Anna thought as she called the hotel switchboard to get a doctor.

Farley lay down on the floor beside Howe and whispered loud enough for Anna to hear, "Texas is our only chance."

"Let's get Rayburn on the phone!" Howe gasped.

"Anna, get Rayburn for me."

When he came on the line, Farley picked up the phone. "Sam, we've got to have your votes now. Otherwise we'll have a deadlock that'll kill any chance of winning in November."

Farley listened patiently to Rayburn, then added "No doubt about it, we can swing it to Garner." A moment later he hung up the phone. "He says, 'We'll see what can be done.' I think that means he'll do it."

The fourth ballot began in an atmosphere of hushed excitement. William Gibbs McAdoo thundered into the microphone, "California came here to nominate a President of the United States. She did not come to deadlock the convention or to engage in another devastating contest like that of 1924."

Anna stood behind the platform and heard a hush spread through the convention hall. Then McAdoo shouted, "California casts forty-four votes for Franklin D. Roosevelt!" Sam Rayburn had turned the tide.

She felt the sweet surge of victory climb her spine, tingle in the roots of her hair. Strange people were hugging and kissing her, and pandemonium had broken loose in the convention hall. When the balloting was finished, Roosevelt had garnered nine hundred forty-five votes. "We've just nominated the next President!" she shouted over and over to everyone she saw.

Dressed in the raspberry suit she'd been married in, Anna sat in the second box from the platform. She held her breath as the nominee was escorted up onto the platform to the strains of "Happy Days Are Here Again." She watched him take his place behind the podium, his leg braces locked, his strong shoulders and vibrant face and dark hair commanding attention. I will remember this moment the rest of my life, she thought.

"I pledge you, I pledge myself," Franklin Roosevelt began, "to a new deal for the American people. Let us all here assembled constitute ourselves prophets of a new order of competence and courage. This is more than a political campaign; it is a call to arms. Give me your help, not to win votes alone, but to win in this crusade to restore America to its own people."

Later that evening, Roosevelt assembled all his workers and thanked each one personally. "Aha," he said to Anna, "I see Farley's converted you to the Democrats, away from Fiorello! Good for him! Thanks, Anna, for all you've done, for giving up your vacation and honeymoon. Are you going to be with us during the campaign?"

"I'll do whatever Mr. Farley wants me to do, Governor Roosevelt, but you can be sure I'll do everything I can to get you elected."

The next day, the Democratic National Committee selected Jim Farley as its new chairman—and Roosevelt's campaign manager.

Before she left for her return trip to Washington, Anna met with Farley to discuss her future.

"I want you working in the Senate. I want you to be my eyes and ears over there. After the election, we'll see about a more exciting job. Meanwhile, Anna, we'll never forget all your hard work."

As the train thundered across the Ohio Valley on its way back to Washington, Farley's words of praise reverberated in Anna's head. If only, she thought, if only I had such good feelings about my personal life with Claude! Why can't I be happy? Something's wrong with me. I'm great in an office, but I can't get through a day without doing something wrong as far as Claude's concerned. And I know it's my fault.

▨ Chapter 16

November 1932

Anna was writing the latest election results on the chalkboard in the dingy, tumultuous campaign headquarters when Eleanor Roosevelt and Jim Farley entered the room. As the workers in the room recognized the popular Mrs. Roosevelt, they fell silent. Seconds later, there was a spontaneous outburst of applause. Work ceased. Jim Farley climbed on top of a wooden chair, while someone whistled for silence.

"In spite of any dire predictions that you may have heard from my friend Mr. Howe, I'm here to tell you we've won this election. And it's a massive victory. It looks as if we'll win forty-two of forty-eight states. That's four hundred seventy-two electoral votes. A huge victory! We're only waiting for President Hoover to concede defeat. Governor Roosevelt sent Mrs. Roosevelt and me over here to express his deepest thanks for all you've done. When Mr. Howe here sees fit to believe the returns, we want him to send you across the street to the ballroom to join the celebration. The President-elect will be addressing his supporters just as soon as we hear from Hoover."

A huge cheer went up, Anna hugged two women who were helping her post returns, then went forward to congratulate Farley.

"Why don't you gals stop working so hard and come back across the street with us? Anna, you talk to Louie—maybe you can convince him we've really won!"

Louis Howe, who was standing behind Farley chatting with Eleanor Roosevelt, managed a weak grin and winked at Anna. "I guess—I guess things do look good," he admitted with a petulant grin. "But I'm gonna stay here awhile, just in case."

"The rest of us are going to join our leader, and I expect you to join us soon," Farley admonished Howe as he took Mrs. Roosevelt's elbow and escorted her through the crowd of young well-wishers.

Anna and most of the campaign staff followed Farley back across the street to the Biltmore Hotel. They milled around, danced a bit, hugged everyone in sight, and gossiped about whom FDR might choose for his cabinet. Finally, after two in the morning, carrying the telegram of concession in his hand, Roosevelt came into the ballroom to thank over five hundred Democratic National Committee workers and his hundreds of friends who had traveled to New York City for the election results.

Anna felt like pinching herself to make sure it wasn't a dream. Only a few short years ago, she'd been a clerk in Hecht's department store. Now she was chatting with two U.S. Senators, Wagner and Copeland, and congratulating the newly elected governor of New York, Herbert Lehman. And she was standing in line to shake the hand and receive the thanks of the next President of the United States and his wife. When her turn came, Roosevelt lowered his voice a fraction, smiled warmly at her from his close-set, deep-blue eyes, and confided, "We're going to be seeing a lot of you in the White House, Anna. You can depend on it!"

The four months between the election and the inauguration of Franklin Roosevelt seemed to Anna—and to the anxious nation—to stretch out interminably. At the year's end, seventeen million people had no jobs and no hope of finding one. A quarter of the people in the nation were somehow surviving on no income whatever. Over thirty million people were receiving welfare.

Those who had jobs were seeking to disenfranchise those who did not. Lewiston, Maine, voted to bar welfare recipients from voting; other communities sought to bar the children of welfare recipients from attending public schools. While outgoing President Hoover did nothing but express his continued belief in the free enterprise system, Franklin and Eleanor Roosevelt made their plans amid a general belief that the nation was not far from a revolution. The well-to-do were becoming genuinely afraid of the hungry.

Anna and Claude accepted Sasha and Louis Bernstein's invitation to their annual New Year's Eve party. Claude had told Anna early in their marriage that they would accept almost all invitations; it would cut down on their grocery bills while at the same time, hopefully, they could turn their social acquaintances into paying patients.

But Anna was apprehensive. An invitation to Sasha and Louis's splendid apartment on Massachusetts Avenue almost always ended in an argument between her and Claude—and New Year's Eve was no exception. The argument started as soon as Claude turned the ignition key to drive home.

"Can you imagine serving fine French champagne to that crowd? I can't believe Louis throws away money like that!" he exclaimed as they drove away from Sasha's.

"Just because they aren't all doctors—"

"Anna, most of his friends haven't even completed grade school, for chrissake!"

"So they aren't educated! They're decent people, trying their hardest—"

"Hoodlums, two-bit gangsters! Where do you think they get the liquor? From bootleggers!"

"And you're better because you buy yours from an ambassador? Either way, it's illegal to drink alcohol, and it's illegal to buy it. One thing's for sure—Sasha doesn't pour cheap wine into expensive French wine bottles like you do, Claude. You can be sure of that!"

"Ah, who knows the difference? I guarantee you the Fricks thought they were drinking the finest Bordeaux last week—and we saved ten dollars. Not so dumb!"

"Oh, Claude! Why must you criticize everything my family does? They try so hard to be nice to you, and they don't even begin to know how to talk to you."

"That's the point—we have nothing in common. They're uneducated, no culture."

"But you accept their invitations because it's a free meal! You certainly enjoyed the caviar and the shrimp and the roast beef!"

"Your sister's a good cook, I'll admit."

"Damn it, Claude, don't go there for dinner and then criticize them all the way home! I'm sick of it."

"You know," he said as he chucked her under the chin to pacify her, "I enjoy talking to Louis. He's sharp. He knows investments. I enjoy him—for about ten minutes. Then he bores me too. All that talk about boxing—God, spectator sports bore me to death! And gambling! I can't imagine throwing money away on horse racing."

"If Mrs. Whitney invited us to Saratoga, you'd be there in a minute, and you'd at least make a pretense of gambling."

"Well, if Mrs. Whitney . . . do you think they might invite us? That'd be swell!"

"I've got more important things on my mind these days, Claude. All frivolity seems wicked when you think of what's going on in the country. I told Sasha to take any leftovers down to the H Street Community Center tomorrow."

"That's nuts! Taking that kind of food to a bunch of bums! If she has food left over, go get some of it for our dinner tomorrow night. Don't waste food like that on a bunch of hoboes! Anna, where's your common sense?"

"Claude, where's your sense of compassion? I thought you were a doctor. Don't you have any feeling for your fellow human beings?"

"Those people wouldn't be in the desperate straits they're in if they'd managed their money wisely when they had jobs. That's why I'm always after you about your spendthrift ways. We've got to save every penny we can, Anna. I can't stress that enough. It's the only way to guarantee our future."

Anna tuned him out and slumped back against the car seat and closed her eyes. He was cold and unfeeling, he seemed to feel no love for anyone. Not even me, she told herself. He pretends to love me when he wants sex. He wants me on his arm at parties. That's true enough, he wears me like an ornament. 'Look, gentlemen, look what I've bought. I now own this beautiful woman.' Damn him! He's an arrogant, miserable . . . but he's my husband. He's my fate. I asked for this. I've simply got to make the best of it.

When they arrived home, Claude was suddenly amorous, as he frequently was after a few drinks and a party where he'd held forth with his brilliant conversation, where he'd wowed everyone with his stories of life in Europe and his knowledge of food and wine.

"Ohh, Anna, my dearest little poochy-woochy! Tonight we'll do it doggy style, what do ya think?" He grabbed her as the door slammed behind them and began thrusting his pelvis into her backside, imitating what he was about to do. Quickly, without so much as a kiss, he began pulling off her chiffon dress, stripping her down to her garter belt and stockings. He bent her over the club chair and held her long hair tightly in his hands; then, without a moment's thought about her pleasure, he took her.

Later, she bathed in soapy water and honeysuckle-scented bath oil while he fell into a sodden sleep, and she let the bitter tears form and trickle down her face. For the first time, she admitted that it had been a mistake to marry Claude. But at least Kurt wouldn't have to feel responsible for her happiness any longer. I've done this to myself. I've no one but myself to blame.

Then, unbidden, as if to begin her new year, she remembered the feel of Kurt's strong hands on her breasts, her thighs, her face. She felt his tongue in her mouth, and she stifled a gasp as she felt molten heat flood her abdomen and make her heart beat in her throat.

On February 4 it came in the mail: a thick envelope of the creamiest vellum. It was addressed in magnificent script penmanship to "Dr. and Mrs. Claude Henri Dunay."

They were invited to everything: reserved seats in the second row behind the Congress for the inauguration, a luncheon in honor of the cabinet, and reserved seats for the parade. Finally, there was a much-coveted invitation to the inaugural ball. Anna felt her heart would explode with excitement and pride. She would be where she had dreamed of being—right smack in the center of things.

As she returned the beautiful invitation to its envelope, she thought of her conversation two days earlier with Jim Farley. He had called her from New York City and told her of his plans to join the Roosevelts in the Mayflower Hotel in Washington for the festivities. He'd told her that Roosevelt had selected him to be postmaster general—a job that usually went to the campaign manager. And he'd told her what she'd been waiting to hear.

"We've arranged, Anna—and I hope you like this—for you to be secretary to the secretary of the Senate. You'll be great at it—arranging all the important events, really running the Senate. I've told Halsey that you're the most competent woman I've ever worked with. He's delighted. It'll be a small raise for you—not much though, with so many unemployed."

"I understand, Mr. Farley." She knew the position well, knew it was indeed one of the most powerful ones in the Senate —at the center of everything.

"We'll be seeing a lot of you over at Sixteen Hundred. The president's secretaries, Missy La Hand and Steve Early, have been instructed to keep in close touch. And you can always pick up the phone and get through to me, Anna. I'll expect you to keep me informed—you know."

"Yes, of course. Mr. Farley, I'm so grateful."

"Now, Anna, this is just the beginning. We're going to help one another, you and I. By the way, I've arranged for you and your husband to have seats directly behind Congress at the swearing-in. And you're on my list for an invitation to lunch in honor of the cabinet. You'll be in my box at the ball."

Anna thanked him profusely, hung up the phone, then called her mother and her sister to tell them her news. She would wait till the end of the day to tell Claude that he was being invited to a luncheon in honor of the cabinet. He would be ecstatic. He would manage to tell every patient for the next four weeks. There would be no end to his bragging.

Well, she told herself, at least I'm fulfilling my end of the deal. I'll help him build up his practice, in spite of his feelings about the poor and hungry.

The sky was slate-gray and threatening snow. Anna was alarmed to see army machine guns mounted in strategic points across the forty acres of park in front of the Capitol's east facade. She and Claude passed soldiers armed with machine guns who were stationed throughout the rows of seats and on the immense platform. They pushed through a crushing crowd —over one hundred thousand anticipated, *The Washington Post* had said that morning—to find the section reserved for VIPs. They watched Franklin D. Roosevelt sworn in as the President who would lead the nation out of the beleaguered wartime atmosphere which had captured Washington.

The whole country, it seemed, was holding its breath. Even the Stock Exchange and the Chicago Board of Trade were closed. Bankers in twenty-one states and the District of Columbia had closed their doors.

Anna, wearing a burgundy-wool coat and Persian fur hat and muff, sat beside Claude, who was dressed in morning clothes, a homburg, and a velvet-collared chesterfield. She watched intently as the new President, hatless and coatless against the winter chill, repeated the oath administered by Chief Justice Charles Evans Hughes. Then the President turned to the speaker's podium, ignored the applause, and drew from his pocket a sheaf of papers containing his longhand notes.

With a grim face he began: "First of all, let me assert my firm belief that the only thing we have to fear is fear itself—nameless, unreasoning, unjustified terror which paralyzes needed efforts to convert retreat into advance."

Anna listened to his ringing voice and felt as if she were praying. Dear God, let the people of America listen to this man. May the tenant farmers, the ravaged miners, the hungry children, and the ragged men freezing outside factory gates hear these words and take them to heart.

"I shall ask the Congress for the one remaining instrument to meet the crisis—broad executive power to wage a war against the emergency, as great as the power that would be given me if we were in fact invaded by a foreign foe."

That night, the Farleys and the Dunays and even Eleanor Roosevelt attended the inaugural ball. President Roosevelt did not. From Jim Farley, Anna learned that FDR had stayed in the White House and worked into the early hours with Louis Howe. Later, more than four hundred fifty thousand Americans wrote the President to tell him they'd been heartened by his words. The Hundred Days had begun.

Capitol Hill felt newly alive to Anna in the week following the inauguration. The sleepy, defeated city had burst into enthusiasm for the new President and his wife. The 73rd Congress was called into special emergency session Thursday, and within thirty-eight minutes, with Mrs. Roosevelt watching and knitting in the gallery, it enacted the first piece of emergency legislation providing for the printing of money, its dispersal to the banks of America, and the reopening of the banks. Individual savings banks were permitted to release ten dollars to each depositor. In New York, the Dow Jones ticker played "Happy Days Are Here Again."

Friday morning, Anna reported to her Naval Affairs Committee office unusually early. She had lots to finish before she left the following Friday to become the top staff member to the secretary of the Senate.

Late in the morning, while she was sorting some files with her back to the door, she felt a silence come over the office, then excited expressions of greeting. Nothing unusual about that, she told herself. All kinds of people make appearances unexpectedly these days. She continued her work without turning around. Then she heard his voice. For a long minute she couldn't believe it. He wouldn't just walk in without warning her! But Naomi was chattering animatedly with him.

She put the files down on the small desk, her hands trembling. Slowly she turned toward Naomi's desk. They were both watching her. Her face began a slow burn, her eyes suddenly teared, and slowly, ever so slowly, she stood and smoothed her skirt. "Kurt . . . Kurt . . . when did you get into town?"

He walked toward her in slow motion. Gallantly, he took both of her outstretched hands in his and kissed her cheek. "You look even more beautiful than I remembered, Anna," he said quietly, conscious that everyone in the office was watching.

She could think of nothing to say.

"I've come to invite you and Naomi to lunch—cancel whatever other plans you have. We're going to the Occidental."

"Oh, wonderful!" Naomi chimed.

"I—I must—go comb my hair," Anna answered weakly, wishing she'd worn a nicer outfit. Her stomach was queasy, and her head was spinning. Kurt Addison was still the best-looking man she'd ever seen. My God! Not even time—or marriage— could erase what they'd had!

"I'll wait," he responded with a wicked grin. Then he turned to Naomi. "Take this pretty lady to the rest room so we can be on our way, would you please?" Naomi grinned back at him and picked up her pocketbook.

"C'mon, Anna. Let's go!"

For a fleeting second, Anna wondered if Naomi had known he was coming to the office. Did he know she was married? She grabbed her pocketbook and followed Naomi out the door.

* * *

She didn't wonder long. No sooner were they comfortably seated in a taxi than Kurt stated, "I understand congratulations are in order. You're married to a prominent doctor, Naomi tells me, and are about to be promoted to the most important staff job in the Senate! I'm thrilled for you on both counts."

They ordered lunch while Anna remained, for the most part, speechless. Seeing him, being in his presence again, had turned her inner world upside down. Everything took on different colors, different vibrations. How could she have married Claude when she loved Kurt? It was an impossible situation. How could she settle for so little when she knew what real love was like?

They talked of Roosevelt, of the bank holiday, of the enormous challenge facing the country. And after they ordered dessert, Naomi announced, as if on cue, "I'm going to take advantage of being downtown by running over to Garfinckels—there's a suit I'm crazy about in the window. See you back at the office, Anna." She bent to kiss Kurt good-bye and whispered loud enough for Anna to hear, "Treat her gently—she's hurting."

No sooner was Naomi out of sight than Kurt reached across the table for Anna's hand. At first she hesitated, then she grasped it with her own. They sat saying nothing, drinking in one another's eyes, feeling their love for one another overwhelm them. After a long silence, Kurt said quietly, "You're not happy, Anna. I can feel it."

"No—I'm fine. It's such a shock to see you again."

"I've been miserable. I've missed you so. I don't think I knew how much I loved you until I was thousands of miles away. And when Naomi wrote me you were married—well, I nearly killed myself with overwork, thinking that would be the cure. Anna, I didn't come here to ruin your life. It's just—"

She had been studying her fingernails intensely, unable to look him in the eyes while he confessed his fervent love. "Naomi wrote you? She didn't tell me."

"She was very concerned, even then. Worried about you. Well, at least your career is going well. I'm pleased about that, though I hate to lose you on Naval Affairs."

Anna looked directly at him, forcing herself to feel the full impact of her own emotions. "I don't think I knew until this afternoon how miserable—" She faltered, unable to complete the thought. It was so disloyal to Claude. She was his wife, after all! "How much I missed you."

Kurt wiped his lips with his napkin, then reached again for Anna's hand. "I have an idea. But I want you to feel free to say no. I have a lovely room at the Mayflower, and a completely free weekend. Is there any way?"

Before he could finish the sentence, she was nodding her head affirmatively. She allowed a broad smile of happiness to envelop him, then slid from the booth with the words, "I must make two phone calls."

She telephoned Claude's office and told his receptionist that she'd been sent to Philadelphia for the weekend to do some political work for Mr. Farley. Then she called her office and told them she was going over to the Department of War for a briefing with Lieutenant Commander Addison. It would take all afternoon; she'd see them on Monday and fill them in. As she walked back toward the booth where Kurt was seated, anxiety lifted from her shoulders and a feeling of deep serenity settled over her. She loved him. She belonged with him.

When they were in one another's arms again, the months melted away for Anna. It was as if nothing had separated them, not time, not distance, not even spouses. Their intimacy was total—physical and emotional and intellectual. Their minds seemed to merge even as their bodies did, and Anna wondered over and over again how she could have ever married Claude.

Not until midmorning Saturday, after they had read the papers and devoured a splendid room-service breakfast, did Anna realize her diaphragm was back in her bedside-table drawer at home. It's worth the chance, she told herself. The "worst" thing that could happen was that she would have Kurt's baby—and wouldn't that be wonderful!

She pushed that thought to the back of her mind and concentrated on enjoying every minute they had together. They would be parted again on Sunday evening, and Kurt would leave for the Pacific on Monday afternoon.

"Roosevelt's so preoccupied with the Depression, he can't even begin to concentrate on foreign affairs," Kurt said with a sigh as he put down *The New York Times*.

"If you were in his job, you'd be too," Anna answered, not really wanting to discuss politics.

"Soon he's going to have to pay attention to foreign affairs. Japan's beginning to bother people besides me, while our military power ranks us sixteenth in the world."

"He's got to put our house in order first. Then he can worry about the world," Anna answered.

"I'd like to get him to Hawaii, give him a briefing on our vulnerability away from the concerns of Washington. It'd be the best thing for the nation, believe me."

"Oh, Kurt, stop being a naval officer and take me to bed again!" Anna whispered as she bent down to kiss his lips.

"How was Philadelphia?" Claude asked as he looked up from his book.

"Arduous," Anna responded, still wearing the same outfit she'd left the house in on Friday morning. "I'm exhausted. What did you do all weekend?"

"I played squash and tennis and rode with David. Then Naomi fed me a delicious dinner of *coq au vin.* I like their home, Anna. We should think about investing in property in Middleburg."

Anna took the pins out of her hair and let it flow down around her shoulders, thinking how totally unsuspicious Claude seemed to be. Naomi surely knew what had happened, but evidently she had kept Anna's secret. What a wonderful friend! "I think we should get a larger apartment or house here in town first, then think about property in the country. After all, we both have to go to work every day, Dr. Dunay!"

She forced herself to bend over and kiss his forehead. He didn't even lift his eyes from his book, such was the state of his ardor. "I'm too tired, Anna. I'm going to turn in soon and I expect you'll want to do the same."

"Yes, indeed. Tomorrow's another day. And I've lots to finish up this week before I move to Colonel Halsey's office."

She left him and headed for the bathroom. A nice warm bubble bath was exactly what she needed to wash away the guilt of the weekend.

⊠ Chapter 17

March 1933

The bold headline in *The Washington Post* read SECRETARY TO A SECRETARY. Beneath a stunning portrait that had been taken the previous day, her first day on the job, Anna read about herself: "First Woman in Job—Mrs. Anna Arnold Dunay is the attractive executive secretary to Col. Edwin H. Halsey, who is secretary of the U.S. Senate. She's the first woman to hold this post but already has made many friends."

She handed the paper to Claude, who was seated across from her finishing his breakfast. "You'll like this, Claude."

"Oh! It's a wonderful picture. You must get the original. It's super!"

"I'll call Underwood Photographers today."

"Yes, order two. I'll put one in my office. That'll impress my patients, you can bet."

"By the way, Naomi invited us for riding and supper on Sunday. Are you free?" She stood and reached for her pocketbook. It was seven—time to leave for the office.

"If I don't have any emergencies between now and then, yes, we can drive out there after my tennis game."

As she rode the trolley to the Capitol, Anna thought about the previous day. For a first day of work, it had been hectic: she had tried to learn everything instantly and handle the many congratulatory phone calls and visitors at the same time. Colonel Halsey had been understanding. She hadn't seen a trace of his famous temper—probably because he had been in and out of the office most of the day. And when he was in, he was on the phone. He had four telephones on his desk, and it seemed at least one of them was constantly ringing.

I like the office, Anna thought. It's majestic and spacious. For the first time since she'd been working on the Hill, she didn't feel crowded. And she loved the big circular window behind her chair. It was refreshing to look out across the broad expanse of green lawn and majestic old trees.

Colonel Halsey was a soft-spoken, tall, well-dressed man who was beginning to turn gray. He wore wire-rimmed spectacles and was just beginning to develop a double chin. Anna wasn't certain, but she guessed his age at mid-fifties. She was sure he wasn't thrilled about hiring her. She guessed that Jim Farley had promoted her in a fairly heavy-handed manner. But I'll prove myself to him. I'll be the best assistant he's ever had.

Farley, in one of his inspired bits of flattery, had delivered to Anna a picture of the President autographed personally to Colonel Halsey. She, in turn, had presented it to Halsey yesterday morning.

His way of accepting it betrayed his feelings. He took it, read the inscription, smiled weakly at Anna, and muttered, "Yes, I understand you are a close friend of the White House."

Does that mean you aren't? Anna wondered, astonished by his lack of enthusiasm for the President. Later, when she entered his private domain, she understood better. His walls were lined with photographs of bill-signings and senators and former cabinet officers, but dominating the room was a large portrait of Senator Alben Barkley, one of the senior powers in the Senate.

Senator Barkley had arrived in the reception room late that afternoon while members of the press were pumping Halsey for information, and Anna had ushered him into Halsey's office. He had sat down next to Halsey's desk and answered questions for over forty minutes—a strictly off-the-record backgrounder. Halsey's inner sanctum, Anna realized, was a place where Barkley could safely leak stories; then his staff could deny he was the source.

After the press left, Halsey had opened the locked cabinet and brought out whiskey and two glasses. Anna had understood that Senator Barkley was Halsey's most important friend, in much the same way that Farley was her mentor.

Even so, she had noticed as she stepped in to say good night that FDR's picture was already hanging on the wall just behind his credenza.

Today, her second day, things were beginning to settle down. She received several letters from the White House—from Grace Tully and Missy Le Hand and Steve Early—and then to her total astonishment, her phone rang late in the afternoon and it was the President himself.

"Anna, that's a wonderful picture in this morning's paper. I'm so proud of you. Jim tells me you'll help us, and I know we're going to need lots of help from the Senate to turn this country around. I'm pleased you're there."

Before she could think of any clever way to prolong the conversation, he had wished her well and hung up. It had all happened so fast, she could barely catch her breath. After she put the phone down, she said over and over to herself: That was the President. The President called me!

Even as she savored her feelings, she recognized that it had been the work of Jim Farley. It was this kind of attention to people that had won FDR the nomination in the first place, and it was this kind of detailed follow-up that would make him a great President.

And I will learn from them both, she vowed.

Claude and Anna drove out to Naomi and David's country home in Middleburg feeling light and carefree, full of the hope of spring. Life in Washington was so intense for both of them that they looked forward to their Sundays. Some days, they rode bikes in Rock Creek Park. Once in a while, they rented horses and rode for hours. But they never turned down an invitation from David and Naomi unless Claude had an emergency at the hospital. Claude, especially, loved any kind of exercise. He played tennis and squash and walked at least two miles every day. And he constantly harassed Anna about getting more exercise. "You spend too much of your life sitting in front of a typewriter. You should take walking shoes to the office and go for a thirty-minute walk at lunchtime. It'd do wonders for your nerves."

Tight with money on a daily basis, Claude had nonetheless insisted that Anna buy proper riding clothes. On this Sunday she was attired in her new taupe riding pants, dark-brown hacking jacket, and black-leather high boots.

They arrived late. David was waiting with the horses already saddled. After quick greetings, they set out across the open field. No sooner had they begun to gallop than Anna felt a searing pain in her lower abdomen, followed by quick, insistent, knifelike stabs. She felt as if she might pass out. She slowed her horse to a walk, then stopped it. The other three riders raced ahead of her, then realized she had stopped. Claude turned his horse and came back to where she sat, ghostlike, on her strawberry roan.

"What's the matter?" he asked as he looked intently at her.

"I don't feel well. Light-headed. And strange pains in my stomach."

"Sounds as if you're coming down with something. You're really pale. Better go back to the house and rest."

"I hate to spoil your day."

"Don't worry. We'll ride for a while. You'll probably feel better after a nap." He turned his horse back toward David and Naomi and galloped off to join them.

Anna climbed down from the horse gingerly, trying not to disturb her abdomen any further. As her feet touched the ground, she was overwhelmed with the conviction that she was pregnant. She knew that she was three days overdue for a period but hadn't paid much attention to it. Now, as she understood the consequences of her weekend with Kurt, she was overcome with nausea and fear. What would Claude say? How serious was he about not wanting children?

She walked the horse back to the barn, took the saddle off, and wiped it down, all the while feeling alternately cold and feverish. If I am pregnant, I hope I haven't damaged the baby. I really don't want to have a miscarriage. The truth is, I'd love to have Kurt's baby!

Not until late May did Anna get up the courage to tell Claude he was about to be a father. She had told no one, not even her mother or Sasha or Naomi. She owed it to Claude to tell him first.

She was still very thin—in fact, she had lost weight since becoming pregnant. It was Claude's insistence that they go horseback riding that finally drove her to tell him the news.

"Claude, my doctor says I can't ride for a while."

He put down *The New York Times* book review section and stared at her. "What do you mean? What doctor? For chrissake, Anna, what the hell is wrong?"

"I'm—I'm enceinte!"

"Oh, shit. Anna, we decided long ago not to have children! How can you be so careless? Damn it, you'll get an abortion—that's all there is to it."

"No, Claude. I won't. I've been thinking about if for a while now, and I would like to have children. You were the one who insisted we have no children, but I never agreed."

"You mean—" Claude threw the paper to the floor, stood up, and began stomping around the apartment. "You mean to tell me, you got pregnant deliberately? Anna, I don't believe you!

You've just been promoted to a wonderfully prestigious job, and you fuck it up by getting pregnant? That doesn't make sense."

He stood directly in front of her with a menacing look in his eyes. She looked at him, then down in her lap at her shaking hands.

He grabbed her shoulders roughly and shook her. "Anna, you must get an abortion! If I have to do it myself, I will. I want you to get an abortion this week."

"Abortion is illegal and immoral, Claude. You know that."

He shook her shoulders again. "God damn it, I want you to get that—that aborted! And you'd better hurry up! If Colonel Halsey finds out you're pregnant, you'll lose your job. We need that fifty-five dollars a week."

"I will not lose my job. That I can guarantee," she lied as she pushed his hands away from her shoulders. "I'll work until a week or two before the baby comes, then I'll hire a nanny and go back to work within a month. You can be sure I've thought this through."

"Anna, you're more of an idiot that I thought you were if you think they're going to let you continue to work while you're pregnant. Halsey will not want a fat woman running his office."

"We'll see about that. That's my department—let me handle it."

"Anna, I'm gonna say two things, then this conversation is over, and I'm going for a walk. First, I don't want a brat spoiling my life and tying me down. Second, we need your income if we're going to do all the things I want to do. *You will not have that baby. Do you understand me?*"

He picked up his hat and walked out the door, slamming it as he went.

Cold hatred permeated their relationship from that day forward. Many nights, Claude did not come home at all, and when he did, he was barely civil. He realized he could not force her to get an abortion after she threatened to report him to the medical society. They continued to face the public as a happily married couple—young, sophisticated, and much sought-after on the party scene.

Anna reported for work every day, determined that her pregnancy would in no way interfere with her work. She watched her weight relentlessly and had her dressmaker alter her clothes and make some new ones that concealed the thickening of her waistline. For the most part, she felt wonderful. She experienced great infusions of energy and optimism. By July, she'd told her family and Naomi, and by early August, her pregnancy began to show. She decided the time had come to confront Colonel Halsey.

She waited until late one afternoon, past six o'clock, when he'd finished his two drinks with Barkley and would be more relaxed. After Barkley left his inner sanctum, Anna walked in and approached his desk.

"Colonel Halsey, could I have a moment of your time?" Anna asked as she placed a stack of letters in front of him for his signature.

"Surely, Anna. My goodness, what are you doing here so late? I didn't realize you were still here."

"I waited. I wanted to talk with you."

"Okay, shoot. Don't tell me you want a raise already?" He lit his pipe and watched her face.

"No, sir, that's not it. I want to ask you how you feel about my performance so far. I originally had the feeling you weren't too thrilled to hire me."

"Oh, that!" He sighed and puffed on his pipe. "It's true, Anna. You're very perceptive, aren't you." He puffed again, keeping her waiting. "Well, the truth is you've really surprised me. You're better than any secretary I've ever had, bar none. I've told Farley that he did me a favor in sending you to me. 'Course, I know you talk to him all the time, I know you're his spy here, but that doesn't bother me none. Fact of the matter is, I've grown to like the President. He's an impressive fellow, knows how to get things done."

"Then you'd like to keep me?"

"Yes, indeed! Now, don't tell me someone's trying to hire you away."

"You're absolutely positive you want me to continue to work for you?"

"Yes, Anna. How many times do I have to say it? You're doing a first-class job. I couldn't find anyone better."

"I'm going to have a baby, Colonel Halsey." Anna didn't give him a chance to interrupt her—she rushed ahead. "I see no reason why my being pregnant should interfere with the work I do for you. I'll look very neat and stylish, you can be sure. I'll work up until two weeks before the baby is due, and I'll be back at work four weeks after it's born. That means I'll need a leave of absence of six weeks."

"Nonsense! I can't have a pregnant woman working in this office! It would look terrible!"

"What's terrible about it? It's perfectly normal. I'm a married woman. Why should my desire to have a family render me unfit to be your assistant?"

"Anna, the public comes into this office! People will see you! How would it look?"

"Colonel Halsey, if you don't want me to continue to work for you, I will simply go to work in the administration. I'm sure the postmaster general will have no difficulty finding me a suitable position. You would have to find someone to replace me, that's all there is to it." Anna stood as if she were about to leave.

"Sit down, Anna." He puffed on his pipe and looked squarely at her stomach. "When's the baby due?"

"October. I plan to take a leave beginning October first. I should be back working for you before Thanksgiving. When Garrick had his heart attack, you held his job for him three months—surely you can hold mine six weeks."

"You mean to tell me you're already over six months pregnant?"

"Yes, sir."

"Well, you've done one hell of a job concealing it. I'll give you that." He puffed again on his pipe and studied her face. "You weren't even out with morning sickness."

"No, sir."

"I must say, Anna, you're mighty convincing. How does your doctor-husband feel about all this?"

"He's very agreeable to the idea of my continuing my career. We've lined up a superb nanny for the baby."

"I see. Well, the truth is, I'd hate to lose you, Anna. It's a busy time here with all Roosevelt's initiatives. If I don't keep you, I'd just be handing you to someone else. I'd be the loser in the long run." Suddenly, he laughed. "I'll be goddamned if you haven't talked me into it. Hope I won't be the laughingstock of the Senate. Who knows what people will say?"

*   *   *

"Anna, darling, he's beautiful. So healthy-looking, and my goodness, what a loud cry!" Sarah stood over Anna's bed, patting her hand and smiling broadly. Sasha stood slightly behind her mother, holding a large box from Garfinckels.

"Mmh . . . I'm still so sleepy from the ether. . . . I feel like I could sleep forever. How much does he weigh?"

"Seven pounds, five ounces. A good-sized boy," Sasha assured her.

"Have you and Claude picked a name yet?" her mother asked.

"We're leaning toward Charles. Charles Arnold Dunay. Doesn't that sound distinguished?"

"The problem," Sasha responded, "with Charles is that everyone will call him Chuck."

"Absolutely not. He will be Charles—I insist upon it."

"That's a good name, *shainele.* Now, you get some sleep. Your papa and I will be back this afternoon."

Sasha opened a box that contained a magnificent pale-blue-satin dressing gown for Anna. Then she kissed her sister goodbye and promised to be back that evening.

Anna lay awake for a few minutes after Sasha left, wondering about Claude. When would he call from Philadelphia, where he was attending a convention? What would he feel when he saw the baby? What kind of father would he be? Would he mellow as he got older?

She wished with all her heart that she could tell Kurt about his son. But that she would never, never do.

▨ Chapter 18

1934

At last her watch said seven-thirty. They had circled the White House three times, so anxious were Anna and Claude to be on time. They drove into the Pennsylvania Avenue entrance and waited while the four cars ahead of them discharged their passengers; then Claude pulled his car directly in front of the huge pillars. A military aide opened each door and assisted them out, while a third soldier gave Claude a ticket and proceeded to park their car.

Anna, dressed in a deep-blue-silk peau de soie ball gown, floated up the grand staircase of the White House on Claude's arm. She was filled with pride: pride in how they both looked— she knew they were a strikingly handsome couple—and pride in the fact that in only two short years, they had been guests at large White House functions six times. Previously, they had been invited at ten in the evening, after state dinners, for musicales followed by punch and cookies in the State dining room. But tonight was different. Tonight they were invited to the main event, the annual Diplomatic Reception.

As they stood in the receiving line outside the Blue Room, Anna nodded greetings to several senators who glanced her way and glanced back again to make sure their eyes weren't deceiving them. She knew they were wondering why a staff person from the Hill would be invited to the White House. Let them guess, she told herself, though she always tried to create the illusion that they were invited because Claude was an eminent doctor—indeed, the doctor for most of Embassy Row. Tonight that made sense.

But the truth was, she had made it a point to tell Steve Early and Missy Le Hand, two of the President's closest assistants, how terribly important it was to her and her husband to be invited to this particular party. This was her payback for being that extra pair of eyes and ears over at the Senate. It was all the reward she had ever wanted, she told herself, as the British ambassador and his wife, who had obviously already been through the receiving line, walked toward them.

"Excellency!" Claude enthused. "How good to see you!" He shook Ambassador Lindsay's hand, then kissed the back of Lady Lindsay's. "Stunning! You look absolutely stunning, my dear. I trust my medicine worked and your cold is gone."

"Yes, Doctor. And you've even managed to prevent the ambassador from getting ill. Those vitamins are wonderful."

Until that moment, Anna hadn't realized that American-born Lady Lindsay was also Claude's patient.

The ambassador took his wife's elbow and guided her in the direction of the dining room. When they were out of earshot, Claude divulged that he'd been trying to get the ambassador to lose a few pounds. "This kind of life is murderous on a man's stomach. Too much alcohol and too many rich foods—and too little exercise."

"Perhaps he'd play squash with you, if you asked him."

"I've suggested it, but he claims he doesn't have time. Ah, here come the Guggenheims. I wonder how they got invited."

As they waited in line, Anna once again felt chills go down her spine. It was hard to believe that she was really standing just inside the Blue Room, waiting to greet the President and Mrs. Roosevelt. No matter how many times she stood in line to shake his hand, she always felt the same thrill. And to be in the White House! It was more than she had ever dared hope for.

An aide asked Claude his name, then announced in a voice loud enough for the Roosevelts to hear, "Dr. and Mrs. Claude Dunay." The President shook Claude's hand warmly, then passed him on to Mrs. Roosevelt.

"Miss Anna! You look beautiful—a beautiful dress on a beautiful woman." He leaned slightly to kiss her cheek. They held the pose a moment longer while they heard several cameras click. Anna knew she would receive an autographed picture in a few days. FDR didn't miss a trick!

Claude then guided Anna toward the huge buffet table in the State dining room. She had never before seen it set with the glistening bronze-doré Monroe mirrored plateau, though she'd read about this fabulous centerpiece. Matching candelabra, each holding twelve white candles, stood on either side, along with great epergnes edged with clusters of golden grapes. Bouquets of roses, baby's breath, and fern completed the magnificent display.

"It's a good thing we ate first," Claude joked as he looked at the petits fours and fancy cookies.

Anna looked around the room, which was now quickly filling with diplomats, members of Congress, and White House and cabinet senior staff persons. "There must be six or seven hundred people here. Missy Le Hand told me they'd invited nearly a thousand. Imagine!"

"No wonder they only serve finger foods and punch," Claude answered as he turned to chat with the ambassador from Ireland.

Meanwhile, Anna wandered over toward Frances Perkins,

the secretary of labor. It won't hurt to remind her of who I am, she told herself.

Working a party like this, while glamorous and fun, was even harder than working all day on the Hill. All the names she had to remember, to match with the faces—it was exhausting. But it was good for Claude's practice—not to mention her own career prospects.

After chatting a moment with Miss Perkins, Anna spied the postmaster general, Jim Farley, and made her way through the tightly crowded room toward him. He was watching the crowd and talking to Tom Corcoran, one of FDR's brain trusters, at the same time.

Farley greeted Anna with a bear hug, then introduced her to Corcoran: "She's my gal over at the Senate."

"Aha! So, what do you think of our leader these days?" Corcoran prodded. "What's the scuttlebutt?"

"Mostly amazement," Anna answered enthusiastically. "After all, with your help, he's saved the banks, rescued the farmers, fed the hungry, and even tamed the mighty Tennessee."

Farley's smile broadened as he listened to Anna's glowing praise. It was all true. They had turned the country around in two short years.

"Now," Anna continued, "if you could just find a way to shut Father Coughlin up and control Huey Long, we'd think you're genuine miracle workers!"

Both Corcoran and Farley laughed heartily, then Corcoran declared, "My God, Farley, she's politically savvy, as well as a sight to behold."

At that moment the Roosevelts entered the State dining room, and people turned their attention to the presidential couple.

"Doesn't the First Lady look wonderful? That burgundy lace is especially lovely. And did you see her necklace?"

"Leave it to the girls to notice things like jewelry!" Farley teased her with sparkling eyes. "She told me on inauguration night that that necklace has been handed down in her family for generations. The truth is, she couldn't care less about clothes and jewels. And now, Anna, if you'll excuse me, I see Senator Borah over there."

Both men took their leave, and Anna surveyed the room for Claude. She didn't see him immediately but spied Mrs. Helm,

Mrs. Roosevelt's social secretary. It might be a good idea to thank her for the invitation.

Later, as the Meyer Davis orchestra played "You're the Top" on the East Terrace and the hundreds of guests danced and chatted and drank punch, Anna found herself staring at a uniformed naval officer. From the back he looked exactly like Kurt Addison—but that couldn't be, she told herself, he was off in the Pacific. She hadn't seen him in over a year, and she thoroughly expected him to walk back into her life any day now. The tall bronze-haired officer turned toward her. She looked at him and didn't recognize him. Both relief and sadness flooded over her. Oh, I miss you so, Kurt. You'll never know how much. But life must go on.

Claude and Anna were among the last to leave the White House. Claude believed in making use of every opportunity to meet new people, potential patients. That was one of the few things in life they agreed on. Making contacts and keeping up acquaintances was fifty percent of anyone's success in Washington. And they had mastered the art, Anna told herself as they turned right and headed down Pennsylvania Avenue toward Fifteenth Street.

That fall, after much looking and calculating, Anna and Claude bought a town house in Georgetown. What Claude liked most about it was the large dining room—a place where he could proudly host the black-tie dinners he yearned to give. By December, the furnishing was nearly complete.

As Anna addressed personalized invitations to their first dinner, to be held in honor of the British ambassador, they discussed their social calendar. She had ordered special stationery embossed with Claude's family crest—she wasn't sure, but she suspected he had invented the crest himself. While she carefully addressed the precious invitations, Claude sat opposite her at their double desk and studied travel folders.

"I think this is the summer, Anna. I really think we can manage it if you continue to save all your salary."

"Manage what, Claude?"

"A trip to Europe. I want to introduce you to my parents, show you the Louvre and all of Paris. Anna, why are you frowning?"

"There's something I must tell you, Claude." Anna put her

pen down and wiped her suddenly sweaty hands on her wool skirt.

"I know. You're going to tell me we can't leave the baby. Well, that's nonsense. Your mother would be delighted—"

"That's not it, Claude."

"For chrissake, what then?"

"I'm going to have another baby. Charles needs a brother or sister to play with."

Claude slammed the folders down onto the desk, stood, and angrily paced back and forth in their small library. "God damn it, Anna! Why do you do these things to us? Can't you see you're tying us down something terrible? You've got one baby! Isn't that mess enough for you?"

"It's a terrible thing to be an only child. I promise you, Claude, after this baby, I won't have any more."

"Oh, shit!" he yelled at her, then stomped out of the library.

She sat stunned for a long moment before she could resume her work. *If you only knew, Claude, if you only knew I did this for you. So you will really have a son.* As if on cue, she heard Charles's call. He was awake from his nap. They had promised him they'd take him for a ride on their bicycles.

Well, Anna thought, *if Claude won't join me, I'll take Charles for a ride by myself.*

Anna's second pregnancy was exhausting. While her first pregnancy had seemed a breeze, the second time she had to cope with severe nausea, back pains, and overwhelming fatigue. The workload at the office seemed burdensome beyond any she remembered.

Her mother pleaded with her to take a leave of absence during the last three months. Anna refused to even consider it. Having judged herself to be a rotten wife and too-busy mother, she resolved to do at least one thing completely right: her work at the Senate.

She dared not give Colonel Halsey any reason to reconsider his extremely progressive decision to keep her on during a second pregnancy. More important, she dared not provoke Claude's wrath by losing her job. As he constantly reminded her, "We need the money if we're going to do the things I want to do. Besides, Anna, you're much too smart to stay home and change diapers!"

* * *

As she lay alone in her hospital bed after her second delivery, she wondered why Claude had chosen this weekend to be in New York and tried to understand his hateful reaction to Charles and now to the new baby, Gilbert. Why had he always been opposed to having children? Why did he ignore the precocious Charles, a toddler who astonished every adult with his verbal ability?

The only answer she could give herself was that Claude was a totally self-absorbed man, incapable of giving love. So be it. I'll have to love our sons for both of us.

With her mother's help and some coaching from Sasha, she was sure she'd be a fine mother. She'd just have to set aside time to spend with them. If only there were more hours in a day.

▨ Chapter 19

Paris, 1937

The Dunays were staying at the États-Unis, the same hotel where Claude's parents had stayed when they had visited him during his student days in Paris.

I've never seen Claude so nervous, Anna realized as she watched him pace from the fireplace to the window, then back to the fireplace. We've only five days in France. It's foolish to spend even an hour here in the hotel room. But his parents will arrive any minute now.

Claude crossed the room to the ancient bombé chest, looked into the Louis XIV gilt mirror, and adjusted his paisley cravat. "The train from Poland is always on time."

"Perhaps they had difficulty getting a taxi." Anna sipped tea from a delicate Meissen cup, then set it back on the silver tray. "I hope they won't be too exhausted. Getting opera tickets for tonight may have been a mistake."

"Nonsense! They wouldn't dream of coming to Paris and not going to the opera. Besides, Mother loves *Faust*. She'll be thrilled. If only they'd—"

At that moment the phone jingled, and Claude rushed to

answer it. "Ah, *merci, merci.*" He replaced the receiver in the cradle, nervously fingered his cravat again, glanced at himself in the mirror for reassurance, then in a raspy voice said, "C'mon, Anna, they're here. Let's go!"

She couldn't help notice the deathly pallor of his face as she joined him at the door. She wanted to reassure him, but he would have found her words patronizing. So instead, she smoothed her hair with a moist palm and consciously assumed a posture of self-confidence as she followed him to the elevator.

Anna recognized them in the lobby before they saw her. Dr. Francine Dunay, a statuesque, broad-shouldered, full-bosomed woman in her sixties, was dressed in a purple-tweed suit, walking shoes, and pearl jewelry. Her dark hair, streaked with gray at the temples, was pulled softly back into a chignon. She carried a large canvas traveling bag and a small black-leather pocketbook.

Dr. Bernard Dunay, a distinguished-looking, portly man in his late sixties, was completing the registration process at the desk. He surrendered their passports, then turned to his wife just as Claude and Anna approached.

"Maman!" Anna heard Claude whisper as he gathered his mother in his arms for a fierce bear hug. He lifted her off the ground and twirled her around in his exuberance. When his eyes met his mother's, Anna saw in them a radiant joy she had never seen before. This reunion, this hug, his mother's approval and forgiveness were the main reasons for their trip, Anna realized with a shock. It had not been to "educate Anna," as Claude pretended, but to win back his parents' love. They had never forgiven him, he had told Anna, for choosing to live in America and for not joining their medical practice here.

"My father has always hated me," Claude had confided to Anna during their crossing. "He was always jealous of my mother's love for me. Besides, he never wanted a child to begin with."

Claude released his mother, then circumspectly turned his attention to the imposing figure of his father. The elder Dunay had refused to look at Anna. It's as if I'm not a human being, not even here, she thought angrily as she watched Claude shake hands crisply and formally with his father.

Dr. Bernard Dunay did not permit even the slightest smile to cross his face. His hauteur and steel-gray eyes announced a coldness that would have been unthinkable between two strangers meeting for the first time, let alone between father and son. As Anna caught the hostile vibrations emanating from Bernard to Claude, she fully understood Claude's apprehension. This father hates his son, she realized, and she wondered if that somehow explained Claude's inability to accept his own sons.

"May I present my wife, Anna," Claude announced in French to his father, thrusting Anna forward to shake his hand.

"Enchantée!" Anna smiled graciously, bowed her head slightly, then continued her rehearsed speech in French. "Dr. Dunay, I can't possibly express how pleased I am—we are—to be here, to spend part of our holiday with you and Mrs. Dunay."

Claude then presented Anna to his mother. Before Anna could say a word, Francine Dunay opened her arms to Anna and embraced her warmly.

"My dear Anna! It is a joy! A pleasure to meet you! You are more beautiful than your pictures. I am grateful to you for making a home for my son." Her blue eyes sparkled with tears. Then she added, "It's been so long—over ten years. Too long for a mother to be parted from her only son."

Dr. Bernard Dunay abruptly interrupted. "They are ready to escort us to our room. Come with us," he ordered Claude and Anna. "We'll make our schedule."

Claude ordered tea to be served in his parents' room. Francine immediately busied herself unpacking, stopping occasionally to pat her son's cheek or hug him again. Claude and Anna sat opposite his father in front of the fireplace, chatting about their plans for the next two days. After the bellboy delivered a tray of tea, small sandwiches, and cakes, Francine joined them and served.

Anna had taken an instant dislike to her cold, pompous father-in-law, and found herself feeling a sudden compassion for Claude. His childhood must have been horrible. No wonder he hadn't minded being sent to boarding school at eight! She remembered the warmth and love showered on her by Jacob and Sarah and counted herself blessed, even though they'd had no money or culture or professional standing.

Francine, on the other hand, fascinated Anna. She was lively, warm, and supremely elegant all at once. Her sparkling eyes glowed with love for Claude—and for Anna too. Her proud, high forehead was unlined, as was her whole milk-white face. Such beautiful skin, Anna thought as she reached out to accept the plate of dainty sandwiches that Francine offered her.

The men were discussing which sections of the Louvre they would concentrate on. Claude argued in favor of Rembrandt and the Italian school, but Bernard was urging the newer acquisitions, the Impressionists.

"We must save time for a stroll in the magnificent Tuileries Gardens," Francine interjected.

Anna looked at her soft, pudgy fingers and imagined her both as a kindly mother and as a sympathetic psychiatrist. How, then, had she allowed such animosity to exist between her husband and her son? But we are so helpless sometimes, as mothers, Anna told herself. Sudden, knifelike pains spread through her chest. We do what we can. That's all we can do.

After the final curtain of *Faust,* the four Dunays made their way up Garnier's Grand Opera House staircases. It was, Anna felt, the grandest, most opulent building she'd ever seen.

"Shall we go to Les Halles for onion soup?" Claude asked as they joined the throngs of people on the Boulevard des Italiens, crowded even at midnight. They walked by the Café de la Paix, where earlier in the evening they had dined, then walked toward the Boulevard de la Madeleine.

"This is where Alphonsine Duplessis lived and died," Bernard stated, displaying his intimate knowledge of Paris. "She was the heroine of Alexandre Dumas *fils'* play, *La Dame aux Camélias.*"

"Oh yes," Anna exclaimed. "I know it as Verdi's *La Traviata.*"

Claude smiled at Anna. She was showing his father that Americans could be well-educated too.

Francine asked, "Do you go to the opera frequently in America?"

"We go to New York to the Metropolitan several times a year," Claude lied, "and when I was a student, I saw the San Francisco Opera Company. Not as good as France or La Scala, but better than nothing."

Bernard, meanwhile, had hailed a taxi to take them to Les Halles. A few minutes later, they disembarked in front of the nineteenth-century glass and cast-iron market buildings. Here the fashionable, well-dressed tourists mingled with the farmers and market porters and ate side by side in the all-night cafés. Claude ordered onion soup and wine for all of them.

Francine patted Anna's forearm and quietly asked in broken English, "Your babies? Did you bring pictures?"

Claude's face inexplicably flushed, then with excitment ringing in his voice, he directed, "Anna, Anna, the pictures! Do you have them?"

"No, I left them back in the room. But I'll show you tomorrow. The boys are adorable! Charles is four, he looks like me. Gilbert, who's two, is the exact image of Claude. And they are both very smart. Like their father." Anna found herself holding Francine's hand, wishing she could magically produce the boys in person.

"I'm so proud. They are my only grandchildren. I wish—I wish to visit America to see them someday."

Bernard growled and looked scathingly at Francine. "I'll wait till they're grown. Children bore me."

Remind me not to invite you, Anna thought as she turned her attention to the cheese-encrusted minitureen of soup the waiter had placed in front of her.

"Be careful not to burn your mouth, Anna," Claude warned. "It's hotter than it looks."

They walked till nearly two in the morning, past the classically beautiful eighteenth-century church of Saint-Eustache, the Bourse de Commerce, and the former home of Jean-Jacques Rousseau. Claude and Bernard seemed to compete with one another as walking repositories of knowledge of French history.

"Liszt's *Missa Solemnis* was first performed here."

"And Rubens's *The Pilgrims of Emmaus* is inside. Too bad it's not open."

"This column is the only surviving fragment of Queen Marie de Médicis' mansion."

It was Francine who demanded, after a long trip and a long evening, that they hail a taxi and return to the hotel. On the ride back, she solemnly clasped Anna's hand in her own as if she could not get enough love and closeness into the two days they had together.

The next morning, Claude ordered a continental breakfast for four in their room. Before his parents arrived, he told Anna to get all her pictures of the boys out. "Didn't you bring the one of Charles on his pony?" he demanded.

"I never dreamed you'd want it, Claude. You always get angry with me for showing pictures of the boys."

"This is different. It's my mother!" he snapped.

"These are the most recent and the best," she said quietly, handing him six pictures. Wonders never cease, she told herself. I've never seen him proud of the boys before. But if it makes his mother happy—

A knock on the door announced the elder Dunays' arrival.

Claude embraced his mother, who in turn hugged Anna. He shook his father's hand, saying with a broad smile, "*Bonjour, Dr. Dunay!*"

A slight smile passed Bernard Dunay's face; then he turned to Anna. "You look very lovely so early in the day, madame."

Anna winced at his formality but was gladdened by what seemed to be a softening of his disposition toward them. No doubt he's a tyrant at home, and that's why Claude is such a despot. He imitates his father without knowing it.

Francine devoured the pictures of her two grandsons, while Bernard pointedly ignored them. Claude's attention, during breakfast, shifted back and forth between them. He glowed with pride while telling anecdotes about Charles, then turned back to his father to comment on political currents in Europe, especially in Germany.

Anna watched with amazement Claude's new-found pride in his sons. If only he'd take those feelings home and let the boys know!

"It's time! We must be off. Mona Lisa awaits us!" Bernard exclaimed as he untucked his napkin and placed it on the table.

The women, walking together behind the men, continued to talk of Anna's boys. Suddenly, with a shy look of pride, Francine pulled a small formal portrait of Claude from her pocketbook. "He is nine years old, in his uniform. Isn't he darling? Your boys might like to see their father."

Anna accepted the photograph. Claude was in some sort of formal military uniform, standing erect and proud, his left hand resting nonchalantly on a chair arm. Even then, at the tender age of nine, he was a self-assured heir of the good life. Already arrogant and proud.

* * *

Five hours later, they emerged from the Louvre, Anna feeling sated and exhausted. Claude and Bernard had spent the last hour arguing about the Impressionists. Anna and Francine had voted decisively in their favor, but Claude had steadfastly claimed the superiority of Rembrandt and the Italian masters.

They stopped at a sidewalk café for an aperitif and late lunch. Bernard began discussing Hitler's Germany with Claude. Anna noted that her father-in-law chose to ignore her in the discussion of world affairs, in spite of the fact that Claude had mentioned her "good connections" in the Roosevelt administration and her position on Capitol Hill.

"Two of my colleagues in Germany have written that they are considering relocating in America. It seems Hitler is making life uncomfortable for the Jews," Bernard declared between bites.

Claude looked at Anna. "Tell him what Ed Murrow told you last week."

Anna cleared her throat, delighted that Claude had included her in this discussion. "One of the CBS reporters, Edward R. Murrow, was in our office just before I left. He was telling everyone who would listen that we must begin to move Jews out of Germany, and other intellectuals as well."

Francine looked hard at Anna. "The stories we're hearing aren't exaggerations, then?"

Anna shook her head and patted Francine's arm. "You might want to think about coming to America if things get worse. There seems to be a wide-open field for psychiatrists there."

Bernard rushed to silence Anna. "Nonsense! We're too old to think of starting over. Besides, the language—"

Claude interrupted his father. "Don't be ridiculous, Anna. You know how long it's taken me to build a respectable practice."

"And," Bernard continued, "no one thinks of us as Jews. We haven't been in a synagogue in years. We're totally assimilated, part of the Polish intelligentsia."

Francine interjected quietly, "I must confess I do worry—but I hope we can visit you soon. I'd like to see America, and my grandsons."

"This discussion is ridiculous," Bernard said angrily. "That crazy Hitler is Germany's problem, not ours. I can't imagine giving up our life in Poland. We have everything. Everything!"

Anna noted how red Bernard's face became when he was emotional—just like Claude's.

Francine looked directly at Bernard as she said, "We do have a wonderful life. Both of us have large, satisfying practices. And we've lived frugally and saved for our old age. We might consider moving to America in a few years"—she turned to Claude —"to be close to you and your children."

A look of alarm crossed Claude's face. Anna suddenly understood that her husband was happier when an ocean separated him from his father. How sad—and how lucky I am to have Jacob and Sarah.

After a late dinner at Delmonico's, the Dunays made a visit —nostalgic, for Claude—to the city's most famous café, La Coupole.

"This is a favorite night-spot of Scott and Zelda Fitzgerald," Claude announced to Anna as they were seated under the high dome. "Once when I was a poor student, I saw Hemingway in here flirting like crazy with one of the bar girls."

Anna watched dozens of avid dancers enjoying a saxophone's lament.

"We never go to places like this in Warsaw," Francine said, her excited eyes straining to see everyone. "But it's such fun in Paris."

Claude summoned the owner, Monsieur René Lafon, over to the table. He reintroduced himself, then asked, "Who is here tonight?"

"The 'famous ones' are a painter you probably have heard of, Picasso, and a bohemian couple who write for our underground papers, Jean-Paul Sartre and Simone de Beauvoir. You will be hearing more of them. See"—he pointed to their far left— "there they are. She's the dowdy-looking woman in dark blue."

"That's the fun of being here," Claude explained to Anna after Monsieur Lafon left them. "The French are fanatic about seeing and being seen at the right places like this."

"Let's dance," Anna suggested, anxious to see who else was on the dance floor.

"Good idea!" Bernard exclaimed as he too led Francine toward the ballroom.

* * *

They parted after two in the morning, with the knowledge that Claude's parents' train to Warsaw left at seven. Francine thanked Anna and Claude profusely for arranging the reunion. "It has done your father much good," she proclaimed, "even though he would never admit it. And I will rest better, knowing my son has such a fine wife. Take my love home with you."

Anna's eyes filled with tears as she watched Francine, a woman she'd become genuinely fond of in two short days, struggle with her parting emotions.

"I shall carry a picture of you in my heart always, dear Anna. God bless you."

Once inside their room, Claude undressed for bed thoughtfully. "Tomorrow we will visit Versailles."

But the rest of the trip would be an anticlimax, Anna knew as she climbed into bed and pulled the sweet-smelling sheets over her tired body.

▨ Chapter 20

October 1941

"The leaves are turning late this year," Anna commented in an attempt at levity as Claude parked in the lot adjoining Normandie Farm, a French country inn in Potomac. While walking toward the entrance, Anna was filled with apprehension. She disliked the idea that she would be the head of their household for the duration of the war they knew was coming. She hated the idea of raising the boys alone even though, when she was honest with herself, she recognized that was what she was doing anyhow. She wasn't keen about keeping up their high-level social life without an escort. But most of all, she was terrified that Claude would somehow discover that she was responsible for his being drafted.

It had been simple. One phone call to the right officer in the Navy, and two weeks later Claude's orders had arrived.

Her motivations had been mixed. Now, six weeks later, she didn't understand why she had done it. The only reasons she could give herself were that doctors were badly needed in the military, and it was the patriotic thing for Claude to do. And she needed a "vacation" from Claude's demands. The truth was, she looked forward to having him gone for a while—or at least she thought she did when she made that phone call.

He'd grumbled and muttered and cursed for a few days, but gradually, as he watched his colleagues close down their practices, he began to feel it was inevitable. He'd even begun to look forward to the adventure of seeing the world at government expense. The only thing that still stuck in his craw on the night before his departure was the money he would lose while he was away "fighting to save democracy."

Anna and Claude were seated in front of the tall stone fireplace at the far end of the large dining room. A young woman clad in a floor-length calico dress, wearing a high peaked hat, placed two golden-brown popovers in front of them and asked for their drink order.

"Tonight's a special night. Our farewell dinner. We'll have a bottle of Mumm's champagne," Claude answered.

"While I'm gone," he continued after the waitress left them, "I most especially want you to keep up our social contacts. Go to parties. Don't worry—hostesses will get used to you coming unescorted. Or grab one of our bachelor friends and have him take you. You know, Anna, we don't have an old-fashioned marriage. I won't be the least bit hurt if you go to parties and balls and the symphony with some of my friends. One thing I don't want is you sitting home alone getting stale. Go to parties and give parties, just as if I were here."

"Oh, Claude, I can barely imagine myself doing that! Lord only knows how long this will go on before we are officially in it."

"Not much longer, I'll bet. Roosevelt will find a way."

"As well he should!"

"Agreed."

"Claude, my greatest worry is your parents. Is there anything we can do that we haven't already done?"

"I don't see how we can help them if we can't even find them. But follow up on any leads you get—I'll have to leave that in your hands, Anna. I won't be in a position to do anything. But I trust your judgment."

The evil intentions of Hitler could no longer be ignored. His troops had entered Warsaw in September 1939. Francine Dunay had written to Claude and Anna, explaining that the Nazi regime had ordered every Jew to wear a white armband with a blue Star of David. "But we don't because we don't consider ourselves religious Jews. If we don't draw attention to the circumstances of our birth, they will let us continue with our practices and our lives, as if they weren't even here."

Subsequently, Anna learned that all real estate and other property owned by Jews had been confiscated. The Jews were prohibited from using the railroad and other public transportation. Jewish businesses were also marked with the Star of David.

Claude received letters from his parents during all of 1939 and up until April 1940. Then the letters stopped. Even though he and Anna continued to write to his parents, they heard not a word. It seemed as if all mail from Poland to America had been confiscated by the Nazis.

"To Hitler's early destruction!" Claude toasted. Then he added, "And to my heroine, who's going to carry on magnificently in my absence. I have faith in you, Anna."

They sipped the champagne slowly, both lost in their deepest thoughts.

"About the bills," Claude said suddenly, coming out of a deep trance. "I sent them out this afternoon with instructions to mail the checks to the house. I've put the accounts-receivable ledger on your side of the desk. You're in charge. Be prepared to send bills again to the ones who don't pay this month and next month—until everything is paid."

"I hope that doesn't go on for too long."

"Some people you may have to call—I always do. I've marked them with a red pen. Keep careful track of everything because you'll have to figure out the income tax this year. If any more bills come to me—and there may be a last telephone bill for the office—pay them and keep careful account."

Anna nodded. "What about Christmas cards? Should I send cards to all your patients?"

"Good idea! I'd like to think of other ways to keep in touch too. It kills me to think of all the years I've spent building a practice; now I'll lose them all. When this damnable war is over, we'll have to start over again from scratch. That's why it's so important for you to be seen everywhere—the White House, embassies, the symphony, and the theater. Hell, you know."

"The boys will miss you, Claude."

"Yes. Well, don't forget to give them vitamins every day. And take some yourself, too, Anna. You should take the boys to your mother's and Sasha's as often as possible—it'll cut down on the food bills. You absolutely *must* save every dime you can. Try to live on your salary alone, and put mine in the bank."

"I'll do my best, Claude. You know that," she answered sharply. Damn him! He's going to war, he may never see his sons again, and all he can think about is money!

"Let other people take you to dinner. After all, you and I are the ones sacrificing for their safety. They can feed you while I'm gone."

"Claude, this is your last night! Let's talk about something besides money."

"Be sure and keep up your French lessons. You're doing really well, almost bilingual now. And read the classics in French. Nothing helps as much as reading a little French every day. Pretty soon, you'll be dreaming in French."

"And when the war's over, you'll take me back to Paris, right?"

"To whatever's left of Paris—and the rest of Europe."

"How long do you think it will take to win this one?" Anna wondered aloud as she sipped her champagne.

"Who can possibly know? Years—perhaps as many as ten years. Anna, be sure you continue to listen to music. It's the most soothing thing you can do after a hard day at the office. I think about your nerves. It's not going to be easy."

"I'll miss hearing you play the piano. I've always loved listening to you play Debussy. I think he's my favorite." Even in our sorry marriage, there have been good moments.

Claude savored the first taste of his veal chop, then reached for Anna's hand. "I'm depending on you, my love, to keep the home fires burning, as they say. You'll manage this as you manage everything else—with a smile, a witty remark for everyone, and lots of hard work."

"Enjoy your meal, Claude." He's trying. He can be gallant. If only I could muster some sort of sadness over his leaving! "It may be the last good one you have for a while. Don't forget—you're going to write where you're stationed under the stamp.

I'll steam it off, and at least have the comfort of knowing where you are."

"Someplace in the Atlantic Ocean, I'd guess. It'll be dangerous out there, but doctors aren't expected to be in the line of fire. Don't worry. I'll be fine."

Monday, December 1, 1941

Dear Claude,

Five weeks since you "flew the coop," and I must admit that I am a bit anxious for some word from you. Having a husband but not knowing where or how he is, is a very strange sensation! Have you been receiving my letters? This is my sixth. I have only been writing of my personal activities, scrupulously avoiding any controversial matters, but now I learn that I can write freely, as my letters are not censored. So I will try to give you a résumé of world affairs as seen from the U.S. Senate.

Giving you the latest news fills space, makes this look like a long letter. The truth is, I don't even want to write you. I don't miss you. Life is so much more pleasant without your daily harassment!

The situation between the U.S. and Japan is very tense. The President came back to the White House this morning from Warm Springs, cutting short his vacation. Kurusu, special envoy from Japan, has been in Washington negotiating with the State Department, but apparently no headway has been made. Saturday's and yesterday's papers were full of news of movement of the Japanese troops and the bombing of the Burma road. Radio commentators yesterday all agreed that the U.S. will move against Japan.

Germany has been routed out of Rostov by the Russians and driven back more than 100 miles. However, the Germans are still pounding away at Moscow.

A contingent of American troops has been sent to Dutch Guiana in South America. They found a lot of Nazi propaganda and a plot for a coup.

Now for the home front. We have had several beautiful days, and yesterday I bundled up in my camel's hair coat and drove the boys out to Middleburg with the top down.

They enjoyed the horses as usual; Naomi sends her love. I wonder if she'll keep the country place going for the duration, with David gone and gas and other things becoming scarce.

I'm preparing a box for you of the medical journals, *Time* magazine, *Reader's Digest,* and several sections of the Sunday *Times.*

I have sent out the bills for your office twice now. Only Miss Simpson, LaR., Backer, and Brady have paid in full, and Mrs. Willett sent half on her account. I hope to have better luck this month.

I've been in touch with the Hebrew Immigrant Aid Society in New York about your parents. I'm also planning to see Mr. Farley next week. Perhaps he can refer me to the right person in the State Department. Your Polish friend Piaskowski, who is in Spain now, writes that he is sending money to your parents and food. The letter is quite unclear —I'm not sure where your parents are or why we haven't heard from them in over eighteen months now. Someone here in the office has told me that Hitler has started slave labor camps in Poland—but I can't imagine that the Nazis are stupid enough to waste the talents of two medical doctors by sending them to a slave labor camp. In any event, you can be sure I'll leave no stone unturned here in trying to establish direct communication with them.

Everyone is anxious to hear from you, all about your trip over and so forth. Senator Truman asks me daily to let him know when you arrive in Iceland. Colonel Halsey, too, is concerned and gave me a long lecture on how I should conduct myself in your absence—as if I didn't know! Besides, he didn't know that I'm going to catch a beau just as soon as I can find one!

I'm sorry I couldn't talk to you when you called—there were five or six people in the office all talking at once, and the other phone rang at the same time.

Last week I went to the Russian embassy, together with about 3,000 others. I suppose you know that Litvinov is the new ambassador. It was jam-packed; saw the usual ones, Henrietta and Herman, the Moyers (they've bought a new house and have asked me to dinner this week), Bob Sevey. I wore my black suit, white blouse, white gloves, my

black Persian lamb hat perched on the back of my head
and my Persian muff—very, very chic! Everyone asked
about you. If toasts and prayers can win this war, you'll be
home very soon.

Well, that brings you up-to-date. I guess this is *au revoir*.
Take care of yourself—I guess I don't have to tell you to be
good—think of me and the boys often and know we are
keeping those home fires burning. Am anxiously awaiting
your letter. I suppose you are missing me??!!

Cheerio, and love and kisses,
Anna

Saturday, December 6, 1941

Dear Claude,

Six weeks today since you left—and it probably feels like
a million years to you.

*Six blessedly peaceful weeks. I'm sure my blood pressure is nor-
mal for the first time since we married. I sleep deeply, awaken
refreshed. Is it wrong for me to feel so good with you at war? Your
life is at risk every day—yet I don't worry about you. What kind
of callous, horribly cold woman have I become? The truth is I
think and worry more about your mother than I worry about you,
Claude . . .*

Your friend Buddy met me at the office this afternoon,
and we went bicycling. He brought along a friend, Gus
somebody or other, from Chicago, who has just come to
work here; an expert on plastics. It was Buddy's first weekend in town, and he asked me to have dinner with him.
Gus came along and we went to Maxime's, the little
French restaurant you and I went to one Sunday night, and
then we went to the Shoreham. It was terribly crowded,
and since we were dressed in sports clothes, we found our
way to the cocktail lounge.

*Why am I writing this? Am I trying to make him jealous? Do I
care? Do I want him to love me?*

A cable yesterday morning from P. asks me to send
some money to HIAS again, who in return will send it to

Lisbon for his passage on January 2. So it looks like our efforts will benefit someone, if not your parents yet. I will be so relieved if I can work out a way to get them here. Farley gave me a lead, a man in the State Department. I have an appointment next week. Everything moves so slowly, even when lives are at stake.

Some money is coming in from the bills. Rowley, Fenton, and Hunter have paid their bills so far.

We've been in recess this past week, and the Colonel has been in New York. What bliss! You can well imagine what this means to me—a chance to catch a real deep breath. But not without anxiety, nonetheless. Dark clouds are hovering overhead, and in our office we don't forget it for a moment. Japan is sounding even more belligerent. The British have sent a flotilla of warships including the *Prince of Wales* to Singapore.

The latest word, as I write this, is that the British forces have been ordered to the Far East. Russia has captured considerable territory from the Germans in the Rostov sector. Britain has declared war against Finland, Hungary, and Romania. I wonder how much longer Roosevelt will hold out, though I must say if it were put to a vote in the Senate, we'd never get into the battle.

Cheerio, love and kisses from
Anna, Charles, and Gilbert

"Mr. Loomis will see you now, Mrs. Dunay," the secretary announced as she opened the door to his inner sanctum.

Anna took a deep breath to steady her nerves, then head held high, she strode into the office of the assistant to the undersecretary of state.

James Farley had called Cordell Hull, the secretary of state, while she sat in Farley's office. Hull had recommended that she see William Bradford Loomis, a high-ranking official in the political section of the State Department. If anyone could help her bring the elder Dunays out of Nazi-occupied Poland, Hull said, it was this man.

She watched him appraise her as she seated herself on the sofa.

He sat opposite her. "The secretary has asked me to help you with—ah—a problem with your husband's parents? Is that it?"

She studied his unlined patrician face. He was relatively young—perhaps in his mid-thirties—and clearly from an aristocratic background. One of the first families of America. Yale or Harvard, she'd bet. Handsome—and arrogant too.

"Yes. His parents, both doctors, live in Warsaw. They are nonreligious Jews. We have not heard from them since April 1940."

"Very little mail is coming out of Poland, Mrs. Dunay. That's not surprising. I don't think you have any cause to worry."

"We have heard about them indirectly, from a friend who is in Spain. But I don't understand why I can't reach them by letter, by wire—I've even tried to place several transatlantic calls, but I get no response. The operator tells me their phone is disconnected, at their home and at both their offices. Something must be wrong." Anna stopped abruptly, afraid she'd gone on too long, betrayed too much emotion in her voice. This man would not take kindly to an emotional woman.

"What would you like me to do?" He reached into his coat for a package of cigarettes, then lit one, waiting for Anna to answer.

"Surely you have connections with an embassy in Warsaw that hasn't yet broken relations with Germany. Going through that embassy, couldn't you manage to smuggle them out of Poland and bring them to America?"

He started to speak, but Anna interrupted him. "Mr. Loomis, please let me assure you, I'm prepared to spend whatever is necessary to bring them here. And I will guarantee that I will be responsible for them when they arrive in America."

"Mrs. Dunay, I realize you are very well connected in Washington, in the Roosevelt administration," he responded in a patronizing voice. "But this request—well, it's simply preposterous! First of all, let me say I think you've exaggerated in your imagination the danger the Dunays might be in. You have no reason to believe their lives are in danger. The worst that could be happening to them is that they might be in one of the labor camps."

"My God! Mr. Loomis, where is your compassion? These people are old, in their late sixties! They couldn't possibly survive forced labor!"

"Will you let me finish?" He waited with a stern look on his face for her to quiet down. "Now, second, we would not even consider making that kind of request of a neutral country. These matters of diplomacy are much too delicate, much too involved, for us to trot off and casually ask Switzerland or Spain or Sweden to involve themselves and endanger their status as neutrals, for two doctors. Impossible, my dear Mrs. Dunay. Impossible."

Anna looked at him in disbelief. How could he be so unconcerned with human life? "If they were Rothschilds, you would do it."

Momentarily stunned, Loomis's face grew pale. "They *aren't* members of the Rothschild family. And I would remind you, Mrs. Dunay, you are not a Strauss or a Warburg." He stood to indicate that the interview was over. "I'm sorry to disappoint you, Mrs. Dunay. There is nothing, absolutely nothing I can do."

"And even if there were, you're not so inclined, are you, Mr. Loomis?" Anna stood and picked up her purse.

"To be perfectly frank, I don't approve of all the visas we're issuing to European refugees. I think Hitler's actions against the Jews have been vastly exaggerated by the Jewish press. I, for one, am not buying it."

"I see I've come to the wrong place." She walked toward his door, then turned back to face him squarely. "For the life of me, I can't imagine why Secretary Hull sent me to see you. You had no intention of helping me, even before I explained the problem."

In reply, he smiled pleasantly and bade her good-bye.

Sunday, December 14, 1941

Dear Claude,

Your first letter has arrived at long last. I had patiently awaited it, not having heard from you since your brief phone call from New York in October.

I'll try to get the things you need and send them as soon as I possibly can. I have not closed the November account, nor will I close the December account, until I receive your expenditures. Never fear!

Listened to a broadcast from Iceland a few nights ago and know that you've gotten the flash of what happened here. Last Sunday will be a red-letter day in the history of the world. While the Japanese envoys, Kurusu and

Nomura, were sitting with Mr. Hull, Japanese bombs were being dropped on Pearl Harbor. A more wanton attack has never before been perpetrated. All week long I've been trying to get a list of the casualties to see if any of the officers I knew when I was with the Naval Affairs Committee were injured or killed.

Or Kurt. I was especially worried about him because he's stationed at Pearl Harbor. But early the next morning I received a wire from him—"Reporting in alive and well. Love Kurt." Only after the telegram arrived did I understand how terrified I was that he'd been killed or wounded. It's so confusing to be married to one man and to love another.

From the moment the first flash came on the radio, you could sense the excitement everywhere. And I am a little ashamed to admit that I got a good case of the jitters too. I suddenly realized how alone I was and would have given anything just to talk with you.

All else has paled into insignificance, but we must take it in our stride and try to live as normally as possible. We've had the most exhausting week at the office. Each evening I come away absolutely limp, and it was with a great deal of effort that I kept my social engagements, as I promised you I would.

Had dinner with Buddy Monday night, and he brought along a young friend from New York who insisted that we stop at the Carlton lounge first. There we bumped into Earl Smith, to whom I presented Buddy and Jim—and there I was surrounded with three handsome gentlemen. From there we went to the Mayflower for dinner and bumped into another friend of Buddy's from New York, a fourth gentleman. Who said there was a shortage of men in Washington? Such attention, such glamour! I couldn't help but be amused and thought you would be, too.

Why do I do this? Do I care what he feels for me? Yes, I do. I want him to love me. And I want Kurt to love me too. Since I can't have Kurt, I'd better hold on to Claude.

Jonathan Herzmark has made me several small pictures of you in uniform, one of which I had framed for my desk at the office. I know that will please you. Everyone wants to know who the good-looking fellow is. —Can you imagine my pride when I reply, "My husband!" I can actually see you smile.

All for now, *mon cher,* soon enough this will be over and we will be together again—thumbs up!

Love and kisses,
Anna

"Senator Landow, thank you so much." Anna beamed her warmest smile at the distinguished-looking first-term senator from Connecticut who had already made a name for himself on the Foreign Relations Committee. "Even before we begin this difficult discussion, I want you to know how deeply I appreciate your staying late to meet with me."

They had been introduced many times before, but Anna didn't feel she knew him well enough to ask for help. Senator Truman, however, had told her that he was actively involved in helping Jewish refugees—and because he was Jewish himself, he was especially compassionate.

The senator sat behind his desk, calmly smiling at Anna. He nodded toward the lovely-looking, prematurely gray-haired woman in the wing chair beside his desk. "I hope you don't mind, Anna, but my wife Esther has joined me for the dinner this evening. Since I knew you wanted to discuss a refugee problem, I asked her to meet with us. She has as many ideas and connections as I do in these matters."

Anna smiled graciously to Esther Landow. "I'm very pleased to meet you, Mrs. Landow."

Looking intensely serious, she answered, "We must make it our number-one priority to bring as many European Jews to America as we possibly can. It—it is crucial. Now tell us."

Anna explained as briefly as possible the situation with the elder Dunays. When she finished, Senator Landow, who had been patiently tapping his long fingers on his desk top, raised his eyes to hers and spoke.

"It's quite possible, even though they aren't religious, that the Nazis have rounded them up and put them in the Warsaw ghetto. My information is that birth certificates are being checked for religion at birth. Even Catholics who were born Jewish but have converted are being rounded up for the labor camps."

"That's exactly what I'm afraid of. They are so old."

"We have two problems," the senator continued, thinking slowly out loud. "First, we have to locate them. Then we have to smuggle them out of Poland, probably using a neutral embassy."

Anna felt her heart skip a beat. At last! At last she had found someone who truly wanted to help her!

"I'll need physical descriptions of both of them. Do you have any pictures?"

"Yes, I have recent pictures, formal studio portraits."

"Bring them to me tomorrow. Realize, however, that you may never see the pictures again. I'll have to pass them along to my contacts in Europe."

"Of course. Then you think there's a chance?" Suddenly her heart felt so light, she could have stood up and danced a jig.

"We must do everything we can. No promises—we've probably got one chance in a thousand. But we *are* bringing people out of Poland. A mere trickle, but enough to know how desperately bad things are there."

Anna stood, aware that the Landows had a dinner engagement. "I can't thank—"

"Don't begin your thanks yet, Anna. We've a long way to go. One thing I must ask of you: Do not share the fact that I'm trying to help you with anyone in the Roosevelt administration. There are lots of people very high up who don't give a damn. They refuse to believe what we are trying to tell them. So don't complicate matters by confiding in Farley or Hull or Roosevelt, or anyone else. If we succeed, it will be in spite of them, not because of them."

Anna felt a sour feeling surge through her chest. It was hard to believe that all those men she held in such esteem were not on her side, on the side of right, in this matter.

She swallowed hard, then reached for his outstretched hand. "Senator, you're the boss. I'll keep it strictly confidential."

"Anna, the call's for you," her assistant called out above the clickety-clack of three typewriters.

Anna picked up the telephone but continued reading from the *Congressional Record*. "This is Anna Dunay."

"Am I speaking to the most beautiful woman in Washington?"

Chills spread through her, and goose bumps raised on her arms—it was Kurt. After a long moment's silence she answered, "Oh my, Kurt! I was so relieved to get your wire last Monday! Thank you for sending it."

"You mean you think it's possible I could have forgotten you? Oh, Anna, not for a second, not for half a second."

"You sound close. Where are you?"

"Here in Washington, at the War Office. I'll be here for a few days." He paused. "I'd like to see you, Anna. Would it be possible for you to—"

"Of course, Kurt. Whenever."

"Tonight? I've a room at the Mayflower."

"I'll be there. After work, about six."

They said good-bye, and Anna replaced the receiver. She felt tears surface in her eyes and, swallowing the lump in her throat, turned back to the *Congressional Record*. Her heart was pounding so loud, she couldn't read the words. Her ability to concentrate had evaporated, rendered impossible by the strong masculine voice out of her past. Oh, how she longed to see him! How will I get through the next few hours? she wondered as she looked at the clock on her desk. Thank God, thank God he's unharmed.

▨ Chapter 21

Anna arrived at the cocktail lounge five minutes early, confident that she looked soignée in her cranberry-wool-crepe dress. She entered the room and strained against the fashionably dim lighting to see Kurt. After a few moments she saw a tall man dressed in a dark overcoat and the peaked hat of a military officer walking toward her from the rear of the room. As he came closer and closer, she felt again his mesmerizing personality, his glowing smile, and his warm eyes, which enveloped her like an aura. Acute excitement blended with serenity. The knowledge of his certain grace, his splendid intelligence, his death-defying patriotism flooded over her. As he swept her into his arms and kissed her fully on the mouth, she wondered again how she could ever have married Claude. Why had she done that to herself?

"Anna! Oh, Anna!" he whispered against her cheek. He held her back to look at her again. "My memory has been playing tricks on me. You're even more beautiful than I remembered. A wonderful sight! Exactly what this sailor needs!" He held her hands tightly in his own, then asked, "Would you like a drink? Or should we go upstairs?"

She laughed at his eagerness. "I choose"—she paused to tease him, then relented—"upstairs."

After the doors of the elevator closed behind them, leaving them alone, he handed her a key. "I'll go up one more floor, then walk down. Let yourself in, then wait for me to knock."

He's so handsome, Anna thought. I forget, while he's away, what an incredible man he really is.

"Here's the eighth floor now, my darling. I'll be with you in a moment."

She left the elevator like a sleepwalker and walked to the room indicated by the number on the key. It's like a dream, she told herself as she opened the door. I can't quite believe he's really here. Safe. Unharmed. And still in love with me.

After she let him in, he took her in his arms again. Slowly caressing her cheeks with the tips of his fingers, he took her face in his hands. He bent to kiss each eye, then the tip of her nose. As he tenderly pressed his lips to hers, she wrapped her arms around his back, pulling him so close, their bodies blended into one.

When he let her go, it was to double-bolt the door.

"I've so much to tell you!" Anna said excitedly.

"Exactly," he answered with a smile, putting his arm around her and steering her farther into the room.

"I don't know whether we should talk or make love first!" Anna dropped her briefcase and purse onto the bed.

"I don't intend to give you a choice," Kurt answered with a lascivious twinkle in his eyes. "It's not even a close call. Oh, you look so good to me!" He reached for her and kissed her again.

"Don't you think we should shed these coats?" Anna teased after a long embrace.

"And lots more too!" He threw his topcoat onto a nearby chair, then began unbuttoning his uniform.

Anna reached for the back of her dress to undo the zipper. Kurt beamed at her as he approached her and gently unzipped the dress, helping it fall to the floor. "It's been so long—so very long since I've had the privilege of undressing you—except in my imagination. And somehow"—he chuckled—"that's just not the same. I love you, Anna. I hope you've never doubted that, even for a moment."

She looked into his moist eyes and felt almost ill with grief that they had to spend most of their lives separated from one another. Never had she felt so complete, so fulfilled, as she did in that moment of watching him desire her. "I love you too, Kurt. I hope you always know that too!"

"I do, my darling. I do."

As in times past, the hotel provided the food and wines, while Kurt supplied the commentary on United States military affairs. As Anna listened to his account of what had happened at Pearl Harbor, she realized that he considered her a safe sounding board for his pent-up frustrations. What he was telling her was strictly confidential, never to be repeated.

"Kimmel and Short, the two men in charge of the Pacific Fleet, refused to believe the intelligence we were providing to them. They continue even today to underestimate the Japs—exactly the way everyone in Washington does. Our officials don't seem to believe that the Japs are capable of mounting more than one offensive at a time."

Anna sipped on the splendid Bordeaux, then set the glass down. "Weren't the Japanese mounting another offensive at the same time they bombed Pearl Harbor?"

"Exactly. Our intelligence knew they were preparing to attack Saigon—they'd massed thousands of troops there. They had troops ready to attack in Manila, Hong Kong, and Malaya. Everything was perfectly synchronized, and their secrecy was damn near perfect. Except for the fact that we had MAGIC— that's the code name we use for the fact that we've broken their secret code. But it doesn't do us a damn bit of good to intercept their messages if our office can't get the admirals and the officials back here in Washington to believe them."

"How badly was our navy damaged?"

"Yamamoto is a damned genius. His objective was to win the war with one strike, by knocking out our navy at Pearl. He almost succeeded. Except for the aircraft carriers that were at sea, they devastated us. Eight battleships and nine cruisers— over two thousand casualties. All at the bottom of the ocean! And it didn't have to happen that way. If only they'd listened."

"What do we do now? Can we beat Japan?"

"Yes. I have to believe that we can win. But it will take all-out mobilization. And concentration on the Pacific as well as the Atlantic. Roosevelt's inclined to make the Atlantic his first priority. I say we've got to make a cold-blooded appraisal of the Japanese threat. We've got to understand that they have awesome hardware. Their men carry two times the ammunition ours do, they carry a five-day ration of fish and rice on their bodies, their ships are faster with bigger guns and torpedos, and the four types of planes they used at Pearl are superior to anything we can put in the air. And now, after what they did to us at Pearl, they have three times the seapower we have.

"Most important of all," Kurt continued, "we've got to understand that every Jap soldier deeply believes that there is no greater glory than to die for the Emperor."

"What I don't understand—what everyone on the Hill is buzzing about—is why Roosevelt didn't suspect the attack in Hawaii. Several senators mentioned to me that we were expecting an attack, but we thought it would be in the Philippines instead of Hawaii."

"Indeed. One more example of how the powers-that-be don't understand the Japanese mind. Every graduate of the Naval Academy in Japan is challenged to describe how he would mount a surprise attack on Pearl Harbor before he is allowed to graduate. Their minds have been fixated on attacking Pearl Harbor for at least ten years now. *We knew that.* But our military and political leaders simply didn't want to believe it was possible.

"Anna, let me tell you, when we spotted the Japanese aircraft on the radar, we still didn't believe it was an attack. We chose to believe those planes were ours, arriving from the mainland. And so even with twenty-eight minutes' warning, we left our planes sitting there. And they were destroyed *sitting on the ground!* Can you imagine that?"

Anna shook her head sadly.

"To answer your question: Yes, we can beat them. But it will take time, and the news will get much worse before it gets better."

"Where will you be stationed?"

"That's subject to change from day to day. But since I'm so heavily involved in intelligence work, I'll probably be either in Hawaii or here. Where's Claude?"

"He's in Iceland, attached to the U.S.S. *Guadalcanal*. He's very bored, I gather. They don't seem to be doing much."

"That's all going to change now, you can be sure."

Anna reached for the coffeepot and served Kurt and herself a second cup.

"The thing we don't seem to understand about the Japanese is that they've won every war they've been in since 1589. They'll never surrender. It would dishonor them as a people. They'll all die, every last one of them, before agreeing to surrender. We've got a long road ahead of us. As a nation, we've got to stop underestimating the oriental mind."

"Part of the problem," Anna stated, "is that we've been concentrating so hard on the war in Europe, we ceased to worry about Japan. Even now, the President and the Senate are more concerned about Hitler than about Japan."

"Right. I'm not saying we shouldn't make Europe our first concern, but we've got a two-front war on our hands, whether we like it or not. And it's not going to be won anytime soon."

"I feel almost unpatriotic thinking about *us*," Anna quietly added. "But will your work in intelligence bring you to Washington more often? Will we get to see more of one another?"

"It's possible. I must confess, I've thought of that too. Being close to you again would be such a blessing. But we'll have to take each day as it comes. And be flexible. And realize how precious these few hours we're together are."

"I agree."

Suddenly, Kurt jumped to his feet and rummaged through his suitcase. He walked toward her with a small white box tied with a blue ribbon. "And now it's present time. You got me so wound up about the war, I almost forgot that I've something special for you."

Anna accepted the box, delighted but blushing. "It isn't necessary to bring me gifts."

"Not necessary, no. But it's my greatest pleasure, my love. And I hope I've picked something Claude hasn't already given you."

Claude's not much for giving gifts, Anna thought meanly as she opened a black-velvet case and found a two-strand, opera-length pearl necklace with a diamond and sapphire clasp. "Oh, my! Oh, my, Kurt! You shouldn't!"

"Seeing your eyes light up like that is worth twice the price, my darling. Now, promise me you'll wear them often and think of me with love."

Anna's eyes were tearing, but she determined she would not break down. It was glorious to be so loved. She had forgotten how wonderful it felt to be cherished by Kurt. And now that he was reminding her, how would she get through the rest of the war? Or the rest of her life? How could she stay married to a man who valued her so little, when this man loved and cherished and dreamed about her from afar?

"I'd give more than a penny for your thoughts, my love. Suddenly, you're quiet."

Her eyes met his as she gently slipped the precious pearls over her head. "Nothing. I was only thinking that I love you even more than I'd realized. I guess I must spend inordinate amounts of time and energy trying not to think about you, about us—about the enormous sadness in our lives."

He stooped and gathered her into his arms. "My darling, don't think about sadness—not now, not while I'm here." Then in an artificially happy voice he demanded, "Tell me about your sons. Do you have pictures?"

"No. I've trained myself not to carry pictures around, not to bore people." She reminded herself of her vow not to tell Kurt that he was the father of Charles, so she quickly changed the subject. "I've an idea. You've still got lots of fans on the Hill among the men who are on the Naval Affairs Committee. Why don't you make it your business to pay a courtesy call on them? You know, for old times' sake and all that—and simply drop into the conversation some of the things you've told me.

"There's a strong resentment of Roosevelt on the Hill. Lots of folks think he somehow got us into this war deliberately. They should hear you talk about the Japanese. It'd do them good."

"As always, Anna, you're exactly right." He reached over

and tilted her chin so she looked directly at him. "And then I might be able to stop by your office and see your glorious face. "

"Hmm." She reached over and caressed the back of his hand. "My thoughts exactly, Commander Addison!"

I'm so glad I started this journal when Claude left for the war. Now I've really got something to write, Anna thought as she stretched her legs out and opened the maroon-leather cover of the book she expected her grandchildren to someday cherish.

Saturday, December 27, 1941

What a grueling week this has been, with Christmas and Winston Churchill dropping into our very midst! Colonel Halsey made a stunning announcement to me Wednesday afternoon, which was Christmas Eve. "I'm sorry to burden you with this project at the last minute, Anna, but I need you. You'll have to sacrifice your Christmas holiday for the good of your country." I was angry. How dare he ask the mother of two little boys to give up her Christmas?

No, I thought, Colonel Halsey, this time you ask much too much. He must have read my mind because then he dropped the bombshell: On Friday morning the Prime Minister of Great Britain will be coming over here from the White House to address a joint session of Congress. You are in charge of issuing all passes and the seating of the Supreme Court, the diplomatic corps, congressional wives, and the military brass. In addition, Senator Barkley is inviting the Prime Minister to a private luncheon after his address. And you, my dear, are responsible for all the arrangements for the luncheon, including telephoning invitations tomorrow—on Christmas Day."

I was in shock. We didn't even know Churchill was expected until the news broke on the 22nd that he had arrived at the Washington airport. So I had only gradually adjusted to reading about his presence at the White House last Monday and Tuesday, and then on Wednesday afternoon after Washington shut down for the holiday, the colonel sprang this on me.

I sound like I hated it. The truth is, I was thrilled right to the bottom of my toes to be in control of this massive undertaking. I was going to meet one of my great heroes—

one of the greatest men who has ever lived. Just knowing that kept me going from six in the morning until long after midnight for the next two days. Now, finally, I'm comfortable in my bed—after soaking my weary, tortured feet!

We held a meeting in our office Christmas morning to determine just how many we could invite, and then everyone scampered off to their Christmas dinners—but me. It was my lot to make all the calls, and as the session was to be held on Friday at half past noon, I was on the phone all day and far into the night calling each person, extending an invitation, and telling them where to pick up their tickets. I addressed the envelopes for the tickets until nearly three in the morning, then fell into bed with fatigue.

Senator Barkley insisted on keeping his private luncheon very small: Vice President Henry Wallace, Colonel Halsey, and the members of the official reception committee, which included three members from each house of Congress. Representing the Senate were Senator Charles McNary of Oregon, the minority leader; Senator Walter George of Georgia, who is head of the Foreign Relations Committee; and of course, the majority leader, Senator Barkley. The House sent the ranking majority member of the Foreign Affairs Committee, Luther Johnson; John Boehme, Jr., of Indiana; and Earl Michener, a Republican from Michigan.

The clerk of the majority, Leslie Biffle, was also included at the luncheon, and Colonel Halsey invited me to sit in on the remarks after everyone was finished eating. He didn't have to ask me twice!

Churchill was amazing. He had entered our office before his address. Senator Barkley presented me to him, and he gave me the warmest smile. He was dressed in a somber three-piece suit, a perky polka-dot bow tie, and a white handkerchief in his breast pocket. He is mesmerizing in person—a man who looks piercingly at you and really seems determined to remember you. He has wonderful sparkling eyes.

A bit of a flirt, I think—or was that my imagination?

We were aware of how historic his speech would be. It was the first time in history that a wartime premier of Great Britain had addressed a joint session of Congress. And Senator Barkley had given permission—also for the

first time in history—for radio broadcasting and motion-
picture facilities in the Senate chamber. (My staff had to
deal with all those arrangements too!) As we entered the
chamber, I was momentarily overcome by the great lights
that beat down on the packed dignitaries. We had managed
to stuff six hundred people into a chamber designed for one
hundred. The cabinet and the Supreme Court occupied the
seats of honor, along with Lord Beaverbrook, the British
minister of supply, who had accompanied Churchill to
Washington. Behind them sat the diplomatic corps and the
members of Congress, former members of Congress, and
the military brass. One amusing thing happened with the
seating: Viscount Halifax, the British ambassador, was at
first seated beside Maxim Litvinov, the newly appointed
Soviet ambassador. After an awkward few moments, our
chief of protocol, George Summerlin, came to the rescue
and moved Lord Halifax a few seats over. The galleries
were filled largely with congressional wives, who had come
as early as eight a.m. to get seats. I've never seen the Senate
chamber so packed and jammed!

And what a speech Churchill gave! Needless to say,
Washington has no lack of splendid orators. We are a city
of connoisseurs of the spoken word. But we have never
before been treated to the likes of Churchill.

When first we entered the chamber, the silence was complete: respectful, filled with awe. But when the vice president announced "the Prime Minister of Great Britain," the
applause and cheering engulfed us. Mr. Churchill took two
bows, smiling warmly at the horde of faces turned toward
him, smiling out at them through a barrage of micro-
phones and hot lights. Then he launched into his prepared
address. We—all of us—were enthralled by his simplicity,
his turn of phrase, his understatement, his humor, and his
lusty words of denunciation for Hitler and Japan and Mus-
solini.

Shortly, I began to notice that the audience nodded with
him at every word. The applause that interrupted him was
at first enthusiastic, then thunderous. Then cheers broke
out—something I have never before witnessed in the Senate chamber. Finally, in midspeech, Churchill was re-
warded with a standing ovation. It made my heart sing

when I saw, at the end of his speech, that the leading die-hard noninterventionists were standing beating their hands together and cheering like schoolboys at a soccer match. And just before he left the chamber for our luncheon, he raised his hand with fingers outstretched in the V symbol he's so famous for. God love and save Winston Churchill! It was a speech I'll never forget.

Then I scurried back to our office to make sure everything was in order. Only minutes later he arrived, escorted by the vice president and Senator Barkley and the colonel. I greeted Churchill and added my words of praise, and he asked me if he might use a phone. I ushered him into Colonel Halsey's office and asked if I could be of further assistance.

"Yes, Mrs. Dunay. If you would be so kind, I understand Senator McFarland's wife is hospitalized and very unhappy that she couldn't be here today. If you could get her on the phone, I'd like to speak with her."

I was astonished. At the moment of his triumph before the Congress and the American people, he was concerned about calling a hospital, calling a senator's wife! No wonder all the world reveres him!

After he finished wishing her a speedy recovery, he used the colonel's bathroom, and I directed him into the luncheon.

I'd arranged a menu of turkey with dressing and cranberry sauce—after making sure Mrs. Roosevelt hadn't served the same thing the day before. I'm told he ate with great gusto and seemed particularly to enjoy the spring onions, of all things—it seems they are rare in England these days. After two glasses of port and a few puffs on a cigar (ugh!), the vice president rose to thank the PM. It was at that moment that I entered the room and took a seat in the back—I'd had Bruno, the headwaiter, alert me when the toasts began. But Churchill didn't respond with a toast. He gave another speech! And I was one of two dozen people present to hear it. Talk about being present when history is being made! I felt like pinching myself to be sure this wasn't one big dream.

First, he warned us against overconfidence and underrating the enemy. Then he said we shouldn't attempt an offensive before "the Army and Navy are adequately equipped with all the modern machinery of assault." He thanked the senators present for all the assistance America has already given to England. "Hitler might soon be tempted to invade Great Britain as a measure of desperation. I am confident, if these events come to pass, Germany will fail. Indisputably, we have superior air power. It remains my hope that Spain will not permit the transit of Nazi troops through the country to strike a blow at Gibraltar."

He reiterated his respect for those members of the Congress who had taken a viewpoint against America's entering the war. "We must respect their opinion and their loyalty."

He is the consummate diplomat!

When the luncheon was over, Churchill personally thanked me again for all my efforts. Halsey had told him I'd given up my Christmas. I took advantage of that moment to ask him to sign the two autograph books I keep on my desk for Charles and Gilbert. He did so with a flourish, then said, "Mrs. Dunay, when this conflagration is over with, as I'm sure it will be soon, you must come to England and let me arrange for you to see our grand country."

"Oh, Mr. Prime Minister, I'd be so thrilled!"

Of course, it will never happen. But what a lovely fantasy to nourish! Imagine having him as my host!

Then he left. After about a half an hour, Senator Barkley stopped back by the office and walked directly to my desk. "Anna, dear, you outdid yourself. Everything came off without a hitch! You handled everything splendidly. I'm just terribly grateful." And then this morning, when I arrived at the office to finish up the loose ends, I found two dozen long-stemmed roses on my desk with a card saying "Thanks again, Alben Barkley."

All in all, it was a Christmas I'll never forget.

Mama and Pa have been taking care of the boys since Wednesday afternoon. I haven't even seen them for a moment. But tomorrow I'm going to dedicate myself to them —and to my parents. I know they are both on pins and needles waiting to get a blow-by-blow account from me. Pa admires Churchill even more than I do—if that's possible.

Addendum (12/28/41): Late this afternoon an impressive package was delivered to my desk from the White House. I opened it to find two leather-bound copies of Churchill's speech, both autographed by Churchill. He had made notations throughout one of them, changing his prepared text to what he actually said. Attached to that copy, he sent a handwritten note: "Mrs. Dunay, my gratitude for your efforts. You decide which son gets the copy with the corrections. After all this is over, I expect to see you in England! Churchill"

Three weeks later, in the late afternoon, Anna's assistant called out, "Anna, Senator Landow is calling you on line three!"

Anna quickly picked up the phone.

"Anna, it looks as if we may have some luck with your in-laws. But I want to warn you, it will be expensive to get them out—lots of palms to be greased, legitimate expenses—"

"Of course, Senator. I expected that. How much money will you need?"

"Five thousand dollars each. I've already advanced ten thousand for you. You can pay me when it's convenient. But I thought you should know."

Anna felt as if a large stone had dropped into the bottom of her stomach. Her entire life savings, since her first job at Hecht's, amounted to a little less than eight thousand dollars. She'd never dreamed it would cost so much. What would Claude say if she spent all their savings?

"Anna, do I sense some hesitancy? You can take a few years—"

"No, Senator, I'll have the money—within a week, I'm sure."

"Fine. But remember, as far as I'm concerned, there's no rush. If we can bring them out, that's all I care about. It's worth every dime."

"Yes." She could hear the indecision and hesitancy in her own voice. Where would she get all that money? What would Claude say? *But it's for his parents, for goodness sake!*

She sat at her desk, a sick feeling overwhelming her. Then she dialed her mother's number. "Mama?"

"Anna, what is it? What's wrong? Are the boys sick?"

"No, Mama. The boys are fine."

"What is it, then?"

"Can I come over for dinner? I need to talk to you and Pa about Claude's parents."

"Of course, *shainele,* come over. What is it about Claude's parents? Have you heard from them?"

"No, but it seems we may have located them."

"Wonderful! Mazel tov! Why do you sound so tragic?"

"It's going to take money—lots of money—to bring them here."

"What's money when human life is at stake?"

"I need . . . Mama, I need ten thousand dollars. And all my savings come to a little bit less than eight thousand."

"So, I'll give you five thousand. Don't worry. Every day your father pesters me for money for the Hebrew Immigrant Aid Society, and I give him all I can spare 'cause they helped us get to this country years ago. But I'd rather give you money for people we really know, people who are kin. Of course I'll go to the bank tomorrow."

"Oh, Mama, you're wonderful! You never let me down!"

"For this purpose, it's a pleasure. I'm so delighted you've found them."

"Nothing is for certain yet, Mama. We've got to hope and pray and keep our fingers crossed."

"What's your connection? Your father will want to know."

"I'm sorry, Mama, I can't talk now. Not on the phone."

"Then come. Come tonight for dinner, and bring the boys."

"Anna, Anna, you look so pretty today! I like that color blue." Senator Harry Truman stood in front of her desk, smiling and holding out an envelope to her. "I'm just back from a weekend military briefing and one of the officers, a Commander Kurt Addison, asked me to hand-deliver this note to you. A brilliant young officer—too bad we don't have more like him. I understand you worked with him when you were on the Naval Affairs Committee staff."

"Yes, indeed. And he was known for his outspoken views

then, I can assure you. How nice of you to bring me his note. Thank you."

"Anytime, Anna, anytime. How are those two boys of yours? One Saturday, when things aren't so hectic, why don't you bring them down here and let me show them around? They could probably use a man in their lives."

"Why, Senator Truman, that's the nicest idea! I may take you up on that."

"We've all gotta pitch in together. War's an awful thing, the way it separates families. And your boys are just the age when a father is so important. What do you hear from Claude?"

"So far, so good. He seems to be spending most of his time advising the ship's cook about how to make their food more edible. And he's always writing asking for more warm clothes. The Atlantic must be awfully cold this time of year."

"Yes, I suppose it is. Well, I'd best be going. Lots of calls to return after being away for three days. Cheerio!"

After Truman left, Anna hastily split open the note and read it. Kurt's words were ominous:

Anna,
You mentioned that Claude's people had disappeared in Poland. I urge you to call in all your chits, leave no stone unturned in your efforts to get them out of Poland immediately. Go to Farley, Hull—anyone and everyone you know —and batter down their doors. It truly is a matter of life and death, no matter what anyone tells you. I love you, my darling. I hope everything is going well with you. I think of you constantly and dream of you at night. God bless!

K.A.

▨ Chapter 22

Late one afternoon, as Anna finished proofing the last piece of Colonel Halsey's outgoing correspondence, the phone rang. "Anna, this is Albert Landow."

"Yes, Senator." Anna felt her stomach lurch. Two months

had passed since she had received Kurt's note with its dire warning. Was Senator Landow's news good or bad?

"My news is not entirely good. We have your mother-in-law. It seems your father-in-law passed away some months ago. I don't know the reason yet."

Anna felt a sudden sense of relief. She hadn't been looking forward to seeing Bernard Dunay again—he was too much like his son. But she felt great happiness at the prospect of seeing Francine. "But you have her? Oh, that's wonderful!"

"Yes, I'm pleased. Now, listen carefully. I want you to leave the office exactly at six. Drive to the alley behind the Spanish ambassador's residence. I'll be there in my car—you can't miss my Senate tags—and we'll go directly into the servants' entrance. If you get there before I do, wait for me."

She followed his instructions precisely and found him waiting for her. Quickly, possessively, he took her elbow in his hand and walked her slowly toward the back door. "You must be prepared for the worst. She may not be well."

"I understand."

They rang, and instantly the door was opened by the butler. With a tense voice he announced, "Excellency is awaiting you, please come in."

The kitchen was a bustle of activity. A number of tuxedoed waiters were preparing to serve a dinner, and several women were huddled over a long wooden table setting canapés out on silver trays. The female cook was stirring something in a large pot on the stove. Next to the stove, sitting in a bent position, was an elderly woman wearing a babushka and a raggedy dark-wool coat. Hesitantly, her eyes searched Anna's. A spark of recognition flared, which Anna caught just as she turned away. Anna turned back, stunned, and concentrated on the old woman. Slowly, stiffly, as if in pain, the old woman stood and held out her arm to Anna.

At that moment the door opened, and in walked the ambassador, clad in a white tuxedo shirt without jacket or tie.

"You're here!"

Even as Anna floated toward the old woman, it registered in her mind that the ambassador had not addressed the senator by title or name. So much the better. The servants in the kitchen wouldn't realize who he was.

"Anna? It is you, Anna?" a hoarse voice whispered as Anna grasp the outstretched hand.

"Yes. Yes. Oh, my God! You're here. You're sick—you've lost so much weight!" She wrapped her arms around the sickly, pale old woman. Her body was so frail, it felt as if it might break like a dried-up twig. What had happened to the pink-cheeked, buxom, cheerful woman she remembered?

"Anna, God will bless you forever for saving me," she murmured in French.

Anna felt the senator's strong hand on her shoulder. "We must leave, Anna. They're getting ready for a party."

Stunned back to reality, she turned to thank the ambassador, but he had already vanished.

"Could I thank the ambassador?"

"No, Anna. You must never mention his assistance to anyone. Not ever. I have thanked him for you. Come, let's go."

The senator took the elderly woman by the elbow and slowly escorted her to Anna's car. "Will she be staying with you?"

"Yes. During the day my mother will have her at her home, at least for a few weeks."

"Good. I must caution you, do not let her speak about her escape to anyone other than you and your parents. If she does, it could endanger our efforts to bring others out. You must instruct Dr. Dunay very carefully." He closed the door on her side of the car and locked it. "Anna, get her to a doctor you can trust tomorrow. She may be carrying God knows what disease or infection."

"Yes, I'd thought of that too."

"And after she's had a few days to recover from her ordeal, I'd like to come by and ask her a few questions about conditions in Warsaw. We need to understand everything we can about what Hitler's goons are doing there. But don't let her talk to anyone else! Not yet."

"Senator, how will I ever thank you?" Anna suddenly felt as if she would lose all composure and break down and cry in front of this dignified man, who had demonstrated his humanity at great personal and perhaps political risk.

"You needn't thank me Anna. Can you imagine what satisfaction it gives me to know that I—no, that you and I together —have saved at least one life from Hitler's death machine? Will anything I ever do on the floor of the Senate equal the feeling I have at this moment, knowing that we have saved this woman's life? Drive carefully, Anna, and give me a call tomorrow afternoon to let me know how she is making out."

Anna climbed into her car, smiled at Francine Dunay, and reached over and kissed her again. Then, holding her frail hand, she drove toward her mother's home, where Sarah and Jacob and the boys were waiting to greet Claude's mother.

Sarah had dinner waiting for Anna and Francine. She had fed the boys and sent them out to the park with Jacob. Mama's usual good judgment, Anna thought. Sarah had realized how precarious Francine's emotional and physical health might be and had arranged for the three women to be alone for a while.

At the front door, Sarah did not even wait for the official introductions. She took one look at the bedraggled, elderly woman and hugged her to her bosom in a tearful embrace. Instantly, the women began talking to one another in Yiddish, leaving Anna out of the conversation. And she had thought she would be translating Francine's French into English for her parents! Wonders never cease. She hadn't realized the older generation would have an age-old language in common.

Now her mother was translating for Anna. "She's telling me that the Nazis built a huge wall, sectioning off a section of Warsaw just for the Jews."

Anna listened to the emotional exchange and watched her mother-in-law's expressive hands outline the dimensions of the ghetto.

"At first the Dunays thought they could avoid being put in the ghetto. They did not wear the armbands with the Star of David, and they continued to use public transportation even after it was forbidden to Jews. All Jews were supposed to be behind the ghetto walls by October 2." Sarah stopped translating to take a drink of tea, then resumed. "They stayed locked in their apartment and their offices for weeks, thinking they were safe, hearing terrible stories of life inside the ghetto. Then one day in December 1940, soldiers came and produced their French birth certificates and herded them off to the ghetto with only the clothes they could carry in one satchel."

Francine's face grew even more pained.

"Once they were there, they found the conditions terrible. Germans and Polish police guarded the gates on the outside, and Jewish militia guarded from the inside. Only those persons who had special permits could enter or leave."

Sarah interrupted her recitation. "Eat, Francine. Slow down and eat. You need the nourishment."

"Ah, ah, you are right. I have not had a decent meal since before we were taken to the ghetto. Only garbage—bread dough mixed with sawdust, potato peels—trash not good enough for pigs. But this—this is so good!" She sipped Sarah's chicken soup again, then took a small bite of the fluffy matzo ball. "After starving so long, this soup is the perfect thing for my stomach. Thank you, Sarah." Suddenly, a shy smile broke out over her face, reminding Anna of the splendid woman she had met in France a few years before. Francine looked closely at Sarah, reached over to squeeze her plump hand, and then said in a quiet voice, "We will be sisters. We will be new sisters, Sarah, you and me."

"Ah, yes." Sarah stood up and walked over behind her chair and bent down and hugged her from behind, planting a kiss on top of her head. "We will be sisters and we will be grandmothers together too. I hear the boys coming!"

The excitement of meeting the boys and Jacob was a bit much for Francine, Anna realized as she watched her mother-in-law visibly tire and slump into the soft chair in the living room.

"I think it's time to go to our house, Mother"—it seemed only right to bestow on her a title of respect; after all, she was Claude's mother. "The boys have school tomorrow, and I know you want to get into some clean clothes. Tomorrow morning, Sarah and Jacob will come get you and take you out to buy some American clothes. We'll make an American out of you in no time."

Francine rode to Anna's home in silence, sneaking shy glances at the boys, who returned glances of their own. Anna realized that these last hours had been a strain on Francine, and on herself as well. They had much to talk about, but it could wait until Francine was rested and on the road to recovery. During dinner, Francine had described the starvation in the Warsaw ghetto, and Anna had understood that her size was due not necessarily to illness, but more likely simply to starvation. She had been forced to survive for over a year on fewer than two hundred calories a day—with inadequate heat, no medical supplies, and a typhoid epidemic that erupted because the streets were strewn with corpses and raw sewage.

While the boys prepared for bed, Anna found nightclothes for Francine and settled her in the guest bedroom. She tucked the boys in, undressed herself, asked Francine if there was anything else she could do for her, then climbed into her own bed and picked up that morning's *New York Times*.

She had been reading for about five minutes when she heard Francine's bedroom door open. Presently, clad in an old bathrobe and slippers of Anna's, Francine stood at her open door and asked, "Anna, may I come in and speak with you?"

"Of course, Mother. What is it?"

Francine was carrying an old soiled and faded corset. A triumphant smile was breaking out all over her face. "Come, we must go to the kitchen. I need a knife, a sharp knife."

Anna's eyes grew large as she looked at the ugly garment and shrank from its fetid smell. "Let's just throw it away. You don't need to cut it up!"

"No, we must go to the kitchen. Come."

Anna reluctantly got out of bed, put on her robe, and followed the frail, indomitable woman back downstairs into the kitchen. She pulled out a large butcher knife.

Francine shook her head no. "A little one. I need a little one."

Somewhat annoyed with this silliness, Anna reached for a paring knife, then followed Francine to the kitchen table, where they both sat down.

With great care and precision, Francine split the fabric down the side of the garment in two places. She smiled at Anna again, then said, "For fourteen months I slept with this on my body. I worked in the ghetto hospital with this on. When I got too thin, I wrapped it around my body even tighter and tied it with twine." With nimble fingers, Francine extracted a long metal stay that appeared to be wrapped in surgical tape. With the knife, she split the surgical tape all the way down the eight-inch stay. As it split, Anna saw that it contained in reality two metal stays—with something wedged in between.

Francine extracted two sets of stays in all, each wrapped in surgical tape, each itself composed of two metal stays with what looked like a long, narrow strip of cotton padding in between. Francine allowed herself another full smile of triumph.

She moved a bit of the cotton aside, picked up something small and shiny, and held it in her hand for Anna's inspection.

"Diamonds! My God! You've brought diamonds!" Anna reached for one of the long stays and began pulling out diamonds: marquise, pear-shape, and an emerald-shape that Anna's eye told her was at least six carats.

"I don't believe it! Wait, let me get a dish." Anna got a cereal dish, and the two women sat picking diamonds, none smaller than two carats, out of the cotton packing.

Francine checked and rechecked to be sure she had every last diamond as Anna put the teakettle on. Francine then examined the cut and quality of each diamond.

Anna brought the tea, two cups, cream, sugar, and lemon, and sat back down. "Mother," she said softly, "tell me the story."

"Ach! Such a story of horrors. I—I don't know where to begin, Anna. The best I can remember, it was after Hitler instigated the draft. I began to have nightmares: dreams of horrible fires, bombs dropping, cities destroyed, always synagogues defaced and destroyed. Trained as a psychiatrist by Freud, I put a lot of faith in dreams. I analyzed myself, and I even went to a colleague to speak about my recurring nightmares. It was as if I were getting a message from someone that didn't really affect me personally—although you can see, of course, in the long run it did affect me and my husband. Well, the message was that Hitler was going to destroy Europe and especially the Jews. I spoke to Bernard, and he laughed at me. I even wondered myself if I was going crazy. We pretended not to be Jews, but who could we kid? We were Jews, we are Jews, we will always be Jews!

"I had a patient at the time who was a wonderful artist. He kept asking me if I would commission something from him. One morning after a bad nightmare, I had an idea. I asked him to copy our fine oil paintings: a Rembrandt, a Claude Lorraine, a Titian, two van Eycks, two Brueghels. One by one, as he copied them, I put his copies in the gilt frames and sold the originals. I never told Bernard, and he never guessed. Then I changed the money into diamonds and went shopping for a corset. After the Germans entered Warsaw in September 1939, I sold everything—the silver, my other jewelry, old coins. For almost a year I changed all the money I made into diamonds, repacking this corset every month. I wore it day and night. Bernard never knew. He thought the stress of the Nazi occupation had driven me over the brink. But I was determined to get out with the clothes on my back—and have a future somewhere. Of course, I was hoping it would be here with you and Claude and the boys. I hoped Bernard would come, too—but even if he'd been alive when your people rescued me, I'm not sure he would have come. I'll never know. Oh, Anna, how can I ever tell you how grateful I am to you for saving me? I love you so much, my dear! Even if I die tomorrow, it won't be at the hands of those Nazi butchers. Anna, they are a breed of monster like the world has never known."

"Francine, if it's not too painful—what *did* happen to Bernard?"

Tears filled Francine's eyes and slowly trickled down her sunken cheeks. "He couldn't adjust to the ghetto, to the filth, to thirteen, fourteen people to a room, no privacy, people having sexual relations in front of others, the loss of dignity. On the ninety-second day we were there, while I was working at the hospital—he refused to help out at the hospital—he injected himself with a lethal dose of morphine. He killed himself, Anna. He just couldn't take it, and he had lost faith in the possibility of escape. Who knows? Perhaps it's just as well. I'm not sure he would have come with me to America. He wouldn't have been able to stand living in the same city with Claude—the competition, the bad feelings between them were so intense. I just don't know."

Anna wiped her own tears from her face and assisted the elderly woman to her feet. "We must get you into bed. Tomorrow we'll talk some more."

Francine handed Anna the cereal bowl of diamonds. "These are for you, for saving my life. I want you and Claude to have them—your inheritance."

"How generous of you! But I couldn't accept them. Tomorrow, we'll get you a safety deposit box in my bank to keep them in. We'll select two or three for you to sell right away so you'll have your own money to buy some clothes and other things you'll need. And you must be sure to tell my mother the story of the diamonds. That's the kind of thing she'd do. She'll love it!"

Long after Francine was sound asleep and snoring, Anna

pondered the tale of horror. She wondered what, if anything, President Roosevelt could do to save those four hundred thousand Jews in Warsaw whose only crime was having been born Jews.

July 4, 1942

Dear Claude,

Last evening we celebrated the six-month anniversary of your mother's arrival with a small dinner at Mama's. You can't believe how close our mothers have become. Every morning your mother takes the streetcar over to Mama's house, they spend the day together shopping, playing cards, going to sisterhood functions at the shul, and visiting with all of Mama's friends. Then your mother comes back home and spends the late afternoon with the boys. It's been so marvelous to watch them become attached to her—she is a joy to behold. I wonder that she wasn't a child psychiatrist, such is her magic with the boys. She is teaching them French—and Polish too! She reads to them, tells them wonderful stories of Europe "in the old days," and does this all without being the kind of nagging grandmother that young boys hate. I feel so much better about the late hours at the office, knowing that she is home with them.

You will be pleased that she has gained back nearly all the weight she lost in the ghetto. She has rosy cheeks again, and a wonderful optimistic outlook. I envy her her ability to put the best face on everything. She says these months of living in Washington and making so many new friends are frosting on her cake! Imagine! Her personality is a real inspiration.

And her cooking! You didn't tell me your mother was such a wonderful cook. Every night, I come home to the most delicious aromas—the smell of freshly baked bread or a big pot of beef bourguignon. And her cabbage soup is positively the best soup I've ever tasted.

She has become something of a celebrity since Senator Landow began introducing her to a select few people he trusts. A celebrity because she knew Freud personally, trained with him, and so forth. Every now and then, she is invited to tea with some of the eminent Washington psychiatrists who are followers of Harry Stack Sullivan and Frieda Fromm-Reichman (who is herself a refugee from Austria). Francine's becoming more and more adept at English and therefore more comfortable with her professional peers. She assures me she has no desire to start a practice again. She wants nothing more than to enjoy the boys and a few friends, of whom Jacob and Sarah are first on her list. All in all, it has evolved into a very comfortable, warm family—you will be pleased when you come home.

I know you're not particularly interested in the boys, but I'm going to tell you about them anyhow!

You'd be proud of Charles. He's growing like a weed, and he's become an excellent swimmer and soccer player. As I told you a couple of months ago, he gets nothing but A's in all his subjects at Beauvoir and exhibits "leadership capabilities," according to Mrs. Blanchard, the principal. His greatest interest, of course, is the war. He follows it on the radio and in the newspapers. In the morning we have a slight tug-of-war over who gets to read the front section first! He's quite a *mensch,* if you know what I mean.

Gilbert, on the other hand, can be difficult. He is stubborn and has a bit of a mean streak. Your mother is working with him—she wouldn't like me to say that, she pretends she's only being a grandmother. But I sense her skills coming into play when I listen to them play chess or checkers. She has the boys help her with reading English—it gives them a sense of importance to be teaching their grandmother. Oh, she's a wizard, your mother is! Anyhow, Gilbert's grades and general behavior have improved a bit since she's been living with us, and I must give her the credit. She spends hours with each of them individually, and then she makes herself available for whatever they want to do together. All three of them love the zoo—they go at least once a week.

As for my social life, it continues much the same. All the gaiety is false. One feels guilty about buying anything new or going anyplace in the car, what with gas so scarce. People seem to be more prosperous, though. The Depression is finally over, I guess, but I hate to think we needed a war to pull us out of it.

Ah, well, I'm sure you don't need to hear all this. Just know that we're all fine, your mother seems to have recovered from the Warsaw trauma nicely, and my parents (though Pa is suffering from lung problems that worry me) are fine too.

There's so much more I'd like to write you—Roosevelt and his men are so frustrating at times—but discretion forbids free discussion in a world at war. I haven't had a letter in over a month. I hope there'll be one soon!

> Cheerio, love and kisses,
> Anna, Gilbert, and Charles

Do I dare write this letter? Anna wondered three weeks later as she picked up the precious cobalt-blue fountain pen that Kurt had sent her and addressed the thin air mail tissue. Well, I'll write it, and then decide if I have the nerve to give it to Admiral Pickford.

Dear Kurt,

I write with some trepidation lest it fall into the wrong hands. When you were here, you seemed to understand so well how to insinuate yourself into the bureaucracy, and I've always prided myself on my ability to squeeze what I needed out of the government, but this time I've come up against what feels like a concrete wall. Ever since Dr. Francine Dunay arrived from Warsaw and I've had first-hand evidence of what Hitler is doing to the Jews of Europe, I've been trying to convey it in a rational, nonhysterical way to the powers-that-be in the State Department and at the White House. Either I can't get a hearing, or if I do, nothing happens. I'm so frustrated and so damn mad at the very same people I've always had such a high opinion of—the whole lot of them, you know who I mean.

Thousands of refugees are being taken out of Europe, primarily through the good graces of Sweden, Spain, and Portugal. So we know exactly what we're talking about. It appears that hundreds of thousands of Jews are simply disappearing—no one knows where. We can't understand why Hitler is shipping German Jews to Poland, supposedly to work in slave labor camps, when there is a labor shortage in Germany. The rumor is that they are being killed with poison gas, but there is no way to get incontrovertible proof. And even if we had it, I don't know what good it would do. The President seems to believe that the only way to help the Jews is to win the war, though others have ideas.

I'm writing all this to you because I thought you might have some ideas for me—or be able to do something through some back doors—and also because I know you really care. You'll be pleased to know my mother-in-law is getting along fine and is a great help to me with the boys.

There's so much more I yearn to write you, but under the circumstances I will follow the dictates of discretion. Take care of yourself and know that my thoughts are with you always.

Love and prayers

⊠ Chapter 23

Spring 1943

Sasha's husband, Louis Bernstein, called Anna at her office with the dreadful news: "Anna, your dear mother has just collapsed and died at the entrance of B'nai Israel Synagogue. They've taken her to George Washington University Hospital, and Sasha is on her way there. Can you go to Jacob? He needs you."

Anna's head began to swim, then a terrible pounding took over. The papers on her desk in front of her swirled in her eyes. I can't faint. Dear God, don't let me faint. It can't be true, I was with her last night, I talked to her only an hour ago, she was getting ready to leave for the synagogue. "Of course, Louis. I'll go right now."

"Thank you, Anna. I'm so sorry. She was a great lady. Our lives will be diminished without her."

The sudden shock of Sarah's death devastated Jacob, who was sick himself with emphysema. During the ensuing days, Anna spent her time comforting Jacob and her brothers while

Louis took over arrangements for the funeral. Francine Dunay, who spoke of herself as Sarah's new sister, managed the food that poured in from friends in Washington's closely knit Jewish community. Sarah had long been a pillar of strength for Jewish immigrants. Now they came in droves to honor her.

After the funeral and after the family had completed the week of mourning, Francine Dunay came downstairs to the kitchen at two one morning to find Anna quietly weeping. Francine got herself a cup and joined Anna at the small kitchen table. After pouring herself some tea and sweetening it with preserves, Francine patted Anna's hand and held it in her own.

"It is good you should weep for your mother, Anna. It's important for your health to let the grief out. She loved you very much. Of all her children, I do believe she was proudest of you."

Anna smiled weakly, knowing Francine's words were true.

"One day she said to me, 'I wonder what would have become of us if we'd stayed in Russia, now with Hitler's troops ravaging and killing. I believe the most important thing I did in my lifetime was take my children and leave Russia. It was a terrible ordeal, driving that hay cart across Polish territory to Germany. And imagine—we thought we were safe when we reached Germany! We believed no one hated the Jews as much as the Poles! But we were wrong—the Germans hate us even more.' You see, Anna, before she died, she had the joy of knowing she had saved your lives."

Anna conjured up her memories of that awful trip. What she remembered most vividly was the hunger and the fear she had seen in her mother's eyes. "Ah, yes, Francine, she was a brave woman, wasn't she?"

"She said that God had put her on this earth to bring her family to America, to save them by bringing them here."

"History may yet prove her right, Mother. By the way, Senator Landow has invited you and me to lunch next week in the Senate dining room. He wants to see you again. He's so proud he was able to rescue you."

"Ah, such a nice man! America is filled with wonderful people, people who don't stop caring."

"Only a few, Mother. Only a few like Senator Landow."

Thanksgiving 1943

Dear Claude,

I realize as I write the date that you've been gone over
two years now. Such a long time to be away from us! You'd
hardly recognize the boys these days, they've grown so.
Charles loves St. Albans, especially the sports programs,
though he does well in his studies too. Gilbert can't wait to
finish up at Beauvoir and join his big brother at St. Albans.
You will be very proud of them.

*I wish it were true. Even now, with them maturing so nicely,
you probably wouldn't give a damn. How many times have you
mentioned them in your letters? Hardly ever. If you knew about
Charles studying Hebrew with my father, you'd be furious. I
must admit, I have mixed emotions about it too. I never intended
to raise the boys with any religion, but I can't seem to say no to
Pa. He's so lonely, so adrift without Mama. It seems the least I
can do is humor him and send Charles over there three times a
week so Pa can tutor him. Charles seems to love it, too, can't wait
to get up and get dressed on Saturdays and go over there for
Sabbath services. Well, it makes Pa happy, and what harm can it
do? Though why anyone would want to announce they are Jewish
in the world we live in today is beyond me.*

It seems the tide has definitely turned—the Allies are
finally winning the war. Actually, the news is better than
we'd had reason to hope it would be by this time. With the
Allies in Germany, it can't be long now before we have the
bastards begging for an end. I never know how much news
you get, so in case you haven't heard, things are improving
in the Pacific now, too, and the Japanese have been defeated at Leyte Gulf.

My good friend, now the vice president, Harry Truman
stopped me in the hall yesterday to ask about you. He
never fails to ask where you are and how things are going.
But he isn't much help on the issue that has us stumped:
What is Hitler doing to the Jews in Europe? They seem to
be evaporating, disappearing by the thousands every day.
Truman doesn't want to talk to me about that either. The
truth is that the Jews have very few friends in the govern-

ment of the United States, even though we'd like to think otherwise.

My social life is very quiet these days. We've all had colds lately—even though we do take vitamins, as you instructed—and I can't seem to find the energy to go to the few receptions I'm invited to. Your mother continues to be a great blessing in my life. She not only is wonderful with the boys, she manages to drop in on my father every day for a short chat, just to make sure everything is okay with him.

Believe it or not, things look so hopeful from the vantage point of Washington that senators are beginning to discuss what we will do in Europe after the war. I only wish it would be over and life could get back to normal!

Though sometimes I wonder if I really want you to come home. Dreadful thing to say! But in spite of the war and rationing and all the inconveniences, our lives have melded into a very comfortable family life. Between Francine and my father, I feel the boys have never been happier or better cared for. Mama's sudden death has made me realize how important family is, something I've neglected for most of my life. Suddenly, it seems so important to me—to keep together what I have, to cherish our quiet moments together, to value these dear elderly people and learn all I can from them before—before it's too late.

This evening we will have Thanksgiving dinner at Sasha's home. It will be the first time ever that we aren't going to Mama's, and it really feels strange. Of course, Sasha included your mother. She is always included in family dinners—everyone loves her. Last evening, she attended a psychoanalytic lecture—the Washington Psychoanalytic Society has been kind enough to put her on their mailing list for lectures and special events, and every now and then she goes. Her English is so good now that she enjoys the give-and-take of these sessions. I'm so glad to see her dipping her finger into her own professional world again, even though she claims that all she wants to be from now on is a grandmother. It seems a shame to let all that knowledge and experience go to waste. But Claude, I love her dearly. I couldn't ask for a finer mother-in-law. And she's so good for the boys!

Well, this is all for now. I hope your turkey dinner with all the trimmings is as good as I know ours will be, but I don't expect that will be the case. Write soon.

Cheerio,
Anna

April 1944

My darling Anna,

I can't resist the temptation to write you a note and say that the four days we spent together in Virginia Beach will give me the strength to get through the next awful months (I hope not years!) here in the Pacific. War is hell! But knowing I am so loved by such an incredible woman makes it possible for me to start each new day with zeal and renewed commitment. I do love you, Anna, and I know it's the kind of love that will last forever. If only the fates had decreed a different future for us—but perhaps I should be grateful for the wonderful times we've already enjoyed. Know that I love you.

K.A.

P.S. After you memorize this note, destroy it!

"Senator Landow, I'm so sorry," Anna whispered as the senator bent to kiss her cheek. She, along with much of the Senate, was attending the funeral of his wife, Esther, who had died an early death from cancer.

"It was merciful—her suffering was horrendous. Anna, please stop by my office late this evening. There's something I want you to see."

"Of course, Senator." Anna reluctantly let go of his hand, curious to know what he was going to show her. The line behind her stretched out, and she understood the protocol of these occasions. Senators were senators, even during a family tragedy.

Later that day, when she was ushered into his private office, she saw the full range of his grief. His eyes were red, the bags under them unusually pronounced, and a gray pallor had settled about his rugged face.

He asked her to sit on the sofa and retrieved a document from his desk. He sat next to her. "What I have here is a report, written by two Slovakian Jews who have escaped from the Nazi death camp at Auschwitz. It is based on their two years as inmates, and it details the geographical layout of the camp, the conditions of daily life, the squalor and filth and starvation and beatings, and—Anna, this is going to be hard for you to understand—the systematic gassing and cremation of as many as twelve thousand Jews each day."

Anna gasped involuntarily, then felt as if she might vomit. She ordered her stomach to quiet down, then looked back at the senator. "Then it's true!"

"I don't like to inflict this on you, but perhaps you can help our effort."

Anna nodded affirmatively, then waited for him to continue.

"It seems they have four large gas chambers—but you'll read it all when you type it. I don't have another copy, so first of all, I need you to make as many copies as you can—perhaps eight? Good. Then, if you will, rack your brain as to who to give it to in the administration. It must reach Roosevelt, and I'm not certain the State Department types will forward this document to him."

"What is it, exactly, that you want Roosevelt to do?"

"Good question, Anna! I love the way your mind works— you always get right to the heart of the matter. We want Roosevelt to order a bombing attack on Auschwitz and on the railroad that leads to Auschwitz. Now wait, Anna, we've thought this through carefully. True, a bombing attack will kill all the current inmates. But we have reason to believe Hitler is preparing to ship all the Jews in Hungary—indeed, the deportations have already begun—to Auschwitz. Anna, that's nearly 800,000 human beings he plans to murder. And we can stop it if we bomb the camp and the railroad leading there. We can save nearly 800,000 lives."

"Forgive me for questioning you, Senator, but how do you know this report can be trusted?"

"First of all, no one would write something so unbelievable if it weren't true. My sources, whom I trust totally, vouch for its authors. Second, it has been corroborated by a non-Jewish military officer from Poland who recently escaped from Auschwitz. It's true, no doubt about it. They are monsters!"

"Okay." Anna ordered her queasiness to go away. She

needed to be clearheaded. "Now, you want me to type as many copies as I can. To whom do you want me to give them?"

"Someone who will give them directly to the President."

"Okay, I'll give it to Steve Early. He'll do this for me, I'm sure. I can't guarantee that the President will read it. We need an executive summary."

"Write it, Anna. I trust you completely. And specifically note that the action required is the bombing of Auschwitz and the railroad leading there. It is clearly within the range of our bombing capability at the present time.

"Now, Anna, you mentioned to me several months ago that you have a good friend in the Operations Division of the War Department. That is where a decision to bomb or not to bomb will be made. Can you get a copy of this to him?"

Anna blanched. She had forgotten that she had mentioned Kurt to the senator. "Yes, I will give him a copy. Are you sure that's where the decision will be made?" Thank God he's been stationed in Washington for the duration. I don't know how I'd get it to him if he were still in the Pacific, Anna thought.

"That's where they make decisions on strategic planning and operations. If Roosevelt is so inclined, that's the office he'll turn to to implement his decision. He may even shift the decision to them in the first place."

Anna returned to her office and called her mother-in-law to tell her she would be home very late. Then she began to type the thirty-page document. She typed without reading it first, but she found herself so nauseated, she could barely finish it. By the time she was finished, it was near midnight. She carefully packaged six copies and locked them in the office safe, then took the top two copies and placed them in her briefcase. Before putting them away, she reread a description of one of the four large gas chambers:

"It holds 2,000 people. . . . When everyone is inside, the heavy doors are closed. Then there is a short pause, presumably to allow the room temperature to arise to a certain level, after which SS men with gas masks climb on the roof, open the traps, and shake down a preparation in powder form out of tin cans, . . . a 'cyanide' mixture of some sort which turns into gas at a certain temperature. After three minutes everyone in the chamber is dead. The cham-

ber is then opened, aired, and the 'special squad' of slave
laborers carts the bodies off flat trucks to the furnace
rooms where the burning takes place."

How can it be? Are there really men in this world who can
gas twelve thousand people a day, day after day, without going
mad? Or must they be mad to begin with?

Anna closed her briefcase, walked briskly down the corridor,
saluted the policeman, and walked out to find a taxi. Tonight,
she thought, after I've a good stiff drink, I must write a cover
memo to Steve Early and to Kurt. Then we'll see what kind of a
man Roosevelt really is.

Delivering the package to Steve Early the next day was simple. She called his office and announced that she was bringing a
document for the President, that it was essential that it be
placed in his overnight reading, and that it was from Senator
Albert Landow. Steve assured her he would do exactly that.

Then she went to the War Department and asked for Captain
Addison. Surprised by her unannounced arrival, his face was
pleased, though a bit pink, when he came into the reception
room to receive her.

"A surprise! Let's go get a drink. My working day is over by
about four hours, anyhow," he said as he glanced at his watch.
It was nearly eight in the evening, and Anna had grabbed only
three hours' sleep the previous night. She wanted to get home,
but she also wanted to impress on Kurt the importance of this
document.

They left for Ebbitt's Grill after Anna called Francine to tell
her she would again be late. "Don't worry, darling, the boys are
playing chess, and Gilbert is beating Charles. You've never seen
Gilbert so excited!" Francine was a gem!

As they settled in the dining room, Kurt announced his own
news: "Your husband's ship captured a German submarine, and
Claude is interrogating the officers, getting us lots of good information. His language ability is phenomenal."

"Ah, so he's a hero!"

"Absolutely! Aren't you proud?"

Anna forced a smile, wondering how much good Claude had
done, wishing she didn't feel so disloyal sitting with Kurt. Then
she turned to the business at hand. She explained the document

and its origins to Kurt, then told him that what was really desired was a bombing attack on Auschwitz.

"It would be feasible," he answered as he tapped his fingers on his glass. "But there's very little sentiment in the War Department for the Jewish people. Unfortunately, most of the officers reflect the populace at large, and that's not good, Anna."

"My sources believe that the decision will be made within the next seven days. If you can possibly influence them to bomb the camp, you will save hundreds of thousands of lives."

"Hey, you don't have to convince me, sweetheart. I'm convinced. It makes all the sense in the world, and we're stationed in exactly the right spot to carry out that attack."

"Then you'll try?"

"I'll give it my best shot. Unfortunately, the brass doesn't always listen to mere captains. Even brilliant ones—just as White House staffers don't always take seriously the suggestions of savvy women like you."

She reached for his hand, needing that human touch, that reassurance of love in a world every day growing more hideous. "We've got to do what we can. I couldn't live with myself if I didn't try."

"Understood. But if we don't succeed—and the chances are about one in a thousand that we will—I want you to know you've done everything you can." He paused, then said, "Anna, dearest, how I wish I had it in my power to reorder the world for you, to make you totally happy. But that's too much to ask. None of us can do that. I love you."

On Monday, June 26, Kurt called Anna to tell her the bad news: "They've decided against bombing because they consider it impracticable. It could work only with the 'diversion of considerable air support, which we consider essential to the success of our forces now engaged in decisive operations.' Basically, Anna, there are offensives in the works that I can't tell you about but that will lead to a German surrender. The feeling here is that the best way to help the Jews—and by the way, we have information that there is more than one death camp—is to end the war as quickly as possible. They're unwilling to divert any forces from that effort. I'm sorry, I truly am, but I gave it my best shot. You should know, just for your own information, that there was no pressure from the White House for us to make any other decision. They simply don't believe the purpose of the armed forces is to rescue people. It is to win this war—period."

"Oh, Kurt. That's terrible!"

"Yes, it is. It wouldn't take much of a diversion of forces to go in there and wipe out Auschwitz."

"Do me a favor, Kurt. Call Senator Landow and explain it to him. Perhaps he can intervene in some way."

"Perhaps, but I doubt it. He's campaigned so strongly for the Jewish refugees, they see him coming. He won't get much of a hearing, either here or at the White House. But I'll call him anyhow.

"And Anna," he added, "my suggestion to you and Landow is that you go to the press—the world press, call 'em all in—with what you have shown me. The press can't continue to ignore your evidence."

"Yes, but by the time the public reacts, those 800,000 Hungarians will have been murdered. That's the tragedy of it!"

Five months later, Anna received a late afternoon call from Steve Early at the White House. "Anna, I'm officially authorized to request a two-week leave of absence for you beginning in late January to accompany the President on a most important mission. You will be reporting directly to me."

"Oh!"

"Yes, I thought you'd be pleased. But this is top secret, and you mustn't discuss it with anyone. I can't even tell you where you'll be going, except that it'll be out of the country—someplace in Europe. So get the necessary shots and so forth. Now, I know you have two boys. Can you arrange for them?"

"Steve, you're so thoughtful. Yes, my mother-in-law lives with me. Between her and my housekeeper, everything will be fine. The rest of my family is here in Washington too. So I'll definitely be aboard—you can count me in."

"Okay. When it gets closer to the time of the trip, I'll square it with Colonel Halsey. In the meantime, not a word to anyone. Now, enjoy your Christmas. By this time next year Claude will be back home with you, I guarantee it."

"I hope so. And Merry Christmas to you, too, Steve."

As she hung up, she once again felt conflicting feelings toward the President she, for the most part, admired but who had refused to save the Hungarian Jews in the face of incontrovertible evidence. A deep sadness crossed her mind: Mama won't be here. I won't be able to share my adventure with her. Mama, Mama, can you hear me? I love you!

▨ Chapter 24

1945

Anna stood huddled with dozens of White House, War Department, and State Department staff outside Washington's National Airport. It was bitter cold. She clutched Sasha's silver fox coat even tighter around her neck to ward off the chill. It wouldn't do to get sick on this adventure, she told herself. She wished one more time that she knew where they were headed so she could at least tell her father. Of course, that was exactly what the White House was trying to prevent. This was a top-secret mission, hundreds of lives were at stake, and they couldn't take the chance that the enemy might discover the President's destination. Everyone knew that German spies had infiltrated Washington—no one could be completely trusted.

"Number 7, board now," the voice over the loudspeaker dictated. That was Anna's plane. She stepped forward and walked as fast as her high heels would permit to the C-54 that was parked about three city blocks away. A naval aide had already confiscated her large suitcase. She carried only a small bag in which she had packed "necessities" sufficient for the next forty-eight hours. "Bring your warmest clothes," the White House directive had stated, and "dress comfortably for the trip, as you will not be able to change clothes for forty-eight hours."

When she arrived at the top of the ramp, a naval steward took her name, then directed her to a seat. Her adrenaline was flowing as she tucked her bag under the seat and settled back to watch the others board the plane. She recognized Assistant Secretary of State Dean Acheson, followed by Secretary of State Edward Stettinius, Jr., and his aide, Alger Hiss. So many people were going on this trip—over three hundred in all, Steve Early had told her—that it seemed the entire government, or at least the foreign policy part of it, was moving out of Washington. She looked around, nodding to acquaintances, smiling to people she didn't yet know. The plane was filling up, but the seat next to hers remained empty. She reached into her pocketbook and pulled her small mirror out just far enough to see her hair—a bit windblown, but still in good shape nevertheless. At that moment, she sensed a man preparing to sit beside her. She glanced up—"My God! Kurt! It's you!"

"You must know I wouldn't miss a chance to sit next to the most beautiful woman in Washington."

"You knew!"

"For about a week now. The Navy is in charge of the arrangements. We're responsible for the safety of all those flying to the conference. Last week, I happened to see the list the White House sent over, and I requested a very special seatmate. Hope you don't mind."

"But when we were together last week, you didn't even tell me. You rat!"

"You didn't tell me either." His eyes sparkled with love and admiration. "So we're even."

"I don't even know where we're going." She watched his face. He *did* know. "Tell me, Kurt, where are we going? What's going on? Is Germany about to surrender?"

"Whoa! Not so fast. I don't think that's in the works, not yet." He tweaked her chin, kissed her lightly on the cheek, and said in a teasing voice, "I'm afraid you'll have to wait till we're airborne. Then I'll make an announcement. I'm forbidden to speak of our destination until that moment—and I do follow orders!"

"Yes, sir, Captain, sir!"

"And I don't abide freshness from colleagues, Mrs. Dunay!" He grinned down at her, then kissed her lightly again.

"You'd better stop that, Kurt. People will see."

"Yes, we'll both have to behave ourselves. But what fun we can have after everyone else is asleep!"

"Tell me, is this really as dangerous as Steve made it sound?"

"You bet it is! It's probably the most dangerous thing you'll ever do in your life. In fact, a strange thing happened yesterday. What we're most afraid of is enemy fire, but yesterday a plane carrying our British counterparts crashed, and seven people were killed. Not a good omen for us. Buckle your seat belt, young lady—or should I do it for you?"

He chuckled and looked at her with so much love, she felt she might melt. *At least he's here with me. I can't think of anyone I'd rather be with in a dangerous situation.* She looked at him and whispered over the roar of the engine, "I love you, Kurt."

He reached for her hand, held it tight, and blew her a kiss as the plane sped down the runway.

Anna looked out the window, watching the Capitol, the White House, the monuments pass under her. *Will I ever see this city again?* she wondered. Yet she felt strangely calm—certain, in fact, that she would return and all would be well.

"Now, my dearest, I'll tell you where we're headed. We're going to Yalta, a Russian resort in the Crimea, for a meeting between Winston Churchill, Joseph Stalin, and Franklin Roosevelt. And to get there, we have to cross the Atlantic Ocean, the Mediterranean, and the Black Sea—all dangerous territory. Now, if you'll excuse me, I've an announcement to make."

Kurt went to the flight deck, and Anna recognized his voice, sounding gravelly, over the loudspeaker. "Ladies and gentlemen, for those of you who have not been informed of the details of this mission, I am now authorized to tell you where we are headed. Later, I'll be walking through the aircraft to answer any questions you may have. First of all, for those who don't know me, I'm Captain Kurt Addison, attached to the Operations Division of the War Department. The Navy Department is responsible for the safety of everyone on this mission, as well as the logistics, the accommodations, and most other details.

"Our first stop will be Bermuda. We anticipate arrival at Kindley Field in approximately three hours. You will be able to stretch your legs in Bermuda for approximately six hours before we are wings up for Lagens Airport on the island of Terceira. Our flight across the South Atlantic will take all night. After a day in Malta, we will leave for the Saki Airfield in the Crimea. We anticipate arrival at Yalta on February 3.

"Please be assured that we have done everything possible to guarantee your safety on this trip. Navy destroyers have been stationed at 300-to-500-mile intervals across the Atlantic, from Bermuda to the Azores. We have planes with rescue equipment on alert in Bermuda. Because of the hazardous nature of the trip, we will maintain radio silence across the Atlantic, and we will be flying with our lights off. We have twenty C-54s making this trip, and they will be flying the same route but at different altitudes.

"One last detail, then I'll come down the aisle and answer your individual questions. We have stationed the U.S.S. *Catoctin* at Sevastopol as our communications ship. Though that is eighty miles from Yalta, we've arranged a courier service to deliver messages. I trust all of you have informed your families that in an emergency, they can contact you through the White House switchboard. Hopefully, none of you will have emergencies back home while we are in Yalta. Now, I'll be coming down the aisle."

Anna thought of her journal. She had packed it, certain that this would be a journey worth recording for posterity. But it was in her large suitcase. She took notes to transcribe into a narrative after they arrived in Yalta. Suddenly, her body shuddered, then broke out in goose bumps. It was truly the adventure of her lifetime, Kurt was right.

After a while Kurt rejoined her.

"Were there lots of questions?" she asked.

"Some."

He seemed preoccupied, very serious. In fact, he seemed quite worried. "Kurt, what's wrong?"

He looked at her, his eyes unusually wet, his skin a gray-white. "I've—I've just received some troubling information. . . . I really can't discuss—oh, hell, Anna, why should I not tell you?" He looked as if he were going to confide in her, but then he changed his mind. "No, it'll just make you worry. No sense in both of us worrying."

"Tell me, Kurt. If I know what it is, perhaps it won't be as scary. You know you can trust me."

"We just discovered that Hitler knows all about the conference—where, who's going to be there—everything. It makes a mighty tempting target for his bombers. I wish I could understand the man, understand how his mind works."

"My God, that's awful! Does the President know Hitler knows?"

"Yes. But the President has decided the conference is too important to postpone or cancel. We're to continue exactly as

planned. Anna, my darling"—he reached again for her hand—
"this is far from a carefree adventure at a resort!"

> *February 5, 1945*
> *Yalta, in the Crimean Peninsula*
> *11:45 P.M.*

It feels so good to stretch out on this bed and relax. I've been up since five this morning, after only four hours of sleep the night before. I can't believe the living conditions: I'm sharing a room with four other women. The beds are lined up like those in a dormitory. But I'm told this isn't so bad. Over at Livadia Palace, where the President is staying, we have as many as seven generals in one bedroom and ten colonels in another! As bad as the bedrooms are, the bathrooms are an even greater problem. We have eleven people using one bathroom here in this guesthouse. Between five-thirty and nine in the morning, people stand in line to use the bathroom.

But I must go back and begin with our arrival at Saki Airfield. After a frightful landing on an ice-coated runway, we immediately repaired to three refreshment tents, where we found buffet tables laden with large glasses of hot tea, vodka, brandy, and champagne (it was early in the morning!), large bowls of caviar, black and white bread, butter, cheeses, smoked sturgeon, and salmon. It was clear from that beginning that the Russians were pulling out all the stops as hosts.

When the President's plane arrived, he stayed aboard until Prime Minister Churchill's had landed. Then he was let down to the ground in a specially designed elevator. He was lifted into a jeep, and he and Churchill reviewed the troops with the Russian foreign minister, Molotov. A crack regiment and a wonderful band that played "The Star Spangled Banner," "God Save the King," and the Soviet anthem (I don't know the name) saluted the President and the Prime Minister. Never have I felt so proud of the President—to come all this way, knowing how dangerous it is, and himself a sick man. He looks deathly ill. I only hope he lives out the war. My friends seem to think the Germans will surrender by midsummer. I hope so.

Churchill looks as sprightly as ever, always chewing on his eight-inch cigar. He seems to defer to Roosevelt a bit. (I didn't get a glimpse of Stalin until this evening. The shocking thing is, he has something wrong with his arm—it's limp, just sort of hangs, and is shorter than the other arm. Strange, I've never read about that in the press.)

After Roosevelt finished reviewing the troops, they lifted him into a sedan, and we all followed after—a long drive, nearly eight hours, to the resort town of Yalta.

The countryside between Saki and the Russian village of Simferopol (hope I spelled that right) was gloomy and uninteresting, mostly rolling hills with very few trees. We saw the remnants of German bombing: burned-out barns, freight trains, tanks, and fields. After we passed through Simferopol, we climbed up a high mountain range—the scenery suddenly turned beautiful—and then we descended to Yalta. Considered the swankiest beach resort in all of Russia, Yalta is situated between the mountains and the Black Sea—it really seems black! We're told the harbor is still mined—that's why our communications ship is docked at Sevastopol. We arrived late in the afternoon, yet we were greeted by brilliant sunshine and a warmer air temperature. The President is staying at Livadia Palace, which is a former summer palace of Czar Nicholas II, built in 1911. That's where all the plenary sessions will be held, and they wanted to make it as convenient as possible for FDR because of his polio.

Meanwhile we peons are living at a guesthouse, crowded into small bedrooms. Our house is guarded around the clock by stiff Russian guards, and we are driven everywhere by Russian soldiers. We simply write out where we want to go, and they make a guttural sound and drive off. I hope it's safe—I don't have much choice.

As for what I'm doing: lots of menial things I would never be called upon to do back in the Senate. For example, we have countless logistical emergencies to deal with. We had to set up a mess hall upstairs in the palace to accommodate the American delegation and staff. There's endless typing to be done. We type a document, then wait for changes, then type it again ad nauseam. And there's cable traffic to record and route to the appropriate officials.

I'd hoped that at some point I'd get to sit in on a session

*with Stalin and Roosevelt and Churchill, but that doesn't
seem likely. Believe it or not, they aren't keeping a steno-
graphic record of the meetings. The men take notes themselves whenever it occurs to them. So there will be no one,
unified report of the meetings, only each person's notes.*

Kurt, however, gets to sit in on some sessions. He partici-
pates in all the meetings of the chiefs of staff of the three coun-
tries. Lucky him! There are times when I dearly wish I were a
man.

*The Russians work all night until five in the morning.
Then they sleep until ten. So the conferences and meetings
don't begin until after ten. They meet all day long in small
groups and have plenary sessions in the afternoon from four
until eight. This afternoon, exactly twenty-three men went
into the room that the czar once used for a ballroom and
discussed the end of the war and how they would divide up
Germany after it's all over. I found out that much from my
friend Averell Harriman. He tells me that Roosevelt is trying to be the arbiter and conciliator between Stalin and
Churchill—that, in addition to presiding over the conference
itself. Churchill is eloquent and skillful, he says, and Stalin
is blunt and sometimes undiplomatically direct. We all call
Stalin "Uncle Joe." I wonder what the Russians call FDR.
The other bit of information I picked up is that Eisenhower
and Montgomery expect to cross the Rhine shortly after
March 1. Hurray!*

*After the plenary session this evening, FDR had Stalin
and Churchill for a small dinner. I skipped out with a
friend and had a late dinner at a small bistro in the heart of
Yalta. Now I'm so exhausted, I'm going to set my alarm for
five a.m. and try to catch some sleep on this bumpy mattress
—and hope the Germans don't decide to bomb us in the
middle of the night.*

"How did you ever get a private bedroom?" Anna asked as
she followed Kurt down into the basement of one of the guest-
houses set up for the American delegation staff.

"I'm good buddies with one of the men charged with accommodations. After I saw your name on the list of White House

personnel, I made a beeline to his office and told him I needed a private room—it could be a hole in the wall, which this is—but I needed my privacy. I told him I snore very badly and didn't want to disturb my fellow officers." Kurt opened the door with his key, kissed Anna's cheek as she walked past him into the room, and added, "I'm not altogether certain he believed me."

"In that case, let's hope he doesn't see us together." Anna was weary. It was nearly midnight, and once again she'd been up since five with not a moment's rest all day. Nevertheless, she was delighted to have a chance to be alone at last with Kurt. She sat on his bed and carefully drew her stockings down her legs. She had to be very careful, as she'd run two pairs already on this trip, and she had only one more perfect pair in her suitcase.

She looked at his face and realized he was just as tired as she was. After removing his coat, shirt, and tie, he sat down beside her on the narrow bed and rested his hand on her thigh. "So how do you feel about being a participant in a Big Three conference?"

"Mainly exhausted. It reminds me of nothing so much as a political party convention—unbearable tension, last-minute changes, lots of big shots to ogle, and lots of work to be done. Not enough sleep, meals eaten on the run—it's a good thing you and I are still relatively young. Oh, Kurt, I'm so tired. Hold me, please hold me."

He held her close, nuzzling her ear with his lips, caressing her magnificent black hair. "Tell me, Anna, why do you seem so down? Things are actually looking up. We in the military are very optimistic."

"I don't really know. Maybe I'm just tired. No, that's not it. I guess—crazy as it sounds—I have mixed emotions about the end of the war."

For a long minute, the silence in the room reverberated in Kurt's and Anna's ears. Then he held her apart from himself and looked into her eyes. "You dread him coming home that much?"

Anna felt her eyes moisten. She would not cry—not here, not now. Besides, this conversation was crazy! "I don't know. I'm not sure I understand myself anymore. I used to know exactly what I wanted. Now I don't. But of course I want the war to end. Everyone wants the war to end."

"I remember when your major goal in life was to become rich. You couldn't wait to have a big house and servants and expensive clothes. By the way, I like your fur coat, I've been meaning to tell you."

Anna shook her head, anxious to set him straight. "That's not my coat, it's my sister Sasha's. I can't afford a fur coat, not on my salary."

"Not even with a husband who's a doctor?"

Anna couldn't hold his gaze. She looked down at her hands and began twisting her wedding ring. "Claude isn't one for spending money." She decided to let it go at that—that was disloyal enough. Impulsively, she added, "Besides, while he's in the Navy, he certainly isn't making the kind of money he would if he were in private practice. Believe me, it's a sore spot with him too!"

"Have you thought about leaving the government and going into a business of some sort? I'm sure you'd do very well."

"The truth is, I love what I do, being in the center of things on the Hill. But I do wish I made more money. I just don't know."

"You're not thinking of divorce, are you?"

Anna could hear the disapproval in his voice. She had never contemplated divorcing Claude, yet she heard herself answering, "Perhaps—we'll see."

"Oh, Anna, that would be so hard on the boys! Why not try a change of career? That might be exactly the right thing for you to do after this mess is over with."

"What will you do?"

"There's no doubt I'll stay in the Navy. When we finish with Japan and Germany, our next enemy will be Russia. Mark my words."

"Yes, I suppose so." Anna paused, sighed, reached for his face, and planted a long kiss on his lips. "I do love you, Kurt, and you are exactly the tonic I need tonight."

"I was hoping you'd feel that way. Here, let me do that for you." He reached behind her to help her unfasten her bra.

They made love with slowly building passion, comfortable with one another and confident that each knew how to make the other feel the depths of pleasure and love. Afterward, as they lay in one another's arms with newly quiet hearts, Anna dared ask a question that had bubbled to the surface of her conscious: "You're going to stay in the Navy—and maintain all your previous vows and responsibilities, then?"

"Yes." He answered slowly and thoughtfully. "I'm sorry if that disappoints you. I wish it could be otherwise."

"I don't know if it disappoints me. If you were willing to desert your wife and children, I'm not sure I'd respect you enough to continue loving you. I don't know—human emotions are so complex. I only know that I love you, and I wish we could belong to one another. I understand why we can't, and I respect your decision. But that doesn't mean I'm happy about it."

"Anna, darling, if you only knew how I yearn to spend the rest of my life with you. But the fates didn't decree it. We didn't meet before I was married and had children. If we had, things would be different. When I'm in your arms, in your world, I find it seductive, and it tears me to pieces to have to pull away again and go back to my little domestic scene. But I have responsibilities, and I don't see that changing anytime soon."

Anna brushed away a tear that had formed in the corner of her eye, kissed his neck, and closed her eyes. She would make the most of the few hours she had left to lie peacefully in his arms. Five o'clock would come soon enough.

When the pilot announced that they were within an hour and a half of Washington, Anna sighed, feeling inexplicably sad, but about what she did not know. She glanced at Kurt, who was sleeping in the seat beside her.

Well, she still had lots to write, she told herself as she opened her journal and resumed her narrative.

The high point of my trip occurred on the last night. I was stationed immediately outside the dining room where the Big Three were to dine with about twelve others. It was Churchill's night to be host. While we Americans were waiting for the arrival of President Roosevelt, Churchill, looking his usual dapper self and puffing on that horrid cigar, came downstairs and approached the table where I sat. I would not have presumed to speak to him, other than to say "Good evening, Mr. Prime Minister." But he came directly up to me and said, "Anna, I've been racking my brain to recall your name. I've caught your eye several times, and only this

*afternoon did I realize that you are the Anna of the
leatherbound speeches. Remember?"*

"Why, Mr. Prime Minister," I said, "I'm ever so flattered
you remembered. That speech enjoys a place of honor in my
library, you may be sure." Perhaps I batted my eyelashes a
bit much, for he continued in a most flirtatious manner,
"Anna, I never forget a beautiful woman. Never! I only
regret we don't have time for a quiet drink together." Then
he left for the dining room to make certain everything was in
readiness.

Well, you can believe that after that, I took a good razzing
from my friends, who were terribly jealous.

When the President arrived a few minutes later, he
looked the worst I've ever seen him. Extremely tired and
chalk-white complexion. I'm relieved to know he's getting a
bit of rest aboard ship now; God willing, he'll soon be safe
back in Washington.

My friends in the military tell me that even though we
expect to defeat Germany soon, it may be 1947 and a million more casualties before we succeed in defeating Japan.
That's one of the reasons why this conference is so important. It seems that Roosevelt was able to convince Stalin to
enter the war against Japan as soon as we secured the surrender of Germany. The good news is that General MacArthur entered Manila last Tuesday. (One of the great advan-
tages of hanging out with the military brass, as I have this
past week, is that I'm getting the inside scoop on what's
going on and what the military prognostications are.)

I'm so tired of typing, I'd like to never see a typewriter
again. The last night, Sunday, we stayed up all night preparing the final documents and communiqués for Stalin,
Roosevelt, and Churchill to sign at lunch on Monday. Then
they left for their various meetings elsewhere in the world,
but we had to clean up everything, cable Washington with
the language and information, and pack our bags.

I got a kick out of the fact that the last luncheon for the
Big Three was held in the billiard room of the czar at
Livadia Palace. It was there that Churchill said, about the
West's former disagreements with Stalin, "The fire of war
has burnt up the misunderstandings of the past." He has
quite a way with words.

If only that were true of my personal life! If only the fires of war could change Claude so that we might be more compatible —but perhaps that's too much to hope for.

After we finished packing, we drove in a long caravan to Simferopol and boarded a train for Saki. We left from the same airfield we arrived at, weary but feeling that it had all been worthwhile if we had truly succeeded in bringing the Soviet Union into a united sphere of action. The military brass are especially happy with the outcome of the conference because for the first time they feel there will be real coordination of military activities between Russia and the West.

At least, that's what Kurt tells me. He seems hopeful that this conference will shorten the war with Germany and save us countless lives. I wonder whether Claude will be expected to go to the Pacific theater after Germany surrenders, or will he be coming home? Kurt has no answers.

The pilot has called for seat belts fastened, so I'll put this away and prepare to see my splendid sons.

"Hmm, that nap did me loads of good," Kurt drawled. He sat up straight, ran his fingers through his hair, and smiled at Anna. "Don't tell me you've been writing all this time!"

"I wanted to record my memories while they're still fresh."

"It's going to feel good to be back in Washington after all this travel. Can you take a few days off?"

"I really don't know. I'd like to, what with my father ill."

"I didn't know, Anna. I'm sorry. What is it?"

"He has lung problems. But I think the larger problem is that he's never recovered from my mother's death. They were very close. My boys spend time with him, and my sister makes sure everything goes smoothly. We've hired a housekeeper around the clock."

"You must have been very nervous about going on this trip."

"Indeed. Every time I saw a courier coming in the building, I held my breath that it wouldn't be a message for me. I'll be relieved to get home and see all of them."

"I know the feeling. Traveling as much as I do is not conducive to family life. I expect it's even worse for a mother."

Yes, Anna thought to herself. And it's worse for me because I've been with you. Now I have to come back to reality, my reality. You, Kurt Addison, are an aberration in my life. I've got to think of you that way. You are not central to my life, only an aside, a parenthetical phrase, not the main event at all. And it becomes clearer all the time that you never will be the main event in my life. I've got to accept that, and stop this infernal hoping. It's gotten me nowhere. My children and my career—I wonder if you're right about a new challenge—are and must be the major interest in my life.

"Penny for your thoughts, pretty lady."

"Oh, they're worth much more than a penny."

He pulled a quarter out of his pocket and handed it to her.

She laughed, and her eyes misted as she looked at him and impulsively said, "I love you, Kurt Addison. I wish I didn't."

▧ Chapter 25

April 25, 1945

Dear Claude,

As I'm sure you've guessed, life is very bleak for me in Washington these days, what with Pa's death, followed so closely by the death of the President. My only consolation is that my dear old friend Harry Truman is now President. He may not be as brilliant or articulate as FDR was, but he has more integrity than almost any public figure I've known. He is your friend too; he never sees me but he asks about you—a deeply compassionate and considerate man. If I believed in prayer, I would pray for him, that he quickly learn all the things he needs to know to follow in FDR's footsteps. I shudder to think of him having to deal with "Uncle Joe"—or even De Gaulle, for that matter.

I get angry when I remember how frail and deathly FDR looked at Yalta. His doctor *had* to know he was dying. Yet no one took any steps to prepare Truman to assume the presidency, and here we are, in the fight of our nation's life against the worst monster the world has ever known—well, I could go on and on. You know how I am when I get my dander up.

The boys miss Pa as much as I do. They had become very close to him in the past few years. Charles spent at least three afternoons a week at his house, and when Pa was up to it, he went to St. Albans to watch Charles's soccer games and swim meets. Pa was really terrific about things like that. He also was great about explaining the war to the boys. He had a world map pinned to the wall of the dining room, and every time the boys visited, he took them in there and showed them where the troops were and what we'd accomplished recently. For a man who learned English late in life, he followed current events religiously.

And he was so looking forward to Charles's bar mitzvah. I never would have considered such a thing, but it seemed to mean so much to Pa. He taught Charles to read Hebrew fluently, took him to Saturday morning services—ah well, it's probably just as well. I never wanted the boys to consider themselves Jewish anyhow. And I know Claude would be adamant in his disapproval if he knew.

It's too bad medical science hasn't developed a pill to help one get over death and grieving—I could use it. Some days I wake up, and I don't even want to get out of bed, and you know that's not like me. But to lose Mama, Pa, and the President in such a short time seems more than I can bear. I never would have believed I could be affected so deeply—I imagined I was beyond all that. But enough of this. I shouldn't be writing to you about death, you see so much of it every day.

Your mother is my bulwark. On days when I feel I can't manage, she finds exactly the right thing to say to me to spur me on. An incredible lady. And now she's trying to be father, grandfather, and grandmother to the boys—and bless them, they are all trying to cheer me up.

And I should be feeling better. You know how the weather always affects my moods. Well, in spite of the war, in spite of death, the dogwoods and tulips are in full bloom again. Spring is nowhere more beautiful than in Washington. Remember the wonderful bicycle trips we took the first year we were married? All over Rock Creek Park, to Haines Point—the terrific picnic lunches we had—ah, it was so nice to be young and innocent and have our whole lives ahead of us. Those were the days!

Now, if you can just convince the Germans it's time to surrender, maybe you can come home soon. We can start over. For that's what it will feel like, I suspect—like starting our marriage all over again.

Do I mean this? What's gotten into me? Well, at least part of me does. That part that listens to Kurt. I've decided I'm going to do my damnedest to pull this marriage back together and create the best possible home life for the boys. Sometimes I feel as if that's all that counts.

By the way, I think your idea of investing in airline stock is a great one. I agree that when this war is over, people are going to want to travel more and more by air. It's the only way. After flying to Yalta, I can tell you I have a whole new appreciation for air travel. I've been trying to talk your mother into investing in some airline stock, as she has a few extra dollars.

I wonder if I should have told him that. He might try to take her money away from her. I've never told him about her diamonds stashed away in that safety deposit box. For the time being, they are probably appreciating in value just as much as if the money were invested. I really should pay more attention to things like that—after all, someday that money will go to Charles and Gilbert. Unless Claude gets his hands on it first.

As I write this, the United Nations Conference has convened in San Francisco to write the charter for the United Nations. Let's hope it all works, so our sons won't have to fight another bloody war when they are young men.

Everyone here sends their love and best wishes. Write soon—it's been over a month since we've heard from you.

Cheerio and kisses,
Anna

Anna glanced up from her steno pad and saw two naval officers enter the reception area. They were in and out all day. She turned her full attention back to the memo she was preparing for Colonel Halsey, only to be interrupted a moment later by the officers.

"Mrs. Dunay?"

"Yes?" She stopped typing and stood up. "What can I do for you, Commander?"

"Is there—ah, a room where we might have some privacy?"

Her heart began to pound in her head. Kurt. Something has happened to Kurt. "Yes, we can use Colonel Halsey's office. He's not here at the moment."

The two men followed her into Halsey's office and asked her to be seated at his conference table. They placed their hats on the table.

Anna shivered, even though it was warm in the room.

"What is it? What's happened?"

"Your husband, Mrs. Dunay."

My husband—yes, that's right. I have a husband in this war, somewhere in the Atlantic.

"He is missing in action, presumed dead. I'm sorry, Mrs. Dunay—he was a brilliant doctor."

Anna tuned them out. She didn't want to hear it, couldn't bear to know what her wishful thinking had wrought. Surely that wasn't it—you couldn't cause someone to die by wishing it, could you? *Could* you?

". . . be happy to drive you home, or to some relatives, if it would help . . . plan a memorial service. We're ready to assist you in any way possible."

Where are my tears? Why am I not crying? Shock. That's it, I'm in shock. Too many deaths, too many.

She had to force herself to speak. "Are you certain? Are you sure there's no mistake?"

"Yes, ma'am. We're certain. Can we take you home? We have a car outside."

"Yes. Yes, I must pick the boys up at school and take them home. I must tell Francine." Then the tears came, flooded her eyes and began to roll down her cheeks. I must tell her that her son is dead . . . her last blood relative—except Gilbert.

I'm all alone now. All alone with my two sons and my memories. This horrible, blasted war!

In the days that followed Claude's death, Anna received hundreds of condolence letters and cards. She singled out three to read and reread.

One was from the White House, a letter from the President.

My dear Anna,

You cannot know my grief in hearing of Claude's death. And when we are so close to victory, I can almost reach out and touch it. My conviction grows stronger each day that history has never experienced such madness. But thanks to brave men like your husband, this cataclysm will soon be over and hopefully, we will be able to create a world at peace—for your sons to enjoy and thrive in.

My prayers are with you, Anna, and thousands of young women like yourself. I only wish that I, as President, could have somehow spared you this grief by bringing events to a quicker end.

Courage, my dear. Eventually you will find joy in your life again.

Fondly,
Harry Truman

Another favorite letter, one she would treasure for her sons, was typed on official naval stationary.

Dear Anna, Charles, and Gilbert,

I am writing to you about your husband and father. I never had the opportunity to know him well, but on many occasions I had a chance to read about his exploits on board ship, and on one very special occasion I did meet him and share with his shipmates his delightful sense of humor. You see, he did an incredible imitation of Adolf Hitler. He wore riding jodphurs, carried a walking stick, and had developed a song-and-dance routine making fun of Hitler that was absolutely hilarious. It became quite famous in the Navy, and he was called on whenever the brass were entertained on the U.S.S. *Gaudalcanal* to perform his imitation.

On a more serious note, he had a wonderful record as a doctor. The men were very fond of him because he not only took care of their health but collaborated with the cook to improve their meals—both from a nutritional standpoint and a taste standpoint.

Perhaps his most significant contribution to the war effort, however, was his amazing language facility. The U.S.S. *Guadalcanal* captured the first German submarine, and Claude interrogated the officers, one at a time and together. From the information he obtained, we were able to predict certain naval maneuvers that the Germans were preparing and counteract them in advance. So you see, he made a tremendous contribution to the victory that is in sight as I write this letter. Someday, if I have the opportunity, I'd like to visit with you in Washington and tell you more about your father's military career.

I know this is a very difficult time for all of you, and my love and prayers go out to you. Be of good faith—everything will seem better in the months and years to come.

> With love,
> Kurt Addison,
> Captain, U.S. Navy

Attached to the long letter was a short handwritten one:

My dearest Anna,

What can I say that will help heal you from the enormous pain you are suffering? I think of you constantly and wish I could be there to offer some words of comfort in person. Even though you may have had ambivalent feelings, I know this is a devastating blow—and you've had too many of them lately. Try to be of good cheer, for the sake of your sons and Claude's mother. My love and prayers are with you. K.A.

And there was yet another letter she cherished:

Anna,

Even though I have the good fortune of passing you in the hall nearly every day, I take pen in hand to tell you my deepest thoughts. After my wife died, you were of enormous help to me. Somehow you understood, without a word passing between us. You have an enormous capacity to give to others—you do it every day. We men all talk about you—I'll bet you didn't know that. You are greatly admired in the Senate cloakroom. But that's not why I'm writing to you.

I want to be of assistance. Your bravery and fortitude are intact. I want to help you regain your rosy cheeks and good cheer. Is there a way I can help you with the boys? I've never had sons, and they need a foster father—perhaps you'll let me borrow them some Saturday for a baseball game or a trip to the zoo or the circus? How about it? I'll wait for a signal from you, but please know, I'd love to see those blue eyes sparkle with laughter once again—and I'd love to help make your life easier in any way that might be appropriate.

> Fondly,
> Albert Landow

"Is that the doorbell I hear?" Francine asked, looking up from her book at Anna, then Charles. "Your mother's so weary, Charles. Be a *mensch* and run downstairs and see who's at the door."

Charles put his biology book down on the coffee table and, with a loving smile to his grandmother, ran downstairs.

"I can't imagine who it could be this time of night," Anna said with a sigh as she put her *New York Times* down and smoothed her hair back off her face. "I'm so tired. It seems I'm always tired these days."

"Yes, we both are. That's a natural symptom of grief. Don't worry, with time it too will pass."

"In that case, the whole Western world must be tired. It's masochism, but I can't stop reading the accounts of the death camps."

"Yes, I'm the same way. They're even more graphic in the Yiddish and Jewish press, which I know you never read. It's probably just as well."

Anna looked closely at her mother-in-law. She, too, had lost weight lately, and her color was unusually sallow. But think of it, Anna told herself, her every friend, every acquaintance, every relative has been exterminated. It's as if, in my case, all the Southwest Jewish neighborhood I grew up in had been razed, everyone there sent to the camps—only multiplied by hundreds of thousands—it's incomprehensible.

From the front door they heard a jovial voice: "Charles, how good to see you, young man! Is your mother home?"

"Oh, yes, Senator. She's upstairs with my grandmother and brother."

Anna recognized the voice of Senator Landow. She stood hurriedly, glanced at herself in the Chippendale mirror over the bombé chest, then rushed to the top of the steps. "Senator, what a surprise. Do come upstairs. Mother is here, too, and she'd love to see you again."

As he walked up the steps behind Charles, Anna watched him affectionately tousle her son's hair. What a nice man he is!

When he reached the top of the steps, he kissed Anna's cheek affectionately, then walked across the room to greet her mother-in-law. "Dr. Dunay, so nice to see you again."

Gilbert, who had been playing with miniature soldiers in the corner of the room, jumped up and ran over to the senator, his hand extended. "Good evening, sir."

"Good, you're both here. Boys, I have a proposition for you. I've got three tickets to the Saturday game between the Senators and the Yankees at Griffith Stadium. How would you like to go with me?"

Anna couldn't help but laugh as she watched both boys' faces light up, then in chorus they asked, "Mom, can we?" She nodded her approval, then listened to the excitement.

"Gosh, Senator, that's really neat of you!"

"Yeah, that's great! Can we get Crackerjacks too?"

"I'm certain that can be arranged! So we've got a date. I'll pick you up here at noon. But now, I've a request of you. I've come to talk with your mom and your grandmother about some political matters, so maybe you'll leave us alone for a while."

"Aw, Senator!" Charles pouted. "I love to listen to politics. I read both the *Post* and the *Times* every day, and I know every battle in the war by memory. You can ask me any question, really!"

Gilbert added, "Yeah—me, too, Senator. Our grandfather taught us everything about the war."

He hugged both boys, then suggested they'd have their own political conversation on Saturday. "What we adults need to discuss is so monstrous, it's difficult even for us. You boys are too young to be burdened with the madness of the world. Now, run along!"

As the boys retrieved their belongings and headed upstairs, Senator Landow eased himself into the blue-brocade armchair. "Anna, do you have any brandy, by chance?"

"I'll get you some."

"Bring one for all three of us. We'll need it."

"The news is that bad, then?" Francine asked as she looked sadly at the senator.

"I've just come from the office. I've been sitting alone reading top-secret reports on the death camps. We on the Foreign Relations Committee are only now getting the full picture of what went on for the past five years. It defies imagination."

Anna returned, carrying a small tray with three brandy snifters filled three-quarters of the way to the top. "It sounds like you need a big one, Senator."

"Anna! How many times do I have to ask you to call me Al? I like to think we're good friends. At least, when we're away from the Hill, you might shift out of a staff mentality."

Anna blushed slightly. He had asked her many times, it was true. But she was so used to being perfectly proper with government officials, it was a difficult habit to break. Besides, he was too dignified to be an "Al."

They all sipped their brandy, waiting to see what he would tell them. He, on the other hand, was nervously trying to decide how to initiate this conversation, how to tell Francine Dunay that he now had positive proof that her brother and his two daughters had been exterminated at Treblinka. He sipped the brandy again, cleared his throat, then began. "Dr. Dunay, you asked me for any information I could get on those who were taken to the Warsaw ghetto. I think I now have a pretty clear picture of the sequence of events there. Are you certain you want to know?"

With steady eyes and a steady voice she answered him. "Senator—ah, Albert, through some miracle you and Anna worked, I am here today, alive and well, and loved by my daughter-in-law and two grandsons. I have a new life in America, I would even say it is a most enjoyable life, if only I weren't hearing daily news of what happened to everyone I knew in my previous life, and if only I hadn't received the news of my son's death. But I am alive, thanks to you. And that is the first law of nature —self-preservation. Yes, I must hear what has happened in Warsaw, and I must work my way through grief after grief if I am to continue to survive with my sanity intact. I must work my way through the guilt I feel for having survived when everyone I knew and loved is now dead. Dead in the most horrifying of circumstances." She paused, sipped on her brandy, and added, "That is what you have come to tell me, isn't it, Albert?"

"Yes. I was today informed that your brother and his two daughters were recorded in the *Totenbuch*, the death book, of Treblinka. It seems that they may have been spared for slave labor for a few months first, then gassed. I'm sorry, Francine."

"I had long since decided it was so." She wiped the corner of her eyes. "Now I can grieve properly."

Anna thought of her sister Sasha and her two children. Francine had lost someone just as close to her—it was pain beyond endurance. Tears filled her eyes. "Mother, what can we do to help you?"

"It is not necessary for you to do anything but be here for me. You have already saved me, my dear, with your love. That's all I need." She turned back to Senator Landow. "Tell me more. Tell me everything you know about Treblinka."

"Is that really necessary?"

"Yes. We must know so we can tell the world, what remains of it. So we never let it happen again. Tell me."

"Between July 22, 1942, when Himmler ordered the Warsaw ghetto to be 'removed,' and October 3, 1942, at least 310,322 Jews were taken to Treblinka and systematically gassed and cremated. In January 1943, he discovered that some 60,000 Jews were still alive in the ghetto. In April 1943, with much resistance by the Jews fighting in hand-to-hand combat, the last Jews were killed or shipped to Treblinka. The truth is that the entire Jewish population of Warsaw was rounded up and systematically murdered."

Anna sat silently stunned, wringing a handkerchief in her hand.

Francine looked steadily at Albert Landow. "I see." She sipped again on her brandy. "Are there any estimates of how many Jews in all Hitler massacred?"

"We have estimates all over the place, ranging from four million to six million. We probably won't know for years exactly how many were killed. The big problem we face now is resettling the ones he didn't kill. That's a battle royal, one we're struggling with every day in the committee."

"Albert, if the time comes, if you should hear of an opportunity, that I might be of assistance to refugees who need help readjusting after being in the camps, I might be able to use some of my old skills, my old training. Would you let me know?"

"Mother, that's a good idea. I hadn't thought of that. But only here in Washington—I'll not allow you to take leave of absence from your duties as grandmother."

Francine smiled softly. "You needn't worry, I have my priorities correct. But"—she looked again at Albert—"some refugees from the camps may be coming into the Washington area. I could perhaps be of assistance."

"I'll be on the lookout. You can be sure."

"How about a refill?" Anna asked.

"I have a good idea," Francine said when Anna left the room to refill the senator's brandy snifter. "Why don't you come back here for dinner after the baseball game on Saturday? I make a good cabbage soup—you'd like it."

"Now, that's the kind of invitation I don't even have to think about twice. I'll be here, and after dinner I'll challenge you to a game of chess."

"Oh, the boys will be very jealous if you play with me instead of with them!"

Anna came back in carrying the brandy. "What are you planning? I only caught a bit of it." After they told her, she suggested a chess tournament. "Play each of the boys, then play Mother. She'll beat you easily. And I'll make book on the outcome!"

Saturday afternoon, while the boys were at the game with the senator, Anna's phone startled her out of a much-needed nap. "Yes, this is Mrs. Dunay."

"Anna, this is Kurt. I'm calling from San Francisco. I've just received orders to the Pacific, shipping out tomorrow morning. I wanted to say good-bye."

"Oh, damn! I'd so hoped the war would be over for you now." She couldn't bear the thought of one more loved one hurt or killed. "How soon will it all be over with?"

"We'll beat those Japs in a year or so, I think. Maybe sooner, if Truman has the balls I think he has. Pardon my language, Anna, but it's the appropriate expression."

"Damn! I wish you weren't going. Why can't you get out of the Navy and find another career, one less dangerous?"

"Don't worry, I'll be back with bells on. You take care of yourself now, and remember how much I love you. Okay?"

"Okay," she responded, close to tears. "Call me whenever you get a chance, and write me. I need your letters, Kurt."

"I will. You can count on it."

After a hearty dinner, which included two bottles of red wine supplied by Albert Landow, and three games of chess between Gilbert, Charles, Francine, and the senator, Anna sent the boys to bed and offered the senator an after-dinner drink.

They drifted into a comfortable conversation about intrigues on the Foreign Relations Committee; Anna's professional reserve had vanished completely. Albert seemed less and less like one of her "bosses" in the Senate and more and more like a trusted old friend.

He unlaced his shoes and took them off, wiggling his toes in relief. Anna removed her high heels and tucked her feet up under herself on the overstuffed sofa. Francine had dozed off, only to be awakened by her own snoring. "Pardon me, I'm so sorry. I'm afraid you'll have to excuse me."

Albert stood to say good evening to Francine.

"No, no—you stay and talk to Anna. She needs the company. I'm going to get my beauty sleep." She offered her cheek to the senator for a good-night kiss, then bent to kiss Anna's forehead. "Good night, *shainele.* Have a nice talk with Albert. It'll do you good."

Albert told Anna stories about the boys at the ball game, then began reminiscing about his daughters when they were young. Anna had met them only once, at their mother's funeral. They were both married with small babies now.

Then their conversation returned to politics, only this time it was the Truman White House they discussed.

The evening grew late, yet Albert Landow showed no sign of leaving and Anna thoroughly enjoyed his company. Suddenly, she yawned. Immediately, he stood. "I've overstayed my welcome—forgive me, Anna. I can see you're tired."

"No, it's fine."

He looked at his watch. "It's after midnight. I didn't realize—"

Anna understood that he really was leaving, so she stood to escort him downstairs to the front door.

"It's been a wonderful day for me, Anna. May I borrow your sons again?"

"Yes, indeed. They seemed to love it. And Mother did, too—she loved beating you at chess."

"That calls for a return match!"

"I'm sure she'll be available—and even make cabbage soup. Anytime."

They reached the bottom of the staircase and stood immediately in front of the door. "And how about you? Do you have the time?" he asked, looking steadily down at her with twinkling eyes.

I do believe he's flirting with me, Anna thought.

"My life is dedicated to making life easier for United States Senators, you know that!" she responded in what she hoped was an enigmatic voice. Then in a softer voice she added, "It's been a lovely evening. Thank you for everything, Sen—I mean, Albert!"

"Good for you! You caught yourself." He bent down to kiss her good night. She began to turn her face to offer her cheek, but his hands caught her face. He turned it up toward his, bent, and kissed her squarely on the mouth.

After kissing her, he looked into her eyes to see her reaction. She was too stunned, too numb to feel anything but surprise. He sensed her shock. Abruptly, he said, "Good night, Anna. See you Monday."

And he opened the door and was gone before she could recover to say anything more to him. As she turned and walked back up the staircase, turning off the light as she went, she told herself, I've always thought of him as a senator—but he seems to think of me as a woman!

Part 5

The Vision Reborn, 1944

Hot young designer Karine Dunay missed seeing Berg-dorf Goodman unveil five windows of her scrumptious evening gowns yesterday. She was in Washington with her family, who are awaiting the outcome of her famous grandmother, Anna Dunay's, abdominal surgery, scheduled for tomorrow.

—Women's Wear Daily

⊠ Chapter 26

"Senator Landow for you, Anna," Brenda called from across the room.

Anna picked up the phone, delighted at the prospect of talking to the senator, who continued to surprise her with conflicting signals. Ever since that Saturday night three weeks ago when he had kissed her, he had been shockingly distant—almost cold—when they'd passed in the hall. Then, this morning, she had almost bumped into him at the revolving door. After insisting that she precede him through the door, he had gone out of his way to escort her to her office and had insisted on carrying her heavy briefcase for her. It had even seemed—she couldn't be sure—that he was flirting with her again as they walked down the hallway.

"I'm in the mood to be seen lunching with a beautiful, brilliant brunette in the Senate dining room today," his deep baritone voice now announced over the phone.

Anna took a deep breath, summoned a bantering tone, and responded, "Did you have anyone particular in mind? There are three women in this office who fit that description."

"Yes, I do. The lady who's been inhabiting my dreams lately has intense blue eyes, a perfect figure. Anna, tell me you don't have any other lunch plans. If you do, I'll kill him."

"My goodness! Such ardor, so early in the day! I didn't know senators were susceptible to spring fever."

"Anna, stop teasing! Meet me at the dining room at twelve-thirty."

"Senator, your every wish is my command. I'll be there."

"Now, that's the kind of attitude I like."

While she waited for twelve-thirty to arrive, Anna pondered the intentions of the senator from Connecticut. Was it simple loneliness? Or was he, from the goodness of his heart, trying to help her get over Claude's death? Was it simply that he missed the warmth of family life and knew her own small family was missing a strong masculine figure? Or was he romantically attracted to her?

That seemed so odd. It had been years since she had felt herself the object of passionate feelings from any man other than Kurt. But perhaps that was because she was so obsessed with her own feelings for Kurt that she had failed to recognize when men found her appealing.

I haven't wanted to appeal to men, she told herself. It's bad enough, agony enough, to love a man who belongs to another woman.

But neither Albert Landow nor I belong to anyone else, not anymore. We are free. Both of us.

He was waiting for her just outside the door of the dining room: tall, elegant in his three-piece navy pinstripe suit, his dark hair freshly trimmed and flecked with gray at the temples. He *was* handsome, and very distinguished-looking, she found herself thinking as she turned her cheek to receive his kiss and allowed him to grasp her elbow in a possessive way. He steered her toward the maître d', who immediately led them to a corner table from which they could see everyone entering the room.

Why is it I'm only noticing his stunning good looks for the first time? she asked herself as the tall black waiter pushed her chair closer to the table.

"Anna, you should wear blue every day. It makes your eyes even more beautiful." Albert Landow reached for her hand and looked deeply into her eyes.

She could think of no smart response in light of his deep sincerity. She murmured a soft thank you, then added, "I'd wondered if I'd upset you somehow—these past weeks. But I guess you've been busy and preoccupied."

A look of surprise crossed his face, then he squeezed her hand and began opening his napkin. "No, Anna, actually I felt that I'd presumed a bit, that perhaps I was intruding in your life —where I wasn't wanted or needed."

"Not at all," she said warmly.

"Since Esther died," he began tentatively, then stopped. "Well, it's a bit lonely. I keep busy all day and into the early evening. But going home . . ."

"I'm sure it's a terrible adjustment. At least I have the boys, and Francine. But there are days I'd gladly change places with you, Albert, days when I wish I could go home to total peace and quiet."

He nodded his head, understanding. "I sold our house. It was too much, too many memories. I've taken a small suite at the Wardman Park that's perfect for my needs."

They ordered lunch and talked of pending legislation and the latest gossip. Then Albert again grasped Anna's hand and urged her to talk about the boys. "I must find a free afternoon soon and take them to another baseball game."

"They'd love it, that's for sure."

"Now tell me, when's Charles's bar mitzvah? I trust you will include me?"

Her face turned pink. She stammered, "Ac-actually, we've decided to forgo that."

Stunned, he let go of her hand and pressed his napkin to his lips. "That's an awful mistake. Now more than ever, a Jewish boy must affirm his identity, must honor the tradition. Why, Charles was looking forward—Anna, you can't mean it!"

At a loss for words, Anna continued to blush.

"I'll help him prepare. I'll make the arrangements. I can't let you make this mistake! Your father would be so disappointed."

"Senator—Albert—you're much too busy. I can't even imagine—"

"Nonsense! Tell him I'll pick him up at eight this Saturday. We'll go to Shabbat services, and I'll take care of everything. Charles Dunay will be a bar mitzvah boy! That's settled."

Anna began to protest again, but he silenced her with his hand. "And there's something I want to ask in return." Senator Landow sipped his coffee, then continued, "I've so many social obligations piled up, I've decided to give a dinner party. I've reserved the Cosmos Club for six weeks from Saturday. And I've made a list of thirty couples."

That would be easy, Anna thought. Only a matter of writing invitations and working out a menu with the chef and arranging for the music. "And I'm hoping, Anna darling, that you will be my hostess for the evening."

Had she heard him correctly? Was he expecting her to be his social secretary—or had he said what she thought he had?

"Oh my, Albert! I don't know."

"I realize it will start tongues wagging. If you think it's too soon after Claude's death, I understand, of course."

She looked at him, trying to discern the feelings in back of his piercing brown eyes. What did he want from her?

"Am I rushing you, Anna? Am I intruding where I'm not wanted?"

"Oh, no! It's just . . . the newspaper columnists . . ."

"Yes, of course. It will quickly become gossip. In this town anything a bachelor senator and beautiful widow do together does. But are you going to let fear of gossip control your life?"

"Albert, I'd be honored, absolutely thrilled, to be your hostess. The gossips be damned!"

His face broadened into a full smile. "I'm so pleased, Anna. I can't tell you. And by the way, I have three tickets to the Boston Symphony for next Wednesday. Do you think Francine would enjoy an evening of Beethoven?"

Anna smiled slowly, reveling in the love she saw in his eyes. "She'd love it. And so would I."

As spring turned into Washington's humid summer, Anna's relationship with Albert began to develop a certain rhythm and routine. At least once a week he treated her and Francine to dinner in a nice restaurant, followed by either a play, an opera performance, or a concert. On Saturdays, he concentrated on Charles and Gilbert. A visit to the zoo or a baseball game at Griffith Stadium was followed by dinner with Anna and Francine—usually, but not always, cooked by Francine. On Sundays, Albert arrived promptly at ten with a bag of warm baked goods and *The New York Times*. After Anna and Albert devoured the Sunday papers, they set out on bicycles—with the boys, if they had nothing better to do—and rode for miles through Rock Creek Park. Late one Sunday evening in early June, as Albert kissed Anna good night, she looked into his dear brown eyes, so sad looking at this moment of departure, and spontaneously asked, "When are you going to invite me to dinner at your place?"

He held her back, looking at her with unspoken questions.

As a slow blush enveloped her, she understood the full implications of her suggestion.

He pulled her body close to his, then, and his strong arms encased her in a warm bear hug. "Soon, my darling, soon. I—I don't want to rush you. I don't want you to regret anything. Soon." He tilted her face up toward his and kissed her fully on the mouth. "You must know by now, there's nothing I want more." His seriousness suddenly vanished. In a voice filled with joy, he informed her that he didn't cook, couldn't even boil water. "But I do know how to order splendid meals from room service! That's the advantage of living in a hotel."

* * *

The following Friday, as Francine, Anna, and Albert were leaving Constitution Hall after a concert, he announced that he would not be staying for dinner the next evening. "I've been summoned to dine with Alice Roosevelt Longworth."

Anna felt an envious twinge in the pit of her stomach. Now, why hadn't he asked her to go with him to that party? That would really have been exciting. But with conscious effort, she kept her feelings to herself.

When he arrived with bagels and lox on Sunday morning, though, she couldn't camouflage her curiosity. He quickly understood and felt a surge of hope. "You know, Anna, I could kick myself. I should have insisted that Mrs. Longworth invite you. I never even thought of it. From now on, when I'm invited to dinners, I'll insist on bringing you. No one would dare turn me down."

She smiled up at him, batting her eyes deliberately. "And won't that start the tongues wagging? Are you ready for that, my dear senator?"

"I can handle it if you can." He bent down and kissed her forehead.

"And what will my boss, Colonel Halsey, say when he discovers I'm dating one of *his* bosses?"

"I imagine he'll be quite pleased. He'll believe it will give him an in with me—as if he didn't already have one with you in his office. I can just hear him whispering about our relationship to his cronies. Capitol Hill is one big gossip factory—you know that, Anna."

"Yes, and think of all the Senate staffers and their envy! Mmm . . . I'm going to enjoy being the object of their curious glances."

Two weeks later, true to his word, Albert Landow took Anna to her first "top echelon" Washington dinner: a black-tie affair at the home of the *Washington Post* publisher, Eugene Meyer.

After a sumptuous six-course French meal, the women retired upstairs to Mrs. Meyer's room, where they repaired their makeup, and the men smoked cigars downstairs in the library. Everyone had been very gracious to Anna all evening. She had especially enjoyed seeing Senator Alben Barkley's face light up in recognition and astonishment when he realized Anna was dating the widowed senator.

"Al, my boy," he had exclaimed, clapping Senator Landow on the shoulders, "you've got a fine young lady there—one of our finest. Why, Anna, here, she's like kin to me, I've known her so long. Now, you be good to her, you old rascal!" Anna had laughed to herself at Barkley's southern bonhomie, so misplaced was it with Albert Landow.

As she powdered her nose and replaced her compact in her evening bag, she saw Alice Roosevelt Longworth approaching her from behind.

"My dear, you must tell me about yourself. I've been hearing rumors of a mysterious lady in Albert's life, but I couldn't get the dear boy to spill the beans. I must say, you are a pretty thing. No wonder he's been keeping you a secret."

Anna turned and flashed her most dazzling smile at Mrs. Longworth, who was dressed in her favorite "Alice Blue Gown" color, an iridescent lace confection. She reached for her frail, veined hand. "Mrs. Longworth, I can't tell you how honored I am to meet you. I've been reading about you and your exploits since I was a child."

"Dear, this is not the way to start a friendship, by reminding me how much younger you are."

Anna blushed, momentarily speechless.

"But never mind, you're allowed one mistake with me. Now, sit over here"—she motioned to a small settee—"and tell me all about you and the senator. My word, how did you catch him? He's only the most eligible, wealthy bachelor in the whole city."

For the next five minutes, Anna gave her undivided attention to Mrs. Longworth, cunningly telling her only what she wanted spread through the salons and cafés of Georgetown. But even as she made small talk and answered Mrs. Longworth's piercing questions, one word reverberated through her brain: wealthy. Was Albert wealthy? If so, why had she never realized it?

I've simply never wondered, she thought as she followed the ladies back downstairs. True, he did upgrade the wines I had chosen for his party next week. And he insisted on having three musical groups instead of the one I had chosen. But I'm good at spotting rich people, and Albert has never displayed any of those characteristics.

"Darling, you look stunning. I'm the envy of every man here tonight. I can tell you, you're the main topic of conversation at this dinner," Albert told her the first moment they were alone and out of earshot of other guests. "You're doing just great. Now, relax and enjoy."

"Albert, you don't know me. I could never relax at a party like this. This is work, the real work of a senator. You know that."

"Yes, I do. But I want you to enjoy yourself."

"Oh, Albert, I am! I'm enjoying this evening immensely!"

Later, as they were driving toward Anna's home and she was wishing she could share the evening with her mother, he surprised her with an invitation that she had already heard hints of from the boys.

"I've a nice old house at Hyannis on the Cape. It's quite nice there this time of year, unless it's stormy, and then it's terrible. I'm hoping I can convince you to bring the boys and Francine and join me for a long Fourth of July weekend."

"Aha! So that's the surprise the boys have been giggling about."

"Yes, they've already accepted. And so has Francine. All of us hope you'll decide to join us."

"I see. Well, sounds to me like you've got everything under control. They'd lynch me if I said no." She nervously tapped her fingers on her evening bag, wondering again about his reputed wealth. Well, perhaps she'd see for herself. "It sounds like the perfect way to cheer up and recover from your big party next week. Of course I accept!"

Anna turned over one more time, shifted her long, damp hair out of her face, and reached for the clock. It was twenty-five minutes after three. Was this what Fitzgerald meant by "the long night of the soul?"

Goodness knows I've enough to keep my mind occupied, she told herself as she adjusted her sopping-wet nightgown and threw off the sheet. It must be a hundred degrees in this room!

When I was seventeen, Albert Landow would have been an incredible Prince Charming in my life. The answer to all my dreams: suave, handsome, cultured, well educated, and to top all that, wealthy and a United States Senator. And he loves me. There's no doubt, he loves me.

What fun it is to be his hostess, to order the finest foods and wine and music, to stand by his side while he welcomes guests —only the most distinguished people this city has to offer.

She had played tennis with him on his private court next to his "cottage"—only eighteen rooms, plus a guest house—on the Cape. She had watched him mix and serve martinis on the porch, all bronze skin, not an ounce of fat in spite of his age. She had seen him deftly handle the sails on his boat and seen the undisguised lust in his eyes when he watched her walk across the sand in her bathing suit.

He was a man who had no negatives. And yet . . .

Kurt.

Kurt was alive (she hoped and prayed) somewhere out in the Pacific, trying to win the war against Japan. Kurt, how I wish I'd never met you! You've spoiled me for all other loves! I just can't stop measuring the love I feel for Albert against the love I feel for you. Such a difference! Who would have thought the love men and women feel for one another could come in so many varieties, such differing textures and intensity?

Because she did love Albert, no doubt about it. She loved his tenderness, his sensitivity, his love for her boys. She loved his dignity and his basic goodness. His feelings for Francine and his consideration of her in everything they did were small examples of his innate decency.

And his wealth—yes, she loved that too. The knowledge that she'd never have to worry about money again, that her boys and she would always have everything they needed, wanted, wished for. Once I wanted great wealth more than anything in the world, would have walked on hot coals to get it, would have sold my soul for Albert's kind of wealth. Strange, now that it stares me in the face, it doesn't mean what it used to mean. Maybe that's maturity. Maybe that's good.

But the truth is that if Kurt were free to marry me, I wouldn't hesitate for a moment. I'd walk away from Albert's money and all his splendid qualities—yes, I'd even hurt him, much as I love him. I'd choose Kurt if I had the choice.

But he belongs to someone else. And there's no changing that.

Anna crawled out of bed, threw on a light robe, and made her way soundlessly to the kitchen. She opened the refrigerator door, took out a pitcher of iced tea, poured a glass, and sat down at the kitchen table. She heard footsteps padding down the carpeted stairs and knew she had awakened Francine.

Francine rounded the corner and came into the kitchen. "So,

is it the heat? Or something else? You need your sleep, *shainele.*"

"I know, I know."

Francine took a glass out of the cupboard, poured herself a cream soda, and joined Anna at the table. Before she sat down, she took Anna's chin in her hand and looked deeply into her eyes. "Would you like a diagnosis from your resident psychiatrist?"

Anna smiled at her, delighted she still thought of herself in those terms even though she refused to set up a practice. "Yes, indeed, Dr. Dunay. What's wrong with me?"

"I believe . . . I think you're conflicted over your relationship with Albert. And I want to settle one matter with you. Immediately. Now." She sipped her drink, then patted Anna's hand. "You mustn't imagine that I am in any way opposed to you marrying Albert."

"Oh, Mother, he hasn't even suggested that yet."

"Perhaps not, but he will soon. I know, I know these things. Anyhow, it would not offend me if you married him this week. After all, my son has been gone from your life for almost four years now. It's not good for a woman in her thirties to be without a man. Anna, women need sex as much as men do—we just feel it differently. If I know anything at all as a result of my training, I know that."

Anna felt herself blush to the core. It felt very awkward to have her mother-in-law say such things to her. There was no way her own mother would have said such a thing.

"Somehow—somehow, though, I don't believe it's loyalty to Claude that's troubling you. Something else, perhaps."

Anna began to protest, but Francine silenced her with her hand. "I do not wish to know the secrets of your inner life. Believe me, Anna, I am not prying. I only want to help you." She paused, sipped her drink, and resumed.

"Let me tell you a story about myself. I've never shared this with anyone. But my husband, my son—both are dead, and soon I will join them. No, don't stop me, Anna, it's a fact. Who can it hurt if I tell you my deepest secret? I know it will end here at this table. And who knows? It may help you sort out your feelings. One thing though, one thing I must say straight out, Anna. I hope you won't hurt Albert. If you find you can't love him, break it off. Soon. It's not fair to that dear man to keep him wondering, not when he loves you so.

"Now, my story. When I was very young—twelve, I think— my parents and Bernard's parents decided we should be married someday. It was arranged—oh, don't be shocked, Anna, most marriages among our people were arranged in those days in the old country. It was a perfect match. We came from identical families, and everyone understood that Bernard would follow in his father's footsteps and be a doctor, and I was a bright child, so my father agreed to have me educated. Of course, in those days, no one dreamed I'd want to be a doctor, too, and no one understood my determination and tenacity. I forced them, I forced them every step of the way.

"But to the point: I was betrothed to Bernard when we went to college and later to medical school. Every time marriage was mentioned, I put it off. Bernard didn't mind because, to tell you the truth, he was having a good time with the gentile girls. He was enjoying himself, and I had not yet awakened sexually, so I didn't even recognize the symptoms, not until much later.

"During my third year in college I met an incredible man in my chemistry class. A Greek god, he looked like to me, though in fact he was a German Catholic son of an aristocratic family. He, too, was planning on medicine as a career, though his first love was painting. His parents insisted he give up his art and become a doctor.

"Well, Anna—I hope I don't shock you too much—he taught me everything I know about sexuality. From him I learned more than I learned in any anatomy class, in any class on Freudian psychology. We were lovers from that time until he died in a freak auto accident in the Alps in 1936."

Anna's slack jaw evidenced her astonishment at Francine's revelation. "Did Bernard ever know?"

"If he did, he never mentioned it. No, it would not be the European way to make a big deal over a love affair. Arranged marriages and affairs of the heart were part of nearly every family's story, it seemed. Anyhow, Frederick and I made passionate love through medical school, through our internships, through our analysis—he became a psychiatrist too. We continued our affair after we both got married, he to a German Catholic woman of high birth, me to Bernard, as our parents intended."

"I'm amazed! You must have been so unhappy much of the time."

"Wrong. Most of the time I was happy and content. Oh, yes, there were moments of supreme frustration. I could never be with him at important times—holidays, anniversaries, birthdays, things like that. And sometimes six months would pass, and we wouldn't see one another. But always when we came together, it was as if we'd never been separated. What a romance! It was a true grand passion, the likes of which few human beings are blessed with. And somehow we made it work. And I made my marriage work too."

Anna sat pensively listening to Francine, wondering how their experiences compared, wondering what she dared to confide.

"Anna, dear heart, I am sharing this with you because it occurred to me the other day that perhaps you love someone with that kind of passion. Maybe that is why you are so slow to love Albert."

Anna sighed, stood up, and carried her glass to the sink. What was it about Francine that she could almost see into Anna's very soul, read her mind with such precision?

When Anna didn't answer and avoided Francine's eyes, she continued, "To my mind, Albert is a most attractive man. Distinguished, brilliant, affectionate, sensitive. He is everything you could possibly want in a man, Anna. I don't understand why you don't grab him."

"I agree with you, Mother. He is all those things. It's just that—well, I've gotten so used to living alone these last five years, and all the deaths have been such a shock. . . . I don't want to rush into anything I'll regret. Most of all, I don't want to hurt Albert."

"But do you love him?"

"Yes. I do love him."

"You say it with such a lack of enthusiasm."

Anna laughed. "I don't think it's the grand passion you describe with Frederick."

"I don't think Albert requires that kind of love. But do you love him enough to marry him?"

"I don't know. . . . I just don't know yet. I hope he'll be patient awhile longer."

"You'd better grab him, Anna, before someone else beats you to it! I may get in line myself!"

"Now, Francine, he already loves you. You'd really be formidable competition! I guess I'd better get on my toes. But now to bed!"

Francine and Anna walked upstairs to their bedrooms, their arms tightly around one another. How blessed I am, Anna thought as she kissed her mother-in-law lightly on the cheek, how lucky I am to have saved her! For myself and the boys!

"Do we have any plans for dinner tonight?" Anna asked Albert, a forced playfulness in her voice. They were seated in the Senate dining room surrounded by his colleagues and their constituents.

"Just cocktails at the Indonesian embassy. But I'm not crazy about all that spicy food, so name it, milady. Where would you like to dine?"

"I've a special place in mind. Are you sure I can choose any place, any place at all?"

"Any place that one tank of gas can get us to—it's gas that's in short supply, not money."

"You promise me, any place I name?"

He looked at her quizzically, a big smile playing on his eyes. "What do you have in mind? Something wicked, I can see from the look in your eyes!"

"Yes!" she nearly shouted at him, then looked demurely down at her soup bowl.

"Anna, the suspense is killing me. C'mon."

"I would like to dine with you at your apartment in the Wardman Park." She watched the expression in his eyes change from a broad smile to a very serious intensity. "If you like, I'll phone over and order the menu. We'll have beef Wellington, green beans amandine, strawberries Romanoff. . . ."

"Anna, you *do* know what you're suggesting. You're not playing games."

"Albert, I am thirty-eight years old, the mother of two boys, a widow who hasn't seen her husband in five years. Yes, I do know what I'm suggesting."

He reached for her hand. She offered it to him, and he squeezed it very hard. "I've been waiting for this. I've even been praying for this, Anna." His face once again warmed into a deep smile. "You can't know how much I've wanted to."

"Do you suddenly have the feeling, Senator, that all eyes and ears in this dining room are tuned in on us?"

He looked around, only to see several of his colleagues staring at him. They nervously looked away, then back, and waved at the happy couple. "Let's finish our lunch and get out of here. You are the very devil, Anna, inspiring me to such silliness right here in front of my colleagues. Shame on you!"

On the drive up Connecticut Avenue to the Wardman Park Hotel, Anna held Albert's hand tightly, willing herself to have the courage to let things happen, willing herself to relax. Albert opened the door to his apartment and ushered her in. He opened a bottle of champagne, poured two glasses, and toasted them with the words, "Anna, I do believe you are as nervous as I am! To our nerves! May this bubbly relax us!"

Simultaneously they set their glasses down and reached for one another. Gently, Albert moved Anna's hair back off her face and nuzzled her neck with feathery kisses. "My God! I haven't felt this excited, this giddy, since high school! What you do to me, Anna! It's unbelievable. I feel like I'm eighteen years old."

Anna grinned at him. "Sorry, I've seen eighteen-year-old boys recently, and they're covered with acne. You must be at least a few years older than eighteen. Besides, I've never been turned on by younger men."

"Hmm . . . you taste so good. I could do this for hours, just hold you close and breathe your scent and taste your neck. Oh, Anna, I love you so. Tell me, do older men—senators—turn you on?"

"One in particular," she answered, kissing him softly on the lips.

"God, I've wanted to do this for so long! Why have you kept me waiting so long, Anna? Do you specialize in torture?" he asked between two long kisses.

Slowly they walked toward his bedroom. "Senator," she retorted, "I seem to recall asking for an invitation to your apartment months ago. You turned me down."

He opened the windows, hoping the night breezes would refresh the humid August air, then adjusted the blinds. "I hope you don't mind, my darling, but I've ordered dinner for nine. I thought there might be something else we'd want to do first."

"I can't imagine what," she teased as she began to unbutton the high neck of her white-linen blouse.

"Hey, that's my job!" He rushed to her and began unbuttoning the blouse while she began untying his tie. Slowly, carefully they undressed one another, stopping to marvel at each other's bodies.

"Anna! You've the body of a teenager . . . so—so beautiful, so perfect."

"And you, sir, the body of a knight. Trim and lean and solid —and oh, so tan! Mind you, all that sun is not good for you!"

"And your skin is like rich cream, so soft, so luscious."

"Because I don't sit in the sun. I cover myself. And I'll look younger longer than all those women who bake themselves every summer!"

"Hush! No sermons now!" He peeled off her panties, and she reciprocated.

"My, I really do inspire you, don't I, Senator? I do believe you've reached new heights! If only your colleagues could see you now!"

"They'd be insanely jealous. They already are. I'm afraid you and I have been the butt of locker-room jokes for months now."

"Well, it's about time we got some enjoyment out of it, right?"

"Right. Now, Madame, allow me to place you on this throne," he said as he picked her up and placed her on the large bed, "so I can properly adore you."

Later, their passion spent, the second bottle of champagne half finished, Anna allowed herself to think through her reactions to Albert's lovemaking. How good it felt to be held and caressed again! How wonderful it was to feel overwhelmed by a man's sheer physical size, to be penetrated by his hardness, all the while experiencing the tenderness of his love, his deep concern! Yes, there were differences in lovers—and differences in love. Albert's love felt good, very good, to her.

After a splendid dinner of beef Wellington—she couldn't believe he had actually ordered the very menu she had made up on the spur of the moment that day at lunch—Albert switched on the evening news. President Truman's somber voice filled the airwaves: "Sixteen hours ago, an American airplane dropped one bomb on Hiroshima. . . . It is a harnessing of the basic power of the universe. The force from which the sun draws its power has been loosed against those who brought war to the Far East."

An announcer stated the hard facts: "This morning, Hiroshima was a thriving Japanese city of 344,000 people. It is estimated by the War Department that at least 60,000 people were wounded or killed by that one atomic bomb. It has also been revealed that the entire Japanese second army was quartered in Hiroshima, all presumably destroyed by this one bomb."

For a moment after the announcer finished, Anna sat in stunned silence, gripping Albert's hand. Then she found her voice. "This is the surprise you alluded to the other day."

"Yes, but I wasn't sure the President would elect to use it. There was a big doubt."

"Will Japan surrender now?"

"If they don't, we'll bomb them again. We have more than one atomic bomb."

"You don't approve?"

"I want the damned stupid war over with. We don't need to lose any more good men over there. But this wholesale slaughter of civilians, wiping out a whole city—I just don't know."

"Too bad we didn't drop it on Germany."

"Yes. If we were going to use such a monstrous weapon to win this war, we should have had it in time to use on Germany. I agree with you on that, at least."

"It should save lots of lives. Japan will surrender soon now, and everyone will come home." *I've just gotten out of Albert's bed, and I'm already thinking of Kurt. I'm disgusted with myself!*

"Our men won't be coming home that soon. Mark my words, we'll keep our officers there and rebuild Japan."

"You really think so?"

"I know so. Plans are already being made."

"Our people haven't spent enough—their lives, billions of dollars—and now we're going to rebuild our enemy? Where will it all end? How much more can American taxpayers be expected to shoulder?"

He took her gently in his arms. "We are now the greatest power in the world. There isn't a nation that can come close to us. And with that comes responsibility. We can't let a whole nation starve to death. But, my dearest, we—you and I—don't have to solve these problems here and now. Besides, I've got a better idea." He carried her back to his bedroom one more time.

▧ Chapter 27

The radio was tuned as loud as it would go, and the static was horrible. But even so, all work was suspended in Colonel Halsey's office, and the entire staff gathered in the front office to listen to the formal ceremonies marking the surrender of Japan. Eighteen days had passed since Japan had admitted defeat in the wake of the bombing of Hiroshima and Nagasaki. Now, as Anna listened to the sonorous voice of General MacArthur, her thoughts flew toward Kurt. She hadn't heard from him in over a month, and in that time her life had turned upside down. She knew that marriage to Albert Landow was inevitable, and with a large part of her being it was what she wanted—unless by some wild chance things had changed in Kurt's life and he was suddenly available to marry her. *If only I could see him for a few minutes, talk to him in person!*

As if wishing it made it happen, less than an hour later her phone rang, and Kurt's familiar voice rang out in victory. "I told you we'd accomplish the mission in less than a year!"

"My God, Kurt! It's so good to hear your voice. Where are you?"

"I'm in San Francisco, and by tomorrow afternoon I'll be in your office, impatiently waiting for you to finish your work and have dinner with me."

Anna felt a deep wound open in her stomach. "Oh, Kurt— it's—it's so good to know you're safe—and the war is over—no more danger. . . ." Tears were streaming down her cheeks in full view of her secretary, who quickly brought her a tissue.

"Hey, I'm okay. No need to get choked up now! C'mon, Anna! Where's that stiff upper lip?"

"Kurt—it's just that . . . well, things have changed."

His voice lost its bantering tone. "I know. We'll talk about that tomorrow evening. You can break away for dinner with a returning officer, can't you?"

"Yes, dinner. But that's all." How cruel! But what else she could do?

"I understand. Let's make it seven o'clock at the Occidental. Okay?"

He hung up, and Anna felt so overcome with emotion that she left her desk and retreated to the rest room. Such are the emotions of war and peace and homecoming, she told herself as she powdered her nose and refreshed her lipstick and perfume. In fifteen minutes she would join Albert in the Senate dining room for lunch with two of his most important political allies from Connecticut. He would expect her to look perfect. He had come to rely on her to examine every bit of political intelligence with her years of experience—and then give him the benefit of her insight. Oh yes, we have become quite a formidable political team, she told herself as she took one last look in the mirror and left the rest room. Walking down the marble hall and then the curving marble staircase she realized one more truth: I love it! I love the way he's made me a full partner in his career. I've been staff long enough. It's nice to be a "principal."

And following that happy thought was a bitter one: Perhaps this is compensation for giving up the love of my life.

The minute Kurt saw her from their favorite corner table, he stood. Tall and elegant in his Navy uniform, he wore all the signs of victory on his face, which broke into a warm, twinkling smile as she came closer. He reached for both her hands, kissed them, and enfolded her in a big bear hug. Silence swept the restaurant, as if all the diners intuitively understood what they were witnessing. After a long moment, waiters moved again, forks resounded on plates, crystal chimed.

Anna found herself thinking, He grows more handsome with age, with a handful of gray hairs at his temples. I forget how devastating he is when he's gone, when he's out of eyesight for a while. Oh, my God, Kurt, I love you so.

But aloud she said, "You look marvelous, Captain Addison! A bit ruddier than I remember, but fit and trim and not at all the worse for the war!"

"And you, my precious darling—you look positively delicious. Ravishing! Anna, I love you! You're the tonic this old sailor needs tonight. Here—sit down, and we'll order some drinks. Everyone is staring at us."

"Let them! Washington's witnessed thousands of reunions like ours these past few months. I'm so glad it's over, so glad Truman used the bomb."

They were both seated, but they continued to hold hands tightly. A waiter took Kurt's order of two double martinis with a twist of lemon, then left them alone to gaze into one another's eyes.

It was Kurt who broke the silence. "I've missed you so these past few months. It's been a positive ache in my gut. I've needed you so, Anna. You're beautiful—you get more beautiful with each separation."

"Kurt, we must talk."

He shifted in his seat, smiled wryly, let go of her hand, and smoothed his napkin on his lap. "Yes. Ah, my buddy Darcy has been sending me clippings from the various Washington papers. Sounds like you've made a real conquest this time. Sounds serious." He looked at her with clouded eyes that hovered on the edge of sadness, awaiting her confirmation or denial.

She held his steady gaze with her own. "It is. Albert Landow is one of the finest men I've ever known."

"And he would be a good stepfather for your boys?"

"He's already very close to them. A marvelous influence on them—better than their own father ever was."

"Anna, how splendidly you will play the role of senator's wife! The political confidante, the Washington hostess, the woman behind the great man."

She looked at him intensely, angry at the cynical tone in his voice while at the same time recognizing it as his way of dealing with his pain. "I would have liked to play that role in your life, Kurt. But it wasn't meant to be. Our fate seems to be to spend a lifetime loving one another but never really to belong to one another." She paused, watching him position and reposition his fork against the side of his plate. It was as if he couldn't bear to look at her. "Has anything changed, Kurt? Anything that might give me reason to hope?"

After a long silence, his eyes again met hers, and she saw tears welling up in them. Finally, he found his voice and said quietly, "No, Anna. Nothing has changed. My life will continue as before the war."

Anna, no longer able to look at the tears in his eyes, now cast her own down onto her fingers, which were twisting and untwisting a handkerchief.

They remained silent while the waiter served the cocktails, grateful for the interruption. Kurt lifted his glass to hers and said, "To your future happiness, Anna. I want you to have whatever it is you want."

They chimed their glasses, and Kurt downed his entire drink in four quick swallows. Anna watched him, alarm growing within her at the sight of his unhappiness.

Nervously, she teased the slippery stem of her martini glass with her brightly enameled fingertips. "You know, Kurt, Albert is too fine a man. I refuse to diminish him by—by cheating on him."

Kurt nodded his head, causing his chestnut waves to ruffle a bit. "Understood."

"Though nothing is certain—not yet, at least. We'll probably get married sometime next year."

"You know, Anna, I've had a restless feeling about you, it was as if I knew. After Claude died, I knew there was a good chance you'd get involved. Hell, I knew men would pursue you —and of course I was in the Pacific fighting the damned Japs and couldn't be here to protect my property. Hell, that sounds god-awful—you were never my property, and I never thought of you that way. But I've always loved you, Anna, since the first day I laid eyes on you."

"And I you. But it wasn't meant to be."

"So this is it, then. The end."

"I didn't mean to greet you with this. But perhaps it's best that we get it over with and stop living on fantasies and illusions. At least, I know it's best for me. I want my integrity back. I desperately want to feel whole again. Do you understand?"

"Yes, I do understand. But that doesn't stop me from feeling bitter, and angry. Right now, I'd like to go out and beat up a few people, or wreck a car, or slam a few thousand tennis balls against a brick wall."

Anna laughed at his rhetoric. "The tennis balls will get you in less trouble."

"Oh, Anna, God damn it all! Why do our lives get so screwed up? I hate this! I hate giving you up! Tell me something—do you love him? Do you really love him?"

"Yes, Kurt, I do. It's not the same kind of love as I feel for you, but I do love him." She put her empty glass down on the table and wiped her fingers, and with a deep sadness in her eyes and voice, she added, "I don't think I can make it through dinner. I'm sorry. If you'll excuse me, I'd better go. I need to be alone."

He stood, almost without thinking, from years of training in an officer's manners. "Before you leave, let me say one last thing. I love you so much that more than anything else, more than my own need for you, I want you to find the happiness that has eluded you ever since I've known you. I do hope—and pray, Anna—that Albert will give you the steady happiness I've never been able to give you." He kissed her lightly on the forehead, then watched, standing almost at attention, as she swiftly made her way through the packed restaurant and out onto the street.

She grabbed the first cab she saw and directed it back to the Capitol. If her memory was correct, Albert would be working late in his office. She willed herself not to cry, corrected her makeup in the darkened backseat of the taxi, and prepared herself to greet Albert.

Within minutes, she was in the reception room of his office. She picked up the intercom and dialed his number. He picked it up, with surprise in his voice.

"Yes?"

"Albert, it's me. I'm back early. Have you had dinner yet?"

"No, darling. What happened to your officer friend?"

"I misunderstood. He was only inviting me for a drink, for old times' sake. I thought the invitation included dinner, but once I realized he had other plans, I rushed back here hoping to catch you so we could be together."

"Darling, I'm delighted. I must admit, I was a bit jealous of your running off to meet an old pal, no matter how innocent. Let's go to my apartment and have something sent up."

"Great idea."

"Where are you now?"

"If you open your door, you'll find me perched on your secretary's desk, looking not one inch like a senator's lady!"

Three weeks later, Albert took Anna to his Greenwich, Connecticut, home for a long weekend. Anna declared that the boys could not miss their classes at St. Albans. Besides, she wanted to spend some time alone with Albert. So much of their time was spent with constituents, other politicians, or the boys and Francine. It would be nice to have a weekend all alone in the Connecticut countryside, about which Albert never tired of bragging. And they had two major functions to attend: a state-wide Democratic party dinner, and a bar mitzvah at the local country club.

Anna had packed with great forethought, knowing she would be put on display for the first time to Albert's hometown friends and to the powers-that-be in the Democratic party, who would naturally compare her with Esther. It was important to Anna that they find her acceptable on all counts—oh, they might not love her instantly, out of loyalty to Esther, but that would come with time. Albert, however, professed to give "not a damn" what anyone thought of her. He loved her, and that was the only judgment that counted.

They were picked up at La Guardia airport by Albert's chauffeur, a huge black man who looked as if he'd been hired for his bodyguard skills rather than for his driving expertise. Roscoe, Albert explained on the way to Greenwich, was married to one of his two maids, Cassie. His butler, an Englishman named Jenson who'd worked for his parents before their death, was married to "the housekeeper," Matilda. "If you believe in their titles, then Jenson runs the household, but in reality it is the housekeeper who rules the roost."

Anna, already impressed to hear that he had four in help, was shocked he also employed a young Frenchman as a chef, Jean Robert. "My goodness, that's a lot of servants for a man who isn't even home very often."

"True, but I'm sure when the boys come up and we begin to do some entertaining, they'll have their hands full."

Anna couldn't suppress the urge to tease him. "My dear senator, aren't you presuming a bit? What's this about 'when we do some entertaining'?"

He reached over and squeezed her hand. "No, I don't think I'm presuming. But time will tell."

He had a surprise up his sleeve, but she couldn't be sure what it was. Truth to tell, she was disappointed that he hadn't formally proposed by now.

Rather abruptly, the car turned off the two-lane country road and onto a long driveway lined with ancient tall oaks and white board fences, not unlike the ones which she'd seen in Potomac and Middleburg. To her right, in the distance, more than a half dozen horses and colts frolicked in the afternoon sun. "Is that a lake? It looks lovely!"

"Yes, indeed, it's a lovely spot. I love to sit and read under that weeping willow. In the summertime we have a full complement of frogs and crickets to sing to us. And if you look closely, I think you can see the swans—we have three couples, and a dozen or so ducks. In the winter the Canada geese frequently stop on their way to Canada. They make an awful racket. But they're a pleasure to behold."

Anna watched out the window of the limousine as it drove around the final curve and came to a stop in front of the most splendid Georgian mansion she had ever seen. She forced herself to sit still and wait for Roscoe to open the door and assist her out. She wasn't used to servants—she opened her own car doors. But she'd learn. Yes, she'd learn quickly.

As she stepped out of the car, the massive front door opened and a tall, elderly man dressed in a formal black butler's suit descended the three steps of the pillared portico. He nodded politely to Anna, then walked toward Albert, who greeted him with a handshake that almost became a bear hug.

"Jenson, I'd like you to meet Mrs. Dunay, who will be our houseguest this weekend."

Jenson bowed in courtly fashion from the waist. "Everything is in readiness, Madame. We are delighted to welcome you to Landow Meadows."

Anna wondered why she hadn't studied up on the proper way to greet servants—but there had never been any need before.

"Thank you, Jenson. I do appreciate all your efforts on my behalf."

"Think nothing of it, Madame. We are here to serve the senator and his friends."

How stuffy! How does Albert stand this? I can't believe this is how he lives! So different from Washington—who would have imagined this great house? "Albert, this house—it's amazing. You didn't prepare me for it."

"Yes. It is, isn't it," he said as he looked up at the roof, where a railed captain's walk sat atop a gray-slate pitched roof. At first glance, Anna thought she saw at least eight chimneys. "I forget how magnificent it is myself when I'm away from it. My parents built it as a country home in 1888, the year I was born. Actually, it was a gift from my father to my mother in honor of my birth."

"I had no idea that there were Jewish families this rich here in the nineteenth century." Anna paused, embarrassed. She'd have to watch her tongue. "If this was their country home, where did they live regularly?"

"They lived in Manhattan, on Fifth Avenue. But they sold that home when I was a teenager. Dad decided it was more pleasant to live here year-round. Besides, Mom loved it so much out here that he couldn't get her to come back into the city. The result was that this is my home, almost the only home I've ever lived in. It holds marvelous memories for me. I hope you grow to love it as much as I do."

He held her elbow as she ascended the steps and walked across the portico into the spacious foyer.

The view inside the house took Anna's breath away. The foyer was larger than her entire living room in Washington, facing a pair of massive marble steps that curved up three floors. On each level a beautifully crafted gallery defined the hallways, which led to bedrooms. On each floor she could see hand-carved moldings, fine English oils, and antique tables that held large mixed bouquets of fresh flowers. At the very top, the stairwell was crowned with a huge stained-glass skylight. She took all this in in a moment, but she could see out of the corner of her eye that Albert was anxiously awaiting her verdict. "Albert, it's splendid, truly splendid. How could I not love it?"

"I'm delighted you like it. I'll give you the grand tour, then we'll have tea on the terrace. Meanwhile"—he turned his attention to the butler—"Jenson, ask Matilda to unpack Mrs. Dunay's clothes. Thank you.

"We'll start with my favorite room in the whole house, the library."

Anna could barely comprehend the size of the library. It was at least twenty by thirty feet with sixteen-foot ceilings, including an upper gallery that was filled from top to bottom, wall to wall, with leather-bound gilt-edged volumes stored behind doors with gilded mesh windows. The room was furnished with a worn brown and beige oriental rug and overstuffed sofas and chairs covered in a fabulous poppy-strewn chintz. On every table sat vases of fresh spring flowers: a dozen red Emperor tulips in an Orrefors vase; a large cachepot with blooming mums; and on the largest glass coffee table sat a huge crystal globe filled with several dozen bright red poppies.

"Such flowers, Albert! Where on earth do you get them this time of year?"

"Jenson works with a fine florist—I told him you love flowers, and he did overdo it a bit, I'm afraid! But I told him to err on the side of extravagance, my darling. Nothing is too good for you."

It took Anna a moment to understand what he was saying: this incredible, overwhelming display of flowers was in honor of her visit!

"Come, I'll show you the living room. It's probably my least favorite room."

They returned to the foyer and took two steps down into a large airy living room with two marble fireplaces and large French doors that led out onto the terrace. "Oh, but I'll bet it's going to be my favorite," Anna cooed as she spied the two massive French Impressionist oils over the wall opposite the French doors. The room was decorated in shades of blue and champagne that perfectly matched the two oversize Kirman rugs, which defined two large conversational groupings of Queen Anne and Sheraton upholstered and wood pieces. The walls were covered in a pale blue watered silk, and the ceiling moldings were a shade darker than the wallcovering. Again, the room was filled with flowers: delphinium, bachelor's buttons, carnations, Queen Anne's lace, Japanese iris, and something Anna had never seen before: lavender roses. "My goodness, Albert, such roses! I've never seen a rose this color!"

"Aha! I'm not much on flowers, but that particular one we grow here in the garden and greenhouse. You'll have to get Jenson to show you. He and Matilda are the horticulturists here. I'm sure, as a matter of fact, that they made some of these arrangements from flowers we grow on the grounds."

"How much land do you have?"

"Twenty-seven acres. And that's after selling off parcels on two different occasions during the past fifty years to developers."

"You won't sell more, will you?" Anna asked, suddenly worried.

"No, my darling. We'll need it for the boys. Bicycle paths, riding trails, hidden places to pitch a tent and play cowboys and Indians."

Anna smiled an enigmatic smile at him. All this—and he still hadn't asked her to marry him!

"Am I being presumptuous again? Sorry. But when you see the tennis court and the stables and the swimming pool and the lake, you won't be able to deny the boys a chance to grow up here. I know you, Anna—the way to your heart is through your sons!"

After they toured the great room, the dining room, the large country kitchen—brimming with antique copper pots and pans and a huge old fireplace—the massive master bedroom suite with his-and-her dressing rooms and an adjoining small den, and six guest-bedroom suites, Albert took her on a tour of the outdoors. When that was finished, they sat down on the terrace overlooking the pool and the entire property and welcomed Matilda's formal English tea of finger sandwiches, small tarts, and sherry. After several bites and a few sips, Anna stretched her legs, removed her sweater, and took several deep breaths. "Oh, the air is so fresh here! And the silence, the peace and quiet, is addictive."

"You think you might be able to call this home, then?" Albert questioned with a broad smile.

"Senator, I'd love to call this home—but only if I have a home in Washington too. I'm a Washington girl—always have been, always will be."

"God willing, and if the voters of Connecticut agree, you'll have a home in Washington too." He shifted in his chair and glanced at his watch. "Anna! It's six o'clock already. I can't believe my tour took that long."

"Does it matter? We're not going out tonight, are we?"

"No, but tonight is a special occasion. I've asked Jean Robert for a celebratory dinner. So I suggest you and I dress for dinner. I've even taken the liberty of buying you a dress."

"Albert, how lovely of you!"

"You haven't seen it yet."

"Nor do I know which bedroom you've put my things in."

"I'm proposing that we take a bit of a nap and then dress for dinner at nine. So let me take you upstairs now—I've a few surprises waiting for you."

Albert knocked on her bedroom door promptly at eight-thirty to escort her down to dinner.

"Oh my, you look so handsome! I love that blue-velvet smoking jacket. And that ascot is perfect with it. I've never been able to master the art of tying an ascot to my satisfaction."

He kissed her lightly on the lips. "I'm delighted the dress fits so well. You look scrumptious."

Anna twirled around to show him the full beauty of the multilayered chiffon skirt. It really was amazing that he'd picked something so exactly to her taste: a royal-blue silk chiffon dress with a scooped neckline and long billowing sleeves, tightly cuffed with matching satin, and a magnificent full skirt that accentuated her tiny waist. With it, she wore her strand of pearls and matching pearl earrings.

He offered her his arm, and they slowly descended the splendid curved staircase. The house seemed even more beautiful in the evening, resplendent in prisms of light reflected from the crystal candelabra and wall sconces. Jenson awaited them at the bottom of the staircase.

"Senator, Madame, I will serve cocktails on the terrace."

"This is like a dream—or a movie set!" Anna exclaimed when they walked out onto the terrace. Floodlights lit the pool and the various specimen trees. Tiny lights were interspersed in the walkways and flower beds leading away from the pool out toward the tennis courts and stables. The silence was punctuated by the sound of a fountain splashing water, and frogs and crickets singing their evensong. "I can imagine a perfect dinner for about thirty people out here, on a gorgeous night like this. What a setting!"

They drank champagne and feasted on beluga caviar. Shortly, however, the evening chill set in, and Albert escorted Anna into the library. There, near the French doors, he had arranged for their dinner to be served. A small table was set for two with a floor-length embroidered organdy skirt and two gold chairs. Six individual crystal vases set atop a circular mirror held gold-toned orchids that picked up the colors in the Flora Danica china. "Albert, I love this setting!"

"But look, there's more," he responded, opening the French

doors out onto a tiny terrace. Just beyond the terrace was a formal English rose garden, bathed now in the light of what seemed to be a dozen full moons, but Anna quickly realized the effect had been created by inventive lighting design.

"The roses smell wonderful! How long do they last?"

"Into mid-October. After that, it's too cool in the evening. I believe Jenson is ready to serve us, my dear." He took Anna's elbow and escorted her back to the table, where she had a perfect view of the rose garden on her right and the library on her left.

They dined on lobster bisque accented with the perfect amount of sherry, a delicate veal with morels, a bibb salad with a perfectly ripened Brie cheese, and chocolate soufflé with a fresh raspberry sauce. As they waited for more champagne to be poured, Jenson arrived bearing a silver compote dish with a blue and white ceramic box. With great flourish he presented it to Anna.

"My goodness—my goodness, Albert! I'll be totally spoiled! A new dress, black-lace lingerie, and now this!"

Nervously, she pried open the lid from the small box. Inside was a blue-velvet box with the word *Tiffany* in gold letters. At that moment she knew, and her hands began to tremble so she could scarcely get the velvet box out of the ceramic box. When she finally did, she set it down in front of her and looked frantically at Albert. "Oh dear, I'm so nervous. Albert, help me."

He squeezed her hand, and in a quiet voice with pleading eyes he said, "Open it. Open the box, Anna."

Slowly, as if whatever was inside might bite her, she lifted the lid.

A blue-white, square-cut diamond solitaire—one of the largest she'd ever seen—glistened against the blue velvet. Her first thought was: I can't wait to show Sasha! "It's beautiful—so big, absolutely a knockout!"

"May I?" Albert reached for her left hand. Slowly, carefully, he slid the ring over her fourth finger. He kissed her on the lips. "I love you, Anna. Will you marry me?" he whispered.

Suddenly, applause broke out. Startled, Anna looked all around, then up to the gallery surrounding the library. There, watching them with no shame at all, were Jenson, Matilda, Roscoe, Cassie, and Jean Robert. Jean Robert aimed a flash camera at them and began shooting pictures.

"Shame on you," Anna said in mock anger, "shame on you for spying on us!" She turned to Albert, "Looks like I'm the last to know."

"I couldn't very well bring you here for the weekend if I didn't plan on making an honest woman out of you, Anna. After all, servants gossip. And I'm a public figure." He reached over and kissed her again. "Now you have your first happy memory in this house. We'll put a plaque here on this spot commemorating my proposal!"

"We'll do no such thing, sir. And if I'm going to be your wife, I'll be running this house from now on. You can be sure I'll not permit any more of this nonsense—proposing to me in front of the servants! Shocking! Who ever heard of such a thing!"

The next few months, Anna felt she was living in a splendid dream. They planned their wedding for the weekend between Christmas and New Year's, to be followed by a honeymoon in Miami Beach. After much back and forth, Albert had the last word about the size of the affair. It would be a small ceremony —only their immediate families and closest relatives—and would be followed by a seated dinner dance for several hundred guests in the grand ballroom of the Mayflower Hotel, with music by Lester Lanin.

Planning the wedding and the prenuptial dinner at the Cosmos Club, and organizing herself for an extended two weeks in Florida, would have kept her busy by themselves. But Albert surprised her one more time by finding "the perfect house" for them in the Kalorama neighborhood, near the French embassy. As Anna walked through the empty house, which was in great need of redecoration, she remembered her first foray into that neighborhood as a teenager, delivering her mother's herring salad. Who would have believed, she mused, feeling the need to pinch herself one more time. Was it all real? But to reassure herself, all she had to do was look straight ahead at the tall, distinguished senator who cherished her every breath.

"Darling, I think we should call Billy Baldwin and simply turn the whole project over to him. You like our home in Connecticut, and he decorated it eight years ago. If you go over color schemes with him and give him a general idea, he'll take care of all the details."

"I certainly would welcome his help, Albert. But not for a

minute would I let him take the fun of making all the decisions away from me. I'm looking forward to it."

"In that case, perhaps you should quit your job at the Senate sooner than you'd planned."

It was the one sore spot between them. Albert had wanted her to quit her job as soon as they announced their engagement in the Washington press. Anna had insisted she'd hold on to it until two weeks before their wedding. She'd been unable to articulate her reasons, but it was clear to both of them that on some level she wasn't sure this wedding was really going to happen.

"Perhaps. I'll think about it, Albert, though I've already promised Colonel Halsey that I'll be there until mid-December."

"I'm sure he'll understand if you up the date a bit. As long as you promise him a good seat at the wedding."

Two weeks later, Anna finally succumbed to Albert's pleas and arranged to terminate her employment in the Senate the first of November. It bothered her no end to give up her job—it had been a great job, with wonderful memories and lots of power. She was troubled that giving it up would make her totally dependent on Albert—and she hated being dependent on anyone but herself. Life had taught her that the only person she could totally trust was "yours truly," and she felt almost superstitious about surrendering her fate to another person. Still, there was no one, besides herself, in the world whom she trusted more than Albert.

"You'll have plenty to do running our three homes and helping me with political advice. And you can give the boys much more of your time," Albert had argued.

But the boys had reached the age when they'd rather be out with their friends than doing anything with Anna. She'd missed that opportunity a long time ago.

"If you still want a career after a few months of not working, simply decide what you want to do, and I'll help you do it."

He was a gem! And she'd hold him to that promise if she found herself bored with Senate wives' luncheons and such.

She stood in the largest dressing room at Garfinckels watching the seamstress pin the dress she was to be married in, and her mind returned to her career. Only six weeks after quitting her job, she was already tired of the endless luncheons, fashion shows, teas, visits to museums, receptions, and dinners. Even for me, she thought, there's such a thing as too many parties. One lost all perspective on life when all one did was go from one party to another, compare food and flowers, compete with the other women, and make endless meaningless small talk. Yes, she thought as she marveled at the exquisite perfection of the reembroidered alençon beige-lace dress that followed so gracefully the curve of her hips, I must give serious consideration to what I want to do when we get back from Florida. I want a big challenge. And I want my own money, money that no one else can claim, money that will protect my sons forever.

Christmas brought the surprise of a full-length mink coat from Albert, and even more important to Anna, the friendship of his two married daughters. In spite of his reassurances, she had girded herself for their hostility, telling herself it was inevitable that they would hate the woman who was taking their mother's place.

Albert, with his intuitive understanding of human nature, had created two generous, irrevocable trusts for thirty-one-year-old Adriane and twenty-eight-year-old Elinor and had divided their mother's jewelry and given it to them. He wanted them to clearly understand that although he loved a woman only a few years older than they were, it in no way diminished his love for them.

Because their father had prepared them, they arrived ready to like Anna. She, in turn, devoted herself to them tirelessly during the week before Christmas, even giving a small tea in their honor at the Cosmos Club.

Their wedding day arrived sparkling blue and crystal clear—a crisp winter day warmed by the sun's golden rays. Anna had deliberately kept the day free of any activity other than packing her suitcases for Florida and being with the boys and Francine. They spent the day quietly in her small town house, hugging one another whenever the spirit moved them, knowing that after this day, this evening's ceremony, their lives would be forever altered. Several times during the day, Anna found herself feeling queasy in the pit of her stomach. The old doubts returned. Was she doing the right thing? Did she love Albert? Was it a love that could sustain a lifetime together? Yes, yes, and yes came the answers from deep within her. I made a mistake with Claude, but this is no mistake. Please, God, give me the strength and wisdom to make it work!

In the late afternoon she dressed slowly, with Sasha's help, in the lace tea-length gown and put the finishing touches on her makeup and hair. The boys, meanwhile, dressed in custom-tailored tuxedos—their job was to escort their mother down the aisle. Sasha would be Anna's matron of honor.

"Such wonderful taste he has!" Sasha gushed as she handed Anna the diamond earrings Albert had given her the previous evening.

"Yes, and there's no end to his generosity. Did I tell you that he's invited Francine to live with us permanently? He's building her a guesthouse of her own on his property in Connecticut. Imagine!"

"I wondered what you would do about her."

"There's never been any question. She's the only grandparent the boys have, and she has no one but us. Besides, the boys are devoted to her. I honestly don't know how I would have gotten along without her these past few years."

"Anna, darling, I'm so happy for you. You're having a wonderful streak of good fortune. I hope it lasts forever. I only wish Mama were here to see your life, to know Albert, to see her adorable grandsons."

"I do, too, Sasha. I miss Mama. So many times I wish I could talk to her, tell her everything. It sounds childish to talk this way. . . ."

"Part of us never gets over being a child, needing our mother. Anna, you look magnificent! Wonderful! Now, let's go before we both get weepy!"

Anna, Sasha, Gilbert, and Charles were met at the entrance to the Mayflower by Louis Bernstein, who would escort them to the Chinese Room, where the ceremony would be held. "Everything is ready. The guests have already had too much champagne—and your groom patiently awaits you."

As Anna followed Louis down the steps toward the Chinese Room, she felt butterflies flutter from deep in her stomach up toward her brain. She was giddy, almost drunk with anticipation—and one more time the dark question presented itself: Am I doing the right thing?

The question hung suspended in her brain and a numbness took over as Louis opened the door and motioned Sasha and the two boys inside. The "Trumpet Voluntary" began, signaling her entrance. Still she waited, the question reverberating back and forth like a swinging pendulum. She stepped inside the room and noted the waiting faces, the sparkling eyes, and the rush of silence that took over the crowd. Sasha stepped forward and began the walk down the aisle. With Gilbert on her left and Charles on her right—the way she had dictated the procession would be—Anna clutched her bouquet of orchids tightly, and head held high, she took the first steps down the aisle. In the sea of faces in front of her, she searched for and found Albert's tall presence, his reassuring look.

Ah . . . there you are.

She breathed deeply.

Yes. The answer came now. Yes, I am doing the right thing.

▨ Chapter 28

Washington, D.C., Spring 1951

The door to the board room opened. Anna's secretary Barbara entered, smiled a general greeting to the men seated around the mahogany conference table, and took her seat at the left of the chair designated for the chairman of the Trans-Continental Travel Agency. The easygoing, early-Saturday-morning conversations about baseball and golf scores resumed. Coffee cups were refilled, and a few more Danish were consumed. It was ten minutes after ten, and Anna was late—an unusual occurrence. She always insisted that her board meetings begin on the dot.

The door opened again, and Anna Arnold Dunay Landow entered, followed by her tall son Charles, who was a sophomore at Harvard College. She flashed a warm, apologetic smile to her three brothers and two nephews. "Sorry, guys. Charles's plane from Boston was a few minutes late."

"Jeez, you came in this morning?" Joel Bernstein asked from the far end of the table.

"You didn't think he was going to give up his hot date last night, did you, Joel?" said Anna's youngest brother, Joshua. "Hell, no—I know my nephew! Rumor has it that the Cliffies are lining up for a piece of the action." Joshua, who was seated directly opposite where Anna would sit, stood up and walked around the table to peck Anna on the cheek and shake Charles's hand.

Charles's ruddy face, wind-burned from running track, colored more deeply as he answered his uncle. He made his way around the room shaking hands with his uncles and slapping his cousins on the back. After he had circled the table, he stopped to pour himself a cup of coffee, fixed another one for his mother, and took his seat at her right.

Anna, meanwhile, was going over some last-minute details with Barbara and Joel, who served as her special assistant in the Washington office. Finally, satisfied that everything was ready, she sat down, sipped her coffee, cleared her throat, and said, "Gentlemen, if everyone is ready, let's begin."

In front of each man was a legal-size folder filled with quarterly reports on the four travel agencies owned by Anna Dunay.

"I've studied each of your reports, and I'm more than pleased. This is the fifth quarter for the branch offices," she said as she looked at her brothers, "and I never anticipated we would be showing a profit so soon. Congratulations! Albert and I both are a bit astounded by this—we had anticipated at least two years in the red before we saw a profit. Our New York office —thanks to your hard work, Josh—has even outproduced the Washington office this past quarter. You must share some of your secrets with us."

Josh put his cigarette out, grinned at his sister, and tugged on his brown-cashmere sweater sleeves, pulling them down his long arms one more time. "I have three secrets: location, location, and location. It was a stroke of genius—one we expected from you, Anna—to put the agency next to the United Nations. Exactly as you predicted, our greatest volume and our largest profits are made on the foreign diplomats. And we've serviced them in such a way that they come to us for their pleasure travel too. And they talk, they spread the word. I'm convinced that in this business, pleasant, competent service is the key to success. Our reputation travels by word of mouth—to all the right people."

Anna smiled warmly at Josh. She tried not to play favorites among the family members who worked for her, but it was damned near impossible. Josh, with his spectacular good looks, his go-getter attitude, and his gregarious personality, had everyone he met eating out of his hands. He had been her first and only choice, when she decided to create a nationwide travel-agency chain, to head the New York office. Simply by virtue of its location next to the UN and the travel sophistication of New Yorkers, it was the office with the greatest potential, and if anyone could make it work, it was Josh. Her instincts had been right, as the quarterly report indicated.

Anna went around the table, addressing her other brothers, each of whom managed a major travel agency: Sam in Chicago, Al in San Francisco.

Al reported, "Things are going well, much better than I thought they would. That letter your embassy clients sent to the San Francisco legations has turned the trick. We're now servicing twenty-seven legations. We have more foreign business; we booked seven trips to Asia this past quarter. What I need, though—and, Anna, you might be able to help us all with this —is which hotels in Asia are up to Western standards. I've had some complaints about hotels and restaurants and general comfort."

"Yeah," Josh added, "we're lacking in information on accommodations elsewhere in the world." He paused, grinned mischievously at Anna, and continued, "I guess the key is for you to send us around the world to search out the best hotels."

"Hear, hear!" Sam shouted to general approval and laughter.

"I'll make you a promise," Anna announced when the laughter died down. "On the fifth anniversary of each branch opening —that's three years and nine months from now, gentlemen—I'll treat each of you and the lady of your choice to a trip around the world at my expense. That's if you continue to show a profit —an ever-increasing profit!"

"Wow!"

"Terrific!"

"Don't get carried away, Anna!" Al cautioned.

"Now," Anna continued, "I don't want any of you to get lazy and rest on your laurels, so I've hatched an expansion scheme." She explained her plan to open agencies in ten more major cities.

"Anna, it's outrageously risky," Al objected, raking his hand through his wavy white hair. "You will rue the day you hatched this harebrained scheme. Christ, I've never seen such an ambitious woman! Does Albert know what you're proposing to do with his money? Is Louis Bernstein a part of this?"

"Albert suggested it," she shot back, "just as it was he who suggested back in 1946 that I should create a travel agency. He's the one who had the foresight to suggest opening branches in San Francisco, Chicago, and New York." Anna turned back to her nephew Joel, who was making the presentation with flip charts and graphs. "Please continue, Joel."

When Joel finished, everyone started to talk at once. Anna intervened sharply. "Okay, one at a time. Josh, you first."

"How much capital have you set aside for this expansion?"

"I've committed ten million dollars, a million for each office. And again, to be on the conservative side, I've estimated two years from each opening for a profit-picture to emerge."

Al raised his hand in protest. Angrily, he blurted out, "Anna, for chrissake, you're talking over a hundred employees—probably close to two hundred, if you have all fourteen offices. That's nuts! I don't think it's manageable!"

"Are you telling me you aren't up to managing four offices, Al? Is that it?"

"Hell's bells, Anna, you're the one who's so hot on family management! Who else is there? Charles isn't going to be ready to do anything for at least four years, and Gilbert's a long way away from this kind of responsibility. Where the hell do you expect us to find managers?"

"My brothers, nephews, and niece will not steal from the business. But that doesn't mean we can't find and train good people to manage branch offices and watch them closely. Guide them, audit their books, make sure they're providing the quality service our name has come to stand for. That's what I expect you men to do—set the example, train your personnel according to the principles articulated in our training manual, exercise quality control on our services, and finally, audit the books very carefully. I think that's manageable, and that's how I want things done."

* * *

"Okay, gentlemen, it's four o'clock, and I promised you we'd be finished by now. Any more questions?"

Al stood up and buttoned his suit jacket. He walked around to Anna, who had just stood herself. Kissing her lightly on the cheek, he signaled his resignation to her expansion plans. "Hard as you work us, dear sister, I do prefer this to taking the trolley to Rhode Island Avenue on Sunday nights to pick up things from the drummers for Pa's store."

Anna's face registered a complete blank.

"Hell, you probably don't remember, you were so young. We used to help Pa get things for the store."

Sam, who was standing behind Al waiting to say good-bye, chimed in, "I sure remember! We've come a long way from Southwest Washington, haven't we, Anna?"

Anna gave Sam an answering hug, then turned to Josh and patted his cheek. "And you, little brother—you probably don't remember much of Southwest at all. Well, all I can say is, I've been poor and rich, and rich is definitely better!"

After her brothers walked out together, Anna turned to her other nephew. "Mark, Josh tells me you're doing a great job in New York. I've already said that I want you to head up our Boston office, so you can make your plans accordingly."

Mark Bernstein, Joel's quiet but brilliant brother, burst into a big grin. "That's super—I can't wait! That's really great!"

Anna knew the brothers were due at Sasha's for dinner, so she hastened to move Joel, who was kibitzing with Charles, out the door. "Joel, you made a superb presentation. I'm proud of you. I may buy you a hotel yet!"

It was a standing joke between them. Joel had trained in hotel management at Cornell University and was constantly teasing Anna about expanding into hotels so he could use his training. She countered by promising him his own travel agency —if she could ever spare him from her corporate headquarters. Eventually, she knew, she would have to let him have something of his own, but she wanted to put that day off until Charles was ready to take Joel's place. And that was four years down the road.

"Okay, you guys. Your mom is waiting. She's having a special dinner for you, so get going. And give them all my love. Tell Sidney that if she'll hurry up and graduate, I'll let her decorate the new branch offices on the East Coast. That ought to put a bee in her bonnet!"

Anna kissed them each good-bye, then sent Barbara home. Only then did she turn her attention to Charles, who had spent the entire day listening to the board meeting, saying very little himself, knowing this was purely and simply his mother's way of keeping him up to speed and peripherally involved in her business.

She finished packing her briefcase and turned off the lights. "So, what did you think, Charles? You must have some words of wisdom for me. Any major disagreements?"

"No, Mom. Basically, you ramrodded things through in your usual way. You showed them one more time who's boss."

"Damn, you make me sound awful!"

"Not awful—just forceful. Competent. The boss."

"Don't forget, my dear son, that your uncles were plodding along with midlevel incomes before I invited them to join me. Now, every one of them is a rich man. You can be sure that no matter how much they may resent my 'bossy' ways, they wouldn't walk away from Trans-Continental. You can bet your life on that."

"What fascinates me, Mom," he said as they rode down in the elevator, "is watching you operate. Your intensity, your determination, your ambition—to be, hell, I don't know, the richest woman in the world, maybe. I watch you throw your heart and soul into this company, and the whole time I know you don't need a dime. Senator Landow has more than enough money to last you your lifetime. I don't understand what motivates you. And that fascinates me."

She reached up and patted his cheek. He was such a dear son, everything a mother could possibly want. When they were seated in her car with Charles at the wheel, she decided to answer his question as best she could. "Though I'm not sure myself of all the factors, I think I understand myself. After I married your stepfather and finished decorating our Kalorama house, I tried to keep busy with the Senate wives' club and with politics back in Connecticut. But as the months went by, I found myself bored, not challenged enough. After all, one can only go to so many parties, do so much shopping, go to so many charity committee meetings. Anyhow, it wasn't my cup of tea.

"And there is something else. Albert has two daughters and

several grandchildren, who will inherit his estate. Oh, I know he'll make provisions for us, too, and we'll never lack for anything. But life is precarious. Life is dangerous. If Hitler taught us anything, it was that we can't trust anyone. Ever.

"There was a time when I needed ten thousand dollars, and I didn't have it. I needed it to save your grandparents' lives, to bring them out of the Warsaw ghetto. I had to go to my mother for the money. Well, it bothered me to take money from my parents, who had sacrificed all their lives. I don't know if this makes sense to you, Charles. I've always made sure you and Gilbert had whatever you needed. You've never known a moment's poverty. But I have. And I simply *must* make my own money. I must make it and control it in order to feel safe and secure, in order to feel that I'm guaranteeing you and Gilbert safety and security in your future. Well, I guess that's why I work so hard."

"Mom, there's more to it than that. Otherwise you wouldn't be expanding like you are. The four agencies you have now could provide security for Gilbert and me. No, I know you. You want to be one of the country's wealthiest women."

"Only because that means I'll have the power to create and define my own life—and to help you and Gilbert."

"No, you also want to be one of the big boys."

"I strike you as that competitive?"

"You do, Mom. You are the most competitive person I know. And you know something? I think it's great. Even if you weren't my mother, I'd think you were one of the world's sensational women. I only wish I were finished with school. I could do an even better job for you than Joel does!"

"Why, Charles, I do believe I detect a tone of envy! Can it be that you're envious of Joel?"

"Damned straight I am. And by the way, what do you have lined up for me this summer? I'm not going to be a messenger boy again, damn it!"

"Is that so?" Anna looked at him and couldn't suppress the smile that formed in her eyes. "Tell me, what would you consider a fitting summer job for a Harvard sophomore?"

"I thought about that during the meeting today. I've never spent any time in San Francisco, and since I know you're not going to give me Joel's job this summer, how about letting me go work for Uncle Al? I'd like to actually be an agent, write tickets, talk to customers—maybe he can send me out to the corporations and law firms."

Anna tapped her fingers on her alligator handbag. "Not a bad idea, not a bad idea at all. Just don't fall in love with a Hollywood starlet—I'm sure he'll involve you in the site selection for the Los Angeles office. You're right, Charles. That's a splendid idea. I'll tell him on Monday that he can plan on you, right after Memorial Day." She paused and reconsidered for a moment. "Of course, Albert and I will miss not having you here this summer. We always love having you home, you know that."

"I know that, Mom. But I'd like to do something real interesting this summer, like explore California. Now, *that* I can really dig!"

Their butler greeted Anna at the front door and announced, "Mrs. Landow, the senator is in the library with Mr. Alsop doing an interview. He asked that you interrupt them as soon as you arrive."

I wonder what's up? Anna thought. She turned to her son, "Charles, be a dear and take my briefcase up to my sitting room. Thanks, darling."

She smoothed her hair in the powder-room mirror, applied fresh lipstick, knocked softly on the library door, and entered.

". . . no question, absolutely no question as I read our Constitution, that Truman was right in firing MacArthur. I give the President my unqualified support." The senator looked at his wife, waved her in, and continued to talk to the distinguished reporter.

When he finished his long discourse, Anna greeted Joe Alsop and added, "I might have known the only subject you two old war-horses would want to talk about today would be MacArthur's firing."

"My dear Anna, you look fetching as always! So good to see you. And now," Alsop said as he stood, "it's time for me to take my long stroll home and digest everything this good man has said. I trust I'll see the two of you at the British embassy this week?"

"Yes, indeed," she said. "That embassy is my number-one client, in addition to being our friends."

Alsop kissed her hand in a courtly farewell and took his

leave. When he was safely out of earshot, Anna asked Albert, "Did you really want me to interrupt you?"

He nodded.

"What's up?" The sudden seriousness of his eyes and the grim set of his jaw struck fear into the pit of her stomach.

"You had a call from Gilbert. He refused to tell me what was wrong. A few minutes later, the headmaster also called for you. Thomas said that Thornbull insisted that it was urgent that you —not me—you call him back today."

"Damn! What mischief is Gilbert into now? I just don't understand that boy. Always in trouble. Well, I'll call Thornbull right now—might as well get it over with. Would you please get me a glass of sherry? I'll probably need it."

Anna sat at the small Queen Anne desk in the library, took out her personal address book, found the number, and dialed the Phillips Exeter school. As she waited, her mind drifted back over Gilbert's previous incidents. Twice caught cheating on exams, several demerits for smoking on school grounds, twice caught with beer in his room. And a lifetime of barely passable grades in spite of his fine mind. All his teachers complained about the same thing: he constantly demonstrated lack of respect for them, he took pleasure in aggravating all authority figures, and he seemed to feel contempt for all adults.

After an annoying wait, Jason Thornbull came on the line. "Sorry to disturb your weekend, Mrs. Landow, but we've got serious problems with Gilbert. This time I think there's no way to resolve it short of expulsion. Can you come up here tomorrow so we can discuss it in person?"

"What is it? What has he done?" Anna frantically swallowed a big sip of the sherry Albert had placed in front of her.

"I prefer to speak to you in person," Thornbull responded tersely.

"Yes, of course. I'll come up tomorrow. But if you don't tell me what has happened, I won't sleep a wink tonight. Please, just tell me that much."

"I really can't. There's no way."

Albert demanded the phone. "Thornbull, this is Albert Landow. Tell me what the boy's done, for God's sake. There's no need to give his mother a nervous breakdown." Albert sat down on the opposite side of the desk and listened, fidgeting with a pencil.

Anna watched his face for clues. His eyes took on a deep intensity, then he clenched his jaw. "Well, I understand your concern. We'll be there first thing tomorrow. No, don't worry about meeting us, I'll have my car and driver. We should be there no later than noon." Anna listened, vaguely aware that Charles had wandered into the room and was also listening intently to the senator's end of the conversation.

Albert slammed the phone down and dropped his head into both hands. For a long moment Anna thought he was crying. Quietly, afraid almost to ask, she whispered, "Albert, tell me."

He looked up at her, aged and weary. He saw Charles standing in back of Anna. "Charles, if you don't mind, I don't think you should . . ."

"Charles, please, darling. Leave us alone."

"Is something wrong with Gilbert?" He loved his brother, in spite of Gilbert's nearly constant hostility to him.

"Yes, something's wrong. But you don't need to know the details. Please leave us alone, son."

Charles, abashed, left the room quickly, closing the door behind.

"I—there's no pretty way to say this, Anna."

Fear gripped her chest to the point that she felt she would explode. Speechless, she waited for the bad news.

"Gilbert—he is charged with breaking into his physics professor's office, stealing the final exam, and sharing it with five of his friends."

Anna let out a loud breath. "Thank God that's all it is. I thought it might be worse."

Albert reached for her hands and led her from the chair to a sofa. When they were seated side by side, he attempted to console her.

"What do we do?" she asked. "Maybe we should have kept him at St. Albans."

"He wanted to go to Exeter, to follow in Charles's footsteps. There's nothing we can do today. He's generally being obnoxious. Sounds like he's got them scared to death of what he'll say next. He begged them not to tell me. You see, Anna, he's scared of me, but not of you."

"What will we do tomorrow?"

"I agree with Thornbull that he needs professional help. The problem is getting him to go to a doctor."

* * *

After a long, sleepless night, Anna and Albert left early the next morning for Connecticut. They had talked the matter over until they had exhausted their thoughts about this troublesome son. By the time they entered the headmaster's office shortly after noon, they had decided on a two-part strategy: professional help for Gilbert, whether he stayed at Exeter or came home, and a last-ditch attempt to convince the authorities to let him stay at Exeter with appropriate discipline and supervision.

Since the school was Albert's alma mater, Anna was content to let him do the negotiating.

After much conversation, Jason Thornbull called for Gilbert. He entered the room looking vulnerable and tired, pale and thin. Anna's first thought was that he looked weak and exhausted. She wanted to go to him, wrap her arms around this sad, errant son, and reassure him of her love. But the next second she felt rage, a cold fury that he could have embarrassed her. What did I do wrong? How and when did I hurt you so? Gilbert, what have I done to you? How did this happen?

"Your parents have been fully appraised of your recent actions, Gilbert. We've been discussing what to do next. They would like you to stay here at Exeter. I will permit you to continue here only on a probationary basis, if you agree to work with a psychiatrist. And *cooperate fully* with a psychiatrist."

Albert looked squarely at Gilbert and in his most authorative voice added, "If you don't, Gilbert, your mother and I will take you back to Washington. We will engage a psychiatrist, and we will enforce very strict discipline, complete with curfews and groundings. I suggest that you might find life here more pleasant."

Gilbert looked at his stepfather with scarcely veiled defiance and contempt. In a steady though husky voice he responded, "You are not my father. You have no authority over me."

"Gilbert!" Anna had forgotten the intensity of his hatred for Albert. Yet if he respected any adult, it was Albert.

"I remind you, Gilbert, that I am your legal stepfather, and you are still a minor. Now, do you want to stay here at Exeter —if they'll have you—or do you want to come home and face our rules and regulations, and miss out on the fine education you'd get here? If you choose to come home, plan on attending public school. It's highly unlikely that we'd be able to get you into St. Albans or Landon after this."

"So you guys think that if I go to a shrink, I'll suddenly become a model prep-school student? You honestly believe a shrink can turn me into a mama's boy like Charles?"

Anna fought to keep her voice calm and reasonable. "We think a doctor can help you figure out what's bugging you and why. Perhaps if you understand that, you can get on with your education. Which is why you're here." She would not let him draw her into a discussion of Charles, though it was clear that his feelings for Charles were a large part of his problem.

"What's your decision, son?" Thornbull asked impatiently. "Your parents have to catch a plane back to Washington this afternoon."

Gilbert's face brightened with a sudden revelation. Somehow they'd fixed it. He wasn't going to get kicked out of Exeter after all. They didn't even seem that furious, only sad. His mother seemed very sad, near tears. But she was a tough broad, she'd never break down. "Sure, I'll go to a doctor. Whatever you guys say. Yeah, lead me to him."

The senator looked at the headmaster. "Well, that settles it. You enforce whatever discipline you want, send me the bills for his doctor and anything else, and we'll keep in touch weekly by phone. And give me at least six weeks' notice for the speech at the Founder's Day dinner. My secretary will find a way to accommodate you, I'm sure." Albert turned to Gilbert. "C'mon, son. Let's you and me go for a walk around the grounds. Anna, find a sofa and stretch out for an hour or so. We'll catch that six o'clock flight."

Albert and Gilbert quickly walked out the door. Anna sighed and tried to smile graciously at Jason Thornbull. Finally, she managed to say, "Raising a son certainly isn't easy. In fact, I think it's the hardest thing I'll ever do. It mystifies me, totally defeats me."

"Mrs. Landow, this has been particularly trying. I'm sure you must be done in. Let me give you a glass of sherry, and you can rest in the ladies' lounge. We have a very comfortable sofa there."

❊ Chapter 29

Honolulu—1952

"Oh, the time has gone so fast! Two more days, and we must go home, Albert," Anna said as he took his seat opposite her on the torchlit terrace of the Royal Hawaiian Hotel in Honolulu. "I'm truly glad you insisted I come. I needed this change of scenery."

He smiled the indulgent smile of a husband who continues to be very much in love with his wife, in spite of her willful ways. "My darling, you should listen to me more often. I am right once in a while. Listen to the ocean—you can even hear it above the chatter of the birds and the music."

Highlighted by flaring torches and moonlight, a native Hawaiian combo played "Blue Hawaii" under the swaying palms. "If I stayed here long enough, I could even begin to like the music. This place is addictive!"

"I suspect we'd like it even better over by KoKo Head—you know, that area called Waialae-Kahala. I wish I could talk you into building a home here and living here several months of the year. Charles and Gilbert would love it."

"Oh darling, thank you, but no. I really can't entertain the idea of a home so far away from Washington. Especially not with this expansion into the credit-card business. I must be there to oversee things. I feel guilty leaving even for a short seven-day vacation like this."

"Anna, have you really thought that through? Are you really certain you want to do it?"

Anna shook her head defiantly. "Positive. I'm absolutely certain that's the direction of the future, especially in the entertainment and travel industry. People want to charge things. They're going to want to be able to cash checks and charge restaurant and hotel bills anywhere in the world. Honestly, Albert, I know you have doubts, but it's the most exciting thing I've done, and I've got the best bank in the world behind me."

Albert sighed in resignation. Then a small, teasing smile began at the corners of his eyes. "Anna darling, at this minute you look like anything but the world's most successful, tough businesswoman. You look ravishing!"

Anna looked down at her dress. It was the ultimate in femininity. She had purchased it just for this trip: an off-the-shoulder confection of pale petal-pink and burgundy peonys on a pristine white-satin background. She reached up to smooth her black hair toward the nape of her neck. "Tell me, do you like my hair like this, or is it too severe?"

Albert scrutinized her profile. Her voluminous hair was pulled softly back to the nape of her neck and fastened there with two large silk peonies that matched the ones in the dress. The coiffure focused one's attention on Anna's eyes, which sparkled like huge star sapphires. And from her eyes to her luscious white shoulders and deep décolletage—"Normally I don't suppose I'd love your hair like that, but with that dress, it's perfect. No, as usual, Anna, I wouldn't change a thing about you, even if I could. Which, of course, I can't! Would you like a mai tai?" he asked as the headwaiter approached their table.

After giving the waiter their drink order, they danced to the lilting melodies of Rodgers and Hammerstein. Then they walked slowly back to their table.

"Now tell me, Albert, what have you decided to do about the hotels? I'm anxious to know."

"I'll decide tomorrow afternoon. We have one more meeting with the two banks and major investors, but it looks good to me. You're the travel expert—don't you think Americans are going to start coming here in huge numbers? Don't you think Waikiki can support four more large tourist hotels?"

"About two thousand new rooms?"

"That's what's on the drawing boards now, according to the men from the banks, who keep pretty close tabs on what's going on."

"No question, tourists will come here in large numbers. And right now, Honolulu doesn't have enough rooms. Yes, it seems to me it'd be a good investment. How much will you put into it?"

"For starters, this time around, probably a hundred thousand in the limited partnership."

Anna's attention was suddenly riveted to the next table. A tall naval officer with the three stars of a vice admiral on his shoulder was being seated with his lady. *It can't be—but it is!*

As he opened his napkin and placed it on his lap, his eyes met Anna's.

In the split second between her recognition of Kurt Addison and his recognition of her, a multitude of images flashed through her mind: the first time she had seen him in the naval affairs office, their picnic in Rock Creek Park the first day they made love, his grief and pain the last time she'd seen him, when she told him she would never make love to him again—but suddenly he was on his feet walking toward her.

He stopped beside her, and his eyes pierced hers with a look of surprise and love and wonder. He reached out his hand and instinctively she put hers in his.

"Anna."

His voice caused ripples of pain to flood through her abdomen, and molten fire coursed down her thighs. I must come to my senses. Albert is watching! "Kurt Addison! What a wonderful surprise! Albert, allow me to present an old friend from my days on the Naval Affairs Committee, Admiral Kurt Addison."

Kurt turned to the senator with practiced deference. "Senator Landow, it is indeed a pleasure to meet you. You may recall we spoke briefly on the phone during the war. The subject was the bombing of the railroad to Auschwitz."

"Ah yes, I do remember. You were in intelligence then." The senator stood to shake Kurt's hand. He remained standing, awkwardly holding his napkin in his other hand. "Are you stationed in Hawaii now?"

"Yes. And this"—he gestured back toward the woman he had been seated with—"is my wife Betty. The joy of this assignment is that my family can be here with me."

So this is the woman who has kept him from me all these years, Anna thought meanly. Well, she's pretty enough, I suppose, but I'll bet she's not all that interesting. Then, listening to her own thoughts, she chastised herself. How rotten of me! How truly rotten! After all, I'm the one who ended our relationship. I'm the one who insisted on being faithful to Albert!

They chatted for a few minutes across the tables, then Kurt took Betty out to the dance floor. Anna was glad for the respite and wished they could leave so she wouldn't have to spend the rest of the evening staring at her beloved Kurt and trying to seem gay and happy for Albert's sake.

Instead of leaving, Anna asked Albert to dance with her every time the Addisons returned to their table to eat. On their third time out on the dance floor, Albert sent chills through her by saying in an offhand way, "You know, Anna, that admiral looks like someone I know. I can't think who it is. It's on the tip of my tongue, but I can't grasp who it is."

"I can't imagine who."

"The eyes. His eyes are exactly like the eyes of someone I know, and I can't figure it out."

Dear God, don't let him realize Kurt looks like Charles. What will I say?

During their seventh dance, Kurt and Betty waltzed up to them. Kurt boldly suggested to the senator that they switch partners, "so I can catch up with my old friend."

Quickly, deftly, he danced Anna to the opposite side of the room. In a deep voice, husky with desire, he whispered, "Are you as uncomfortable as I am?"

She looked into his eyes for the first time. "Kurt—oh, Kurt, why did this happen? I was doing such a good job of forgetting you."

"Hush! I don't want to hear that. I still spend sleepless nights remembering our love. I'm famished! Anna, I'm starved for you! I need you so!"

"Please, Kurt, you mustn't."

"I still love you, Anna. Nothing will ever change that. Not seven years, not seventy years."

Anna stopped dead still. "I must go back to the table, Kurt. I really must."

He enclosed her in his long arms again and kissed her temple. "I'll take you back to the table if you'll meet me somewhere tomorrow. I simply must talk to you, Anna. We'll just talk."

"No."

"I insist. What time can you get away? There's a small bar down at the end of this block, the Blue Willow. It's dark and quiet, no one would recognize me or you."

"Three o'clock. I shouldn't!"

"You should. We both need to talk. Now that's settled, pull yourself together, and let me hold you for a few more minutes."

Slowly, with great self-confidence, he held her in his arms and whispered his love. Then they returned to their tables for dessert.

"You did manage to slip away! Good!" Kurt exclaimed as he led Anna, clad in yellow shorts and a shirt, to a booth in the back of the bar. After they were seated across from one another, he studied her anxious eyes. "Anna, for chrissake, I'm not going to bite you!" In a softer voice he added, "Or rape you, though I'd sure like to."

"I didn't sleep a wink last night, Kurt. I must have remembered every word you've ever said to me, every place we ever went together."

"I know. I didn't sleep either. Do you realize it's been seven dastardly long years since—"

"Yes. And twenty-four years since that fateful day you walked into the office. A lot has happened—to both of us."

"Tell me about your travel agencies—everything, I want to hear it all." He reached for her hand and held it while she recounted the highlights of starting her own nationwide company.

"And the boys? What are they doing now?"

"Charles is at the Harvard Business School, and I can't wait for him to finish—I need him badly in the business. Gilbert is in his last year at Exeter. He wants to go to Brown University and then law school. Yes, the boys are fine and quickly becoming men. And your children?"

"Do you have pictures?"

"No," Anna lied, "I never carry pictures. I can't abide it when people foist their pictures on me, so I've never carried my own. Where are your children?"

"Kurt Junior finished up at Annapolis a few years back, and he's out in the Pacific having a ball. Monique is married, and Elise is married, too, and has one little boy and is pregnant again."

Anna laughed. "I can't believe it! You, a grandfather!"

"Yes, and let me tell you, it's wonderful. I recommend it highly."

"You're the sexiest grandpa I've ever met!"

Kurt preened, then squeezed her hand. "Care to find out exactly how sexy I am?"

"No way. I promised myself. This time around, I'm doing everything right."

"By the book."

"Exactly."

He paused, then asked the question he most wanted her to answer. "You seem happy, Anna. Are you?"

She forced a bright smile. "Very much so. In fact, my life seemed perfect until—until last night when I saw you sitting down at that table. Seeing you again—it triggered memories, sensations, dreams. But, Kurt, I'm telling you the truth, my life really is perfect these days."

"You love Albert?"

She sipped her Coke, put it down, and looked him directly in the eyes. "He is an incredible man, the most decent person I've ever known. A wonderful father and husband. Everything I always wanted. Albert is it—everything."

He released her hand, wiped his brow with his napkin, and sipped his Scotch. "I'm glad. Happy for you, Anna, that you got what you wanted. That's good."

But she heard unhappiness and even dismay in his voice.

Suddenly their conversation seemed to end. They had said everything they had to say to one another. It was over. Really, finally, for sure. It was finished.

"I've got to get back. Albert's at a business meeting, but he'll be back by four. So I must go."

He stood and kissed her lightly on the lips, then signaled the waiter for another drink for himself. Anna walked away, out the door, down the street, and back up to her suite.

It's over. It really is.

"Hawaii has turned you into a little sex kitten, Anna," Albert teased as he rolled over and pulled her into the crook of his arm, placing her head just beneath his chin.

"Hmm. Something in the air I think—or maybe it's those damnable birds and their incessant chattering. I don't understand why they get so noisy late every afternoon."

"How can I keep you here? Or get you to come back? I love it here. I could give up the Senate and retire out here!"

Anna lifted her head and looked at his face in alarm. "You can't be serious! What an awful idea!"

"My darling, you forget how much older I am than you. I could very easily retire and be happy managing a few investments and playing some tennis and golf."

"Sounds terrible! I can't imagine what I'd do with myself if I didn't have an office to go to! Why, I'd go crazy."

"We could make love three times a day, like we do here."

"You know, Albert"—Anna giggled— "a few years ago, I

honestly thought men your age—well, you know—we're too old for all this sex. I mean, really! Three times a day! How long do you think you could keep up that pace?"

"Indefinitely, if you pranced around in the nude like you've been doing here." He tweaked her nipple with his fingers, making it stand straight up.

"There's something about a hotel room—no servants, no children, no inhibitions."

"If I retired from the Senate, I'd be free to travel with you anytime you wanted to investigate a new hotel or a foreign country or a new ocean liner."

"Albert! I forbid you to talk about resigning your Senate seat! I won't ever let you do that."

"I *do* think you married me because you wanted to be Mrs. Senator Landow!"

"And you know something? I'm so honest that I'll even admit that your being a senator is one of the things—only *one* of the things, mind you—that I love about you. So get rid of any ideas of retirement!"

"Yes, ma'am! Whatever you say, ma'am!" He ran his fingers up and down her flat stomach, and with his index finger he drew the words *I love you* across her pelvis.

▩ Chapter 30

1956

"Surprise!" Anna exclaimed as she threw open the heavy walnut door to reveal Charles's office, which she had strategically placed next to her own.

Slowly, Charles walked in. His feeling of expectation was replaced by astonishment. Not only was the office huge, it had a magnificent view of the city stretching south to the White House and the Washington Monument. Directly beneath the broad expanse of window, he could see old men and women in the Farragut Square park feeding the pigeons. After studying the scene below, he looked back at his mother, who was watching him from just inside the door.

"Mom, Mom, it's great! But don't you think you've overdone it a bit?" He gestured toward the tufted leather sofa, which was upholstered in a warm antique brown, the glass and brass coffee tables, and the Bakara oriental rug that defined the conversation area beyond his burled walnut desk. "I mean really, Mom, this office is designed to make everyone at Dunay hate me."

"Nonsense! Sit down, Charles, and we'll talk about that. I want to set you straight right from the start." Anna picked up the phone, pushed the intercom, and asked Barbara for two cups of coffee. She settled back on the sofa, ran her hands over the smooth cashmere of her skirt, and engaged Charles's undivided attention with her piercing, demanding eyes.

"I didn't create this multimillion-dollar nationwide corporation so my son could start at the bottom. No, you've served your time, Charles. Every summer since you graduated high school, you've worked in a different job. You've never missed a quarterly board meeting. I've sent you every monthly report on every agency. You've a notebook full of the history of this corporation. And you've recruited two fine young men from Harvard Business School to join our credit-card operation already —and they're doing a superb job. No, it was always my intention that as soon as you graduated, you would become my executive vice president. And starting today, that's your title."

"But Mom, won't that make Al and Sam and Josh outright *hate* me? Not to mention Joel and Mark and all the other senior guys who aren't family?"

"No," Anna answered with steely determination as Barbara delivered a cup of coffee to each of them and quickly departed. "I've never promised any one of them that they would someday run this organization. They have always known, since day one, that I was building this corporation for you and Gilbert. You have to remember that being a graduate of Harvard Business School gives you all kinds of clout and prestige. After all, my brothers graduated from a dinky little business school—basically they're accountants, no more, no less. You, on the other hand, have the finest business training that money can buy."

"Well . . ."

"I don't like your hesitation, Charles. Don't forget, I'm the boss here. This is a dictatorship, not a democracy. When we have a board meeting, I can have seven men against me, but my one vote outweighs them all."

Charles laughed. His mother was quite indomitable. No wonder everyone in the company was intimidated! "By the way, Mom, you haven't told me what my starting salary will be."

A small smile twinkled at the edges of Anna's eyes. "What's the going rate for first jobs for Harvard graduates?"

"Some of my buddies—those who were at the top of the class—are making twenty thousand."

Anna tapped her pen against the notebook she had taken out of her purse. She began to add and subtract figures.

Charles's eyes drifted to the painting over the sofa, a scene of an Indian pueblo in the Southwest. "Mom, I like that painting. Where'd you get it?"

"Sidney found it in Taos. Isn't it wonderful? I thought you might like it. Sidney did a superb job of making this look like a young executive's office, don't you think?"

"Like everything else you do, it's overwhelming. Guaranteed to stir up envy among the troops. I don't know about you, Mom." He paused, brushed his brown hair back off his forehead, then added, "Of course, I realize you aren't rational where Gilbert and I are concerned—you never have been."

"That's not true, and I resent it," she shot back at him. "Thirty thousand a year, plus two percent of the gross as a bonus. And I expect this to be kept between me and thee and our accountant. There's no reason for anyone else to know what your compensation is."

Charles swallowed, then grinned. "That's very generous of you, Mom. Maybe I can afford the payments on that Thunderbird I've been looking at. Gee, that's terrific! Thanks!"

"You interrupted me before I could say that you're entitled to a company car." Anna couldn't help herself. She was enjoying this moment so much. She grinned broadly and finished, "A company car of your choice. Something appropriate for an executive vice president."

Charles couldn't help himself—he hugged and kissed his mother in gratitude. "Wow, Mom, you're the greatest! I can't wait!"

"Charles!" She tried to sound stern. "It is generally not an accepted business practice for vice presidents to hug and kiss presidents at the office during business hours." She looked up at him mischievously. "But I'll let it pass this time. And from now on I think you should call me Anna, rather than Mom."

He nodded. "Now, what do I do for this vastly inflated salary —work eighty hours a week?"

"I want you to make a weeklong visit to each of the fourteen travel agencies. Look at them through the eyes of all your training in efficient management practices and what you know about public relations. Then I want a comprehensive report in writing, with suggestions for streamlining our operations. And there's another matter I want you to work on simultaneously. I need about three or four energetic young graduates—two with strong banking and financial backgrounds—to join up with us. So rack your brain and sound out anyone you think would be appropriate and might be interested."

"Anna," he said, with a twinkle in his eyes, "one thing I'm going to study hard this next year is what makes you tick. Why are you so anxious to build and expand?"

"That's simple. Power. Money equals power in our world. Do you have any idea what it means to be powerless? When you're powerless, when you don't have enough money, the Hitlers of this world can discriminate against you, throw you in ghettos, cart you off to concentration camps. And even though there are millions of powerless people in the same situation, without money they remain powerless. Not a single Rothschild died in the Holocaust. I'll bet they didn't teach you that at Harvard."

"Mom—Anna—you're getting upset. Let's talk about this another time."

"No, son. I learned a valuable lesson one day in the early forties. I learned that the Jews who had a lot of money were able to buy their way out of Hitler's Europe. Those who were only upper-middle-class died by the millions. One thing I promised myself: My sons will have the kind of money that the Rothschilds have. My sons will never be powerless. That, my darling young man, is what makes me tick. I merely want to guarantee the survival of my family through all future cataclysms."

"Wow, that's a heavy way to start this job."

"Indeed," Anna said as she stood and reached for his hand. "Welcome aboard, Charles. This is a very happy day for me. Now"—she turned her sternest look on him—"get to work!"

The Landow family were greeted by the maître d' of Abetone's Restaurant as if they were dear old friends, and were seated immediately at a table for four. While they waited for the waiter to return with their drink order, they nodded to acquaintances at neighboring tables whom they had met the previous two years while skiing in Aspen.

"Cheers!"

"L'chaim!" Albert toasted. "And I'd like to welcome Emily. We're delighted that Charles has finally brought you home to meet the family! He's done a pretty good job of keeping you a secret for the past—what is it, eighteen months?"

Emily smiled shyly at Charles, waiting to see what his answer would be.

"Actually," Charles began, "we met and began dating in the fall of my last year at Harvard. It's sort of been on-again, off-again since then. But—well, we're pretty serious, I guess you could say."

Anna looked closely at the young woman seated opposite her. Her best feature was her gorgeous hazel eyes flecked with gold. At moments they looked almost brown, and at others they looked blue or turquoise. Her porcelain-perfect skin was framed in a soft dark-brown pageboy haircut. Though she had arrived in Aspen only hours before, Anna had instantly sensed an inbred refinement, a kind of inherited cultural background. Charles had told her only that Emily was a pianist, an opera freak, and a history major who had graduated summa cum laude from Radcliffe the previous spring.

Emily was exactly the kind of girl Anna had expected Charles to fall in love with, she realized as she studied her shy, quiet demeanor. But Loomis—what kind of a name was that? Surely not Jewish. Not that that had ever been a big issue with Anna. She had sort of expected Charles to bring home a Jewish girl—but what the hell, it didn't really make a difference—except perhaps to Albert.

After the second round of drinks arrived and dinner was ordered, Charles cleared his throat in a way that Anna recognized meant that he was about to say something important. "We have a problem, Mom and Dad." He reached for Emily's hand and held it as he continued, "I've asked Emily to marry me. She's accepted," he said with a quick look at her. "But her father is adamantly opposed to our marriage. He's threatened to disinherit and disown her."

Anna felt as if someone had socked her in the stomach. "What is your father's objection to Charles, Emily?"

"My father is unfortunately intensely anti-Semitic, and he objects to my marrying a Jew." She quickly sipped her champagne, then looked straight at Anna. "I'm sorry."

Albert quickly declared, "My dear, you cannot be blamed for your father's feelings. Please understand that we know that."

"What about your mother?" Anna asked. "How does she feel about this?"

"My mother died the day I was born," Emily answered without emotion. "My father raised me with the help of a governess."

"Do you have brothers or sisters?" Albert asked.

Emily shook her head. "No one else. There's only me, I'm his only child. Perhaps that's one reason he's acting so horrible. He won't even *meet* Charles."

"What business is your father in, dear?" Anna continued.

"He's a lawyer in Philadelphia. Our money is inherited from generations ago."

"You have to understand," Charles interjected, "Emily's family traces its roots on two sides back to the *Mayflower*. They are truly a first family of America."

"The worst kind," Anna muttered.

"That's not fair, Anna," Albert stated. "You cannot make generalizations like that."

"What are you planning to do?" Anna asked with a sigh. She had so hoped her sons could avoid experiencing anti-Semitism, but it was not to be.

"Emily has decided—"

"Let her speak for herself, son," Albert interrupted in a kindly voice.

"I've—well, we've been trying to get him to mellow for the past year. Charles asked me to marry him a year ago at Christmastime."

Anna looked in astonishment at her son. He had kept this secret from her for over a year!

"I've made no progress at all. If anything, he's become more determined to prevent the marriage, so . . ."

Emily's voice trailed off, as if she could not finish the sentence.

Charles picked up where Emily left off. "We're going to get married in spite of him. And we hope we have your blessings."

Both Albert and Anna answered at once: "Of course!"

"Darling, you know we'll stand by you in whatever you decide to do. But I hope you've given long and hard thought to how you will feel, Emily, if you never see your father again."

She nodded her head sadly. "I have. Believe me, I spend many nights tossing and turning, wondering how I'll feel ten years from now. It's a tough decision." She looked triumphantly at Charles. "But I've made my decision. I'm going to spend the rest of my life with Charles."

"Perhaps—perhaps I can go see your father, talk to him," Albert volunteered.

"No, Senator, no disrespect intended, but my father hates you."

"Ohh!" Albert broke into a broad grin, wondering what bill he had passed that had offended this man who saw himself as one of America's patriarchs.

Charles tugged on the sleeves of his sweater. "Seems you voted wrong on some tax legislation. He'd like to do away with all taxation on those who make over fifty thousand a year. He's about as reactionary as they come, from what Emily tells me."

"Well, in that case," Anna stated, "I'll go see him. I've never met a man yet who I couldn't have a rational conversation with."

"It's worth a try at least, Anna. Yes, I think you should go see him." Albert patted the back of her hand.

"I don't mind you going to see him," Charles said. "But I want you to understand that regardless of what he says, we're going to get married."

"Understood," Anna answered. "But it would be hard on Emily to get married under that cloud. Let me try to resolve the situation first."

The first week in February, Anna flew to Philadelphia, then rode through ten miles of Mainline Philadelphia in a chauffeured limousine that she had hired specifically to impress Emily's father. When she arrived at Bradford House, she was taken aback by the size and grandeur of the seventeenth-century French château that was Emily Bradford Loomis's home.

The butler admitted her to a grand foyer with stone walls,

marble floors, and a curving staircase of marble with bronze and iron railings. He ushered her into an immense cherry-paneled library filled from the floor to its sixteen-foot ceiling with leather-bound, gold-embossed volumes. She was staring at a large ancient atlas on a pedestal desk when William Bradford Loomis entered the room. Hearing the soft patter of his shoes, she turned to face him.

He walked with a certain hauteur; tall, patrician, elegant. Even handsome, she had to admit to herself. And I've seen him, known him before—but where?

"May I offer you a sherry, Mrs. Dunay?"

He's tight, Anna thought, as nervous as I am. Tight as a strung-out rubber band. This is not going to be easy.

She nodded, and he quickly crossed the room and poured her a sherry.

"This library is truly magnificent," she said admiringly.

"Indeed. It was designed by Lucien Alevoine et Cie and imported from France, as were the ballroom and the dining room. The chandeliers were handmade in the Baccarat factory over a hundred years ago. Come, I'll give you a tour."

Anna followed him out the library door, back into the foyer, understanding that he was stalling their confrontation by giving her this grand tour. He was also showing her the life-style Emily had grown up accustomed to. It was a clear attempt to intimidate and manipulate her.

"The house was designed by Horace P. Trumbauer. The foyer designed by Jean Delafosse. And the seven acres of formal gardens were originally designed by Frederick Law Olmstead, Jr."

As they walked through the ballroom, it hit Anna—this was the same man she had met at the State Department back in 1941, when she had been trying to save Bernard and Francine. She had suspected his anti-Semitism then, but now she could confirm it. He was the same arrogant, cold bastard.

"Now, Mrs. Dunay," he continued as they sat in the library and she picked up her sherry, "you can see how my daughter has lived. And I hope that she will come to her senses and realize this business with your son is foolishness." He took out a package of cigarettes and lit a long brown Gauloise.

"Your daughter is a very lovely young lady. The senator and I have grown very fond of her."

"Yes, I understand how you might feel. But I've always been of the impression that Jews don't want intermarriage any more than we do."

"We prefer it if our children marry in the same faith—for many reasons, including the survival of our people. So many were lost during the war."

"Quite so. A tragedy."

"However, let me assure you that we are ready to accept Emily and love her as if she were our own flesh and blood." Anna sat back on the sofa and sipped her sherry.

Loomis seemed alarmed, disconcerted for the first time during the interview. "I see. You think you're getting a prize, a rich girl with blue blood."

"What I see when I look at Emily is a lovely, well-educated, deeply cultured, sensitive young woman who loves my son very much and would make a splendid wife for him. I believe we have to honor their love for one another."

"Bosh! That's ridiculous. She'll fall in love half a dozen times during her life. As far as I'm concerned, marriage is a social-business arrangement. Love and sex have nothing to do with it. Emily will not marry your son, by God, even if I have to cut her off from every dime she's going to inherit. So help me, Mrs. Dunay, I expect you to cooperate with me and help me bring these kids to their senses."

"I have no intention of cooperating with you, Mr. Loomis. That's not why I came here today."

"Why, then, did you come?" he asked with a sneer.

"I came here to do you a favor. To tell you that if you do not accept Emily and Charles's decision to marry, you will lose a very precious daughter—your only child. And you will regret it the rest of your life."

"Let me tell you something, Mrs. Dunay. When I die, Emily will inherit something like eighty million dollars—if she marries someone I approve of. If she marries a Jew, she will be completely disinherited. Not a dime, not a penny."

"Yes, I know. Emily and Charles have already told me that."

A look of amazement crossed Loomis's face. "And you think Emily should throw away that inheritance? For your son? Come now, Mrs. Dunay, surely you don't—"

Anna crossed her legs, watching his eyes follow the movement. She sipped her sherry again. "You don't remember me, do you, Mr. Loomis."

He looked intensely at her, snuffed out his cigarette, and said contemptuously, "Should I? We've never met before."

"As a matter of fact, we have. During the war you were in the office of the undersecretary of state. Is that correct?"

"Yes." He nodded. "But I don't remember—"

"No, I don't suppose you would. You probably had many requests like mine. I expect you handled most of them as arrogantly and inhumanely as you did mine."

Loomis stood up abruptly. "What in hell are you talking about?"

"I came to ask you to help me get my in-laws out of the Warsaw ghetto. They were still alive then, and you might have helped me smuggle them in through one of the embassies. But you told me that we Jews were exaggerating the danger our families were in. You didn't believe Hitler would do anything more than conscript them for labor camps. Mr. Loomis, you had to know even as you uttered those words that they were being incinerated by the hundreds of thousands. You knew about the death camps, and you did not do one thing! Not one thing!"

He had paced to the window and was looking out. When Anna had finished, he slowly turned to her, and in a voice that she could barely hear he informed her, "The only mistake Hitler made was that he didn't kill them all. It was a shame. He might have finished the job."

Anna stood, shaken to the core by this living, breathing version of evil. "Does Emily understand the role you played in the State Department? Does she know how you feel about Hitler's 'final solution'? Could she even want the money or the name of a man who can utter such an obscenity?" Anna picked up her purse. "I will leave now, Mr. Loomis. We have nothing further to say to one another. But I will tell your daughter of your sentiments. I'll make sure she understands fully what her choices are."

"You do that, Anna Dunay. You make sure she knows."

Anna let herself out the massive oak doors and ran down the steps to the waiting limousine. When she was finally out the driveway, she took a deep breath, exhaling the venomous air she had breathed, promising herself she would make sure Emily and Charles inherited far more than Loomis's money.

In Emily's case, it wasn't only what she would inherit, but what she would escape from. She must get away from that disgusting, loathsome man. She must have the opportunity to experience a full, healthy love. She must create a family to fill the vacuum she must have always felt.

Emily, I will be your mother. I will see to it that you have everything material your father might have given you—and much, much more. You will have a close, warm, loving father and mother who will cherish you. I will not let that bastard ruin your life—that arrogant, murderous son of a bitch.

No wonder she's desperate to escape from him, no wonder they're in such a hurry to set a date. Well, I'll help them. I'll give the wedding, and it will be spectacular! Everything Charles and courageous Emily deserve!

"Exquisite, Anna! An absolutely delightful affair!"

"The food was divine! The best wedding cake I've ever tasted!"

"You must be so thrilled with Charles's choice of bride—she's lovely."

"The flowers, Anna, my God! Who ever saw topiary trees of yellow roses—and on every table! Utterly magnificent!"

Anna's shoes were pinching, but there were only a few more guests waiting to say good night. In the background she was vaguely aware of dozens of waiters clearing the tables of their embroidered organdy cloths, and Meyer Davis's band was packing up. Albert was tipping the banquet manager and making arrangements for the gifts to be stored overnight at the Willard, the finest old hotel in Washington, and delivered to their home the next morning, along with all the flower arrangements.

When at last they were ensconced in the gray-velour comfort of their limousine, Anna kicked off her shoes and reached for Albert's hand. With a deep sigh, she murmured, "It was lovely, wasn't it Albert?"

"Absolutely perfect, Anna, even prettier than our own wedding."

"Emily seemed so pleased through everything. I wondered how she was going to hold up through all the emotion."

"She has amazing poise for someone that young. Absolutely impeccable social manners. Her father may be a bastard, but someone trained her well."

"The amazing thing is that her basic orientation and philosophy of life are so different from his."

"Probably the result of Radcliffe. She got a liberal Ivy League education. Makes a difference—I can attest to that." Albert removed his black tie and unbuttoned the top button on his dress shirt. "You haven't breathed one word about Gilbert's surprise. What do you think of her?"

"Oh, dear! I haven't had a moment to talk with her. But she certainly is sensational to look at. She sort of reminds me of that movie star Marilyn Monroe—only she looks about twelve years old."

"A sort of budding nymphet."

"Oh, Albert! We mustn't be too hard on her. But what did you think of her? I noticed you dancing with her after you finished all the obligatory dances."

"Anna darling, every man in the place was mesmerized by Winslow. She's got the kind of sex appeal that Helen of Troy must have had. Men would declare war over a woman like that!"

"Come, Albert, you're exaggerating."

"I'm not, Anna. That young lady is hot stuff—and she's got her claws into Gilbert pretty good, from what I could see."

"You talked to her. Is she intelligent? Well educated?"

"She's so sexy, it's hard to concentrate on what she says. I'm sorry, Anna, I'm simply giving it to you straight. But she's in her last year at Sarah Lawrence. She must be bright."

"What do you know about her family?"

"Nothing. Not one thing. But I'd guess she's not Jewish."

"I'm sure she's not. But that didn't seem to be a problem for Emily. I can't believe how quickly Rabbi Brickner converted her!"

"Emily's another matter. She's dedicated, really cares about religion, about being an integral part of our family. Hell, she'll end up being a better Jew than Charles is, mark my word."

As the limousine came to a stop in front of their door, Anna kissed Albert lightly on the lips. "You were a splendid father of the groom, my darling! Thank you for helping me so much with

this wedding, and thank you for being such a wonderful father
to my sons."

Albert wrapped his arms around her, ignoring the chauffeur
who stood holding the car door. "Thank you, my darling, for
being everything a man could ever want in a woman. I love you
so very much!"

"Hey, Mom! Any chance Winslow and I could have lunch
with you today? Or are you going to the office?" Anna set her
coffee cup down and looked up at Gilbert. He was standing in
the entrance of the solarium clad in gym shorts with a towel
around his neck. She repressed the thought that he was surely
one of the sexiest men she'd ever seen. Mothers weren't supposed to have those thoughts!

"Gilbert, I'd be delighted to have the two of you for lunch.
Why don't we eat right here? I'll order up something special,
and we'll gorge ourselves on desserts left over from the sweet
table last evening."

"Great!" He walked a few steps toward her, flicked his un-
combed brown hair back off his forehead, and asked in a hopeful voice, "So what do you think of my girl?"

"She's a knockout. I understand every man at the wedding
wanted to steal her away from you."

Gilbert's color intensified, and he smiled proudly. "Yeah,
she's something! Wait till you see her in a bathing suit. Sen-
saaaational!"

Anna laughed, enjoying his pride in his newest acquisition.
"Lunch at one, then. Right here in the solarium."

"Right-o!"

The two young people came to lunch straight from a vigorous
tennis game, laughing and teasing and still slightly winded. It
was a joy to watch them, Anna thought. They took their seats
at the small table that faced the large glass wall, permitting
them to enjoy the profusion of blossoms on the flowering crab
tree just outside on the patio.

"Early May is my favorite time in Washington," Anna exclaimed. "Just look at that tree and those glorious dogwoods
and tulips! Soon the azaleas will be blooming."

"Yeah," Gilbert answered. "Y'know, Mom, this is Winslow's
first visit to Washington."

Anna looked at the slim but voluptuous blue-eyed blonde seated across from her. No question she was a knockout, every which way. "You came at the best time. You'll have to come back sometime when I can show you around a bit, when we don't have all the excitement and confusion of a big wedding."

"Actually, Mom, that's what we want to talk to you about."

A tiny pain flickered across Anna's forehead and settled into her temples.

"But—but you have three years of law school ahead of you, and you still have a couple of months—I'm sorry. I'm a bit weary this morning, after Charles's wedding yesterday. I'm not thinking clearly. First, let me say congratulations—are you that serious?"

Winslow smiled a broad smile at Anna that seemed to say yes. Then Anna looked at Gilbert to confirm it.

"Actually, Mom, if you can arrange it . . ."

Anna realized that Gilbert was buttering her up, being gracious and polite and utterly charming. He used those skills well when he wanted something.

"We'd like to have a small wedding sometime in the next three or four weeks."

"Three or four weeks! My goodness, what's the rush?"

Anna sipped her wine and watched Winslow's creamy face turn bright red. Winslow looked at Gilbert frantically, then at her hands, then gulped a large swallow of water.

It dawned on Anna that Winslow was pregnant.

"We do feel an urgency to get married, Mom. We're in a hurry."

Anna eyed Winslow sternly. "What do your parents think of this?"

"I haven't told them yet. I don't live with my parents. They're divorced, and each of them has been remarried and divorced again. Mom lives in Wyoming with a rancher, and Dad lives in Florida."

"I see." A broken home, no decent family life, no role models. *Oh, Gilbert, why? Why?* But Anna asked, "How old were you when your parents divorced?"

"I was three. I've been raised by my grandmother, who is now near eighty and not well. She lives in Boston. She's really the only family I've ever known. And she's the one who's putting me through Sarah Lawrence."

I'm going to get two daughters in short order, Anna told herself. And a grandchild? Well, it must be faced.

"Tell me why you're in such a hurry to get married, Gilbert. Surely you can wait until after graduation. We could have a wedding in late June or early July."

Gilbert smiled sheepishly at Anna. He took Winslow's hand in his, looked directly at Anna, and informed her, "Winslow's two months pregnant. The doctor confirmed it two weeks ago, but we decided to wait till after Charles and Emily's wedding was over to tell you."

Anna continued her hard, stern glare at Gilbert, deliberately avoiding Winslow's terrified eyes. She swallowed hard, then asked, "When exactly are classes over?"

"Exams are finished for both of us in two weeks. Graduation is the last week in May."

Anna turned toward Winslow and stared at her. "Winslow, tell me something. If you weren't pregnant, would you still want to marry Gilbert?"

"Oh, yes, Mrs. Landow! I love him. I've wanted to marry him ever since the first day I met him."

"When was that?"

"Last fall. We met at a Brown football game, and we've been so in love ever since."

"I see." She looked back at her son. "And you would want to marry Winslow this summer even if she weren't pregnant?"

"Yes, Mom. She's made a different person out of me. Haven't you noticed the difference? I'm getting great grades now, and I haven't been in any kind of trouble in ages. Winslow is magic—she's made me grow up. Can't you see the difference? Mom, I'm happier now than I've ever been, and Winslow is the reason."

"That's good news. Okay, I'll have a small wedding in the garden right after you both graduate. Winslow, you must phone your parents and grandmother and discuss this with them. I don't want to offend anyone."

"Oh, thank you! Thank you so much, Mrs. Landow!" Winslow gushed as tiny tears trickled down her face.

I can't believe this is happening, Anna told herself as she tasted her asparagus vinaigrette. But I'm glad Gilbert's gotten serious about life. I've got to give credit where credit's due. I'm going to be a grandmother—my God! Wonders never cease!

⊠ Chapter 31

The First Night of Passover, 1958

"May the spirit of this festival remain with us throughout the coming year, and may we be imbued, at all times, with its lofty and exalted teachings.

"May Zion be blessed with peace, and may our brethren and all mankind live in harmony and contentment. Amen"

Charles closed the prayer book, smiled warmly at Emily, then his eyes met his mother's: "Good Yuntif, Happy Pesach, Mother." Then he looked at his stepfather, who had helped him conduct the Passover seder: "I have you to thank for the fact that I can still read the Hebrew, Dad."

Albert Landow returned Charles's affection in full measure. "Me, your Bubby Francine, and your Zadye and Bubby Arnold."

Albert turned his attention to Emily, who was seated at the opposite end of the dining-room table from Charles. "He may have conducted the service, my dear, but I know who's responsible for this wonderful evening. It does my heart good to see you so enthusiastic about the holidays. We're proud of you, Emily."

Emily blushed, radiant with happiness. "It's my greatest pleasure, Dad. Think of it—for the first time in my life, I have a big wonderful family, and we celebrate family holidays together. You can't imagine how special all this is for me."

Gilbert, seated to the left of Emily, sipped on the holiday wine. He had refused to have a bar mitzvah, had never learned Hebrew, and had been unable to join in reciting the prayers with his brother and stepfather. "I've never liked gefilte fish," he began with a teasing voice to Emily, "but tonight since you made it from scratch, I'll try it."

He looked across the table at Winslow. All this was strange to her. Not only had she looked as bored as he'd been during the hour-long ceremony, but it was her first seder. She understood none of the symbolism or the weird foods she was expected to eat. "Winslow, if Emily continues to be so religious, you and I are gonna have to take Hebrew lessons to keep up."

"It's not that I'm religious, Gilbert," Emily tried to explain, "but I want to perpetuate family traditions—and the best traditions are based on religious observances, no matter what your religion is."

"Well," muttered Gilbert, drawing out the word as if he were a southerner, "I think we're gonna become Unitarian or something. All this Hebrew is too—I don't know, foreign, ancient, dead."

"I used to feel that way," Anna said softly to Gilbert, "but I changed my mind after the war, after my parents and Bubby Francine died. Maybe it's just that I'm getting old."

"You! Getting old? That's a hoot, Mom! You've still got more energy than any three people I know," Gilbert interrupted.

Anna looked at Gilbert with surprise. You never knew what your children thought about you. "As I was saying, the older I get the more I remember about my childhood. And I was never religious. But my favorite memories are the family dinners—mostly seders, Sabbath dinners, the dinner on Rosh Hashanah eve."

"Do you remember Russia at all, Mom?" Charles asked.

"Oh, yes. Vividly. My mother's father—Reb Joshua Siderman was his name—stands out most clearly in my mind. He wore a black-felt skullcap over his long white hair. Oh my, he had hair falling down his shoulders"—Anna gestured with her hands—"and a long flowing beard like silk, and a moustache. And he wore little wire spectacles."

"Was he a rabbi?" Emily asked, her voice filled with awe.

"No, he was a Talmudic scholar, a very learned man. My mother always insisted he was very progressive, quick to adapt to modern ways. After all, he let her marry the man of her choice, Jacob Aronowitz, and that was rare in Russia in those days. Usually, weddings were arranged by matchmakers."

"All I can say," Gilbert interjected, "is, I'm sure glad your mom and dad didn't miss the boat!"

Everyone laughed except Anna.

"And when you realize what happened to the Jews who didn't emigrate, the Jews who stayed in Pinsk, you should really say prayers of thanksgiving," Albert admonished.

"What happened to them?" Emily asked.

Anna had teased Emily that she was writing a book, she seemed so avid for family history and mythology.

"Anna," Albert gently commanded, "would you tell your

sons what would have happened to you and your brothers if Sarah hadn't had the courage to bring you to America?"

"I'm not sure that's fitting conversation for dinnertime."

Charles insisted, "No, c'mon, Mom, tell us. We should know."

"When Hitler's officers marched into Pinsk on August 4, they marched eight thousand Jews outside the city. They forced them to dig graves at gunpoint, then they executed all of them. The next day three thousand more were executed in the same way. However"—Anna paused for effect—"three people clawed their way out of the graves and fled into the forests, where they survived like wild animals until the war was over. Then"—Anna paused to sip her wine—"they told the world about the massacre of Pinsk. The Great Synagogue, where I was named and where my grandfather was a renowned Talmudic scholar, was burned to the ground."

"Wow! That is a heavy story!"

"Jeez, Mom! You mean no one survived?"

"Only three people. As far as I've been able to find out, only one of my relatives was still there when the Nazis came. The rest had emigrated to the United States, to somewhere in Europe, or to Israel."

Emily looked as if she might cry, but she summoned her strength for a question. "You mean, if your mother and father hadn't come here, this family—Charles and Gilbert, and our babies—"

"None of us would exist, with the exception of you, Emily, and Winslow. And I guess Albert's family was here shortly after the Civil War."

"Mom, Bubby Aronowitz always tried to make me believe Zayde was some kind of hero back in Russia. He fought against the czars or something. Tell us what you know."

"My father was a labor leader, part of what was called the Bund. His workers struck against the factories and businesses in Pinsk, even against some business interests of my grandmother's family. He was responsible for changing the workday from fourteen hours to ten hours a day. In fact, that's why my father was forced to come to this country. The czar's cossacks were out to get him, and my grandfathers—both of them—insisted that my parents come here. Thank God, I say!"

Gilbert perked up, fascinated. "Hard to believe the grandfa-

ther I remember was a political organizer. He seemed like such
a mild man."

"I'm not sure, but I think my father's personality changed
radically after he arrived here. My mother told me that he was
never quite the same again, became very disillusioned with com-
munism, sort of lost a lot of his spark. But what I remember
most vividly was the cossack slapping my mother. It was on a
night like this—we were gathered for a Passover seder—the
cossacks broke into the house, and right off the bat one of them
slapped my mother. I was in her arms at the time, must have
been two or three, and it scared me to death, I'll tell you."

Winslow, who had been quietly listening, was shocked. "And
you remember it? I find that amazing! I don't remember much
of anything before my fifth birthday."

Anna looked intensely at her beautiful, blond daughter-in-
law. She could not say what came into her head: that Winslow
had blocked out the unhappiness of her first few years, those
years when her parents were still married and fighting all the
time. It was so terrifying, she had repressed the memory totally.
Poor child. *So I have two daughters-in-law with miserable
childhoods. Lots of repair work to do.*

"I remember my grandfather dispensing groschen from his
money box after we found the matzo," Anna added, anxious to
turn to happier memories.

"Well, my dear little bubby," Albert teased from across the
table, "we have about two years to wait before Larissa and
Elliot will be able to hunt for the matzo."

The maid Emily had hired to serve the dinner came in and
cleared the plates from the soup course. While she served the
turkey and matzo stuffing and carrot *tsimmes,* Anna began to
compare the two young women her sons had married.

Emily, who had never cooked before marrying Charles, had
become a dedicated gourmet cook, specializing in traditional
Jewish foods. She even baked fresh hallah for the Friday Sabbath dinner.

She had declined Anna's offer of a full-time maid to help with
the house and baby Elliot, insisting she didn't want someone
underfoot. Finally, after much urging by Anna, she had agreed
to employ a cleaning woman once a week. It seemed that Emily's only ambition was to be the world's greatest wife and
mother. Charles was to be envied, Anna thought as her eyes

rested on the Steinway concert grand that took up nearly a third of the living room. Emily was refined, cultured, and a wonderful pianist, the kind of woman who had never even considered social climbing. Her idea of happiness was to have an opera playing on the stereo, a book in her hand, and the baby sleeping quietly in his crib.

Winslow, on the other hand, had no domestic interests. She had lost no time convincing Gilbert that she needed a maid who could clean and cook—and now, baby-sit. But she seemed to have an amazing talent for organizing social functions. She was —already!—on the board of the Boston Symphony and the Boston Museum of Fine Arts. She had joined the Junior League— perhaps they didn't realize Dunay was Jewish, it sounded French—and she'd served as chairman of a recent cancer luncheon in Boston. Yes, Winslow was an avid social climber and seemed to make all the right moves. One day Anna had suggested that since they were moving to Washington after Gilbert finished Harvard Law School, this Boston activity was all a bit of a waste. "Practice!" Gilbert had responded. "She's getting in fighting trim to storm the social walls of Washington. This is just practice!"

Anna had asked Sidney to help Emily decorate their first apartment at Pooks Hill in Bethesda. Anna had paid the bill—it was her wedding present to them. Having done that, she could do no less for Gilbert and Winslow. But—shockingly—Winslow's taste ran to expensive oriental rugs, genuine antiques, and Scalamandré silk, while Emily had wanted only wall-to-wall carpeting, contemporary durable furniture in wool and linen, and a few nice reproductions. "We'll wait for serious furniture until we build a home," she'd told Anna. Winslow, it seemed, was as frivolous and impractical as Emily was practical.

And they were both lovely-looking tonight. Emily was dressed in a soft peach-wool dress, accented with her mother's double strand of pearls. Winslow was dressed in a gorgeous mint-green Originala suit that must have set Gilbert's bank account back at least three hundred dollars! Such extravagance for a law student—but their whole life was an exercise in extravagance. Where had Winslow gotten such notions? Such habits? Anna looked at her jewelry: a bulky gold bracelet, a matching necklace and earrings. On her right hand was the eight-carat diamond Gilbert had insisted upon; circling her left ring finger was a wedding ring set with eighteen rectangular diamonds.

But I'm as much to blame as anyone, Anna told herself. I'm the one who can't say no—and who thinks up new luxuries all the time.

Gilbert had confided that Winslow wanted a fur coat for Christmas. He couldn't afford to buy her one, given all their other expenses and the fact that his only income was the very generous salary Anna paid him for attending board meetings once a month at Dunay. One day, being in a particularly indulgent mood—what with two new grandchildren and all—Anna had bought each daughter-in-law a fox fur coat: red fox for Emily, and a flashy silver fox for Winslow. What she did for one of them, she made a point to do for both of them.

"Hmm—your matzo balls are wonderful, honey. Really good!" Charles beamed, waiting for the others to praise Emily's cooking too.

"One of the things I remember about Mama," Anna said, again in a nostalgic mood, "is how proud she was that in their home in Russia, they'd always had a wood floor. It seems that was quite a status symbol. Pa's family, the Aronowitzes, had a dirt floor. But Mama's parents and Mama herself always had a real floor!"

"Actually, Anna," Albert began in a teasing voice, "I've been meaning to talk to you about the floor in our country house in Potomac."

"Yeah, Dad! That's a great idea. Give Mom a dirt floor!"

Anna looked up from her plate, her face animated. "They're beginning the landscaping this week. The pool is finished—and Winslow, you'll be delighted to know the tennis courts are complete."

Winslow's eyes burned with brightness. "I can't wait, Anna! I'm so excited. When will you move in?"

"Hopefully, in about two months if Sidney manages to get the furniture and draperies—well, everything in place."

"And then, my dear," Albert addressed Emily, "you and I will do some serious shopping for horses. We'll find ourselves a stud and some good brood mares, and we'll be in business."

"The plans for the stable look marvelous. I just hope you've left enough land untouched for trails."

"Don't worry, my dear. I'm looking out for you every minute."

"Let's see now," Charles began, "we've put in tennis courts for Winslow and Gilbert, and a stable for Emily and Albert and Anna. Who's the swimming pool for?"

"It's for Larissa and Elliot!" Anna announced.

"Speaking of which, I think I hear one of them," Charles said, rising from the table.

Winslow followed Charles into the nursery and returned carrying little Larissa, whom she deposited in Anna's lap. "I'll warm her bottle."

"What a little doll you are! Oh, what fun it is to have a little girl! Look, Albert, watch how she holds on to my hand!"

Who would have thought I'd enjoy being a grandmother? And I'm not faking it, either, Anna told herself as she gave tiny Larissa her bottle while conversation continued around her. You've got your mother's eyes and your father's hair, and the glorious skin of a baby.

"Anna, don't you think the girls would love spending a month in Rehoboth Beach this summer?" Albert smiled broadly at Winslow. "We'll get a nanny to care for the babies, and you girls can sit in the sun all day, play lots of tennis. Charles and Gilbert can come down Friday afternoon and stay until Monday morning."

"What a marvelous idea, Dad!" Gilbert enthused. "We accept —count us in."

"Don't you think the babies are awfully young to take to the beach?" Anna frowned, thinking of the gritty sand and all the towels. "Besides, all that sun isn't good for the skin. Ages one awfully."

"Oh, Mom, don't be so stuffy," Charles interjected. "It'd be the best thing in the world for Emily. And you and Dad could spend the whole month there and let me and Gil run things at the office."

"I don't know." Anna was furious at Albert for bringing it up. She was of no mind to turn the company over to Charles to run, not yet.

"Aren't you going to the Cape?" Emily asked.

"No," Albert said. "I've given that house to my two daughters, and they've scheduled houseguests for the whole summer. Meanwhile, I want to spend the summer with your mother.

And the four of you. And your babies. If your mother will agree to take a vacation, for a change."

"Well, I don't know, Dad," Charles said with a grin. "It seems to me that if you can give her that palatial mansion in Potomac, the least she can do is give you the pleasure of her company for a month in the summer. That's not too much to ask."

Albert smacked the table, causing the crystal and china to shake. "That settles it, Anna. These young people want to do it, so I'm getting a real estate agent on it tomorrow."

Anna put Larissa over her left shoulder and began to pat her back, hoping for a burp.

"Would you look at that, kids? Your mom is burping a baby against her Chanel suit. Wonders never cease! This summer we might even get her to the beach."

"Only if Larissa and Elliot are there for me to play with."

"Mom"—Charles laughed—"I need a camera, this moment. I'm going to take a picture of you with the babies and frame it for the boardroom."

"You'll do no such thing! And if you're not careful, I'll find a new executive vice president! I expect respect around here!" At that moment Larissa burped and slobbered milk over the back of Anna's suit. "Help! Help!"

As they drove down Wisconsin Avenue toward home, Albert took Anna's hand in his own and said, "I signed my new will today, darling. I'm glad that's over with."

"Ah, so you finally made up your mind about everything."

"It really wasn't that difficult." He patted her hand comfortingly.

"Well, you can forget about it now. It's done with."

"Aren't you curious?"

"I have the distinct feeling you're dying to tell me."

"I gave the house on the Cape to the girls to share. If they ever decide to sell it, they can split the money fifty-fifty. I enlarged their trust funds considerably. And—" He paused, trying to see her eyes in the darkness.

"And?"

"I left everything else to you."

"You did?" Anna was aghast—and surprised.

"I finally decided that neither of my daughters would ever

want to live in the house in Connecticut—their lives are elsewhere. I want you to have that house and give it to one of your grandchildren someday."

"Oh, Albert, I don't need another house!"

"Perhaps you do. You may want to have a legal residence in Connecticut someday."

"What in the world are you talking about, Albert?"

"It occurs to me that if you gave me the word, I could arrange for you to get the nomination for senator in 1962—no, Anna, hear me out. I'm getting awfully old. I've had all the joys and heartaches of being a senator. You'd make a glorious senator."

"Albert, don't be ridiculous! I've more than I can do with the business."

"But you've told me yourself that Charles is a genius at it, and we're talking four years from now."

"Even so." Anna's mind slipped into fantasy. Yes, it would be fun to be a senator. After all these years of working in the Senate, holding that institution is such reverence and awe, to be a part of it. "No, Albert, I wouldn't dream of letting you give up that seat. Besides, who's to say the people of Connecticut would want me in that job?"

"Name recognition, my dear. It's the name of the game. Don't forget, I won with eighty-six percent of the vote last time. The Landow name is magic. If you wanted it, I could swing it. Everyone in the party hierarchy owes me one. Yes, I'm quite sure I could swing it."

"Albert, you're a dear sweet man, and I love you to death, but I've more on my plate than I can deal with. That's ridiculous. But I do love our home in Connecticut. It holds many happy memories for me too. Who knows? Perhaps someday little Larissa will want to live there. We'll have to keep it for her."

"Knowing it would stay in our family would make me very happy, very happy, Anna dear. I love you."

As he kissed her, Anna saw the chauffeur watching from the mirror in the front seat. Oh my, what a lucky, lucky woman I am.

◈ Chapter 32

"Anna! Come out here and enjoy this gorgeous evening with me," Albert called from the terrace. She'd been on the phone catching up with Sasha, but he'd heard her cheery "Talk to you later!" which was the way the sisters always ended their nightly calls. It had never ceased to amaze him that those two women were so close; they lived in such different worlds. Anna's life was consumed with business and politics, while Sasha devoted herself unswervingly to Louis and her three children, who were now grown and married. Sasha seemed to live vicariously through Anna—she ate up all the political gossip and loved hearing about Anna's social life. Well, it was wonderful for sisters to remain so close over a lifetime.

"Oh, it is beautiful, isn't it!" she enthused as she opened the terrace door and stepped out. "So warm for April. I feel bad, Albert, that you didn't let me make a bit of a fuss for your birthday. Everyone's asking me why we aren't celebrating it this year."

"My dearest," Albert began as he pulled her closer to himself on the double chaise, which was positioned at the perfect spot to enjoy the panoramic view of the Potomac River, "this is what I call perfection. Just the two of us alone, the occasional sound of a plane overhead, a darting bird or the hoot of an owl. It's so rare that I have you all to myself, and strange as it sounds, Anna darling, I never get enough of you."

"My goodness, Albert, you sound—I don't know—like we're newlyweds or something."

"That's what I feel like. I've never gotten over my amazement that you married me. You were so beautiful, such a prize —still are, of course. The youngest-looking grandmother I've ever seen. No, Anna, there's nothing that special about being seventy. It's just old. I'm feeling old and tired, and if it didn't mean so damned much to you, I'd retire from the Senate. I'd like nothing better than to spend the rest of my life out here on this terrace, watching the seasons change."

Anna smoothed her hair against the slight breeze that was blowing. "I understand that, really I do. Some days I come home so weary, I find myself wondering why I do what I do. But the next morning, I can't get to the office fast enough."

"I know. It's in your blood. You love it."

"I do. But on the other hand, I'll be glad when Gilbert graduates and I have him to rely on too."

"The end of next month—it's coming up soon." Albert sat up a bit, and Anna noticed that he cringed. The bulging disc in his back was obviously giving him some pain. "The truth is, I'm worried about Gilbert," he said.

"Why? He seems to be fine—they're having a grand time in Boston."

"Let's just say you don't know everything I do, and leave it at that."

"Oh, I know Charles tells you things that neither of you want to trouble me with. But generally speaking, I think Gilbert is doing fine. He wants me to support that young Jack Kennedy. It seems Winslow has infiltrated their social set and is quite agog about the Kennedys."

"Young Kennedy's not a bad sort, but I'd prefer that firebrand from Minnesota, Humphrey. Anyhow, it's not Gilbert's political friends and affiliations that worry me. It's his gambling. His debts get bigger and bigger, and he borrows from Charles. I'll say one thing for Charles—he's a damned loyal brother. Never says no to his younger brother."

"Then give me some credit! I've done something right in the way I've raised my boys."

"Oh, Anna, I give you lots of credit. There isn't a more straight-arrow guy in the world than Charles. He seems to know what he's doing with your business. But Gilbert—well, he's another matter. I'd recommend that you not give him too much responsibility too soon. I hate to say it Anna, but I'm not sure I'd trust him."

"Albert! What a terrible thing to say! He's my son, my very own flesh and blood!"

"And you continue to be blind to his faults."

"Albert, for God's sake, tell me what you know so I can judge for myself!"

"You know about his weekly poker game. You know he has a weakness for horses. But do you realize he's borrowed over a hundred thousand dollars from Charles over the past three years, most of it to support his gambling habit?"

"My God! I had no idea."

"Did you know that he and Winslow have developed a fondness for marijuana?"

"But that's against the law! I know a lot of young people are trying it—but Gilbert?"

"I'm afraid so. I wonder at his stupidity, though. He tried to tempt Emily and Charles into using it with them the last time they visited in New York."

"Oh dear, and Emily pregnant—I hope she didn't."

"You know Charles isn't going to let his wife do anything illegal or unhealthy. No, Charles has better sense, and he's furious with Gilbert. He threatened to tell you, but Gilbert begged him not to. So now I've gone and done it."

"Well." Anna stood up and paced back and forth on the flagstone terrace. "I don't know what I'll say. I guess I'll pretend I don't know unless something comes up. I want those two men to get along. I want them to share the responsibility for running Dunay Enterprises. In fact, I think Gilbert has a knack for commercial real estate. I like those two pieces of land he talked me into in Boston, and I want him to take a look at some property in London and Paris as soon as he finishes school. I've got big plans for him."

"I know you do, darling. I only hope he doesn't become more of a problem than an asset."

"Don't be silly! If there's one thing I know how to do, it's keep my employees in line."

"Yes—when they're not your sons."

Anna waited expectantly in the executive office that she had designated for the general counsel of Dunay Enterprises. As she sipped on her second cup of coffee, she tapped her long fingernails against the glass-and-brass lamp table.

Yes, it was perfection. Sidney had done it again. It was decorated differently from Charles's office, yet it was every bit as nice—and the view was even better, since it was two floors higher. Imagine, she thought, we've expanded to five floors! And when I originally signed the lease for two thousand square feet, I wondered if we'd really need all that space. Well, so be it. I firmly believe in growth.

She picked up the intercom and buzzed Barbara, who was in her own office two floors below. "Has Gilbert called in?" she impatiently asked Barbara.

"No, Mrs. Dunay, not a word."

Perhaps something important is holding him up—though I

can't imagine what. He certainly lives close enough. I should have stopped by their house and picked him up on my way in.

Gilbert and Winslow had chosen to live off Massachusetts Avenue in a three-floor town house that sat high above Rock Creek Parkway—it was ten minutes' driving time from the office. Damn it, he knows I'm a fanatic about being on time! She paced across to the window that fronted on the Farragut Square park. Already Miss Reedy, the "bag lady" who seemed to live in the park, was feeding the pigeons that clustered about her feet.

"Good morning, Mother. Sorry I'm late, but Winslow got me involved in a conversation with Steve Smith about the arrangements for the Democratic Convention. That woman lives, breathes, eats, and sleeps that campaign. She's become an addict."

"Ah, so that's what's going on. I must say, I wondered. You know I can't stand people who are habitually late." She smiled broadly at this tall, roguish man who still seemed to have the round face and tousled hair of a boy. He was sexy—she could see why all the women fell over him.

"Don't worry, I know that's one of your fetishes. I'll do my best."

"Well." Anna gestured toward the large room. "What do you think?"

"Great! Sidney did a super job. I love it." He moved behind the huge modern desk—actually, it looked more like a glass-and-brass sculpture than a desk—and sat down in the silver-gray-leather Mies van der Rohe chair. "Yeah, even the chair feels good. I like it, Mom. You done good!"

"Gilbert, I can't abide that awful slang, you know that!"

"Let me tell you how I want to begin," he said. "First, I want to visit all the travel agencies, then the hotels. I need to know the players and be able to visualize the offices and hotels."

Anna, taken aback by his take-charge attitude, started to interrupt, then held her tongue.

"Then I'd like to spend about two months familiarizing myself with the credit business—that's the area I feel weakest in. High finance has always mystified me."

"That's the area Charles is most comfortable with."

"Yeah, I know. Then I want to see firsthand all the properties you've bought."

"Yes, exactly! That's your strong suit, Gilbert. I trust your judgment. Remember, I'm interested only in property with commercial potential—land that will become office buildings, hotels—or better yet, suburban shopping malls. We spent last Saturday out at the Seven Corners shopping area in Virginia, and I tell you, it's amazing. I'm certain that's the wave of the future."

"I couldn't agree more, Mom—Anna, sorry. Charles warned me that you don't like being called Mom down here."

Anna smiled, tickled with this handsome young man. He was shaping up after all.

"As far as being head of the legal division, I'm really not too keen on practicing law."

"You have a staff of six fine lawyers."

"Yeah! And I see my job as managing them. But this other stuff is more important—buying property, keeping an eye on the other operations. Oh, have you hired a secretary for me yet? I hope not."

"Actually, Barbara had begun to interview. Do you have someone special in mind?"

"Yes. So if you don't object, I'll give her a call and bring her on."

"Fine." Anna marveled at his natural take-charge manner. It was amazing in someone so young, just out of school.

"By the way, Anna, Winslow asked me to talk with you about using Pennyfield Manor for some political dinners—perhaps a large cocktail party for big givers."

Anna paused, trying to think how to respond.

"You know that I want all of you to feel free to use the house to entertain in. But in deference to Albert's position of not endorsing a candidate before the convention chooses the nominee, I'm going to ask that you hold off until after the convention. If Kennedy wins, you and Winslow can use the house for whatever entertaining you'd like to do."

He didn't look pleased with her response, so she hastened to soften it. "Of course, if Winslow wants to have a tea or cocktail party for any charitable group—cancer or the symphony or the —no, I don't suppose the Junior League would be interested."

"You're too sensitive about that Jewish nonsense. The Junior League isn't like that anymore. But the truth is, Winslow's totally immersed in the Kennedy campaign. She won't come up for air until after the convention. If Kennedy wins the nomination, we won't see her until after the election."

Anna smiled, stood, and walked behind the desk. She kissed Gilbert lightly on his forehead. "Darling, wish her luck for me. I remember how much I enjoyed Roosevelt's first campaign. I couldn't get enough of it. Ah, those were the days! Tell her I'll do anything I can to help as long as it doesn't compromise Albert. We must honor his feelings."

"Yeah, I suppose so. Well, thanks for this office, it's terrific. I'm going to go meet my staff!"

Anna sat alone with Emily in Emily's bedroom. Out in the living room, some thirty guests were assembled for the ritual circumcision of Emily and Charles's second son, who had been born exactly seven days before. He had been named Douglas.

"I'm sorry, I just don't have the stomach for these things. I can't fathom why you didn't just have it done in the hospital—and be done with it."

"Mother, we're just going to have to teach you Jewish ways," Emily teased with a slight smile.

"Oh, I know, I know. Albert thinks you're exactly right. We've had more than one discussion about this. But to each his own—if you and Charles feel this way, then it's right for you. I can't imagine having all these guests when you've had a baby only seven days ago. I remember how exhausted I was after each birth."

"I have times like that, too, but I have gusts of energy—and right now, I feel grand. Isn't he darling?"

Anna thought about her third grandchild. Even at one week, he was the spitting image of his biological grandfather, the man he would never know. Astounding! All she had to do was look at that baby, and images of Kurt flashed through her head. Elliot actually looked more like Emily's father, that son of a bitch. Too bad. But Elliot was still a handsome little boy—and there were moments when he smiled a certain way that he, too, reminded her of Kurt.

Albert knocked and entered the room, beaming with pride. "It's over, ladies. You can relax. The mohel is bringing your little darling in right away. All the ladies are cooing over him. He didn't cry for a moment, Emily—but he sure did like that taste of wine!"

Emily stood. She was dressed in a flowing sea-foam-colored robe, and her hair was tied back in a soft ponytail with a satin ribbon that matched the robe. She wore the small diamond earrings that Charles had given her to celebrate the birth of their second son.

"Are you sure you feel up to this?" Anna asked, nervous about Emily's pallor.

"Of course—this is a celebration! Let's go."

Sasha had volunteered to manage the party, and Anna had been delighted to let her—that was her forte. Now, Sasha surged forward from the crowded room to congratulate her sister and Emily. "He's adorable, absolutely adorable! I volunteer for baby-sitting services!"

"I'll take you up on it, Aunt Sasha, you can be sure!"

Charles excused himself from his conversation with his uncle Sam and came rushing over to Emily. "Darling, everything went fine. He's performing beautifully for all the women. I do believe he loves every minute of it. Now, let's find a chair for you. I don't want you standing up so much." He led her away to the sofa.

Albert took Anna's hand and put his other arm around Sasha. "This is a grand day. I'm so grateful to you two wonderful ladies for giving me such a wonderful, warm family."

Sasha looked up at him, surprised by the tone of his voice. "It is wonderful, isn't it? We have so much to be thankful for." She looked at Anna. "Don't you wish Mama and Pa were here to see this day?"

"Yes, I found myself thinking the same thing last night as I lay in bed thinking about today. Mama would be so pleased."

It was a steaming day in mid-July when the call came from Senator Landow's office. ". . . appears to be a massive heart attack . . . ambulance . . . to George Washington University Hospital."

Barbara summoned Charles; Gilbert was away in San Francisco. Together, Charles and Anna rode to the hospital, but they arrived too late. Albert had never regained consciousness.

After that, everything became blurred for Anna. She vaguely realized that her brother Joshua and Sasha had taken control of all the details, and Charles, himself functioning only minimally, okayed their decisions.

Anna, for the most part, talked quietly in her bedroom with Emily and Charles and—when she could break away from the telephones—Sasha. Winslow had been summoned home from the campaign, and Gilbert was flying in from the West Coast.

The calls came in by the dozens. Anna took only those that she couldn't refuse: President Eisenhower, Senator Lyndon Johnson.

When Sasha told her that the governor of Connecticut was on the phone, Anna thought it was a condolence call, one she had to accept.

"Anna, dear! What a shock! You can't imagine the impact this has had up here! My phone hasn't stopped since it broke over the radio. We're inundated."

Anna listened with half an ear, wishing this call would hurry and end.

". . . know it's awfully soon to bring up such a thing, but you're a pro, Anna. You know politics never takes a holiday. The press is already badgering me about naming a successor. I've had three calls from men who want to be named, but I'd like to honor Albert's wishes. He asked me to name you in the event. It almost seems as if he knew."

The governor suddenly had her full attention. What was he saying?

"Anna, I'd like to be able to go to the press with the story the day after the funeral. That's about as long as I can hold everyone at bay."

"I'm sorry, Governor. I'm not sure I understand."

"We've—I've decided to appoint you to serve the remainder of his term of office."

"But that's impossible! My business—"

"Anna, he insisted that you would do it. He told me your sons could run your business."

"I—I just don't know! It's all so sudden."

"Yes, I'm sure you're still in a state of shock. But please consider it—and remember it was Albert's wish. He was a dear friend to me in addition to being a political colleague. I want to honor his wishes."

"Could I talk to you tomorrow night?"

"Yes, let's talk then. Meanwhile, think very hard on it, Anna. And remember, Albert wanted this."

* * *

Seven days later, *The Washington Post* ran a full-page story about the amazing life and career of the newest member of the United States Senate, Senator Anna Arnold Dunay Landow.

❖ Part 6

The Pinnacle, 1960

Winslow and Gilbert Dunay, dinner guests last evening on Malcolm Forbes's yacht, reported that his mother, the former senator from Connecticut, is recovering slowly from major abdominal surgery.
                    —*"Page Six,"* New York Post

Chapter 33

*Then peace came deep in me. I lay in the silver heaven
between dreams and day.*
                                    —*Rainer Maria Rilke, 1898*

March 1961

The Connecticut reporters were gathered in Senator Anna
Landow's office for their weekly off-and-on-the-record chat. It
was a custom Albert had initiated, and Anna had been disin-
clined to end it, though it had always required intensive homework the evening before.

"Senator, how do you feel about President Kennedy's first
eight weeks in office?"

"Wonderful! He captured the mood of the nation, especially
the young people, with that splendid inaugural speech. As you
know, last week he announced the formation of a Peace Corps
—exactly the thing our young people need to dedicate themselves to, and what the Third World needs. I applaud that, and I
will give every ounce of support to make the Peace Corps a
permanent program."

"What do you think of him naming his brother-in-law to
head it? Doesn't that smack of nepotism?"

Anna laughed. "Gentlemen, I'm a great believer in nepotism.
Three of my brothers, two nephews, a niece, and my two sons
all work for me in Dunay Enterprises—along with dozens of
other talented young people. As far as the President appointing
Sargent Shriver, consider for a moment. The Kennedy family is
very wealthy—Mr. Shriver doesn't need the income. So that's
not nepotism in old-fashioned Tammany Hall terms. No, it's
simply the President choosing a man he has confidence in to
run a program that is dear to his heart. I fully approve."

"Senator Landow, how does it feel to be one of two women in
the Senate?"

"It feels wonderful. But I wish I had several dozen more
colleagues who were women so we could really make a difference."

"What do you see as the major issues facing this President
and this administration?"

"As the newest member of the Foreign Relations Committee,

I'm gravely concerned with foreign policy, as my husband was. We must be concerned about what is happening in Cuba. While rejoicing, on the one hand, that a dictator like Batista has been overthrown, we must not make the mistake of thinking Castro is the answer to Cuba's problems. That bears close scrutiny. Conceivably, our actions—and reactions—to Castro could cause him to become more and more aligned with Russia. I hope we're smart enough to prevent that."

"Where else in the world do you see trouble spots?"

Anna smoothed her hair back off her face and recrossed her legs. "Gentlemen, I'm also deeply concerned about our increasing involvement in Southeast Asia. This week, the President sent additional advisers to help train the Laotian army to back the Royal Laotian government to the hilt. I'm troubled that everywhere in the world, we seem to back incumbent governments, even if they are headed by savage dictators, against what appear to be civilian revolutions. Time and time again in closed committee hearings, the State Department and our military officials go to great lengths to demonstrate that these rebellions are Communist-inspired. I'm not convinced—I just don't know. But I'm particularly concerned about our activities in Southeast Asia right now. It's more a gut feeling than anything else—call it woman's intuition—as I said, we need more women in the Senate."

"Gentlemen"—Steve Turner, her press secretary intervened —"that's all for today. Senator Landow is already fifteen minutes late for her next appointment. See you next week—same time, same place."

Anna greeted the reporters by name, asked about their wives and children, sent "hellos" back home to mutual friends, then departed for a meeting in Senator Humphrey's office. As she strode down the marble corridor, flanked by her aides, she once again marveled that she—Anna Arnold, who as a young woman had worked in the Senate mailroom—was now a United States Senator. The crowning achievement of a thrilling, fulfilling life—thanks to Albert! Oh, I have so much to be thankful to Albert for. Dear blessed heart of my heart, how I miss you! Does the pain ever go away completely?

The children missed him dreadfully too. She'd been so touched by Gilbert's grief—Gilbert, who she'd imagined hated Albert. "But Mother, he's the only father I've ever known.

Even though we had our spats, I always respected him and, yes, loved him. I can't believe he's gone!" Yes, Albert had left a huge empty space in their lives.

Anna turned the corner, opened the massive wooden door, and was greeted enthusiastically by Humphrey's administrative assistant, Herb Waters. "Come in! Come in. Senator Humphrey will be delighted you've come, Senator."

Several weeks later, on a Sunday afternoon, Anna sat on her terrace overlooking the Potomac, waiting for Charles to arrive. He had phoned her at her Senate office on Friday and told her he had to speak to her privately about a business matter. From the sound of his voice, she knew it was bad news. She'd been on pins and needles since then.

One of the major problems she had struggled with immediately after Albert's death was how to continue to run her companies while serving in the Senate. After conferring with lawyers over conflict-of-interest laws and thinking through the ethics of it, she'd determined that Charles must be made chief executive officer and president of all her companies, with her brothers and nephews in charge of the day-to-day operations of the separate entities: the travel agencies, the hotel chain, the credit company, and the international holding company. Gilbert, meanwhile, as general counsel, had legal oversight of all the various operations.

She had cautioned Charles that she wanted to know nothing, to make no decisions, about acquisitions, mergers, or transportation regulations, or about the tax implications for her companies of various bills pending before Congress. Finally, she had set up a mechanism whereby her brothers Joshua and Sam and her son Charles would together make decisions regarding her personal stocks and bonds and invest her share of the profits from Dunay each quarter. She would not be consulted or advised; she would simply receive a substantial check each month, to supplement her Senate salary.

She wanted to be able to vote on every issue on its merit, regardless of its effect on her business. If, by chance, she discovered that pending legislation would affect her business, she excused herself from voting on it. So far, she'd had no trouble adhering to her own high standards. She hoped that whatever was on Charles's mind this afternoon wouldn't compromise those ideals.

"Mother, you look splendid. Even rested. I guess it all agrees with you." Charles bent to kiss her forehead and took a seat opposite her on a bright chintz-covered wrought-iron sofa.

"Would you like a drink, son?"

"Only because I think you're going to need one before we're finished, and I can't let a lady drink alone."

Anna rang a small bell on the table next to her. Antonio quickly appeared to take their order.

"A sherry for me, Antonio, and a Chivas for Mr. Charles. And would you also bring a small plate of crackers and some of that wonderful Brie? And perhaps some grapes."

She turned her full attention to Charles. "Your voice sounded grave on the phone, Charles. Tell me."

"Our controller, Phil Levine, has discovered some relatively serious problems regarding Gilbert's travel and entertainment vouchers."

"Oh, for Pete's sake, is that what this is all about? Something as petty as that I'd expect you to handle in house, without bothering me. I don't believe this, Charles!" Anna stood angrily and paced back and forth between the edge of the terrace—which jutted over the river—and the sofa.

"Anna, hear me out before you jump to conclusions."

Grudgingly, Anna muttered, "Go ahead."

"Gilbert has been traveling a good deal since he joined Dunay three years ago. In fact, he's hardly ever in the office."

"Get to the point! I authorized that travel."

"From his very first forays out to the agencies, Phil noticed unusually high requests for reimbursement for cash expenditures. Like a thousand dollars for taking the entire staff out to dinner."

"That *is* a lot."

"A month later, his credit card voucher would arrive, and it would show that he'd paid for that dinner with the credit card, not with cash, as he'd claimed." Charles ran his hand over his scalp, trying to puzzle out his brother's behavior.

"After this happened seven different times, with varying amounts of money claimed, Phil called him in and sat him down and questioned him. Gil got hot under the collar and threatened to have Phil fired. That's when Phil brought it to my attention. I told him I wanted to see all of Gil's vouchers and requests for cash reimbursement before they were paid—but not to tell Gil that."

Charles paused to take a large gulp of his Scotch.

"So?" Anna impatiently demanded.

"Well, I was so astonished by the amounts Gil was requesting for reimbursement that I personally checked them out. To make a long story short—Mom, I'm sorry to have to lay this on you—"

"I hate that slang, Charles. Just tell me what you know."

"It seems that Gil has a woman in every city he visits. He wines and dines them and buys them expensive gifts—jewelry, for example—and sends them on exotic trips or cruises as 'goodwill' for Dunay. All these expenditures that don't seem appropriate are for Gil's women—dozens of them, it seems, and all at Dunay expense."

Anna sat down, and a feeling of nausea rose in her stomach. For a while she was speechless, her mind in tumult. She twisted a linen napkin, then looked up at Charles, nearly in tears. "And Winslow's going to have a baby any day! What does Winslow know or guess about all this?"

"I confronted Gil with that. His response was that they had a special relationship. They had both agreed to give each other 'lots of space,' whatever the hell that means."

Anna's disappointment turned to fury. "It means they're both having affairs, both being promiscuous. Damn! I'd hoped for better things."

"I'm sorry, Mother."

Anna twisted her napkin again, in agony. Finally, she looked at Charles. "What do you suggest?"

"Only three people know about this: Levine, me, and you. I don't know how long that will continue to be the case. But we can't afford to let the rest of the company know about this—it would undermine morale terribly if they thought you and I sanctioned such a thing, if they believed our exalted general counsel was so unethical."

Anna sipped her sherry. "I'm so disappointed. I'd really begun to believe Gil would work out okay."

"What I suggest is that you write a strong memo to Gil, for his eyes only, with a carbon copy it to me so he knows I've seen it. Then we'll wait and see what happens."

Anna nodded, then added thoughtfully, "You know, Charles, who Gilbert sleeps with is no business of mine, or yours, for that matter."

"I agree. That's between him and Winslow."

"But the fact that he's financing his amorous adventures with company money—and not very cleverly disguising it—well, it's as if he wanted us to find out. It's as if he's flaunting his power in front of the staff, telling them he can get away with anything because he's my son. I find it disgusting and shameful!"

"Do you want to write the memo, or shall I draft it for you?"

"No, just leave me the documentation, and I'll write the memo tonight. Where is he, by the way?"

"He's in Las Vegas, looking at some land he wants us to buy for a hotel and a casino."

Anna shot out of her chair. "Damn it! I told him I would not consider property in the state of Nevada! That state is controlled by Meyer Lansky's mob, and I'll have no part of it! Get him on the phone, Charles, and order him home. I will not spend one penny of Dunay money inside the state of Nevada!"

"He went there knowing that. I suspect he's planning to invest some of his own money."

"What money, for Pete's sake? The only money he has is the money I pay him!"

"Not true, Mother. He has money Bubby Francine left him, and now the money Albert left him."

"But the provisions of Albert's will say he can't have the principal until he's thirty."

"He can use that as leverage to borrow whatever he needs. Don't doubt for a minute that he hasn't figured all the angles. I don't think you can control how he spends his inheritance."

Anna's hand flew to her forehead, and she grimaced in pain. "Charles," she said weakly, "do you mind, darling? I need to be alone to think this through. I'll call you this evening and drop whatever I write by to you tomorrow morning. I'm sorry."

Charles rose to leave. "I'm sorry to have burdened you with this, but dealing with Gilbert has become the most difficult part of running Dunay. I really don't know how much longer we can continue."

Anna waved him away. She didn't want to hear what he was going to say. It was too painful—too, too painful.

* * *

The idea for the midsummer dinner-dance hit Anna as she was riding home late one afternoon. An incredible amount of backbiting and duplicity was marring the Kennedy-Johnson administration. It was such a shame, when they could be spending all that energy on productive activities. It wasn't so much the two men themselves, the President and the Vice President. It was their staffs, who were constantly deliberately frustrating one another and literally sabotaging each other's efforts.

This was not the way to run a government, Anna told herself. But she also realized "it was ever thus," from time immemorial. What we need to do is get them together in a social setting and force them to get to know one another.

In truth, the backbiting was understandable. Kennedy and Johnson had been mortal enemies during the primary and preconvention process, and even after Johnson accepted the vice presidency, Kennedy's people found themselves wishing he'd turned it down, as they'd expected he would.

Johnson had saved the whole election by carrying Texas for Kennedy. Without Texas, Nixon would now be President. A sobering thought, that. One Kennedy's men should remember every morning when they began to bait the Johnson fellows. Ah well, such is life, such is Washington—but perhaps I'll experiment.

That weekend she assembled Emily, Winslow—who now had a second baby girl, Karine—and her secretary Barbara for a planning session at Pennyfield Manor. After explaining her purpose and the basic idea—which caught fire with Winslow, to the point that there was no holding back her exuberance—Anna declared, "Staging a party like this one, on this scale, is like a theatrical production."

She would send Winslow to New York to order the invitations at Tiffany and sixteen matching scalloped-bordered circular tablecloths from Porthault: "In a multicolored floral, very bright and gay. We'll use the white china with the gold border and fill the center of the table with rustic baskets of multicolored spring flowers."

Barbara was responsible for tracking down the addresses of all the guests, engaging the services of Peter Duchin and his orchestra, and arranging for a harpist to play during the cocktail period.

To Emily fell the responsibility of making a huge seating chart—sixteen tables of ten—and overseeing the work of the florist who would decorate the ballroom and terrace.

"The four of us will do the final seating arrangement the night before," Anna stated. "My intention is to seat one Kennedy assistant and one Johnson assistant at each table; one senator or member of Congress; one member of the press; and one representative of old established social Washington—plus five wives. And we will not seat wives at the same table with their husbands!"

"Oh, what fun!" Winslow cooed. "This will be the most coveted invitation in Washington! Please, Mother, *please* let Gil and me make a list of our friends. I know everyone who counts in the Kennedy circle."

"I know you do, Winslow. You'll be a great asset. Yes, make a list—but mind you, not too long."

"Are you having any family?" Emily asked.

"Only a few. Sasha and Louis, Sidney and her husband. My lawyer, Adam Grenville, and my stockbroker, Hal Morganstern. But that's it. Everyone else is political, press, or social Washington."

Anna patted Emily's hand. "You make a list with Charles and let me know who you would like to include."

"What about the President and Mrs. Kennedy?"

"Yes, indeed, we'll invite the Kennedys and the Johnsons. But you mustn't feel bad if they don't come. It's highly unlikely. Go ahead, Winslow—use your charm to try to get them here. Fine with me!"

"What will you serve?" Winslow asked.

"I haven't given it much thought yet. I think saddle of veal Orloff for the entrée, and a big seafood bar out on the terrace during the cocktail hour. You know—shrimp, crab claws, oysters, though that's a bit messy to eat in black tie and long dresses. On another table we'll have gravlax with dill sauce and a big bowl of beluga caviar. Don't worry, Winslow, it will be splendid. And champagne! I'll have a full bar, plus tubs of the best French champagne."

Barbara took notes of all Anna's decisions. It would be her task to check on Emily and Winslow to make sure each detail was complete—a job she had perfected over the years.

* * *

Nature cooperated by providing a spectacular setting sun the evening of Anna's big dinner-dance. As one hundred and sixty guests gathered on the forty-foot terrace four floors above the cliff overlooking the Potomac River, as the harpist played a medley of tunes from *West Side Story,* Antonio whispered in Anna's ear, "Madam, the President has arrived."

Calmly, appearing cool and totally collected, Anna turned away from the sunset, from her guests, and glided back across the ballroom floor toward the elevator in the hall. All around the house, at every entrance, and throughout the yard, Secret Service agents were stationed. Winslow had succeeded, Anna told herself, smiling softly, as she approached the elevator.

The Vice President had seen her in the Capitol three days before and stopped her in his courtly, southern-gentlemanly way to tell her, "Bird and I are surely looking forward to your big party next Saturday!"

This evening, he had timed his arrival so that he was lionized before the President arrived. Now, as Anna had anticipated, the President would make the rounds, say hello to everyone, hold up her dinner, then take his leave so that she could finally seat the guests. This meant that everyone would have already had so much to drink, they would hardly taste the exquisite dinner she had arranged. So be it! It's worth a few ruined appetites to have the President in my home.

"Mr. President!" Anna gushed as the tall, handsome man came off the elevator.

"Senator!" He bent to kiss Anna's cheek. "Hmm, I love kissing senators," he whispered, "when they're as lovely as you."

The attorney general and his wife, who had arrived with the President, greeted Anna, and a moment later she heard Winslow's and Gilbert's voices in the chorus of hellos, with hugs and kisses all around.

Anna, in a self-consciously regal walk, escorted the President —Mrs. Kennedy was vacationing with the children on the Cape —into the ballroom and across to the terrace. The crowd parted to admit them, then spontaneous applause broke out. "As you can see, Mr. President, I've assembled a few of your most ardent fans!" Anna announced as she released his arm and let him circulate among the guests, all of whom he presumably knew at least by name.

Ted Sorenson and Pierre Salinger followed closely behind him, ready to prompt him with names or otherwise refresh his memory.

As Anna watched the President make his way through the crowd of guests, Gil, his face beaming with pleasure, rushed to her side. "Mother, let's ask Duchin to play some dance music! This crowd loves to dance."

Anna was reluctant to give in to Gilbert's wishes. "I thought we'd begin his music when dinner is served."

"But the President will be leaving soon, and several of the ladies are dying to dance with him. What can it hurt?"

"All right. If they want to dance now, go ahead."

Gilbert was right. The minute the music began, dozens of couples took to the floor. She turned back to the seafood bar to sample a shrimp.

"Anna dear, this is truly a magnificent home! I'd no idea such beauty existed out here in the country," Patricia Walsh, an "old Washington" type, exclaimed. "What a group you've assembled here tonight!"

"Yes, wonderful, isn't it? Such a young, attractive, and brilliant group of people the Kennedys have assembled around themselves."

Even as she made polite conversation with her guests, Anna kept an eye on the dance floor. Yes, indeed. As she'd anticipated after Gil's request, Winslow was dancing with the President. There would be no holding her down now! And now Bobby's cutting in! Rich! What fun!

Then the President was striding directly toward her. In response, she found herself walking toward him. "May I have a dance with the most beautiful senator in America before I have to leave?" he asked as he swept her into his arms and they glided together to the dance floor.

"Such a home! And a wonderful family! But I miss the counsel of your husband."

"Yes, he left a void. We all continue to miss him."

President Kennedy suddenly became serious. "Anna, I read your comments about aid to Laos. I'd like to send one of my best people over to discuss it with you. I need your support, your vote on the committee."

"Mr. President, I'd be happy to listen to anyone you'd like to send. But I must confess, I'm worried about what you're doing in Asia. I just don't know."

"Damn!" He smiled broadly at her and winked as he said, "I could always count on Al's vote. Looks like I'll have to work to get yours—or spend more time dancing with you!"

And then the attorney general cut in on his brother. It seemed to be a routine they'd perfected. But as Anna realized, the President was about to leave. "Bobby, I must escort the President downstairs—please excuse me."

"Mother, I've got to hand it to you. It was absolutely the most fabulous party I've been to—ever!" Gilbert's face beamed as he sipped his cognac.

The five of them were gathered in the library. It was nearly two in the morning. Emily looked especially weary to Anna— but no wonder, she was expecting her third child and was only now beginning to get over three months of morning sickness. She looked wan and exhausted as she nestled in Charles's arm, her high heels kicked off, her bouffant hairdo beginning to look a bit messy.

"My friends will be talking about it for weeks! I hope we do it again soon," Winslow enthused, kicking off her shoes too.

"Not too soon!" Anna answered. "It's a lot of work."

"I've never seen so many gorgeous dresses," Emily said.

"Or such jewels! The 'sparklies,' as the press calls your bunch, Winslow, really do compete, don't they?" Charles added.

"Speaking of jewels, Winslow, I've been looking at your necklace and earrings and bracelet all evening. Are those real diamonds?" Anna asked.

Winslow's hand flew to her throat, and Gilbert's face turned crimson. "Ah—ah, yes. A gift from Gilbert. To celebrate our wedding anniversary. I was so surprised—and so thrilled!"

"I'll bet you were," Anna answered, her voice tinged with sarcasm. Then to Gilbert she said, "Wherever did you get that kind of money? That jewelry had to cost nearly a hundred thousand dollars. Do I pay you that much?"

Gilbert cleared his throat, sat straight up in his chair, and looked steadily, defiantly at Anna as he said, "Actually, I've made some good investments these past two years, and they're beginning to pay off."

Anna realized that Charles and Emily were staring at Gilbert with overt hostility. Winslow suddenly stood and announced, "I'm exhausted, Mother. I think it's time we went home. You give wonderful parties!"

▨ Chapter 34

"Yes, Barbara?" Charles answered the call on the interoffice line.

Although Anna was officially "chairman emeritus" of Dunay Enterprises while she served in the Senate, Barbara retained her position at Dunay. Barbara's first responsibility was to serve as a sort of social secretary for Anna; her second was to help Charles in any way he designated.

"Charles, are you aware of an Adams Company here at Dunay?" she asked. "The girl who's substituting for Gil's secretary just called me. She's had four calls in the past two days from a man in Paris who insists that Gil gave him this phone number and mailing address for the Adams Company."

Charles had given Barbara only a bit of his attention until he heard the words *man in Paris*. "Hmm—no, Barbara, I can't think of any. Tell you what, get the name and number of the man, and I'll return the call. It might be important."

"I can't imagine it's something you should waste your time on."

"Barbara, do me a favor. Don't worry so much about my time. Just get me the man's name and number." He put the phone down, instantly regretting the tone of voice he'd used with Barbara. Damn! What's Gil up to now?

There's something about Adams . . . and a man in Paris . . . and Gil . . . Hell! Adams is Winslow's maiden name! I'd forgotten.

The phone rang again, and Barbara gave him the name and number.

"Barbara, please accept my apologies. I didn't mean to snap at you a minute ago. It's just—"

"Don't worry, Charles, I understand. Let me know if I can help with anything."

"Sure thing. And thanks for being so understanding."

He looked at the name on the piece of paper: Jean Pierre Gillet.

Charles did something he'd never done before. He called Gillet, pretending to be Gilbert. What he found out chilled and disgusted him. Gilbert had been buying real estate in Europe for Dunay International at vastly inflated prices, then receiving a cash kickback. Gillet wanted to know where to send the hundred fifty thousand to Gilbert. He also discussed a similar deal in Portugal. If Dunay paid thirty-one million for some ocean-front property, Gilbert would take a cool million off the top.

So that's where Gil gets all his extra spending money. Ripping off his own mother!

He balled up the paper with Gillet's number on it and threw it across the room. He pounded his fist on the desk three times, then dropped his head into his hands. Utter contempt for Gil washed over him.

How am I going to tell this one to Mom?

How many times has he done it? How many times has he inflated the price of land at Dunay's expense? Mother is so damned proud of his unerring judgment about commercial real estate! Hell's bells! My brother's no better than a criminal!

He rang the intercom. His own private secretary, Nancy, answered, and even as he asked her to pull certain files, his mind was reeling with the understanding that he alone could conduct this investigation. No one—not even his uncles or cousins—could know what Gilbert was doing. This was family: Anna, Gilbert, and Charles. No one else could ever know.

Because Mother will want me to, I will spend the rest of my life protecting and defending that piece of trash who is my brother!

Six weeks later on a Sunday night, Anna convened a meeting of her two sons—alone, without their wives or children—in the library of her Kalorama home.

Gilbert arrived first, deeply tanned from his month in the Mediterranean, seemingly in a splendid mood. After fixing himself a cognac, he took a seat on the muted-turquoise-velvet sofa opposite Anna, who had not greeted him beyond a lukewarm "Hello, Gilbert."

She sat regally, a file on her lap, in a softly upholstered wing chair at the far end of the sofa. Next to her, on a skirted lamp table, was her customary sherry and a pair of reading half-glasses.

Gilbert appraised his mother's appearance and mood. "You're looking tired—and grim. Politics must really be getting to you, huh?"

"No, son. It's not politics that wears me out. It's my family."

At that moment the doorbell rang again, and the butler admitted Charles, who came immediately into the library. He nodded curtly to Gilbert and walked across the room to plant a kiss on his mother's forehead. In a somber voice he intoned, "Good evening, Mother. I hope we can make this short—you look exhausted."

Anna said nothing. She opened the file on her lap, glanced at the top page, then slammed it shut as if it might bite her. In a harsh voice she snapped, "Let's get started!"

Charles poured himself a Scotch straight, sat down, and opened his briefcase.

Gilbert looked from his mother to his brother, sensing fireworks, then back to his mother. "What's the subject, if I may ask? Or do we have a formal agenda?"

Anna held her hands together in front of her, making a steeple with her fingers. As she tapped her fingers against each other, she said in a quiet, steady voice, "The subject—the subject, Gilbert, is ethics. Your ethics."

"Good God! What is brother Charles whispering to you about now?" He took a deep swallow of cognac and set the glass down heavily.

"As it turns out, it isn't your brother Charles. It's your French business partner, Jean Pierre Gillet."

Gilbert's bronze face flushed a deeper shade. He looked directly at Charles, then back at his mother. A slow smile broke out on his face. "So—so I've been found out."

"Did you imagine you could go on with it indefinitely and we'd never discover anything?" Charles asked in a gruff voice.

Gilbert, playing for time, wondered exactly how much they knew. He walked back to the bar and poured himself a second cognac.

Anna and Charles watched him, wondering how he would try to wiggle out of this one. Anna half hoped he would come up with a plausible, somehow understandable explanation of his activities. She wanted—desperately—not to believe he was deliberately stealing from her.

Gilbert returned to the sofa, sat with a despairing sigh, and uttered, "I guess I always knew you'd find out sooner or later." Then he looked from Anna to Charles, as if he were a little boy waiting to hear what his punishment would be.

A sudden thought illuminated Anna's mind. Before she thought it through, she asked, "Did you always intend for me to find out? Did you have two motives? Is it true not only that you wanted the money—because there is never enough money to satisfy your greed, Gilbert—but that you also wanted Charles and me to find out, so you could hurt us?"

Gilbert said nothing, but a look crossed his face that seemed to indicate that her guess was correct.

Anna opened the file and glanced at the top page. "According to my calculations—if Charles's investigation of your activities for the past few years is complete, and I'm not convinced it is—you've cost our company nearly half a million in inflated land prices. And you are currently negotiating with Gillet to buy land in Portugal that will also be inflated by a million dollars, half of which you will receive."

"Mother, I'm not sure we should go ahead with that."

"Damn straight we won't go ahead with that! You can bet your life on it!" Charles shot from his chair. Then he abruptly stood and walked to the bar to pour another Scotch.

"Whether we go through with that deal is not important for the purposes of my meeting with you tonight, Gilbert. Remember, I'm a United States Senator. I'm not involved, nor do I wish to be, in the decisions of Dunay. I'm not even terribly troubled by the amount of money we're talking about—though I grant you it's a huge sum.

"No, Gilbert," Anna continued in a voice so quiet that both men had to strain to hear her, "it's not the money. But I am deeply wounded by the knowledge that you would steal from me and from your brother. All these years"—Anna's voice broke, and she steeled herself against tears—"all these years I've made it a point to put my brothers and my nephews in positions of responsibility in my companies. I've made each of them millionaires. But the truth is, it was for you, Gilbert, and Charles. Everything I've done, all the companies, all the long hours, the financial risk—" Anna stopped to blink away the tears that had formed in the corners of her eyes. "The reason I've worked so hard ever since you boys were born was so that you would never know a moment's poverty, a moment's pain. And now this. . . ." Her voice trailed off, and her eyes asked the question, Why, why Gilbert, did you need to hurt me like this? But she couldn't get the words out.

Both men sat silently, staring at the Aubusson rug, at their trousers, at their fingernails.

Anna wiped her eyes and sipped her sherry. "Charles will make arrangements with you to pay back the money you've appropriated from the company. I want it paid back within the next five years."

Charles crossed his legs angrily and muttered, "Damn!"

Anna shot him a look that seemed to plead for patience. Then to Gilbert she said, "Under the circumstances, our chief executive officer has determined that you will no longer be involved in any part of our real estate operations. Your responsibilities will be solely those of general counsel and board member."

Gilbert gave a small sigh of relief and seemed to relax a bit.

Anna looked at Charles and saw eyes of steel and a madly beating pulse in his temples. She knew he was furious.

"It had always been my intention that after a few years, the two of you would have equal power and equal responsibility— and an equal income, in spite of your younger years, Gilbert. But you've put me in a position where I can no longer justify that kind of trust."

Gilbert's head reared up, and anger suddenly replaced apprehension in his eyes.

"Gilbert, you've done it to yourself! Surely you see that!" Anna remonstrated.

"The hell I do! What I see is you continuing to favor Charles! He's always been your favorite—everyone who knows our family knows that. Hell, my friends all comment on the fact that you favor Charles. Because he kisses your ass all day long every day! Well, I've a mind of my own, and I never was a mama's boy, and I never will be. I've got more business sense in my little finger than he has in his whole brain! For chrissake, Mother, can't you see that?"

Anna sipped her sherry, never taking her eyes from Gilbert's.

"Would you prefer to be relieved of all your responsibilities at Dunay? And your income from Dunay?"

Taken aback, Gilbert stared at her, realizing the full implications of her words.

"That can be easily arranged," Charles growled.

"Yeah," Gilbert sneered in his direction, "I'll bet you'd love that, wouldn't you?"

"What I would like"—Anna stood and smoothed her skirt, placing the folder on the footstool in front of her—"is for the two of you to work out an arrangement whereby Gilbert can pay back, over time, the money he has borrowed from Dunay. And I would like the two of you to work out your differences and get on with the business of running Dunay. I have more important immediate concerns, like foreign aid. The last thing I needed, Gilbert, was to learn that my own son is not to be trusted. Now, if you'll both excuse me, I've some homework upstairs. And hopefully, a night's sleep. I've agonized over this business since Friday, slept hardly a wink."

Suddenly, impulsively, she stooped and kissed Gilbert on the forehead. "I still love you, Gilbert. I hope you know that."

She headed toward Charles, and he stood. "Mother, I . . ."

"I know you probably don't believe I've handled this right, darling. But try it my way. Let's try to make it work. We *are* family, after all. We need to learn to forgive one another."

Whatever Charles had intended to say, he squelched. Stiffly, formally, he kissed her good night, then snapped his briefcase shut and followed her out of the library.

The chief of naval operations was carefully working his way around the table, dancing with each woman in turn and then returning her to her place with a flourish. His eyes had nearly burned a hole in Anna during dinner; in a few minutes, he would be claiming her for a dance. And in her heart of hearts, she knew he'd done something about the seating arrangement. Somehow he'd influenced the White House social secretary to seat him at the same table as the junior senator from Connecticut.

Yes, after all these years of carefully avoiding him, of staying away from committee hearings at which she knew he would be testifying, of declining invitations—which arrived every couple of months—to the big house on the hill on Massachusetts Ave nue, now finally, she would have to talk to him, dance with him, permit him to hold her in his arms again—and it would feel so good!

Oh, Kurt! Kurt! Can't you ever leave me alone? Must you torture me for the rest of my life? Where is your wife tonight? Why isn't she here at this state dinner?

And then he was standing behind her chair, gently pulling it back as she stood. Her eyes met his, and a smile of resignation to the inevitable lit her face. He was resplendent in his full-dress uniform; she, a stunning beauty in deep-purple faille.

They said not a word to one another as she followed him to the dance floor. She found her old place in his arms, felt warmth flooding from his body to hers, felt his moist lips against her temple. She heard his voice whisper, "I love you, Anna. Nothing has changed. I'll always love you."

A hard, cold wall she'd erected over the years crumbled. Inside her, everything became fluid—all her emotions, all her thoughts. She could barely hear the words tumbling out of her own mouth: "And I love you, Kurt. Always." The world melted around her, and shimmering jewels and gowns and music and crystal faded away. Concerns about protocol and appearances and appropriateness evaporated.

Their arms around one another, they swayed mindlessly to the music, hoping it would never end, that this moment would go on forever. And forever.

Their bodies parted, but they did not leave the dance floor when the music stopped. Kurt looked down the front of his uniform, grinned mischievously, and asked, "What do you think the President would say if he looked closely at his chief naval officer now?"

Anna suppressed a giggle. "This President would understand completely!"

"Since you put it that way, you've got a point. And I've got a bone to pick with you."

"Oh?" Anna said warily. "What's that?"

"Why didn't you attend my swearing in? I personally hand-addressed the invitation." His eyes were boring into hers. This was no laughing matter.

"Yes," Anna paused, "I recognized your handwriting. And I thought long and hard." She sighed, and he took her back in his arms when the music started up again. "I guess it's a simple matter of self-preservation. I couldn't bear the thought of seeing you in all your glory with"—she hesitated, it was so difficult to get the words out—"with her at your side, when I so badly wanted to be there myself."

"So you didn't come, and I didn't even get a note from you. Tsk! Tsk! Anna, what's happened to your manners?"

He pulled her closer and kissed her forehead. "I'll think about forgiving you—if you'll let me take you home tonight."

Anna felt something in her stomach tighten like a fist. Could she bear to let him into her life again? Could she deal with that kind of frustration? "No, Kurt. I've a car waiting—and I don't want to begin something again, something which would only hurt more and more. . . . I think we're both too old to deal with—what can only be a difficult situation."

"You're sure?" He looked down at her, trying to gauge the real feeling behind the words.

"I am certain, Kurt. Absolutely certain."

On Christmas Eve afternoon Anna summoned her two sons to Pennyfield Manor. They joined her in the sitting room next to her bedroom, and she handed each of them a sealed envelope. She began to speak as they read the checks enclosed.

"I've given each of you half a million dollars to build a home. Your children need private rooms and space to play in, and your wives deserve a lovely home to entertain in."

"Mom," Charles enthused, "this is wonderful! Emily will be thrilled! She's really gotten the house bug lately. But this—this will buy quite a house!"

"Thanks, Mom," Gilbert added, pocketing the envelope.

Anna looked sternly at Gilbert. "Notice that the check is made out to Winslow and Gilbert Dunay. It's to be used for a home and furniture, and nothing else. Not for your gambling debts—or some floozie."

"Mother!" Gilbert pretended shock that his mother dared bring up such subjects.

"Oh, I know a lot more about you than you'd like me to know, Gilbert. I'm no dummy."

"No one ever said you were a dummy—certainly not me, Mom." He smiled his most devilish smile at her, a smile that always tore at her heart.

"And," she continued, "I've decided to make a dramatic increase in your salary and bonuses. From now on, each of you will receive a basic salary of six hundred thousand a year, plus bonuses twice annually." She looked pointedly at Gilbert. "That should cover all your living expenses. That's even more than *I* draw from the company. That should be enough for Winslow."

"Grand, Mom. She'll be pleased. And I am too."

"Well"—Anna warmed a bit—"see that you deserve it." When she looked at Charles, she saw that he was fuming silently.

"Gilbert, be an angel and go bring up that bowl of fruit I left in the kitchen. I've given all the help this afternoon off."

When Gilbert was out of earshot, Anna asked Charles what was troubling him. "Be as blunt as you care to, son. I can handle it."

"Mom, I hate to put it this way, but if you don't get him out of the business, I'm quitting. I mean it. I don't want him around, meddling in things. I want him out. *Out.*"

"But what else would he do?"

"I don't give a damn *what* he does! I don't care if he spends the rest of his life on a yacht doing nothing. I don't care how much money you give him. I don't want him meddling in Dunay Enterprises."

"I see." The truth was, she'd never seen Charles so upset, and she believed he was in earnest. She had tried his patience long enough with her insistence that Gilbert be given responsibility. "Give me two or three months, darling. I'll work something out."

Gilbert came back into the sitting room, carrying a crystal bowl. "Here, Mom. These pears look good, and the grapes seem to have been washed."

"Thank you, Gilbert. Now, let's pack the children's gifts in your cars. I've put them in large shopping bags with each child's name."

They made several trips to the cars carrying packages and platters of Christmas cookies that Anna's cook had made for the grandchildren.

"I'm so sorry you won't be with us tonight when we open gifts," Anna said to Gilbert as he prepared to depart. Almost as an afterthought she added, "Where will you be?"

His face flushed slightly. He finished putting on his soft leather gloves and smiled wryly at his mother.

"You might as well hear it from me first. We—Winslow and I —have . . . converted to the Episcopalian religion. We'll be attending services with the children."

Anna was speechless. She felt as if he had punched her in the stomach or struck her face. She had never made a big deal about religion . . . but Gilbert—her son, Sarah and Jacob and Francine's grandson—had disavowed his Jewish religion.

Anna turned quickly so he couldn't see the tiny tears in her eyes. "Wish everyone a wonderful Christmas for me. Give Larissa and Karine a big hug—I hope Santa is good to them. Cheerio."

But as the front door closed behind her, she felt anything but cheery.

It was late February before the attorney general came through for her—and she swore him to secrecy. It wasn't a surprise, although she acted as if it were, when Gilbert came to see her at her Senate office two days later.

He was already standing inside the small, private office, in front of a wall of pictures and plaques, when she returned from a floor vote.

"Gilbert, how good to see you! My goodness, how tan you are! It looks splendid on you. I swear, you could be a movie star. I hope Winslow appreciates that."

"You can be sure, Mother, that she beats the other women off with a stick!"

"Hmm." Anna's eye was caught by a telephone message lying on her desk. A call from the attorney general. It could wait. "So, sit down, Gilbert. What's on your mind? I'm sure this isn't a social call."

"No, Mother. Actually, I'm a bit nervous."

"With me? Don't be ridiculous. Sit. Now, talk!"

Anna, meanwhile, sat in a wing chair rather than behind her desk.

"I've been offered a wonderful opportunity. Actually, I think it's because all of Winslow's socializing has finally paid off— anyhow, she's claiming the credit."

She would, Anna thought, but she said nothing.

"The attorney general has offered me a job on his senior staff."

"Wonderful! Oh, Gilbert, that's wonderful! I'm so happy for you! I know you've wanted to be in politics. This is a perfect place to begin to build a reputation."

"It doesn't pay much."

"But I'm sure he knows you don't need the money. The Kennedys understand things like that."

"You don't mind, then?" Gilbert seemed genuinely astonished by his mother's reaction.

"Son, I'm so proud of you. I'm thrilled for you. Nothing could make me happier."

"I sort of hate to leave Charles in the lurch like this, I mean with you here at the Senate—he needs me there."

"Don't worry about it. I'll be back at Dunay in ten months. Albert's term expires then, and I've no intention, as I've said all along, of running for this seat again. No, the governor wants to be senator—and I'm so grateful to him for honoring Albert's wishes and letting me be a senator for two years. No, Gilbert, don't give it a second thought. Charles can manage just fine until I get back there myself."

Gilbert's face broke into a big smile. "I'm so pleased, Mother. I didn't know how you would take it. You've made it easy for me. Winslow will be so happy, too—she was concerned."

"Yes. I'm sure she was concerned about living on the salary of a government employee."

"Well, she didn't think you'd cut me off completely. What will you do, Mother? How much will I make from Dunay?"

"I'll speak to Charles. We'll arrange to keep your income at its present level. We'll consider you on leave from Dunay—you can come back whenever you choose. But you might decide to run for office, the state legislature or something."

"That's a thought, of course. But we'll just have to play it by ear."

"My sentiments exactly! Now, there's a call I must attend to."

Gilbert left the room beaming, even as Anna picked up the phone and dialed the attorney general to thank him.

"Actually, Anna, I was calling about something else," he responded. "The President asked me to explore with you whether you'd be willing to take on an ambassadorship when you finish Albert's term this December."

"I—I don't know. Of course, I'm terribly flattered by the President's confidence, but my business—"

"Anna, don't make me have him call you. He's so damned busy with this Cuban trade embargo and the peace march coming up. Anna, just say yes so I can report back to him, one more mission accomplished."

"Oh, Bobby, you know I never could say no to you. Of course I'll do it. I'll do whatever you folks want me to. But when you see him, tell him how pleased I am, Bobby. Truly pleased."

Anna placed the phone in the cradle. Then, in a whisper, she said, "Albert, do you believe this? Do you believe it?"

And in her imagination she saw his soft smile and heard him say, "Of course I believe it. I arranged for it—from here!" And then she heard his wonderful laugh.

▧ Chapter 35

Vienna, the United States Embassy, 1963

Anna bade her second secretary good evening at the front door of the residence, nodded to the butler who held the door for her, and walked directly up the long staircase to her private quarters. It was only nine in the evening, early for her to be returning from the obligatory social rounds of an ambassador. But tonight had been a light night—only two cocktail parties and a movie premiere to benefit the International Red Cross. She'd done her bit by showing up for the reception preceding the premiere; there had been no need to sit through the screening, she told herself as she entered the softly glowing sitting room, illuminated now by a blazing fire in the fireplace.

"Good evening, Madame," her personal maid, Josephine, greeted her.

"Ah, you've tea ready! That will hit the spot!" Anna handed her fur coat and evening bag to Josephine, then went into her dressing room to change to more comfortable clothes.

As she slipped the short, cut-velvet cocktail dress off her shoulders, she glimpsed her pale face and tired eyes in the mirror. "This is not my favorite job," she said aloud to her reflection. Not by a long shot. I'd rather be back in the Senate—or back at Dunay, for that matter. These parties are so wearing, and I wonder what we really accomplish."

She scrubbed the makeup off her face, gave her shoulder-length hair a good brushing, and wrapped herself in a navy-velvet lounging robe. She went back out to the sitting room, where Josephine was waiting to serve her tea.

"Would you like something more? A sandwich, perhaps?" Josephine asked, knowing that the ambassador rarely ate much at the stand-up parties she attended.

"No, I'm too weary even to eat. And look at that stack of reading material I've got to get through! My goodness!"

Anna sat in a large wing chair near the fireplace and reached for the first of a stack of papers that had arrived that afternoon in the diplomatic pouch from Washington. She sipped her tea and had read several documents before Josephine returned from the bedroom, where she'd been no doubt putting Anna's clothes away and straightening the bathroom.

"Will there be anything else, Madame?"

Anna felt a momentary impulse to ask her to stay, simply for company. But that would be ridiculous! I'm turning into a dotty old woman, she scolded herself. Besides, I've got all this work to do.

"No, Josephine. I've everything I need. Thank you."

But wouldn't it be nice, Anna thought as she watched the door close behind Josephine, if I were close enough to the boys that I could have a nice visit now! Ah, this is a lonely life, and it's getting lonelier and lonelier.

Albert, I miss you so. And let me tell you something: Keeping busy is not the answer. Nothing replaces the loss of someone you love. It's an irreparable loss. Don't let anyone kid you. . . . I really am turning into a dotty old woman. Soon I'll be talking to myself!

She put the documents on the footstool, picked up *Time* magazine, and leafed through it, stopping to read the national and international pages. Then she skipped back to the columns about the theater and newly published books.

What's wrong with me? I'm so damned restless or something,

tonight. Hell, I'll read *The New York Times*, catch up on what's doing in the theater and on Wall Street.

Maybe I'll call Charles after I finish the paper. I could do with a nice long chat with them. Emily's baby is due in a month. . . . She's such a wonderful mother. I'm so pleased we rescued her from her father.

She flipped through the front section of the *Times,* stopping to read the editorial page and glance at the letters to the editor.

I miss politics, the politics of Connecticut. And the politics of Washington. I miss the excitement the Kennedys brought to Washington. It's so far away here, and it doesn't seem quite real.

She picked up the second section and scanned the pages. She stopped on the obituary page, automatically looking for Connecticut names.

"My God!"

Her hands began to tremble, then they became icy as she stared at the bold headline: BETTY ADDISON, WIFE OF CHIEF OF NAVAL OPERATIONS, KILLED. A long story accompanied by a picture told the story of Betty Addison's death at the wheel of her car. "In addition to her husband, Admiral Kurt Addison, Mrs. Addison is survived by her son, Kurt, Jr., two daughters, Mrs. Elise Caufield and Mrs. Monique Easton, and four grandchildren."

Something about the story struck Anna as strange. She read it a second time, then realized what was bothering her. "The medical examiner stated that the results of the autopsy will not be released." What was it Kurt had told her years ago? Something about drinking too much, mixing pills with alcohol? Poor Kurt. He must be devastated! And the children. . . .

Anna put the paper down and picked up her teacup. She held it in both of her icy hands, trying to warm them. Feelings of sorrow competed with joy. Visions of Kurt as she'd first seen him flashed across the screen of her mind. He'll be so lonely . . . he'll need me now. We're both free—but I hurt him so much last time. . . . He'll look for a younger woman, I'm too old already. . . . He'll need me, I've got to be there for him— no, no, I can't do that, I can't let myself go running to him, not after all these years!

Anna stood and paced the length of the room and back again,

hugging her arms to her body, unable to feel warm in spite of the blazing fire.

Instinctively, she walked to the tall secretary desk and took out a handful of her personal stationery emblazoned with the Dunay family crest.

I will write him a condolence note.

"My dearest Kurt," she began. Then, thinking of those three adult children who might be opening condolence letters, she crumpled the page into a ball and threw it into the fireplace.

"Dear Admiral Addison," she wrote at the top of the second page, then stared at it. He'd think she'd lost her mind if she wrote him so formally. She threw that page into the fireplace too.

My darling Kurt I love you you'll never know how much I've missed you all these years and now perhaps we can be together I love you please tell me you feel the same. . . .

"Damn!" she said aloud as she stood again and paced back and forth. What to say?

She sat back down and began again. "Kurt,"—that would have to do.

"I've just read the horrible news of your wife's death in *The New York Times,* and I'm so sorry for you and the children. I can only imagine . . ."

She wrote for two pages, pouring out her sympathy, which suddenly felt genuine. She could relate to his loss of Betty because she still felt the pain of having lost Albert. It was as simple as that. They had both lost someone they loved. They would both now be alone. Unless . . .

Without rereading what she'd written, she licked the envelope and closed it. It would go out first thing in the morning.

And she'd wait to see if he responded.

Charles and Emily arrived for a visit in late June, minus their four children, who were safely ensconced in their newly completed Potomac home with a nanny and Sasha's daily supervision. Emily brought Anna a volume of pictures that had been taken just the previous month, pictures of six-year-old Elliot, five-year-old Doug, red-haired Sonia, who was driving her brothers wild with her determined babble, and the new baby, one-month-old Brad.

Anna paged through the album while Emily and Charles related stories of temper tantrums and toilet training and sleepless nights when the little ones had the flu.

Anna smiled at her dear daughter-in-law. "God knew what he was doing when he made parents young. I don't think I could handle sick children with such patience as you have, my dear."

"Oh, it's awful when they're ill. If Charles is out of town, I *really* feel his absence then. But when they're all well and happy, I can't imagine there's another person in the world as blessed as I am. They're each unique, and it's such fun to watch their personalities unfold, and wonder—wonder what makes them tick!"

Anna reached over and spontaneously hugged Emily. "I can't tell you how good it is to have you here. I hadn't realized how very much I miss my family, all of you."

"Well," Charles declared, "we've only five days here. So if you two women can tear yourself away from baby pictures, I'd like to see the charms of Austria."

"And I want to hear what's going on at the office," Anna responded. "You can brief me while I give you my best sight-seeing tour."

There were days when Anna wanted nothing more than to pack her bags and go back to Washington and resume her position as head of Dunay International. But when she thought of how much Charles was enjoying being at the helm, she found she couldn't deprive him of that pleasure. Truth to tell, he turned everything he touched to gold. No, she had no complaints about his management. She only worried about whether his health would hold up under such a heavy load and whether he was paying enough attention to his wife and children.

No sooner did that worry cross her mind than she remembered herself at his age. No one could have convinced her that she needed to spend more time with her children and Claude. It was her career that mattered—wasn't it? How could she preach to Charles now? She had only to hope that Emily herself would demand whatever attention she needed, that Emily would bring the same patience to being a wife that she brought to being a mother.

"You must tell me about Gilbert and Winslow too. I'm actually surprised they haven't come for a visit yet. I had thought they might."

"He seems to be enjoying his work in the Justice Department enormously. I've never seen him so full of himself!" Emily exclaimed.

"Ah, yes! I'm delighted," Anna said as she remembered when he'd told her that Winslow's connections were responsible. Little did he know.

"I wonder about the little ones," Charles interjected. "Anna, you should see Karine—she's really something. Looks like the pictures of you when you were a toddler. And her newborn, Scot, is adorable. Anyhow, Winslow's riding the crest of a social wave that seems to have the whole world in thrall. The Kennedys are incredible in their ability to garner public attention. Winslow and Gilbert seem happy, really in their element, I suppose. But those poor children—that's another story."

"Oh, I'm sure they're well cared for."

"Mom, of course Winslow's got nannies and maids and chauffeurs," Charles snapped. "That's not what I'm talking about. But she sleeps till noon and is gone the rest of the day far into the night. Those kids are lucky if they see her an hour a week! I'm not kidding!"

Charles's face turned red when he got angry, and it was red now. Anna looked at Emily. "Is it really that bad, Emily?"

Slowly, sadly, Emily nodded. "What they need is a bubby in Washington. You'll have to come home soon."

"Believe me, I think about that every now and then. Six grandchildren growing up, years of their lives I'm missing and can never replace—I'd like to be closer to all of you. Yes, Charles, someday soon you may have to give up the exclusive title to that executive suite and let me have a little office again."

"Anytime, mother. Anytime. With pleasure."

She looked at him. He seemed to really mean it—he'd welcome her back. Well, that was good to know, consoling to tuck away in the back of her head.

The servants were awaiting her arrival at Pennyfield Manor. The moment Marc stopped the car in front of the portico, in spite of the near-zero cold, Antonio opened the door and rushed out to greet her, followed closely by her personal maid, Josephine, and the cook, Rosa.

It was early evening and dark, but the house looked as magnificent as it had in her memory: lights blazed from all the front windows, and the exterior was lit with artfully placed flood-lights.

Looks like a movie set, she told herself as she alighted from the limousine. Why am I wasting my time in Austria when I could be here, at home? Although she had come to Washington the month before for President Kennedy's funeral, she had had little time or inclination then to enjoy her home.

"Mrs. Landow, we're so pleased you could come home for the Christmas season!" Antonio exclaimed.

Anna looked at him dubiously. "You are? When it means you must give up your own holidays to take care of my family? My stars, such loyalty!" Then she softened her tone. "Antonio, please tell the others how pleased I am that you've agreed to be here while I'm home for ten days. I expect you to be sure every-one gets appropriate time off after I leave.

"Now—are any of my children or grandchildren here?"

"No, Madame. Mr. Charles asked me to tell you they'll all be coming for brunch tomorrow at noon. He wanted you to have a chance to rest after the long flight."

"I see. Well, that's fine. Now, Josephine, you and I have quite a job of unpacking these bags."

Anna glanced around the foyer and into the library. The riotous color and the scent of fresh flowers and the potpourri, which Rosa had made from pine needles and cloves, filled the house. Yes, it was as wonderful as her imagination had told her it was—it was home!

"Rosa has prepared some of her minestrone for you. Would you be interested in a steaming hot bowl right now?"

"Ah, yes! That would really hit the spot. And I'd like a bit of wine and some warm, crusty bread. Do you have a fire going in the small dining room? If you do, that's where I'd like to eat." That's where Albert's portrait hangs, and I'd like to be alone with him for a while. Aren't I the funny old woman!

Anna wandered through each room slowly, letting memories seep through her, recalling happy and sad times, remembering Albert's voice as if he were speaking with her even now. She let her hands caress favorite porcelain figures and bronze sculp-tures. She stood transfixed beneath her one Monet canvas, not noticing the subject matter, simply letting the peaceful muted blues and greens and violets soothe her.

Ah, it's so good to be home. Home . . .

* * *

Shortly after their arrival at noon the next day, Charles pulled his mother aside and handed her an envelope from Gilbert. "He asked me to give this to you," Charles said with no further explanation.

Anna opened it and began to read.

Mother dear,

I know you'll understand our absence during the next two weeks. Only yesterday we got a call from Frank Sinatra's secretary. They have invited us to be house guests in Palm Springs for the season. You can imagine Winslow's excitement—parties with the Sinatras, the Annenbergs, Bob Hope, the whole Hollywood political crowd. So she bought everything Garfinckels had to sell, and we're heading west.

I've instructed the governess to bring all the children to Pennyfield Manor as soon as you're home and rested, so you can enjoy them to your heart's content. If they exhaust you, just send them back! We'll call on New Year's Day.

Much love from Winslow and me. Have a wonderful vacation.

Anna sat down in the wicker chair. Her hand flew to her forehead to push back her hair. She had been rendered speechless once again by Gilbert and Winslow's selfishness and thoughtlessness.

"The nerve of him—deciding to go away the one week of the year when I can be here!" she muttered quietly.

Emily, who had silently taken it all in, quietly asked, "Would you like me to call Constance and have the children brought out this afternoon?"

So furious she could barely think, Anna looked up at Emily. She felt as if someone had knocked the wind out of her. Finally, she grasped what Emily had asked. "Yes, please, let's see how soon they can get here. That way Larissa and Karine can enjoy Elliot and Doug and Sonia. It would be good for them all to play together, don't you think?"

"Yes, indeed," Emily laughed. "But you'd better decide on one room and limit them to that room. Their play could be devastating in a house like this."

"Here"—she gestured to include the room they were in—"we'll let them play in here, in the solarium. After all, this house was built so that my grandchildren could enjoy it. If they mess something up or break something, we'll jolly well fix it. Yes, I'd like to see them all together."

Emily left to call Constance, Charles picked up the Sunday paper, and Anna sat immobilized by her thoughts. Do you suppose—do you suppose he's punishing me for never being home when he was a child? He's deliberately not here when he knows I want him to be here . . . knows it would mean so much to me. Is he going to spend a lifetime getting even with me? Oh, that's ridiculous. If I were their age and had been invited to such glamourous goings-on, I'd be there too! Still—I am his mother, and they haven't seen me in exactly a year.

"I know you've just arrived, darling," Anna said to Charles, "but I've suddenly spiked a bad headache. If you'll excuse me, I'm going upstairs for a half hour. I'll rejoin you in time for brunch."

Charles put the paper down and looked at his mother intently. "I'm sorry, Mom. Sorry that Gilbert can't seem to stop himself from hurting you. We want this holiday to be wonderful and relaxing for you—all the things you want it to be."

Anna stood. "I know you do, and it will be. We'll have a grand time in spite of Gilbert and Winslow. After all, we'll have their little ones. Now, excuse me."

When everyone finished eating, Anna looked up and down the long table. It was, as Emily had predicted, a mess! Anna hadn't realized what it meant to eat at the same table with seven children under six. And two of them were only babies, of nine months and seven months.

Not only was food spilled on the tablecloth, but splotches of baby food decorated the floor. Thank God it was only varnished wood; it would wipe up instantly. Toys were scattered throughout the room, and Sonia and Karine were competing to see who could talk the most and the loudest. Sonia was winning at the moment.

Five-year-old Doug and six-year-old Elliot were anxiously waiting permission to go outdoors and practice their baseball skills. Each dressed in a Washington Senator's minisuit with matching cap, they had tyke-size bats and gloves and a ball that Anna hoped was softer than it looked.

"Blame your brother Josh for all this baseball nonsense," Charles stated. "He's the one who's outfitted them and stirred them up. A frustrated ballplayer himself, determined to turn his grandnephews into professional baseball stars!"

Anna laughed, remembering Josh's enthusiasm for baseball when he'd been a boy. "I have other plans for them. Elliot will replace his aging father as CEO, and Douglas will become head of the credit-card division." Anna's eyes roamed back to Sonia, who was telling Karine that she was putting the wrong dress on her paper doll. Sonia was so bossy for a two year old—and so verbal!

"I think we'll put Sonia in charge of all the travel agencies. She's going to be a real shrew! Forgive me, Emily." Anna's eyes twinkled with delight as she planned aloud her grandchildren's futures.

"Yeah, Mom, great dreams! But what are you going to do when none of them want any part of the business?"

Anna looked at Charles with shock, then realized he was only teasing her. "I can't believe, Charles, that you'd even give them an opportunity to do anything else. What kind of father are you? Don't you have a firm grip on your children's lives?" Anna laughed at her own silliness, then caught a glimpse of Larissa.

Sweet, calm, good-natured Larissa of the wavy butterscotch hair and tortoise-rimmed glasses sat quietly in the far corner of the sofa, ignoring everything going on around her, reading a book. And she was only six!

Anna stood and walked over to her. She sat down and snuggled closely, reaching for Larissa's hand. "What are you reading?"

"My favorite, *Winnie-the-Pooh*." Larissa's velvet-brown eyes seemed magnified behind the thick glasses. But they were such sweet, confiding eyes!

"If there's a book you'd like to have that you don't have, I'd like to get if for you. Is there a special book that you could remember your gram got for you?"

"Oh, yes! My friend Maria has *The Wind in the Willows*. Could you get it for me?"

"For sure, tomorrow. Do you think you and Doug and Elliot might like to see *The Nutcracker* ballet?"

"Ugh, Gram. Not the boys, they don't behave at the theater. But you can take me—I'd love to go with you!"

"Okay, I'll order tickets. But what could I do special with the boys? Any ideas?"

"Oh, you can take them to any old movie—they're not choosy."

Anna touseled the little girl's hair, then bent down and hugged her.

She walked back toward Charles and Emily. "I must say, watching them all, seeing how they've grown in the past year, makes me have second thoughts about staying much longer in Austria. Seems I'm missing a lot. I think I'll make it a point to come home in August, and we'll all go to Rehoboth for the month. Maybe Gil and Winslow will join us for a while there."

"If they don't have a more important social engagement."

"Charles, don't be hard on them! Just be glad your Emily has different values. I heard a new expression the other day: 'Different strokes for different folks'! I thought it was funny—and it surely applies here."

"I'm going to take the boys out and give them some batting practice. Mother, why don't you and Emily ride? The horses need exercise."

Anna looked at Emily expectantly. "Are you game?"

Emily's face beamed with pleasure. "I'm game, if we can trust Charles and Constance to look after all these little ones."

"Don't worry, Emily. I'm still boss enough to give him orders." Anna winked at Charles, then said, "I expect you to be in complete charge during your senior officer's absence. If any one of these children has a complaint, you'll be severely reprimanded!"

Charles saluted his mother smartly: "Aye, aye! Ma'am!"

The day after New Year's Day, as Anna was returning from a visit to Dunay International, she heard startling news on the car radio: *"The Navy Department has today acknowledged that the son of the chief of naval operations, Lieutenant Kurt Addison, has been killed in action in Vietnam. This is the second tragedy to strike the Addison family in a year. Last March, Admiral Addison's wife Betty was killed in an automobile accident."*

Anna's clammy hand reached inside her purse for a handkerchief. Tears filled her eyes. That poor man! So much to bear, in addition to carrying a huge load of responsibility on his shoulders. I would be there for him in a minute—but I've heard not a word, not a word! I must write him another note. What could hurt worse than the loss of one's only son . . . only son? But Kurt—you have another son!

▣ Part 7

Happiness—A Life Fulfilled, 1966

. . . a setback, a bout of pneumonia, which complicates her recovery from major surgery," said Charles Dunay in response to a call from a reporter from Newsweek.

—The Washington Post
"Style" Section

▨ Chapter 36

Vienna, March 1964

Anna sat at her magnificently appointed formal desk and reviewed the dinner chart Erika had placed in front of her fifteen minutes before. If she moved the minister of culture to table four, she'd have to move at least six other people. Damn! How could Erika have placed him next to his mistress?

It's such bad form! After all, I can't make it look like I approve their relationship. It's my fault to begin with—I shouldn't have invited the Bendheims. And I wouldn't have, except that he's a prestigious columnist for the most important paper in Austria. Why can't his wife stay in his bed? It would certainly make seating a dinner party easier.

Of course, if I move Jacques Berard here . . .

She toyed with the chart, moving people in her imagination, trying to guess whether they already knew one another, what the dynamics of the conversation might be if she moved this man next to this woman.

Finally, when she had the seating worked out to her satisfaction, she put it aside and picked up a stack of correspondence that had been prepared for her signature. She was signing the third letter and beginning to feel hungry when Erika came in.

"A very distinguished-looking gentleman—an American—is here, and though he has no appointment, he insists you will see him. I tried to tell him you're having a dinner party this evening and your entire afternoon is tied up, but he's very insistent. He asked me to give you his card."

Anna put the fountain pen back into its crystal holder and accepted the card from Erika.

ADMIRAL KURT ADDISON, USN, RET.
PRESIDENT AND CHIEF EXECUTIVE OFFICER
FAWCETT DAVIDSON COMPANY

The vision of his face when she'd left him in that bar in Honolulu flashed into her mind: resigned, hurt, still in love with her . . .

In a voice so low that Erika could scarcely hear it, Anna managed to say, "Yes . . . I'll see . . . please tell Admiral Addison I'll be with him in a moment."

Panic flooded through her. Her hair looked terrible. She hadn't done anything with it that morning because her official appointment schedule was light, and besides, she was having it done that afternoon before the dinner. She'd taken no time at all with her makeup. What would he think of her? She'd aged so since Albert died!

"Oh my, oh my," she muttered to herself as she extricated a compact and lipstick from her purse and quickly tried to fix her face. Her hands were trembling and had turned to ice.

She ran a comb quickly through her black hair. At least I haven't let it go gray.

She stood and smoothed the pebbled wool of her chocolate-brown suit. Then, head held high, she passed from behind the ornate desk and through the formal sitting area of her gorgeously elaborate office, which had a marble fireplace and gilt moldings. She opened the door to the reception area. Slowly, deliberately, praying for her composure to return, she walked toward the tall man who stood with his back to her, leafing through a newspaper.

"Kurt . . ."

He turned. His questioning steel-blue eyes bored into hers. He said nothing; he simply looked at her.

She held out her hand in an instinctive reflex. A moment of fear flooded through her. "Won't—won't you come in?" She gestured toward her private office.

"If—if you're sure you can make the time." His voice sounded like gravel, hoarse and low—almost cruel.

He followed her without another word, though he took the liberty of closing the door as he passed through it.

Two green-leather wing chairs flanked the fireplace. A settee backed up against her desk. Anna gestured toward one of the chairs and seated herself on the settee facing him and the fireplace.

"What a surprise!" she babbled, trying to think what to say.

He looked her up and down and took in the opulence of the office. He relaxed back into the solid leather chair, his eyes never leaving hers.

"Kurt—you look wonderful! I mean, considering what you've been through—only a few more gray hairs."

"The truth is"—he laughed, relaxed now—"I'm grateful for the gray hairs. Better than no hair at all, and it's really thinning out." His eyes had changed from cold to warm, from appraising to loving.

Anna felt a surge of confidence return. "What brings you to Vienna?"

"Anna, you make me laugh! I can't believe you even asked that question. What brings me to Vienna, indeed!"

She wanted to reach out and touch his hands, she wanted to hold his face in her hands and kiss his eyelids, slowly, slowly. . . .

He stood and walked toward her. When he was standing directly in front of her, he reached for her hands, and she offered them to him. But she remained seated, her eyes afraid to meet his.

"I came to claim you."

Something in Anna's chest plummeted to her abdomen. She couldn't find her voice.

"I hope I'm not too late. I hope I haven't waited too long."

She raised her eyes to his. Two deep-brown orbs twinkled down at her, then pleaded for an answer.

As she didn't stand, he sat next to her on the settee, never releasing her icy hands.

"Mm, cold hands."

"Means I've got a warm heart." She melted into his eyes, calling silently for him to take her in his arms.

"Yes. I seem to remember—a long time ago you had a very warm heart. And body."

She wanted to reach over and pull his head close to her own. She was desperate to kiss him, to feel his arms around her. "Why—why did it take you so long to come?"

"Anna, darling! You're glowing, you know that? This minute, you're absolutely glowing—a kind of incandescence. Anna, I love you. Is it possible—could we be lucky enough to finally . . ."

But he didn't finish the thought. Instead, he pulled her into his arms and held her tightly, breathing in the sweet fragrance of her skin and hair. When his heart felt as if it would burst from his chest, when the pounding in his temple demanded release, he lifted her chin, looked into her eyes—which now held tears—and kissed her softly on her parted lips.

"Anna, could it be?" he breathed in wonderment.

Her eyes answered yes, even if she could not make her voice speak.

"I waited—perhaps too long—out of respect for Betty's memory and for the feelings of my children. And Kurt Junior died in Vietnam. A lot has happened. I couldn't come racing over here to marry you instantly. I disciplined myself, held my feelings in check for exactly one year."

Anna suddenly laughed, a tension-relieving laugh that broke up the molecules of anxiety inside her. "Oh, Kurt! That's so like you. Everything by the book—always, everything exactly the correct way! I don't believe it!"

He stood and paced toward the fireplace and bookshelves. He picked up a leather-bound edition of Proust, looked at it carefully, put it back down, then turned and faced Anna.

"It takes a lot of nerve for a fellow who is worth at most a few million to court one of the wealthiest women in the world. A woman who has made it all herself. A dazzling woman who has charmed presidents and senators and foreign potentates!"

"Oh, come now, Kurt, that's ridiculous. An exaggeration, to say the least!"

He walked slowly back toward the settee. "The only reason I even hope, my darling, is because I remember how much we loved one another when you were a mere secretary on the Naval Affairs Committee. If any part of that fabulous woman still resides inside your skin, maybe I've got a shot."

Anna felt herself flush, felt her body warm with a sudden rush of passion. Was this the dream she'd dreamed for years? Or was it really happening?

He reached for her hands and pulled her to her feet. "Tell me your favorite restaurant, the most romantic, glamorous, expensive place in all of Vienna. That's where I'm taking you for lunch, my darling."

"And now, believe it or not, the credit-card business is the most lucrative of all. I swear, sometimes I think plastic will totally replace real money."

Kurt laughed heartily, thrilled to hear of Anna's successes in the heady world of business. "Now that you're a grandmother, I don't feel so elderly. You really had a great time teasing me in Honolulu. Remember?"

"Of course. I couldn't believe such a sexy man could be a grandfather. Goes to show what I know."

"So tell me, how many grandchildren do you have?"

"Charles and Emily have three boys and a girl. Gilbert and Winslow have two girls and a boy. And I adore them all! I'm enjoying them so much more than I did my children."

"So why on earth are you here in Vienna?"

"I ask myself that about three times a day." Anna sighed a weary sigh. "I guess I never could say no to a new challenge, a new adventure. But I've about had it with this one."

"Then you wouldn't mind terribly if I whisked you back to America?" His eyes, suddenly deeply serious, bored into hers.

She felt such happiness, she was afraid it might disappear, he might disappear, if she dared let herself believe what he was suggesting.

"What? No answer?"

"Oh, Kurt, Kurt . . . it's just so—sudden! You coming unannounced. I think I'm in shock. You'll have to give me a few days to get over the shock. And I've got this dinner tonight. Lord knows how I'll ever get through all that protocol. You will come, won't you? I can make a phone call and get you a tux."

He reached for her hand. "I'll come. If only because I don't want to let you out of my sight. Ever again."

She grinned. " 'Fraid you'll have to, sailor boy. I've got to get my beauty sleep, and my fairy godmother has to fix my hair. I'm afraid I'll have to expel you from my sight until exactly eight o'clock tonight. And then"—she squeezed his hand tightly— "you'll have to promise not to distract me during dinner. I really must do this right."

"You mean, I'm not allowed to make eyes at you or wink?"

"No way. In fact, I'm going to seat you as far away as possible so I can keep my head about me."

Anna watched her butler for the signal that everyone had champagne. Then she rose to toast the director of the Metropolitan Opera, in whose honor this dinner was being given. As she stood, her glance fell once more on the small card that rested near her water glass: "Love, like the moon, has many phases. K.A." The butler had delivered the card to her between the fish and the meat course. "Admiral Addison asked me to give this to you," he'd said with disdain, indicating her last-minute guest's lack of manners.

And what will he think when I take Kurt upstairs later tonight?

It was all she'd been able to think of during dinner: that when this lengthy bit of official business was finished, she would fly upstairs with her very own knight, she would capture him once and for all time. And she would never let him go.

Well, only another forty-five minutes or so to get through . . .

The last guest departed, and the butler was making the rounds, turning off lights and double-checking the locks on the windows and doors.

And Kurt seemed to have disappeared. Anna knew he couldn't have left without saying good-bye, yet the three sitting rooms were empty, and the ballroom was being vacuumed. Where on earth had he gone?

Damn him! she thought as she went from room to room. She glanced into the library, lit by one small desk lamp. Just as she had decided he was not there, she heard his voice materialize from a chair at the far end of the room.

"Is everyone gone?"

"Kurt! There you are! I've been searching for you. What are you doing in here with all the lights off?"

"I'm planning a military campaign. I always do my best planning in the dark. Come here."

She walked over to the chair where he was seated. He pulled her down onto his lap.

"Maybe it's not a *military* campaign. But it is a campaign of sorts. You see, I'm trying to figure out how I can sneak upstairs into the ambassador's bedroom without a whole houseful of servants knowing I'm there."

"Aha! And what does the ambassador think of this idea?" She kissed his forehead lightly.

"I don't know, but I'd sure like to." He nuzzled her neck, then bent to kiss the warm flesh where her breasts began.

"The ambassador thinks that if you don't quickly follow her upstairs, she might rape you right here in the library. Think of what a scandal that would be!"

* * *

Anna opened her eyes slowly. Yes, he was there, next to her in bed. Still asleep.

The dream was real.

She smiled, looking at his thick brown eyelashes. He looked so vulnerable when sleeping—exactly as she'd remembered.

Sunlight was filtering in through the lace curtains, even through the embroidered organdy draperies that enclosed the canopied four-poster bed. Our pleasure bed!

This bed will forever symbolize our renewed passion, she told herself as she recalled the lovemaking and endless talk. They had talked until four-thirty in the morning, and only then had they drifted off to sleep in one another's arms.

She looked at Kurt in wonderment. He was real. She could have him in her life, in her arms, in her bed, for the rest of her life, if she only had the courage to make the decision.

What would it mean to Charles, to Gilbert, to her grandchildren to discover this father, this grandfather?

"Hmm . . . you look as if you've spent the night making love. Not exactly what I'd expect of our ambassador."

"Kurt!" She purred, and reached over to caress his face with her hand. She moved closer and kissed him.

He responded with a deeply passionate kiss and said, "I will only make love to you this morning if you promise me I can spend every night from now on in your bed." His eyes twinkled as he waited for her response.

"Having spent a lifetime fighting my addiction to you, Admiral Addison, I'm ready to surrender and simply accept my fate. You are my fatal weakness!"

"I like that!" He reached for her breast and began teasing the nipple, even while he continued talking. "What time is it, anyway? I feel like it's lunchtime already."

"That's what happens when you spend the whole night making love like a teenager."

"Making up for lost time." He pulled her body even tighter against his, forcing her to acknowledge his hardness.

Anna reached for him, teasing him. "Pretty good for an old grandfather—all night, and then again in the morning."

After satisfying their passion, they showered together, soaping one another, enjoying the sight of their still-firm bodies.

"How do we manage breakfast without the servants knowing

what we've been up to?" Kurt asked as he shaved with Anna's razor.

"I've just ordered a large breakfast. We'll share it, and then I'll sneak you out," Anna answered mischievously, enjoying every minute of his concern about propriety.

While she put on a minimum of makeup, he disappeared into the adjoining sitting room. In a few minutes he was back, standing behind her in the bathroom, holding a framed picture. She could not see which of her many family pictures he was holding, but fear froze her heart as she tried to imagine. The confrontation she was so dreading would come sooner rather than later. Perhaps it was best to get it over with.

"Anna, who is this young man?" His voice was low, pained, and serious.

She turned away from the mirror, a tube of mascara still in her hand, and faced him squarely. She glanced at the high school graduation portrait of Charles that he was holding in his hand. "That's Charles, the year he graduated from Exeter."

Kurt looked from the portrait into Anna's eyes, then back at the picture.

She could stand the silence no longer.

"Yes, Kurt, he's your son."

Kurt's eyes filled as if he might cry. They bored into hers, asking dozens of questions.

"I've spent a lifetime dreading this moment, wondering if, when you finally found out, you'd understand . . . if you'd be able to forgive me for never telling you."

He stared at the picture again, unable to look at Anna's fearful eyes, her trembling hands. "This . . . Charles—the Charles who runs your companies—is my son?"

"Yes, Kurt. And he's a magnificent man. Brilliant, compassionate, incredibly competent. The mirror image of you, in every way."

Kurt turned abruptly and walked out of the bathroom, back into the sitting room.

Anna laid the mascara on the sink, ran a brush through her hair, picked up a tissue, and followed him into the sitting room.

He was standing in front of the bookshelves, staring at all the pictures of Charles and Emily and their children. Anna approached him from behind. "You will love Emily too. She is bright and warm and loving." Kurt didn't respond, and terror flooded Anna's heart. "The children are adorable—so smart and lively. I can't get enough of them."

Slowly, looking devastated, Kurt turned and faced Anna. "I guess—I guess what hurts most, Anna, is that you never trusted me enough to tell me over all these years. Why? Why?"

She faced him directly, and he reached out for her, yet kept her at a distance by holding her elbows in his strong hands, forcing her by the sheer magnetism of his eyes to speak the truth.

"If I had told you, would it have made a difference? Would it have absolved you of responsibility to Betty and your children? I didn't want to burden you. I didn't want you to leave Betty because of Charles's existence. If you were going to leave her, I wanted it to be because of me, because of your overwhelming love—and need—for me."

He pulled her close, wrapped his arms around her, and soothed her trembling body. "Anna, Anna! It was never a question of loving her versus loving you. That was not the issue. It was the responsibility I felt for her and the children. They were in my life before I ever met you. I couldn't see my way clear to destroying their home, their sense of security. I couldn't do it."

Anna looked up into his tear-filled eyes. "And I, in my saner moments, didn't really want you to, Kurt. I wouldn't have respected you as much if you had left them. But that didn't change the fact that I wanted you to. Wanting something you know is wrong is part of being human, I think. I've never been able to will a change in my feelings, and you've always been rational and disciplined enough to do the right thing. A fine pair we make!"

"Anna, darling, I do love you."

"Then will you forgive me for not telling you about Charles? I was so thrilled when I discovered I was pregnant and knew it was your child. Claude wanted me to get an abortion—he never wanted a child—but I knew it was your child, and there was no way—absolutely no way—I'd let your child be taken away from me. And oh, Kurt, what a splendid son he's been—and how I've longed to tell you all about him. You'll never know how sorely I've been tempted. But I knew if I told you, you'd never know a moment's peace again, you'd be so torn."

Kurt released her from his arms and turned again toward the

pictures on the bookshelves, picking them up one by one and asking Anna to identify all her family.

Finally, seemingly exhausted, he dropped into a chair. They stared at one another for a long minute. Then he asked, "Does Charles know? Does he even suspect that Claude was not his real father?"

"So far as I know, he's never suspected anything. But the two men could not be more different."

"How do you think Charles will take it when we tell him I'm his father?"

The grip of panic in Anna's stomach suddenly dissolved. He didn't hate her. He would somehow forgive her for the years of deception, for depriving him of his son. She felt a slow warming of her hands. "Then you still—"

"Yes. Forgive me, Anna, if I seemed angry with you. I'm in a state of shock to discover that I have a son I've never known— especially after losing Kurt Junior in Vietnam. You've given me a great surprise this morning, a great gift—a son! I feel so many different things, I can't even sort them out. But predominately, greater than any other emotion, I know I love you dearly, and I want to claim you. And my son and my grandchildren—all of you. I'm a greedy son of a bitch, and I want all of you. I need you, my darling. I never guessed how hard it's been for you all these years, keeping this hidden from me. When I remember all the times I've asked to see pictures of the boys and you've always refused to show me . . ."

Anna nodded her head. "Yes, I knew that if you took one look at him—after all, he's the spitting image of you, and so is Douglas. Little Doug looks like a miniature Charles, and he looks even more like you than Charles does. Oh, Kurt, I'm so relieved to finally have the truth out. You can't imagine what I've felt!"

Anna's maid knocked, entered, and delivered breakfast and newspapers. Anna resisted the impulse to explain Kurt's presence and decided to act as if he were simply her husband of long standing, visiting her in Vienna. And as the thought passed through her mind, she realized there was truth in it. Kurt was her husband, had been ever since that day long ago in Rock Creek Park.

After the maid left, Anna served Kurt hot chocolate as only the Viennese make it, fresh hot croissants, and eggs Benedict, saving only a bit of orange juice and half a croissant for herself. "After all," she told him laughingly, "if I'm to be a bride again, I must watch my figure!"

The U.S. Ambassador to Austria and Admiral Kurt Addison were married three weeks later in a private ceremony performed by the chief rabbi of Vienna. Afterward, they sent a cable to Anna's sons and to Kurt's daughters.

"Sending a cable seems so impersonal," Anna protested, "but I'm not sure I have the courage at this moment to call Charles and Gilbert. Gilbert especially. He'll be furious!"

"He'll think I've married you for your money?" Kurt said with a wry smile. He held her hand while they sipped champagne and looked out over the quiet Danube from their hotel suite. Kurt had insisted they spend the weekend away from the prying eyes of the embassy staff.

"Precisely! Knowing how Gilbert's mind works, that's exactly what he'll think. In fact, that's probably what he'd do himself—marry a woman for her money!"

"Wow! Them's strong words for a mother about her son. Is he really that bad?"

Anna looked pensive. "I don't know, I honestly don't. I won't tell you any more about Gilbert. I'll let you judge for yourself. He's always been a mystery to me."

"I'm looking forward to meeting my children and grandchildren. As far as I'm concerned, Anna, I'm prepared to love all of them equally. Both Charles and Gilbert."

"Well, I'm glad of that. But we'll see. I don't know, but I imagine Gilbert will take the news about you being Charles's father very hard, very hard indeed."

"How do you intend to break it to them? Have you figured that out yet?"

"First, I'll tell Charles. In fact, we'll have Charles and Emily to dinner at Pennyfield. I can't wait for you to see Pennyfield Manor—it's absolutely the most exquisite home in existence, and I apologize, I know I'm totally immodest about it."

"I can't wait. If it's a creation of yours, I know it's splendid. Just like my bride."

⊠ Chapter 37

Potomac, Maryland

Charles and Emily were apprehensive as they drove out River Road toward Pennyfield Manor. Emily had been trying to soothe Charles's ruffled feelings ever since the cable had arrived. Yes, it was certainly out of character for Anna to do such a thing—marry a complete stranger whom she'd only known a short while, without any of her family present. But after all, she was a mature, sophisticated woman. She was known for her competence in dealing with cunning, manipulative men. Surely there was more of an explanation than they'd had yet.

Charles had been hurt, then angry. Then he had found himself in the ridiculous position of trying to defend Anna to Gilbert and Winslow, who were outraged and didn't care who knew it.

The *Washington Post*'s gossip columnist had got hold of the news and printed a story indicating that "after a whirlwind romance, the glamorous widow of Senator Albert Landow, now our Ambassador to Austria, has married the dashingly handsome and brilliant military expert, former chief of naval operations Admiral Kurt Addison." After that story, their phone hadn't stopped ringing with reporters and old friends and acquaintances, and of course the whole family—Anna's family—who wanted to know what Charles and Emily knew.

It had been a wretched week. But at last Anna and her new husband were at Pennyfield Manor. They had arrived early that morning, and now Charles and Emily were on their way there for a private dinner. There was something strange about it, Emily mused, because Anna had not invited Gilbert and Winslow and had specified that she didn't want her grandchildren to come. "I want all of you to come back on Sunday for a big brunch—so Kurt can meet all his new grandchildren!"

Anna sounded so happy, so thrilled. So in love.

Charles, meanwhile, had spent the week researching this stranger his mother had married. Over the years he'd read the newspaper accounts, and he had a passing familiarity with Addison's career. But after the cable arrived, he'd sent Barbara to the Library of Congress to make copies of all the newspaper articles, of the story from *Time* when Addison had been their cover story, of the major piece in the Sunday *New York Times Magazine.* Charles had read them all, hoping to find a clue, a tiny bit of understanding of this impulsive action of his mother's. It was *so* out of character for her.

All the newspaper and magazine stories portrayed Addison as such a straight-arrow character. A man, Charles thought, he'd probably like very much.

Antonio, the butler, welcomed them and said, "Mrs. Addison is waiting for you in the solarium."

"Charles!" Anna gushed when they walked in. She rushed to his side to kiss him on the cheek, then she kissed and hugged Emily.

"Congratulations, Mother. You look marvelous!" Emily said with enthusiasm.

Kurt had followed Anna across the room, and Charles shook his hand, saying only, "Admiral."

Anna turned from Emily at that moment and watched the two men. They were sizing one another up. Kurt was looking at his dynamic, ruggedly handsome son—exactly his same height and build, the same twinkling eyes.

"You are everything your mother has told me—a most impressive young man!" Even as Kurt said the words, he reached over to Anna and, placing his arm around her shoulder, pulled her toward himself.

Then he turned to Emily. She extended her hand, but he bent down and kissed her cheek. "And Emily, your mother-in-law couldn't love you more if you were her own flesh and blood. She's been telling me about you for the last four weeks. It seems Charles, here, is a very lucky man."

Emily felt her heart melt as she looked in his eyes. She had resented Anna for her impulsive remarriage because she had been so fond of Albert Landow. Albert had been a substitute father to her, and she had felt a sense of betrayal on his behalf. But now, as she felt the full force of Kurt's personality and recognized his warmth and basic decency, her emotions shifted one more time.

"Come, make yourself a drink, Charles, and make one for Emily, and let's sit down." Anna was more nervous at that moment than she'd ever been in her life. She'd felt Charles's coldness. It was an emotion she'd seen in him before, but never directed at her.

While Charles poured a drink for Emily and himself, Emily kept the conversation going by exclaiming over the daffodils lining the long driveway to the house.

"Yes"—Anna laughed—"I think we planted over five thousand bulbs down that driveway. And they give me a lift every time I see them. I only wish spring would last forever in Washington!"

"So," Charles began as he sat down, "tell me all about this whirlwind romance we've been reading about in the papers." His face was still bereft of a smile, and his eyes were like steel.

Anna couldn't find her voice and was grateful when Kurt jumped in. "Actually, it's not such a whirlwind. Anna and I have known one another well ever since Anna was a clerk on the Senate Naval Affairs Committee in the late twenties. As I recall it, we met when I was working on the investigation of the destroyer *Paulding*'s collision with a submarine off the coast of Connecticut."

Anna saw questions in both Charles's and Emily's eyes. She took a deep breath, swallowed, and interrupted Kurt's narrative. "Actually, Charles, Kurt and I were lovers before I married Claude. We were very much in love almost from the first moment we met. I would have married him then, but he was already married and the father of three children."

The room was absolutely still. The silence reverberated in Anna's ears.

Charles looked from Anna to Kurt as if he expected Kurt to deny what Anna had just confessed.

Anna began again. "Don't think badly of Kurt. I knew he was married and had children, and still I loved him so, I nearly begged him to have an affair with me."

"Well," Kurt interjected, "you didn't quite beg. But the time came when all my discipline went up in smoke, and with great trepidation, we . . ."

Emily laughed and broke the tension. "I think it's wonderful! A classic love story! After a lifetime of loving one another, you can finally be married. It's grand!"

Anna appreciated Emily's vote of confidence, but the worst—or perhaps the best—had yet to be told. Again, she swallowed hard, and the words she'd been rehearsing for a lifetime came out. "Kurt is your father, Charles."

The two men stared at one another. Kurt tried to understand the emotions Charles was desperately trying to hide.

"My God!" Emily exclaimed. "That's why you look so much alike. I've been wondering about it ever since Charles brought home that old *Time* magazine last week. The one with pictures of Admiral Addison when he was a young man."

Very calmly, in a low voice, Charles asked, "But I thought I was born well after you were married to Dr. Dunay?"

"You were. Kurt and I ended our affair—at least, we thought we had ended it—when he left for the Pacific. I met and married Claude a few months thereafter. I guess you could say I married him on the rebound. Some months later, Kurt came back to Washington for a week. By then, I was vastly disillusioned with Claude and with marriage in general—and I must admit I couldn't resist my feelings for Kurt. Even though I knew it was wrong, that it was adultery—I did it. A few weeks later, I discovered I was pregnant, and I immediately knew the baby was Kurt's."

"But," Kurt interrupted, "she never told me, Charles. She never told me you were my son. I never knew, over all these years, until I saw your picture at the embassy four weeks ago. Had I known, I don't know how I would have handled it over the years. I just don't know."

Charles stood. "I need another drink."

Kurt followed him to the bar. "I do, too, as a matter of fact. And I expect Anna could use another sherry. How about you, Emily?"

Emily shook her head and moved over to where Anna sat on a white-wicker love seat. She sat down next to her and took her hand in her own. "I understand, Anna. Truly I do. And I'm happy the two of you can be together now. It must feel like such a burden is lifted."

"Oh, right you are, my dear. I've wanted so to tell you over the years. I've longed for Charles to know his real father."

"And Gilbert?" Charles demanded, walking back toward where Anna sat. "What about him? Who is his father?"

"Claude is his father. I've never told you this, but Claude never wanted children. I more or less agreed to go along with that. We were both going to have terrific careers, make oodles of money, and forgo what we thought were the doubtful joys of parenthood. But after I got pregnant with you, Charles, and refused to abort—I might tell you that was quite a fight—I thought you shouldn't grow up as an only child. I also felt that it would only be fair to Claude to really have his child. My thinking was strange, I recognize that."

"So this explains why Gilbert and I are so unalike, hardly like brothers at all. I've always wondered."

Anna was sick at heart. Charles was taking it so hard—he seemed devastated. "You've always had me on such a pedestal, Charles. It must be difficult for you to realize I am a passionate, normal woman whose emotions have occasionally gone out of control."

Charles stared at the drink in his hand, then finally looked to Anna. "So this affair went on all these years, nearly forty years?"

"Not quite," Kurt answered.

"No. When I decided to marry Albert Landow—because Kurt still wasn't free to marry me—I told him we would not be able to see one another again. And we never made love again. Not until . . . now."

A wry smile began to form on Charles's face. "I see." He sipped his drink. "You know, Admiral, it's strange to listen to my mother talk about her love life. You'll have to forgive me for not enjoying it!"

Kurt nodded. "I understand. Perhaps it would help if you and Emily would call me Kurt and cut the Admiral bit."

Emily looked squarely at him. "Would it be all right with you if we just called you Dad?"

Kurt's face filled with happiness. "I'd like that even more!"

Antonio came into the solarium to announce dinner. Kurt quickly took Emily by the elbow and ushered her toward the dining room. This left Charles to escort his mother. Before they left the solarium, with Kurt and Emily out of earshot, Charles hugged his mother hard, kissed her forehead, and whispered in a hoarse voice, "Mom, I only wish you'd told me a long time ago. It explains so much, answers so many questions I've had all these years."

Anna could find no voice for her gratitude—she only squeezed his hand tighter.

* * *

Why is it that I feel so lighthearted! Emily wondered as she savored the delicious lobster bisque. But she no sooner asked herself the question than the answer flooded over her.

Anna's confession had somehow lifted a burden from Emily too. If Anna could conceive a child outside of her marriage and still be the wonderful woman I know she is, then perhaps I'm not such an awful person either. Perhaps I should stop condemning myself.

It had happened, she knew with the wisdom of hindsight, at the worst time of her marriage to Charles. He had been awfully busy, preoccupied with the business. Right after Anna took over Senator Landow's Senate seat and left everything in Charles's lap. It had seemed for a year or so that she no longer mattered to Charles. He had worked around the clock and was out of town more often than he was home. Emily had been hurt by his lack of attention, had begun to feel he didn't love her anymore, had even begun to imagine there might be other women in his life.

Admiral Addison and Charles are talking up a storm, hardly aware that Anna and I are even at the table. Well, it's good to see them getting on so.

We only made love three times, Dr. Kramer and I, but it was enough for me to get pregnant. And for Sonia to be born with that blazing red hair, hair that reminds me every day of my life of my horrid infidelity, my lack of morals . . . But somehow Anna's confession tonight—well, if she could do that and still be the person she is after all these years, I should stop worrying so about myself and Sonia. Charles loves me, and he loves Sonia, and he's never suspected for a moment. I'll never ruin things by telling him. Because I didn't love Dr. Kramer, he was just a momentary diversion—a sop to my ego. It's Charles I love.

Anna interrupted Emily's reverie. "Emily dear, I do hope you'll plan on being here early for tomorrow's brunch. I've a feeling I'll need all the moral support I can get, what with Sasha and Louis and all their children and grandchildren, and brothers Al and Sam and Josh and all their questions! Do plan on coming early. I know I can count on you."

"Of course, Mother."

* * *

Dinner over, they were seated in the library sipping after-dinner drinks. The men were discussing the relative merits of various ski resorts, comparing notes on the most difficult runs. It was as if a dike had been opened, Anna realized. The two men had so much in common, thought so much alike. In fact, it was hard to believe that Charles hadn't been raised by Kurt, so similar were their ideas and principles and hobbies.

"Anna, I've a wonderful idea. You and I have spent too much time together these past few weeks. I think you should go back to the office for a week and get reacquainted. The next week, Charles and I will take a minivacation and go spring skiing at Aspen while you mind the store."

Oh, Kurt, you're brilliant, Anna thought. How perfect! A way for the two of you to really get close, with no distractions, doing what fathers and sons do, competing! On the ski slopes. "That's a splendid idea! And after the two of you are back, Emily and I may just find something special to do together." Anna reached over and squeezed Emily's hand, as if sealing a pact.

"I think the two of you should buy the family a house in Aspen while you're there. Then we could take the children and go several times a year. It's even beautiful there in the summer," Emily added as an afterthought.

"We'll look around a bit. What do you say, Charles?"

"Sounds good to me, if Mom likes the idea," Charles answered.

"Oh, come now, we don't need her approval on everything, do we?" Kurt responded with a huge wink at Anna. "If we find a place we like, we'll just go ahead and buy it. In fact, it will be my gift to my new family. How's that?"

How can they not love a man like this? Anna reassured herself as she rose to say good night to her children.

"Where's Winslow?" Anna asked Gilbert when he strode into the library the next morning without his wife.

"She's coming in her car. She has to leave early—a beauty-shop appointment at Saks. I told you, we're going to the Cancer Ball this evening. She's determined to be the most beautiful woman there—and she'll be competing against half a dozen movie stars."

Anna linked her arm in Gilbert's and walked him toward the terrace. "It's such a gorgeous day and so warm, I thought we'd lunch out on the terrace."

"It is beautiful. Where's—your new husband?" Gilbert said the words with unconcealed distaste.

"He's out looking over the horses. I never knew he had an interest in horse breeding, but he's amazingly knowledgeable, much to my surprise."

"Perhaps you wouldn't be so surprised if you'd gotten to know him before rushing into marriage."

They stepped out onto the flagstone terrace, startling two squirrels who were feasting on acorns. Anna let go of Gilbert's arm and faced him. "Is this a prepared sermon, something you've been storing up this past week?"

She seated herself on a wrought-iron sofa that enabled her to look out on the Potomac River for several miles in each direction. The trees were just beginning to sprout leaves; in another two weeks, much of this view would be obscured.

"Damn it, Mother! I've always considered you so mature, so responsible. This is such an irresponsible act!"

"Am I late? I'm sorry," Kurt said as he walked quickly onto the terrace from the side of the house. "Gilbert! I'm delighted to meet you." He looked at Anna for any signals, then turned back to Gilbert. "Where's your wife? I've only seen pictures, of course, but I'm anxious to meet the family beauty!"

Gilbert extended his hand in a cold greeting, refusing to smile in spite of Kurt's genial manner. "She should be here soon. She has to leave early for an appointment—and we had other plans anyhow this morning. We had to cancel them."

"Yes," Kurt answered pleasantly, determined to make this meeting as positive as possible for Anna's sake, "I understand you are about to announce your candidacy for the Maryland House of Delegates. How can we help?"

Anna put in, "Charles told us that you've decided to run for the legislature. I think that's marvelous."

Gilbert smiled for the first time since arriving. "Yes, I've decided to give it a shot, for the Democratic nomination. It'll be a tough race, but I think I can win the nomination. And the election."

"Charles says you've got some top names on your advisory

committee," Kurt said as he poured himself a vodka and added tonic and a bit of lime. "Can I make you a drink, Gilbert?"

Gilbert joined him at the small bar. "Somehow, it seems I should be offering to make you a drink. I haven't quite accepted the fact that you married my mother last week. What was the rush?"

Anna's crisp voice preempted Kurt's answer. "I think I should be the one to answer that question, Gilbert. Kurt and I have known one another for nearly forty years, since the late twenties."

The two men sat down facing Anna, their backs to the river view.

"In fact, we were lovers before I married your father, Claude." She watched shock register in Gilbert's eyes. "And though we had no intention of resuming our affair after I married Claude, I too am only human, my dear son. When—"

The door from the house opened suddenly, and Winslow, dressed in a cerulean-blue-leather miniskirted suit and high heels, her long blond hair tumbling in disarray around her shoulders, bounded onto the terrace. "Sorry I'm so late folks, but I got held up in traffic in Bethesda. Driving on Saturday morning in Bethesda is really the pits! You must be Admiral Addison." She smiled provocatively at him and softened her shrill voice. "I'd read about you—but I didn't know you were a friend of Anna's."

Kurt was instantly on his feet, walking toward Winslow. He bent to kiss the cheek of his new daughter-in-law. "And you are an apparition! You definitely live up to your advance billing!"

Winslow, momentarily taken aback by his mesmerizing charm, self-consciously brushed her hair back off her forehead to give him a better view of her dazzling blue eyes.

"Turns out," Gilbert's angry voice boomed from his chair, "these two have been lovers for most of Anna's life. It's not the innocent whirlwind romance the papers have been writing about."

"Really?" Winslow's face glowed with the anticipation of scandal. "How delicious!"

She headed for the bar, followed by Kurt, who rushed to make her a drink.

Meanwhile, Gilbert continued his interrogation of his mother. "So you've been lovers all these years, is that it?"

"Not exactly. And I would caution you both"—Anna looked severely from Gilbert to Winslow and then back to Gilbert—"people who live in glass houses shouldn't cast stones."

Winslow registered Anna's meaning and laughed riotously. "Forgive me, Anna, forgive me. But I simply can't imagine you —of all people—carrying on a clandestine affair. It's so outrageous a thought."

Kurt, suddenly angry, looked at Winslow, and in a measured voice he said, "What Anna and I have had all these many years is a deep love for one another, coupled with an overriding sense of responsibility to the other people in our lives. We have spent a lifetime denying ourselves the happiness we might have enjoyed, in order to protect my first wife and my children, and in order that she might protect Gilbert and Charles from any hint of scandal. I think it's time all of you understood the sacrifice Anna has made over these years. Her first consideration has always been what would be best for Charles and Gilbert."

Gilbert was on his feet, ready to do battle with Kurt. "I don't understand what you mean. How did this involve Charles and me?"

"Let me, Kurt." Anna waved Kurt down into his chair, pleading with her eyes. "Gilbert, I'm going to tell you and Winslow something very personal, something that I could continue to keep secret from you. I told Charles and Emily last evening, and now, because I love you both very much and want to be honest with you, I'm going to tell you." She took a deep breath. "Kurt is Charles's father."

It took a moment to sink in—a moment when the only sound was the rustling of the branches and the intermittent song of the birds.

"Shit! Jeez-us Christ! What do you mean?" Gilbert exploded.

"After your father and I were married awhile and I found myself miserably unhappy—and Kurt came back to Washington for a week—well, we got together, and I became pregnant."

"So who is *my* father?"

"Claude was your father—there's no doubt about it. Absolutely none."

"So. This shit-faced bastard seduced you, knowing he couldn't marry you, and even after you had his baby, he let you fend for yourself."

"You're misconstruing things, Gilbert, and I won't stand for it."

"Well, I won't stand for him coming into our lives now, in a blatant attempt to bilk you of our money. Hell, Mother, can't you see what he's doing? He's married you now, now that you're one of the richest women in the world. You weren't good enough for him when he was aspiring to be a great military hero. Hell, no—he didn't want you then. At least not enough to marry you. But now that he's had his hot-shot military career, now that he's ready to have some fun, he wants your money! Can't you see that? Or are you so blinded by his charm . . ."

Anna stood and walked toward Gilbert. "Shut up! Shut up! You cannot stand here in my home and insult my husband like that!"

"I don't intend to stay here! I'm leaving right now. C'mon, Winslow—we're outta here! Right now! And when you get this parasite out of your life, let me know, Mother. Maybe then I'll have something more to say to you."

"Gilbert!" Anna cried out as he grabbed Winslow's hand and pulled her reluctantly through the house.

Kurt put his arm around Anna's waist and moved her toward his lean body. "Don't worry, darling. He'll get over his temper tantrum—as soon as he needs money for his campaign. He'll be back, hat in hand. You'll see."

She turned to him, letting him hold her close and caress the back of her neck and shoulders. "Oh, Kurt, I was so afraid of this, I was so afraid he would react badly. He's so hurt that you're not his father too."

"Yes, I suppose. We have to try to understand." He released Anna from his arms. "Let me make you a drink. You need one."

Anna sat back down and looked out over the river. "Well, so be it—he's always been my nemesis. Tell me, what did you think of Winslow?"

"She's breathtaking! There's no other word. The amazing thing is that she stays married to him. What do you suppose keeps her there?"

"My money, I suspect. If the truth be known, I'm *sure* that's it. After all, what can't she do? He lets her do anything she wants to, and he supports all her habits. Why should she even think of leaving—short of a real affaire de coeur—and I'm not sure Winslow is capable of a grand passion."

"Helen of Troy comes to mind. She's the kind of woman men would fight wars over, a true femme fatale. And Gilbert strikes me as her perfect foil, the man who will keep her for what she contributes to his image of himself. Ah, Anna! Let's forget about them for a while. Let's enjoy this magnificence, let's eat that scrumptious lunch and retire upstairs. I've a thing or two I'd like to do with you, my love."

⊠ Chapter 38

1975

Anna and Kurt heard the crunch of tires against gravel and the screech of brakes, then braced themselves for the slam of the car door.

"He's here, and he's angry," Kurt stated matter-of-factly.

It was early Saturday morning in late March. Anna had invited her eldest grandson, Elliot, out to Pennyfield Manor for breakfast. Actually, "summoned" would be a better word, Kurt thought as he put on a cardigan against the early-spring chill and bounded down the front stairs to open the door for Elliot. It would be best to warn him about his grandmother's mood.

Kurt greeted Elliot with "Morning, son."

"Hi, Gramps! How're things?"

He was dressed in his usual faded, tattered jeans, worn-out sneaks, and a nondescript gray T-shirt. He needed a shave and looked a bit hung over.

"Your bub's fit to be tied. You're gonna need every ounce of charm you can muster." He looked at Elliot, a deliberate twinkle in his eye. "Too bad you didn't shave—it might have helped."

"Aw, Gramps, shit, I'm only gonna go to practice this morning. I'll shave before I go out tonight."

Kurt put his arm around Elliot's shoulder and walked with him toward the breakfast room. "Now listen, my boy, we're gonna have to fight this battle together. You try to follow my lead, okay?"

"Yeah, I guess. Shit, Gramps, Mom and Dad are furious too. I've never seen them so mad. Whose life is it, anyway? I hope you'll talk to them today. I need all the help I can get. Hell, I feel like leaving home, not even waiting until next fall."

"Okay, you two. Stop all the plotting. Don't think I don't know what's going on!" Anna said as she walked into the breakfast room and gave Elliot a half-hearted hug. She glared at him with piercing eyes. "I don't need to tell you, young man, how disappointed I am. I can probably still fix things up with Harvard—"

"No!" Elliot's voice boomed.

"Calm down," Kurt cautioned. "Anna, let's eat, then talk. This young man is still growing in spite of his size, and if he's gonna beat Walter Johnson High this afternoon, he needs some food in his stomach."

Elliot looked at his grandfather questioningly. "Are you coming, Gramps?"

"Sure thing. Wouldn't miss it." Then Kurt smiled at Anna in an attempt to soften her attitude. "Unless your bubby wants me to do something else. You know, she always comes first with me."

"You bet—except when Elliot's playing baseball," Anna said. "You two go ahead with your plotting—that's okay. And when I write you out of my will, Elliot, I hope you can convince your grandfather not to leave you penniless."

Rosa and Antonio served a hearty breakfast. Elliot and Kurt ate in silence, occasionally looking at one another meaningfully as Anna scanned *The Washington Post*.

When they were finished, Kurt suggested they take their coffee and adjourn to the solarium, where they could talk without the servants hearing what was bound to be a very heated discussion.

"So what do your parents have to say about your turning down Harvard?" Anna began after they were seated.

"They're pretty mad, I guess."

"Hmmph! As well they should be. When I think of the thousands of young men who'd give their eyeteeth to have your opportunities, and you say no to Harvard—I wonder what's

come over you. I've always had such high hopes for you, Elliot."

"Anna," Kurt intervened, "let's give him a chance to tell us
his thinking. I'm sure he's given this decision a lot of careful
thought. Let's hear him out. You promised me!"

"Okay," Anna grudgingly agreed, making an annoyed face at
Kurt.

"Well, Bub, you know I've always wanted to be a professional
baseball player."

"I didn't know that. I thought all this baseball nonsense was
just kid stuff, something you'd give up after high school. If you
ask me, you've already devoted entirely too much energy to it."

"Anna, please!" Kurt remonstrated.

"Bub, I've wanted to be a baseball star since I was three or
four. And I'm good. I'm going to be all-Met. I've already had
professional scouts at practice."

"I can't believe you're planning a career in baseball!"

"Bub, at least I'm willing to *go* to college. I could sign up
now on a farm team and not go to school at all."

"In a pig's eye, you could! Your father and mother would
never allow—"

"Anna!" Kurt warned again.

"Please listen, Bubby. In the southwestern conference they
play more games per year than any other conference. So I can
play ball, go to school, and get a degree, and if I'm good
enough, when I graduate, I can play pro ball."

"But that's ridiculous. How does any of that prepare you to
work with your father at Dunay?"

"But that's the point! I don't *want* to work for you and Dad.
I want to play ball!"

"Anna, listen to me for a moment. Elliot's only eighteen
years old. Ninety percent of the people in this world don't know
what they want to do with their lives when they're that young. I
say let him go after his dream—at least he's willing to go to
college. A few years from now, he may feel different. He may
give up baseball, or if he's a big star, so much the better. He can
always come to work for Dunay. After all, the company isn't
going to disappear. It's not as if he has to make a living immediately."

"But Harvard! How can he give up Harvard?" She turned
back to Elliot. "Can't you play ball at Harvard?"

"Bub, how many scouts do you think go to Harvard to look at the talent?"

"He's right, Anna. If he wants to play baseball professionally, Harvard is not the right school."

"A lot of help you are," Anna sneered at Kurt. "A fine grandfather you've turned out to be!"

"Well, someone has to be on the boy's side. This battle's pretty one-sided, if you ask me."

Elliot smiled broadly at his grandmother. "Bub, you don't need me. Douglas and Scot and Brad can't wait to work for you. Probably some of the girls want to work with you too. Don't worry—you'll get lots of help from them. Not me, though. I'm no brown-noser, and I can't see myself sitting behind a desk like Dad. Nope, that's not for me. But I love you anyhow, Bub," he said as he stood to leave and came over and kissed her on the forehead. "I know you won't stay mad at me long. Gramps promised me he'd take care of you, right, Gramps?"

Anna knew she was defeated, but it was a bitter pill to swallow. She remained seated as Kurt walked Elliot toward the front door. She was devastated. She'd spent her life building up a company for her sons and grandchildren, and now Elliot wasn't interested in being a part of it. And to give up a chance to go to Harvard—it was unthinkable!

Kurt came back in the room and sat next to her on the sofa. He reached for her hand. "Anna, darling, I know you're disappointed."

"That's an understatement."

"Will you take some advice from an older, more experienced grandparent?" He nuzzled her neck with kisses as he talked.

But Anna was not to be humored. "I don't understand you. I don't see why you're on his side. I'm furious that you're siding with him. What kind of a grandfather are you? Encouraging him in this nonsense!"

"Try for a moment to see things from his point of view. He has this famous grandmother who's excelled in everything she's touched. A grandfather who was the nation's leading naval expert. A father who is a genius in the world of business. How is he going to compete with those three people? How is he ever going to measure up?"

"Not for a moment do I believe that Elliot hasn't the talent and brains to achieve everything we have, and go to even further!"

"That may be what *you* feel, and you may even be right. But *he* doesn't have that kind of self-confidence yet. No, he has confidence in only one area: baseball. And he's good, he's damned good. Good enough to play professional ball, and I wouldn't be encouraging him if I didn't believe it. At least give me some credit, Anna. I convinced him to go to college. He could be finishing high school this May and leaving for training camp the next day. At least he's going to college, even if it isn't the school of your choice. And who knows—he may tire of it and change his mind, and he can always transfer to another school. No, my darling, try to understand. This is Elliot trying to become a man in his own eyes by excelling at something his grandmother and grandfather and father have never done. You've got to let him do it his own way. It's very important."

"Oh, Kurt! You're probably right. But it's so painful! I'm so disappointed! I've had so many dreams and expectations for the grandchildren. Beginning with Elliot. He's so smart and so good-looking. He's so like you, my dear sweet husband. I love you, Kurt, and you're probably right."

"Thank you. And now, I'd like to propose a Saturday morning walk to the stables. Perhaps even a nice long ride."

"Good idea. But what's the rush? I feel lazy."

"The rush is that I've a date with a young man at the Churchill baseball field at two o'clock, and I've got to take care of his bubby first!"

Kurt opened the door to admit a former marine lieutenant who'd been detailed to his office fifteen years before. Every now and then, one of the men who'd worked for him would call for a favor—usually a job recommendation—and he made it a practice to always have time to see them. They'd served him well in his time, and now he felt nothing but gratitude to the men who'd served so loyally under him.

Bob Peterson—balding, still stocky, with piercing dark eyes —held out his hand. "Admiral, you're lookin' good, man!"

"Bob! How ya doin', big guy? Come in!"

After the two men were seated in the library and Bob had been served a beer, Kurt asked, "What brings you out to Potomac on this scorcher of a day?"

He began with hesitation. "I think I mentioned to you that I'm working for the Drug Enforcement Agency, out of Baltimore."

"Yes."

"Am I right in believing that State Senator Gilbert Dunay is your wife's son?"

"Yes, indeed. Why?" What the hell kind of trouble is Gilbert in now? Kurt wondered as he steadied his hand against his glass of iced tea.

"I feel a bit like a rat fink, doing this. I've spent several days and nights trying to decide where my loyalties lie—with you, my former commanding officer, for whom I have great respect, or with the cause of controlling drug trafficking. Shit, I never did have much truck with sting operations, and . . ."

"Yes—tell me," Kurt encouraged, understanding the man's dilemma.

"DEA has set up a sting operation for next Friday night, and they're gonna trap Senator Dunay. I thought—I thought if I told you, maybe you could prevent him from being there, or something."

Kurt groaned aloud. "How heavily is he involved?"

"I'm not sure. I don't know if he's done any previous jobs. But when our undercover man offered him a chance at this, he grabbed it. Seems he hangs with a bad bunch of people over in Baltimore. Partly mob, partly just trash, some of 'em pretty high in the state government. He's got big gambling debts, and his broads are expensive to keep."

"Tell me the details. When and where?" Kurt asked as he walked to the desk to pick up a pen and pad and returned to his chair.

"Thing that surprised me is how greedy he is. Grabbed a chance at two hundred fifty thousand. Hell, that must be chickenfeed in this family!"

"Yes, well . . ." Kurt didn't want to discuss Gilbert's character flaws or his wife's wealth with this former marine, no matter how beholden to him he felt for supplying the information.

"We're gonna make the pick-up at the Lift-Off Motel on Reisterstown Road next Friday night just before midnight. Dunay and two other members of the legislature are gonna be picked up." Peterson watched Kurt's face. "I sort of figured you'd wanna know and try to prevent it."

"You're right. And I will—you can count on it."

"Yeah, I figured. Keep him outta drugs in the future—it's a nasty business. Not the right milieu, if you read me, for an aspiring politician."

"I couldn't agree more, Bob. And I thank you for alerting me. If I can do anything for you . . ."

"No, sir, that's not necessary. You were always a great officer. I respected you more than any other commanding officer I ever reported to. That's why I couldn't let this happen to you or your lady." Peterson stood. "You'll take care of it, then."

"You can count on it."

Kurt saw Bob Peterson to the door, then returned to the library and picked up the phone. He dialed a number at the Pentagon. "Bill, I need to see you and Jack. Can we meet this afternoon at eighteen hundred, the cocktail lounge in the Marriott Key Bridge?"

Gilbert stepped out of the shower, humming a tune from *West Side Story* and thinking about the pretty little thing he'd left just an hour earlier. Only seventeen, and sassy as they come. He liked her kind of brassiness. And she loved the dope he gave her! A month's supply, for chrissake!

He dropped the towel and reached into the drawer for his shorts. At that moment the door to his bedroom burst open, and he turned to face two masked men with guns pointed at him. "What the fuck?"

"Get dressed. And no funny business," the shorter of the two men thundered.

"My wife's jewels—they're in the guest bedroom."

"That's not what we came for. It's you we want. Now, shut the fuck up and get some clothes on, unless you wanna leave this fuckin' palace in your birthday suit."

"Is anyone else home? Any servants? Any kids?" asked the tall blond intruder.

"No. No, the servants are gone. My wife's in Greece. And the kids are with their grandparents at Rehoboth Beach. Shit, even the dogs are at the kennel!" As Gilbert pulled a cotton sweater over his head and pulled on his trousers, it dawned on him. "Hell, is this a kidnapping? Do you know who I am?"

"Yeah, we know who you are. Heir to a massive fortune, right? S'matter of fact, we expect your mom'll pay big dollars to get her little boy home safe and sound. C'mon—move it!" He shoved the gun in Gilbert's ribs and steered him out the kitchen entrance into a dry cleaner's van. Once inside the van, the two men bound Gilbert's hands and feet with rope, blindfolded him, and placed him on a mattress in the back of the van. The tall blond man guarded him, while the short stocky man drove the van.

After driving for more than an hour, they stopped the van and herded the still-blindfolded Gilbert into a house and down a set of stairs into a damp, dark unfinished basement. While the blond man continued to guard him at gunpoint, the short man went out for sandwiches.

They removed the ropes from his wrists and the blindfold to allow him to eat, then tied his wrists again.

"I don't understand what you guys want with me. Have you sent a ransom note to my mom? For chrissake, what's going on?"

"Patience, buddy. Just be patient. In due time, you'll understand everything."

His captors smoked and drank beer and had pizza delivered, made a few phone calls, and had a long conference upstairs while he cooled his heels in the basement.

Later—much later, in the middle of the night it seemed to Gilbert—he heard the door upstairs open and close, heard voices that sounded familiar, and watched four sets of legs emerge and come down the basement steps.

To his utter amazement, the newcomers were his brother, Charles, and his stepfather, Admiral Kurt Addison.

"Thank God you've come! How much do they want?" Gilbert said gratefully as they removed the ropes from his wrists. Still, the blond kept his gun trained on Gilbert.

"We're not going anyplace. Not yet. Not until we talk," Addison said gruffly as he sat down on the hard chair in front of Gilbert.

"What's going on? Let's get outta here!"

"Sit still," Charles commanded his brother.

"For chrissake, pay them off and let's get outta here! What's wrong with you guys—are you crazy or something?"

"No, but we wonder if you've completely lost your marbles,

Gilbert. Tell me, where were you supposed to be at this time tonight?" Kurt demanded.

Startled, Gilbert stared first at Kurt, then at Charles. A thin film of perspiration covered his face. "What do you mean?"

Charles answered, "Gilbert, you were supposed to be in Baltimore, weren't you? You were going to pick up a cool quarter of a million dollars for distributing some Colombian coke, giving it to some of the Dumphy gang. Am I right?"

Even in the dim light of the basement, they could see Gilbert's face turn ashen. "What do you know about that?"

"Everything," Kurt stated flatly.

Fear replaced surprise on Gilbert's face. "Does—does Mother know?"

"No," Charles said, "and I'd like to keep it that way. If—and it's a big if—if we can cure you of your addiction to making big money with the underworld—if we can somehow beat some sense into you. . . . Shit, Gil, how could you take a chance like this? How can you do it to yourself, let alone Mom and me and—the admiral?"

"How the hell did you guys find out?" he managed to ask.

Kurt looked at Gilbert with cold eyes. "It doesn't matter how we found out. What matters is that we prevented you from being picked up tonight by the Drug Enforcement Agency. Your other friends—they're history. Yes, Gil, it was a classic sting operation, and you were their sitting duck, you were their fool. How would that have affected your political career?"

"I don't see any point in waiting around here, Dad. Let's take him home. We can talk on the way." Charles looked at the blond man. "You can put that away now. I'm sure he'll come peacefully."

Gilbert looked in amazement as the blond man tucked the gun into the top of his pants. "You mean"—he looked back at his stepfather—"you mean these thugs are working for you?"

"Yes, Gilbert. They kidnapped you on my orders, to save you from a federal narcotics-trafficking charge. To save you from a certain prison term. To save the entire family from a devastating scandal. But don't misunderstand my motivation. I didn't do this to save your ass. You deserve any punishment you'd have received. I did it for your children, and for your mother."

The three men began to climb the stairs. When they arrived

at the top, Kurt turned to his friends Bill and Jack, thanked them quietly, and said, "I'll be talking to you."

In Charles's car, Kurt sat in the front seat and Gilbert in the backseat. Kurt turned to Gilbert. "This is the last time, Gil. Next time I'll let you twist in the wind, next time I'll let you rot in jail. I'm sick and tired of saving your ass. From now on, you'd better watch it. This is it! Positively the last time!"

But later that week in a private conference with Charles, he cautioned, "Charles, I won't be here forever to protect your mother. Make sure Gil has whatever he needs in the way of money. It's the only thing that'll protect her from a scandal that would ruin her life, destroy everything she's worked so hard for all these years. I'm counting on you, Charles. Not only must you keep the business running smoothly, you've got to protect yourself and Anna from Gil. Don't let your guard down—not for a minute."

"Bub, when I grow up, I'm gonna make movies. I'm gonna be the writer and the director and the producer." Fourteen-year-old Sonia lay on the floor of the living room at Anna's Rehoboth Beach house. All the other grandchildren were asleep. It was raining outdoors—thunder and lightning occasionally made the house shake. Anna had candles at the ready in case the electricity went out.

Anna put down the book she was reading. She looked at Sonia. Her bronzed legs were akimbo, and she was lying on her back, holding a movie magazine high up in the air as she read it, as her red hair fanned out behind her head.

"You're certain you wouldn't rather work for me? We could arrange for you to manage a magnificent resort hotel, perhaps in the Caribbean. Maybe on St. John's."

"Ugh! Who wants to do that? No, Bub, the only thing I can imagine myself doing for you is taking promotion pictures and designing your brochures. But that's not the same, that's not working with film the way I want to."

"Some days I regret ever having given you that first camera. What were you, eight years old?"

Sonia sat up and put her magazine down. "Yeah, I was eight, and I took pictures of Jennifer. And I won prizes. Remember, I started off winning prizes that same year! And even you admit my horse pictures are some of the best you've ever seen. The ones I took at Chincoteague are spectacular."

"Hmm. The ones from last year's International at Laurel aren't bad. No, my dearest, I admit you do take spectacular pictures. But that's not the same as directing a movie."

"Will you invest in my company?"

"Sonia! You're only fourteen! I don't think we have to settle the matter of my investing in your career until you graduate from college—at the very earliest!" Anna remembered Kurt's advice: "Find out what they want to do, and encourage the hell out of it!"

"No, Bub, I need to know now. I need to be able to plan. After all, I've scriptwriters to line up, actors to hire—"

Anna laughed out loud. Sonia was so programmed, so organized. She was always organizing her brothers and sisters and cousins, always planning for the next day, for tonight, or for the next dozen years.

"Well, Bub?"

"Of course I will. I'll gladly invest in anything you want me to, darling. You know that. . . . I can't understand where your grandfather is. I've called home three times. He didn't tell me he was going anyplace. Your father's not home either, and it's nearly midnight."

"Oh, Bub, stop being such an old lady! They're just out with friends. Don't worry. You know Gramps likes to go out with Bill and Jack and play poker until the wee hours. But I'm tired. C'mon—let's go to bed, and you can talk to Gramps first thing in the morning."

Sonia stood up and approached her grandmother. "Bub, Mom told me that someday I should make a movie of your love story with Gramps. She says it's the most romantic she's ever heard!"

"Oh, it's no such thing! Your mother shouldn't be putting ideas like that in your head."

"Will you tell me someday? Please—please, Bubby. Promise me that when I'm eighteen, you'll tell me your love story."

"Don't be silly. There's nothing to tell. I don't understand why Emily would say such a thing—and to you, of all people. Such a romantic! My goodness, the boys won't stand a chance around you."

"Don't be so sure! Michael hasn't even noticed me yet."

Anna glanced again at her smiling, shiny-eyed granddaughter. "That's good. You're a bit young for Michael—after all, he's in college." She stood. "I guess your gramps has forgotten all about his wife tonight. Let's go to bed."

The two headed for the bedroom, their arms around one another.

⊠ Chapter 39

Aspen, Colorado, New Year's Day 1984

Anna looked down the long table at her nine grandchildren—now young adults. Tonight, they were bursting with the anticipation of a week of skiing before they had to return to school or work. They were handsome, vigorous, and healthy specimens all. And they were grown-up enough now that she could imagine what they would look like for the rest of their lives.

She took a taste of Rosa's caviar roulade. It was marvelous! With dismay, she realized that all her grandchildren did not share her opinion. Jennifer, Rick, and Elliot had taken only one taste and laid their forks to rest on their plates. Even so, everyone else seemed to be devouring the delicate dill-flavored, caviar-filled roll.

"What's wrong, Elliot?" she demanded of her eldest grandson, who was seated on her right.

"C'mon, Bub. I'm trying to be polite. You notice I didn't make any nasty remarks. I just don't like all this fancy stuff."

"My dear," she said with great patience, "that's caviar you're *not* eating. Russian caviar."

Elliot grimaced, then grinned mischievously at her. "I hate anything that tastes fishy. And this sure as hell does."

"You must develop a more sophisticated palate, even though you insist on living in the wilds of New Mexico. For the life of me, I can't understand why you persist in staying there."

"Bub, let's not have this discussion again. I love the horses and the mountains and the hunting and the fishing."

"But darling, I've told you I'll buy you a wonderful place in

Virginia—Middleburg, or somewhere like that. You could have horses and hunting and fishing and the Blue Ridge Mountains."

"Aw, Bub, c'mon—I love the Southwest. And believe me, that's where the action is these days. I'm doin' great, and I love livin' there. You can't complain—I'm making some damned good investments for Dunay. That's one hell of a resort complex we're building in Santa Fe. You should be thrilled."

From the opposite end of the table, Kurt tinkled his spoon against one of the hand-blown wine goblets that Anna had commissioned from Santa Fe glassblower Josh Simpson. Her heart fluttered with fear that it might chip—and how she loved those cobalt-speckled-with-gold glasses!

How smart Sidney was to talk me into making this home a showplace for American craftsmen! I resisted and resisted, but Sidney prevailed, and I'm thrilled with the results, she thought as she watched her tall, handsome husband stand up at the far end of the table.

"If I can steal the floor from my lovely wife, I've an announcement to make," Kurt began, when everyone had quieted down. "There are so few occasions these days when we have all of you gathered together at one table, that I decided this afternoon—and your bubby doesn't even know about this—that I would tell all of you together about the arrangements I'm making for my estate."

Suddenly, Anna noticed, the expectant faces turned grim. Even though Kurt was eighty-two years old, he was still in splendid health, due in large measure to his routine of exercising and eating properly. Everyone—certainly his grandchildren —thought of him as invulnerable, as a man who would live forever. But she knew his own mortality had been much on his mind lately.

"After much thought and consultation with our lawyers, I've decided to create nine living trusts with a principal of one hundred thousand dollars. One for each of you."

There were smiles and gasps of delight all around the table. Charles and Emily looked at their own children's faces, at Gilbert and Winslow's children's faces, and back to Kurt.

Anna wished, for the umpteenth time that day, that Winslow and Gilbert were present. Why do they have to spoil everything by refusing to participate in family occasions when Kurt is going to be there? At least their children ignore their silliness!

"You will be able to access the interest when you are twenty-one, the principal when you are thirty. But you, Elliot, for example, can borrow against the principal now for some of your real estate deals."

"Wow!" Rick exclaimed. "But it's four more years before I'll be twenty-one!"

"Jeez, that's just great, Gramps!" Sonia beamed. "I can borrow against it when I get ready to start my movie company next year."

Sonia, who was currently working for Sherry Lansing at Paramount Pictures, was determined that after she spent two years "apprenticing," as Anna called it, she would have her own film company.

"I suspect you'll need more than that." Kurt chuckled. "You'll have to speak to your bub, and she'll have to speak to her bankers."

"And I can use it to start my dress-design company too," Karine bubbled from her seat next to Emily.

"We'll have to have a bit of a conference later this week, girls," Anna responded to both Sonia and Karine.

Jen, her violet eyes gleaming, shyly asked, "Does that mean I can't use any of the interest this summer? I won't be twenty-one for two more years."

Kurt sat down, then reached over to his youngest granddaughter, who was seated on his right, and patted her hand. "What did you want to do this summer, sweetheart?"

"I want to work as a stagehand at the Santa Fe Opera company. Dad said maybe yes since Elliot lives nearby. He can sort of keep an eye on me."

"Sounds good to me. Maybe we can make special arrangements—I don't think that's out of the question." Kurt looked at Emily and at Charles, to make sure he wasn't agreeing to something they disapproved of. Then he added, "If it's okay with your parents. If they say yes, sweetheart, you come see me, and we'll make the financial arrangements."

"Gosh, Gramps, that's terrific! Thanks!"

All she has to do is smile at him, and she can have anything she wants. She's his favorite angel, Anna thought as she watched the interplay between Kurt and Jennifer. She thought of how he always called her his "little angel" in their private conversations.

And Sonia is my own weakness. She can have anything, anything at all. I must be so careful not to let those feelings show! I must be fair to Karine and Larissa and Jennifer! God knows I love them all!

"Gramps," Douglas enthused, "that solves my problem about this summer. I really want to go to Israel, and that'll do the trick for me. Super!"

Darn! Anna said to herself. I don't want you to go to Israel. It's just not safe! That's why I haven't offered to pay your way. And I know that's why Charles and Emily have been reluctant, even though you deserve it. As a graduation present, before we start you out at Dunay. Well, Israel and Greece are two great places to visit, I suppose.

Antonio and Rosa finished clearing the plates from the first course and prepared to serve *veau à l'orange aux quenelles* on the handmade porcelain dinner service specially made by Lyn Evans for Anna's Aspen house.

I love creating the ambience—that's my specialty here, Anna told herself as she looked at the glorious table. Everyone else skis, and I create this magnificent atmosphere. Instead of flowers in the center of the table, blown-glass sculptures by Dale Chihuly. Instead of eighteenth-century paintings, wall hangings by Christina Bergh and Kozikowski. Indian pottery by Maria, champagne goblets by Randy Strong. And these glorious clusters of black wrought-iron candelabras standing in groupings around the dining room instead of electric lights. It's glorious—absolutely the finest America has to offer! How I love this house and the people gathered around this table! If only Winslow and Gilbert were here, it would be complete—but they do so love to run with the Reagan crowd. I suppose New Year's in Palm Springs is more appealing to Winslow—and to Gilbert, too—than being here with their children. A false set of values . . . but, oh well.

"Would anyone like to know what I've decided to do with this house?" Kurt glanced expectantly up and down the table, his eyes twinkling. "I'll bet you thought I would leave it to Anna. Wrong! She's not a ski enthusiast, never has been. Besides, she already has too many homes. Nope, I've decided that this house belongs, from this day forward, to Charles and Emily."

"Oh, wow! That's terrific! Can I control the calendar, Mom?

I'll book it year round. And all you other cretins"—Sonia grinned at her siblings and cousins—"will have to deal with me."

"Hey, Dad, that's not fair! You're not gonna let Sonia control—" Brad, who'd spent his young life being ruled by Sonia, objected.

"Don't worry," Charles interrupted. "Your mother and I will handle the scheduling." He looked pointedly at Larissa, Karine, Scot, and Rick. "And I want you kids to know you're welcome to use this house too. Anytime you want to, you just call Aunt Emily, and she'll make the arrangements. Even though Gramps is legally changing the title, it belongs to all of you, to all of Kurt and Anna's grandchildren."

How like Charles, Anna thought as she smiled approvingly at him and Emily. How like him to be good to Gilbert's children.

Two hours later, after much more champagne and a divine coffee-and-chocolate-flavored charlotte, Kurt and Anna retired to their master suite to watch the late evening news on television and to snuggle together in the warmth of their bed. The lights were turned out and the draperies drawn open, revealing a magnificent panorama of snow-covered mountains twinkling with the Christmas lights of houses and condominums basking in the silver light of a full moon. The snow, which had been falling all day, had now stopped, leaving a crystalline covering on the pine tree that hovered against the far edge of the window. A strong wind caused the windows to shudder, and Anna looked thankfully at the smoldering fire in the corner fireplace. "Fires smell so much better out here, don't you think, Kurt?"

"Hmm . . . that's because of the mesquite and piñon wood they use. Yes, it's very nice." He put down the Thoroughbred horse magazine he was reading and snuggled close to Anna. "How does it feel to have all your little chickadees under one roof again? You seemed deep in thought during dinner."

"They really are wonderful, all of them. Not a lazy one among them. In spite of our wealth, they've turned out okay. They'll be productive human beings. If only they didn't wear those horrid jeans! You'd think they came from poor families, to see the way they dress. But they're wonderful kids. I can't get enough of them."

"Anna, darling, those jeans are the style."

"I suppose that's true enough. But when I was that age, I

took pride in how I dressed. I didn't have any money at all, but I always looked smart."

"Have you noticed how much you and I both think about the past these days? We must really be getting old. I never thought I'd see the day when I spend so much time remembering instead of looking forward."

"Dearest, we aren't exactly young anymore. What with you almost eighty-three and me—goodness, I'm so vain, I don't even like to admit it to myself—only three years away from eighty!"

"But all things considered, we've had a wonderful life. If things can just continue . . ."

"I'm sorry Doug is going to Israel. I've spent years trying to ignore his pleas, ever since his bar mitzvah, when that rabbi put the bug in his head. I don't think it's safe."

"I know. I've always wondered that you aren't terribly proud of your heritage. I wish I could claim to be Jewish myself, in fact. I understand Doug's feelings. He even seems obsessed with the idea. Sooner or later, he'll go, and it might as well be after he finishes his MBA and before you load him down with responsibilities at the office. Besides, a good travel executive *should* see the world. He's already been everywhere in Europe and Asia. It's a miracle you've kept him out of Israel this long."

"I suppose so. Of course, Charles and Emily don't share my views completely. They've been ready to let him go for years."

"I don't think it's his physical safety you're so concerned about. I think you're afraid he might decide to stay there."

"He's such an idealist! He reminds me of you, when I first met you. But then, you had a strong practical streak too. I'm not sure he does. Like you once did, he feels he can single-handedly change things. I'm afraid he'll get over there, make the State of Israel his new cause, and never come back to Dunay. I don't think I could take it if he refused to work with Charles. I'm counting on it so!"

"I don't think you really have much to worry about. And Brad and Scot are coming along—both of them expect to work for you."

"Yes." Anna glowed. "Someday Brad will be the general counsel, and Scot will be chief financial officer."

"And what will Doug be?"

"My dearest, I see Doug as a reincarnation of you. He looks

exactly like you when I met you. He has your brains, your drive, your idealism. He'll be the chairman of the board and chief executive officer. Whenever Charles is ready to slow down or retire, Doug will run the show. That's what I've decided."

"And Elliot? What about him?"

"Elliot chooses to stay in the Southwest. He'll play whatever role he wants and make a ton of money, but unless he relocates here, there's no way he can run the show. He knows that. It's his decision."

"I see. And the girls? What about them?"

"I'm following your advice to the letter with the girls, Kurt." Anna grinned mischievously at him. "I admit, I've not followed it with the boys, I've been a bit heavy-handed. But with the girls, I'm doing exactly what you told me to. I find out what they want to do, and I encourage the hell out of it. So . . ."

"So?" Kurt pulled Anna closer and began playing with her breast.

"So I'm subsidizing Larissa's writing. I'm so proud of those two stories she's published! If I knew how, I'd bribe a publishing house—but I guess she'll have to earn that on her own."

"I hope they accept her at the Iowa Writer's Workshop this summer."

"Your trust fund will make it possible for her to spend whatever money is necessary and concentrate on being creative."

"Yes, she seemed pleased."

"And when Sonia and Karine seem ready for their own businesses, you can be sure I'll invest the appropriate amount of money."

"And Jen? Do you imagine you can buy her a spot in the chorus of the Met?"

"Oh, Kurt! Stop making fun of me! You know as well as I do that you can have all the talent in the world, but if you don't have connections, you spend a lifetime without ever being recognized! I intend to do what I can for Jen, but first we have to see how her voice develops. After all, she's only nineteen."

"But you've been told by several teachers that she has a splendid voice!"

"No question, she does. But for me to push her opera career is about as questionable an enterprise as it was for you to push Elliot's baseball career. It's a one-in-ten-million shot."

"You haven't mentioned Rick. What future have you planned for his music?"

"How can you even use the word *music*? That incessant noise of his drives me wild! I don't know how his parents have stood it all these years. And he needs a haircut!"

"If you're going to be a rock star, you need that kind of image."

"Actually, it's the environment I worry about. The people he'll be associated with. They all use drugs."

"This old grandfather is getting tired of talking about sexy young men and beautiful young women. What I need is some affection from a beautiful young grandmother."

Kurt reached up and pushed the buttons that closed the draperies and turned out the lights. Then he snuggled closer to Anna and whispered into her ear, "Are you mad at me because I gave this house away without consulting you first?"

Anna answered with put-on hurt, "You could have at least waited until I'm finished with it! I intend to continue to come here for the next twenty years!"

Kurt laughed. "You'll have to speak to Sonia first, and get her permission!"

Anna laughed, too, then asked, "And what about your daughters? What are you doing for them?"

"Leaving them everything else—at least a million apiece. Knowing you, in spite of their nastiness toward you, I imagine you'll leave them a little something."

Anna smiled up at Kurt, then kissed his lips softly. "Yes, you do know me well. I've already made plans to be sure they—and their children—have a secure future."

Sonia and Karine carried two trays of champagne glasses and four bottles of champagne from the kitchen, through the foyer, and into the great room. This much champagne will put all of us to sleep—and give us rollicking hangovers tomorrow, Sonia thought, as she passed the huge Alan Hauser sculpture of an Indian woman with a baby that dominated the flagstone foyer. Hmm—I wonder if Gramps is giving Mom and Dad all the furnishings, too, and the art and sculpture and pottery and glass. I hope so!

They set the trays down on the glass-and-brass table in front of the deep sofa, which provided seating for all of them together.

Scot was talking about Gramps's decision to give the Aspen house to Charles and Emily. ". . . really pleased! If he'd given it to Gilbert and Winslow, it's a cinch Dad would sell it and spend the money on broads and gambling."

"Yeah," Rick chimed in, "this way, we'll always be able to use it. *Your* folks will make sure we get equal time!"

"Just remember, buddy," Sonia said with a broad smile, "you're gonna have to clear it with me."

Elliot interrupted angrily, "Shit, Sonia! Dad said Mom is going to control it. If you think I'm gonna call you for permission before I bring a chick here, you've got another think coming. Besides, I live closest to Aspen—it's just a quick plane flight here, and I'll use it most."

"The reality is," Larissa drawled, "most of the time it will go unused. All of us are too busy. On the other hand, it would be a great writer's retreat."

"Anytime. Just let me know!" Sonia beamed at her cousin.

"Yeah, Cuz! Just call me first to make sure I'm not shacked up here. Though there are lots of bedrooms."

"You're so tight with Gramps, Elliot," Larissa continued, "I'm surprised he didn't give it to you."

"Yeah, well. Bub still hasn't forgiven me for not going to Harvard—even though, thanks to you creeps"—he looked pointedly at Scot and Brad and Doug—"she'll get three Harvard graduates yet. Three out of nine ain't bad!"

"So after all that fuss about baseball, why'd you give it up?" Karine asked Elliot.

"I guess I realized I wasn't good enough to make the majors, and I didn't want to spend the rest of my life sitting on a bench. There comes a time . . . you guys who are trying to be singers and musicians and writers—hell, you've got about as much chance at succeeding as I did. It's a long shot. We probably should all of us just join Dunay and make a pile of money and find some good hobbies."

Sonia was concentrating on Elliot, staring at him.

"What the hell are you staring at me for, Sonia? Have I grown horns?"

"No I'm just wondering if your sexiness would come across on film."

"Aha! A little incestuous thinking going on here!" Scot wisecracked.

Larissa took up for Sonia. "She's right. Elliot *is* sexy, like Gramps and Uncle Charles. But I can't see any of Emily's genes in him."

"And Doug," Karine joined in, "is the exact reincarnation of Gramps. I've heard her say that. That's why Gram is so determined to groom him to be head of Dunay."

Doug's face had colored, and he shook his head modestly.

Rick, in a sarcastic voice, asked, "Are you gonna find jobs for all us guys who don't make it as entertainers and artists? Are you gonna be our savior?"

In response, Doug threw a pillow at Rick. "Anyone but you, Rick! No jobs for long-haired musicians!"

"Rick, don't worry," Sonia said. "You can work for me in my movie company. I'll make you music director."

Elliot perked up. "When's this movie company I've been hearing about for a dozen years gonna get off the ground? Have you convinced Bub yet?"

Sonia smiled a secretive smile. "Big conference is on the agenda for later this week. I've got to catch her in a good mood."

"Shit! She's always in a good mood with you, Miss Brown-noser!" Rick shot back.

"Are you really sure you're ready? You've only been at Paramount for two years," Jen asked.

"I'm ready to try my wings. I only hope I don't go bankrupt and lose all the money Bub and Gramps and Dad are willing to invest. It takes millions."

"Exactly how many millions?" Doug demanded.

"Three to five to start up, with a profit about five years down the road," Sonia answered.

Karine brightened. "That's about what it will take to start my dress-design company. I'm scared shitless to ask Dad and Gramps and Bub to back me—that's so much money!"

"Not really," Elliot said. "Not a hell of a lot considering what Dunay is worth. Bub could write out a check to each of you and never even miss it."

"But she won't!" Doug stated flatly.

"Hell, no! She'll set it up in such a way that you bear the lion's share of responsibility. It'll be your operation, and if you lose the money, it'll be your problem too. All you'll be losing is your own inheritance. So don't do it until you're sure you're ready. That's all I've got to say to you girls. It's a dog-eat-dog world out there, and you're trying to play in the big leagues mighty young."

Larissa looked at Elliot skeptically. "So are you! For God's sake, building a twenty-six-million-dollar resort complex out in the middle of nowhere! That's playing in the big leagues!"

"The difference is that Dunay has some experience with hotels and the travel industry. What the hell does Bubby know about creating a movie company or a dress-design company?"

"What we know," Sonia answered calmly, "is that you hire the best possible people and give them their head. I've got some of the best scriptwriters ready, a terrific cameraman, and a fabulous set designer all lined up ready to come to work for me when I give them the word. You hire the best, pay them what they're worth, and let them be creative. That's the name of the game."

Scot set his glass back on the table. "I hope to hell you know what you're doing, Sonia. I'd hate to have to pick up the pieces after you go bankrupt."

"I fully expect to get expert advice from my cousin, the graduate of Harvard's business school—advice for free, in fact! In exchange for—let's see—four weeks' use of this house each year. How's that?"

Scot laughed. He was, by family agreement, the best skier among them. He spent every weekend on the slopes and made it a point to ski in Chile in the summer—when he wasn't traipsing around Europe with Brad.

"What about actors, Sis?" Brad asked with a wink. He was renowned for his prowess with women, fancied himself a real lady-killer. And, Sonia mused, with his infectious smile and laughing eyes and worldly sophistication, all the rumors were probably true.

"Bub would kill me, simply kill me, if I diverted you away from Dunay. Nope, Brad, your future is signed, sealed, and delivered. You will be the general counsel. Sorry, Brother—no way out for you!"

Doug, always sensitive to people's feelings, turned to Larissa. "Why don't you become a screenwriter for Sonia?"

"Hey! Good idea!" Sonia enthused. "What are you writing now? Why don't you try your hand at a movie script?"

"I'm working on my skills right now, and looking for stories wherever I can find them. Like here, in my family. I need to live awhile first, experience things. Then I'll be able to write about them."

Elliot, who had been looking at Larissa intently, asked, "Have you ever thought of wearing contact lenses? Or do you like the intellectual image?"

"My glasses!" She took her owlish horn-rimmed glasses, which had been perched on top of her caramel-colored hair, off her head, folded them, and laid them in her lap. "Actually, it's never been an issue with me. I'm comfortable with glasses, and my appearance has never meant a damned thing to me."

"Having Winslow for a mother explains that," Brad interjected.

"It would seem to me," Doug began cautiously, "that you have quite a laboratory right at home, what with Winslow and Gilbert to study."

"I don't live at home anymore."

"Right! I'd forgotten. By the way, how does it work, with Bubby 'subsidizing your creativity,' as she puts it?"

"Simple. She pays me sixteen hundred a month. That's plenty for me to live on. I write all day long, every day. Someday it will pay off."

"All of literature seems to be about the relationships of men and women. Perhaps what you need most of all is some experience with love. I don't mean to be offensive. . . ."

"No, Doug. I understand exactly what you mean, and I agree with you. But that can only come with time. In the meantime, I'm working on skills. Most of what I'd like to write—well, it's too painful right now, and I can't seem to get the proper distance and perspective."

"Hey, guys, I don't want to be a killjoy, but if we're gonna hit the slopes by noon tomorrow, we should turn in. It's almost one o'clock," Scot admonished. "We can continue this exercise in family analysis and group therapy tomorrow night, same time, same place!"

"Good idea!" Elliot said as he yawned. "Only tomorrow night I don't expect to be here. By this time tomorrow evening, I'll have found myself a woman!"

"From your mouth to God's ears!" Brad said. "May we all be so blessed!"

"Hush!" Sonia scolded. "Such talk in your bubby's house! Shame on you! And in front of Jennifer!"

"Oh, Sonia, stop being the little mother. I'm tired of that shit!" Rick said as he walked past Sonia and buzzed her on the cheek. "Good night, all!"

"You've got to be ruthless in pushing them, Elliot," Anna admonished. She was speaking to him from her office at Dunay International in the Watergate office building. As she spoke, she doodled on a lavender-colored pad that Karine had given to her specifically for that purpose. "I insist that the resort be opened in time for the opera season—it's as simple as that. You need the exposure and the publicity. Get the construction crew in there overtime and on weekends, and tell Sidney it's a top priority with me. She's never let me down yet."

"Bub, I'll do my best. You know that. But I want you to put your mind to work on the gala opening. Call in some chits. I'd like a few Hollywood celebrities, the two senators and the governor—maybe even some Las Vegas entertainers. We need to make folks—especially the summer crowd here in Santa Fe—sit up and take notice."

"Okay, I'll plan the opening. We'll make it a weekend of festivities. I'll speak to Neil Simon . . . and Liza Minnelli. I'll be back in touch in a couple of days. Meanwhile, you ride herd on your vendors. And spare no expense with the landscaping! I want it to be beautiful. Absolutely the most beautiful resort in all of the Southwest!"

"Understood! Bye, Bub. Talk to you tomorrow."

"I love you, Elliot."

"Yeah. I know, Bub. Bye."

Anna replaced the phone. She stood and walked to the window. Below her spread the Potomac River, to the right the spires of Georgetown University, to the left the Lincoln Memorial. Traffic was speeding by, even though it was only midafternoon. Elliot's good, she thought, darn good at what he does. I wish I had ten more like him.

The door to her office opened suddenly, and she turned to face Charles. He was walking toward her hesitantly, his face the color of pale ashes.

"Mom . . ."

"Charles! What is it?"

He wrapped his arms around her and held her close. She felt his body shudder. "Charles, tell me," she implored.

"Doug . . . it's Doug."

He held her away and looked down into her face. "Mother . . . it's awful. The Israeli ambassador just called me. He's been killed in a terrorist attack on a tourist bus."

"No—no, it can't be! Some mistake . . ." Anna felt all the blood in her body rush to her feet, and Charles's face began to spin. "I—I must sit."

He held on to her elbow tightly and guided her to the sofa. When she was safely seated, he sat next to her and held her hand. Tears brimmed in his eyes.

When Anna could find her voice, she said, "We must call Elliot. He'll come home."

"Yes, I'll call Elliot." Charles, looking more stricken than Anna had ever seen him, squeezed her hand. "Mother, you must come with me. I've—" His voice cracked, but he managed to continue. "I've got to go home and tell Emily. God knows where I'll find the strength."

"Oh—oh, my . . ." Anna's mind was suddenly racing, and her adrenaline was pumping again. She willed herself to cast aside her grief—it couldn't be true, anyway, it was too monstrous—surely it was a terrible mistake.

"Before we leave, I think we should call Dad. He can be here in a couple of hours."

"Yes, and Sonia too. Emily will need her. I'll need her. Kurt and Sonia can come home this afternoon, together. Yes, darling, get your father on the phone, and then we'll call Sonia together."

Charles placed the call to his father's office in New York City and told his secretary it was an emergency. He was put through immediately and signaled Anna to pick up the phone. After telling Kurt about Doug's death, he listened to his father's orderly mind take control.

"We'll send Elliot to Israel in one of Dunay's planes to pick up the body. I'll arrange a military escort to help cut through any red tape. Meanwhile, let's get all the children home and out to Pennyfield. Anna and Emily will need to be surrounded by them. Hell, all of us will need whatever solace we can find. Hell of a thing. . . . Charles, how's your mother?"

"She's right here beside me, Dad. Holding up, like the trooper she is."

"Kurt," Anna whispered hoarsely into the phone, "get Sonia, and come as quickly as possible. I need you here. Beside me."

"Yes, darling. I'll be there in less than two hours. Meet you out at Charles's house."

Anna hung up the phone and once again allowed herself to be cradled in her son's strong arms. She understood that the very act of comforting her gave him strength. She tried to force the fog of grief from her mind, tried to compartmentalize it and set it aside for later, but her iron-willed discipline failed her.

I'm too old now, she thought, too old for this tragedy. Oh, why couldn't it have been me? Or Kurt? We've lived our lives. No grandmother should live to see her grandson's life snuffed out, so needlessly, so horribly. Maybe there's some mistake.

But there was no mistake. As the afternoon turned to evening, Kurt's connections in the State Department and the Defense Department confirmed that the identification of Douglas was beyond question.

Kurt helped Charles with the awful task of telling Douglas's sisters and brothers while simultaneously trying to console Emily and Anna. Kurt made all the necessary arrangements for Elliot's trip to Israel, and shortly after five in the morning, Elliot, having flown in from Albuquerque, left on a Dunay jet for Tel Aviv.

Sasha, blessed Sasha, arrived at Emily's, and after detailed consultation with Charles and Kurt, she took over all the arrangements for the funeral.

Anna and Kurt retired to Pennyfield Manor with Sonia in tow. Her job was to take care of Anna. Jen and Brad remained with Charles and Emily. The funeral would be held three days thence, as soon as Elliot was back in Washington.

Telegrams and flowers poured in from all over the world. Two Dunay staffers were detailed to do nothing but answer the phone at the two residences. Anna insisted that she be shielded from the calls and the well-intentioned would-be visitors. She wanted no one but Kurt with her—and Sonia, who, God bless her, remained steadfastly upbeat in spite of her breaking heart.

"I never wanted him to go to Israel. It's as if I had a premonition. Ordinarily I don't believe in things like that."

Kurt paced back to where Anna was sitting, reached for her hand, and said, "What will be, will be. There are things in life we have no control over."

"Bub, Doug was such a neat brother! So good-looking, and so nice. He seemed to be able to read our minds, find our particular pain, and assuage it. He was the most sensitive man I've ever known—perhaps he was too sensitive for this world." Sonia reached for the handkerchief that she had taken to carrying in her blazer pocket.

For once, Anna noticed, Sonia was not in jeans. She looked very nice in a tailored linen blazer and skirt, her hair restrained in a large ivory barrette. It was a comfort just having her in the same room.

"Ah, yes. I guess we all noticed that about Doug, his sensitivity." She felt a small smile creep over her face. "Perhaps someday you'll write about him. Maybe you'll even use him as a character in one of your movies. He was a splendid young man. Reminded me so much of your gramps." A wistful, nostalgic tone took over Anna's voice.

Her mind flew back over the years: How clearly she could see that young military officer standing in front of her desk in the Naval Affairs Committee! The image blurred, changing from Kurt to Douglas, then back to Kurt again. She let her eyes fill up with his image, retreating deeper and deeper into memory. Yes, Kurt. I do love you. I can never give you up. She felt the sudden warmth of his arm around her shoulders, felt him tugging her head against his chest, heard him whisper, "Anna, darling, I'm here. You don't have to give me up. I'm right here beside you."

She opened her eyes and saw Sonia sitting opposite her with a look of deep concern in her eyes.

"Bub, can I get you anything? Would you like a snack? You didn't eat much at lunch today. Or would you like a bit of sherry?"

"Your Bub's going to be fine, honey. She needs a bit of a nap, I think. What do you say, Anna? A little nap before dinner?"

She looked at the man who held her against his chest. Yes, it is you, it is you, isn't it, Kurt. "Yes, that's a good idea . . . a

nap. This shouldn't happen to a grandmother. I never wanted
to live this long . . . to see Douglas murdered . . . it's too
awful."

▨ Chapter 40

Potomac, Maryland, March 1985

"Sonia's been up there with your bubby a long time," Kurt said
to Jennifer as he put another log on the fire in the family room.

"That's 'cause Bubby promised to tell her the whole story of
your romance. Sonia's going to make a movie of it." Jen put
down the crossword puzzle she'd been working and looked at
her gramps. "Was it really terribly, terribly romantic? Like
Mom says, one of the greatest love stories ever?"

Kurt sat down on the sofa next to Jen, affectionately touseled
her black hair, and answered, "Depends on what you call romantic, I guess. I'm not sure it'd be so special to your generation."

"Sonia says you've loved Bubby forever!"

Kurt chuckled. "About sixty years, I guess."

"That *is* forever!"

Kurt heard the front door close and recognized the voices of
Karine and Scot. "Your cousins are here. Bubby will be happy
to see them."

He stood and walked to the foyer to greet them. "How's
Gram?" Scot asked anxiously.

"Better, much better. I'm about to let her out of prison. Her
fever's been gone for three days now. But it's been rough. The
worst case of flu I've ever seen."

"I'm so glad she's better," said Karine, relieved. "Can I go
up?"

"Sonia's up there with her, but she's been there nearly two
hours. Anna's exhausted by now. Yes, Karine, go on up and tell
her Scot's here and that we'd like her to come down and join us
for tea."

Jen, who had followed Kurt into the foyer, hugged Scot and

asked, "Will you practice with me? I've got the score to *Butterfly* and *La Bohème.*"

"Sure thing, doll-baby. But first I've got to talk with Gram. That's why I came. Then we'll have some fun!"

Kurt gave Scot a sharp glance. "I hope you're not going to upset her with anything, Scot. She's been sick. It's not the right time."

"Jeez, Gramps, I really need to talk with her! Karine insists I can't make any changes—hell, I'd really like to transfer out of Harvard to Juilliard."

Kurt put his arm around his tall blond grandson and steered him into the family room. "Why don't you and I talk about it, see if we can't work something out? Then I'll speak to your grandmother for you. I really don't want to upset her right now —she's still on the mend."

"The more I think about it, the more I'd like to switch from business to music—piano and composition. That's what I love."

Kurt sighed, understanding the young man's dreams but knowing full well that his grandmother needed to believe her grandsons were going to take over her business.

"Let's see. You're two semesters away from your master's degree, as I understand it."

"Right."

"Why don't you stay the course, finish up, and then go on to Juilliard? Get a second degree in music composition or whatever. Anna won't object too strenuously if you delay joining Dunay, as long as she knows you've finished your education and could come aboard on short notice. Meanwhile, during the next two semesters, find the best teachers in Boston and spend your free time working on music. How's that?"

"You really think she wouldn't raise hell if I enrolled in Juilliard?"

"I'll talk to her. If you finish up at Harvard, you're certainly entitled to go on to Juilliard. After you've learned everything you can at Juilliard, decide what you want to do with the rest of your life. Besides ski!"

Scot grinned mischievously. "Yeah. Considering that I might have become a ski bum, she can't complain if I become a great musician instead."

"Exactly."

"Wow! What a story! It's sure to get me my first Oscar,"

Sonia exclaimed as she burst into the room. She plopped down onto the sofa next to her grandfather and hugged him. With twinkling eyes, she looked at him and said, "You old devil, you! I never would have guessed!"

"I can't imagine what you're referring to, Sonia. Don't forget, old people tend to embellish their memories. You really don't believe everything Bubby's told you, do you?"

Sonia laughed at her grandfather's sparkling eyes, a dead giveaway that everything Bubby had told her was exactly true.

"Is she coming down for tea?" he asked.

"Yes—if she can get Karine out of her closet. Right now, Karine's prancing around, modeling that gorgeous necklace you gave Bub. Some necklace! Those tanzanites are scrumptious, the most gorgeous color I've ever seen!"

"You like it, then?"

"Like it? Hell, I'll fight Karine for that necklace someday!"

"Don't let Bub hear you say that. One thing she doesn't want is any fighting between her grandchildren."

"Yeah," Jen interrupted. "Besides, she told me I get that necklace. It matches my eyes. Isn't that right, Gramps?"

Kurt looked at his beloved Jen, so shy and vulnerable. "Yes, it does match your eyes, but I've no idea who Anna will give it to. Seems to me she has enough jewelry to go around for all you girls. Speak of the queen, here she is! You look lovely, darling," he said to Anna as she floated slowly into the room wearing a sapphire-blue-velvet floor-length robe trimmed with a white-lace collar and cuffs. "Almost completely well. The color is back in your cheeks for the first time in weeks."

"All from a bottle, my dear," she said as Kurt met her halfway across the room and put his arm around her waist. He kissed her cheek, then guided her to the sofa so she could be surrounded by her grandchildren.

After she was seated and Sonia covered her with a mohair throw, she patted Scot's hand. "So good to see you, dear. How are things in Cambridge?"

"Fine, Gram. Still cold up there, though. It's much nicer here."

"I wouldn't know how nice it is here. Your grandfather hasn't let me out of the house in four weeks. I'm a houseplant, for goodness' sake! Now, where is the tea?" she asked, just as Antonio and Rosa entered carrying trays of pastries and fruit and sherry and tea. After she had been served tea, Anna said, "Antonio, when you have a chance, please put some Debussy on the stereo."

"Yes, ma'am."

"If you ask nicely, Anna, I think Scot and Jen might give us a live concert. You could hear some Debussy—and maybe a bit of Puccini too."

"Only," Jen teased, "if Gramps will play Lieutenant Pinkerton. Then I'll do Butterfly!"

Karine pranced into the room at that moment wearing a stunning red Oscar de la Renta ball gown. "Gram, what do you think? Terrific, isn't it?"

"Beautiful!" Kurt pronounced before Anna could comment. "Movie-star beautiful. You could be a model, Karine!"

"Yeah," Scot said, smiling proudly at his sister, "I tell her that all the time. She's as good-looking as Winslow."

"Where is your mother, by the way?" Anna asked Scot and Karine.

"She's in Paris buying clothes. I can't wait to see what she gets."

Winslow got along better with Karine than her other children. Anna thought, At least they have something in common —their love for high fashion. "So, my dear, when are you planning on wearing that gown?"

"I don't have plans, Gram. But if something fancy comes up soon, can I borrow it?"

"Certainly. You know you can borrow anything you want."

"Except the tanzanite necklace and earrings," Sonia snapped. "Those have my name on them."

"No fighting, girls! I'm really not up to it at the moment," Anna cautioned as she picked up her glass of sherry. Then she added, "I guess your dad's in Annapolis. The session won't be over for two more weeks. I haven't talked to him in ages, simply ages."

Kurt winced inwardly. Such a son! Months went by between his phone calls, yet Anna catered to his every wish. And I can't tell her anything about him. She won't hear it, simply won't hear it. Anna's fatal flaw—her son. Well, I guess she's entitled to one major fault. Mother's love is blind.

* * *

"The rain's finally stopped," Charles said when he arrived several hours later to pick up Sonia and Jen. "Thank God. It's a mudhole out there. The driveway is going to need some work this spring, Dad. I hope you've got someone to fix it up."

"In another month or so," Kurt answered. "Come see your mother—she's been asking for you. She's much better."

"With you as warden, I don't wonder."

Charles greeted Anna with a hug and a kiss. "We don't even miss you at the office. In fact, the staff is hoping you'll stay away for a few more weeks—that way they won't have to answer your questions."

"Fat chance! I'll be back Monday."

"Maybe half a day."

"Mom, listen to the boss. He says only half a day, and I think that makes sense, given how sick you've been."

"Yes, but I'm bored silly. If I don't get back to the office, I'll die of boredom! I can only read so many books and listen to so much music. I'm going stir-crazy."

"We're about ready to do the deal in Australia. If you come in on Monday morning, you can sit in on the briefing. I think you'll get a kick out of it."

"Elliot's worked it out, then?"

Charles beamed in spite of himself. "Yes, I have to admit that my son's turned into one helluva negotiator. And I've come to trust his judgment. That's going to be a big money-maker in years to come."

Anna smiled back. "I told you—give him his head, and trust his judgment. That boy's got a good business head on his shoulders."

Charles looked at his nephew Scot who was listening intently to the discussion. "I can read your mind, Scot. You're wondering if there's skiing in Australia."

"You caught me!" Scott's face reddened. "Elliot says it's a wonderful country. Maybe Brad and I will check it out this summer."

"Scot," Anna began in a scolding tone, "you know I don't want you two traveling together. It's too dangerous. I can't bear the thought of anything happening—"

"Gram, Australia isn't Israel. Australia isn't dangerous, no way!"

"But take separate trips. Each go your own way."

"Gram, we're not only cousins, he's my best friend. We enjoy traveling together."

"I know I'm being a silly old grandmother, but since we lost Doug—I need you boys even more. I don't know what I'd do. . . ."

"Bub's trying to say she thinks you should be traveling with a woman instead of Brad," Sonia teased.

"Hush! Sonia, you say some of the darnedest things!" Anna scolded.

"Listen, while you kids torment your grandmother, I've got some business to talk over with Dad. So if you'll excuse us . . ." Charles looked pointedly at Kurt, and the two men left for the library.

". . . don't know if I should be doing anything to warn him or not. Christ, I don't need another thing like this."

"You're keeping a dossier of all this?"

"Hell, yes! But I don't know what for. What good does it do me, his brother, to have all this documentation?"

Kurt pondered. He crossed his legs again, then picked up the detective's report. After the drug incident, Kurt had instructed Charles to hire a detective to follow Gilbert for one week out of every year, to keep an eye on what he was up to. The reports were varied: illegal gambling, cocaine purchases, several mistresses. Sooner or later, it had to happen: sooner or later, he would bring disgrace on the family name. There didn't seem to be any way to stop him.

Kurt sighed and looked Charles in the eye. "I'm too old, and I'm too tired of his living on the edge of disaster. I don't know what to tell you, son, except I hope you'll always protect your mother. Look out for her welfare first. That's what you've got to do. It might also be a good idea if you told Gilbert that 'some friends' in the police department in Baltimore have recognized him. His political career does seem to matter to him. Maybe if he's scared, he'll ease up."

"Maybe, for a while. But he seems to need to live on the edge. He courts disaster. I don't understand it—hell, I wish I did! I wish there was some way we could help him."

"I feel I'm a big part of the problem. He hates me with an unbelievable passion."

"No, Dad. He was a problem long before Mom married you. He's always been a problem. Things have just gotten worse since you and Mom married."

"You guys finished yet?" Sonia interrupted. "We're ready to go home, and I've got a hot date tonight."

Kurt smiled, relieved to be interrupted by his auburn-haired granddaughter, whose enthusiasm for life never failed to lift his spirits. "We're finished, but I want to hear more about this hot date. Anyone I know?"

"No, Gramps. But he's almost as sexy as you!" Sonia planted a kiss on Kurt's cheek and ran for the front door before he could ask any more questions.

"Then he's definitely dangerous!" Kurt shouted as the door shut.

"Mrs. Addison, ma'am, there's been an accident. You better come. . . . The admiral—well, you'd better come." The trainer, calling from the stables, was barely able to spit the words out.

Anna swallowed hard, then answered, "I'll be there in a few minutes. Have you called an ambulance?"

"Yes, ma'am. First thing I did. Should be here in a minute."

"I'll be right there."

Anna threw on old slacks and a sweater, called down to Nick to pull a car up to the front door, bundled herself up in an old raincoat, and tied a challis scarf around her head. God, let him be okay. Let him be okay!

But even as she prayed, an awful intuition came over her: Kurt has been wounded, mortally wounded.

I didn't want him to go riding after this rain! Even Charles said the place was one big mudhole! But Kurt had to ride his new toy, his new stallion. God, let him be okay!

Nick drove the station wagon slowly down the bridle path, following closely behind two police cars, their lights flashing. Anna's despair deepened. He was badly injured, maybe even— no, it couldn't be. She wouldn't let herself even imagine the worst.

The accident scene was quiet bedlam. Medics were loading Kurt's still body onto a stretcher, two policemen restrained the Arabian stallion several yards away, and a second ambulance was careening toward them down the narrow bridle trail.

Murphy, the trainer, recognized Anna and ran forward. "A terrible accident, Mrs. Addison. Something spooked the horse. The admiral was thrown against that tree over there."

Anna walked steadily toward the stretcher as Murphy explained. The medics, seeing her, set the stretcher down.

The blanket was over his face. What did that mean? Were they trying to smother him? "Take that blanket off his face!" she demanded in a hoarse voice.

One pale medic, hands shaking, gently pulled the blanket down to Kurt's chin.

"Mrs. Addison, I'm afraid . . ."

Anna knelt beside the stretcher and reached out to touch his cheek. It was ice-cold. Her hand slipped down to his neck, and she pressed to feel his pulse. "He's dead. I'd hoped . . . it wouldn't be . . . this bad."

"Mrs. Addison." One of the medics was holding on to her elbow.

"Yes." It was like a movie, or a nightmare—it wasn't real. "Yes. We must get him to the hospital."

She let them raise her to a standing position, then walked beside Kurt's body as they loaded it into the ambulance. They assisted her into the ambulance and began to close the doors.

"Wait—wait a moment." She leaned out the door and spoke to Nick. "Call Charles, and have him meet me at the hospital. Tell him what has happened. And bring the car."

I will not collapse. I will take care of Kurt, nurse him. . . . This is a bad dream. It will end soon. Charles will come. And Elliot and Douglas—no, not Douglas. . . . I will sit here beside Kurt, and when he wakes up, he will find me holding his hand.

"Oh, Kurt darling, I love you so much. Like I told Sonia this afternoon, there hasn't been a day in my life since I met you when I haven't loved you. But you knew that, didn't you? Yes, you old rascal, you've always known that!"

⊠ Part 8

Happiness Restored, 1988

*Rick Dunay canceled his appearance scheduled for to-
morrow night in London's Palladium to fly to Washington and be with his grandmother, former U.S. Senator
and Ambassador to Austria Anna Dunay.*

—Entertainment Tonight
April 2, 1988

⊠ Chapter 41

April 1988

Exactly one week after the glorious dinner at Pennyfield Manor, which ended suddenly when Anna fainted and was rushed to the hospital, Anna felt she had recovered her strength sufficiently to talk to Gilbert. She thought she'd better have it out with him now, if she was ever going to. So she asked him to come in Sunday evening for a talk.

After Gilbert kissed her on the forehead and seated himself across from her bed, Anna took a deep breath. She opened the manila file that had been on the table next to her bed. She smiled softly at Gilbert. "It's been a long time since you and I have been alone for a chat."

Gilbert, his palms cold and sweating, cleared his throat nervously. "Yes, well . . ."

"I shan't keep you too long, but I promised you I'd tell you about my will. I haven't done that yet, have I?"

"No, Mother. But you've certainly been generous with the children. Especially Karine and Larissa. Giving Karine Senator Landow's home in Connecticut—that was certainly a grand gesture. Winslow's had her heart set on that house for years now."

"Karine will enjoy it as a weekend home as long as her business is in Manhattan. If she's going to be a dress designer, Manhattan's the place to live, though I never liked it much myself."

"Do you have any idea what the Kalorama property—and the art and books and antiques—are worth? My God, Larissa's hardly the person to appreciate that house."

"She'll love it, especially the books. Mind you, I made these decisions very slowly, very carefully." Anna paused. "And now for you."

He cleared his throat again, crossed his legs, and leaned back.

"I have not cut you out of my will, though you have every reason to believe I might."

"I didn't say—"

"Hear me out, Gilbert! I can't stand being interrupted!"

Anna continued imperiously. "I'm deeply concerned about your plans to run for the United States Senate."

"What does that have to do—"

"Don't interrupt me!" Anna rang for her private nurse, asked for a glass of ice water, and resumed. "I do not believe you have the moral character or the ethics to hold high public office, neither in the Senate nor in any other federal body."

She quietly waited for that to sink in.

Finally, Gilbert responded. "I don't know what you're talking about. I don't see what my Senate race has to do with the disposition of your estate."

Anna reached for the black notebook that was sitting on the table next to her. "This book," she began, "contains the record of your—ah, misconduct, I think we'll call it. Dates. Names of witnesses. Sworn affidavits."

"Explain what you mean by 'misconduct.' Surely you're not talking about a few love affairs—not you, Anna," he added in a sarcastic voice.

"To my great dismay and utter horror, I'm talking about charges far more serious than adultery. Repeated and frequent purchases of cocaine. And most repugnant of all, for a man who wants to be elected to the Senate, conspiring with foreign drug traffickers in an import scheme."

"Let me see that notebook!" Gilbert roared.

"No! And don't even think of overpowering an old lady! Charles has the duplicate of this notebook."

"I knew it was the two of you together—it always has been, ever since I was a kid. So what are you going to do about it?"

"I want you to withdraw, publicly withdraw, from the Senate race by Tuesday evening. I'm scheduled for surgery this Thursday, and I'll be signing my final will on Wednesday at noon." Anna paused, studying his face. "I've asked my attorney to prepare two versions of the paragraph that deals with my bequest to you. If you agree to withdraw and never run for public office again, I will leave you twenty million dollars. If you do not agree to withdraw from the race, I will leave you exactly ten thousand dollars, and I will release this dossier to the press."

"You wouldn't!"

"Try me!"

He stood and angrily walked out of the room.

Anna sat quietly, waiting, amazed at her own clearness of mind and deep feeling of tranquillity.

He stormed back into the room. "I don't for an instant believe you'd release that garbage to the press! And if you did, who'd believe you?"

"I have sworn affidavits from the men who kidnapped you the night the DEA was prepared to arrest you, the night Kurt saved your skin."

"So you've known all along. I always wondered . . ."

"No, I didn't know about that until the weekend of the Pennyfield dinner, when I saw this notebook for the first time. Your stepfather and your brother never told me. All these years, Charles has been signing checks for you, millions and millions of dollars for you, to throw in the sewer, to poison yourself with. Cocaine! Gilbert, how can you be so sick? So crazy? How can you take such chances?"

Mother and son stared at one another, their faces filled with despair.

What have I done to you? What kind of a mother have I been that you would destroy your life like this?

Suddenly, Gilbert broke the silence with a nervous laugh. "How do you imagine I'll live the rest of my life on twenty million?"

Softly, Anna answered, "You could try working. It's good for the character. At one time you had a fine mind, and you received the best possible education. You're still licensed to practice law, aren't you, in spite of this?" She waved the black book at him.

"Shit. You really give a man a choice! Twenty million, or ten thousand and disgrace. God damn."

"You have until Tuesday night. I'd like to see the press conference on television and read about it in the *Post.* You can withdraw "for personal reasons," or because you need to participate more fully in the family business. I'm sure Brad or Scot can find something useful for you to do. By the way, I've named Charles, Sonia, Scot, and Rick as the executors of my estate. They will be sure you live up to the terms of our agreement—whatever it is. And your sons will be fully briefed. I've decided the time has come—it probably did long ago—to stop making excuses for you, to stop trying to protect you. From now on, if and when you break the law, no one in this family will come to your aid."

Gilbert tapped his fingers on the table. "Just out of curiosity,

Mom, not that I can't guess, what else does your will provide
for?"

"I've left all my business interests and personal investment
portfolio to Charles and the remaining eight grandchildren in
nine equal shares, to be managed by a special board. I've given
my jewelry and homes away, and specified other personal items
for various people."

"And if I decide to contest the will?"

"My lawyer assures me that that will be impossible. He's put
in an *in terrorem* clause. I guess you know what that means."

Gilbert nodded his head slowly. "And Winslow?"

"I didn't specify anything for Winslow. I thought you might
share your twenty million with her." A small smile played
around Anna's lips.

"Well, I guess that about settles it, then." He stood to leave.

"I need an answer by noon on Wednesday."

"Yeah. I'll think about it."

"One last thing you should know. I've left a videotape in
which I explain my reasoning on all these matters. It's in the
safe in my attorney's office. He has explicit instructions about
the use of that video."

He turned and looked at Anna with complete contempt.
"Thought of everything, haven't you? Smart lady. I always have
admired your smarts." With a final sneer, he left the room.

Anna's hospital room had been filled with flowers even before
the surgery. Now, as she waited for her lawyer and Gilbert to
arrive for the signing of the will, Charles, Scot, and Rick paced
the room inspecting the cards and flowers.

Her maid, Josephine, sat in a nearby corner, ready to answer
her every need, and Barbara had come in specifically to witness
the will, along with Josephine. When Adam Grenville, her lawyer, arrived, he quickly pointed out that they couldn't be witnesses since she'd left them each a bequest. He summoned two
nurses from the corridor.

The last person to arrive was Gilbert. He nodded curtly to his
sons and brother, shook hands with Grenville, and handed his
mother a note. She opened it and read it quickly—it was his
promise never to run for public office.

But this was old news. She had seen his withdrawal press

conference the evening before and had read about it in the morning paper. The note was anticlimactic.

Surrounded by these witnesses, she signed the will with a flourish. Suddenly, she felt exhausted. "Now, everyone leave me be a bit. I need a nap. An old lady like me needs a beauty sleep once in a while."

They filed out one by one, until only Gilbert stood looking out the window. When the room was quiet, he approached Anna's bed. "Mom, I'm a little late saying this. I've been doing a lot of thinking since Sunday night. . . . I want you to know I hope you"—he waved his hands helplessly—"I hope this surgery isn't so bad, that they get it all." He bent down and kissed her on the forehead. "God damn it, Mom, I'm trying to say, I hope you get well and come home. I do love you, Mom."

Anna reached for his hand. She squeezed it, then held it a moment longer. "Oh, Gilbert—you always could charm the socks off a person when you tried. I—I'm old enough . . . and fool enough, I suppose . . . I almost believe you."

He looked at her with an expression so sad, she thought he might cry. He bent down one more time and kissed her forehead, then turned quickly and headed for the door.

"Gilbert," she called out, "I do love you. Nothing destroys a mother's love for her son. Nothing—remember that."

▨ Chapter 42

June 14, 1988

Carrying her brown alligator briefcase and wearing a smart beige-linen suit, Anna Dunay entered her office at Dunay International. It was her first day back on the job since late March when she had entered the hospital for colon surgery.

Oh my, it looks so good! she thought as she crossed the magnificent navy Kirman rug to her desk. A bouquet of red, white, and blue flowers topped with an American flag awaited her. She picked up the card: "Happy Flag Day and welcome back. We love you." Signed: "The employees of Dunay International."

Wasn't that nice of Barbara! A truly thoughtful touch!

She sat down and punched the intercom. "Barbara, the flowers are beautiful, dear. Thanks so much. You know, I'm in the mood for some Rachmaninoff—perhaps a piano concerto. Can you find that tape?"

She opened her briefcase and removed a black notebook and a videotape. Standing on tiptoes, she moved a painting from the wall behind her desk and slowly, carefully turned the dial on her small wall safe. She placed the video and the notebook inside, closed the door, and sealed the safe.

"I won't be needing these anytime soon," she said aloud to herself.

That accomplished, she sat down and opened her desk drawer. In the small magnifying mirror, she checked her hair and makeup. Pretty good for an old lady who's just come out of major surgery! She applied a bit of blush to her cheeks, then picked up her telephone and punched the numbers for Charles.

"Good morning, Charles."

"Mother! You're here! Wonderful! Now, don't try to do too much the first day."

"Charles, it's mighty quiet in here. I'd like you to call a senior staff meeting this afternoon. I want a complete report on the Santa Fe resort, the occupancy rate, and projected profits. Everything. And I want to plan the groundbreaking ceremonies in Australia. After all, this is Dunay's first excursion onto that continent, and I think we should make it a memorable event."

"Yes, Anna."

"Now tell me, what news do you have of Gilbert? I haven't heard from him in two weeks."

"The latest—shocking as it may seem—is that Winslow is divorcing him. Seems she doesn't want to be married to a man who isn't going to be a senator. And she considers his future financial prospects poor. Seems she has bigger fish to fry."

"Amazing!"

"Even more amazing is Gil's reaction. He seems somehow relieved. He's spending more time with his sons—had them out to dinner separately and together twice in the past few weeks. And wonder of wonders, he's investing in Karine's business."

"I think I'll call him and see if he's available for dinner tonight."

"Don't be disappointed."

"Charles, let me worry about my own relationships with my family."

"Mom—you sound wonderful. Absolutely spectacular! Completely well!"

"Yes. I want you to send Scot in to see me. I need some money, and I think he can probably find it for me."

"What do you need money for?"

Anna heard a touch of impatience in Charles's voice. "Rick's doing a benefit for the Hopi Indian scholarship fund, and he needs some seed money. And Jen tells me the San Francisco Opera needs help with some new sets."

"Anna, Anna, you are incorrigible!"

"Charles, I think you should be more generous with Emily. She told me yesterday about that orphanage in Israel."

There was silence on the other end of the phone, Charles laughed. "Speaking as the chairman of Dunay, I wonder if we really *are* happy to have you back."

"You know, Charles, you can be replaced! Mind your manners, or I'll fire you and replace you with Brad!"

They both laughed heartily, knowing it was a miracle that Anna had recovered so quickly and was back on the job. Then in a soft voice, Anna added, "Charles, I love you dearly. I don't think I tell you that often enough. Being so close to death—it helps one understand how precious every moment is."

"Mom, we're all so glad."

"Hush! Let me finish! There's a lesson I've finally learned, and I want to share it with you. There is nothing, *nothing* in life as important as taking care of your relationships with your loved ones, your children, your spouse.

"When I was young, my ambition sometimes got in the way of my responsibility to you and Gilbert. It's my major regret in life, but it's not too late.

"What's important to me is you and Gilbert, and all the grandchildren. Nothing else matters. Remember that!"

FREE FROM DELL

with purchase plus postage and handling

Congratulations! You have just purchased one or more titles featured in Dell's Romance 1990 Promotion. Our goal is to provide you with quality reading and entertainment, so we are pleased to extend to you a limited offer to receive a selected Dell romance title(s) *free* (plus $1.00 postage and handling per title) for each romance title purchased. Please read and follow all instructions carefully to avoid delays in your order.

1) Fill in your name and address on the coupon printed below. No facsimiles or copies of the coupon allowed.

2) The Dell Romance books are the only books featured in Dell's Romance 1990 Promotion. Any other Dell titles are not eligible for this offer.

3) Enclose your original cash register receipt with the price of the book(s) circled plus $1.00 **per book** for postage and handling, payable in check or money order to: Dell Romance 1990 Offer. Please do not send cash in the mail.
   Canadian customers: Enclose your original cash register receipt with the price of the book(s) circled plus $1.00 **per book** for postage and handling in U.S. funds.

4) This offer is only in effect until March 29, 1991. Free Dell Romance requests postmarked after March 22, 1991 will not be honored, but your check for postage and handling will be returned.

5) Please allow 6-8 weeks for processing. Void where taxed or prohibited.

Mail to: Dell Romance 1990 Offer
        P.O. Box 2088
        Young America, MN 55399-2088

NAME_____

ADDRESS_____

CITY_____STATE_____ZIP_____

BOOKS PURCHASED AT_____

AGE_____

(Continued)

Book(s) purchased:_____

_____

_____

I understand I may choose one free book for each Dell Romance book purchased (plus applicable postage and handling). Please send me the following:

(Write the number of copies of each title selected next to that title.)

☐ **MY ENEMY, MY LOVE**
Elaine Coffman
From an award-winning author comes this compelling historical novel that pits a spirited beauty against a hard-nosed gunslinger hired to forcibly bring her home to her father. But the gunslinger finds himself unable to resist his captive.

☐ **AVENGING ANGEL**
Lori Copeland
Jilted by her thieving fiancé, a woman rides west seeking revenge, only to wind up in the arms of her enemy's brother.

☐ **A WOMAN'S ESTATE**
Roberta Gellis
An American woman in the early 1800s finds herself ensnared in a web of family intrigue and dangerous passions when her English nobleman husband passes away.

☐ **THE RAVEN AND THE ROSE**
Virginia Henley
A fast-paced, sexy novel of the 15th century that tells a tale of royal intrigue, spirited love, and reckless abandon.

☐ **THE WINDFLOWER**
Laura London
She longed for a pirate's kisses. . . even though she was kidnapped in error and forced to sail the seas on his pirate ship, forever a prisoner of her own reckless desire.

☐ **TO LOVE AN EAGLE**
Joanne Redd
Winner of the 1987 *Romantic Times* Reviewer's Choice Award for Best Western Romance by a New Author.

☐ **SAVAGE HEAT**
Nan Ryan
The spoiled young daughter of a U.S. Army General is kidnapped by a Sioux chieftain out of revenge and is at first terrified, then infuriated, and finally hopelessly aroused by him.

☐ **BLIND CHANCE**
Meryl Sawyer
Every woman wants to be a star, but what happens when the one nude scene she'd performed in front of the cameras haunts her, turning her into an underground sex symbol?

☐ **DIAMOND FIRE**
Helen Mittermeyer
A gorgeous and stubborn young woman must choose between protecting the dangerous secrets of her past or trusting and loving a mysterious millionaire who has secrets of his own.

☐ **LOVERS AND LIARS**
Brenda Joyce
She loved him for love's sake, he seduced her for the sake of sweet revenge. This is a story set in Hollywood, where there are two types of people—lovers and liars.

☐ **MY WICKED ENCHANTRESS**
Meagan McKinney
Set in 18th-century Louisiana, this is the tempestous and sensuous story of an impoverished Scottish heiress and the handsome American plantation owner who saves her life, then uses her in a dangerous game of revenge.

☐ **EVERY TIME I LOVE YOU**
Heather Graham
A bestselling romance of a rebel Colonist and a beautiful Tory loyalist who reincarnate their fiery affair 200 years later through the lives of two lovers.

TOTAL NUMBER OF FREE BOOKS SELECTED ____ X $1.00
= $_____ **(Amount Enclosed)**

Dell has other great books in print by these authors. If you enjoy them, check your local book outlets for other titles.